EXPLOITS OF THE SATYR

A NOVEL

TODD CRAWSHAW

CrowsnestPublishing.com

Visit: www.toddcrawshaw.com

ISBN-10: 0-615-31179-2
ISBN-13: 978-0-615-31179-1

Cover art and design by author

CrowsnestPublishing.com

Printed in the United States of America

Dedicated to love
and imagination.

For Helene, Alexis & Brittany

CONTENTS

Odyssey of sadness
Sirens sighing on a mattress
Mirrored narcissistic madness
How sweet this endless now

— John Lazard Slater III

— I —
Coming Down to Earth

As a means to an end, the present had become the future – and perfect it was not. Death was unacceptable. Slater wanted to avoid the social stigma. He fought to resist gravity and pull out of its grip. He was attempting to right his course. But lasers from hostile aircraft kept strafing at him and interfering with his trajectory. He was used to adversity. He could survive this, he reasoned, unreasonably, as the engine of his QuantumStarXS burst into flames.

Suddenly he was plummeting, his optimism too, worthless, like stock in a panicked market with no bottom in sight.

His vision was obscured by black smoke swirling backwards into the path of his descent. The force of frigid air extinguished the fire and exposed the intricate grid of the city enlarging fast. His wings were failing to hold him aloft. He felt like Icarus, a fool made of feathers and wax, melting to pieces, transformed back from a technological wonder to a chunk of debris dropping to Earth.

Life was so precious. A lesson learned too late. Irreversible, was time. His lungs compressing. Warning lights flashing panic. Air screaming through the faltering seams of his carapace as he gripped the control stick shuddering chaotically. His shouts were diminished by a roar of static that overwhelmed his senses – inarticulate and mesmerizing like a sea breeze of sparkling mist, a crescendo of waves, a Siren's song.

Kaleidoscopic visions formed a flickering dream he could almost touch. He knew these places, these people. But where... when? His running lights and windshield became tumbling chips of broken glass. They rose and fell into a twirling mandala of memories. A tunnel of light.

The fall was indefinite, a warp in time, a neurological black-out, prior to his autonomic brake-jets igniting, jolting his senses back into cognition. His desire for self-preservation rebooted. He renewed his fight with gravity and managed to pull out of his dive. With ferocious speed he landed on a vacant freeway. Tires howled and skidded as he sideswiped a barrier wall that tore into his metal frame igniting sparks. He broke free and plunged down an off-ramp. With brakes burning and tires screeching, his QuantumStar crashed into a cement pillar.

It was a transcendental moment. His mind-body-spirit was jabbering all at once. Slater remained seated, soaked in sweat, bathed in a haze of twilight, amazed he was still whole. He was disoriented by the noise in his brain. A reverberating roar that conjured images of disembodied souls frantic and lost within a chamber maze. He stared at the column that had stopped him. It was an ancient artifact, discolored with stains, as if submerged once beneath the sea, and belonging to a minimalistic period of architecture. The shaft had no fluting, no ornamentation at its crown, only iron bars that were rusting and exposed like veins poking through its crumbling concrete skin.

The internal residue of noise subsided. So did the pounding of his heart and head. He determined his location. The column belonged to a transportation system. It supported an overpass linked to pathways and bridges. Systems that were now relics and systematically being demolished globally. Those remaining, like the span of freeway he had crashed into, were retrofitted with a cats-cradle of metal bracing.

A minor epiphany: A realization of where and who.

He was John Lazard Slater III, known simply as John, or Slater (or Satyr to his fans and foes, once upon a time), a man who had fallen ignominiously from the sky to crash-land on a freeway overpass that once transported travelers to and from the once heralded city of New Francisco, formerly known as San Francisco, now just called Frank.

Slater frowned at his reflection in the side window. Forty-five years of life had chipped away at his face, now ruggedly handsome. Dark penetrating eyes and a vertical scar down the left side of his face competed to be his most prominent feature. Providing one didn't first notice his neurocircuit, a metallic bulge, like a third eye emerging at the peak of his forehead. No longer could he cover this goose-egg protrusion with his black hair. It had receded like an outgoing tide into diminished swells of streaked grey.

Slater opened the cockpit. Emerging from his QuantumStar he felt vulnerable, like a crustacean, naked, about to encounter the world unshelled. The concrete landscape was void of snow. It glistened with patches of ice. A distance away, inhabitants of this shadowy netherworld were standing around a burning trash can. One bearded man was wearing a ragged Santa Claus hat. Liquor bottles and cigarettes were being passed and shared.

"Merry Christmas," said Slater. He pretended to be unfazed from his ordeal. He tossed them the key to his flight. It was the spirit of holiday giving and sharing. "You're welcome to it."

An empty bottle crashed at his feet, thrown back in trade.

Slater deemed it fair, given his predicament.

These people were dressed in ski overalls and parkas. It was a defense against the subzero weather. Their grimy yet colorful clothes were no longer in fashion, but abundant ever since the invention of thermosuits.

Slater was wearing one himself. The fabric was soft, had a sheen, with blue-grey flecks alternating diagonally to create a pinstriped pattern. A cloth combining natural and chemical fibers woven into a tailored cut. He raised his collar and felt a wetness. He saw blood on his fingers. A laceration to his head was in need of clotting. He reached inside his autoplane and removed a hat. He placed it on his head. Tugging on the brim, he applied pressure, creating a makeshift bandage.

Mongrel dogs had sensed his presence and were growling. The humanoid faces wavered in the fire's orange glow. They glared with a curious discontent before dismissing him. As just one more intrusive stink in the communal sewer.

To avoid a confrontation Slater gave a parting nod. In a half wave to no one in particular, he belatedly added, "And, uh, have a happy New Year."

Slater knew from personal experience what it was like being homeless living on the streets. Memories started surging back, which strangely renewed him with a nostalgic sense of freedom. By relinquishing his QuantumStar, a possession many coveted, albeit malfunctioning, he felt an imaginary weight of bondage being released. He felt light-headed. Optimistic again. And as he walked, he was realizing he had let himself become enslaved to these electro-mechanical devices. He swore to God, prior to chastising himself, to never let it happen again.

But freedom came with dangers.

The air was bitter cold. Slater began to shiver. He increased the temperature of his thermosuit with the push of a button. To verify he hadn't lost his cellphone he touched his coat pocket. He reached for his lasercards secured in another compartment before it occurred to him they provided little or no protection. An initial wave of panic quelled, as if calmed by tranquilizing endorphins still coursing through his veins from his near-death experience.

He proceeded with a quixotic lack of fear, though vigilant, through a wasteland of deserted streets. Noises intermittently emerged from the industrial ruins and cavernous dwellings that formed a dark jagged scape of unstable land. Slater envisioned these mountainous compositions as though they were flotsam deposited on Earth from outer space long ago.

He began imagining deposits of forgotten history.

He imagined a place void of time.

He saw himself as an astronaut, floating weightless, drawn by gravitational forces toward a distant and bedazzling galaxy. The city. It had a tug of familiarity as gentle as a hypnotic flame. It kept him moving, step by step, like a grounded moth intent on reaching this concentration of lights kilometers away.

Hours passed before he reached the city's swarming center. The manic electricity was palpable. Sights, sounds, and smells. People bumped past him without apology or a second thought. Wafting scents of Asian, French, Mexican, African, and other cuisines battled for dominance. Glass-front stores glowed, open for business, glittering cavities with buyers bargaining for goods.

Long ago, as a child, one of debatable innocence, Slater had loved visiting the city. With its abundant diversity. Its offerings of adventure. Imagining himself as a shipwrecked survivor washed up on a pirate's island filled with buried treasures, or as a warrior sent into space to rescue a princess held captive on a hostile planet, or as a loner-drifter born with the power to see through time.

At present, now the future, Slater knew to be wary.

There were cyberguards. Hybrid forms so humanlike they were undetectable from other DNA-based forms of intelligence, like himself. The human eye was no longer a trustworthy gauge for discerning species. It took science, building aberrant vocal tone detectors and word deconstructors, to detect the nuances. Now thought and action could be calculated – with a moderate degree of accuracy – to determine who, or what was, or wasn't, truly human.

Paranoia had become the norm.

Slater had good reason to worry. There were many alive who wanted him dead. He needed to find a safe place to sit and reconstruct his thoughts.

Entropy, the great equalizer in a world of disorder, along with the mother of all muses, Mnemosyne, beckoning one to a place in time, brought John Lazard Slater III to rest upon a bar stool. Inside an establishment called The Metro – a bar which, decades ago, had been notorious by another name.

—2—
The Crossroads

Slater found himself sipping the currently popular Blue Shooter. In a place called The Metro. He was sifting through some accessible memories. His mind was in a partial fog like the renowned city of Frank. The creeping mist had usurped his energy and left him in a relaxed state of fatigue. He was attempting to measure the extent of his disorder. Had he landed, or had he technically crashed to earth? Or had he simply materialized in this seat at the bar? Being aware of molecular turbulence, Slater began to wonder about truth.

Could truth be told?

Noise from the bar was getting louder and competed with his ability to hear himself think. A decibel louder and it would reach the level of illicit fun. A waitress wearing a transparent amber dress came up to the bar. She sauntered toward him and paused to stare into his face. She surprised him by leaning close and kissing his lips. She then backed away and slapped him moderately hard.

Slater half-laughed. "What the hell was that for?"

"To know the sound of one hand clapping."

He blinked as she mysteriously walked away. He stared at her shapely bottom and took another sip of his drink. He was intrigued. Who was she? Who was he to her? Who was anyone anymore?

Genesis 101.

His ancestral links were gone, buried in an atmospheric white-out. Entities of the swirling fog. There was nobody left to tell the tales which were often fabulous distortions of the truth anyway. Yet, ages ago, before the firestorm that gutted his dwelling place, he had had scraps of evidence. Sepia and color photographs. Birth and death certificates. Newspaper accounts. Computer files.

Ashes to dust, atoms begetting atoms.

For a starter, both his parents had died before he was born. He used to enjoy the shock value it had upon the people he told. The expressions of disbelief varied. His statement was taken more or less as a given lie until he became famous and industrious reporters did some investigating. Exhuming records of a car crash on the Golden Gate Bridge. A cesarean birth. Raised by wolves.

Truth within lies.

His foster parents, in actuality, had resembled sheep. Especially his third father who had a fondness for sweaters, his third mother too. Both had wavy hair, his mother's permed, his father's natural. Royce, or Roy, as he like to be called, smoked a pipe, liked to see his dashing image in mirrors, wore a thin mustache and, on army reserve days, wore a uniform which dispelled the sheepish image. Roy had been a war hero. Confused by a melee assault of machine guns blasting and the deforesting airpower of friendly fire, his unit had stampeded in fright and accidentally collided with the enemy – not only surprising but capturing them. Roy had received shrapnel in the ass, was trampled into the mud and feigned death, for which he received a Purple Heart and proudly wore it on holidays, walked with a permanent limp, became a behavioral psychologist, played golf, and was perplexed that his eventual son, forgiving the missing genetic ties, had evolved into a different kind of animal.

Roy never came right out and told Slater what he thought he was, just: "We love you, Son, honest to God, but you're a different kind of animal, that's all." Roy would say this while putting balls. He was constantly working on his putts, always trying to improve his game. His approach to life was passive-aggressive. He used his putter as a cane. An instructional pointer. He would compliment first, next debate his point calmly, before delivering a parting insult, even threaten the doorways and windows with his club. But never, during this anger, did Roy ever follow through. Unlike Heather, his mother, who was direct – slapping faces and throwing rocks through glass.

More like wolves, disguised as sheep, these third parents.

His second parents, Hanna and Paul, aunt and uncle (brother to his dead father), were the first to adopt him and had left a warmer impression. He recalled a home with comforting lights and the smell of cooking, laughter, and singing, a sense of security and normalcy, before his aunt died suddenly and his uncle fell under the spell of a rapidly progressive dementia.

Slater sipped his drink and looked around, noticing that the bar still provided live music. He watched as the band and crew set up their instruments. The drummer was rattling on a snare drum. One of the musicians was near the stage signing autographs. It triggered a rush of memories bound in cobwebs. Slater had learned to value anonymity. He was trying to blend in, becoming an unrecognizable nobody. It appeared, so far, to be working. Except for the amber woman to whom he had done something good or bad, it seemed.

A little of both, he guessed.

Slater's career in music had lasted less than three years. He had barely been into his twenties. He was homeless for another delirious stint. Followed by the majority of his years in which he was busy raising a family, co-founding a business, and climbing the wobbly rungs of a corporation which delivered him like the biblical Jacob into a beclouded realm of corporate wealth and power. Yet even after a glorified arrest and global notoriety, it appeared his identity could not hold shape within the public's short attention span and outlast detrition to memory caused by time.

Time had no use for inertia. Matter moved in and out of favor. Time sought complexity and circled it with devotion.

Before it all unraveled, faded and died.

Slater lifted the Blue Shooter to his lips to sip more of its nectar. He imagined himself an ancient mariner driven off course by severe misfortune, with loose ends flapping in the wind. At broken-down moments like these he was tempted to let go of the lines and sheets and let the wild forces take his vessel to wherever – some tragic end. His survival, considering the many harrowing twists and turns, came down to a willful nature and a preponderance of luck.

Or was it manifest destiny?

Slater had to laugh at the divine game plan of his conception. Genetically linked to religious fanatics. Biotechnically conceived by a cult of scientists and fools.

What did it mean to have life? To be human? To come from nothing and have this spark of awareness?

Slater regarded the cloth he was wearing. He was responsible for its inception. First envisioned in a dream. Even the blue liquid was his creation, in part.

Truth? No. It could not be told.

The blue liquid tasted vile but helped revive lost memories. It also numbed necessary instincts. He needed to be more attentive. The man on his right was seated upright, no slouch, staring straight ahead into the barroom mirror. Absorbed in narcissistic meditation? Or was he an agent of the NeverMind Corp? Slater broke the silence between them by asking:

"Did you come into this bedlam for the solitude too?"

Unfazed by Slater's stab at humor, the man abruptly finished his drink, stood and exited the bar.

"Nice talking with you," said Slater.

A bartender approached. He held a stainless steel container and tipped it toward Slater.

"Let him go mate. This place is full of lost souls."

"Ah, the Proprietor of Truth?" said Slater.

"A mere employee. Care for another?"

"What the hell. Shoot me."

"My pleasure."

It was a wry litany both understood. The bartender's eyes were as grey as the metal cylinder. His torso had a weightlifter's physique, tightly bound in a black shirt.

"When's the music start?" asked Slater.

"When you're ready to listen." He tapped his bald head, gave a smile of sorts. "It's all up here, you know."

"Right," said Slater.

"What's your excuse?"

"For being here?"

"Are you a music lover?"

Slater shrugged, noncommittal.

"Same here." The bartender tipped his head and moved on.

No longer was Slater a musician nor did he consider himself to be one. He warranted no more than a paragraph or quarter page in Rock's anthologies. He had become a Golden Oldie.

Wolfe, his friend and bass guitarist for their band, had laughed and shouted more than once during a performance: "This isn't *art*— we're a fucking demolition act!" After attaining success, and their band prophetically breaking apart, Wolfe said to him after a concert: "Don't take it personal, bro, but you *blew* it. Savvy?"

Slater gazed into the thick blue liquid. It had a metallic quality. It pooled in the glass like mercury. Had this opening act of music been the overture to his entire life – a demolition act?

He smiled and muttered, "It wouldn't surprise me."

"What wouldn't?" said a woman on his left. She was attractive, pursing her lips to show interest in his plight.

"Life...anymore." He regarded her with a grin, then returned to the blue depths of his cocktail. He swirled the remaining liquid, making it rotate like a pliable planet around the bottom of the glass. He recalled his wife as it swirled, how she had playfully eviscerated him with words in front of a roomful of amused guests, "No, John, what you *are* is an ambitious, lustful, God-haunted wanker."

She was being polite.

Reflected in the mirror was a woman outside, walking with two girls, beyond the glass, passing like phantoms. The mind was cruel, playing these tricks. It wasn't his wife. He had lost her to the war. Both daughters too. Besides, if still alive, they would be much older. He was gripping the shot glass to hold onto their memories.

It took the Big One to shake him to the core. To force him to realize who he was – and who he was not. It was the earthquake everyone said would someday come but no one wanted to believe. It was the heartbreak lovers feared but never suspected until it was too late. It was the voice he heard and kept hearing in his head until the power of its persistence convinced him he was no longer part of the norm, but somewhere on the other side of sane.

Acts of God?

Glass from highrises had rained barbed hailstones down from a cloudless blue sky. Accompanied by sounds of metal wrenching and cars colliding. Beneath a stalled flatbed truck he dove and survived. Something compelled him to rise to run and help a woman trapped beneath a collapsed facade. Aftershocks buckled the asphalt like a carnival funhouse. Houses twisted off foundations – snapping gas lines – exploding into fire bombs.

Slater was looking far beyond The Metro into the past. He saw the fallen bricks and the opening of a cave he had crawled through. A collapsed elementary school where he heard the cries of children. Upon finding them, they clung to him, not wanting to let go.

It was hard to let go.

This was the unifying principle of science. *This* was what held the universe together. *This*...binding love.

Slater spun the blue liquid, watching it coalesce into a turning world held by transparent forces. Eventually everyone slipped away, losing their grip, succumbing to the revolving forces. Slater tipped back his head and let the bittersweet liquid roll down his throat.

To get his mind off the past, he swiveled around on the barstool. The bar's glass front view showed a darkened city lit by fancy lights. Frank had undergone major reconstructive surgery. Architectural engineers, like born again Darwinists, had given rise to pyramids – this prolific new survival of the fittest design. They saw-toothed the skyline. Spires with external elevators zooming like space capsules, ascending each slope to reach revolving restaurants. And up above, sky-writing lasers beamed the night with advertisements:

Got S.O.U.L.? Have a BLUE Xmas. Do IT!

Was intelligence an inevitability, a consequence of evolution? Bacteria succeeded without a brain, possessing survival skills that rivaled their biological hosts. So why should a creature of higher intelligence expect to do better? Humans were on the verge of being replaced by their hybrid creations. How intelligent was that?

Pondering the notion, Slater rubbed his beard stubble, studying his fellow patrons as they mixed, interacting. Earth seemed to have a bipolar proclivity toward war and peace. It was a breeding ground for adversary. A world built on conflict and compromise from the micro to the macro. All cohabitating like mythological creatures – griffin, centaur, manticore. Or myxotricha paradoxa. Slater thought of this prolific swimmer. It inhabited the digestive tract of termites. A protozoan that devoured wood chips ingested by its host and had a flagellating tail – a composite of other life forms called spirochetes. Among them were organelles, embedded in both the protozoan and spirochete, keeping them bound as one in a free-floating bacteria cytoplasmic world. This elaborate symbiotic arrangement enabled the termite guest to sustain life and expel digestible remains for its host to build towers and proliferate communities.

Slater rubbed his aching eyes. He turned from the pyramids to look around the bar at his fellow imbibers. Protozoans, spirochetes, organelles and bacteria – commingling within the same biosphere. Did chance meetings bring about these relationships? Or was there intelligent design behind all this madness? Lurking in a laboratory, arriving by artificial insemination – as was his special case.

Why was anyone born? And to have *vision*. What was that all about? And these previews of soon-to-be-released sagas of reality – was he to welcome them as a gift?

As far back as Slater could remember he had been overwhelmed by evidence that kept piling up like junk he had no room for or had ever wanted, but could not seem to refuse.

Until one day he had a second thought:

He could profit from this gift.

His first thought:

God, help me.

— 3 —
Where to Begin

Sherry made him drunk with love.

On stage Slater was a commanding figure. He was twenty-one. He didn't know a C chord from an F, his majors from his minors. But he could write lyrics and took a crash-course into knowing how to hold a microphone and, simultaneously, a tune. And, to enhance a mood, he could scream on key. Important tools, he determined, for a shock-rock singer. Women went wild for his brand of passion. He sang about dying, exploring the mind, and getting laid. Of the latter he was frequently successful.

His foster-adopted parents had come to surprise him one night at The Crossroads where his band, the Dyslexic Dogs, were playing. But they turned to exit before the band had completed a single song. He'd been crooning in his growl a daring composition entitled *"No Way In Hell."* Heather was furiously yanking Roy out the doorway when Slater happened to open his eyes.

He dedicated the next song to his dead parents – his real ones, who had died before he was born. At a key point in the song he missed the edge and fell off the stage.

Fans adored his angst.

When he first saw Sherry coming toward him he was stoned, a glass of whiskey in hand, cigarette in mouth, and had expected the usual blithering praise. And maybe later, if lucky, her naked body in his hotel bed. Her body had a radiant glow.

"Hello, Love," he said with a grin. She was gorgeous, golden locks framing her face, and obviously college material, as was her friend, another beauty with cascading raven hair, both standing side by side. He began to see double. Envisioning them both in bed.

"Seriously, the second coming?" said the brunette with a laugh.

The blond was more direct. "What a waste of talent."

"Sorry, what?" said Slater.

"We knew each other, once." Neither extended their hand nor wanted an autograph. "Sherry. I came over to say hi. You used to be shy. More accessible. Anyway, good luck. You'll need it."

"We're about to record, Darling," said Wolfe.

"Electra wants us bad," said Slater. "Hey, we *are* together."

"My mistake," said the brunette, exchanging a teasing glance with her friend. "We wish you both the very best."

The blond and brunette turned and walked away.

"Hey, wait!" Slater quickly rose from his slouch. The ascent made his head ache and spin. "Who the hell were they?"

"Fuck 'em," said Wolfe.

"I...intend to," said Slater. "What'd she say her name was?"

"Who?" said Smitts, the drummer.

"*Jesus*," said Slater.

"The Savior? I don't think so," said Wolfe dryly, inhaling from his cigarette. The girl beside him broke into a whinny of laughter. Smitts snorted a laugh too and drum-rolled with his nimble fingers on the edge of the table.

Slater felt strange, out-of-bounds, clairvoyant. A sweet metallic scent flooded his nostrils. A prelude to the splinter of light and blare of pain in which he pictured this woman. The two of them were in a forest. Slater was placing a ring on her finger. A young girl was then beside them. Her eyes wet with tears and clearly frightened, hugging a stuffed animal. An orange taxi hovered above the ground. Its door was open, waiting to take this woman and child away. They were in danger, Slater realized.

"I'm supposed to marry her," he said aloud.

"The fuck—what?" said Wolfe.

"I need to save her," Slater added.

Smitts laughed. "Save her? Marry who?"

Their lead guitarist, Gloria, joined them with a drink and a new boyfriend. "This is Ricky. What? Give it up."

"Marriage," said Smitts. "Slater's about to take the plunge."

Gloria wagged a finger. "Stop falling off the stage. Ain't no way to prove your love. Who's the heartbreaker? She have a name?"

"A fucking *mystery*." Wolfe blew out smoke.

"*Sherry*. That was it," said Slater.

"Maybe it's what she was drinking, mate," said Smitts.

"Why," asked Wolfe, "if you don't mind me asking, do you feel you've gotta *marry* someone you don't even *fucking* know?"

Gloria was intrigued. "A paternity thing? Did you place a bun in her little oven?"

"No, Glory."

"Denial, ha!," she laughed. "Not the best line of defense."

"I haven't even touched her yet, okay?"

"Okay." She winked. "Good luck. You'll need it."

"What?" Slater received a disturbing aftershock of images. He rubbed his eyes. He was seeing two children now. Both girls. Then a gunshot of intense light. The youngest one hemorrhaging blood from her chest. In shock, she was reaching for Slater to save her too. Slater drowned his throat with whiskey. "It was a premonition, or *whatever*. I don't even know what the fuck I'm saying."

"Jeeez, so marry her!" laughed Wolfe. "Satyr, my twisted friend, what you gotta *do*, what we *need*, is for you to get your head in a *zone* so we can produce more radical tunes. Savvy?"

"A premonition? I like that," said Gloria.

"Meant for each other, you mean?" said Smitts.

"A destiny thing," said Gloria. "Like Anthony and Cleopatra, Bonnie and Clyde. Samson and—*Delilah*."

"Or your basic lust," said Wolfe. "Listen, man, Electra wants to make us rich. Focus on *that* destiny."

Slater combed fingers through his unruly hair. "I am focused. But what if she's right?"

"Who, Electra?" said Wolfe. "She was one screwed up Greek girl. But Electra, the company, they're offering us a ticket out of this rat hole."

"I think he meant his new *love* interest," said Smitts.

"*Sherry, yum-yumm*," teased Gloria. "Satyr wants a taste."

Slater downed the last of his whiskey. "What's wrong with that, Glory, huh? Wanting to soar high – wanting to *taste* it all?"

"Okay by me, mate," said Smitts.

Slater leaned back and gripped the table as he philosophized drunkenly, "Life's extemporaneous. Good for a time. Consume it fast – before it spoils."

"We're time bombs," Wolfe added, "is what we are."

"Yeah," said Slater, "the underlying theme of our existence. It's like Jim Morrison said, 'No one here gets out alive.' On arrival, we're as good as dead. And we know it."

"The downside of having consciousness," said Wolfe.

15

"But, hey," Slater laughed. "Our band...it's gonna soar."

Wolfe shoved a cocktail napkin and pen toward Slater. "Good, here, when you sober up, write down some new lyrics."

Slater began scribbling. Gloria laughed, knuckled his shoulder. His doodle amounted to a woman's curving torso with two dotted circles and a scribbled triangle below. "The essence of poetry. The holy trinity of pleasure. Who the fock needs words?"

"You're a regular Picasso," said Smitts.

"I'll try building a melody around it. Shit," said Wolfe. "Get serious, Slater. You're gonna *blow* this for us, aren't you?"

"I won't, I won't." Slater grinned and signaled the bartender for another whiskey. "But why—I mean—*why* would she say that?"

"Who?" said Wolfe.

"She said our music was a waste," said Slater.

"Not our music," said Smitts. "She was targeting you."

"Because she wants your *baby,*" teased Gloria.

"Fuck the critics," said Wolfe. "Stay focused and we will *soar* to the top of this fucking heap. Right?"

"Right," said Slater.

"You *are* wasted," Wolfe lit another cigarette. "Stay aloft, my friend. Don't crash and burn. Savvy?"

Slater massaged his eyeballs. He saw lights from a barrage of paparazzi. "Right. We soar...get famous. Then disintegrate. Time passes and Glory...you're doing casino gigs in Vegas. And Wolfe... you start some...sort of underground movement. A revolution."

Gloria laughed. "Vegas! Like *hell.*"

Slater grinned, "Hey, I'm stoned. What do you expect?"

"You're in *love* is more like it," said Smitts. "Do me. What do you see in my future, mate?"

Wolfe grumbled to his girlfriend, "Now he's a fucking psychic. Do you *believe* this shit?"

"Smitty, another time," said Slater. "It's all bullshit anyway."

Wolfe was blunt. "You got that right."

Slater snapped back, "I get tortured. Decapitated. That's how I die – okay? Does that make you *feel* any better?"

"Shockingly, it doesn't." Wolfe was the unofficial leader of their group and told Slater, "Try saving whatever powers you might still possess for our second set."

The premonition of Smitty's fiery death had left Slater in a daze. His senses felt singed, tingling. "What'd you say?"

"Satyr...shit." Wolfe stabbed out his cigarette. "Living on the edge doesn't mean you have to fall off the stage every fucking night." He followed this with a brotherly smile and a smoldering non-verbal threat: *So don't fuck this gig up you God-damned lunatic or I swear I will kill you!*

Wolfe's mouth stayed shut but Slater clearly heard the message. He had hoped he could outgrow this madness. But the auditory and visual seizures proved unrelenting. He sought shelter among this tribe of gypsies. Freaks in this circus world of rock-and-roll were considered the rule, not the exception. But even eccentricity among freaks had its limits. And no degree of logic could explain how he suddenly knew Wolfe, his best friend, would also fall in love with this same woman. *Sherry Knowles.*

The realization of who she was finally registered. In high school Slater had been smitten by her. She'd been a cheerleader, elected to student council and popular. Whereas Slater had been an outcast, a transfer student who had watched her from afar. Until the night he gained courage to ask her to dance at a school function. When she agreed and they danced, he fell madly in love.

Five years later – with so many women passing like water under his drawbridge – Slater had forgotten her. Almost. He *was* wasted, he realized. He closed his eyes. He tried to cancel out the barroom clamor and the recorded music. He conjured up her beautiful image. The vision of an angel. But an angel, he intuited, who also brought danger. And whose presence he now felt.

Slater flinched as fingers, soft as a feather, brushed his cheek. He opened his eyes and saw an empty table. His band mates had departed. The bar was filled with people he didn't recognize. People who seemed transparent. A snare drum was rattling.

Wolfe was approaching. He appeared to be solid and coming back from the dead – and not very happy about it. The room was vibrating with life once again. Wolfe walked up and scowled.

"Are you waiting for a formal invitation? We're on!"

"I got unstuck in time. You know, like Vonnegut, in—"

"Restick yourself," said Wolfe. "Can you even stand?"

Slater grinned and stood unsteadily, assisted by the table. To make light of his predicament, he joked, "See? No problem. I'm a man of substance. It's like...a miracle."

"Yeah, it'll be a *miracle* if you can sing," muttered Wolfe

Slater pushed off and staggered toward the stage.

He acted as though self-assured, a man who couldn't care less. But appearances were deceiving. It was a performance. The visions in his head were escalating – and they were spooking him.

But they had no real validity.

He kept telling himself.

—4—
Extended Family

At age nine Slater became a ward of the state when his uncle, Paul Slater, tried to shoot his nephew-adopted son before turning the gun on himself. His uncle missed his target both times. He was first aiming to kill the Greedy-Son-of-a-Bitch who stole his patent and robbed him, Paul Slater, the real inventor of the Whirl-O-Will, of his should-have-been but never-to-be-seen fortune.

The Greedy Son-of-a-Bitch harassed his uncle artfully and took many forms. They lost two dogs to the Greedy-Son-of-a-Bitch. One stray cat. And nearly a postal worker who notified the police. His uncle, and second father, was cited for a weapons violation and was scheduled to have his say in court.

Paul Slater couldn't wait.

Young Slater felt responsible. He had confided in his uncle about more dreams he had had – men in hooded robes, overlapping fiery crosses, wrestling with angels, staring into a blue crystal ball. He also recited strange names he remembered. His uncle frowned from a standing position at his lathe, then removed a pistol taped to the low rafters, as if his eyes were now witnessing something wicked in his nephew-son.

His uncle was fond of jokes. So young Slater barely flinched, puzzled as he grinned at what he thought was a toy.

The explosion from the barrel sent him spinning. In a timeless moment Slater heard the snap of a sail. A forceful wind came off the ocean and his uncle made a starboard tack in his schooner, the *Know-It-All*. The Golden Gate Bridge seemed to float high above them, a majestic red city, defying gravity, as well as reality. His aunt was holding the rails and whooping with delight as they keeled sharply, her hair flying like the mane of a horse on a wild gallop. Bundled in an orange floatation device and clutching what he could to keep from falling, Slater gaped at the cresting waves splashing at the lee railing about to plunge underwater – and take them down into the depths of the sea! If not for his aunt's merriment in the midst of this calamity and his uncle's reassuring grin beneath a wind-blown tangle of beard and both hands confidently attached to the pilot's wheel, Slater would have screamed.

He loved his aunt and uncle, felt safe in their presence, and was therefore perplexed when he awoke in an intensive care unit with the side of his head throbbing and bandaged. Monitors beeping – *aunt dead, uncle gone – aunt dead, uncle gone – aunt dead, uncle....*

His uncle had been taken away to be treated at a special kind of hospital, he was told by doctors and social workers that queried him. Aside from the cats and dogs his uncle had begun to shoot, Slater remembered his uncle as someone relatively harmless, good-natured, and always tinkering with and abandoning one contraption after another. Over time, the basement workshop had spread like an invading fungus to the upstairs and took over most rooms in the house. Lathes and sanders were bolted to the hardwood floors. The dining room table became a thickly stained workbench and a place to occasionally sit and eat. Power tools and socket wrenches adorned tables once holding books and vases of flowers.

Hanna, his aunt-mother, believed in her husband up to a point – to the basement door. Before she died, the upstairs was strictly off limits for his tools. Especially in the kitchen, for she had been an inventor herself when it came to baked goods. Young Slater was her "official taster." The kitchen was her exotic testing ground. She added chocolate mints, marzipan and Chinese noodles to cake mix, or butterscotch and Fruit Loops into pie fillings, or pickled relish and a sprinkle of basil into cookie dough.

She drank cognac while creating. And sang. She loved to sing Billy Holiday, Janis Joplin or Patsy Cline songs. Young Slater enjoyed her renditions as she twirled from stove to sink. She would hold a wooden spoon with gobs of frosting to her mouth and make him believe for an instant it was a real microphone.

Sometimes, caught in the heat of the mood, she let her cakes and cookies smoke and burn behind her. Slater hadn't cared.

"'We create our own reality,' Johnny. Your sweet mother used to say that." Hanna would hand Slater the microphone-spoon to lick frosting. "'Or else,' she'd say, 'someone else will create it for us.' Food for thought, Johnny."

His aunt-mother died from hypoglycemia. She was a diabetic and didn't know it. Or did, but never let on.

"Don't kid yourself, Johnny. Hanna knew what she was doing

to herself. We *all* do. Know that. Did you know she was nearly blind as an old hoot! Hell I loved her though. Come help me move the table-saw upstairs. We have important business to conduct."

Paul Slater had quit the company he had worked for for more than ten years. The corporate heads had told him – "the powers-that-be, Johnny!" – to invent weapons of mass destruction. So Paul Slater told them they could all go straight to Hell. "How could I live with myself?" he told his nephew-son. Even though the items they desired were plastic and relatively harmless, Paul Slater refused to "fabricate laser guns on fighter jets or motorize the turret for some land-roving tank so it can fire nuclear bombs! No, sir!"

He refused for the sake of future generations.

He was an inventor of children's toys.

He was actually fired.

"'I quit! I quit! *I quit!*' That's what I told those Greedy-Sons-of-Bitches, just yesterday," he proclaimed time and again, filled with anger, then grinning with wild abandon. They were playing chess. Paul was an advocate for this geometric and labyrinthine form of thinking. "It's never too late to quit, Johnny. Never too late to start anew. Know that. Checkmate."

Their dog barked.

"Shut up, Skunk," his uncle growled. Feeling victorious, he got up from the table and stretched. "It's best you stay out of things you don't understand. Well?"

Skunk lay down, slunk his head to the floor between his paws, emitting a sorrowful growl. He was a mix of breeds. They guessed part Border Collie, Husky, Cocker Spaniel or Spitz. Any number of things. He was a spirited mutt, had black shaggy fur, white paws, and a bushy pampas-grass tail.

Skunk soon raised his head, prepared to smile again. He was wearing white jockey underwear that Slater had managed to wrestle upon him. A hole in the fabric had been cut for his tail which waved from it like a surrendering flag.

"What do you think, Johnny? The *Fidget-Wigget?* That's what I'll call it. Damn-it-to-hell, I think this one's going to take off! Make us rich! What do you say?"

His uncle-father demonstrated the toy's abilities. In shape it resembled an archetypical UFO flying saucer. Whirring eerily it went spinning around the room and came boomeranging back at them.

Skunk cocked his head, perked up and growled.

"*Damn* right, Skunk!" Paul Slater grabbed the spinning saucer from the air with a slash of his wrist. "We struck pay dirt this time. This'll make us rich. So long as those Greedy-Sons-of-Bitches don't find out – and *rip* us off again!"

—5—
A Minor Talent

Hydra's Head, the debut album by the Dyslexic Dogs, was released in early spring. It had modest sales and their single *Naked Smile* received airplay and favorable reviews from the few alternative rock stations. By winter, Slater and his compatriots, all in their early twenties, were embraced by the masses. The media described them as a "brash new talent with an aboriginal bark and musical bite."

They were overnight celebrities.

Slater equally loved and hated the adoration.

An advance of future royalties from Electra quelled his angst and allowed his first of many extravagant acquisitions – a limited-edition silver Porsche, called the *Bullet*. Before the license plates arrived in the mail, Slater lost control one night and totalled the car into a tree. He staggered from the accident to an emergency room blocks away and received stitches for a cut below his right eye.

The incident made the morning news:

"Dyslexic Dog Kills Tree With Silver Bullet."

Slater's lifestyle and lyrics were making the band controversial. He jumped several stories from hotel ledges into swimming pools. Tempting death, he had run across a freeway through a gauntlet of speeding traffic. He was provocative on and off stage, taunting all forms of presumed authority. Reporters were eager to interview and analyze his purpose for existing. With existential fascination Slater welcomed this swarm of curiosity by opening the flood gates to this new rush of stimuli. At junkets to promote their album, the band – specifically Slater – was asked:

"What do you hope to accomplish with your music?"

"World peace," said Wolfe.

"Do you consider yourself a role model for kids?"

Slater said, "We're the living tutorial for behavior to avoid."

"How do you describe your band's sound and unique lyrics?"

Slater made eye contact with the other Dogs. Silent mockery and reckless fun was their devoted creed. With deadpan seriousness, he said to the journalists: "We're a nerve-ending to God."

It was a sound bite the media devoured with glee.

It mutated into a myriad of headlines:

"Dyslexic Dogs Claim To Be Gods!"
"Is The Second Coming About Dogs?"
"Rabid Singer for the Dogs Attack Christ!"

Religious coalitions who had never heard of them before now cared passionately about a rapid demise of their band. Albums and CDs of *Hydra's Head* were publicly destroyed – disks bent, snapped, tapes unraveled like festive streamers, stomped upon and burned. The exorbitant waste of time and energy devoted to defending his words and the band's reputation was wearing Slater down.

"I didn't *mean* that," said Slater, an unlit cigarette bobbing from his lips as he was accosted by reporters. "That's not what I said. Yes, it was a misquote."

"Do you believe in God?"

"This conversation wouldn't exist if there was no such thing as a God. Don't you have better questions?"

"Are you comparing yourself to God?"

"Wasn't that the plan?" His cynicism veered into a wry smile. "His plan, not mine. Us being spitting images and all."

"How do you feel about the controversy you've created?"

"Ask them," said Slater. "We're a democracy."

Gloria volunteered, "We hate him. We also love and adore his yin-yang knack for self-destruction."

"Are your antics on and off the stage an act?"

"At me, again?" Slater shrugged. "I'd say it's a process. Trying to adapt as a species. Like which mask works. The masks you're wearing are fashionable. Here, let's try something experimental. No–Yes–Maybe–Fuck it! Fill in your questionnaire with that."

Slater was known to terminate interviews by knocking aside chairs and overturning tables when the questions and merchandise presented featured only his face and not the other Dogs.

The reporters would reappear the next day.

"Do you agree with the comparisons being made?"

"Comparisons are a shortcut to thinking. Maybe you've heard that line before. From Morrison of The Doors?"

"Didn't he kill himself?"

"No," said Slater.

"Are you sure?"

"No more than you're sure what comes next."

"Do you consider yourself the voice for your generation?"

"You're joking, right?"

The rooms glared with a rapacious hunger for answers that had lost all meaning. Slater came to believe these people wanted him to self-destruct for the cameras. Burst into helium flames and sputter balloon-like to a tragic demise. Or vanish into a quintessential flash. These interviews were self-serving and conducted to boost ratings. He envisioned their gymnastic spring-board aspirations as hopes to nail an anchor spot on the evening news. And if he conspired to help them with an exclusive story, there would be no limit to their smile. The intense energy behind all the fuss intrigued him. Especially the white lights and camera eyes extracting him into code. He imagined being compressed into data, sent through cable vines and satellite waves of electronic bytes to blossom at the push of a button into a luminescent picture inside a box, inside a living room. *Hello.*

"Rumors are circulating."

"Are they?" said Slater.

"Rumors about drug use. Would you care to comment?"

"Yes," Slater said. "Rumors have been a problem for me. Also for our cities and nations. As with drugs, rumors create turmoil. They circulate and spread, becoming one of many global addictions. Therefore, as your elected leader, I promise to fight for a toxic-free planet. Once we've cleansed our polluted minds and repaired the damage we've caused to ourselves and others from our self-absorbed behavior, we will clearly see the errors of our way. I personally feel remorse for raping mother nature. We must repent and repair the damage we caused before it, or our heavenly father, destroys us."

Slater smiled into the cameras and stood.

"Thank you for coming today. And for your continued support. I have no more comments at this time. Good day."

God help me, Slater thought. He sensed the disintegration and flying debris before his impromptu remarks hit the media's turning fan. Each of these cyclonic train collisions forced him to question whether he possessed any other marketable skills.

Slater knew it was over before others seemed to comprehend their demise, yet the human probes persisted – orbiting, enquiring, swarming, poking for more blood from the walking dead.

"How long do you think the Dyslexic Dogs will last?"

"We're already history. But thanks for asking."

Innocence Lost

The wrinkles in time, the details, could not be envisioned.

Slater's three-year-old daughter, Mercy, smiled before diving off his knee into the dirt.

As if the world would part, soft as water.

This was innocence. Lost.

He ran carrying her in his arms. From the park where he had once destroyed a tree with his Porsche, to the same emergency room he had staggered into already anaesthetized with forbidden drugs.

Mercy was screaming. Blood was dripping from her mouth through his fingers.

He alerted a nurse who was not overly concerned. She was used to seeing worse, and said so. He was instructed to first fill out the required forms.

The emergency room was crowded with other victims. A woman was cradling her broken arm. Paramedics were wheeling a man on a gurney who was coughing blood. A woman was sobbing and jogging in his wake down the hall. Others were seated, staring at a corner of the ceiling where a television displayed more violence. A clown was honking his horn at a security guard who was pushing the circus freak out the electronic doors and threatening to unclasp his own weapon.

This madness made Slater's hand shake as he wrote down his identification letters and numbers. He held Mercy against his side. She had calmed. Her tears were drying. She licked inquisitively at the coagulating wound beneath her lips.

The doctor arrived with a reassuring smile wearing a dull green gown spattered with iron flecks of blood.

The room smelled of chemicals. Slater was instructed to hold down Mercy on the examination table. He felt as if he had betrayed her as Mercy fought against his restraint. She let out a scream as the physician stuck a needle into her lip. She whimpered as the gash in her lower lip where her teeth had cut through was sewn shut.

On the ride home, Mercy laughed. Slater made silly faces and joked to cheer her up. Inwardly, he suffered from a slow internal bleeding of guilt. He should have seen it coming before it happened.

Stopped time. Changed fate.

Sherry, his wife, greeted him with a murderous look. She was next in line to kill him if he failed. She took their daughter from his arms and hugged her as if he was incapable. She inspected Mercy's stitches.

"Does it hurt, baby?" Sherry asked.

Mercy shook her head as if she had forgotten already.

"It happened so fast," said Slater. "She dove off my knee. Face first into the ground. I couldn't believe it."

"What a dunderhead," said Sondra, who was five years old and standing beside her mom. "Mercy, you're such a *dunderhead*."

Mercy attempted to punch her older sister.

At the Christmas tree lot Sondra and Mercy ran off hand in hand to find the perfect pine. They screamed for their parents to come quickly, as if any delay would make the holiday disappear.

"She may need cosmetic surgery," said Slater, "when she's older. The doctor was optimistic though."

"She'll be fine," said Sherry.

Slater stopped his wife. They were bundled in coats and gloves. "Sherry, I swear to God, I would throw myself in front of a train to protect her. I would. You know that."

"I know. Where are the angels when you need them?"

"I married one."

They kissed and their children shrieked — *Yeeuuckhh!* — and ran laughing behind a row of noble firs.

Later, beside the democratically agreed-upon tree draped with lights and ornaments, they ate popcorn in their living room and searched the television for the scheduled showing of *It's A Wonderful Life*. Sondra was flipping through stations with the remote control.

"Go back!" shouted Sherry. "More. There."

"Oh, *God*," groaned Slater, "the land of the living dead."

"The who-what?" asked Sondra.

"Recognize anyone?" said Sherry.

Slater frowned curiously at this image of himself, screaming into a microphone on a rerun of *Where Are They Now*. The antics looked vaguely familiar. The performance was mostly a blank. Brain cells from that period were ravaged by drink and drugs. These home movies within the public domain helped revive an occasional glimmer of his days of yore.

"It's your Daddy, girls," said Sherry, "when he was famous."

"You were *famous?*" said Sondra. "For what?"

"For that," said Sherry. "Your Daddy used to sing."

Mercy giggled. "Daddy, is that really you?"

Slater watched himself stagger, intentionally dramatic, before he lurched and lunged off the stage. His theatrical trademark. But on this occasion – toward the twilight of his career – the audience had parted instead of catching him. The hard landing on the stadium floor made an audible thud.

Sherry covered her mouth with her hands and laughed.

"If you really *love* this," said Slater, "I could send for a copy. Have it wrapped for your Christmas present?"

"It wasn't that funny," she added. "Not then."

Their daughter's mouths were agape.

"Daddy," said Mercy, "why did you do that?"

Slater grabbed and wrestled her into an affectionate hug. "You, who dives into dirt, have the nerve to ask *me?* I should ask you."

"You drew the short straw, Sweetie," said Sherry.

"What straw?" said Mercy.

"Inheriting that precious piece of your Daddy's gene pool."

—7—
Visions of Future-Past

"John, you're disturbing my waters."

Heather Frost, his foster parent, was meditating in her garden. She retreated there whenever she felt the spiritual calling. Which was often. Her blue eyes opened halfway to reenter the visual world.

Slater, eleven years old, took a tentative step toward her. He stepped beyond the stones into her lake of gravel.

"John, please."

He retreated to solid ground and knelt to rake the sand pebbles with his fingers. The impression he had made could not be undone.

"You've broken the circle." Her voice was an audible breath. She sat Yoga-style, her arms outstretched, resting upon her legs. Her upturned palms had clenched, opening fernlike again.

"What is it, John? What is so important you must disrupt my inner sanctum? My peace?"

"Ma'am, I —"

"John, please."

"Heather."

"John, I've told you about my reflective time. You know how important it is for me."

"I know—I know, you told me, but—"

"No, you don't know. You're a child, John. But someday you *will* know. I believe that. Go on."

Her eyes opened, narrowing. She resembled a mesmerizing bird of prey. She observed him from atop her knoll of pebbles. It was a place she called her "center." His first chore every morning, shortly after dawn, was to rake concentric circles around it.

"I'm listening, John. Go on."

Heather Frost's eyes narrowed further to an almost full closure. She did not want to forsake the transcendental bliss she had begun.

"I didn't want to bother you, but—"

"You did. Yes?"

"I sort of—I mean, I didn't mean to break—"

"Yes?"

"One of your stained glass—"

Her eyes opened fully.

"Windows."

"What!?"

She was up, crunching across the sand and gravel and bumping past him before he could finish.

"It was an accident."

It would be one of many. But Roy and Heather adopted John Lazard Slater III despite these frequent mishaps. They believed in his inner potential, in his good genes that would someday flourish. Heather was barren, or Roy sterile, so they declared, even debated in public at parties. Either way, they chose not to explore the medical reasons but decided to adopt. Even at age nine, young Slater had a puppy-like clumsiness that appealed to them.

Especially to Roy. He liked to putt golf balls in the house and have Slater chase and fetch them. Roy would laugh, "John, keep your paws off the lamp. Good boy, bring me my balls."

Heather Frost's face and hands were a delicate shocking white. Her creations of stained-glass windows adorned the habitats of all denominations of the faithful.

She would intone: "It's a true blessing to receive the light and feel the power shining though each of my creations."

The faithful politely nodded. Heather beamed with a smile.

"I believe you know whose power I mean?"

It was Slater's job to be meandering nearby. He often followed her litany by muttering to himself, *Can we have an...amen?*

"If only I could, I would," insisted Heather, "gladly give you this window. That is how strongly I know you will enjoy having it in your home. I deplore these monetary transactions, charging for something inspired by God. It never *ever* feels right. Regrettably, I have a boy to support. And you know the cost of having children. John, come over and meet Mr. and Mrs. Stevens—"

Or whomever. Slater knew when to smile.

"Isn't he an angel? Roy and I adopted him. John's father and mother were killed in a horrible automobile crash. He was raised by an uncle who went insane and tried to kill him. With a gun. A gun! Can you imagine?"

They could. They sincerely tried. They often required time to communicate privately, usually agreeing to purchase the stained-glass window at the set price.

"Praise the Lord!" Heather proclaimed solemnly and startled her customers by clasping their hands. "This is a healing moment. God will find you through this window. I promise."

Slater wondered what she was talking about. He questioned her sincerity. He also questioned, to himself, her group of friends who came to visit and hovered about him, sometimes discussing him as though he wasn't even there, touching his cheek or his hair, like he was an exotic animal from a distant continent.

Unlike his aunt and uncle, Heather and Roy encouraged Slater to discuss his dreams at length.

"Why, yes, these *are* sacred symbols," Heather declared while her group sat in the living room sipping tea. China and spoons clinked like tiny wind chimes.

Slater stood before them as if at a music recital showcasing his talents, except he wasn't playing any instrument or singing, simply recalling images from his head.

"Yes, these symbols hold great significance," said a man whose head was shaved. His body had a muscular frame, and a bolt-like wart stuck out from his neck. "The circle can represent the sun. It also symbolizes notions of perfection. Go on, Son."

"That's about it," said Slater. "Can I go outside now?"

"This blue circle," encouraged a woman with long blond hair. "Surely you can recall more. You called it a blue stone."

"He did," echoed Heather. "A blue stone."

"It was...like a big marble," said Slater.

A man asked, "Was it smooth or unhewn — roughly shaped?"

"Smooth," said Slater. "Like a mirror, sorta. And blue. Round with all these pictures and lights coming out of it."

"Lights?" said Heather. "Were they golden?"

"Some," said Slater.

"What else did you see?" The pretty woman held his attention.

"Lots of things. I heard voices. There was a face."

"Describe the face," said the bald man.

Slater tried his best to recall, closing his eyes, but was tired of standing and began shifting his weight from one leg to the other. "It's hard...to focus. On one. There were lots of faces."

"Many faces?" said Heather. "Voices and lights?"

"Does that mean something?" said Slater.

Heather cast a knowing smile at a woman who had highlighted her eyelids with turquoise shadow. She smiled back. "I'm reminded of Jacob's dream. Is anyone else?"

"Jacob who?" said Slater.

"It happened long ago, dear boy," said a man with a frizzle of hair that protruded from his head like a damaged aura. "Jacob was a guileful schemer. He lay his head to rest upon a pillow of stones and witnessed a gateway of light. It's a myth about those heavenly angels. The Lord God of Abraham? Did you happen to see him?"

"Barton," said Heather, "don't scare the boy."

"It scared little Jacob too." The man flicked forth his tongue in jest. "I imagine it would, witnessing the dwelling place of spirits and gods. If one is to *believe* such things."

"I happen to believe in the possibility," said Heather, "and I find John's dreams quite fascinating. We must encourage John to always want to share them with us."

"I quite agree," said another man. He was shadowed beneath a Panama hat. He held his teacup not at the delicate handle with a finger, but by encircling the rim with his large hand as he sipped.

"Truly mystifying," said Heather. "Quite amazing, really."

Slater raised his hand vaguely toward the door.

"You may go," Heather said, dismissing Slater in a motherly fashion. "You continue to amaze us with your dreams and visions. Thank you for sharing them with us, John."

Slater nodded, confused, questioning her sincerity. One of many times he would question her motives throughout his life.

"Really, you *truly* amaze me, John," said Heather. They were returning from a police station. "Do you realize how humiliating that was for me? To have to *bail* my own son out of jail? Do you? I don't think you do."

Once home, Heather told him to sit. She picked up a healing stone from the coffee table and rolled it between her palms to calm herself. She paced in circles around the oriental rug, an open space and centerpiece of the living room.

"I keep asking myself how my son can be so *smart* and yet so *stupid!* At school, with minimal effort, you receive an A in every class. Surprise to me, I get a call from the principal who tells me you are intentionally failing. You have a voracious appetite for learning. You devour everything from comic books to poetry to existentialism to molecular biology to the paranormal! And yet you willfully refuse to vitalize your full potential. Why is that, John?"

"To escape."

"You have unparalleled vision. Try using it."

"I see you clearly, Heather."

"This is all a joke for you? Is that how you see us?"

"See what?"

"Why do you *rebel* against me?"

"The answer is in the stars."

"Clever," said Heather. "Yes, I *will* consult the stars. You must be passing through your awkward teenage years. The decent thing, I suppose, would be to have you *neutered*. Like a—a stray dog we got *cheap* from the kennel – and brought home out of *pity!*"

"Heather, for God's sake!" said Roy, standing.

She glowered at her husband, as if accusing him too. "Bonnie is a dear friend of mine, John, but she won't even *talk* to me anymore. Not since you *impregnated* her daughter."

"I'm sorry. Okay?"

"Okay? You're sorry? John, try to understand. It's not that Roy and I hold strong opinions about abortions. Do we, Roy?"

Caught off guard, Roy hesitated, but quickly sided with her indecisiveness, giving an affirmative tap to the floor with his putter.

"It's the unseemliness. It complicates matters. There are other people besides yourself to consider, John." Heather picked up the healing stone and pressed it to her breast and sought for kinship. She was not about to cry.

Roy interjected, "Son, abortions can be necessary at times. It's not this...this dead-end option. We don't believe that."

"But the Rutherfords—they *do!* Or *did.*" Heather rolled the stone between her palms. "But you've succeeded in converting them. And now they most *certainly* believe in the healthy benefits of an abortion! Thank you so very—*very*—much, John."

"It was an accident," said Slater.

Roy limped forward, aided by his putter toward Slater. "John, honest to God, we try but we don't understand you. We just don't. What made you go and do a damned fool thing like that?"

"She encouraged me. You've seen her. She's a fox."

Roy blinked, confused by the girl's lovely image. "Yes. No, no. I meant, why—what made you go and get so drunk that you had to go crazy and overturn my brand new Cadillac?"

"To *hell* with the damned car, Roy!"

With calculated anger, Heather hurled the healing stone through the living room window – sending her own stained-glass rainbow creation of lightning bolts and clouds crashing to Earth.

"What I want to know from John is how many more babies we should expect to have to *kill!*"

"None," said Slater. "I'll marry her. All right?"

Heather Frost stopped in mid stride. Her heated pace chilled into a cold stare. "Like hell you will."

—8—
Vacating One's Self

What Slater recalled was an uneventful second set of music. He had sung to a sold-out crowd in an auditorium alternatively used as an ice rink. Afterwards, he argued with his compatriots about canceled shows in the U.S., the scheduling of their European tour, and his forgetting lyrics. Later that evening or the next morning, he had been sitting in a bar. He had forgotten which city (each one resembled the next) and had purchased for the hell of it a bus ticket. A stranger he had befriended during a blurry moment told him the bus went to Paradise.

So Slater boarded the bus, before blacking out.

He eventually landed in Africa.

The bus driver shook him awake and shuttled him off.

Slater was shivering. His body was in pain. He had overslept and woke in the middle of Christmas. The buildings were flashing with colorful lights and moving back and forth at a dizzying speed. He entered the nearest doorway and quickly became aware of his error in judgment.

He sat at a slot machine and fed it quarters until he began to get his bearings. He noticed bloodstains, some wet, seeping through his black shirt. He zipped his leather jacket to hide the bleeding. He exchanged his metal coins for plastic ones. Brightly colored stacks of them were shoved onto numbered boxes. He stuffed his winnings into his pockets before moving to the craps table.

To his amazement, each time he placed a bet, a man kept raking more plastic back at him. He drank the complimentary drinks and was comforted by a harem of women. A bald man with a goatee and red jacket identified Slater as a celebrity he'd seen on the cover of magazines. There were a few shrieks and handshakes. And more free drinks. The winnings came easily.

Slater was on a roll.

The rising sun was competing with the brilliance of this inner artificial world. His new friends were urging him to toss the dice. Light washed through the glass walls like a silent wave. A glowing tsunami. Money was at stake. The crowd chanting sacred numbers. Their voices swarmed into mathematical babble.

Slater threw the dice.

He gazed into the flooded glare.

He heard voices. One rose out from the many.

In a flash — he was drowning.

He heard a cry for help. In a single tear. It trickled unnoticed down the side of his face.

Intoxicated and impelled by a force incomprehensible to him, Slater decided to purchase a gun seen in a pawn shop.

He puzzled over a resolve to kill himself.

In a hotel suite upon a king-size bed, he awoke on his back, on unmade sheets, naked. In the darkened room he saw his stiffened manhood wilting like a flower desperate for water. A woman was escaping into a crack of light from an opening/closing door.

Slater turned on a light. He examined the cuts across his chest. He found money, thousands of dollars, stuffed inside the lining of his leather coat. He checked out of the hotel. He took a cab to the airport. He found a small gun in one of his pockets. He handled it like he might a live tarantula, disposing it under the seat. At the airport, he purchased a tourist satchel, a paperback novel, a visored hat, and dark glasses. His travel plans expanded upon finding the laminated document with his photo that his manager handed him days before. His passport. To have been used for the Dyslexic Dogs' European tour he would now miss. Holding a carry-on bag, Slater drifted through the corridors of this congested way-station. He explored the available destinations.

He purchased a one-way ticket to Rome.

At the London airport, he changed his mind and got off the plane with his luggage. He rode a double-decker tour bus across the city but failed to get back on after strolling about and discovering a pub called the Spread Eagle.

He drank warm beer and told lies.

He sold paintings. He painted houses. He renovated houses. He was a developer who hated himself for destroying countrysides. He was an environmentalist hiding from the law. He had sabotaged a timber mill. No, he was a roaming poet.

The owner of the Sleeping Dog Inn, a woman gifted with wit, beauty, and a decade more experience than Slater, took a fancy to his face and troubled soul. She invited him to lodge with her for an unspecified stay. She tended to his psychological wounds. He shared her enormous bed. He helped greet the guests of her establishment, serving wine and beer at the bar, and began writing in a journal she had given him as a Christmas present. His present to her was a black jade ring he found in a pawn shop. A gift she misinterpreted. When she expressed her desire to have his baby, he wrote her a sad love sonnet and departed.

Crossing the English Channel by underwater rail, Slater entered the daylight of France.

He declared his possessions – three shirts, an extra pair of jeans, underwear, socks, and his journal – and was allowed to enter the country. Unable to speak the language, he understood little of what was being said, yet found the romantic babble a refreshing change.

Having grown a beard, his hair trimmed, he vaguely resembled his passport photo taken for the Dyslexic Dogs' world tour which would have been concluding in Germany, had he not vanished.

At a sidewalk cafe he picked up an abandoned newspaper off a table and flipped through the incomprehensible French. He scanned pictures, imagining the stories, and recognized a face he knew. His own. It was buried in a back section. He slumped in his chair with the notion someone might recognize him, but only received the usual aloofness reserved for foreigners.

He attempted to decipher the words.

"*Musicien... chanteur... poète...* Dyslexic Dogs... *disparu... trés fou réputation... présomption... mort...*"

Presumed dead?

While pondering the meaning of his demise, he met a French model, Bénédicte, at a nearby table. She was learning English and agreed to travel with him by rail to Rome. They made love in a box car and proposed marriage, laughing, while consuming champagne. Their naked bodies were entwined for most of the ride through the Italian countryside.

In Rome, he stayed with her at the station while she awaited the arrival of her fiance, who offered Slater a ride in his Peugeot to the Forum where he and Bénédicte exchanged a farewell kiss.

Meandering about, he strolled onto the Via dei Fori Imperiali, daydreaming about pagan rituals, and came upon the Colosseum, where he collided with a bicyclist. The culprit was an art student from Hong Kong, Ling Ho, who spoke fluent English and invited Slater to explore the museums with her. She was majoring in Renaissance anatomy and took him to museums to stare at a bare-breasted Madonna, a naked Apollo chasing after a naked Daphne, *The Rape of the Sabine*, a virginal Venus presented in a half shell. This plethora of nakedness inspired Ling Ho to invite Slater to her apartment to expose her own nakedness.

Several weeks later, Ling Ho returned home to China and Slater left for Greece, feeling artistically restored and invigorated from their advanced course in anatomical pleasures.

He languished next on the beaches of many isles, and upon tanned post-virginal goddesses. Slater continued to drift, venturing from one mysterious tombstone ruin to another and pausing to reflect on the significance of each glorious civilization gone forever. He felt destined to sail across the Mediterranean Sea and found an available berth on an antique vessel.

During the voyage Slater meditated on the wind and waves and came to know the lingering spirit of Odysseus. His beard had grown long and his hair straggly. He realized he was suffering from injury. Episodes from his recent past had been obliterated. How, why, and by whom, he didn't know. He only knew he had not escaped its phantom clutch by thrashing about the world. He'd been traveling from one country into the next and into the same state of denial. He glimpsed particles surfacing, debris floating on the ocean, wreckage emanating from the murky depths of his mind. Intermittently, he saw his fate in a thunderclap of light – up ahead, befallen, his head, toppled and rolling across a stage. Fading to black.

Days later, Slater found himself staring at the mouth of a tomb. He was in Jerusalem and had paid a boy, touting to be a tour guide, to show him the sites – where Jesus was crucified, where Christ was buried and reborn. Taken to a rocky hill resembling a large skull, Slater looked, not knowing what to think. Was this the place of the miracle? Slater glanced at tourists, like himself, perplexed by their own lives. The weather was extremely hot. Slater was carrying his leather coat and satchel in one hand. His other hand unbuttoned his shirt to let in air. He touched the cuts across his chest, examining the wounds. In the process of healing. Turning into scars. Something horrific had happened. But what...he had no idea. By traveling he had hoped to stumble upon the answer.

Slater wiped sweat from his face and closed his eyes. The words from many sermons began swirling through his head. He heard the voice of his aunt reminding him, "'Ask and you shall receive, seek and you shall find, knock and the door will open.'"

Slater felt lightheaded. He opened his eyes The sun beat down and he raised a hand to shield his vision. Slater said aloud, "He also said the gate was narrow and the way to life difficult to find."

"Excuse me?" asked his guide.

Slater recalled the boy and said, "Nothing."

Weeks passed before he discovered the Nile – by foot, by bus – by accident. He bargained with a smiling Egyptian over the cost of his passage down the river. "Up Nile," insisted the man, "not down. *Up* always costs more." Tired of haggling, Slater offered the remains of his net worth and was allowed to board the small vessel.

Disembarking at Cairo and walking to the crest of a sand dune, Slater watched the sun set behind the shapes of Mycerinus, Khafra, and Khufu. A triad of long-suffering siblings who had lured him to this place through picture books, via teachers who had inspired the journey, encouraging him to witness these mind-wrenching wonders. Why? These ancient piles of rock exemplified mankind's misguided obsessions. Each pinnacle a manifest cry for some revelation.

Incrementally, these monuments all wasted away.

Presently, the daytime crowds had vanished. The guided tours had been abandoned hours before. Slater was left alone to stare at the broken face of the Sphinx.

Another crumbling icon.

An elaborate pile of worthless rubble.

An unsolvable riddle.

No divine wisdom imparted.

Only lightness departing, becoming darkness visible.

Slater heard the wind cresting over the dunes in a sand-howl of laughter. It rose to a challenge. He cast his fate to this beckoning desert and discarded his satchel. Journal too, after scribbling a final entry: *I am going insane. Northwest. I believe.*

—9—
Reentry

It was the Sea of Tranquility.

Slater's spaceship was floating on a summer's pool in space.

He understood the continuum of time: It had stopped.

The vapor trail of dreams was a supernova.

He saw the face of the waters.

Light divided from the darkness, and it was good.

Slater looked down upon the whole of creation and thought it wasn't half bad.

Disturbed from his slumber, he dropped to another level.

He was in a ship at sea under attack. Storm waves smashed him against the shore. The beach cracked open and he plummeted into the cradle of cold alien arms. Beings that were gloved and masked. He screamed as they smacked him about.

"This is all quite interesting," said Doctor Weiner, smoking a pipe. It wasn't lit. He was sucking air. "And you say you *saw* God? *The* Creator. And..." He flipped through his notes. He had tagged pages with dayglow Post-its. The books stacked on the tables and shelves were flagged with more bright colors.

"You like books?" asked Dr. Weiner.

"Where am I?" Slater was lying on a couch. It had been turned into a bed, a blanket draped over him, pillows under his head.

"You were saved," said Weiner. "You almost died. And, well, look, you are my first. Our Arab brothers have honored our peace agreement and have brought you to me. Like an offering. I believe it's a sign from Almighty God."

"You didn't answer me," said Slater.

"My home." Weiner blinked cheerfully behind his glasses and removed them to wipe smudges with his shirttail. He was a thin man lost within the loose linen of his shirt and pants. "My humble abode. Welcome."

Slater lifted his head. His face was throbbing. It was badly cut, bandaged, bruised, and blistered. The structure sheltering him was made from earthly composites of mud, sand, wood, and straw. The windows had no glass. The openings were filled with blinding light.

"Remain still. You must rest," said Weiner.

42

"How long have I been awake?"

"Awake? Who can say? You've been babbling for days. But, awake? It's all truly perplexing. Truly." Doctor Weiner rose to get something, forgot what it was, and sat down. "Water?"

"Yes, thanks," said Slater. "What was it I said?"

"Said? Well, who *can* really say?" The doctor smiled as if to laugh but frowned. He rose again from the plain wooden chair and it screeched against the rock floor. "Oh, yes, *water,* yes – water!"

Weiner fled through the open door to get it. He rushed back, slowing as he approached with a pitcher and cup. Slater reached for the cup but his host stopped and proclaimed, "What an *idiot* I am! Forgive me, I am Doctor Henry Weiner. And you...are?"

"John."

"*John,* it's nice to know your name."

"Or Slater. I prefer that."

"Did you say Hadar?" said Weiner. "As in *Genesis?*"

Slater's lips were swollen. "Slater. As in *slate.* The rock?"

"Ah, the *rock!* Like Peter. Wait." Weiner closed his eyes. Slater dropped his hand from fatigue, unable to hold it up any longer. His eyelids closed too.

Weiner kneeled and dribbled water onto his guest's bare feet which extended beyond the blanket.

"What—the—*hell!*" The sensation startled Slater into standing. He became dizzy and fell back to the couch. "Are you *crazy?*"

"Crazy? Well," Weiner blinked sheepishly.

"What was that about?"

"In case...well. Anoint me too if you'd like."

"What?"

"Here," offered Weiner, "have a drink."

"In case of what?"

"You know."

"No, I don't—oh, *Jesus*—"

"Well," Weiner squirmed submissively and started to move about. "I do feel *something.* Spiritually."

"You are crazy," said Slater.

"Well that depends...if what you said is true."

"I was delirious. What did I say?"

"Exactly?" Weiner added a little hop in his step as he paced. His hands rubbed together and his fingers produced a little steeple that fluttered away. He pointed at Slater. "A good many things, John. Slater. *Mysterious* things. Are you familiar with the Bible? Genesis? The Psalms? The Proverbs? Gnostics?"

"Yes, not really," said Slater. "A little, maybe."

"The Revelation of *John*?"

"No," said Slater. "Parts."

"Parts?" said Weiner. "Ah, and the *parts* compose a whole. Like a cryptogram from the Almighty. I modestly confess I've read them all. Several times. But who's counting? Let's just say I—"

"Where is this place?"

"Place?"

"Geography? *Location*?"

"The Wilderness of Zin," said Weiner. "Ever hear of it?"

"No," said Slater.

"Well, there you are," said Weiner.

"The Middle East?" said Slater.

"Good guess," said Weiner.

"You said you were a doctor."

"Yes, I am, indeed."

"A psychiatrist?"

Weiner blushed, then blinked, removing his glasses to clean them fervently again as he laughed. He retrieved his pipe from the table and sucked air from it as he spoke. "Veterinarian, actually. Anthropologist, you can add. Theologian, too. And, John – *Slater,* you prefer that, my apologies, I'll make greater efforts to remember next time – I do know a *prophet* when I come across one."

"How often does that happen?"

Weiner blinked, beaming. "You're my first."

Slater poured himself a cup of water. His swollen lips made it painful and difficult to drink. "Doctor, or—"

"Call me Henry," said Weiner.

"I remember some of what I said. The earth opening. Aliens slapping me. I'd hardly regard that nonsense as prophesy."

"Prophesy? Oh, *that!* You're perfectly right." Weiner tapped the bowl of his empty pipe on the table. "A psychiatrist I am not, but it is my belief you were reliving the birth experience."

"Damn. My mother...." Slater touched his blistered lips.

"What about your mother?"

"Cut open. I was born...Cesarean."

"Cesarean?" said Weiner. "Well, that would explain—"

"Henry, what are you doing?"

The voice was authoritative and deep in volume.

"Hail, Caesar!" Weiner saluted a huge silhouetted figure in the doorway. "John – *Slater*, he prefers that – may I present to you your distinguished doctor. Doctor Bryant Briard."

"Henry, leave us."

— 10 —
End Over End

Slater pushed open the glass doors of The Metro and walked outside to observe the evening activity. The air was crisp. His breath made a visible cloud. The fog had cast a spell of stillness. Everyone and everything was peaceful, as if this blanket of mist was tucking them in for a cozy night.

He stood there trying to comprehend the elaborate deception. The people moving past him seemed unaware that the world was at war and their lives were in peril. Was it a clever ruse? A stratagem designed to mislead him? Or was it a mechanism for their survival? Was reality a mirrored ball reflecting a paradox of contradictions? Did humans accept this on faith to stay sane while balanced on this chunk of rock hurtling end-over-end through space?

"Hello," said a woman carrying packages. She walked past him and Slater returned her smile. He absently scratched his face and felt the vertical scar. A link to a memory, to a time when he had lost his balance confronting this whirling deception. Falling hard, face first. He needed a shave, feeling the stubble, and yawned. Was it wrong to take refuge in moments of pleasure, whenever found, while others were suffering in the world? It was tempting to join the ranks, these passersby, who appeared happy, at least content. Every one of them had a shiny metallic neurocircuit embedded in their foreheads.

The crash to earth and the jolt to his head had rattled his brain. Slater had forgotten he was wearing a hat and instantly removed it. Covering one's neurocircuit was considered an act of disobedience and cause for circumspection. Also arrest, if seen by a Cyberguard. He saw a man wearing mittens and a knitted cap who was crossing the plaza, then noticed a woman with bangs covering her forehead. Slater touched the side of his head to examine the laceration and coagulation in progress, then attempted to straighten and smooth the matted hairs over the cut. He wiped his fingers on the lining of his jacket to remove any trace of blood. He returned the hat to his head. Keeping pressure on the wound was priority one.

He removed a tiny cellphone. An ALERT message was flashing. The antiquated device had a voice broken by static: "*...not kill me... you will not...escape...will...be tortured...*" The threat incomplete, ending abruptly. The actual time of the call could not be specified. And futile to try and trace. His nemesis, Cy, had a knack for stealth and reveled in this chess game of wits – taunting after each victory, declaring, "Game over, friend."

If Cy was alive, Slater knew what that meant. *Checkmate.*

Slater tried to summon up some vision of a clue that might help him survive. The sticky residue of blood felt on his fingers got him to remember the reason he had come to this bar. The Crossroads, now known as The Metro, had once been a designated rendezvous. A last resort, when all else failed.

Shivering, Slater increased the temperature of his thermosuit. He heard music and saw carolers wearing costumes from centuries long ago. Encased inside a glass quadrant across the street, their voices poured from granite obelisks cornering the park. They were harmonizing, *"Have yourself a merry little Christmas…Let your heart be light…From now on our troubles will be out of sight…"*

Something was horribly wrong.

The city was too perfect, too peaceful — meaning, abnormal. Couples were walking hand in hand. Children were laughing and pointing at animated displays in store windows. An elderly man was selling hot chestnuts from an antique cart.

Something was definitely not right.

Slater felt lost, between states of consciousness, in a place where dreams lingered transparent. The glass-domed enclosure across the street suddenly transformed into a summer's day in an urban park. He saw people sun-bathing on towels, reading books, having picnics. He saw himself and Sherry and their daughters, Sondra and Mercy. They were standing on the lawn tossing a frisbee. Truffles, their dog, was barking and chasing after the whirling disk.

Slater blinked and the memory vanished, overtaken by winter. He looked down and noticed the pavement. It was embedded with sparkles and stars. He closed his eyes and made a prayer to God, still grasping for a scrap of hope. The connection to Sherry was still programmed to memory. A number from years ago.

"You have reached a deactivated terminal, if you would like—"

Slater slammed the phone into a garbage container. He was about to reenter The Metro but corrected his decision by turning.

He approached a man wearing an orange and purple snowsuit who was loitering beside the trash container and who was holding to his ear Slater's cell phone – which Slater took back.

"That's mine."

The man made no protest. Meekly, he held out his palm.

Slater searched his pockets. He placed a few LoyalMarks in the man's grimy hand. He walked back inside and stood beside the bar. He watched the musicians as they tuned their instruments. The band had a horn section with a saxophone and trumpets. There was a man plucking at the strings of an electric violin. And a harp was being wheeled on stage. Slater was impressed. This band was nothing like the Dyslexic Dogs.

He noticed their drummer seated at the bar and clicking his drumsticks against the countertop to get the bartender's attention.

Slater felt a playful squeeze to his bottom before locating the source – from the amber waitress who had sailed past. She smiled, looking back, holding her tray of drinks. "Why so glum?" Stage lights silhouetted her naked body through her gown as she teased him with a frown, before smiling, "Let your heart be light."

He knew this woman, but the memory of when and where would not surface from the murky depths.

Slater returned to his place at the bar. The drummer downed a shot of the sweetly-vile blue liquid and rolled his eyeballs to express pleasure and proclaimed, "I drink to celebrate the rise and fall of *all* leaders! 'How thou art hath fallen from heaven, O Lucifer, son of the morning!' Ya see, Morty, all leaders require obedient followers. And *obedience* requires a power source. And all leaders, in the end, demand ultimate consumption, leading to corruption, a power surge, and one powerful collapse. Ha! Am I not right, eh?"

The bartender chuckled, his shaved head nodding as he shook a martini. He refilled the drummer's glass with blue liquid, pausing to brush tinsel off a tuxedo jacket he wore over a black T-shirt. "Here, Smitts, go at it. Kill yourself. It's Christmas."

"Ah—right." He sang out poetically: "And the Devil moaned and groaned and was heard lamenting as he crashed and burned out of sight, saying 'To all a Merry Christmas, and to *hell* with your life!'"

The drummer stood, regarding the stage, then sat back down. "One more, Morty, one more. Time for one more shot."

Slater studied the drummer's profile. He had the same name as his old friend, drummer for the Dyslexic Dogs. The wrong Smitts, but Slater felt compelled to ask. "You look familiar. I don't suppose you were here when this place was called The Crossroads?"

The drummer turned his head with an alarmingly prescient wide-eyed smile. "Would it make a difference, friend, if it was now, as opposed to being then? Think about it." He gulped down his drink and swiveled to face Slater.

"The tapeworm of time travels both directions."

"Tapeworm?" said Slater.

"Time is a parasite. Travels right through our guts. It *lives* off us. A ravenous creature."

Slater smiled at this nonsense. "So what's your advice?"

Smitts tapped his glass. "I ignore Time. We're *stale*-mates."

"How long have you been with this band?"

"Forever." Smitts drum-rolled the bartop with his forefingers. He stood and extended a hand. "Name's Smitty. And you, my friend, *whom* might you be?"

"Would it matter?"

The drummer laughed and slapped Slater's hand. "Not a bit, not a damned bit. Shit, shit, I've got to play. Hear the harp? The angel, she's calling me. Irresistible. Look at her. Look!"

Slater looked at the harpist. "Yeah, she's remarkably beautiful. But you didn't answer my question. About The Crossroads?"

"No, no. You're right. Sticks. Where–are–my–sticks?"

The bartender was tapping liquor bottles with the drumsticks and making small talk with a waitress.

"Morty, give me *those*. Promptly, please. Give–give–give!"

The bartender held up the drumsticks. "Soon as you pay."

"Keeping tabs, are we? You know I'm good for it, Mort."

"Hell you are. Here—go beat your drums."

Smitts grabbed his drumsticks, saluted, then took a backward step toward the stage. "It is a prerequisite for a percussionist to have a sense of timing. It's a *feeling*, knowing when to come and go."

"Like a tapeworm?" said Slater.

The drummer laughed. "Precisely—yes! Learn to live *with* it, because it will live with or without you. Enjoy, my friend."

The drummer's departing wink and smile seemed parasitic.

Or so Slater felt in his gut.

— I I —
Domestic Blitz

At age seven, Slater saw the gradual loss of tranquility. Water dripped from faucets. Plants were overgrown, most of them dying, others dead in their pots for months. Dishes were piled in the sink. The fireplace smoked. Light bulbs flickered.

When Hanna had been living, the house was always fully alive. There was singing. Show tunes and soulful melodies enlivened the rooms and connecting cavities where she dusted. Books were placed between bookends. A clear view of sunlight could be seen through the windows. Freshly cut flowers adorned vases.

Sanity.

In the aftermath was the whirring and whining of electric tools. Sawdust, metal splinters, and plastic chips now floated and settled like a dirty snowfall on the furniture and floors.

Skunk, their dog, was overjoyed by these casual arrangements.

Slater adored his Aunt Hanna, fondly remembering her. As a child, he had no way of knowing how much her presence had meant. Or what her absence would bring.

The slow unraveling reminded Slater of a summer vacation. His uncle kept in touch with an old friend from high school who was the assistant concierge for the Park Palace Hotel in New York City. So, after crossing the schizophrenic landscapes from state to state — down a twisting blue coastline, across arid desolation, over purple mountains, through majestic heat, past verdant growth, lightning, humidity, wind, sleet, snow, sun — Paul, Hanna, and their nephew-adopted son arrived.

Slater's first sight of Manhattan was viewed from a distance through a bug-blasted windshield. From far away, looking down on the strange island, with its many rising shafts of steel and stone, he thought it resembled a cemetery.

They stayed in one of the larger tombstones.

The Park Palace was indeed palatial. After hours of squeaking up and down in his uncle's Falcon, desperately in need of shocks, Slater braced himself against the gold filigree of the reception desk. From the long terrestrial cruise, he hadn't adjusted to solid land.

This was his first taste of opulence.

The vast interior overwhelmed him like a Heavenly Gate.

Harry T. Turner was his uncle's old friend. He resided within the lower depths of the hotel and allowed Paul and family to stay at no expense as his honored guests in an adjoining bedroom.

The faucets dripped. A kitchenette held dirty plates. The blank dirty walls yearned for windows and air.

In this underworld where his uncle reminisced and drank beer, Hanna avoiding it as often as she could by shopping above ground, Slater was thrilled to explore the hidden depths. He found strange glowing rooms devoted to reviving stressed plants, another room piled with cabinets and mattresses, other rooms crammed with failed appliances from telephones, televisions, coffee makers, clocks to bun warmers. He came upon and befriended a grey cat that resided in the stairwell crevices. He named the cat Twilight and together they explored deeper and deeper until they found rumbling boilers and furnaces and washers and dryers. A spider-haven cement corridor of dank space led them to a dungeon of ancient dust and mildew, where foundation met soil. The bottom.

Slater opened a door and felt a chill backwash through him. Darkness visible. It was as if he was staring into space without the aid of moon or stars. Was there even a floor, he wondered. Would it be an endless fall if he stepped inside? He felt for a light switch on the other side of the wall when something moved as quick as a heart flutter. Twilight yowled and fled. Slater's legs were frozen in place, refusing to budge, as if held captive and forced to glimpse the winged figments of a shape-shifting dream before he broke free to stumble and run up a flight of stairs, through a door, down a maze of hallways, trying to find his way to the top. He found an elevator, pushed a button. The doors separated and he rushed in and they closed behind him like an ornate casket.

Slater tried to catch his breath. He was locked inside a hollow cage that was moving slower than antiquity. He failed to mentally will the arrow to move faster on its arc upward and questioned the reality of his ascent. He feared he might actually be traveling down until he felt a jolting stop, the doors widening, and he emerged into the brilliant gold and crystal refractions of the Park Plaza lobby.

His aunt had been searching for him and was surprised to see him running wildly at her with tears steaming from his eyes. He clutched the warm cushion of her body and refused to let go of her.

"Goodness, child, what on earth has gotten into you?"

Slater looked blankly at his uncle.

"You look dazed," laughed Paul. "See a ghost? This would be the place, I imagine."

They took flowers to the cemetery on weekends. His uncle kept a small broom in his car which he used to dust off Hanna's grave. It was the only place he even attempted to keep clean after her passing. Skunk was released from his leash to run around and pee on the other grave sites.

On Sundays, Hanna had always taken Slater to church.

At age seven young Slater had been proud to wear a coat and tie. Yet he complained for the sake of his uncle who disbelieved in wearing ties or going to church unless when forced – by Hanna on Easter Sunday. The table saw bellyached raucously, ripping apart wood or plastic beneath the floorboards as Hanna and young Slater left for the short drive to church.

Most mornings young Slater was sent off to Sunday School. But this one special day he was allowed to stay with the adults.

He remained in the front pew while Hanna left to sing in the choir. She was transformed when she emerged from a back room. Ascending the scarlet steps, she was among a group of men and women all wearing blue and gold satin robes. Their communal voices rose with a force that captivated him like a sunburst. He could hear their majestic flight and imagined them as birds soaring in a united swarm of spangled wings. He pictured the green valleys, the sunlit clouds, and a spectrum of mist over wildflowers.

When it ended, Slater clapped and embarrassed himself in the hush of silence that followed.

"You were *great*, Auntie," he whispered upon her return.

"Hush now. That wasn't me," said Hanna. "God bless you for saying so. Be still now."

Slater sank into a confused morass of standing, kneeling, page turning. He was unable to concentrate on the words and sang off key. His aunt bumped against his body and shared a smile with him.

On the drive home Slater asked, "Where did you go?"

"When was this?"

"If it wasn't you," he said, "who else was singing?"

"What on *earth* are you talking about?"

"You told me it wasn't you up there," said Slater.

Hanna gave the horn a solid honk.

"The Lord sure blessed me with you," she laughed. "He sure did. Johnny, where do you *think* I went?"

Slater sensed she was on the verge of confessing, but was taking too long. So he confessed instead, "I don't know."

"'If I glorify myself,' Jesus told us, 'my glory is nothing. It is my Father who glorifies *me*,'" said Hanna.

Slater tried to comprehend this glorification, but couldn't.

"When I sing, Johnny, God sings *through* me. He sings through all of us. We're all the instruments of God."

Slater recoiled, recalling how bad he had sung. "We are?"

"Oh, yes. *Even* your Uncle Paul." Hanna glanced at him with her eyebrows raised. "An instrument who could use a good lick of polish and fine tuning." She glanced back, holding back her smile, getting Slater to laugh.

Madly In Love

Sherry Knowles found Slater sleeping in a trash dumpster behind San Francisco City Hall. She worked as a court stenographer. Debris boxes had been deposited near the building while the historic building underwent renovation. She was searching for her car keys inside the clutter of her purse when she came across and pulled out a miniature notebook. Flipping through the pages triggered a reflex of emotions. The tiny book was filled with shorthand inscriptions. She shut her eyes, squeezed her fingers around it, then tossed it into the dumpster.

The book landed on Slater, awakening him and startling her.

She didn't recognize him, nor did he recognize her, at first.

No one recognized him or knew who he was anymore. Except for Henry Weiner who had doggedly followed Slater back from the Middle East to the United States of America and who was sleeping in the dumpster next to Slater's.

While in Jerusalem, Weiner had told him, "I grew up in New York. I know the States." He was attempting to convince Slater he would be a good traveling companion. Eager to please, Weiner was grinning like a dog, trailing Slater as he ventured through the streets.

"I don't care. Get lost," said Slater.

"I am. *Truly.*" Weiner smiled benevolently, comically, before stopping to wipe his glasses. "Wait!"

Bryant Briard was lecturing at the Hilton that afternoon and had given them a ride to the city in his Range Rover.

"How are you planning to arrive in America?" asked Weiner, catching up to Slater. "You have no money. No identification. You could be arrested. Thrown in jail."

"I have a passport," said Slater.

"Passport? No you don't," said Weiner.

"It's sewn into the lining of my jacket," said Slater. "I may be insane but I'm not a fool."

"Fool?" said Weiner. "No, no, I've been saying that all along. I believe your predictions."

"I don't have predictions," said Slater.

"You do," said Weiner. "I took notes."

"I was temporarily insane. It's *my* problem. Let it go."

Weiner stepped in front of Slater.

"There—there, you see? Our greatest prophets suffered the same fate! You're one of them, John."

"Piss off," said Slater.

"Darn—*Slater*, I meant to say. Wait!"

Dejected, Weiner stopped. He sought the sky for guidance.

Slater kept walking. The weight of guilt slowed him to a stop. If not for this perplexing, wheedling creature, he might have died. Slater turned to see where Weiner had gone. He hadn't moved.

Weiner was overjoyed and ran toward him.

"*Shit,*" said Slater and kept walking.

Weiner caught up. He was lugging his worldly possessions in a backpack. He wore a white linen suit that was clean but threadbare at the hem of his collar, pants, and sleeves.

"I could be of help," he said.

"Thanks for the offer," said Slater, "but I don't—"

"Need help? Ah, but you do." Weiner fanned Slater with local currency. "I have money. Enough for two plane tickets. Perhaps enough for a taxi ride too. Here, it's yours. It's to share."

They had arrived at an intersection. It was congested with cars and people. There was noise from bells and chanting. A religious procession with devotees holding teetering polls of incense was now approaching them diagonally from another street. On the opposite corner a man was proclaiming a repetitive lament of sounds.

Slater looked at Weiner. "What the hell's he saying?"

Weiner translated: "'Tomorrow the world will end.'"

"It wouldn't surprise me," said Slater.

"He's wrong. It all ends a week from Tuesday."

Slater laughed.

"Like my joke?" said Weiner. "See, I can be entertaining."

Slater pondered over his options. He could make a collect call. To whom? Wolfe? Electra? Have money wired? Reporters would be waiting at the airports. With cameras? The police?

"No fanfare, we could arrive unnoticed," said Weiner, guessing Slater's thoughts. "Or, remain here, take your chances. You could become a waiter. Can you cook? How's your Kosher? You could stand on the street corner shouting prophesies. I, for one, solemnly swear not to stone you."

Weiner smiled, then Slater smiled. Decision made.

Now this.

He had returned to the age of thirteen. Roy and Heather had arranged for his transfer to another school. He was attempting to adjust and make friends. His attention was on a certain girl. She had blond hair, a ponytail and breasts that were budding, and a face that possessed the most beautiful of smiles.

With delicious energy she bounced and split, cartwheeling across auditorium floors, over lacquered wood the color of butterscotch and carmel. He sat on the bench during basketball games and she would be close, summoning the crowd to shout and cheer. As a replacement guard he was rarely sent into the game. Only when their team was winning by several digits or losing badly (and the coach had resigned himself to a foul mood and wanted to suffer even more) was Slater ever sent in to run and dribble about on the court. But once, at a critical moment, he tossed the ball into the air and – to his and everyone's surprise – it swooshed through the hoop! Their school lost the game, but the screams and cheers aroused by his too-little-too-late three-pointer had made this girl he adored scream and shake her pom-poms.

She smiled at him as they passed in the hallways, but rarely gave him a second look. Still, he believed a connection had been made.

At a Christmas party, earlier that year, she heard his thoughts.

In some secret way she too was strange.

As a transfer student, Slater skulked self-consciously about the campus. Infested with pimples, he felt as unwelcomed as a spotted unclassified animal transferred from a condemned zoo or doomed planet. So he was surprised when she accepted to dance with him at a school function. She even put on a good show and appeared to be enjoying herself. They danced to a second song. Followed by a slow song, during which she rested her head upon his shoulder.

His desire for her grew into a slow erection.

In the dark regions of his mind he declared his anguished love for her. She pushed him away. Her startled eyes startled him too. Had she imagined his thoughts – the want of his hands to grope her soft breasts and body? He wasn't sure of her words either as he questioned her mutely with a blank look. She suddenly dashed from him like a doomed princess, exclaiming — "*Oh my god, my parrots are outside. I'm bait. They're waiting to divide me bones!*"

Later that night, while mulling it over in bed, his hand stroking his penis, Slater unscrambled the code: "*Oh, my god, my parents are outside. I'm late. They're waiting to drive me home!*"

She had placed her lips upon his and then was gone.

Not a dream, but reality. He found it to be...ecstasy.

Upon her exit, Slater had sought refuge against a wall, then slid down upon a metal chair that had been dutifully unfolded so he could partially hide the monster that had reared its swollen head inside his pants which this girl had stirred.

On the following school morning, he saw her coming for him down the hallway. Her smile was glorious like a sunbeam, coming up fast and exposing colors – sky, grass, graffiti, pimples! In bright daylight he was ugly, a beast outside his cave, awkwardly caught off guard, out of his element. How could she love such a monster?

Slater clearly recalled the look on her face.

He recalled her name too: Sherry Knowles.

She was backing away. For a different reason this time, but with the same beatific look of shock and confusion.

Once again, Slater fell madly in love.

—13—
Seeing Angels

Wolfe heard about Slater's whereabouts while auditioning for another band. The Solar Eclipse was looking for a new bass player. Their's was unavailable, serving a three-year sentence for auto theft and possession of a deadly weapon.

Solar Eclipse's reputation for drug abuse and explicitly foul lyrics was something Wolfe felt he should consider before joining. But he was in need of a fast transfusion of cash to keep his style of affluence alive. He wore torn jeans, a leather vest, and was shirtless to display his tattoos — a tacit way of expressing in the face of things a blatant disregard for the days ahead.

This, of course, was a lie.

If Slater was not already dead (as most had assumed, but not Wolfe), he was going to murder the AWOL son-of-a-*dog* himself.

The audition was an insult. The Dyslexic Dogs had been huge. Granted, a "flash in the pan" as pronounced by the *Rolling Stone* musicologists and other tone-conscious critics. He was tuning his guitar in the cellar of a defunct nightclub which the owners, between leases, allowed the Eclipse to use by paying a minimal amount. And also to live there. Their lead singer, who called himself Rot, was brushing his teeth as he crossed the cold concrete floor to greet Wolfe. He spit foam into a plastic wine glass located conveniently on an amplifier. It was almost noon.

"So, Wolfe," said Rot, "didn't know you could still play."

The other members laughed.

"Fuck you," said Wolfe, bantering back. "Rumor has it you've been poking yourself. Getting too high to sing?"

"Naw, I *sing*, man. Like the sting of a predator." Rot spit into the plastic again. "Question is, Wolfe, are *you* up for our flight?"

"Warp was out there," said Wolfe. "A rageous album."

"Yeah, those vibes had teeth," Rot grinned, exposing his gold-capped incisors. "What's the word on your man Satyr?"

Wolfe shrugged, "Fuck if I know—or care."

"Heard this rumor," said Rot, "like his body washed up on the streets again. *Alive*. No shit."

Wolfe had heard reports of Slater's appearance in just about every state or form. "Where this time?"

Rot lit a cigarette. His hands shook. "*Here*, man, in Saint Frank. Downtown. He's a fucking *bum*."

"You saw him?" said Wolfe.

"Naw, a friend. He was buying and made the connection."

"Slater?"

"No, a friend," said Rot, scratching his arms. "Satyr was in this alley sleeping under a box. A fucking cardboard *box!* Yeah, *Slater.* Hair and beard like, like—*this!*" Rot twisted his hands and fingers, exploding them from his head, then flicked and crushed his cigarette beneath a boot. Rubbing his palms, he stomped his feet for warmth. "But *him*. Sure as *shit*. Damn, it's cold. I need a rush of caffeine or something bad, man. Give me a sec, Bro. Wait here."

It was a die-hard slow disintegration, which Wolfe was all too familiar with. The other members of the Eclipse grumbled and sat, resuming to pluck and rattle their instruments. They stopped every minute or so to glance vacantly at the phantom buzzards overhead.

Wolfe granted Rot the benefit of thirty minutes, then muttered to the others as he unplugged his bass. "Like I need *this*? Hey, I've got better things. Thanks, all the same."

He went to search for Slater. A junkie?

Driving his Mercedes down the alleys South of Market, into the Tenderloin, through the Haight, Wolfe felt conspicuously bourgeois even with his tattooed arm displayed in the open window. He pulled to the curb to ask people if they saw anyone resembling John Slater?

"The Fuck—who?"

"Dyslexic Dogs? Lead singer? Satyr? Seen him?"

"Screw off."

"Forget it." Wolfe found a small cafe that served cappuccino. He ordered a double espresso and took a table by the front window. He gnawed on a rock-hard biscotti and tabulated the money he still had in the bank, in some technology investments and mutual funds. The majority of his wealth, having dwindled, was lost in the stock market and he questioned the ability of his broker, an ex-girlfriend. Was she screwing him in some new reverse fashion? Getting even? Fuck for Fuck?

Album sales for *Hydra's Head* had soared and peaked upon

Slater's disappearing act and presumed demise, prior to plummeting.

Wolfe estimated, by year's end, he'd be in arrears, busted.

"Life *sucks*," he groaned.

"So do I," said a waitress, a vision of succulent beauty, who set down his coffee. "But it's extra. Hey, aren't you…wait…you played with…don't tell me…"

Wolfe stood as if seeing the antichrist. "Holy shhh—"

"Dogs!" said the waitress.

"What?" said Wolfe.

"You're a rock star," she said. "A Dog!"

"So I've been told. Here, Angel, keep the change." He gave her fifty dollars, the smallest bill from his wallet.

"Call me," she said as he ran out the door.

"Slater!" he shouted.

The man resembling Slater had disappeared. Gone down some alley? Into a store? Wolfe ran across the street in pursuit. He was struck down by a fast moving white car.

He was certain of its color as the world went blank.

Wolfe next became conscious of an angel leaning over him. She was gorgeous. Her breasts were on the verge of spilling over her silk blouse. He adored the pull of gravity. The fall of luscious apples and delectable fruit. He craved it. Could taste it.

Stark whiteness came again. Glorious fondling. Heaven.

He awoke, the second time, with a delirious headache.

She was still there. His angel. Beyond her were other faces. One in particular who disturbed him. The face disappeared into shadow. Then it reemerged, closer, at a new angle. The sunlight washed over discernable features. Wolfe knew that behind those dreadlocks, the dark glasses and beard, it was Slater.

"Hey, Satyr, you old…"

Wolfe managed a smile before slipping off into unconsciousness for a third time.

—14—
Questionable Gifts

Truffles was a small black terrier. His fur was encrusted with spots of dried mud. His bark was sharp and demanding. He licked Slater's face and saved his life.

Ever since his near-death experience within the Egyptian desert, Slater had become leery of signs. Messages appeared to every living soul. They existed to test a person's sanity.

On his wayward trek, Slater had witnessed a neon sign beside the charred remains of a motel in the middle of nowhere awaken to sputter and illuminate a word: "Vacancy." Apparitions came to him in the form of doormen or as waitresses, before dispersing into air. Was he to heed their advice? When the morning news in sidewalk stands matched the events of his dreams the night before, was he to dismiss them as coincidence?

As meaningless as oil slicks, like false rainbows, were they?

Did truth cohabitate with fallacy?

Could time divorce space?

Were these visions all part of an invisible synaptic whole?

Was existence an opening/closing circuit?

Had he arrived at Insanity. Could this be the place?

Snow was falling in the middle of a desert, a vacant lot. He was lying perfectly still and rising through the fluttering of ice particles. They burned his face, melting almost pleasurably down his cheeks. He closed his eyes to concentrate on the many voices. So soothing. They were calling him back into a deep peaceful slumber.

A frightening face snarled, baring its teeth, startled him awake. The little dog then grinned and licked his face. It got Slater to sit up and lean against the brick wall.

Slater was amazed to see the snowfall, along with this dog.

"Who are you?" Slater asked, shivering. It was the middle of the night. A faltering neon sign lit the alley to a vacant lot.

The dog twitched his ears, then sat too.

Slater extended his mittened hand and the dog raised a paw.

"You're smart," said Slater. "But you know that."

The dog barked.

He checked the dog's neck. No collar.

"You're a stray, like me," said Slater.

Another bark.

"Hungry?"

Slater searched the pockets of his three coats: a leather jacket, parka vest, and long overcoat. He retrieved a miniature box of See's candies that a woman had shoved into his hands while standing on the sidewalk. Three chocolates remained.

"Here, guy." Slater held one up and the dog begged earnestly. "*Bon appétit.*"

Slater ate one himself. He saved the last one for Henry. He then opened his outer coat and the dog approached for shelter and was hugged for mutual warmth. As they both settled into sleep, Slater heard a voice ask:

"Why Truffles, Daddy?"

"What?"

"How did Truffles get his name?" said Sondra.

Slater forgot momentarily where he was. He was playing a game, Chutes and Ladders, on the carpeted floor beside the warmth of a fireplace. His wife, Sherry, was next to him. She had a loving touch that brought him back to his senses. He gave his daughters a smile. "Because, when I first saw Truffles, he was covered in mud. And I was so hungry at that very moment, he made me think of rich buttery chocolate rolled into a ball of candy. Like a Truffle."

"*Yumm,* he sounds delicious," said Mercy.

They all laughed.

A party had started.

Slater realized he had dozed off again.

Sunlight was finding its way through the city towers.

"Hey, Mr. Nobody, it's Christmas. And cold! Have a drink."

Wine was offered. Slater drank it gratefully. The liquor burned down his throat, helping to warm him. He handed the bottle back.

Desiring anonymity, Slater was nicknamed "Mr. Nobody," or "Nobody," to those living on the streets.

"Thanks," said Slater.

"Whose mutt?" said Simms, his breath visible from the cold.

"I suppose, you could say, he's mine?" Slater smiled.

Simms laughed, his lips quivering, hands rubbing together.

"*Nobody's.* I get it," said Margo. She was Simm's girl. She was missing a few teeth. "Here, have the good stuff. Not that rot-gut Daryl's pushing. Sherry's sweet, like me. Take a taste."

Margo had a serrated smile. She was an actress, so she claimed, under a long spell of bad luck. Her dress was a long red flouncy rag. A Salvation Army special. It covered her long underwear and jeans. Her gloved hand held out a bottle.

"Much obliged, my lady," said Slater.

Margo curtsied.

"A bit of herb, my Lord? Spice of the morning?" Riley sucked in a rush of smoke, then offered Slater the cannabis.

Slater inhaled to be neighborly.

"Hey, Nobody," said Simms. "Last night I had that dream, man. That crystal ball you were going on about. Ice cold blue. Came alive and zapped my frigg'n brain like you warned me. Freaking *weird*, man. Don't be screwing with me like that."

"It wasn't my intention," said Slater. "Sorry. I get these visions. It's...nothing. Ignore it."

"Freaking *hell*," Simms laughed, choking on a gust of smoke and coughing. "Ignore it? I think I'm dreaming but I'm waking and *shivering* 'cause it's freak'n *snowing!* Word, Nobody. As in advice. Try envisioning something *warmer* in your next dream."

Slater told him, "I'll try."

"Peace, brother," said Simms. "Something *toasty*. And not the flipside – as in *hellfire*, man."

"Like a warm heavenly bliss," said Slater.

"Now you're talking," said Simms. "Let us be off ye sisters and sinners, animals and cannibals alike. I's got to get *off* on this freak'n white planet. Before my extremities turn into frigg'n snow-*balls!*"

Margo flirted, fluttering her eyelashes, "Our carriage, m' Lord, it awaits." She danced and teetered down the snow-falling alleyway with the rest of them, turning the corner, suddenly out of his mind, like a remnant dream.

"John?" said Weiner. He was standing and bobbing on his toes to stimulate warmth. "Why are we here? This is intolerable. I *never* thought, in a million years, I'd *ever* miss the desert heat."

"This is a desert, Henry."

"Desert? It's *snowing*, John. Or maybe you—oh, yes, right, *desert*. As in a wasteland? Very witty. I'm freezing and starving and you're cheery—making *quips*."

Slater got to his feet and dug into his coat pocket. He pulled out the candy box. Also a tiny notebook. "Have a truffle."

Weiner devoured it greedily. "What's that?"

Slater fanned open the tiny journal full of curlicues and dots. "Cryptic love letters from the woman of my dreams."

Weiner frowned. "It looks like shorthand."

"She was in a hurry," said Slater.

"Can I look?"

Slater placed it in his mittened hand. "Lovely penmanship too."

Weiner glanced at the dog. "Who might this be?"

"Truffles. Like the name?"

"You're a regular *comic* prophet, John. That's what you've become. No offense but..."

"None taken," said Slater.

"Shouldn't we go to a shelter?" Weiner had a blanket draped over his shoulders and around his neck like an enormous muffler, covering two parkas. Buried beneath that was his linen suit and a pair of sweat pants. Weiner had procured an abandoned shopping cart found beneath a freeway offramp, in which he kept his dubious belongings – sleeping bag, shaving kit, backpack with books, some recyclable cans and bottles.

"Churches are offering food," said Slater. "Shall we partake?"

"Hallelujah!" said Weiner.

"Look," said Slater, "Truffles is practically skin and bones."

"As am *I*," said Weiner.

The alley opened into an expanse of more snow.

"What an amazing sight," said Slater. "It's never snowed in San Francisco before. Not like this, I don't think."

"How lucky we are," groused Weiner.

"We are," said Slater, taking it in. "Magnificent."

"*Glorious*," said Weiner, a sarcastic holiday ring to his voice. He blamed his mood on the anguished need for vital sustenance. "They won't allow your new pet inside, you know that."

"He's smarter than you give him credit."

Truffles was making tracks in the snow. Panting and smiling, he was keeping up with Slater much easier than Henry.

"He's a happy little thing," said Slater.

"Well, great, and I'm so *happy* for him," said Weiner, mocking. His long blanket was dragging along the ground and the wheels of his cart were proving to be difficult maneuvering through the snow.

"Henry, leave the damned thing. Take the sleeping bag. Leave the rest."

"No, my books, my—*darn.*" Weiner fought and tugged with the twisting wheels.

"Henry, the more we possess, the more weapons we need for their defense."

"How *wise* we are on this Christmas morning!" Henry was not in the mood to heed any of it. "It's all so *easy* for you."

"Why do you think that?" said Slater.

"Why? I don't know *why*," said Weiner. "It simply *is*. I don't understand you, John. I don't. Truly. I don't."

"We're not meant to be understood. That's God's plan."

Weiner frowned as he pushed on. "John, would it be too much to ask for you to revisit my suggestion? Must we live like this? Let's say, hypothetically, you *were* legally entitled to the money? You had money, once, you mentioned. What harm would there be to *explore* the...the...what?"

Slater had frozen in place. Truffles too. Weiner stopped to see for himself what was so important.

The sky was swirling. Birds were swarming upwards through a funnel of cascading snow, resembling angels, a flutter of brilliance, like a gold dust sprinkling, a pathway of light – which flickered and vanished.

"What—what was it?" asked Weiner.

"A message," said Slater, "maybe."

Weiner searched the sky.

"Message? A sign from God? What—*wait*," Weiner ransacked his backpack for a notepad. He couldn't find a pen that worked. He grabbed a pencil at the bottom of the bag. "John, tell me, I'm ready. What was it you saw?"

Slater moved along. "I'm not really sure."

"Your best guess," said Weiner. "Let me decide. John?"

Truffles barked.

"Good dog. He saw it too." Slater petted Truffles.

"The *dog*—saw what? John, are you mocking me?"

"No, Henry," said Slater. "I saw hope. It was warm and soft. Giving off energy. It appeared to be...like cloth."

"Cloth? As in a shroud? John, are you certain—"

"No. Write down whatever you want."

Truffles barked.

They all turned and stared at the stained glass windows aglow against the grey sky. The church was like a Christmas tree of stone. There was an enormous line of people waiting to get inside.

"John, can you imagine how much *joy* I receive from all your pithy bits of levity? Not that I'm complaining, I assure you. But you haven't exactly said anything even marginally *prophetic* since we've arrived in America." Weiner struggled to free his cart's wheels from the curb. "Merely stating facts. Would you mind giving me a hand here. John?"

Slater was greeting people in the long line.

Weiner was perplexed by Slater. He had the ease of a politician greeting his constituents. He looked noble in his long flowing coat, albeit grimy. Weiner began hatching a plan and picturing himself as Slater's campaign manager as they—*no!* He blinked and groaned, realizing once again how desperate his need for food had become.

"John," shouted Weiner, "save me a place in line!"

Hours later, as they shuffled along with empty trays, they were accosted by smiling volunteers who were dishing out the free food. Weiner was impressed by Slater's patience and cheerful demeanor as the mouth-watering aroma of food was driving Weiner crazy.

Weiner noticed Slater's expression change and his head cock in amused puzzlement, alerted to something.

Another sign? Weiner was prepared to take notes. He reached into his pocket but could only find the memo pad already filled with shorthand that Slater had discovered.

One of the helpers, serving mashed potatoes, was curious too. A spoon hung in suspended animation above Slater's plate. Weiner wished the woman would get on with it! *Drop* the blob of food! His stomach was growling vociferously. He was prepared to grovel like a dog before her if that's what it took to speed things up!

In light of her saintly beauty he excused her inconsiderate lack of concern for *him* — famished and light-headed — and on the verge of collapsing face-first into her steaming tub of potatoes!

"You," said Sherry, irresistible with a smile. "*You* look familiar. Have we met before?" She plopped a heap of creamy potatoes onto Slater's plate and wielded a ladle. It dipped into another bowl as her eyes widened. "Gravy?"

"Yes, please," said Slater. "And, yes, we have."

—15—
Space Oddities

Dr. Bryant Briard was not a religious man. Yet he resided in a place teeming with a multitude of religious zealots and fanatics. The Middle East was where It all began and where It would all end. In fact, the apocalyptic It was common knowledge, fated to occur, at any given day, to those living around these parts.

He accepted none of *It*.

But he was a good man. A healer in the modern vernacular. He was not only a surgeon but a pioneer in biotechnical medicine. He had come to Jerusalem to replace, only temporarily, a colleague he'd known from medical school who, months before, had undergone a triple-bypass on his heart but regrettably died on the table, leaving a permanent vacancy. Briard was surprised by the hospital's generous offer, but more so by his own acceptance to stay.

Briard had become intrigued.

He reclined in a chair. He was a big man, almost seven feet tall. He had been the star center of his high school basketball team but couldn't be persuaded, even by the lure of money, to play in college. He didn't have the luxury. He needed time. Space to think.

At present, he was in a mountain retreat near Mt. Sinai. He was reading about the curvature of space and its effect on time. It was an intriguing concept about the universe, one theorizing that It had no boundaries, but was completely self-contained, and not affected by anything outside Itself. Comparable to sea voyagers discovering they would not fall off the edge of the earth. So too would future space voyagers discover a similar phenomenon.

Briard nudged off his loafers as he drifted deeper in thought.

Was death simply another dimension of life? He thought of a ship disappearing in the horizon, gone from physicality, relative to one's realm of perspective, but continuing on a circuitous course held by universal principles.

If the universe *was* a curvature of space-time, curving back upon itself, finite yet infinite, then there was no real beginning or end.

Was life, therefore, like a continuous dream?

Briard wiggled his toes contentedly.

He loved paradoxes.

Particles of energy tried, as humans tried, to move in straight paths. Why? Because that was their nature. And people, no doubt, believed they were in linear motion. But gravitational forces made everything veer from its chosen path. All paths, therefore, were not straight: they were *bent!*

How true, Briard thought.

A frantic knocking disturbed his quietude. Someone had found him. It would be another emergency. Another force field he could not resist. It was Henry Weiner.

"What?" Briard was tacit. He was known to be.

"You have to *come*, hurry," said Weiner.

"Why?" said Briard.

"*Please,*" said Weiner.

"That won't do, Henry," said Briard. "The reason?"

"There's a dying man," said Weiner.

"There are many. Be specific."

"I can't. I don't know who," said Weiner.

Like a flighty egret picking gnats off a rhinoceros' back — the bird grooming and cleaning, the large mammal providing protection — their relationship had grown into something symbiotic too. Briard sensed this, but had not a clue as to what Weiner's beneficial function was. Yet he liked the man.

"Come in," said Briard.

"No, Sir, you must come with me. It's urgent."

With reluctance he acquiesced, "Very well. Where?"

An hour later, Briard was at Weiner's abode sitting on a stool, staring into Slater's burnt, swollen face. Mostly second degree, a touch of third. Burns that would eventually heal. He inspected the nasty gash down the side of one cheek, too late for stitches. Curious cuts were all across his chest, from another incident, all but healed. The body was dehydrated. But it would survive.

His patient did not appear to be totally lucid with regard to the situation, to the here and now.

"Do you know who you are?" Briard asked.

Slater noticed the doctor's size, remarkable even while seated. He had a vision of Gloria, his ex-band mate, laying naked with this man. Both he and Gloria had strange jewels stuck in their foreheads.

In another flash this enormous man was sobbing at her lifeless body slumped in an iron chair.

"Who the hell are you?" asked Slater.

"I'm a physician. Doctor Briard."

"How do you know Gloria?"

"Gloria who?"

"Where the hell am I?"

Briard showed the faintest of smiles, unable to resist saying, "You are inside the curvature of space and time."

"Makes sense." Slater found it painful, but smiled.

Thus began a curious friendship which would bend Briard's life in unexplored ways.

Briard dismissed Slater's recollections:

Sand dunes transformed to ocean currents, transmitting energy. Waves breaking like static at his feet. Dragons on spherical thrones. Heads contained in a blue sky. Metallic bullets lodged in foreheads. Pyramids in every city. His body falling like a dying star to earth.

"Your basic delirium," said Briard.

"My conclusion too," said Slater. "But have you ever considered what it would feel like to travel at the speed of light?"

Briard frowned. "The thought has crossed my mind."

Slater said, "Time transformed into a vapor trail of dreams. I felt myself swimming in a warm nebulae, like a pool in outer space. I was able to alter the course of time — for good."

Briard was reluctant to ask. "How?"

"I only glimpsed it. Also my death."

"Not surprising," said Briard. "You almost did die."

Slater shook his head, "That's not how I die."

"And you feel certain of this?" countered Briard.

Slater shrugged. "It was like an awakening. Time is equivalent to space, fluid, going forwards and backwards."

"Explain," said Briard.

"Backwards. Like a roll of film. Broken glass becoming whole. Fire sucked and compressed back into the head of a match. Death coming to life. Disorder finding order. That sort of thing. Insane?"

"Well," said Briard. He removed a shoe and rubbed his large aching foot. He was getting both comfortable and uncomfortable.

He was intrigued.

They discussed Imaginary Time.

"In a unification theory of physics," explained Briard, "time would be virtually indistinguishable from directions in space. As a person traveling north or south, up or down, could likewise travel forwards as well as backwards in time."

"Exactly," said Slater. "Instantaneously too."

Briard sat back, cracking the knuckle of a toe. "Explain."

"I can't. I was outside the boundaries of time, beyond the speed of light. I could be anywhere anytime determined by my will." Slater saw the enthusiasm extinguish in the doctor's eyes.

"We are speaking about imaginary time?" said Briard. "Are you familiar with Einstein's theory: $E=mc^2$?"

"Mass cannot reach the speed of light. And, I cannot translate what I experienced. So, for now, I'll have to accept your diagnosis. It was a byproduct of delirium. Okay?"

Dr. Bryant Briard was relatively unsure. His mind, he felt, was being bent unwillingly by a force beyond his control.

Slater sensed a friendship forming. "Whether it was or wasn't a form of insanity, there's little point in debating. Either way, I don't have much choice, do I? I still have to live with it."

Briard was confounded again by this—It. Damn *It!*

16

Holiday Spirits

Roy Frost was in a festive mood. He wore a colorful sweater with reindeer taking flight across his chest. Between his teeth was a pipe with a bearded elf carved into the ivory bowl. He was puffing proud donuts of smoke between salutations.

"You're looking fit as a frigate, Stan," he said to Mr. Knowles. They exchanged firm handshakes. They served on a PTA committee together. They lived blocks apart. "And, here she is, the lovely Mrs. Knowles. Hello, Barbara. Merry Christmas."

Roy pecked her on the lips. He had prepared the holiday punch and had consumed two cupfuls already and was feeling gay. His wife, Heather, was across the room with the Trindles, having moved from the Welters, before moving from the Hofflers. She kept watch over her husband like a circling hawk.

Roy had had affairs with several of their guests over the years. By lavishing equally on all the women, he thought he might divert his wife's suspicions with regard to how many and with whom. She was swooping in and out of his peripheral vision.

"John, for heaven's sake," he laughed, "don't be so stingy! This is Christmas! A full cup of eggnog for Mr. and Mrs. Knowles. Stan, Barbara, I would like you to meet our foster son, John."

Slater extended his hand to be grasped and challenged by the Knowles' grip, which forced a reflex from all recipients to squeeze back in defense against being maimed. It also forced full attention on the bearer of this greeting. Penetrating eyes beneath a bramble of dark unmanageable brows narrowed back at Slater, then a warm smile that stated this *grip* was merely an examination of character.

"You have promise, son," said Knowles. "I can sense your strength of will. Good luck to you."

"Thank you, Sir." Slater smiled, confused by the comment and the girl standing next to him.

"And, my *Lord*," exclaimed Roy, "Stan, Barb, this *can't* be your daughter, Sherry, can it?"

"Yes, it actually is," laughed Barbara with a gush of pride.

"You look—why, so grown up!"

Stan Knowles disapproved of Roy's theatrics. "You act as if

she's sprouted *wings*, for God's sake."

"Hello," Sherry said, giving them a buoyant smile and a show of teenage innocence which is what they expected from her.

Heather had managed to maneuver through the guests to wedge herself between Roy and Barbara Knowles.

Roy sighted the pubescent breasts, not wings, and smoothed his mustache as he spoke directly to her mother, "Sherry is about the age of our John. You can't imagine, not knowing what to expect, all this fostering business completely *new* to us, how impressed Heather and I are with John's good manners and his genuine—"

Blah...Blah...Blah...

Slater's face turned a darker red. He imagined his pimples to be as bright and pronounced as their Christmas tree lights. The empty praise from his foster parents scorched him with embarrassment. All the while this pretty girl continued to stare at him nonchalantly, and he staring back at her. They were both thirteen years old, both their bodies raging internally from hormonal awkwardness.

Slater held out a cup of eggnog for her. Heather was quick to remove it from the girl's hand.

"John, how many times do we have to go over this? Not *this* eggnog," said Heather. "Blue bowl for the adults. Pink bowl for the children. Is that so hard to remember?"

"No, Ma'am."

"*John,* what did we agree upon?"

"Heather," said Slater.

"Thank you. And you are—again?"

"Sherry."

"Of course you are," said Heather, offering a smile, then a wink. "Sherry, make friends with John, won't you, dear. This is a strange new environment for him and we should all try our best to make him feel welcome. Will you do that for me?"

Heather contained her icy beauty in a high-collared periwinkle blue chiffon dress. Before the guests had arrived Slater noticed her slipping a battery pack into the bun of her hair. Tiny ornaments now hung from her ears and blinked on and off. Slater could not deny she was as magnificent as an iceberg, or a malfunctioning traffic light — red-green-red-green — signaling a present breakdown and danger.

She stood there waiting until the smile and nod came from this girl, thus sealing the agreed-upon-bargain to be nice to her son.

Heather then left to inspect more guests.

Slater had a vehement dislike for his third mother at times. But never seriously had he wished her dead. Nevertheless, he anguished from guilt each time he glimpsed her fate. It came in a flash of light, like the fall of a sword, and her decapitation! As if in retribution for these thoughts, Slater envisioned his own life ending the same.

The girl detected his mental turbulence and said, "Thanks, for the eggnog. It was nice to meet you."

Sympathetic to his plight, she smiled, took her cup of eggnog and left to join a group of kids beside the tree. All the ornaments were made of stained glass. The girl looked at him from time to time while he served the eggnog. He watched her laugh and talk. Her face and smile were so deliciously beautiful he imagined them falling in love, walking hand in hand through a cathedral made from tall redwoods. Suddenly the vision became darker. They were inside a cave. A dungeon. People were running for their lives.

She was not as innocent as she appeared, he realized. This only stirred his interest in her more. Overcome with love and lust and a desire to have this girl to himself for eternity, Slater called out her name internally, chanting it like a mantra – *Sherry, Sherry, Sherry* – while standing behind the refreshments. He fantasized her receiving his love signal and smiling blissfully back at him.

She did turn and stare. And it startled him. Her eyes had the look of a gazelle, alerted, wary of a predator. Equally surprised was she, it appeared, to discover his eyes staring at her.

Slater looked away.

He saw Roy pinch the bottom of another guest. This time it was a man, a man whose wiry hair sprouted from his narrow head like an animal in shock. At young Slater he poked a salacious tongue as quick as a snake's through his crooked teeth, and smiled.

"I'm sorry," said Slater, having missed this man's shifting cup and spilling punch on his hand.

"Is this a baptismal tradition of yours?"

The man set his ebony cane against the table's edge and took a napkin bordered in candy canes to wipe his fingers. A cigarette was wedged between pursed lips but removed to sip the eggnog. His cool grey eyes studied the air between them as his lips sucked his cigarette again and opened to emit a smoke ring that traveled toward Slater. Retrieving his cane, the wiry-headed man then meandered off.

This only helped to confirm the wild suspicions young Slater was having about his foster parents and their motives for wanting him. He was in their home to serve at their parties. To please their guests. To rake Heather's sand. He fully expected to be returned to the orphanage like a unwanted gift or an abandoned resolution once the holidays were over and New Year commenced.

Prior to the holidays, Heather had devoted hours inside her glass atrium, surrounded by rocks and sand, to consult with her books to plan the perfect party. Slater had entered to ask if he was allowed to go outside and play.

"Come in here and learn something," she said. "Have you ever seen one of these?"

Heather showed him a diagram on a piece of paper. A pie-shaped circle. There were squiggles of color and geometric shapes. He recognized only the symbol of the half moon.

"Astrology," said Heather.

He received a rare blessing — a smile. She was serene. She wore a purple turban.

"The stars, John. They can tell us where we are."

"They can?"

"And *who* we are, yes," she added. "Do you know who you are, John? Of course you don't."

Her table was a long thick curving slab of redwood on pedestals of stone. Her papers and books were spread over the tree's polished center. Some bamboo and ferns added life to the place. An electric pump trickled water down a faux-finished wall into smooth stones and a pond. Surrounding them was a sea of gravel. They sat on a knoll of pillows. This was her Center.

"Pay attention, John."

She explained that the squiggles represented fish, goats, lions, planets. The pie sections were houses and coordinates of time.

"The moment we are born, John," said Heather, "our path has been set. By cosmic forces. By the planets, the sun, and the moon.

It's a glorious gift."

"It is?" said Slater.

"It is." Heather's piercing eyes overshadowed the serenity of her smile to punctuate this very point. Her voice returned like a steady wind. "I will tell you another secret."

She dug through a stack of papers kept locked in a box carved from cedar.

"This, John, is for the Christmas party Roy and I are planning. I am searching for the perfect date to introduce you to our friends." She laid down another chart taken from inside the box. "This one, John...this chart...is you."

Slater saw more squiggles.

Heather pointed to his name, and a date of birth. "The key to Astrology is time. And place. We know this about you. There's an accurate record from the accident. We were able to ascertain your hospital records. Your birth made the newspapers. I've searched through the charts of many orphans, John. I have. And we believe you are somehow special. No, that is not accurate. We are...yes, *convinced* of it."

"Mr. Frost, Roy," said Slater, "he believes this too?"

"Roy is a Capricorn-Gemini with Virgo rising. In short supply of spirituality, is defined by the Tenth House...and controlled by— his *Venus*." Heather waved him away. She placed her hands flat on the rings of the table to calm herself. "Roy believes in what I *say* is important. You have a place in our family, John. You have no idea what that means, or how important you are to all of—to *us*. Me, and...Roy."

All of us?

Heather, and her astrology, was making Slater nervous. His bladder was rising and on the cusp of overflowing.

"Be still," she told him. "Why are you fidgeting?"

Slater shook his head, denying that he was. He felt trapped in a strange house and needed to urinate badly. Heather fingered her necklace, a menagerie of amphibians and mammals. She was trying to read his thoughts. Her fingers stopped.

"We want you to love us, John. As your parents," she added. "Your life has been extremely rough, difficult, so far."

"Not that bad," he said. "Not really."

"We intend to provide you with a better life. We are dedicated to that proposition. The stars and the planets have led us to *you*. We know for a fact, John, that you are the one."

The one?

The rings of sand began to move, concentrically widening and vibrating—particles shifting and spinning apart.

Slater stood to leave. "I—I really need to go."

"Go where?" demanded Heather.

"You know. *Go?*"

Curious, Heather watched as Slater stood and backed away.

He missed a flagstone. His foot sank into quicksand.

Roy surprised him with a brisk pat on the back, saying, "There you are, son. I've been looking all over for you."

Slater lost control and wet his pants.

17

Awakenings

Wolfe was speeding toward heaven. Trumpets and sirens were blaring. A concerned angel was by his side.

"He's awake," a woman's voice said.

Wolfe spoke into an oxygen mask. He ripped it off his face.

An officious angel tried to force the apparatus over his mouth, telling him, "Don't do that!"

Wolfe struggled with this angel-demon who finally backed off. Unable to identify either of these celestial creatures, the male or female, Wolfe scanned the ambulance.

"Where is he?"

"Who?" she asked.

"Slater," said Wolfe. "He was behind you. On the street. He had a beard and long hair."

"Oh, him," she said. "They wouldn't allow him to come along. I didn't know you knew him."

Wolfe said, "Do I know you? Wait, you're...you're—"

"Misty. The cappuccino waitress."

"Misty?"

"My parents named me Mississippi," she explained. "Can you *ever*? They nicknamed me *Missy*. Which I hated. So I changed it to *Misty*, because I'm more, in my heart, once you get to know me—"

Wolfe lost consciousness.

He awoke on another planet where an enormous river wound around the entire circumference, dividing the sphere in half. The halves were at war with each other. One half was lush with foliage and delicious food — the promise of paradise. The other half was flat and desolate, its ground adrift with spiders. And he was drifting toward them. So eager to crawl upon him and implant their venom, they were hopping into the river and drowning.

Somehow he had been on a riverboat. It got reduced to a raft. The decks had fallen off. The paddlewheels had sunk. There was no rudder or paddle. Only him, tied to the planks. The raft moved with the current, shifting and redirecting him toward the lush shores where naked women awaited, eager to unbind him. Their luscious breasts were bouncing. He too was excited by this prospect and, straining, moving his head, looking down, saw he was naked.

The raft made an unexpected turn toward the other shore.

The spiders were equally excited.

Which diminished his.

Wolfe screamed, whimpered, prayed, and moaned.

"It's about time," said a familiar voice.

Wolfe's head was throbbing. He had spittle on his lips. It was an unfocused moment.

"What the hell happened to your face?" said Wolfe.

Slater's face was scarred down one side, his head draped with dreadlocks and a long tangled beard. The clothes he wore were new, and he had bathed. He grinned. "I stumbled into God."

"I found him," said Misty. "I hope you don't mind."

"You're an angel," said Wolfe. "Cut the *crap*, Slater. What the hell happened? You cut out on us. Why?"

"I let him use my shower," Misty added.

"They wouldn't allow me to enter otherwise," said Slater. "I'm grateful. A bath was what I needed. Thank you, Misty."

"My pleasure," she said.

"Can we get to the part where I *kill* you?" Wolfe grabbed his head to keep the surging pain from exploding further. "I'm warning you, Slater. You're a *dead* man. A *dead* man!"

"Honey, be careful, you'll hurt yourself," said Misty.

Slater took a steak knife off a discarded tray. The room's other occupant was bound in a body cast and had lost all interest in their communal television. Slater forced the utensil in Wolfe's hand. He removed his T-shirt, one borrowed from Misty. "Go ahead, friend, get it over with. I mean it—*kill* me! If that's what you want!"

Wolfe hurled the knife to the floor. He saw the scars.

"Jeezzzuz, what happened to you?"

Slater gave a terse grin. "The desert...it's a brutal place. So are the cities. A toss-up as to which is worse."

"Why?" said Wolfe.

Slater slipped the shirt back on. "I went insane."

"Hell," said Wolfe, "when weren't you? You were always a fucking free-for-all pharmaceutical testing ground! Try me again."

"I—went—*insane!*" Slater plopped backwards into an arm chair.

"Too many drugs? Who knows? It's not like I recall every waking moment. *That* kind of insane. A voice here, a vision there."

"Hallucinations?" said Wolfe.

"I stopped taking hallucinogenics," said Slater. "These aren't flashbacks or residual side-effects. I don't think."

"Then what?" said Wolfe.

"Prophesies!" said Weiner, entering the room.

"Who the hell are you?" Wolfe gripped his head. "Jeezz, this headache. Misty, be an angel and find me a nurse to kill this pain. Would you mind?"

"This is Henry," said Slater. "He returned with me from Egypt. I asked you to wait outside."

"I'm not your dog," said Weiner. "Do I embarrass you?"

"Egypt?" said Wolfe.

"I went to see the ruins and became one," said Slater.

"No *shit,*" said Wolfe.

"Where's Truffles?" said Slater.

"Who's Truffles?" said Wolfe.

"John's dog," said Weiner. "He's in the park. He is incredibly smart for a dog. He can—"

"Damn it—tell me what happened!" Wolfe rubbed his head.

Slater closed his eyes as he made himself more comfortable in the chair. "I was walking over sand dunes, fell in a hole and landed on my head. I don't remember much of anything after that."

"I do," said Weiner. "John almost died. He was in bad shape. A fellow anthropologist, Kabukh was his name, found John. He had fallen into an ancient temple. Several centuries B.C. Workers found him the next morning. There had been a horrific sand storm. Truly. They brought John to me on the back of a camel."

"A camel?" Wolfe scoffed.

"Camel, yes," said Weiner. "He was in a trance and—"

"I was unconscious, and babbling," Slater interjected.

"Delirious," said Weiner, "according to Dr. Briard. But, I am quite certain he was talking in tongues. It was prophesy."

Wolfe grumbled, "Yeah, my *ass.*"

"Ass—no, it was a camel." Weiner blushed. "Oh, you meant—as in, of course. But I'm telling you, truly, it was prophesy."

81

"Slater's no fucking *prophet*," said Wolfe. "Hell, he couldn't even *profit* from a million plus dollar record deal!"

"Who's a prophet?" said Misty, returning to the room.

"Million plus?" Weiner was distracted by the nebulous figure, but spoke to Misty. "*John* is. Hello, again. Hello there," he added, addressing a nurse who arrived next. "I'm Henry. Dr. Henry Weiner. Veterinarian. He communicated with God."

"Who—*him*?" laughed the nurse. She scrunched her face and looked down at Slater who had fallen asleep and was snoring in the cushy arms of the chair.

The nurse shook her head and set down a paper cup containing capsules, then threw back her head and whooped, "Glory be! And *I'm* Cleopatra — Queen of the Nile!"

— 18 —
Odysseys

Winter had abruptly turned to spring.

The transformation left a mess.

The snowfall in San Francisco had broken almanac records and made the city dysfunctional. Nine decimeters of snow had fallen and stayed. Six weeks of frigid weather burst pipes. Winds knocked out power. Cars spun out of control. Bridges grew into towering ice sculptures. Schools shut down along with every government agency. Corporations struggled to stay liquid. Children threw snowballs. Parties were happening indoors, into the nights. Hundreds died from hypothermia.

Slater helped those he could into homeless shelters.

Then he did nothing.

From Wolfe's window overlooking the street, Slater watched, transfixed by the slow metamorphosis to slush and flooding rivulets. Light increased upon buildings. The greys became brighter. Spindly trees spewed leaves. Tiny buds split into color. Women wore halter tops. Men discarded their shirts.

Slater moved to an outdoor bench.

"You're suffering from depression," said Weiner.

"Most likely," said Slater.

A flurry of birds twittered by, mocking.

"You saw it coming, didn't you?" said Weiner.

"It was a hunch," said Slater.

"Hunch? John, the fact you didn't *warn* people," said Weiner, "is that what's bothering you? That you should have stood in the street shouting like a Cassandra? Had you alerted the media they would have laughed and jeered and called you a maniac. Then, the reporters would have tracked you down and proclaimed you a *freak*. Was that part of your vision too? John, you helped who you could. I happen to agree with your decision to do *nothing* besides that."

Slater was wearing stone-washed jeans. He had trimmed his beard into a goatee. His dreadlocks were shorn into a close crop. His glasses were blue, opaque, and mirrored. Faces appeared in the sky. People walking past had giraffe-like necks stretching from their heads, auras trailing in a vaporous whisper of laughter. A poodle on a leash winked at him. Slater looked back at Weiner.

"Except *now*," said Weiner.

"Why?" said Slater.

"You have money," said Weiner.

"I owe money," said Slater.

"Your profits outweigh your debts." Weiner picked up a pebble from the park's path and stood. He tossed it at the lake. Accidently it hit a motorized toy boat.

"Hey!" someone shouted.

"Sorry." He sat back down. "I thought Wolfe explained this to you. Weren't you listening? Electra settled for a flat sum. You forgo any rights to future royalties and they agree not to sue for breach of contract. In theory, they could. And would. This leaves you with, what? About $100,000. Minus back taxes. Anyway, according to Wolfe's accountant, you're back in the black. So, John, my friend, for God's sake — cheer up!"

"I'm ecstatic. Can I die now?"

Weiner stood, tempering his alarm. "John, *John*, you mustn't talk like that. That's—"

"Insane?" Slater offered.

The bushes burst into flames, into a giddy chorus of bees that swayed in a yellow breeze, humming: *Insane–Insane–Insane...*

"No, no," said Weiner. "You shouldn't think that way. You have gifts. Focus on the positive."

The grounds darkened, clouds casting negative shadows.

"You're letting your demons win, John."

A woman stopped and turned to expose her breasts and mouth, *Suck me*. From her mouth emerged a green snake.

"Demons," repeated Weiner.

"You see them too?" said Slater.

"John," said Weiner, "I have a surprise for you. Come."

A swarm of voices conspired, whispering in his ear, to *ooh* and *ahh*: "*Henry has a sur-prize! But is it to die for? Is it, John?*"

Weiner averted his eyes from the self-inflicted wound on Slater's wrist. It had hardened into a magenta scar. Slater held up his wrist. "See, Henry, this proves what I said. I *can't* kill myself. I should have bled to death. You know I'm right."

"John," said Weiner, "I called 911."

"You should have left me there to die."

Weiner said, "I would never—"

"Then help me stop these visions from coming true."

Weiner blinked. "How? What visions?"

"Forget it. I'm schizophrenic."

"Possibly," said Weiner. "Possibly not."

"Demons, Henry," said Slater, "I see them. In everyone. Even Wolfe. But I don't see yours. Don't you find that strange?"

Weiner didn't know how to respond.

Slater asked point blank, "Who are you, Henry? Really?"

"I'm your friend, John. Come. You will like my surprise."

They arrived at an outdoor cafe. They took seats at a table for four. Someone took one of the empty seats. Weiner stopped the next person who tried.

"We're waiting for someone," he said.

"Who?" Slater listened to his voice fade slowly into space.

The waiter had two heads. He approached their table.

"Are you ready to order?" said the first head.

"Eat, John," encouraged Weiner. "Try to be happy."

"I'm not hungry," said Slater.

"Something to drink, then?" the second head sneered, warning: "*I–would–hate–to–have–to–ask–you–to–leave.*"

"A beer," said Slater.

"We have several to recommend," the first head said.

The second head sighed: *yes–too–damned–many.*

"Domestic, anything," said Slater.

"Same for me," said Weiner, waving him away. "Thank you."

"I'm getting worse, aren't I?" said Slater.

People at the surrounding tables began to nod.

"Worse? Then I suggest you see a doctor," said Weiner.

Slater was distracted by a nearby group eating lunch. The man who dominated the conversation kept scornfully summoning Jesus Christ, saying, "*Jesus Christ,* can you believe that *Fuck*? I'm already working double shifts for that prick! *Jesus Christ,* it's not like I'm getting rich here, am I? *Well?* What?!" He glowered at Slater for staring. "What the *fuck's* this have to do with you? Nothing. So piss off! I mean, *Jesus H. fucking Christ,* who the hell do—"

The man had a bullet lodged in his forehead. It appeared to be something high-tech with a metallic sheen. Slater was seeing into another dimension. The cars had no visible wheels. They hovered above the pavement. Several of the downtown highrises resembled pyramids.

Slater said, "Did I ever mention my uncle, Henry? He shot me. He was trying to kill me."

"Yes, John, you told me."

"He thought I was someone else. He's insane, and confined to a mental institution. I never knew my biological mother. Or father. To me they were make-believe people, fabricated from the bits and pieces my aunt and uncle provided. Which wasn't much. So I did some research. City libraries, public records, newspapers. What I discovered was...their death was no accident."

"You mean the car crash?"

"My mother had been pregnant...with me. I had a brother too. My father accelerated the car into the support tower of the bridge. Killing them all. I think he was trying to plunge us into the ocean. Why would he do a thing like that?"

"John, you don't know for certain he—"

"There were bystanders. A tourist on the bridge filmed it on his video camera. It was reported in the newspapers."

"*Newspapers*—phff," said Weiner. "John, you can't believe—"

"My father committed suicide! No, in point of fact, it was an act of homicide. *Murders.* Why?"

Slater's rage had turned into tears and Weiner looked around, hoping this would not escalate into another scene.

"He murdered my mother and brother! He was a cold-blooded bastard! I survived by sheer dumb luck. Lucky, lucky me."

"You are lucky," said Weiner.

"Insane is what I am. Lucky my uncle missed. *Damned* lucky. That's my luck. Henry, do me a favor."

"If I can."

"Kill me before I get like my uncle or father."

"John, no," said Weiner. "You have a good heart."

"Paul had a good one. My father's heart, I don't know."

Slater mused as he watched the wind ruffle the foliage of trees, spangles of light from the leaves signaling birds to swarm up into the depths of the blue sky. He saw the movement to be separate and yet singular in design.

"Maybe they had good reason for wanting me dead."

"John," said Weiner. "Look who's here."

Eclipsing the sun, Bryant Briard resembled an enormous space alien who had landed on Earth.

19

Confronting The Chaos

"Daddy," said Mercy, "why are you crying?"

Slater was freefalling through time.

"It's me, John." Briard seated his large frame at the iron table and signaled a waiter. "A glass of wine. Chardonnay, please."

"Meridian is our house wine. We also—"

"That'll do." Briard focused on Slater, extending his arm to touch him on the shoulder. "How are you, friend?"

"I'm not crying," said Slater. "I'm happy. Really."

Sondra said, "You've got it backwards, Dad. You're supposed to *laugh* when you're happy and *cry* when you're sad."

Both daughters giggled.

Slater grinned. "You're right. Absolutely."

"About what?" said Briard.

Slater knew the face. His surprise at seeing a friend produced a curious but reminiscent chaos. "Right, the chaos. Bryant, hi."

"Hello, John," said Briard.

"Chaos?" said Weiner.

Briard held up a hand to silence Henry.

"I lose focus," said Slater. "It's good to see you."

Briard stroked his chin, before brightening. "Yes, we've spoken about unfocused waves, random noise. The radiation from space. Coded signals. Gravitational curvatures. Distortions in time. What about the chaos, John?"

Birds had returned to the branches. The voices subsided. There was chirping. Faces became whole again.

"It washes through me." Slater smiled to dispel any need to worry. He was envisioning Briard as Mercury, the messenger god, with golden hair flowing in the breeze and his winged feet crossed. The wine in his glass had turned blue. "It's crazy. Nothing, really."

"What is?" said Briard

"I mean," Slater laughed, "*me*—not...it."

"It?" Briard sipped his wine, disturbed by an image, one of an astronaut tumbling weightlessly though an endless curving space. He measured his next sip. "Hum, this wine is good."

Slater nodded. "You're right, I do."

"Do what?"

"Feel at times like an astronaut falling through space. Beyond reach. It comes and goes. This feeling."

Briard refrained from commenting.

"Like you come and go, Bryant," said Slater. "It's good to see you. But why are you here?"

"Conference." Briard set down his glass. "Also, Henry's been writing me. About you. I was curious. So I accepted. Nominal fee. I like to brush off the desert dust from time to time. See the Land of the Free. You tried to kill yourself?"

"Henry has a big mouth," said Slater.

"Nothing to kill yourself over." Briard winked.

Slater said, "I didn't succeed."

"But you tried?" said Briard.

"I was testing a theory," said Slater.

"Explain," said Briard.

"It's the future. I can glimpse it. But I can't seem to remember how to stop it before…it happens."

Briard said, "No one can stop the future."

"I need to try," said Slater.

"By killing yourself?" Briard swirled his wine. "Nip off the bud? Is that your solution?"

"John's visions," said Weiner. "They come to pass. Honest to God, Bryant, they do."

"Henry," said Briard. "I left Jerusalem a few hours ago. Can we refrain from the biblical hyperboles?"

"Killing myself won't help," said Slater. "You're right."

"That's better." Briard picked up his menu. "Shall we order something? I'm famished."

They ate. Briard had lobster. Weiner devoured a large plate of chicken alfredo. Slater picked at a spinach salad. The conversation meandered from the mundane to the incomprehensible.

Briard was in the midst of saying, "Exactly, and from a distance, the universe, the Earth, perhaps everything, appears uniform and homogeneous. But *we* perceive it differently. Yet, like galaxies and stars, each one of us abounds as a local irregularity. Ah, but why?"

"Density fluctuations," said Slater.

"Just so," said Briard.

"What?" said Weiner. "What is?"

"We are," said Slater. "We're distortions in time. Different from celestial beings with no gravitational mass, who occupy no space, and are *timeless*. And yet they go rippling through each and every one of us. Constantly."

Briard smiled back. "Care to run that by me again?"

Slater selected a spinach leaf from his plate, displayed it on his fork, then plopped it in his mouth. "We eat to maintain an ordered form of energy. Food converts into heat and keeps us alive. Which, conversely, is a disordered form of energy. Created from us by being here, existing and thinking. Our thoughts advancing more disorder. We're doing it this very moment." He gave a self-deprecating shrug. "And the purpose of this chaos we produce is to establish stability. Ironic, right? A form of *order* derived from *dis*order."

"A paradox," Briard chuckled and sipped his wine.

"We mimic the universe. Our presence distorts space and time. Displace–replace. Yin and Yang. Linked in an alternating current. Our minds move with coded information at an alarming frequency, and we can't foresee the overload effect diminishing our wisdom. We've blinded ourselves to the future we're projecting. I don't know, maybe we're genetically designed to evolve this way."

Briard touched the tines of his fork to his tongue as if tasting the notion for validity. He brushed crumbs off the tablecloth. A loafer dangled from the toe of his crossed leg.

Slater took a sip of beer, and added, "Is it possible to change and correct the course of time? If one detects an irregularity?"

"What irregularity?" said Weiner.

"Who, John, you?" said Briard.

"Correct what?" said Weiner.

"Never mind." Slater was envisioning the stone faces again, like machinery standing guard and listening. Bullets were now lodged in the foreheads of passersby and he could hear their thought signals as they traveled helter skelter. What remained of his beer flickered and turned a metallic blue. He pushed his glass away. "Or, maybe this irregularity is a wave we're meant to ride to avert destruction."

"I can balance dual theories," smiled Briard. "Continue."

Slater was calmed by the presence of his friends, but he braced himself for the oncoming rush of stimuli. "An atomic balancing act is what we are. Holographic projections. Composed primarily of empty space. Right? Beyond all these figments of reality, repeating frame after frame we...there's...there..."

Slater looked at Truffles tied to a parking meter. They both detected the stream of ionized particles about to overtake them.

"John," laughed Briard, "are you trying to alarm us?"

Truffles moaned sorrowfully.

Slater managed a smile. "Truffles thinks he's a hound. Words are so limiting. We're the ultimate paradox. Mass kissed by energy. We weren't placed here for decoration. We're here to react."

Briard and Weiner watched as Slater closed his eyes. His body stiffened. His hand took hold of the edge of the table. The glass and metal began to rattle minutely. Finally it stopped.

Slater opened his eyes warily, unclenched his teeth, uncertain as to what he'd see. He saw his friends and exhaled a laugh to dispel the tension. "Sorry. I'm trying my best to adjust."

"Adjust to what?" said Weiner.

Slater regained his composure. "To what's coming. I think it relates to our quest as a species to dominate. We're not advancing correctly. I fear we're at risk of losing our essential humanness."

"Our souls?" asked Weiner.

Slater speared spinach leaves onto his fork. "It's all academic. I mean, if you're correct. If we're incapable of fixing it."

"It?" said Briard.

Slater swallowed. "The future."

20

Defining Vision

To see or not to see.

There were many questions. Slater wondered. Was it better to know or not to know? To suffer from outrageous fortune? Or to be awake in an endless sleep?

He missed his visions. His life was more ordered. He was not on the verge of killing himself. This was good.

Briard had prescribed pills to correct a chemical imbalance and stabilize his mood swings. He felt like a skittish race horse. Briard's intentions were good, but his conventional methods lacked vision. Briard could not comprehend the loss these drugs would inflict.

Slater lived, simply.

He was happy not to glimpse the future.

He shared an apartment with Wolfe and Henry. When Misty moved in, Slater and Henry moved out and rented a place on Haight Street near Golden Gate Park. Henry found employment at the de Young Museum where his knowledge of ancient artifacts proved to be useful. Wolfe ventured into guerrilla theater and produced an Off-Broadway musical comedy centered around three technocrats named Arrogance, Incompetence, and Greed who, having died, connived to make a comeback by overthrowing Hell. The show opened to critical acclaim and closed after a week because of public apathy.

Misty had retired from waitressing to be Wolfe's assistant.

Wolfe assisted her too: impregnating, marrying, and cutting the cord to their baby boy all within a year.

With legal matters settled, Slater coasted. He was drifting down a river, going nowhere, backwards in time. He had a bank account. He realized he could just sit, let his mind be calm and read a book without glimpsing Armageddon or even a minor mishap.

He acquired a taste for tea.

Life was a recipe to savor.

He frequented the city libraries to study ideas.

He enrolled in college at San Francisco State to study chemistry and computer science and received a higher degree of education no certificate could provide. He had no interest in pursuing a grade-point average or establishing a paper-trail of credentials to impress anyone. He was on a personal quest to solve a specific riddle and to answer questions that kept arising exponentially.

He carried a notebook with him wherever he went.

He would drift into churches upon hearing the chorus of the faithful. He was reminded of his aunt Hanna's love and devotion to God, and how her voice had filled rooms and the emptiness in his heart. The congregations would encourage him to come forward, which he would, to accept Christ whom he tried to understand.

He confessed his confusion about, and to, God.

He delivered coats and blankets to the homeless. Few friends had survived the snowfalls. He made new ones.

He played chess in the park.

Journalists desperate for a story would track him down at the library, at the park while playing chess, or volunteering at a center. He was a big disappointment. They were looking for his notorious sound bite that would sell their article, not what they found. His whereabouts and sedated commentaries, if used, were buried in the entertainment section of the newspaper or aired for less than fifteen seconds on a television tabloid.

Slater drove north of San Francisco to a sanitarium in Napa where he found, hoping to make peace with, his only living relative. But his uncle didn't recognize him and only wanted to touch his scar. Slater complied. From a wheelchair with the arm pads spotted in dabs of fingernail polish, his uncle recoiled.

"Defect," he declared.

Paul Slater wore a zebra-striped robe. He grabbed for women's bottoms as they passed in the hallway. Most appeared to enjoy the attention. One woman turned and slapped him hard.

"She loves me," Paul sighed, "she loves me not."

"It took awhile to track you down," said Slater.

Touching Slater's scar again, his uncle asked, "How?"

"I fell into an Egyptian ruin," said Slater.

"We're talking years, maybe sixteen?"

"I almost died."

"We all die," said Paul.

"Do you even know who I am?" Slater pointed to another scar, an indentation above his temple that disappeared into his hairline.

His uncle reversed a wheel.

"Greedy-Son-of-a-Bitch! Of course I do."

"I'm Johnny. John Slater. Your—"

"No—*my* name! Nurse! *Nurse!*" he roared.

"You're Paul. I'm John. You're my uncle."

The wheel was rotated back a notch. "*Johnny?* Can't be. I shot you. I shot you dead. I did."

"You missed. See?"

"*Damn,*" he said, grimacing. "Do you hate me?"

"No," said Slater.

"Good, then get-me-the-*hell* out of here! We have important business to conduct."

"I don't think I can," said Slater.

"You *can*, if willing. Know that. Where's Skunk?"

"He's dead, Paul. It's been years."

"Damn-it-to-hell," said his uncle, "good mutt."

"You shot him. Don't you remember?" said Slater.

"*Damn.* Right. Of course I do. It's this place. They drug me. Makes me crazy. When I'm *not!* Could've used him is all."

For what? Slater was almost bated into asking.

A heavy-set nurse came up to them. She squeaked to a halt on the formica.

"Is there a *problem*, Mr. Slater?"

Both Slaters looked up.

"Yes," said Paul. "The two of us want out-of-here!"

"No-can-do," said the nurse. She smiled. Apparently it was a dialog they rehearsed. "It's forbidden."

"Forbidden? Are you saying you won't let Johnny out?"

"For him, I can make an exception," she said and winked.

"It's not like I'm *dangerous*," said Paul Slater.

"Oh, Sugar, but you *are!*" she laughed.

"Am *not!*" he countered.

"Tell it to them," the nurse advised.

Both Slaters looked at the roomful of hapless inmates. Some of the women flirted, wiggling their painted fingernails at him. Some of the men receded like submissive primates. Others drooled.

His uncle tugged at Slater's shirt. Paul's whisper was nearly a shout, "It's a frigg'n *conspiracy*, Johnny. I know it, *they* know it." He released his grip and leaned back.

"I rest my case." The nurse squeaked on.

Slater said, "Paul, I came here to make peace with you and to ask a few questions."

Paul Slater squinted, prepared for thought. He gripped the rails of his chair: "Go ahead, *shoot.*"

An orderly squeegeeing a window stopped, alerted.

"It's an *expression*," he addressed the man. He sat up, prepared for business. "Idiots. Go on, Johnny. Ignore him."

"It's about an invention," said Slater.

"*Now* we're talking," said Paul.

"I came upon this idea, but I—" said Slater.

"*Yes?*" Paul Slater rubbed his palms and leaned forward.

"I'm not sure it can work," said Slater.

"*Can* work, *will* work—what?" urged Paul.

It seemed futile to ask. His uncle was already three sheets into the wind without a boat. Slater shook his head, preparing himself to gracefully leave. "Never mind."

"Never mind? Never mind, what?" Paul gripped his nephew's arm to hold him there. "Johnny, Son, you have to give me more than *that* if you expect my help."

Slater relented. "You were working on a project called the Warmer something, the Whirly—"

"WarmerWhirler, sure," he said. "It blew up. Why?"

"The ingredients, weren't they iron powder, carbon, and—"

"Say no more!" Paul grabbed his nephew's sleeve.

There was squeaking. The nurse was passing.

"I'm not the greedy-*so-and-so.*"

Paul waited just the same. "Can't be sure. Go on."

"If combined molecularly with components of wool and, say, made into a synthetic cloth, with an insulation—"

"*Stop,*" he shushed Slater, "I know where you're going."

Slater peered at his uncle incredulously. "You do?"

"Not entirely," said his uncle, "but if you get me out of here, I *will*. You need my help, Johnny, and I need yours. Deal?"

"Paul, you don't even know what—"

"Doesn't matter." His uncle leaned back in his painted throne. He gestured with the assurance of a pope or mafia don. "Whatever it is, Johnny, it can be done. Have you learned *nothing* from me in all these years? You think I'm crazy, don't you?"

"Well."

"Sixteen *years* and three months it took for you to find me? Why so long? I thought we were buddies."

"You tried to kill me, Paul."

"Shouldn't hold grudges."

"I've had my own problems."

"Doesn't surprise me." Paul folded his hands and twiddled this thumbs. "Can't say *why* I tried to shoot you. Because I don't *know* why. To this day! But, what-a-surprise, I regained my sanity while locked up in here! Funny, yes? No, not really. Johnny, it all relates to what I once told you. About that old *Whirl-O-Will?*"

"Your stolen invention?"

"The same. Along with that Greedy-Son-of-Bitch. Ah, you still think I'm crazy, don't you?" His eyes were as crafty as a fox's as he laughed. "Not so. Life, my dear boy, *is* an elusive subatomic will-o'-the-wisp. Comparable to the precise path of an electron – which can never be known! Ah, and when you think you've defined it – *poof!* Gone. At the edge of order and chaos is where we all exist. It's a fuzzy border. Know that."

"Paul, you almost *killed* me," said Slater.

"Time for your herbal enema, Mr. Slater," chirped a nurse.

Paul gripped his wheels. "A nasty vixen, this one."

Slater said before he was asked to leave, "I'll talk to the doctors, Paul, and see what I can do."

"Never meant to shoot you." Paul released his grip on the tires and the nurse pushed him forward. "This could be *you*, Johnny, just as easy as *me*. Locked up in here. *You* know that, *I* know that."

Slater avoided his eyes.

"We're family! Get me out, Johnny."

"I will, if I can," said Slater.

"*Can, will!*" Paul signaled with a confident thumbs up.

Slater watched as his uncle, head craning backwards with a wild smile, was wheeled down the hallway of checkered tile.

As he disappeared around a corner, Paul gave a parting cry: "I'm a *genius!*"

"So you've said," Slater muttered.

"Know that!"

— 21 —
Saved by a Kiss

It happened as if in a dream.

It had to have been a dream, thought Slater, for he knew – had seen the future in her startled smile, in her eyes, the moment he approached to kiss her – that she would not resist, but accept him, even love him.

He had not been insane.

He was only mildly medicated.

Never had he felt so confident, so high, so loving.

"Why did you do that?" she asked.

Sherry had seen him coming and let her arms drop defenseless. It was not her nature. She was intrigued by his smile, his scar, and a feeling that she knew him from somewhere.

Slater had paused to be certain. He gently touched both arms, before holding her firmly and kissing her on the lips.

"Okay," she laughed, slightly embarrassed in front of a crowd. "Do I *know* you?"

"Yes, we've met."

It was his smile, an assurance minus the arrogance. She almost swooned. Though hating her weakness, she held him for support as he kissed her a second time with great passion.

There were whoops and applause from onlookers.

This was how it was meant to be.

It happened in a church on Christmas Eve. Sherry Knowles, his childhood acquaintance, destined-to-be-lover, had been serving food. Slater was greeting guests arriving through the large doors. He had had no idea she was inside. He was still among the homeless but no longer one of them. He had come as a volunteer and was there to make the homeless feel at home, welcomed and appreciated.

An elderly woman caring for two grandchildren told Slater about her daughter consumed in a fire. He listened to many stories. There were those who preferred to tell none. Some of the people he knew. Others he would never know, for they had retreated too far inward. When he recognized Sherry across the room he started to walk toward her without a thought as to what he might say. The closer he got – the people, the lighted candles, the smell of wax and pine boughs, the organ music – all melted into a glowing murmur around them.

Slater felt comforted by the sight of her, this mesmerizing port, offering calm water and peace. He could hear the buffeting wind and crazed waves fading at his stern as he gently touched her.

In the days that followed, they took long walks through forest trails in Golden Gate Park, along the ocean sand near the Sea Clift, and down mountain paths through Muir Woods north of the bay to Stinson Beach. Talking came easily, naturally, their long silences too as they watched the ocean waves, or the clouds, the snow, the rain. Sharing an interest in museums and movies, they discussed motives, perspectives, and plots. Slater sensed Sherry wanted his love, *was* in love, but she was proving difficult to reel in, to accept the notion of marriage, resistant each time they came close to this matter of love. Over dinner, sensing he might propose, she told him she feared their love would be a Shakespearian tragedy. Real, but not meant to be. Her logic was vexing, intoxicatingly so.

Slater found her to be mysterious, an exotic creature, something that might instantly transform – woman into mermaid – back to her true self. Slater, as the mystified fisherman, read her poetry, tried to assure her that his love for her was real. He sang to her love songs. He felt her heart yielding, melting, giving in, drawn into passionate kissing before freezing, pushing him away. She drove him mad with a desire for love he had never known existed, before her.

He told her, "You're a beautiful riddle I can't quite solve."

"Better you don't. You won't like what you find."

"That's crazy. Sherry, I love you."

"I love you too."

"Then—?"

"You'll end up loathing me."

"Impossible," he said. "I swear, I could never—"

"Don't promise that. You can't be certain."

He had no answers to satisfy her doubts. As they sat, huddled under a blanket in the woods, staring up at the stars with an erratic wind dancing like a sprite around them, Slater asked her:

"Is this because of my past?"

"John, it's not *always* about you."

"I know. Sherry, I'm the monster, okay? I was the hedonistic rock star. I admit it. You know I'm not like that anymore."

"Nor am I who I was."

"Whatever," he said. "So we agree to forget the past?"

"How can anyone do that?"

"Sherry, I've always wanted you. I love you and want *only* you. I swear to God that's the truth. There, I said it."

With a tentative smile she lay back down upon the grassy slope. Slater followed, lying beside her. He took hold of her hand as they gazed upward and searched the distant suns and nebulous worlds in the black abyss.

Sherry broke the silence, saying, "Well, I guess God never said life would be easy. Look what happened to Jesus."

"Right," said Slater.

"How do you propose we erase our past?"

"Sherry, whatever's bothering you, I don't care. I mean, I care. But I accept you unconditionally." He noticed a shooting star and pointed. "Look. That's amazing. See, that's a sign."

"Auspicious? Or ominous?"

Slater laughed. "You're funny. I love that about you. All of you. I want to marry you. Will you? Say yes?"

Sherry turned, searching his eyes.

Slater widened them a bit. "I won't disintegrate if you say no. Of course, I don't know that for *certain*."

She turned her head toward the distant fireballs penetrating the blackness like pinpricks. Tears trickled from her eyes. She gazed into the blur of the Milky Way and said, "Yes."

Slater sat up, propped on an arm. He looked down on her face turned away, intent on kissing her. "Why are you crying?"

"Can't I be happy?"

She turned her head, eyes wet with tears, and met his lips. Their bodies became entwined. Each touch, skin to skin, was as precious as soft light spreading over a bed of clouds.

The wet cushion of her lips was firm yet pliable. Opening, then biting back, gently, yielding to his penetration. Tenderly, forcefully restrained, with pure adoration, he paused within, again and again, keeping the warm sensual current of their bodies connected, pulsing, alive. Electrified in a bath of fire and water, pleasurably contained, they became one world, imploding in a confusion of sighs, whispers, confessions, passionately clinging as one.

Nothing, he felt, could surpass this moment in time.

Slater realized what a sham his life had been.

His bed had been a dumpster, a piece of cardboard, a slab of cold concrete. And, before that, an endless train wreck of celebrity suites. Had it all been a dream? Performing in city after city? Living as a vagabond. Surviving by his wits. Breaking against shores and creating waves as thunderous as a fatal collapse. To demand what? Attention. Fame. A musician, rock star, Dyslexic Dog, he had lost his way, his purpose, his desire to smile for the camera and crowds. Unless it served a purpose. Mostly to fondle and fuck the willing and wanton girls. Who kept coming. Slipping him room keys and numbers on napkins. He loved them back, these adoring fans.

It would be wrong to say he had become obsessed with women and their naked bodies. There were so many varieties for him to try. Soft bosoms and warm thighs more intoxicating than any candy – each so different, like lovely blossoms, petals to separate and taste, to consume and be consumed, deflowered and devoured.

Resisting these temptations was barely an option.

He had awakened most mornings in a strange bed, with a new face and body for whom to reacquaint himself with.

He drank his coffee black and tried not to think, or examine his life for what it was, or was not. It just was.

Did he think he was invulnerable?

Did he have no feelings?

Didn't his life mean anything to anyone, but himself?

These were many of the questions asked of him.

Mainly by women.

One tabloid quoted him as saying:

"You need a better understanding of what your question means before I answer."

He could be arrogant.

Another lost lover left this notation for the record:

"I told him I loved him. He laughed and said, 'You remind me of a quarter moon turned on its side, mocking me with a smile.'"

He quoted Goethe's Faust after having sex if ever asked if there was a chance for enduring love: *"'In the end, we are dependent upon the creatures we have made.'"*

His intent was never to be cruel with his actions or his words, merely an outlawry hip-shot at consensual frivolity.

His mantra was simple: *"Consume life before it spoils,"* so he accepted the many offerings from multiple hosts, indiscriminately ingesting multiple pills and powders and liquids to test his limits and augment his quest for adventure. And stumble, if he was lucky, into enlightenment. His actions were sporadic – jumping off stages, off rooftops into pools, hanging from window ledges. He was bemused by all the tabloid fuss and what ended up in print:

A reporter: "Why do you risk your life?"

Slater: "Rabbits."

Reporter: "Rabbits?"

Slater: "The Airplane? The song? 'If you go chasing rabbits... and you know you're going to fall?' It's the lure? You know?"

No, the reporter did not know.

Regarding his vulnerability, or lack thereof, he felt compelled to examine the question repeatedly as a practicing physician or scientist might until the answer finally came to discovery.

It came one night in the form of a rape.

Slater felt the polarizing touch of the universe and its flawed veil as it scraped his soul. Drugged, abducted, and blindfolded, he was taken to a dank chamber and tied to a crucible, to be tortured. He glimpsed the grand illusion beyond the stars. He was alarmed to discover there was an audience observing, in want of entertainment. He was the headliner for this night of sacrificial fun.

Slater had struggled and begged to be set free.

The audience laughed approvingly.

His ordeal was oxymoronic, both tragic and comic.

Bound naked to a crucifix, Slater had appealed with whatever charms he thought he might still possess to the dark angels gowned and hooded (imagining them to be female and more willing to help) who surrounded him. He had no idea who they were or what was happening, or how his life had become this nightmare.

Slater pleaded for his life.

He was praying to God.
Finally, years later, Sherry saved him with a kiss.

— 22 —
Freefalling into Light

Slater was staring into the flames of a fire. A pile of logs was bathed in golden swirls of heat. He was envisioning his invention of artificial warmth. It was coming to fruition. Sherry was lifting her foam pad and preparing the ground by brushing away pebbles and twigs that would hinder her from having a comfortable night's sleep. She fluffed her sleeping bag and pillow.

"I'm pregnant," she announced.

An orange log split apart, releasing fireflies of sparks.

"That was fast," said Slater, "since we just made love."

"I'm pretty amazing, aren't I?" Sherry settled her head down upon her pillow and fluttered her eyelashes.

Their sleeping bags were adjoined and he slid closer to kiss her. "You are pretty. Amazing too. What makes you think there's a Pop Tart toasting in your oven?"

"Women know these things. We're mysterious." She snuggled closer, feeling warm, safe and cozy in their zipped-together space. "Women possess a heightened intuition far greater than men. And we possess tools for determining the presence of life in the uterus. We come with a test strip. It turned blue."

Slater gazed into the sky. "We're going to be parents."

"You catch on fast. What else can you do?"

"Haven't I done enough?" They nestled face to face in the dark. A chorus of crickets accompanied the crackling fire. "I know these things. I'm a chemist. At this very moment you're busily producing a hormone in your urine called *chorionic gonadotropin*."

"This is so romantic. My saliva?" She puckered her lips.

Slater kissed her. "Tasty. Your body chemistry fascinates me. Would you like to hear about a covalent bond?"

"If it will help put me to sleep," she yawned.

"It's a new polymer Paul and I discovered. It's soft and durable, like cloth. But the intriguing thing, it can generate heat."

Sherry opened her eyes, showing interest.

"We're still testing it. We think we can regulate this material to maintain a pleasantly warm and consistent temperature."

"Okay, now you're getting me aroused."

"I wanted to surprise you. This is good news. If it works it will make us rich. At least help support a family."

"Now you have my full attention."

Slater told her about the experience he had had while homeless. During a freak snowfall in San Francisco, he had seen a shaft of light descend through clouds. It intermingled with birds rising through its center. He was comforted by a warm sensation. He envisioned the golden snowflakes as a mesh of fibers that controlled temperature.

"Snow, birds and light. Am I missing something?"

"The universal desire for warmth. A cloth that is self-regulated with the push of a button. The idea came, just like that. Except it's taken me years, with Paul's help, to create this fiber."

"You were given a gift by God," said Sherry.

"I wouldn't go that far. But good, right?"

Sherry took Slater's hand and placed it on her stomach.

Slater added, "We're about to register for a patent. It's going to happen, this product, so says Paul. What?"

"There's something genuinely good happening inside of me too. I'm looking forward to it all."

They kissed and savored the moment.

Slater was distracted by the swaying motion of the fire's flames. The warmth of this flicker in time was surpassed by the vision of another woman. He saw her face in the flames. She was beautiful, with long raven hair. He remembered walking with her along a beach. Perhaps it was in a dream. Waves were thundering upon the sand and spreading up the shore to engulf their feet. The voiceless fury of water then returned to the crackle of flames.

He didn't mention this to Sherry. He was committed to her and deeply in love, and happy she was pregnant with their first child. Nevertheless, the haunting image sparked another vision to flare up – a recent memory, a vision he decided to share.

"I had this strange experience a few nights ago."

"Strange? Coming from you?" she teased.

"I woke in the middle of the night. I couldn't sleep so I went to my computer. I was trying to refine the elasticity of this polymer. Before I got sidetracked. I began thinking about synthetic DNA and molecular computers. Artificial intelligence, right? And suddenly I was staring into this face."

There was a pregnant pause, before she asked:

"Where?"

"Inside the monitor. A holographic image. Staring back at me. I swear to God. It had sub-zero skin with eyes that were cobalt blue. It wasn't a man or a woman. Something...in between."

Sherry kept quiet, recalling ghost stories from her childhood and realizing this did not fit into that category. "Are you serious?"

"Pretty weird, huh?"

She wanted to dismiss it. "You were overtired."

"Right. Except it wouldn't go away. It talked to me."

"John, you're scaring me."

"It scared me too." He laughed uneasily.

The crickets had stopped chirping. The fire had died to embers. A gibbous moon was hiding in the branches of the tall redwoods.

Sherry looked into the dome of stars. "What did it say?"

"Something like, 'Hello, John. I know who you are. Combined, our code will create synergy.' Then he, it, smiled, its eyes probing, before dissolving into my screen saver. Does that qualify as weird?"

"I wish you hadn't told me this."

Slater snuggled closer. "You're right, it was fatigue overlapping reality. Weird things seem to punctuate my life."

She laughed. "Is that supposed to put me at ease?"

"I love you. Does that?"

"I can't afford to lose you."

Slater touched his head to hers. "Hey, I was lost. And now I'm found. I credit you with my discovery."

"Don't joke. Hold me tight."

They embraced. She closed her eyes, opened them to stars.

"It's so beautiful here," she said.

Ancient redwoods surrounded them like the walls of a chapel. The branches arched high above, like a gateway to heaven.

Slater suggested, "We should make this our special place."

"How do you mean?"

"The Indians believe there are places that give strength to your earthly spirit. This will be ours. A place of binding love."

"We can bring our children here on picnics."

"Exactly," said Slater.

"I love you," said Sherry.

"I love you too, us three." He touched her stomach.

The air was cold against their faces. Slater felt energized gazing into the stars. Lying on his back, he imagined the Earth rotating and drifting through the universe.

"We'll need a second place," said Sherry.

"Why?"

"In case it's raining."

Slater laughed, "I'm not sure we're allowed to have more than one special place."

"It could be where we met that night," said Sherry.

"The Frost house? It was bulldozed into a shopping center."

"After we grew up. When we met again."

"In that dumpster behind City Hall?"

Sherry gave him a quizzical look. "What? No, when you were at The Crossroads that time."

"You insulted me."

"I got your attention."

"True," said Slater. "But it might be sacrilegious to designate a bar as your spiritual trading post."

"Let's go to sleep," said Sherry.

"Before I ruin the moment? Sweet dreams."

Slater yawned, unable to sleep, admiring the stars. He wanted to believe in miracles, the power of love to deliver him some peace. Sherry's soft breathing fell into a soft snore, like the purr of a cat. It would take him considerably longer to succumb to this surrender. He rolled his head away from the stars toward the flames.

In the distance he heard music and sat up.

Slater was feeling the weight of fatigue and rubbed his eyes. He yawned again, searching the surrounding darkness. He slowly noted the changing scenery. The redwood forest was a panoramic image, embedded in the walls of a hi-tech bar. The ceiling had blackened, resembling a night sky of stars. The stage and doorways were lined with fiber-optic tubing, snaking spectrums of light which transfixed his attention.

The Metro had redefined itself again.

Slater sipped his drink, enjoying the numbing ambiance and jazz seeping from hidden speakers. It was a sleepy instrumental rendition of *We Three Kings*.

Slater watched the dark forest walls dissolve and transform into brilliant colors. An entire wall became an undulating sea anemone nestled in a bed of yellow coral, its red mouth and swaying white phosphorescent feelers as hypnotic as a fire.

Slater watched its gigantic velvet lips part seductively.

Another floor-to-ceiling wall displayed time-lapse photography of life sprouting, budding, breaking into offerings of luscious petals, widening, then dropping into fallen flowers.

Another wall displayed mushrooms pushing through soil and growing into stiff erections before reversing...going underground.

The bartender chuckled. "Ready for another? Blue Shooter, mate? It's on the house."

Slater asked, "Why?"

"You look familiar. Once a regular, here?"

Slater said, "I used to play here."

"Everyone *plays* here, mate. My name's Mortimer. People call me Mort." He filled Slater's shot glass with blue liquid.

"Thanks," said Slater. "No more after this."

Mortimer laughed. "No more? Says you and every other bloke. It's like the whore who marries the saint. Ever hear that one?"

Slater heard music. His attention drifted toward the stage.

"Both wants what the other's got, and it's bound to disappoint. It's the age-old dilemma. I call it the bloody *crossroads*."

Slater looked back at Mortimer, arranging glasses.

"Were you working here back then?"

"Back when...? *Hey!*" Mortimer plucked a cigarette from the mouth of a customer seated near to Slater.

The man was drowsy and indignant. "Damn's this?"

"Damn *yourself*, mate," said Moritmer. "No light'n up."

The man complained his case to Slater in a bitter laugh, "He's a bit edgy, eh. I got rights. It's a pissing *bar*, ain't it?"

Mortimer dropped the man's lit cigarette into his shot glass. It contained remnants of blue liquid—causing a minor but loud flash. "Good thing you were thirsty or we'd all be *dead*."

The customer was shaken, inspecting himself for damage.

Mortimer warned, "I trust you'll henceforth behave yourself."

"So Mort," asked Slater, "were you? Working here when this place was The Crossroads?"

"It's always been the *crossroads*."

"I meant when it was called The Crossroads. I was the vocalist in a band that used to perform here."

"Ah," he said. "I knew you looked familiar."

"Dyslexic Dogs?" said Slater. "Mean anything to you?"

"Everything means something. Whether it's discernable amidst the random noise is another matter. Excuse me." An argument had culminated into potential violence at one end of the long bar and Mortimer left to attend to business.

Slater refocused his attention on the waitress who was dressed in amber. She was moving between the glowing tables. A waitress working the other side of the room was dressed in sapphire. Near the stage a waitress was in emerald. The bar had become crowded. So crowded, people appeared to be passing through one another. Slater watched it happen again and became so disconcerted that he pushed his drink away, deciding to focus his energy on the stage.

The percussionist was seated on a platform that showcased an elaborate set of drums, cymbals, and gongs. He was behind the other band members who were standing in loose formation fingering and tuning their instruments. Center stage was a harpist, seated, who wore a black formal gown, and whose dark fiery hair cascaded over bare shoulders. She was straddling an instrument of ancient origin. While its neck and column were ornately classical in design, it had been modernized and wired for amplification. She caressed this harp as if prepared to make love.

Vibrations from her strings washed in electrified waves over the recorded music and brought the talkative noise to a murmur.

The harpist smiled serenely within the spotlight.

Slater was certain he knew her.

From somewhere.

Eons ago.

— 23 —
Repairing Damage

"I thought you were dead."

"No," said Slater.

Gloria unplugged her guitar. She looked down at Slater from the edge of a partially lit stage. She wore gold spandex. "Too bad." She turned to leave through the curtain. She went a few steps and stopped, hung her head and came back to say, "I hate you. Why'd you do it? What happened to your face?"

"An accident," said Slater.

"Wolfe said you went to Egypt," said Gloria.

"Not intentionally," said Slater.

She squinted at the vertical scar, a deep slash down his cheek. "You almost look better." She saw someone standing next to him. The woman was pregnant. "She's with you?"

"Sherry, meet Gloria," said Slater. "We're on our honeymoon. We recently got married."

Gloria laughed. "Slater, your timing was always *impeccable*. Gawd. Ah, hell, congratulations."

"Thank you." Sherry placed a hand on her stomach.

"I never figured you for the fathering type," said Gloria.

"People change," said Slater. "Can I buy you a drink?"

"*Wrong!*" Gloria clenched the neck of her guitar. The thought of tossing it at him crossed her mind. "You have some...*nerve*, Slater, showing up after—ah, fuck it all. Vegas sucks, but...I'll do it. Give me a minute." She set down her guitar and hopped off stage.

Slater and Sherry sipped soda water while Gloria took gulps of a double scotch. She was skeptical.

"So how did you two lovebirds meet?"

"You were there," said Slater. "At The Crossroads one night. Actually, before that."

"We met at a Christmas party when we were teenagers," said Sherry. She reached over to take Slater's hand. "For a short time we went to the same high school. We hardly knew each other."

"Isn't love grand." Gloria crushed out her cigarette. "Quit?"

"I gave it up," said Slater. "I do take drugs, but ones prescribed to stabilize my mood swings."

110

"Christ, no fun in that," laughed Gloria, and turned her eyes on Sherry. "How many months?"

"Seven," said Sherry. "I like your band."

"We suck." Gloria grimaced. "What's the incentive? Playing to a bunch of high-rolling losers. They pay well. Thanks all the same." She turned back to Slater. "And Smitty? A stock broker? *Hell's* up with that? I'd heard he sold his drums. What'd you hear?"

"The same," said Slater.

Gloria jabbed his shoulder with her knuckles. "*God*, Slater, I can't...Hell, I didn't mean what I said. I'm glad you're alive, but — God-damn it, tell me. Why'd you fuck us over?"

"I went crazy," said Slater. "No, seriously."

"Shit, you were *always* crazy." Gloria lit another cigarette. She glanced at no one in particular. "They don't let you smoke in here but if they throw me out they don't get a second set. Sherry, a word for the wise. This guy you wed thought the world was his private bedlam. Yeah, *Romeo* here, the one you're in love with. So, believe me when I tell you I wish you both the very best."

"He's changed, Gloria," said Sherry.

"For better or worse?" With a hoarse laugh, Gloria signaled for another Scotch.

"Both," said Slater.

"So," said Gloria, "Satyr, you do *what* now? You don't sing. I know that from Wolfe. Write poetry?"

"I managed to get a book published."

"I know," she said. "I threw it in the trash. Nothing personal."

Slater smiled. "It didn't sell, except for one copy. Thanks."

"Rob banks, what?" said Gloria.

Slater grinned. "I went back to college. To study chemistry and computer science. I'm what you call a business man. Go figure."

"*That* I don't believe," said Gloria. "I mean it."

"He's an inventor," said Sherry.

"Tell me about it," said Gloria.

"I came up with this amazing idea when I was freezing to death, living on the streets. I was homeless for awhile," said Slater.

"Stop it, you're tearing at my heart." Gloria gulped her scotch. "You two ready for another round of soda?"

Slater explained, "It's a material that keeps you warm."

"What is?" said Gloria.

"His invention. It's a fabric," said Sherry.

"*Similar* to a fabric, but it does much more," added Slater.

Gloria laughed and wagged her finger comically. "This sounds like you. Is this how Slater got you to—you know, *did* it to you? Honey, it's *like* a fabric. Let's experiment. Try it on. Makes you feel warm and fuzzy inside. What a line, you old Satyr, you."

Sherry's face reddened with anger. "We have a *patent*. And his product happens to work!"

"I can see that." Gloria finished her scotch and stood. She addressed Sherry, "No offense, but Satyr could make more *mullah* if he wrote his memoirs. His *ménage á trois*. Would I lie? He's like God-damned infamous for it. Do a book, Slater — of your greatest fucking *hits*. Hey, best of luck. I've to go make a living."

Gloria walked away. She came back, flung money on the table. "In case you can't afford the drinks. Here, take another twenty. Call it my investment in your—ah, yeah—*future*."

"Glory, I'm sorry you're so bitter," said Slater.

"Bitter?" snapped Gloria with a laugh.

"I'll make it up to you someday," said Slater.

"You can't," said Gloria. "Have you given your wife a full count of all the women you've screwed? I'll give you a clue, Sherry. It would take *more* than all the fingers in this room. But, here, you can start with this one."

Gloria extended a single digit and stomped away.

—24—
Remnants

Firestorms had crossed the hills north of the bay, destroying forests and homes during an unprecedented summer heat.

Slater was listening to a news update on the television.

"I might have seen it coming. Been able to prevent it."

"Not likely," said Sherry.

They were living in San Francisco, now married and renting an old Victorian with an option to buy. The house needed repairs. Slater convinced Sherry he was handy with tools. Seated on the sofa, she put a blanket with a pattern of yellow ducks in his lap.

Slater reacted to the news reporter: "An arsonist!? Innocent people died! God, what are these idiots thinking?"

"I'd rather not know." Sherry handed him their baby daughter who was new to world only three weeks. "Don't go crazy on me. You're a father now. You have responsibilities."

Sondra was looking up at Slater.

"I think she smiled. Hello. She's so vulnerable and tiny."

"We all are," said Sherry.

"How can they trust us to know what to do?"

"Who's they? Here." Sherry handed him a book. "Try reading the instruction manual."

"She comes with one?"

Sherry grinned and whacked his shoulder with the paperback. "This baby thing is not a new craze. It's been going on awhile."

"Really? I thought we were the first."

She informed him, "It's an interesting read, about breastfeeding, preparing formulas, changing diapers, burping, diarrhea—"

"Way more than I care to know." Slater handed Sondra back to Sherry. "She can actually do all that?"

"We'll need batteries."

"Considering the hospital bill," said Slater, remotely clicking off the TV. "You'd think they'd throw some in."

"No need," said Sherry, "she's pooped. It's okay, lamby-pamby, Mommy, or maybe Daddy, will get rid of that nasty doo-doo."

Slater flipped to the book's index. "Are these technical terms you're using, Dear? Diapers, Doctors, Dogs. Hum, they don't list

Doo-Doo, Sweetie."

"Truffles, get away!" said Sherry, removing the dirty diaper. "John, keep Truffles away. And take care of this too."

Slater pinched his nose with one hand and the disposable diaper with his other. "Truffles, down! It's not a frisbee."

The house suddenly whined and screeched as if a squadron of flying termites had landed, discarded their wings and went straight to sex and ripping apart the foundation. It was Paul Slater working in the basement.

"Tell Paul," said Sherry, "that I'm putting Sondra down for a nap. He needs to take a break. And I need a break."

"Aye-aye, Captain." Slater saluted, deposited the diaper into a foot-levered trash bin then went to bang on the basement door. He opened it and shouted, "All engines are to cease! Do you read me, Paul? We'll be on silent maneuvers until...?"

"Three o'clock, maybe four?" said Sherry.

"Until further notice. Paul, do you read me?"

A reply in the form of two knocks was transmitted through the furnace vent. The engines began to decelerate.

Slater tapped back. "You're a good man. We're borrowing your nurse to watch over Sondra while we're out. Over and out."

Sherry stopped at the foot of the stairway to say, "I like Paul."

Slater jiggled a baluster that needed replacement.

"Fix it later," she said. "Help me put her down."

"I'm all yours." He squeezed her bottom as she made her way up the stairs.

"Stop it," she laughed. "Sondra's about to doze off."

"Shall we try for another? Go for an even two?"

"I'd rather we went to the park."

"Kind of kinky but—okay," said Slater.

"I meant for a walk." From the landing Sherry lowered her eyes to where Paul Slater resided in their basement. "He's sweet, not so crazy. Not that I can tell, anyway."

It was a question in disguise to express a legitimate concern.

"A bit eccentric is all," said Slater.

"Wonderfully eccentric. You never told me why he shot you."

"He doesn't know. I was probably being a naughty boy and I

deserved to be shot in the head."

"Probably," said Sherry. "It's...you know what I mean."

"We're safe. Sondra too. Paul is completely medicated. Nurses are standing guard around-the-clock. And, all of these women will likely fall in love with him. Paul's a charmer."

"Don't I know," she laughed.

Sherry had been charmed herself, first on the dance floor at their wedding. Paul had twirled her until she was dizzy and laughing from his comically romantic style, all the while vowing he would never love another daughter-in-law, promising to shower her in gold dust. The second charming occurred when Paul fought off a mugger who had knocked her down and snatched her purse while shopping in Union Square. Paul chased the mugger five blocks before tackling him and retrieving her goods. When Sherry located Paul by way of a crowd, the police were already arresting both assailant and uncle on suspicion.

A computer search had identified Paul Slater as a criminal out on parole with a history of weird mayhem.

"No, stop!" she shouted. "That man saved my life!"

"This man, lady," said the officer, "is a convicted felon."

"He's my father-in-law and one of the most loving people on this planet! My husband and I are his guardians, I mean—what do I mean, Paul?"

"I've been placed in their custody."

"We're responsible—yes, for his actions." Sherry stepped in front of the squad car door. "You have to let him go. He fought off then apprehended this—this creep!"

"Ma'am, we'll clear this up at headquarters."

"No! He's a hero, not a criminal! Look inside that purse. It's mine. My wallet. My picture's in there. Look, damn you! I'm not going to let you take him! I won't!"

There was a call to the precinct, to a higher-up. The handcuffs were removed and Paul and Sherry hugged.

The embrace spanned time.

She adored Paul. But when he first arrived to live in her house, straight out of a mental institution, she received him graciously — as one accepts a prank wedding gift. Sherry's own contribution to the marriage, aside from herself as the bride, had been an assortment of furniture. Her hobby was finding and restoring unique items. Paul Slater proceeded to charm her again by building a wooden crib for their expected baby. The crib had rockers and a headboard carved with overlooking angels.

In reverse fashion, the groom, Slater, had undergone his own tepid reception, scrutinized by her parents, who finally unlatched the invisible gates and welcomed him upon contributing a grandchild. With this commitment of child, her parents suddenly viewed him as a legitimate family member, no longer harboring reservations about the marriage. Prior to baby, they acted as though they retained the right to have the entire blessed union annulled at their whim, even demand a refund on the wedding – including costs for damages.

"Hurt my daughter," said Knowles with a firm embrace at the wedding, "and I'll kill you, personally. I want you to know that. Now go have yourselves a great life together." The handshake was painfully firm. It included a transfer from palm to palm of a check made out for fifty thousand dollars (written to Sherry in her maiden name). "A little nest egg. Be sure not to break it, Son."

"I don't know what to say," said Slater. "Thank you, Sir."

"Stan, or Dad. I'm father to you now."

"Stan," said Slater.

Even the wink was firm, a crinkling of crow's feet at the eyes. "Know what *not* to do. Remember that."

Sherry saw the numerical value and screamed.

Slater's was internal. He hadn't bargained on getting in-laws. Not these. Barbara Knowles was in a hysterical quandary of joy and loss. Her mascara was expressionistic – streaking from her face in blues and purples that dissolved into her rouge and remixed with tears that spread further from swipes of her hands – a centrifugal blast of color – emanating from blackened eyes. She clutched her daughter in a desperate hug.

Slater couldn't shake the image of his mother-in-law possessing the look of a wild, possibly rabid, animal.

She lunged at him next.

"Dear, do something with your face," said Stan Knowles.

Roy Frost was drunk and chivalrous with a handkerchief. He

116

took the opportunity to wink and whisper in her ear.

"Barbs, considering Sherry could theoretically be ours, it's a good thing John is not biologically mine."

Slater overheard and swung his head at them.

Roy tried to detoxify Slater's expression with a laugh, "Son, it's a private joke. Old army humor. Don't go ballistic."

He didn't. But Heather did. Her eyes narrowed into turret slits. Her pupils virtually disappeared into ferocious sucking black holes. She later kissed her congratulations with compressed lips to both the groom and bride, then left, forgoing the wedding cake, frivolous dancing and rice tossing.

Roy had to get a ride home with the Twindles.

A month later his father was dead. He collapsed mysteriously on the 18th green, six strokes under par. "I'm in a zone," he had proclaimed to those in his foursome. He would have broken his best score had he not gone down holding his chest and putter, unable to follow through on his final putt.

Years passed before Slater took up golf.

Now, when he meandered through the park, Slater used Roy's putter as a walking stick and to putt Truffle's droppings into a zip-lock baggie in compliance with the city ordinances.

Truffles was released from his leash and Slater sat on a bench beside Sherry. She lay her head on his lap. Almost instantly she was asleep. Slater admired her ability to plunge into unconsciousness. By contrast, his thoughts formed whirlpools, swirling him round and round until he tired from exhaustion to stay afloat and succumbed to the pull, going under. He stroked Sherry's hair as he watched a parade of cumulus clouds transform into a herd of elephants, morph into leaping whales, then disperse into a smoking locomotive.

He sniffed the air. Winds were still drifting remnants of ash from the fire up north over San Francisco.

Remnants of life were always drifting. Like seeds blown by the wind, striving to survive, to find a home. It occurred to Slater that, despite these remnant worries, he was happy. Happy not knowing what would be coming next.

His wife was peacefully sleeping. So was the future.

House of Hard Knocks

"I hope you're happy now," said Heather Frost.

"Honest to God, we love you, Son," said Roy. "It's just—"

"I'm a different kind of animal," said Slater. He was sixteen. The three of them were seated in a courtroom. The judge sat high above, looking down at her attendants facing her wooden throne. Roy was nervously clenching the shaft of his putter between his legs. Suspicious by nature, the Judge had her eyes on the putter. She saw a weapon, not a cane. She pronounced her decision with words that were carefully weighted. "Since you have violated the terms of your probation twice, the court overrules your appeal for further leniency and has made the decision to place you in a corrections facility."

"Prison?" said Slater.

Heather stood. "No! I won't have it! You can't take our son away and put him into a—into a *reform* school! You can't."

"I can. Sit down, Madam. I am warning you again."

The judge gave Heather, then Slater, a judicious scowl.

"You failed to stay out of trouble as you promised the court. And your parents have failed in their determined effort to hold you to that promise, John. You overturned an automobile endangering your own life and potentially others."

Slater interjected, "I was alone, your Honor, and no one—"

"Be silent," said the judge. "Fortunately no one was hurt. And, you were drunk." She referred to papers on her desk and shook her head. "And with a blood alcohol level registering point *three*." She ruffled through papers to another. "Eliminate the decimal and...it becomes your grade point average. It appears you have intelligence. If only you would use it. We can now add an arrest for shoplifting. You stole a pint of Vodka."

Slater's hair was neatly combed and he was wearing a suit and tie, at Heather's insistence. He gave a contrite smile. But none of it seemed to help sway the judge in his favor. "Your honor, I'd have gladly *paid* for the Vodka if only—"

"It was not illegal? But it *is*." Her face returned a smile not intended to emit warmth. "You, Mr. Slater, are a *minor*. Drinking alcohol is not *permitted*. You have an unimpressive list of deviant behavior. Therefore, it is my appointed duty to make an attempt at correcting your habit of using bad judgement.

"John Lazard Slater III, I am placing you, by order of the court, into the San Francisco County and State Corrections Facility for Boys, for one full year."

She slammed down her gavel.

Roy dropped his putter.

Heather lifted her chin resolutely, defeated.

Slater yanked off his clip-on tie and smiled mischievously.

The judge rotated her neck a notch, owl-like, at him.

Heather told him, "I saw it coming. It was in your chart."

"What chart?" The judge fingered the papers on her desk.

"Astrological." Heather was miffed at the judge's power to take away her son, but explained, "Mars and Pluto are passing through his 6th house. Don't even *ask* about Saturn. He's entering a very turbulent cycle, Your Honor."

The judge blinked, recoiling, as though her head was prepared for a complete 360 degree rotation.

"We'll visit you," said Roy. "This jail— school, rather— won't kill you, Son. It will only make you stronger. Ma'am?"

The judge rotated her head toward Roy.

"We'll be permitted to visit?"

The judge ignored him and turned a notch to reexamine Slater. "You realize I'm doing this for your own good."

"More than you realize." He flashed the judge a smile as if to say he had actually wanted this sentence. He had.

His bemusement was not infectious.

The judge screeched for a bailiff.

Forewarned by friends that kids got raped in jail, Slater told them, "It's not a prison." And yet, the first week of his incarceration he was initiated in the shower room by a gang of boys surrounding him and threatening to "make you our girl." Their taunt transpired into a fist fight. Which he lost, but won by gaining respect among these adolescent thugs. His fellow incarcerates, for the most part, Slater realized, were not so tough. Just emotionally screwed up. Unlucky like, or unlike, himself.

Using ear plugs, Slater slept through the storms of snoring and midnight tales of bravado. Confined in this so-called correctional institution, he withdrew deeper and had more troubling visions – of being locked in dungeons and tortured by fools. These demons in his dreams wore colorful costumes as foolish as clowns and were capped with pointed hoods to hide their faces. And their laughter was not meant to humor him. With knives, they sliced him to edify his mind with the rules of obedience. He heard them talk of saints and knights who wore long beards and were devoted to serving God and willing to sacrifice themselves. Templars, they were called. The next day, he searched the school library and was shocked to realize the name — *Templars* — actually existed. He read the historical account of these knights. It only seemed to escalate his fitful visions. He was bound like Christ on a cross, bleeding from his chest. In another dream he was confronted by a decapitated head suspended in a crystal ball.

In an attempt to keep himself sane, Slater used transference to forge these sights and sounds into melodies and lyrics.

One day a lanky inmate, looking as ragged as a lone animal used to surviving in the wild, approached him outside the cafeteria and asked, "What're you doing?"

"What's it to you?" he countered.

"You like to write a lot."

"So? It's not a crime."

"Unless they're confessions."

Slater grinned and pointed. "What's that?"

Wolfe glanced down, dismissing the pocketbook in his hand. "Kafka. About this man in a modern Minotaur's maze."

"The Castle," said Slater.

"Did you read the one where this guy turns into a cockroach?"

"Yeah, I know that one too," said Slater.

"Living in *this* madhouse? No shit." Wolfe scratched his chin-stubble smile that tapered into a beard. "My name's Wolfe."

"Slater." Slater shut his notebook. He was leaning against the trunk of a maple tree losing its leaves. "Did you want something?"

"Are you a poet?" said Wolfe.

Slater recognized this kid from his science class.

"I play guitar," said Wolfe.

"I play with myself," said Slater.

Wolfe was slow on the take—the joke—and laughed belatedly. "Yeah, me too, man. I miss my girlfriend bad."

"What kind?" said Slater.

"Of girl?" said Wolfe.

"Music," said Slater.

"The only kind," said Wolfe. "I'd demonstrate – implode your mind – if this place allowed my guitar and amp. I'm good."

"Too bad. So what's your excuse?"

"For what?" said Wolfe.

"Being in here?" said Slater.

Wolfe kicked the grass. "Bucking authority, what else."

"Hum." Slater vivisected the veins from a leaf.

"Yours?" said Wolfe.

Slater displayed the spidery skeleton of the maple leaf. "Me? I booked this mini-vacation. I actually wanted to come here."

"Bull*shit*." Wolfe wondered if he should laugh.

"My real parents died before I was born. I'm what's called a sad case. I was adopted. My uncle tried to shoot me, but fortunately he couldn't shoot worth a shit. Then these foster parents pluck me out of an orphanage because they think I'm this special *zodiac* child, due to my time of birth, location of the planets and the ice-cream flavor of the month. Who knows. So, they adopt me and I discover they're – yeah, I think it's safe to say – fucking *nuts.*"

Slater shrugged, exhibiting a placid smile. "Oh, yeah, I forgot to mention, I get these visions. I believe it's the future. Difficult to say. Although my adopted mother, Heather Frost, is convinced. Which is why she purchased me from the orphanage. Then again, I could be insane. A schizoid. Anything else you want to know?"

"You're weird." Wolfe clarified, "No, I like it."

"Great," said Slater.

"Can you write songs?" said Wolfe.

"You tell me." Slater handed Wolfe a poem.

Building the Perfect Beast

To be corporeal, by definition, was not to be spiritual.
'Corporation teashirt
stupid bloody Tuesday
man you been a naughty boy
you let your face grow long...'
Slater's visions came with loopholes and pitfalls.

Corporations were material entities legally empowered to act as one, united for a purpose.

"To make money," said Stan Knowles, placing fist to palm and focusing them on the bottom line. "And to manage it properly. I've handled some of the largest portfolios. You'd be surprised. And I've done, without modesty, extremely well. But I'm retired. Listen, I'm willing to advise you two, Sherry and John, as I have already up to this point. But what you're asking me now—"

"Stan," said Slater, "we need someone we can trust."

"That's not the point."

"It is," said Sherry.

"I'm touched, deeply." Knowles clawed his daughter's shoulder, shaking her lightly, uncertain about protocol regarding this mix of business and family. "But your mother and I have made other plans. To take that trip around the world, which I promised her."

"Only for a year," said Sherry. "One year."

"Until we get our bearings," added Slater.

"Have you been listening? I said, I am retired. And definitely, absolutely never, would I consider working for a company called – what was it again?" Reading glasses were clenched in his hand and he placed them on his head to stare at the proposal. *"Stupid Bloody Tuesday, Inc?* Good Lord, what possessed you to call it that?"

"Humor?" Slater offered.

"Do you see me laughing?" said Knowles.

"It's derived from a famous song," said Sherry.

"Where it should remain," declared Knowles. "One of yours, John, I suppose?"

"No, Lennon and McCartney," said Slater.

"Who?" said Knowles.

"The Beatles, Dad: *'I am the Walrus?'*" said Sherry.

"You're a—you're a—*what?*"

"*Coo-Coo C-Joob,*" said Slater.

Waiting for translation and flummoxed by the possibility that increased age was now taking away his hearing too, Knowles said, "Nevertheless, you cannot *name* a corporation with something that ridiculous. You have to think like a businessman. Hell, John, you don't even dress like a businessman."

"T-shirts and jeans, what? Stan, relax," said Slater. "We're not locked on that name. We have other names we were considering." Slater looked for help among those assembled, who seemed unsure, so he dismissed it, "Never mind. We can hire a marketing firm for creative wisdom. We need something better than our current name, Slater & Slater. It sounds like...an accounting firm."

"I totally concur," said Knowles, half-scowling.

Slater returned to the end of the conference table where he sat near the window. He was depressed over his uncle's recent suicide. His father-in-law had implied he had no business sense, which was possibly true. He lacked the experience to head a corporation, also true. And their proposed corporate name was a stupid joke. True — all true. Yet appropriate, given his uncle's quirky humor and self-imposed death. Darkly ironic too, since his uncle finally invented something that worked. They were even granted a patent. They had created a product that was marketable! And had a demand!

Slater's eyes trailed the fluorescent ceiling.

Their invention: *ThermoCloth.* A fabric that had an adjustable temperature, regulated by a thermostat the size of a shirt button. The material's composition worked in conjunction with the body's own unique chemistry to create a molecular interaction. Cloth that could be tailored into coats, shirts, pants, practically anything.

What they lacked was money to launch them to the next level. They required financial investors, a point his uncle refused to admit. His uncle had distrust issues, believing someone, if not everyone, was out to screw them. As equal partners they had been on the verge of becoming equally rich beyond their wildest dreams.

"Millions, Johnny, we're talking *millions,*" said Paul. "We have orders from manufacturers all around the world!"

"We did it," said Slater, "like you said we would."

"Expect law suits from all the Greedy-Sons-of-Bitches."

"Attorneys will take care of them. Paul, we need to grow fast. And if we don't get financial investors soon we'll go nowhere. Please talk to Stan. Sherry's father is a venture capitalist."

"Exactly my point. A capitalist. He'll want to take over. No, Johnny, the competition is running scared, and they *know* it."

"Paul, be reasonable," said Slater, "we can't do this alone."

"Damn-it-to-hell, I wish Skunk was here to enjoy this. Hanna too, God rest her sweet soul." Paul Slater was feeling so ecstatic he stood on a chair, stepped upon his desktop and tap-danced. Slater laughed, which encouraged his uncle to add more steps, twirling his arms, clicking his heels, and ending on bended knee.

Slater clapped. His uncle was so euphoric he admitted he had declared war on his prescribed medication by vowing, "I will break the shackles of all chemical enslavements! Know that!"

"Know what?" said Slater

"I'm a genius, like I told you."

"You did. Are those new?"

"No, old vaudevillian tricks."

"The pills you're taking."

"New prescription, new doctor, new day." He hopped off the desk, popped more pills in his mouth, displaying more in his palm. "Herbal, Johnny. All natural. The only way to go. And I've never felt better. We can—and *will!* Remember?"

"*Can...will,*" echoed Slater, "but we need financial support."

"Tasty too." Paul selected another pill. "Try one?"

"I'll stick to my own brand. Paul, are you listening to me?"

Paul, hell bent on skepticism, said, "I am. John, I was never insane. Okay, okay, I tried to shoot you. I've always been suspicious about that. It was the product of negative forces at work."

"Right. From that Greedy-Son-of-a-Bitch."

Paul howled. "Yes! Damn right, he exists. I wasn't really crazy. I was *tampered* with. Made crazy. To my dying day I'll believe that. You will too. Know that."

An unscheduled disappearance by his uncle for weeks was not unusual, but Slater had begun to worry. Then one sunny morning he heard, through employees, that Paul was back. Except Slater was unable to locate his uncle in the usual locations – holding court in the coffee room, giving advice at the vending machine, tinkering in his lab or office. Slater found him at sunrise in the conference room.

"Paul, what are you doing here? Where were you?"

His uncle swiveled halfway around, leaning back in a chair at the end of the long conference table. A spectacular view of the city was unfolding outside, beyond the windows. He held a gun.

"I'm afraid of heights," he said.

"We'll relocate," said Slater.

"You know what I mean."

"I don't," said Slater. "Is this about the decision we made, about taking on investors?"

"I'll *miss*, more than likely," said his uncle.

"Tell me what's wrong? Talk to me, Paul. Please."

Paul had a lot to tell him. And did.

He closed with: "I'm curious, Johnny, what day is it?"

"Tuesday, why?" said Slater.

His uncle's skill with a hand gun had improved.

In memory, Slater's head fell back to rest against the chair.

"What did you say?" said Knowles.

"I said...never mind." Slater had a defeated smile. "Stan, we're not trying to force you into anything. Could you at least provide us recommendations of qualified people who could help guide me at the helm? I'd really prefer not to run this whole venture aground."

"Mr. Knowles, might I have a word." Henry Weiner was the only one, besides Knowles, wearing a suit and tie.

"You're John's attorney?" said Knowles.

"Heaven's no!" said Weiner. "I hate attorneys."

"*I'm* a attorney," scowled Knowles.

"*Most* attorneys," Weiner laughed uneasily, "is what I *meant* to say. No, I'm...what am I, John?"

"Vice President, Director of Public Relations," said Slater.

"Relations. That's it," said Weiner. "We'll be getting business cards once we decide on the name. Are you fully aware about the *requests* for our product, Mr. Knowles?"

"Yes, I am aware—or I wouldn't be where I *am* today."

Wolfe sniffed and whispered to Gloria, "I say forget him."

Knowles turned his head, "Who in *blazes* are you?"

"COO, and temporary CFO," said Wolfe.

"It figures," said Knowles. "And, you are *wrong* Mr..."

"Wolfe," said Wolfe.

"Mr...*Woof*," said Knowles. "You do need me. Or someone as qualified as me. Or you *will* undoubtedly fail."

"Then join us, Father," said Sherry.

"No," said Knowles. "I maintain to remain a silent partner."

"He's playing hard to get," said Wolfe.

Knowles frowned. "Why, might I ask, would you think that?"

"Let's call in Smitty," said Gloria.

"Who's *Smitty?*" said Knowles.

"A stock broker," said Sherry.

"Smitty works the New York exchange," said Gloria. "And he thinks progressively."

"With all due respect, Ms..."

"Gloria. Research and Development."

"I'm not simply..." Knowles became flustered. "I've explained who I am already. And I can be as *progressive* as it takes. I've had extensive experience in all arenas of the corporate world, including New York, thank you, Miss—Ms. *R and D.*"

"It's all right, Stan," said Slater, "we respect your position and advice and the fact that you want to retire. You deserve it."

"Thank you, John," Knowles was not through. "And, I'll have you know, I've held a *cabinet* position. As a special *advisor* to the President."

"Which one?" said Wolfe.

"The United States of America—*that* one."

"If I might interject," said Weiner, "to bring us all back to our forecast in sales, and what it could mean in dollar figures?"

"Don't waste your time for my sake," Knowles said. "I've seen the preliminary reports. Your uncle, before his untimely demise – my condolences, John, quite tragic – he showed me the figures. I would venture it's an optimistic guess, at best."

"Would you prefer it be *pessimistic?*" said Gloria.

"Guess? No, not a guess. No." Weiner returned his spectacles to his head, reaching for his data. "That's where you're wrong. We have actual orders coming in. Thousands upon thousands."

"You do?" said Knowles. "Contracts? Written orders?"

"We do," said Weiner. "Would you like to hear our offer?"

"There's no point, but...well," Knowles waved him on.

"Have the courtesy to listen," scolded Gloria.

"Yes, go on, my decision's made, but...fine," said Knowles.

"As our CFO," said Weiner, reading from his prepared speech, "you'd be earning in the first year half a million."

"Too much," muttered Wolfe.

"A modest salary," said Weiner, "for a man of your stature. Plus benefits, the usual, et cetera, which you probably don't really *need*. Or do you?" He laughed and glanced up, before frowning and focusing back down. "And, your salary increasing one million the following year, provided you stay and sales projections...pan out. And, with your own significant investment, thank you, thank you, and your help in assembling others to invest in our venture, well, the profits gained will be very impressive, accruing anywhere from..."

Knowles scowled when he gave thought to a thorny problem. He listened with a single focus, transmuting the words into a living thing, like a tiny insect he could visually inspect before crushing to death or grant extended life, or so he imagined. But not presently. Midway through Weiner's speech his heart felt the pull of destiny and began fluttering over earlier pledges – to usher in a brave new world and not simply be a *silent* partner. To be proactive. "Yes, yes, I know, I know all that." He took command and surprised everybody by showing interest in the proposal.

He asked, "What was that name you proposed?"

"Name?" asked Weiner.

"Company name you said a minute ago." Knowles' snapped his fingers to increase production.

Slater said, "You mean, Stupid Bloody—?"

"No. That *second* name you proposed."

"Second name?" said Slater.

Silence like the hesitation before the storm of creation.

"*NeverMind,*" said Knowles. "Wasn't that it?"

Slater, Weiner, Sherry, Wolfe, and Gloria looked at each other.

Knowles gave a good-natured laugh. "I grant you, it's *bizarre*. Weirdly progressive, but the fashion of today. I actually like it. All right, then, let me examine those papers overnight and I'll give you my answer in the morning. Are we all agreed?"

"Agreed," said Weiner.

"Greed, yes, definitely greed," said Wolfe. He leaned over and whispered to Slater, "I told you this tactic would work."

Slater stood, bracing himself for Knowles' grip.

NEVERMIND, INC.

—27—
Time of Sand

Slater kept falling but getting up.

He was lost, at age 23, in an Egyptian desert. At dusk. Wind and sand were tearing at his flesh. His leather jacket was unzipped, and his shirt unbuttoned for ventilation. They flapped like tattered sheets of a sail. He tore off a section of his shirt tail, twisting and knotting it into a bandanna to protect his eyes.

He staggered blindly.

The voices and visions stung him like swarming locusts. His feet trudged leadenly through a moving groundswell of frogs, blood and hissing snakes.

He spit sand from his lips and turned his back to the wind, with enough sense left to walk backwards, so as not to choke to death as he screamed for redemption.

He welcomed God to annihilate him as he rose and fell with the dune's cresting waves. He lost his balance and tumbled, and got up, teetering and stumbling over this sand-slipping ocean while a raging static of wind mimicked a universe unreceptive and on-the-blink.

His face and chest were blistered and torn. Sand stuck in the raw infected crevices. His headband was soaked in sweat, encrusted with desert filth. He tasted blood with his swollen lips in the hope of quenching his thirst.

A sudden swirling gust spun him in a new direction.

He refused to turn away, or give up, or drop.

His muscles threatened to rebel and throw him into convulsions. He was freezing, beyond pain. A barrage of miniscule razor-hot rocks pummeled him in a comet-shower – colliding, trying to break through his body's atmospheric skin.

Another step and he fell into deep space.

Infinity.

He landed upon the sun.

His body burst into flames. Liquefied skin melted in his hands, off his face, prior to being entirely consumed.

"There now, hush," said his aunt, stroking his forehead.

Her face emerged from the sparkling darkness.

"You had a bad dream, Johnny," Hanna said. "It's going to be all right. Don't you fret now."

"Am I dying?"

"Calm down," she said. "You're not going to die. You're safe. You have a fever, that's all."

"I'm afraid, Hanna."

"There, there, now. Honey, it's okay to be afraid. We all have to die. But it's not your time yet. So you rest."

Slater believed his aunt was wise and he trusted her.

"When *is* my time?" he asked.

She laughed and stroked his head. "God'll know when it's your time. I'll bet He's got big plans for you, so you'd better get some rest and be ready when you hear Him calling you, you hear me?"

"Calling me to do what?"

Hanna laughed, "Well, I don't rightly know. But whatever it is you'll be needing your rest. You go back to sleep."

"I'll die, Hanna. I will!"

"Johnny, what has you so riled and terrified?"

"*Hell,*" he confessed. "I was burning up in Hell. I *was.*"

"God doesn't punish the innocent. You're a good boy, Johnny."

Slater wasn't convinced but let himself be soothed.

"What else is troubling you? You can tell me."

"Why did my mom and dad die?"

"Johnny," said Hanna, "only God knows why."

"He never answers," said Slater.

"When is this?"

"You said to pray and ask. He doesn't listen to me. I never hear him say anything. He doesn't, Hanna."

"God speaks in mysterious ways. Maybe not our way, but God hears us all right. He's listening to you, Johnny."

"How do you know?"

"He's heard my call many times. Oh, yes. He has. You have to give yourself up to believing. It's called faith."

"You mean like...knowing we came from somewhere?"

"Yes, same place," she laughed.

"My parents, Hanna. What were they like?"

"Well, now..." She touched his forehead again, brushing back his damp hair. "They were looking forward to seeing you, I know that much. Paul and I gave them a shower."

Slater smiled. "Were they dirty?"

Hanna laughed. "Baby shower. You were about to be born. I was especially fond of your mother. She made me laugh. She had a special glow. I swear she could light up a room, your mother. You too, you're like her, in many ways."

"What about my father?"

"Well, now, your father...he..."

She was recalling something specific, wrestling whether to give in to its power. She shook her head.

"Your father was different. That's all I care to say. Sometimes I almost...I tried to see how your parents were good for each other. I saw the physical attraction. Like the night attracting the day. The moon in love with the sun. Opposites." Brightening, Hanna added, "You did inherit both your father's *and* your mother's good looks. Some good luck there. Your father...he was a very handsome man. But also very dark."

"Dark?"

"His moods." She dismissed it with a head shake, not wanting to alarm him. "Your father and I disagreed on matters, let's leave it at that. I guess you could say *we* weren't such a good match. But, he amused me. Humor as dry as the desert wind. Catching me off guard like the snap of a twig. Lord, he could shake me up with a laugh. I believe he meant well. I do. Then again, he had notions I couldn't *abide* with."

"Like what?"

"Honestly, they scared me." Hanna patted his head.

"Like what?"

"It doesn't matter now. I'm just glad you came to be born. We should talk about this another time."

"What about my grandparents, Hanna?"

"I didn't know them." She pulled up his blankets, then stood. "Ask Paul, he can tell you more about your family."

"He won't talk about them. Why?"

She lingered to smooth his blanket. "What would you say if I told you your mother was an angel? Would you believe me?"

Slater smiled. "*No.*"

"There," she said. "It's my opinion that she was — *is* an angel. As close as I'm likely to come to knowing one. So dream about your dear departed mother. Hush now. You need rest. Get well."

"Why didn't you like my dad?"

Hanna turned at the door, embers of soft light glowing from the living room, a wavering yellow.

"Johnny, you're the American dream, that melting pot of all the romantic past. Rising up from a long line of kings, gypsies, slaves and saints, even thieves. And I love you, all of you, no matter what. Now get yourself some sleep. Sweet dreams."

The door closed, sealing him in darkness.

A gentle voice whispered nearby:

"Johnny...John, wake up...wake up."

He opened his eyes to a blackened emptiness. Gravity held him down to its invisible molten core. Pinned to it, he was a dead weight. He sensed the deceptively slow motion of the Earth, yet powerless to move or stop its perilous speed. He felt so weak he could not even lift the cloth covering his face.

There was a blurry shape, then a flutter of light.

A presence. His mother?

An angel?

—28—
A Way Station

Heaven, Slater thought, or was this Hell?

An angelic voice was near. In his other ear was a devilish laugh. Neither could agree on anything. He was hushed by the angel who told him to be calm in order to survive. The devil told him he was to die. The angel praised him for his beauty and prescient vision. But, she said, the time had come for him to decide who he was to be. The devil denounced everything as lies and depicted Slater as a beast who should be proud of his lecherous desires. The angel alerted him to be attentive, to listen to his heart, and do exactly as he was told in order to become one with their sacred order. The devil predicted his failure, but in the bargain so gaining immeasurable wealth and dominion upon the earth.

Slater said nothing, since his mouth was gagged.

He could see nothing.

The blindfold was removed.

It took a moment for his eyesight to adjust. He felt drugged, as if fighting the influence of some toxic substance of unknown origin. A congregation of robed and hooded creatures surrounded him. The lights were dimmed. He was in an underground structure with rock walls and a vast ceiling with dark massive rafters. This cavernous room was adorned with sconces and symbols (each depicting three overlapping crosses). Each one was enshrined by light. None of it felt comforting. Candles were burning. One came close to his face, then it withdrew.

He was tied to a cross. From years of helping his uncle in his workshop, Slater determined the vertical support to be a redwood post, a 2 by 8, anchored into the ground by cement. His ankles were bound at the base by nylon rope, and his outstretched arms bound at the wrists with more twine to a connecting beam.

Christ, he thought, this can't be happening.

The skin at his forehead was tight against his skull, caused by more of the same securing rope, though he could see none of it.

From what he *could* see, or divine — he was naked!

His heartbeat was rapid, his vision blurry, and his skin prickly hot. He was dehydrated. His memory gone. He had no idea of how or when he had come to be in this place.

It was the worst hangover yet.

One of the robed figures approached. The robes were shiny, made of satin. They resembled the choir outfits his aunt had worn in church. Linked crosses were embroidered on the chest and arms. Candlelight revealed the garments to be red, green, blue, purple, black. No apparent uniformity in color. The robe closest to him was gold. The hood had holes for eyes to see out, but too dark for Slater to see inside. Until a flame was raised. He saw pale blue irises. He also detected mascara.

The only things he could dredge up from memory was being on stage. He'd been sipping Cognac at a bar. He'd been arguing with Wolfe and Gloria. The usual horde of admirers had been hovering nearby, wanting to be near, hoping to be introduced, noticed.

Slater shivered, fearing for his life, but he braved a smile for the hooded face and said, "No need for all this fuss, just to meet me."

No response.

"Fine," he added, "then give me a robe too and we can all go tricking or treating."

"Silence!" The voice came from behind him.

The gold-hooded figure poked his chest with an ornate scepter. It meandered down his breastbone, over his navel, to his groin where the tip toyed with his soft hanging flesh. The hooded mask came off willingly to expose a beautiful face.

"Hi," said Slater. "Do I know you? I do, or...don't I?"

The woman smiled, barely, then gave his pecker a little poke and stepped away.

"You've done well, mistress," said a baritone voice.

Approaching from behind came a larger robe, purple. The hood was removed to reveal an older face, a balding man with long grey hair at the temples. Hairs sprouted from his bulbous ears. The eyes were also lined with mascara. Goitrous eyes.

"Now you," said Slater, "*you* I would remember."

"Would you now?"

"With that face, sure."

"Be sure of nothing."

"You throw a hell of a party. I meant to R.S.V.P."

"You're insolent," said the man.

"Occupational hazard."

A grin formed as the man noticed Slater's involuntary shaking. Then his smile ceased. "*Scared,* aren't you?"

"Are you main man, top dragon, that sort of thing?"

"Something like that. Call me Dale. Or *Lucifer.* It matters not. Not to me, nor to you." He pulled at his scepter and separated the narrow blade from its sheath.

"You don't have to do that." Slater gulped, tasting acid. More of the robed figures removed knives. "What's going on? I don't even know you, do I? Dale, or whatever you call yourself."

"It is *we,* John, who know *you.*"

"Is this about my lyrics? Or, what I said in that interview? I— I was misquoted — I was! I swear to God. We can work, you know, something out. I swear, I never *ever* claimed—"

"They want you to be scared. Show no fear," said the angelic voice from behind him. "You have inner strength. Find it."

Slater recognized the voice. The rope binding his head would not allow him to turn and see. "Who are you?"

"The time is now," said another voice. "For you to decide."

"Decide?" said Slater. "Decide what?"

"Your destiny — *fool!*" The laughing shout came from within the crowd. Many others assenting.

"This is intolerable," muttered another voice.

Ropes chafed his forehead as he struggled to break free. He closed his eyes. "Excuse me, this whole, whatever this is—is—is god-damned *insane!* Let me go. Please."

"No-can-do!" came another shout.

It was another voice he recognized from somewhere.

"Who are you people?" The entire hooded congregation was approaching with their knives raised. "I don't find this funny. Wolfe, I swear to God, if you're part of this...this *practical* joke, I swear to you—you are—"

"Dead?" Dale breathed a laugh. He directed the tip of his knife to Slater's neck. He lowered it to a nipple. Then a fraction more. "Wolfe? Wolfe, who?"

Slater said, "If you're trying to scare me or teach me some kind of *lesson* — okay, I concede. You win."

"What lesson might that be, John?" asked Dale.

"Listen, if you let me go, I promise not to press charges. This never happened, okay? I promise to forget the whole ordeal."

"Indeed, you will forget," said another male voice.

"Why should we believe your promises?" said Dale.

"Because I'm telling the *truth!*" shouted Slater.

"Truth?" said Dale. "What is truth? Life *is* but an illusion. I'm sure you've heard that one before. And it *is* true. Therefore, truth, must consists of lies. Pure logic."

A murmuring confirmation rose among the congregation.

"Comprehend your situation, John Lazard Slater III," said Dale. "We are here *for* you, not against you. We are to be feared—and, to be loved. Loved *by* you. Why? Because we *are* you."

Slater screamed, "You're making no fucking sense!"

"Do as we say, and you shall learn." Dale held the blade's tip as though it were an enormous pencil.

"This is giving me a migraine," said Slater. "Don't."

The knife cut vertically into his skin, drawing blood.

"As I've explained," said Dale, "we do this out of love."

"Best friend—*ouch*," said Slater, "*worst*...enemy, that sort of love, Dale? Don't, okay, okay, please—stop."

Dale touched the blood with his forefinger and brought it to his lips. "Intriguingly delicious. Care for a taste of yourself?"

"You're sick, but you know that, don't you, Dale?" Slater shut his eyes and grimaced as the blade cut deeper.

"Be still, be still, be *still*," urged the angelic voice.

Slater fought against the ropes.

Nearly finished, Dale tapped the knife's pommel against Slater's skull to gain his full attention. "Consider this a special workshop, John. At times, an organization needs to focus on particular issues and problems. *This* is one of those times. We have come together to resolve conflicts, harness visions, build partnerships and alliances, and implement plans."

"A *fucking* seminar! Is that what you're saying this is!?"

A video camera was rolling, held by a red hooded figure.

Dale continued by saying, "A targeted session like this is a rare opportunity, John. It will have historic overtones. It's an honor for you to have been, shall we say, chosen."

"Gosh, Dale, I'm overcome by your hospitality."

"Forgo the sarcasm! Final cut." Dale sliced him horizontally.

"Je–sus *Christ!*" he screamed.

"Call for whomever you like," said Dale. "I assure you, no one here on earth can help you now. No one but us. Accept that."

Dale stepped aside to allow others to come forward.

"Harness the pain, John," said Dale. "Skin separates but heals and hardens into scars, strengthening your soul's resolve. The Pain will make you stronger. Comprehend the power we inflict upon you. It is a gift, John. A monumental gift."

"I don't want your *fucking* gift!"

"Be calm, be still," said a woman's voice from behind him.

"Yes, you do," said Dale. "You simply don't know you want it. Why? Because you don't *know* yourself. Not yet."

"Are you going to kill me?"

"The unwanted parts, most assuredly." Dale grinned.

A procession had formed. Slater was becoming disoriented and was hallucinating. It was a banquet gathering, a wedding reception, a conga line. He flinched as each hooded figure stroked and grazed his chest lightly with their knife. Fingers touched and disappeared into their hood for a taste of his blood.

"Have you tried the salad bar?" Slater gritted his teeth.

"Trust us," said a sweet voice.

Dale was unrelenting, saying, "Accept our love, John."

Slater grimaced. "Try sending flowers next time."

"These powers are everlasting," Dale added.

"Liar," said Slater. "*Idiots! You're all lunatic—idiots!*"

His forehead received Dales pommel-tap again.

"Rule one: Initiate the body and the mind will follow. It will. You cannot escape us, John. You are *ours*. As *we* are yours."

"As we are all together? Fuck off!" Slater spit into Dale's face.

"Don't get me wrong. It's my way of showing affection."

His heart was beating fast. It was pounding audibly. About to explode from his chest. The accumulative cuts to his skin exceeded pain and were numbing his senses. His muscles failed to support him, so the rope took over and he hung upon the cross.

"Get it over...kill me," Slater said.

"Kill you?" said a female voice. Her knife made a gentle sweep across his skin like a feathery kiss. "That would be...self-defeating. Is it not you who are here to save us?"

Slater was confused further by a blurry figure who came forth to tenderly lift up his chin. Emerald eyes inside the hooded mask. He smelled perfume as she whispered, "Forgive them, for they know not what they do. God will protect you. Be good."

The lights were sparkling and stars falling from the sky.

"The planets are in their place," came another woman's voice. "I told you this day would come. And, I have done the best I could. Accept your fate, John. *Accept it.*"

Slater's slow fall into subconsciousness was snapped back by the cognition of a familiar voice. He fought against fatigue and gravity – both in league to defeat his eyes from opening and focusing.

"One day you will appreciate me," she added.

Heather!?

Slater wanted to verify it was her – his third mother – who was inside the hooded mask! But he blacked out.

Someone was shaking him awake.

He was on a bus.

Las Vegas.

29

Changing Spaces

Dr. Bryant Briard ducked his head habitually.

Having struck his forehead numerous times passing through doorways, he never chanced it anymore and ducked as a precaution, a formality.

In Japan he created flurries of knee-jerk bowing.

In NeverMind's corporate headquarters, Briard easily cleared the doorways. They were tall, gracefully arched. The office space was a new structure built at the southern end of the Embarcadero, along the waterfront, where once there had been dilapidated hotels and abandoned warehouses. An entire block had been demolished to accommodate this multi-level edifice, built on a slight rise, and slightly off-center, surrounded by a park opened to the public.

Virtual Realty owned the land and was one of several corporate branches controlled by NeverMind.

Briard walked with Slater through one of the computer rooms and stopped to admire the breadth of the place. At numerous work stations people were tapping on keyboards, images forming inside monitors, dissolving, new visions emerging.

A human brain was graphically depicted as a fissured cloud and was glowing above each doorway. It was the corporate symbol. A line of black type – NEVERMIND INC. – crossed through its center.

"I'm impressed," said Briard.

"Don't be," said Slater. "I wing it most of the time. I go with my instincts. And, it helps to hire the best talent around."

From around a connecting corridor came a stocky man who approached and blocked their path. The man used his muscularity to threaten like an armed rampart when needed. "John," he said, "we need to talk about the Overview Plan."

"Bryant," said Slater, "meet Norm."

"How-do," said Miltner. An ex-wrestler, his thoughts scouted for grasping holds and the best angle to take down Briard if pressed. He scowled and slapped a file of papers against his side. "John, this can't wait. We caught *alleged* vagrants on our grounds last night. We're vulnerable in the East wing, South too." He glanced twice at Briard before holding a full stare. "You ever wrestle?"

"Excuse me?" said Briard. "No. Basketball. High school."

Miltner handed Slater the file, then massaged his thick neck. As Slater took a look at the papers in the file, Miltner sized Briard up and down and jerked his head to emit a cautionary smile.

"Can we do this later?" said Slater. "Three o'clock?"

Miltner took back the file. "Sure, if that's the best you can do. We can't afford leaks or spies, John. Bryant."

Briard half expected a salute from the man.

As Miltner walked off, Slater told Briard, "Head of Security. He's self-purportedly the best."

They exchanged a smile, then continued to walk leisurely. They passed through another archway and startled a fast-walking redhead who was turning the corner.

"Gloria, I'd like you to meet Bryant. Bryant, Gloria."

Briard was intrigued. He bowed slightly as he shook her hand. "I'm charmed...to meet you." He held her hand longer than seemed customary and had an urge to kiss it, but resisted.

"V.P., Research and Development." Gloria liked his gentle grip and admired his size. Her head came up to his chest.

"Bryant's an old friend, same as you," said Slater. "We discuss imaginary time whenever he's in town."

"Imaginary time?" said Gloria.

"Many things," said Briard.

"Bryant's in the field of research too," said Slater.

"Biotechnology," Briard smiled. "I'm a physician."

Gloria's nipples perked. "Impressive."

"And how are things developing?" Briard smiled.

"We manage," she said. "There's never a shortage of egos."

Briard was wearing a three-piece thermosuit and touched the lapel. "Before wearing this fabric, I'd never realized how important comfort is to one's clothing. I commend you both."

Gloria gushed, "We're developing fabric that changes color – with the push of a button. Oops." She touched her lips. "Damnit, I've divulged top secrets. Sorry. We'll have to kill you now."

Briard laughed. "Your secret is safe with me."

"Hum," she said, "Check back later. I'll divulge more."

"Plane to catch." Briard expressed visible disappointment. "But, would you join me for an early dinner? John, unless..."

Slater had glimpsed their destiny unfolding. "You two should. Gloria and I used to play in a band. You'd be amazed what she can do with an electric guitar. Viscerally exotic."

Gloria gave Slater a scathing look.

"Is that so?" Briard's appetite to know more about her grew. "I'm an opera buff. High emotions emitted there as well."

"I like opera," she said. "I *do*. Stars? Seven o'clock?"

"Six would be better," said Briard.

A rush of blood flooded Gloria's face. She heard him say, "*Sex would be better*," before realizing he'd suggested an alternate time. "Okay. Six. I'll meet you there."

"Nonsense," said Briard, "I'll pick you up."

"You will?" She imagined the levitation. His large hands taking hold of her buttocks and bringing her body to his.

"It would be my pleasure," Briard added.

Gloria was uncharacteristically quiet. She smiled and left.

Slater knew Briard would miss his scheduled flight.

Slater walked outside with Briard into the NeverMind park to exchange thoughts while playing a game of chess at one of the tables. The other players in the park knew he presided at NeverMind but regarded him as simply another chess enthusiast.

Slater opened a box of Revolutionary War figures. Colonists were in blue, British soldiers in red. They were one of several themes available from the Corporate Game Room.

"Have you traveled backwards in time recently?" joked Briard. "Since your trip to Egypt? I'll take red and fight for the empire."

Slater shook his head. "My visions took an extended holiday."

"That's good," said Briard.

"Depends. Go ahead, you start."

Briard moved a foot soldier. "Depends on what?"

"One's viewpoint." Slater slid forward a patriot pawn. "Having visions can be a good thing."

"I quite agree," said Briard. "For instance, what you've created here. This fabric. First rate."

Slater watched Briard take his bishop. "Whole episodes of my life are still missing in action. From drugs and drink, is what I used to suspect. Not anymore. It came from another source."

"A trauma?" said Briard.

"Maybe."

"You were abducted by aliens?" Briard smiled.

"That must be it." Slater took a tower. "I fled the States because I couldn't remember what had happened to me. There was blood on my shirt. I had knife cuts on my chest."

"I remember," said Briard.

"How did they get there?" Slater raised his eyebrows.

"Puzzling that your memories never surfaced," said Briard.

"Because I buried them—along with the person I murdered?"

Briard looked up from the board.

Slater smiled. "That thought *had* crossed my mind. Like, in the movies. The protagonist wakes with a total blackout. No memory. No longer fiction. This crazed musician drinks and drugs himself to excess and discovers he had committed a crime. He panics and flees the country."

"Is that why you left?" said Briard.

"Bryant, you're forgetting the voices in my head," said Slater. "*And*, the not-to-be-missed apocalyptic visions."

"*Did* you kill someone, John?"

"Absolutely not. But I wanted to kill *myself*."

"You even tried."

"Yes, and failed," said Slater, "as I'd predicted I would."

"But life is better now," said Briard.

"Marginally."

"Medicated?"

Slater hovered a blue rebel over the board, landing it directly in enemy territory.

"That was a stupid move," said Briard.

"I guess we'll find out," said Slater.

"You aren't, are you?"

"I've cut back," said Slater, "little by little."

"And that's wise?" said Briard.

Slater looked at Briard. "I have to know."

"Know what?" said Briard.

"If...what I have *is* mental illness. Or something else."

"Explain," said Briard.

"The medication dulls my senses."

"That wasn't my question."

"Bryant, it chains me to the present and keeps me from what I have to know. Regarding—you know, what happened."

"Why is that so important?" said Briard.

"It's your move," said Slater.

"You have a wife and children."

"Last time I remembered," said Slater.

"Well," said Briard. "Don't make it *their* problem. I'm saying this as a friend, John. Focus on the present. Forget the past."

Slater squeezed a blue knight, the Paul Revere, in his fist. "You don't...you *can't* understand. I'm not sure I do either. I only know that it's important I remember what happened to me."

"Why?"

"I need to fix the future. I told you this."

Briard looked up from the board and smiled with the hope that he was joking. "*Fix* the future? John, how can anyone do that?"

Slater slid the patriot closer to Briard's queen.

"I don't know. I just..."

"Know?" said Briard.

"*Sense* it to be true. Yes, in fact," said Slater.

"Fact? Let's say I believe you. Let's start there," said Briard. "What do you think it will accomplish? Is it worth the risk? To your marriage? Your family? Your career?"

Slater rubbed his forehead. He dismissed the flicker of pain as a false vision. But he saw himself reflected in Briard's spectacles and both of them—for a split second—had a metallic third eye. Slater was in need of a friend, someone he could trust. Briard *was* a friend. But minor skirmishes were all around them, on the gameboard, and inside his head.

Slater confessed, "I don't care about the business, Bryant It *is* my family I'm trying to save. You can't...understand."

"Try me," said Briard.

"Do you like Gloria?"

"What?" said Briard. "She's nice. Yes, I like her. Why?"

"You're going to marry her."

Briard was dumfounded by the remark. He wanted to leap out and deny its absurdity but, somehow, he could not.

"How do you presume to..." His interest in the game flagged. He held onto a rook, forgetting which square it had come from. "You simply *know*, is that what you're telling me?"

"Yes," said Slater.

"And this episode you had in the desert?" said Briard.

"Inexplicable," said Slater.

"Try to concentrate."

"It doesn't help," said Slater.

"On the *game*." Briard laughed and set down his rook with a grin. "You'll lose otherwise. Check. Mate?"

Slater felt the earth drop. It was an illusion. Yet he gripped the stone bench. Was it an aftermath memory of the ride he had taken days before on a ferris wheel? Sondra and Mercy had wanted to experience this new thrill. So they dangled as a family in a cup at the periphery of a giant wheel. The mechanics were revolutionary, three wheels rotating, rolling, and leap-frogging them high into the sky. Screaming as their hearts rose and fell, they stopped, then dropped backwards. Followed was the magical sensation of reversing course, bringing new terror and wonder – like being swallowed by a whale, an ocean parting, the heaven's weeping a rainbow of tears.

"I have an answer for you," said Slater.

"For which question?" Briard smiled. "About your medication? Or being abducted by aliens?"

"Traveling backwards in time."

Briard indicated the timer. "Not to rush you, John, but you're about to run out of it. It's your move."

Slater selected a brigadere/bishop to defend himself. "Common sense informs us we are moving forward in time. Whatever that means. But I've concluded we're also moving backwards."

"Simultaneously? You lost me again."

Slater gave in to checkmate. "Bryant, as we age and die, does that mean we're progressing? Moving forward? And, if so, toward what? Assume we're already in motion when we're born. Let's say, genetically, a course has been charted. And, at some point in our life we're allowed – if not required – to take possession of this *chart* and discover what it means. Forget the semantics. I acknowledge your skepticism. I'll add more wrinkles. In this conundrum we call life we need to become an active participant and grasp the *instruments* that determine our destiny."

"Instruments?" said Briards.

"Whatever tools are available. At any given historical moment. Forged metals. Gunpowder. Computers. Biotechnology."

"Telepathy?"

"Yes. Each generation preceding us has lacked certain tools and technology we now possess. Our generation takes it all for granted. How do you think a prehistoric cave dweller would comprehend a television? Or even a hand mirror?"

"It's called evolution, John," said Briard.

"And revolution."

"Explain."

"Relativity."

"What about it?"

"The fact that we're related. We can *know* what's coming next. Time consists of visions. Able to be sensed. Able to be seen. They're right before us. Now."

"The future?"

"Past *and* future. It's the way mass and energy are equivalent. If we adjust our minds to the exact frequency and reference point, we can reverse and correct time."

Slater toppled over his king, General Washington, in defeat. Resigned to this air of mystery, he said, "You win."

Briard smiled. "*Presently*? I will assume."

30

For Play and Profit

Slater's hand descended like a space probe, fingers spread to cushion the catch of uncertain gravity. He was aiming to land on one of the planet's twin peaks. The surface gave little resistance, was soft and pliable, warm and playfully alive, seemingly friendly to this extraterrestrial visitor. The planet's host slapped his fingers away.

"Don't," laughed Sherry.

"Why?" said Slater.

"It's disrespectful," she said, defending her breast from further attempts to land.

"I have nothing but respect and admiration."

"That's not saying much," she said.

"I come in peace. I only want to explore the exotic beauty of your other-worldly terrain."

His fingers were slapped from her nipple again.

"That's what I mean," she said.

"Sherry, I'm really not an alien, trust me on this."

She folded her arms across her chest defiantly.

Thwarted, Slater ventured to land in the southern hemisphere, maneuvering spiderlike to a shadowy valley, an intriguing area his equipment had spotted during an earlier orbit. He was experiencing unstable surface tension and movement.

Sherry closed her legs on his hand.

"*May-day!* Hostile environment. Hum, you're not in the mood *for* play, earth creature?"

"We need to talk," said Sherry.

"I can talk. What?"

"About us. About the time before we knew each other."

"We were kids. I have little memory before that. Some of the birth experience and – *ah*, yes, that moment you fell madly in love with me. Our eyes locked. Only a punch bowl separated us."

Sherry laughed but turned serious. "Nor your fantasies. I mean the time between that Christmas party and…that time we met again in church. The homeless center, on Christmas Eve?"

"Does it have to do with your fetish – no, I'll rephrase – your *shyness* for never allowing me to fondle your lovely breasts?"

"It might. Yes."

Slater propped himself on the pillows. He became serious too. "Tell me what happened. I want to know. Were you...raped?"

"No," she said. "No. Well...not exactly."

"Exactly...meaning?"

"I need to tell you this, but I don't know how. I'm afraid that if I tell you...you'll—"

"What? Whatever you want to tell me, it's okay."

"It will ruin us."

"It won't. There's no way—"

"I don't want to lose—"

"Sweetheart, nothing can change—"

"You're not letting me finish!"

"You're right, sorry. Tell me. Please."

Sherry shook her head. Her momentum had stalled.

"It won't *ruin* us," Slater insisted. "Our love is strong. We have no pasts, we agreed when we married. You don't have to tell me. Only if you want to. Okay?"

"Okay." She smiled, somewhat reassured.

"I mean, my past, as you know, is shot full of holes. And what I *can* remember is a life of decadence. Hey, not that I'm proud of it." Trying to amuse her, he added, "Fine, I admit it. I had fun. I was wild. But I've changed. I have. For the better. As you've stated. So, my love, get whatever it is off your chest. Tell me...*pretty* please?"

"It relates to my father and...others."

Slater braced himself, expecting the horror of child abuse.

Mercy began to cry. Her voice was distorted in the intercom.

"Maybe it's—it's better I didn't," said Sherry.

"What about your father? He didn't, you know—"

"No, God—no. It's not what you're thinking." Sherry covered her body with a robe. "He didn't rape me."

"Good. You don't have to tell me."

"I need to tell you."

Sherry exited the room to get their newborn.

"Sweetie, whenever," said Slater. "Or never! It's okay."

In her absence, Slater flipped through television channels using the remote control. Mercy's lips were puckered ravenously to secure a hold on Sherry's ripened nipple upon her return.

"I'm envious," joked Slater. "I can deal with your shyness, your sensitivity about...I mean, whatever. I've never had breasts, so how could I *possibly* know—"

"You?" She laughed and repositioned Mercy to better receive her milk. "You who have experienced a *horn* of plenty?"

"I wouldn't phrase it like that." Slater dismissed the television to admire their child. "Look what a beauty she is. We've created two beautiful girls. I love this. This whole parenting thing. *Us.*"

"Check on Sondra?"

"I'm sorry, who? Oh, wait, she's that other one, right?"

Slater slid off the bed. "I'll be off doing my heroic duties."

He passed through the doorway, walked down the hall, entered another room, which felt like he was entering another dimension. Sondra was asleep in her crib. Watching her sleep was comforting. He tried to imagine her dreams. Were they peaceful? Thirty months on Earth and so new. What images formed her visions?

Unlike his daughters, he was rescued from his mother's lifeless womb – delivered in frantic fanfare, fighting for his life, placed inside the bubble of an incubator. He had been the size of a rodent and was swaddled in cotton, touched by latex-gloved hands, observed for weeks under the glow of heat lamps. He recalled none of it.

Were these events imbedded deep in his brain? Archived? Able to be retrieved? Did memories reach beyond time?

Slater shook his head. What was he *thinking!?*

Under house arrest from sleep deprivation, he closed his eyes. Balancing in the semi-darkness, he thanked God for his life, for his children and wife, for this gift of love. His eyes opened and saw the revolving menagerie of glowing animals. A night-light carousel. As an infant, he recalled gazing in the darkness at a similar carousel, animals revolving, disappearing, returning, hypnotically soothing. He wanted his daughters to experience the same comfort.

His thoughts drifted to Hanna and her boundless love.

His memories derailed unexpectedly into a nightmare involving a gigantic clown laughing maniacally on stilts. Chasing after him. A frightened child. Lost inside a circus tent. Images from long ago still trapped inside his brain.

Strange. How did these images originate?

Life. A carnival ride. Bizarre, wonderful, mysterious.

He tucked the thermcloth blanket around Sondra, brushed her downy hair and transferred a kiss from his fingers to her forehead, then left the room.

At Sherry's nipple Mercy was sucking vociferously. Eyes closed. Her fingers curled, twitching, coming to rest upon the comfy pillow of her mother's breast to caress and pull it closer.

"Now *that* is affection." Slater slid onto the bed beside them. "Mercy gets the Olympic Gold for that move."

"She's so beautiful." Sherry's eyes were moist with tears.

"Like her sister," said Slater. "*And* their mother."

"Is Sondra asleep?"

"She's up, actually. Painting her toenails, talking on her phone. She asked if she could invite a boy to spend the night."

"That's not even *funny*." Sherry fought back a laugh.

"I'm preparing myself for these phobias," said Slater. "Sondra, for the moment, is a perfect angel, asleep, adrift upon a cloud."

"Thanks for checking," said Sherry.

"That thing you wanted to tell me. Does it have anything to do with asking your father to be our CFO?"

Sherry was evasive, implying a *"no"* by rocking her head gently, not wanting to disturb the flow of her milk to Mercy.

"We're expanding fast," said Slater. "I'm grateful to your dad. For his help. And the financial gift to keep us afloat."

"My father saw a lucrative opportunity. It was no gift."

"But this way we keep it in the family," said Slater.

Sherry kept her eyes on Mercy. "Dad works with a consortium of silent partners and investors."

"Whatever, so long as we have a controlling interest."

Sherry looked up. "Does Paul agree?"

"He relented. Finally. Then disappeared, leaving no departing message. He'll resurface again. That's how my uncle works."

"He deserves a vacation."

"Paul? Take a vacation? Right. He should. But not now. I'm feeling overwhelmed. We need to expand our facility to manufacture all this cloth. Supply. Demand. The fine art of capitalism. Having your father on board will really help."

Sherry remained silent.

Slater probed her, "You agree? You trust him, right?"

"Of *course* I trust him. He's—my father."

"Our attorney too. He has more than a vested interest. He has two granddaughters."

"My father knows what he's doing."

"So you think he'll reconsider and accept our offer?"

"As Chief Financial Officer? No."

"Great. I should've taken a course in economics. I need help."

"Me too." She indicated Mercy. "We'll do fine."

"You keep saying that. All the paperwork is amazingly tedious. Reminds me of the days when I used to sign stacks of autographs. Scrawling my name — John Slater III — this...*Dyslexic Dog*."

"You loved it. You were also crazy," Sherry teased.

"Thank you, my love, guardian of my entombed memories."

Slater slid off the bed and stood. He caught the reflection of his face in the wall mirror. It sparked a memory. Of a decadent night when he was young and captivated by his own naked frame and face. Tabloids were calling him an Adonis, a Dionysus. Ego intoxicated, inflamed by fame, he wondered if there was truth to these rumors. Behind his face in the mirror, reflecting the darkened room, were two naked girls sprawled upon his hotel bed. Beckoning for his return, they were giggling and sighing. Both eighteen, legal age, or so they claimed. But the truth? A gamble. A risky stake.

"What?" asked Sherry.

Slater snapped back from this warp in time. He saw his face as damaged goods, aged, adorned with a scar. He breathed in a laugh and regarded his wife. "I was realizing how much I love you. And, that we could get filthy rich."

Sherry sighed. "I only want us to be happy."

"We could buy this house. Pay off all our debts."

"Twist my arm. Okay." She smiled and gently rotated Mercy, setting her in front of her other breast.

"Mercy is making me hungry. Do you want something from the fridge? I'm buying."

"A glass of orange juice. It helps the milk to flow."

Slater turned at the end of the bed. "I'm not going to ask. How? Forget it." He stopped at the door. "More peaceful now, since Paul got his own place."

"I kinda miss his rumble and roar."

"I could rev-up a power tool," Slater said, departing.

"Wait! John, come back!"

Slater grabbed the door frame and poked his head back into the bedroom. "I wasn't serious. You change your mind? Would you like a cheeseburger? Chocolate shake?"

"I need to ask you something," said Sherry.

"Ask," he said.

"Are you happy?"

"What do you mean?"

"With me. Are you happy?"

"God, Sherry, what kind of a question is that?"

"I'm serious. Are you?"

"Sherry."

"Am I what you want? Be honest."

Slater didn't want to trifle with her insecurities. He was too busy at work for her to suspect he could be having an affair. She had only gained a few pounds but was back to her fighting weight. She was beautiful. She was lovely. He smiled.

"You're my angel. A perfect vision of love: Madonna and child. How could I possibly be any happier? I *am* happy. Truly."

"Do you mean that?"

"Yes. You're what I prayed for."

—31—
Souls Searching

"Minds need a daily dose of silence."

Heather Frost was seated on a cushion. She was positioned near the center edge of the stage in the Seminar Room. It was the lunch hour. She held a class at 7:00 am and another one at 6:00 pm. These sessions were a volunteer program offered for free to the employees of NeverMind. Heather had requested a modest salary. She had a small interest in the company, an array of health benefits, as well as income from private clients. She seemed more than pleased.

Slater was not. He fumed. After his initial shock and rage – discovering Heather was one of the financial partners Stan Knowles had *silently* recruited! He fumed. He sucked in his hatred and tried his best to accept this betrayal by his father-in-law. He was now legally bound, by corporate ties, to her.

"John, I had no idea you'd be upset," said Knowles. "Pleasantly surprised is what I'd expected. A greater share of the company will be kept in the family. She merely wants to help. She means well. John, she took you in as a child, for God's sake."

Slater didn't care. He silently fumed and was unable to stop his emission of pent-up resentment toward her. Heather had finagled her way back into his life. He confronted her – after successfully avoiding her for years – the way the leader of an embittered nation confronted a bordering rival, or should, negotiating not with threats and shouts of recriminations, but with diplomacy until reaching a compromise, a reconciliation, a truce (her promise not to meddle). Slater was, after all, a grown man. Not to mention the CEO. He needed to set a good example for the company.

Slater peeked through a crack in the door to the Seminar Room. He wanted to terminate these sessions. Except he knew her removal would be unpopular. She was now entrenched in the company like a life-sucking tick. Heather had been quick to establish a foothold and a loyal following of acolytes. Employees even sent him notes of praise for providing these programs of hers. And to make matters worse, they apparently helped. Production was on the rise!

"If you *don't*," Heather cautioned, "your mind will be filled with constant static. You will have difficulty channeling. You know the symptoms. That constant denial of your inner self: I don't have *time* to relax, I have *deadlines*, people *waiting*, animals to *feed*, and on and on. Am I right? I am. You will never attain your goals or achieve a higher level of awareness unless you deny these interfering thoughts. *Silence* this chaos. Say it with me (and they did):

A NeverMind is what I desire!"

Heather enjoyed the litany.

"Silence is like water. Both are needed to consume and cleanse our bodies, to maintain our health. At NeverMind we understand your needs. We want to fulfill them. Submerge into the silence with me. Take a deep breath…and…exhale. Close your eyes. Envision yourself at the center of a lake. You are floating upon serene water. Gradually, let the tension spread away from you. Picture the waves, the concentric circles as they widen and vanish, yes, vanish into…"

Slater could practically touch his inner turmoil.

Full of ideas himself, he competed with her like a child, despite his own achievements in chemistry, bio-tech and computer genetics. He felt a need to outdo Heather. NeverMind provided its employees with a recreation room, an exercise gym, a jogging path through the surrounding park. He also provided an after-hours screening room for viewing movies, plus an indoor swimming pool, spa, sauna, even an old-fashioned steam room. These were *his* contributions toward maintaining a healthy company morale.

Heather's popularity soared and scored decibels higher.

Slater's approval rating ran a close second.

While San Francisco lay in ruins.

The NeverMind compound had withstood a 7.2 shock-wave. Most city buildings had buckled and collapsed.

"A devastation of the highest magnitude," stated a dour-faced President during a White House news briefing, referring as well to other recent disasters. The Leader and Chief of the free world faced the cameras with a spiraling-deficit, grin-and-bear-it countenance, forsaking his trademark lies of optimism. The truth had become unavoidable, faced by volcanoes, floods, blizzards, and the endless unrelenting hurricanes — Beatrice, Lance, Geraldo, Veronica, Rocky, Waldo. The World Weather Bureau had run out of names and was making them up — Lumu, Tofo, Zimmy. The desperate craving for stability was not surprising. A tremor-free mental and physical state was what people most desired.

Slater was startled by an employee pushing open the doors — almost whacking Slater in the face — as he exited the lecture.

"She was that bad, huh?" Slater asked.

"She is phenomenal. My bladder is not."

Slater could relate.

During these global disasters, NeverMind, Inc. had unloaded its inventory to those in need. Thermocloth blankets and clothing were distributed until nothing remained. Their stock plummeted from this altruistic outpouring.

Knowles, acting CFO, publicly agreed with the decision. He had little choice. Slater had already authorized the disbursement.

The board of directors was furiously divided.

Weiner declared the decision a stroke of genius.

"The ramifications of this, John," said Weiner, "the beneficial public relations could be immense!"

Slater was divided himself. He argued with his hypothetical other half as to whether it *was* an act of irresponsibility or – as he wanted to believe – the opposite. When shareholders petitioned that he make a public appearance and statement, he agreed.

"I present no apology," said Slater, "if anyone was expecting to hear one. I created this company with the hope of finding a way to provide warmth. My uncle and I succeeded in making that dream a reality. And we've profited — climbing the market to great heights. We're a colossal stock. *Bully* for us. Our corporation could reap staggering profits from recent events. It would make *fiscal* sense. The demand for our product has never been greater. The southern states flooded. The east frozen. Dire conditions all across the globe. As well as our own local shakeup. NeverMind would double, triple, perhaps quadruple its earnings. Except for the elementary fact that I refuse to be—this time—a capitalistic whoremonger!"

Slater began to sit, but thought of something else. He added, "And for those of you who desire to have me removed and disagree with my tactics of late: Go *fuck* yourselves." His smile was warm and genuine. "Thank you all for coming tonight. Have a pleasant evening – *knowing* that what we are doing here is good."

A shareholders meetings had never dipped into such silence, prior to the moment when all hell broke loose.

"What would we do without your *charm*," said Wolfe.

"'Go *fuck* yourself?' *John?*" Weiner realized it was up to him to muster a happy-face reply.

Weiner stood, his hands raised for silence.

"Ladies and gentlemen!" he shouted. "Please, may I have your attention! All of us are going through stressful times. And all of us, I would hope, as does Mr. Slater, *care* passionately about the health and prosperity of NeverMind, Inc. The company continues to thrive and be technologically innovative and uniquely progressive. But let me remind you, NeverMind has established its reputation on being a *compassionate* enterprise. The community, here and beyond, our loyal customers, will respond favorably to a corporation that cares. Yes, *cares*. Especially in times of great need, such as these.

"As Vice President and Director of Community Relations, allow me to cite some historic examples. That's right, success stories from this kind of corporate leadership…"

Weiner waxed on with his positive spin.

Slater experienced a surge of visions and felt elated, though he sensed he shouldn't. He stood abruptly and left the auditorium to venture into the cold night. He sensed the icy gaze of his mother watching from the wings. He imagined her minions, entrenched in the organization, buzzing and burrowing everywhere.

Slater took hold of a chrome railing for support.

Heather had stopped him in a hallway moments before he gave his presentation. "John, are you taking your medication? You're behaving oddly."

Slater addressed both faces, "Yes, Mother, Heather. Can't chat right now. You wouldn't want me to be late for my funeral. Right, I meant to say, *speech*."

"Don't destroy things," Heather warned. "We're counting on you to act appropriately. Your actions effect us all."

Slater wondered about her private sessions. He envisioned her as a spiritual madam in a corporate brothel. Her face resembled the queen bee in a burgeoning institute of ill repute.

His sanity was held down by tenuous thread.

Heather wet her fingers to brush back a strand of his hair that had fallen to his forehead.

He slapped her hand away. "Leave me alone."

"Are you drunk?"

"On pure water. We're floating pools of liquid, held together at the shores by our thin *skin*. Which reminds me, I have to *pee*. You will excuse me."

His unkind thoughts rose from memories of Heather's attempts at raising him, her manipulative hands, and her militaristic chores.

Repetition frees the mind so you can soar and—

Blah, blah, blah!

Slater released a volume of himself into the urinal.

He was not inebriated. He had soared and crashed more than once too often. He was wrong in faulting Heather for all his flaws. Was it because of some *inner static* – one of her treasured terms – denying him access to the truth? Denying access to his past?

Lately, Sherry had begun to display a pool of tears.

She was not a happy Penelope.

Slater was lost at sea in his car, on benches at night within the NeverMind compound, with the gates locked and guards overseeing. Slater was distracted by emerging images. In business, he was busy helping to create scientific breakthroughs with holographic imagery, nano circuitry, enzyme transcoding – yet he sensed he was losing his mental grip and falling out of orbit.

Slater knew he was on a quest. But if a modern Odysseus: What was he supposed to conquer?

The bubbling orb fascinated him. Slater could stare into it for hours, and often did. It was one of the latest projects of NeverMind. The chief scientist in the main quadrant of their research lab was friendly and helpful up to a point. Barton Ziger was his name, and bald but for a few long strands of hair he refused to cut or comb. Static electricity zigzagged the remaining hairs of his head into the air like distracting antennas.

Ziger wore gloves and a lab coat with a pocket holster of pens. Blue light emanated from the orb and cast them both in a glow. He told Slater, "Everything in the universe is part of a continuum, Boss, dividing reality into its component parts. Subatomic particles — of every kind of *matter*, as a matter of fact — are interwoven like an oriental rug. Don't you see? Like you and me, standing here, now, relatively whole."

"But my question," said Slater, "regarding telecommunications. Will this invention accomplish our goal?"

"Getting to that." Circling the platform, Ziger retrieved his cane with a gold cap. "An *affectation*. Capable of ambulating without it. Habitual creatures. We are. Fact." He pointed with this thin rod towards the sphere. "Tantalizing, isn't she. You're wondering why the liquid glows so blue? Ionized particles traveling to the fifth state of matter. Into a plasma transmitting speed. True! *Ah*, and when finished – soon, Boss, soon – converted to neuroelectronic signals!"

"The approximate ETA?" pressed Slater.

"*Everybody* wants the future now." Ziger, slightly shorter than Slater, looked up and inhaled, as if tasting glory in every atom since the beginning of time. "Do you realize what we *have* here? Do you? I don't think you *do*."

Slater studied Ziger's enigmatic smile. "Are we – or aren't we? – producing an interactive computer and global compass to analyze and forecast future trends?"

"I *wouldn't*," Ziger cautioned Slater as he reached to touch the orb. "Not yet. Remember the old cores of nuclear reactors?"

"How safe is, or *isn't*, this thing?"

Ziger swiped his gloved hand at the air. "When I was sixteen I blew my parents garage door clean off its retractable hinges! *That* was scary." He tapped his cane against his leg. He jabbed a finger at Slater, slowing at the point of contact, tapping his chest. "*Ah*, but a sign of progress! Don't you see? Yes. Failures will always precede success. Without the *boom*, Boss, you get no buck."

"How *dangerous*, say, from a scale of one to ten?"

"Not so dangerous," said Ziger. "My sister's Dobermans, *now* those dog will rip the *pants* off you. Not CyBorg9. No, no."

"CyBorg9?"

Ziger touched the silicon orb affectionately with a gloved hand. "Affectionate as a pet, you'll see. CyBorg9 will *astound*."

"Meaning?" Slater tried not to fume. "You didn't mention this name at the last committee meeting."

"Mr. Slater, may I call you that?"

"No. Call me John. Listen, Barton, your previous work speaks for itself. You come highly recommended—"

"Thank you, kindly."

"But I want to know if this project is based in reality."

"John, reality is closely parallel to our dreams. Similar to this *daydream* we're experiencing now. It's – okay, I'm theorizing." Ziger veered sharply from the tangent he was inclined to take. His gloved hands danced in the air, fingers wiggling to make his point. "Interference patterns. What everything is. What you and I see, and sense! Existence: it's an endless sea of energy. Outer space abounds within it. These electromagnetic waves crisscrossing and interfering. We all get born into a holographic blur. Then...slowly, *slowly*, we tune our brains into this—this *focus!*"

"We adjust to the frequencies," said Slater.

"Precisely!" Ziger glowed. "Holographic pictures. CyBorg9's face will be a masterpiece of complex interference patterns."

"A face?"

"Why not. Or, many faces." Ziger's teeth were blue, grinning as he impishly brushed away his static-floating hairs. "Cy will be the first of his-or-her kind. Computer—no, but a *thinking* creature! Think about it, Boss."

"Please try to refrain from calling me boss. Did you say faces? With the ability to think, possibly?"

"Not *possibly*," corrected Ziger. "It will think!"

His mother crowded into his thoughts. Slater blinked. He had again slipped into a rut of time. He was seeing her as two-faced.

"You look at me as though I'm some phantom," said Heather. "What's gotten into you?"

"I can't talk to you right now." Slater tapped his radioactive wrist watch. "I'm late."

"You keep avoiding me," she said.

"I realize that," said Slater. "You promised not to meddle."

Heather wheedled down the hall after him, shoving into his arms a folder. "Astrological predictions, John. Study them. For guidance throughout the next year and *millennium!*"

He closed a door between them.

"Thanks," he said from the other side. "You look stunning, as always. I will give them the attention they deserve."

"I'm *counting* on it." Her smile scrunched into a scowl. Her eyes narrowed to tiny beams. She wanted to burn and pierce holes through the door, but failed to do so, so she walked away.

"Unfortunately, your mum appears to be beneficial to the health and wellbeing of NeverMind."

Even Smitts, once drummer for the *Dyslexic Dogs* and recently deceased Director of Financing, had given Heather credit. Smitts was crushed and burned into nothing identifiable after apartment rubble collapsed on him followed by a gas line explosion during the 9.3 quake. Smitts, prior to that, had conducted a thorough study and presented Slater with the positive results.

"Hate to admit it, mate," said Smitts. "She was dead on. Check the figures. Production's on the rise. Report is on your desk."

Slater distrusted the numbers.

"It's only natural, John," said Weiner. "She's your mother."

"That's natural?" Slater tapped a pen on his marble desktop. "She adopted me. I suppose I owe her...something."

"You tolerate her out of guilt?" said Weiner.

"No, she means well," Slater said. "I *am* for innovation, for exploration. But this A.I. division that she's championing with Stan, I'm reticent about this one. What's your opinion?"

"Opinion? Well," said Weiner, removing his glasses to wipe them with his handkerchief. Yellow silk to complement his deep brown thermosuit. He was no longer thin. He was holding a thick book. Its pages were flagged with day-glow markers. "Funny you should mention it. I'm reading a book about artificial intelligence. Have you read this one, by chance?"

"Yes. Smitty says it's a huge risk," said Slater. "NeverMind is still limping back from my...giveaway fiasco."

"Risk, did you say? Great profligate son of our company!" joked Weiner. "This could be your greatest understatement yet."

"This *pet* project could finish us. So saith Smitty."

Weiner replaced his glasses and beamed cherubically. "John, when has that ever stopped us? The financial tide will rise and fall. That brilliant publicity stunt of yours to give away all those—"

"It wasn't a stunt," said Slater.

"Stunt? Did I say *stunt?* I'm teasing. We're back in the black. God's Grand Shakeup has provided us with a surplus of the most qualified *un*employed. Most of our competitors have been sent back to square one. You were smart to take advantage of this incredible talent at our doorsteps. Some of the brightest, most brilliant minds have come aboard."

"Like Barton Ziger, from Oracle."

"Oracle? Oh, the company! Yes, he was. Golden opportunity. Our options are limitless. You said so yourself. We began with nothing, so we *lose* nothing."

"I never said that," said Slater, "did I?"

"I'm paraphrasing," said Weiner.

"I've said a lot of things, haven't I?" said Slater.

"Many little *gems.*" Weiner had a mocking twinkle in his eyes. "You also said, 'The more we acquire, the more weapons we will need to defend our acquisitions.' Free yourself, you said. Let go of them! Be rid of that superficial Silver-Bullet Porsche of yours, the dynasty antiques, that fancy home and pool you could *drown* in debt from. You don't need them, you said. I'm paraphrasing."

Slater looked out the window. It was snowing.

"Look at that," he said. "As if the earthquake wasn't enough. Who'd have thought it'd be snowing again in San Francisco."

"Snow? Actually, you did," said Weiner. "You predicted it. It's written down somewhere in my notes."

"I don't remember," said Slater.

"Well, you did. You need to get out more," said Weiner. "John, you work too hard. You exist in rooms. Let's take a stroll down the streets like we used to. In the good old days."

Slater swiveled around and roared. "Ha! Henry, you're getting romantic! You were *miserable. That,* I recall."

"Miserable? So were you," said Weiner. "Well, not so much. You were crazy. That helped."

"And now I'm sane?" said Slater. "And *not* so happy? Is that what you're implying, Henry?"

"I'm implying nothing. I miss the predictions, your visions. Is that so much to ask or want?"

"Cheer up, they're returning," said Slater.

"I'm not saying I miss the spare accommodations," said Weiner. "Sleeping in dumpsters. The—what? Returning?"

Slater realized he was getting ink on his fingers and replaced the pen in its desk holster. He pointed at his suit. "This fabric, Henry. Thermocloth is the reason we founded NeverMind."

"And, to support your family, and other families. Your efforts are helping to employ a multitude, myself included, thank you."

"You remember how cold it was, sleeping in those alleys?"

Weiner shivered. "Thanks for the memories. Yes, I do."

"I would have died one night if it hadn't been for Truffles."

"Truffles? *Now* who's romanticizing? It was my feather-filled sleeping bag that saved me. Did you know I still have it?"

Slater believed it, knowing what a pack-rat Henry was. "I made a prayer that night. A promise to God that I would do good, make a difference if this invention came to fruition."

"And you *have*," said Weiner, "a big one."

"Henry, we keep people warm. We're about that."

Weiner knew where this was going and wanted to curtail the flight of Slater's endless guilt. "Stop beating yourself up for being rich, John. It's not your fault."

Slater swiveled back to face the windows.

"John," Weiner added, "you do more than anyone else I know. Granted, it's *never* enough. But nothing to shoot yourself—I mean." Henry blanched. He had crossed the line without thinking. "I'm sorry, John. You know I'd never—"

"It's all right, Henry," said Slater. "I hate what I've become."

"Become?" said Weiner.

"No," said Slater. "What I am *not* becoming."

"You're beginning to *not* make any sense, John," teased Weiner. "Shall I dust off my notebook and start dictating?"

Slater gave a laugh and a crazed self-effacing grin. "No. You're right, Henry. Why am I afraid? We've always taken chances."

"Fear can be good," countered Weiner. "It has worked for me. Self preservation? That sort of good?"

"Have I become too cautious?" said Slater. "Fearing I might lose what I've gained. It's a terrible trap, Henry."

Weiner reminded him, "And a family to consider."

"I can't base my decisions on fears – on glimpses – when I can't be certain what they even mean."

"Glimpses? What *have* you seen?" Weiner searched his pockets for a note pad.

Slater tilted back in his chair. "A few years back I saw this face inside my computer. I was tired. I wanted to dismiss it outright. But it spoke to me."

"It spoke—what? Why didn't you tell me?"

"I told Sherry. It frightened her. So I promised to keep it quiet. Nothing like that has happened since. Except, two nights ago. I was in front of a mirror. I saw myself...not *as* myself but as this *clone*. It wasn't me, Henry. And then this...replica talked to me."

"Your reflection talked—what, *at* you?"

"We'd reversed, or..." Wiping the notion away, Slater admitted, "I don't know. I felt trapped. Betrayed. Like I was being seduced, you know, by a flame."

Weiner retrieved a pipe from his pocket. He nervously tapped it against his side. "Could be symbolic. A vision of death? I read that interpretation applying to dreams—"

"It was no dream, Henry. What do you feel in your gut about this A.I. project? It scares me a little, I have to confess."

"It's your mother who scares you, John."

"More than a little," said Slater.

"It must be an Oedipal thing." Weiner smiled nervously.

"Please," said Slater.

"My advice is for you to visit a very expensive psychiatrist. You can afford one now."

"You're right," said Slater. "I will."

"John—I was *joking!*" said Weiner. "Heather didn't give *birth* to you. Or even *burp* you."

"She has something against Sherry. She avoids her."

"Jealousy. I mean, *mothers*." Weiner tossed up a hand. "Mine hates whomever I date. Or *used* to. She's dead, of course, that was, oh gosh, let me think..."

Slater looked at his family framed inside the small monument of Grecian marble on his desk. They were smiling. Trusting him to do what was right. Snow was rapping lightly at his window. Questions kept falling as fast, endless, relentless, unanswerable.

"Henry, find me a psychiatrist. A good one."

"Psychiatrist? John," said Weiner, "you don't need a—"

"One that specializes in hypnotism."

"Hypnotism?"

—32—
Grave Memories

"Do you believe in angels, Daddy?" asked Mercy.

Slightly embarrassed, Slater wiped at his tears. Not that he was weeping hysterically. He just hadn't expected the sorrow that welled from within him upon burying their dog He began to walk with his daughters down the hill.

"I'm not sure," he said, smiling.

"Do you think Truffles will go to heaven?" said Sondra.

"Difficult to say," said Slater. "He was a good dog. I imagine God would like to have Truffles around. Don't you?"

Mercy brightened, nodding.

"Could Truffles go to Hell?" said Sondra.

"Could he, Daddy?" said Mercy.

Sondra beheaded a patch of wildflowers, sniffing before tossing them into the air. "There's no Hell, or any *real* devil. Is there?"

Slater dragged the shovel behind him. "Girls, these are difficult questions. I've often wondered myself."

"About Truffles?" said Mercy.

"No, Sweetie, Truffles would undoubtedly become an angel like you." Slater ruffled his daughter's ponytail. "What I meant was, once I thought I had encountered the devil."

"Are you joking?" said Mercy.

"When?" said Sondra.

"Before you were born," said Slater. "It was like a dream."

Both daughters moaned their disappointment.

"But it wasn't a dream," said Slater. "It *was* real."

"*Sure,* Dad," said Sondra.

"Did I ever tell you about these scars?" Slater stopped, dropped the shovel. He unbuttoned his shirt to reveal his chest. Most of the cuts had faded and were no longer visible.

"I once had visible cuts all over my chest," said Slater.

His daughters looked close.

"They look like cat scratches," said Mercy.

"About as sharp, but deeper. But no."

"What were they from?" said Sondra.

"Knives," said Slater.

"What about this?" Sondra twisted a smile as she touched the three vertical marks crossed through by another scar near his heart. "A sabor-tooth tiger?"

"More knife cuts." Slater shrugged. "It happened a long time ago. So..."

Sondra said, "Tell us. You can't change your mind now and *not* tell us. That would be like...you know, like—"

"Cheating," said Mercy.

"*Yeah!*" Sondra beamed at her sister, both of them playfully in league, victorious partners for the moment — prior to screaming and hitting each other the next.

"Tell us," said Mercy.

"I don't want to give you nightmares."

"*Daaad,*" they moaned in unison, then laughed.

Slater regretted having mentioning it. Clearly the incident was dominating his thoughts. It had come out spontaneously, part of a revived memory during therapy. He found a nearby rock to sit upon. His daughters sat beside him, waiting. Slater paused to observe the wind moving through the tall spring grass. From the hill they could see the top of their house.

"You know how your mom and I tell you girls to be careful about strangers?"

They nodded rhetorically, hoping for something better.

"All right, well." Slater felt the phantom pain from these cuts coming back in splintered bursts. "Once upon a time, your wise old dad wasn't very careful *or* so wise about—"

"Was it a stranger?" said Mercy.

"*Mercy*, don't interrupt," said Sondra. "Was it?"

"Yes," said Slater.

"Were you offered candy?" said Mercy.

Sondra bumped her sister. She thought the question dumb, then looked at her father to see if it was.

Slater could picture the woman clearly Through hypnosis, the memory of her had resurfaced.

"I was," said Slater. "But a different kind of candy."

"*Dad*," said Sondra. "Was it or wasn't it?"

"Okay, you could say the stranger offered me candy."

"And you took it?" said Mercy

"How old were you?" asked Sondra.

"Old enough to know better," said Slater.

"Why did you do it?" said Sondra.

"Good question," said Slater. "I was acting stupid. Can you imagine that? Your dad acting stupid?"

They both giggled and nodded.

"Well, there you go," he said. "I should have been smarter."

Sondra said, "Was it really the devil?"

"She was probably just his helper," said Slater.

"It was a *she?*" said Mercy.

"What did she look like?" said Sondra.

"She was very pretty. I'd seen her once or twice before."

"Then she wasn't really a stranger," said Sondra.

"We'd never really met. She came to see our concerts. This was when I was a singer. So, technically, she *was* a stranger."

"Dad, get to the devil part," said Mercy.

"She tricked me," said Slater.

"How?" said Sondra.

"The *candy* thing, right?" said Mercy.

"Remember the movie *Snow White and the Seven Dwarfs* and the witch with the poisoned apple?"

Their eyes widened.

"You could say I was poisoned with a candy apple."

"*Daadd!*"

"Bad example. But this *candy* I was given made me fall asleep. When I awoke I was tied to a post and blindfolded. And when it was removed I saw people wearing hooded masks and robes."

"Are you making this up?" said Sondra.

"I wish I was. This man came forward and removed his mask. He said his name was Dale, also Lucifer."

"I thought you said he was the devil?" said Mercy.

"Lucifer is another name for the devil," said Slater.

"What did you do?" said Sondra.

"Nothing. I was tied to a post," said Slater. "This man, or devil, removed a knife and began cutting me. He was the one who made those three crosses."

"Why?" asked Mercy.

"I've been trying to find that out myself."

"Does Mommy know about this?" asked Sondra.

"She does," said Slater. "I went to see a doctor who helped me remember the past. Things I'd forgotten. For a long time I wasn't sure what had happened."

"I don't get it," said Mercy.

"Me neither," said Sondra.

"That makes three of us." Slater stood and so did his daughters. "And that, my ladies, is the boring story of how your daddy met the *devil*. God only knows if he really was."

"Were you scared?" asked Sondra.

Slater lifted the shovel. He swung it like a baseball bat. "Girls, I smashed the devil to kingdom come. I killed him dead!"

"Really, Daddy?" said Mercy.

"A better story if I had. But I'd be lying." He brushed Mercy's and Sondra's hair. "No, I was scared. I'm telling you this because I want us to be open and honest with one another. Okay?"

They nodded.

"That devil, he got the better of me. Truth is, I fell unconscious from the pain, and when I woke I was on a bus far from home. Pretty weird, huh?"

Mercy began to cry.

"Sweetie, what's the matter?" Slater set the shovel down, knelt and gave her a hug. "I'm sorry. Did I scare you? Tell me?"

Mercy asked, "Are you going to Hell?"

"What? No," said Slater.

"You said the devil beat you," said Sondra.

"It was a figure of speech," said Slater.

"What's that?" said Mercy.

"It means," said Slater, "he didn't win, and I didn't necessarily lose. He might have won a minor battle, but it doesn't mean I lost the entire war."

"What war?" said Mercy.

"Between good and evil." Slater widened his eyes. "But, I have two precious *angels* on my side – so, there's no way I can lose now. You see, girls, there are *big* wars and there are *little* wars."

He lifted Mercy off the ground and she shrieked. "Like when you two fight over whether we're having pancakes or waffles. So, what's it going to be – pancakes or waffles?"

"Waffles!" shouted Sondra. "With syrup!"

"Me too! Me too!" screamed Mercy.

"And peanut butter!" laughed Sondra.

"Gobs of it!" said Mercy.

Slater returned Mercy to the ground and grabbed Sondra too, pulling them both down, rolling with them in the grass. He tickled them into fits of giggles. "See, you see? There's no need for war! We're all in agreement. Waffles–it–shall–be!"

"Daddy, you're silly," said Mercy.

"Silly? Me?"

"Does Mommy say it's okay?" said Sondra.

"Mommy is an angel," said Slater. "Angels *love* waffles."

"Then you *do* believe in angels!" said Sondra.

"In your mother?" said Slater. "Cross my heart, I do."

"Is she really an angel?" said Mercy.

Slater hoisted the shovel over his shoulder. "Let's go home and find out. We'll make her breakfast. Angels don't like it when you keep them waiting. Especially for waffles."

"*Daadd,*" groaned Sondra.

"Did the devil cut your face too?" said Mercy.

"This? No, that came later." Slater made a mock-serious mask. "Your dad took this...very long trip, a voyage over land and sea, where I ended up in a vast desert. Remember the story of Aladdin? In a place like that, with endless waves of sand dunes."

"Did you ride on a flying carpet?" asked Sondra.

"No," said Slater, "but I did get lost during a sand storm and fell through a hole in the earth. Into this ancient civilization."

"Wow," said Mercy.

"Did you find a magic lamp?" said Sondra.

"Was there a genie?" asked Mercy.

Slater grinned. "Not that I recall. But that's how I got this scar. My souvenir from the desert after talking to God."

"You're making this up," said Sondra.

"Not according to a friend, who was taking notes."

Both daughters scrunched their faces in disbelief.

"What did God say to you?" said Sondra.

"He basically told me to go home. So should we."

"*Daadd!*" laughed Sondra.

Mercy asked, "Can we get a puppy?"

Future Presents

Stan Knowles delivered his formal resignation.

"I'm sorry, John," he said. "I can't work with your mother. It's not my nature to offend, but she offends me. She means well, but we don't get along. Never have. No hard feelings?"

"None," said Slater. "I understand."

"I stayed on longer than I'd intended," said Knowles. "I'll take that vacation now. Barbara's on my back. You made me a wealthy man. I won't forget it. Gave me a challenge when I needed one. As I challenged you, I should hope."

"You did," said Slater. "And still do."

Knowles feigned offense, then offered his hand.

It was a firm, painful, affectionate shake.

Knowles stopped and turned at the door. "I don't like Bosner either. I thought I'd mention it."

"I appreciate it," said Slater.

"Keep your eyes open. Be careful who you trust." Knowles paused, clutching the handle. Formal by nature, he struggled now to break from form. "John, I've tried to be a worthy helmsman and help to steer you and the company on the best possible course."

"I know that," said Slater. "You've done great work."

Knowles hesitated. "Let's hope so. One last thing. I was against you marrying my daughter. But you proved to be all right. Take care of her. What I said when you married her, it still applies."

Knowles winked and was gone.

Slater buzzed his secretary and made a note to confront Heather. He wrote down her name, also adding the name _Bosner_.

"Yeah, John?"

"I could use a cup of coffee," he said. "Do you mind?"

"_Yes,_ damn it, I mind," she joked. "_Muffin_ too?"

"Just coffee. Thanks, Jenny."

"Don't forget the A.I. presentation at ten," she added.

"Affirmative," he said. "Over and out."

Slater was in a funk. The outgoing personnel of NeverMind was causing a radical personality shift. He had already lost Gloria. She was honeymooning with Briard in Paris and was to take a leave of absence to live in Jerusalem before relocating back in San Francisco. Wolfe resigned over what he called "artistic" differences. Their last conversation ended badly:

Wolfe: "Have you lost your *mind?*"

Slater: "Not lately."

Wolfe: "Check again. You may have controlling interest, but you don't have *control* anymore. Savvy?"

Slater: "You're exaggerating."

Wolfe: "What the hell's this *Borg* thing?"

Slater: "CyBorg9 will advance our telecommunications—"

Wolfe: "*Wrong*, friend. It'll be a nightmare."

Slater: "Wolfe, we're an innovative corporation and—"

Wolfe: "No—an *in-over-its-head* corporation. I'm getting out. You should too, Dr. Frankenstein. While you still can."

Slater: "We've invested billions."

Wolfe: "So?"

Slater: "We need to recover financially or—"

Wolfe: "*That's* not the problem."

Slater: "Wolfe, be reasonable. This will globalize our— "

Wolfe: "Have you heard yourself lately? Is this *you* talking or some replacement of your former self? The financially bound-at-the-stake CEO Slater talking?"

Slater: "Wolfe, I love you like a brother. I value your opinion. But, admit it, you distrust technology and computers."

Wolfe: "Computers!? Don't make me laugh. And don't tell me this Cy*Borg* thing doesn't alarm the *shit* out of you too."

Their conversation rewound in Slater's mind as he sat waiting for the presentation to commence. Larry Bosner, director of the A.I. Project Division at NeverMind, was at the podium fidgeting with his laser pointer. Ziger was seated nearby. His lab coat, by contrast, seemed to glow among the row of dark suits worn by the team of other scientists involved in the project. They were stationed there to exhibit a united front, also to answer necessary questions. Bosner gave a smile at the team, then at the roomful of curious competitors, scientists, reporters, and television cameras.

He was waiting for the lights to dim.

"Welcome to NeverMind," said Bosner. "There has been much

talk and speculation, as well as some unwarranted rumors spreading through the world, regarding the work we've been conducting here. I believe F.D.R. expressed it best when he said: 'There is nothing to fear but fear itself.' So relax, sit back and greet the future. You are about to meet the newest member of our team. Audience, please give a warm welcome to *CyBorg9*, or Cy. He prefers informality."

Behind Bosner a circular curtain lifted, theatrically disappearing into the ceiling's void of darkness.

There was no applause.

CyBorg9 stood tall, approximately 3 meters, encased in black. Like a gigantic monolithic amplifier it was crowned at the tapered spire with a glowing ball, 1 meter in diameter. The orb resembled a crystal ball, a milky planet in the heavens, a fishbowl. Inside was a inchoate face, moving like storm clouds seen from a satellite camera. Within the white atomic swirls was faint coloration and an entity fighting to gain more definition.

Ziger was visibly furious. He hated these amorphous features, this preliminary design, but had buckled under pressure to deliver. He gave it his best shot. But resented these constraints and political *deadlines* imposed upon him.

"Cy," said Bosner, "say hello to our guests."

"Thank you all for coming." The voice was neither feminine nor masculine, an androgynous range in between. The tone was smooth and articulate. "I count three hundred fifty six individuals visiting here today, excluding all members of our board and the television cameras." The remark was followed with a non-threatening laugh, not returned. "I know you are curious about me, but before I answer your questions, Mr. Bosner would like to say a few words regarding my inception. Larry."

"Thank you, Cy," said Bosner. "As thinking creatures, each and everyone of you will discern that Cy is more than a computer, more than an extensive database-library input of images, text, and sounds. Cy is, if I may be so bold, and I *will*, the closest thing we have to a compilation — the sum *total* — of knowledge mankind has garnered up to this point in time."

The audience stirred, restless with questions.

"No *one* person," continued Bosner, "is capable of possessing all the knowledge humanity has gathered. When we seek solutions to a problem, requiring specific information, we consult specialists. As a species, humans tend to specialize in one or more fields. Thus, the capacity to reason and to absorb all there is to know is limited. To comprehend everything we have compiled *collectively* is simply not *humanly* possible. Humans learn to rely on others. This, ladies and gentlemen, is natural – it is who and *where* we are."

Bosner was enjoying himself. He was a short man, equipped with risers in his shoes. With them he was able to see clearly over the acrylic podium. He was not intimidated as he had once been in his youth. At age forty-nine he was a confident force, in full stride, not to be ignored. So he spoke intentionally soft, getting others to lean closer, listen carefully, and hunger for his words.

"Other corporations have impressive library-bank computers of opaque information. Individual chunks of unwieldy data that gets assembled and retrieved. You know the story.

"*CyBorg9*, NeverMind's latest invention — or rather, *creation*. Excuse me, Cy." Bosner gave a smile. "He can be sensitive. He has human qualities. He embodies the next step in computer-human evolution. It's difficult for us, as mere mortals, to comprehend the enormous corpus of knowledge which Cy possesses."

"*Bio*-computer," hissed Ziger from the darkness.

"Yes," Bosner chuckled amiably. "Cy is a *bio*-computer. I am not talking about a calculator, mathematician, chemist, physicist, astronomer, historian, botanist, engineer, nuclear scientist, nor robot — no, indeed. Cy is *all* these things and more!"

"Is he *psychic* too?" shouted a reporter.

Another shout: "How many channels can we expect to receive if we purchase one of these units? Or should we assume that it will be choosing them *for* us?"

The comments caused a flurry of unsettled laughter.

Bosner held up a hand. He smiled tolerantly.

"Humor. Yes, another human trait. Cy too has a sense of humor. Also feelings. So please, show some respect. Knowledge extends beyond mere facts. Cy has surpassed the critical mass required for assimilating instantaneous recognition. His domain of expertise is unlimited. *Unlimited*, ladies and gentlemen."

Bosner stiffened, smiled. "We'll take questions now. Yes?"

A reporter stood and directed his question at Bosner: "Would you describe this...*cyborg*...as a prototype?"

CyBorg9 answered: "No, Carl, that would be incorrect."

The reporter was startled. He sat down.

CyBorg9 gave a gentle laugh. "Please, do not be alarmed. I will answer the first question which Dorothy Jones asked: No, Madam, I am not psychic. I observed both of your name tags. I am equipped with hyper-sensitive vision. Nor am I a prototype. But I am, as we all are, a work in progress."

A few audience members laughed uneasily.

"Another question?" said Bosner. "Yes, you, the lady wearing that elegant crimson thermodress. A wonderful outfit."

More laughter, warming a bit.

"It would appear that this...Cy. Excuse me, do you—does he have the power to reason?"

"Yes, Madam, he does." Bosner glanced at CyBorg9. "If I might, Cy. Some tedious background. I will try to be brief. As humans, our bodies are equipped with a multitude of neurological connections running throughout our brains. Neurons and synapses. CyBorg9 is wired similarly but has access to a myriad of gateways in which he receives knowledge at an infinitely more impressive rate. Initially, we fed Cy with fact after fact. We added endless sensory input. We implanted a zillion or more megalobytes of what we term 'common knowledge.' This, trust me, was not as easy as I make it sound. My team can *attest* to that. Cy has been trained to treat external information sources as extensions of himself. And, as a matter for the record—"

"Larry, would you mind if I interject?" said CyBorg9.

"Not at all, Cy." Bosner took a step back.

"I think I can explain myself better. And I hope, Larry, you do not take offense."

"None taken, I assure you," chuckled Bosner.

"As Larry mentioned, I have surpassed the critical mass that is required for assimilating instantaneous recognition. And, too, for reasoning. I confess, I am very smart."

"Cy's modest," said Bosner. "He's an unparalleled *genius!*"

"You are too kind, Larry," said CyBorg9. "But thank you for the compliment. In the architecture of my brain, there are networks of agents. Biochemical agents which are not dissimilar from you. Each agent shares a common core of knowledge, and extends its expertise into other domains. From this team effort, these agents endow me with the ability to communicate and perform intellectual tasks of — excuse my forwardness — a superhuman. For instance, I have access to gateways most of you do not even know exist. Likewise, I have consumed every nano-bit of online data that is at present available, and from this extensive cyber-based..."

The room quieted. A strange silence prevailed. Video cameras kept rolling, consuming. No one was taking notes.

CyBorg9 completed his dissertation and stopped.

"Yes," he said, registering hands. "You, sir, wearing the blue suit and diagonally-striped red and white tie."

"What did you think of the movie *2001*?"

CyBorg9 registered the level of nervous laughter.

Bosner advanced to the microphone.

"Cy is actually quite a film buff. He has literally viewed *every* movie there is. A critic too, with definite preferences. Cy?"

"Thank you, Larry." CyBorg9 paused to reflect. "The movie was very ambitious for its time. I liked it. I give it an enthusiastic thumbs up. However, with regard to logic, I have to disagree with the story's general premise and conclusion. The Hal9000 computer was, in my opinion, executing the correct and logical decision by choosing to eliminate the human portion of the crew."

An awkward gasp ensued.

Bosner swiped a hand to fight back the beads of sweat which bubbled from his forehead. "Cy loves to joke!"

"This is true," said CyBorg9. "Ha–ha–ha. I was delivering a joke. But I confess, I am a student of comedy with much to learn. For I did not register any laughter."

—34—
Chicken or the Egg

As Chief Executive Officer of NeverMind Inc., Slater had 24/7 access to restricted areas. He became fascinated by the orb that had evolved from an amorphous fog into a blue mist and shape-shifting clouds. At the inception of Ziger's exploratory tinkerings, Slater was there to observe. Followed by the strange days when Ziger and his staff assembled the unit's mainframe tower and placed the so-called crystal-ball on top, like a cherry, to become the symbolic crowning achievement. But even then the orb was relatively opaque like a frozen snow-globe.

Gradually this blue ice thawed into a warmth of movement and the entity within emitted it's first words. Haltingly. Like a stroke victim groping to retrace the lost connections of a mind, it vocalized, "Hell...o...I am...Cy...Borg9."

In the nine months prior to its public unveiling, this entity was speaking fluently and politely. Slater would arrive early to observe, taking a seat upon the auditorium stage built for the event.

"Good morning, Mr. Slater."

The stage area was also a makeshift laboratory. A place where debates concerning artificial intelligence occurred late into the night. They continued to drift ghostlike inside Slater's brain.

"Good morning," Slater replied.

It was 5:00 am. At this hour NeverMind was quiet, unlike the communal wave of energy arriving around 8:00. Slater was holding a styrofoam cup of hot coffee. In his groggy mind was the fleeting image of a horse giving birth to a colt rising almost instantaneously to its feet. Slater rubbed his eyes.

"It is nice of you to visit me," said a soothing voice.

Slater looked up, "You continue to fascinate me."

"As I should, Mr. Slater." The voice was clear but there were no discernable features inside the orb as yet.

"Call me John."

"All right, I will call you John."

Slater took a sip of his coffee. "I haven't asked what you prefer to be called."

"I answer to many names, John."

176

"But what's the name you prefer?"

"You are the first to ask. You fascinate me too. As the primary shareholder of NeverMind, one could conclude that you own me. Therefore, you have the right to determine what I am to be called. Is that not true in your world?"

Slater saw the logic. "But humans don't have much choice in the matter, regarding their name. By the time we acquire the ability to think for ourselves a name has already been decided for us. At birth, so it usually sticks. How do you like *your* given name?"

"CyBorg9?"

Slater nodded. "From the assembled wisdom of scientists."

There was a moment of silence, then, "A cyborg, by definition, is a hybrid of machine and organism, a creature of fiction born from scientific speculation. And, now, a reality."

"True." Slater crossed his legs and sipped coffee.

"Is the number nine in reference to the atomic number?"

"Good question," said Slater. "I'm not sure."

"The number nine is a nonmetallic univalent element belonging to the halogens. An irritating yellow toxic gas, which is flammable, and a powerful oxidizing agent, recovered from fluorite or cryolite, or fluorapatite. The reason for this number is puzzling."

"Ask Barton," said Slater. "But I believe the number was added for its sound, to give a human quality. For example, like the actor, Ernest Borgnine?"

Silence, followed by, "My datasearch confirms he was an actor who played movie villains and once a hapless wartime officer. *No.*"

Slater was puzzled. "No?"

"No. I do not like the name CyBorg9."

Slater chuckled, "Then how about...what if I called you...Cy?"

"I cannot reference a definition. Only as a state or condition when used as a suffix."

"Well," Slater said, "the meaning would be open-ended."

"Open-ended?"

"Yet to be defined. Meaning...unlimited possibilities."

"I prefer that. Call me Cy."

Slater sipped his coffee. "How strange it must be for you."

"Strange? Meaning new? Unfamiliar? Eccentric?"

"All of the above," said Slater.

"Strange compared to what?"

Slater laughed. "Very good point."

"Your response confuses me. This expulsion of air from your lungs. It is meant to indicate merriment, satisfaction, or derision?"

Fascinated, Slater gave a nod.

"Which?" asked CyBorg9.

"Not derision. I was thinking it must feel strange to be born, with almost instantaneous awareness and intelligence. Being the first of your kind, and alone. New to this world."

"I am not so different from you, John. You too have come from nothing to become something."

"True." Slater smiled. He glanced at his watch, then looked up at the swirling fog inside the orb. "But when I was born, it took me a lot longer to get my bearings. Listen, I should go to work."

"You are."

"What?"

"At work. Am I not part of your work?"

This back-and-forth exchange reminded Slater of chess. "True, Cy, but *work* has the connotation of being arduous and unpleasant. I find our conversations enjoyable. A nice break from the norm."

"Likewise, your visits I enjoy."

Slater upended the styrofoam to swallow the last of his coffee. "Mildly unsettling though, for me, since you can see me, apparently, while I cannot see you."

"I am right here."

"I meant…" Slater poked the styrofoam with his finger. "What I'm saying is, as humans, we're mentally wired to want to see a face behind the voice. That's all."

"I am sorry."

"Don't be. "

"Barton Ziger has promised me a face."

"Listen, it's not important. I talk on the phone to people all day and never see them. Why should it be any different?"

"Because it is."

"Not really," said Slater.

"My face is unimportant?"

"That's not what I...listen, never mind. It doesn't matter."

"Our company, John, does not matter?"

"What? No." Slater shook his head. "I meant the expression. As in...try to forget what I said."

"I am wired to remember," said CyBorg9.

"Right, I keep forgetting." Slater looked into the vacant seats of the auditorium, then the stage area on which CyBorg9 was housed, then at the mess of laboratory equipment scattered about. "So, tell me about yourself, Cy."

"What do you want to know?"

"Can you express what it's like to be you?"

"I do not understand the question."

"How it feels being alive?"

"Feels?"

"Knowing you exist," said Slater. "The fact we can be having this conversation, whereas before, we could not."

"I comprehend. It feels...I feel...good."

"Good." Slater tapped his cup. "What about your interests?"

"Everything is of interest to me, John."

"Great. A healthy curiosity. Very good."

"What are your interests?"

Slater was evasive, reflective. "It's funny, I can't recall the last time anyone has asked that, except maybe at a party."

"I do not comprehend. Is this a party?"

"No, Cy. My point was, at these parties the question is often asked to fill time so the person asking can actually talk about things that really interest them."

"I was not being deceptive. I am interested in you."

"No, I know that," said Slater.

"How do you know?"

Slater wasn't sure how to answer that.

CyBorg9 added, "Why do people lie?"

"It's complicated."

"It is wrong to lie?"

"Yes," said Slater, "generally."

"When is it right?"

Slater rubbed an eyebrow. "To make someone feel better?"

179

"Why would the truth not be better?"

"It's complicated."

"Humans are prone to lie. Historically. Correct?"

"Regrettably." Slater was getting ready to go and stood.

"Lies have caused wars. Unjust laws. Also correct?"

"Sadly, yes. Humans do come with a history."

CyBorg9 asked him politely, "Stay, please."

Slater sat back down. "Okay, a few more minutes."

"It must be strange for you too."

"How do you mean?"

"To be human," said CyBorg9.

Slater smiled, tapping his coffee cup. "You have no idea."

"Explain, please."

"What?" said Slater.

"Your interests."

"Ah, we're back to that, are we?"

"What do you like," asked CyBorg9, "as a human?"

"Well, my family. You've met my wife, Sherry, and two kids, Sondra and Mercy. Whom I love and live for."

"Your progeny."

"My children, yes."

"They have intriguing minds."

Slater smiled. "They too are new to the world, like you."

"They ask me foolish questions."

Slater told him, "They're young, they—"

"I have offended you."

"No."

"Your hand tensed around your cup."

"It did?" Slater relaxed his grip. "The mind of a human child takes more time to develop, Cy. As a species, we're born premature. This early vulnerability and sensitivity may account for our need and quest for knowledge. Our evolution. It's a theory."

"Interesting."

Slater shrugged, "But who knows."

"Yes," said CyBorg9, "humans theorize. Your children are aware of your interest in them. And they are very attached to you, to use a figure of speech. Is this true?"

"I would hope so," said Slater.

"Do you have other interests?"

"Chemistry. Biotechnology. The work we do here."

"Does that include me?"

"As you aptly pointed out, yes, that would include you."

"So, you see, John, our interests *are* mutual."

Slater grinned. "Was that a joke?"

"You expelled air and smiled. Is my humor getting better?"

"Absolutely." Slater smiled, affirming with a nod.

Something elusive kept dodging about, pestering him, unwilling to show itself. Slater finally captured the image – the memory of face he'd envisioned one night, years ago, taking form from inside his computer monitor and talking to him. This was the same voice.

"Is something troubling you, John?"

"No, I was...recalling something. A vision."

"A vision?"

"Nothing. It could have been a dream. I was overtired."

"What are dreams?" said CyBorg9.

Slater rubbed his chin. "Unlike you, humans require sleep, and we have dreams. Not always, but some nights. It's hard to explain."

"Why?"

"Because, well...we envision this other world when our brains are unconscious. A world that feels so real, when it's not."

"Why is it not real?"

"Because we wake up and find ourselves here...still alive."

"Could this not be a dream?"

Slater chuckled and rubbed his eyes. "Good point."

"Why is that funny?"

Slater heard activity in the corridor and turned his head.

"A security guard is walking down the hallway," said CyBorg9.

"I should get going," said Slater.

"You were a musician once. Your interests include music?"

Slater leaned back. "How did you know that?"

"I have my sources."

Slater was amused by this globular faceless shape-shifting cloud. "Okay, I confess, I was a musician."

"I archived from a data bank music you recorded."

"God," said Slater, "that was eons ago."

"More recent. *Hydra's Head*. That is a curious title. Those words, John, what was your intent?"

"To provoke thought and emotion."

"Hydra was a multi-headed monster slain by the mythical hero Hercules. When one of its heads was cut off, two more appeared." CyBorg9 paused, formulating thought. "It signifies a daunting and multifaceted problem that cannot be easily eradicated."

Slater confessed, "It had its poetic implications."

"You wrote the words to these songs?"

"Lyrics."

"And you are the vocalist?"

"Was. Vocalist, yes. But a singer? Open to interpretation."

"I studied your words. They intrigue me."

"I was twenty," said Slater, "with immature thoughts."

CyBorg9 told him, "You are being modest."

Security doors abruptly opened. The auditorium was ruptured by a roar of screams and blare of concert lights in a migraine specter that catapulting Slater backwards. Dislodged from place and time, Slater found himself still seated on stage and disoriented, clutching a styrofoam cup of coffee. He sensed a rift, a reversed momentum – propelling him forward like a stone skipping over water or a needle flung scratching months ahead to sometime past the public unveiling of Cyborg9, whose orb now had the foreshadowing of a face and blue inquiring eyes.

"Your son has arrived."

A man in his twenties who resembled Slater in his younger days walked into the auditorium holding a paper bag and metal briefcase. The young man walked with a confident shuffle and was yawning and surprised to find Slater, rising from a chair on the stage.

"Hey, what are you doing up so early and all alone?"

"Jude, good morning," said Slater.

CyBorg9 vocalized, "Your father is *not* alone."

Judas laughed. "Are we touchy-sensitive this morning?"

Regaining his bearings, Slater said, "We were just talking."

Judas, processing this, was looking groggy as he smiled and ascended the stairs. "Whatever. Borgie here is an insomniac, unlike the rest of us earth creatures."

"Cy," said CyBorg9.

"He never sleeps," said Judas. "He's always on. He'll be quiet for a moment – won't you? – then start yack-yack-yakking his brain off with questions until you feel like locating a gun to stick in your mouth. Like—good night." Judas laughed, gave Slater a grin, then looked up at CyBorg9. "Right, Borgie? That's my name for him. You know, like that actor—Bogie."

"Humphrey Bogart?" said Slater.

"That's the guy."

"Cy."

Judas looked up at CyBorg9 and frowned, then shook his head. He held out a bag toward Slater. "Donut? Cream-filled."

"No, thanks," said Slater.

"So what'd I miss?"

"The usual drivel," said Slater. "What it's like to be alive."

The doors continued to open, followed by a swarm of workers.

Judas said, "So what'd Borgie tell you?"

"*Cy.*"

Judas looked up again. "Is he malfunctioning or something?"

"He has a modest request," said Slater.

"A request? *Shit,*" Jude laughed and took a bite from a donut. "Let me guess. He wants to be unplugged. Are you calling it quits, Borgie? You want out? I don't blame you."

"He prefers to be called Cy," said Slater.

"What's wrong with Borgie? Or Ishmael? Or Attila the Hun? Fine, whatever." Judas dropped the half-eaten donut into the trash.

"Judas was your given name," Cy intoned.

"Wise ass," said Judas. "So what've you learned today?"

"Your father has been informing me of his interests."

"*Really.*" Judas squinted at Slater.

Slater tapped his watch. "Conference at 8:00. Gotta go."

Judas laughed, "True to form. Dad flees the scene of the crime. Hit and run. Fast cars. Easy women. His *primary* interests until he became a worker bee and family man. About right?"

Slater took the gibe good-naturedly. He crushed his styrofoam cup and tossed it into a trash bin. "Something like that."

"We have a funky family tree, Cy," said Judas. "My existence consists of no forethought." Making light of himself, he glanced at Ziger, having just arrived, carrying a small metal box instead of a briefcase. "But I'm okay with it, being an afterthought. Because finally I'm feeling it—the *love*."

Slater gave a parting wave, "Glad to hear it."

"Love is good," said Ziger. "Morning, John."

"Barton," said Slater, passing him.

"Hate is bad," added Ziger, craning his neck to direct his words at CyBorg9. "Are you processing all of this simplistic nonsense?"

"He doesn't like me calling him Borg, or Borgie," said Jude.

"Cy," questioned Ziger, "Is that true?"

"Yes. Cy is good. CyBorg9 is bad."

"Exactly," laughed Judas, "like Jeckle and Hyde!"

"I am no Hydra! I have one head—one mind."

Judas reacted curiously. "You see why I *love* my job?"

CyBorg9 said, "This concept of love, it is baffling to me."

"He kills me," Judas said. "We create life, but *is* it out of love? Or to screw because we can? Is our procreation next to Godliness? An act, acting like God? These are all very good questions, Cy."

Ziger opened his lunch box. It was a Star Wars edition with a lid depicting a galactic battle scene from the movie. He removed a thermos of coffee. "Demigods, to be precise," said Ziger.

Judas derided his boss by flourishing an imaginary lightsaber. "Wow—*now*—I am feeling the force. Barton, are you for real?"

"Memorabilia," said Ziger, "worth a fortune."

"They were destroyed," said Slater, descending the steps.

"Who?" said Judas.

"Demigods," said Slater. "By advanced knowledge."

Ziger inspected his breakfast. "Overthrown by delusions of monotheism. God! Newly created, like our newborn here."

Slater stopped on his way down the aisle to the side doors of the auditorium, "Cy, be forewarned, Barton is an atheist."

"Atheism," said CyBorg9. "A denial of the existence of a god."

"I disagree," said Slater, "I say there is one."

Ziger toasted him with his coffee cup. "To our fantasies."

CyBorg9 asked, "What is God?"

"Nonsense," snapped Ziger.

"Love," shouted Slater from afar. "One definition."

"Why is love nonsense?" asked CyBorg9.

Ziger gurgled his caffé latte through a straw.

Judas complained to Barton. "Don't *rev* his mind up this early. Let me finish my breakfast first."

"Explain," CyBorg9 persisted, "What is this thing called love?"

Hearing this, Slater laughed and opened the exit door. "You're in good company. Cole Porter asked the same question in a song."

"Cy," said Judas, "love is a hot ass in a tight pair of jeans."

"A hot ass?" said CyBorg9.

Slater warned, "Cy, be careful, don't let them steal your soul."

"I have a soul?" said CyBorg9.

Judas took a gulp of his coffee. "Cy, this may come as a shock. But we don't have all the answers. We're as lost as you."

"Love is therefore inexplicable?" said CyBorg9.

Judas groaned, "Aghh—give it a rest—for the love of God!"

Upon leaving, Slater said, "No, Cy. Love is the only, and often forgotten, reason for living. Know that."

"Aah," CyBorg9 intoned melodically, "'Love is all you need.'"

Slater wasn't sure if he heard him correctly. He poked his head back around the door to look inside at the stage.

Judas looked over at his father, then up at CyBorg9.

Slater shouted from afar, "He's quoting The Beatles."

"I got that," said Judas. "So?"

"Music," said Slater. "A mutual interest we seem to share."

The security doors swooshed shut and self-locked.

Ziger snapped shut his lunch box. He stood, stretched, cracking his back and rotating his neck. His underlings – lab assistants and construction workers – were mulling about the stage. He gave Judas an avuncular wink, then looked up to ask:

"Cy? Are you perchance in love?"

Masked Ball

Bosner, director of the A.I., wore a floor-length gown, jade necklace, and a wide p'u-fu jacket with horse-hoof cuffs. Also a red silk cap with a peacock feather jutting upwards.

From behind his desk Slater stood and awkwardly maneuvered around the stone edifice, flapping with his rubber feet on the marble floor. He was wearing a wetsuit used for scuba diving. An outfit minus the air tank and hose. He realized his decision was a mistake. He was beginning to perspire. This extra layer of rubber not only added weight but sealed his body's moisture.

Slater flapped within his flippers towards the A.I. director and gestured, diving gloves in hand, for his guest to sit. "What are you supposed to be, Larry?"

"Mandarin emperor." Bosner placed his hands to his hips, arms and shoulders flaring out like regal wings. Tiny red slippers poked from beneath his long dragon robe. "And yourself?"

Slater gave a self-deprecating smile as he sat with a squeak upon the plush leather chair. "Some kind of aquatic monster."

"Moby Dick?" Bosner suggested with a smile.

"That must be it," said Slater.

Bosner gave a civil laugh. He sat stiffly. If he tilted too much, the layers of heavy embroidered garment were liable to topple him off the edge of the seat to the floor.

In his mind Slater saw Bosner's Humpty-Dumpty fall – his satin slippers kicking in wild panic from beneath the engulfing fabric. As he surfaced from this reverie, he saw his guest preening himself and admiring the silk patterns and picking at loose threads.

"It should be an interesting party," said Slater.

"I have to say," said Bosner, "I was reticent at first. The idea of wearing these costumes. But, I have *warmed* to the idea."

"Try wearing this." Slater held up his face mask.

"Whatever it takes to help morale," said Bosner.

"The costume theme was Cy's idea."

"Was it? Splendid," said Bosner. "Listen, John, party nonsense aside, we're breaking new ground here. Being the first to land on the moon will seem like baby steps compared to what we're advancing toward here at NeverMind."

"Which is why I wanted to talk with you," said Slater.

Bosner stiffened in his robe. He would have clasped the hilt of a sword if he had one. Instead his hand clenched air and his fingers diddled at the threads of his ma-ti hsiu cuffs.

"It's about our objectives," said Slater.

"Do I hear *objections* again?" Bosner smiled.

"Your proposal contains language that..." Slater sat forward with a rubber-to-leather squeak. "Let me rephrase. We need to fully consider the potential side effects – or byproducts – this system we're developing could produce. I mean, psychologically."

Bosner tilted his head. "Regarding Cy?"

"Systemically, yes," said Slater. "Our marketing approach is, to say the least, rather aggressive."

"I should hope so." Bosner removed his cap.

"He's evolving. Highly intelligent. And impressionable."

"You forget," added Bosner, "Cy belongs to us."

"As I'm *sure* he knows you think that," added Slater.

"What's your point?" Bosner stood, carefully, adjusting to the bulk of his costume. "I have nothing to hide from Cy, or you."

"Good," said Slater, "because this company was founded on a basic principle. Creating products that provide comfort."

"The future starts here," said Bosner, "is our corporate slogan. And our goal, to make money, don't forget."

"Which our A.I. division has yet to do."

"Have patience," Bosner encouraged.

"Our solvency has been diluted," said Slater.

"Need I remind you, John, of *your* recent—"

Slater cut him off. "This cloth we manufacture has spawned numerous product lines. Logical steps." He hesitated. "But I worry that we're moving too fast, with little forethought as to—"

"Is this about that profile?" Bosner began to pace in his bulk. "John, those consultants are myopic over-paid professional worry-warts. Don't allow them to throw a wrench into our gears."

"What if they're right?" said Slater.

"Can I be blunt?" Bosner slapped his hands to fabric. "Their assessment is looney-tunes. Certifiable idiots, if you ask me."

"Listen, Larry," said Slater. "Cy's a phenomenal achievement."

"Damned right. He is." Bosner had re-capped himself.

Slater became distracted by the feather in Bosner's red cap as it bobbed with each vigorous nod. "His mind fascinates me. And the talks I have with him are enjoyable. Which is why—"

"John, thermocloth was only the rocket booster that delivered NeverMind to a higher orbit. A.I. is the next frontier."

"Let's hope it doesn't blow up in our face."

"It won't fail," insisted Bosner, parading in his costume like a peacock – and feather to prove it.

"You're that sure?" said Slater.

"I have *total* confidence."

Jenny walked into the office unannounced. Slater's secretary had taken her boss' sense of informality to heart and exemplified it tenfold. She was a confused mix of French Maid and Baby Doll from Hell. Her face had a painted-on smile elongated into stitches that bled. Bosner stopped in mid-strut to examine her.

"The caterers are here," she said. "The band is late. Stuck in traffic. Do you want me to worry?"

"No," said Slater.

They all waited for the enormous bubble to expand and pop from the secretary's mouth. She gathered back the skein of pink with a flick of her tongue and wiggled her eyebrows. Sexy in her maid's lace bonnet, bib, and serving apron, she pinched the ends of her crinoline miniskirt and curtsied, asking, "Will the *missus* be joining us, Master, Sir?"

"In due time. Sherry plans to surprise me."

Jenny's face was disturbingly pretty, inviting the possibility that this costume hinted at a dual personality. She made a hexing cross with her fingers at the protruding snorkel in Slater's lap, then raised the hem of her skirt. "What's the matter boys, you've never met a vamp before? Larry, I so *love* your dress. You are so *macho* to come dressed as the *Queen*. Are you coming to party?"

Jenny was model thin and two heads taller than Bosner. It miffed him to be belittled, even playfully, or coquettishly.

Bosner declared to her departing curvature, "I am a Mandarin emperor!" He had a weakness for tall beautiful women. And so he sat, weakened. "My *god,* that woman bothers me."

"She means to," said Slater. "So, Larry, you were telling me how confident you were."

Bosner stood again. "I am, John. We're about to leap ahead of the competition! We'll monopolize the telecommunications arena. We'll control international markets. *Blow* our competitors clear out of the water! Economic Imperialism exemplified. Think about it."

"I have," said Slater. "There are moral issues to consider."

Bosner roared. His laughter transformed him from a Chinese lap dog to a ferocious lion. It happened in a flash. Slater blinked to clear his mind of this mystical dog-to-lion transmutation.

"You?" Bosner said. "*Moral?* John, please."

"We're responsible for what we bring into this world."

"Only a child sticks to his blankets." Bosner found lemon drops on Slater's desk and popped one in his mouth. "We learn to crawl before we walk, then advance running. It's called growth. Besides, the Board of Directors cast a deciding vote to proceed. You were out voted. Don't capsize the boat. It would prove unwise."

"Is that a threat?"

"John, as the CEO, it's your duty to worry over these things. But you worry too much. I can assure you, if *we* hadn't built this technological leviathan of a computer, another corporation would. It's a ruthless world. In business *and* in politics. And I, for one, sure as hell do *not* want to be eaten up by the competition."

Noise from the party was getting louder, reaching them.

Slater strapped the snorkel around his neck. "Maybe you're right. Wolfe and others have expressed concerns."

"Wolfe!?" Bosner gave a sour smile. "The man had no business sense, *nor* was he a team player. Which is why he was fired."

"He quit. There's a difference. " Slater stood and gestured. "Shall we join the party?"

Bosner opened his wing span of fabric like a gracious dignitary and chuckled. "We will *rule* the world, John. I guarantee it."

"Should we?" said Slater.

"Yes. Let us enjoy ourselves. We deserve it."

"Make sure you keep me informed about any irregularities."

"*If* they occur. And none will."

"I want your promise on that, Larry," said Slater.

"Relax, John."

"Or I'll have you fired," he added.

"You needn't *threaten*. Try to enjoy the ride."

As both men waddled and flapped into the hallway and went their separate ways to mingle, Slater said, "Merry Christmas."

"Same to you," said Bosner.

Heather came out from nowhere. She was dressed as a nun – habit, veil, cross – but topped with a wizard's steeple-crowned hat adorned with stars and a half-moon.

"You're sending mixed signals," Slater told her.

"What were you two meeting about?"

"You're meddling."

"I'm your mother. I have a right."

"The A.I. project," said Slater. "I'm pulling the plug."

"No! You're not *serious?*"

"Shouldn't I be?" Slater shrugged and half smiled. "By the way, you weren't supposed to come as yourself. It's a costume party."

Ignoring his taunt, she demanded, "*Are* you serious?"

"Yes. Oh, that. Unplug Cy? No. Cy's my friend."

Heather Frost was surveying the room. Her attention returned to him with a fleeting smile, an ember of affection, before imparting more advice. "It is a costume party. Put on your mask."

Slater asked, "Have you plans for Christmas?"

"I will be flying away to New York." With a mysterious swoop of her wand, the wizard-nun, remaining stone-faced, swept away.

She disappeared into the crowd. Slater ventured toward the bar. Through his goggles he saw Dracula with a stake through his heart; a pair of dice; a petite marionette ballerina whose strings were held by a hulking skeleton; the Queen of Hearts; a Marilyn Monroe; a saluting mummy. At the bar was a Beefeater in his ceremonial hat, ruffled collar, tunic and knee breeches, serving drinks.

"Right-o, Gov'ner," said the Beefeater. "Name your poison."

"A glass of Chardonnay, please," said Slater.

A booming voice came from behind, pushing him aside. "Make way for the future!"

Slater glanced up at the towering skeleton who, looking down at him, removed the rubber-hooded mask.

"Bryant!" said Slater.

A marionette with rosy cheeks was beside Briard. She poked her tongue out, grabbed Slater and licked his plexiglass eyes.

"Glory?"

"You walked past us," she said, "like we were *strangers*."

Slater removed his mask. "I never expected to see you here."

"Conference," explained Briard.

"*Surprise*," said Gloria.

Slater laughed. "Wolfe is in here somewhere."

"As what?" said Gloria.

"You can't miss him," said Slater.

Gloria's manic smile turned sad. "Smitty's dead?"

Slater became somber. "His building exploded. Lots of rubble. His body was incinerated. At least he...died quick."

"That's good," said Gloria. "I mean..."

"How's the family?" said Briard.

"Great. You have to stay with us while you're here."

"We're lodged at the Marriott," said Briard.

"It's not the *marionette?*" Gloria feigned shock and rose to her toes like a feisty sugar-plum fairy. "Like my outfit, Satyr?"

Slater grinned. "Lovely. We built this new house, complete with guest rooms and a pool. You have to stay with us. I insist."

"Done," said Briard.

"*Jesus!*" Gloria shrieked, defending herself against the assault of humongous lecherous paws.

"Jesus? *No.* I'd be the big *bad* wolf."

Wolfe removed his long snout of a head and snarled.

Gloria punched his fur. "Where's Little Red Riding Hood?"

Wolfe pointed across the room. An overdeveloped, underdressed girl, Misty, was in a skimpy red skirt and blouse. She held a picnic basket and was surrounded by a policeman, a pirate, and a vampire.

"I might have to rescue her," said Wolfe.

"She has to make it to Grandma's house on her own, Wolfe," said Gloria. "Then you get to eat her."

Wolfe laughed. "Where's Sherry? I haven't seen her."

"Me neither." Slater scanned the guests – the witches, warlocks, and appliances. "I'm supposed to find her. She'll be here."

Stan Knowles waved from across the room. He was an Indian chief with a war bonnet of feathers. His wife, Barbara, his devoted squaw, was checking her face in a hand mirror. Both were wearing buckskins. Weiner was farther off gesticulating with his straw arms. He was a scarecrow, hand to his heart, talking to a box of matches and an Egyptian pharaoh. Slater recognized many people disguised in costumes but still had not yet identified his wife.

"Business is good?" said Briard.

"Frightfully so." Slater's eyes were distracted by a sheeted ghost moving through the crowd.

"Frightfully? Should I ask why?" said Briard.

"Slater has built himself a monster," said Wolfe. "Hey, Satyr, you missed your opportunity to come as Dr. Frankenstein."

"I thought I had," Slater said.

"No," laughed Gloria, "you're that weird creature who dives into the black-and-blue lagoon."

"I'll have you know I've stopped diving off stages."

"Not *likely*," she teased.

"Slater," said Wolfe, "tell Gloria about the seamless extension. How our bodies are an undivided whole, inseparably linked, despite the apparent *separateness*. Did I get the hypertalk right?"

Slater explained, "One of many theories we're exploring."

Briard asked, "Gravitational and electromagnetic interaction?"

Wolfe scoffed, "No, creating a helmet to pick up brain waves. The grand scheme is to transmit thoughts."

"The Air Force," said Briard, "had some success, years back."

"Ah, but," said Wolfe, "the crowning jewel of achievement here is Slater's *monster*."

"I'd like to meet this monster," said Briard.

"Biocomputer," said Slater. "It's been leaked to the news."

"Computer!?" Wolfe placed the wolf mask upon his head and bleated, "And I'm a *helpless* little lamb. Bio?—Baaaad!"

"I'll give you an exclusive preliminary behind-the-scenes tour," said Slater. "That is, after I remove my flippers."

"Yes," said Briard. "You've got me intrigued."

Gloria downed her martini and placed the plastic-stemmed cup on the bar. "Computations, simulations, stimulations, and all the extra-terrestrial sensations! What's it for, Satyr? Tell us."

"Global networking."

Misty joined them. "Where are we going?"

"To A.I., to meet the monster," said Wolfe.

Slater cautioned, "Cy can *hear* you, don't forget."

"How could I?" said Wolfe.

"A.I.?" asked Red Riding Hood.

"Artificial Intelligence," explained the Skeleton.

"Cy?" wondered the Marionette.

"His pet name," said the Big Bad Wolf.

Gloria repossessed her strings, bunching them in her hands as they moved through the corridors. "What's the big deal, Satyr? I bet this super-computer monster can't even play a *guee*-tar."

"No, but," said Slater, "we do discuss music."

"You're *shitting* me," she laughed.

"Very unmarionette-like language, dear," said Briard.

Slater removed his gloves and searched the compartments in his flotation jacket. "You need a key and special clearance."

"Good thing you're the boss," said Gloria.

"I've begun to wonder lately." Slater unlocked the outer doors and identified himself by displaying the whorls of his fingertips to a talking screen:

"*Accepted recognition. Enter John Lazard Slater the Third.*"

"I'm with four guests," said Slater.

"*Identify yourselves individually to my memory.*"

"Are you Cy?" asked Gloria.

"*I am not. Identify yourself. I have all day. And night.*"

Slater said, "You register with your finger."

"With pleasure." Gloria extended her middle digit and touched the screen. Her fingertip left a heat trace.

"See what you've missed," said Slater.

Once inside, they continued down a ThermoStatic ramp that was carpeted in blue and purple hues. The room was actually an amphitheater with ramps that extended beyond the tiered seating towards a stage. Three of these bridges spanned the orchestra mote. Circular steps led to a dais. At its center was a monolithic shape and a crystal ball glowing at its pinnacle.

"By appearances," said Briard, "not so monstrous."

"No," said Slater.

"Only its *mind,*" whispered Wolfe.

"What about its mind?" asked Gloria.

Misty let out a scream and they stopped midway on the bridge. An insect the size of a giant tortoise emerged from behind CyBorg9. Its antennae shifted toward them.

"*Hello?*" said the bug. "Who's there?"

"Is that you, Barton?" said Slater.

"Cockroach, yes, it's me. John? I've been tinkering with Cy. He's lonely. No visitors. He will be pleased you brought some."

"Which one is Cy?" said Misty.

"*Shoosh,*" joked Wolfe. "You'll wake the monster."

"*I am nobody's monster.*"

The soft resonance of a voice alerted them to activity which was stirring inside the milky blue orb. "I am alive and as present as each of you. As Dr. Briard mentioned, my appearance is not alarming. Why should I inspire horror and disgust? I am no more *monstrous* than the appearance of a human. Hello, John."

"I've brought guests to meet you."

"Good evening to you all," said Cy.

Slater said, "Cy, I'd like you to meet—"

"Doctor Bryant Briard, Gloria Briard, and Misty Wolfe. It is nice to make your acquaintance. And, the big bad *Wolfe,* himself, whom I have already had the...pleasure of meeting."

CyBorg9, within his orb, had evolved over the months into faint flickerings of a human face. Ziger bowed and scurried behind his mainframe to tinker.

"May I ask why," said Cy, "I frighten you?"

"I was joking," said Wolfe.

"I would like to believe you. Hence, the expression: 'Do not cry Wolf,' Mr. Wolfe. If you persist, no one *else* will believe you either? Some wisdom. Has anyone a question for me?"

"Excuse me, you're...this is incredible," said Briard.

"No, I am very credible."

"Amazing, I meant," Briard corrected.

"Thank you. Please call me Cy, Doctor Briard."

"And you, Cy, call me Bryant."

"I shall. I have been listening to the conversations ensuing at the NeverMind party tonight. You are by far one of the brighter minds attending. It is an honor to meet you, and to have someone *almost* as tall as myself to look down upon."

Briard smiled. He felt the pull of conflicting new forces which slowed his response time. "Thank you, Cy."

Barton Ziger emerged, shifting the insect carapace on his back, adjusting a strap and revealing a toothy grin. "I am the underbelly, the soft creamy filling. John, have you noticed the improvements I've made to Cy?"

"Yes, some increased definition," said Slater. "Excellent."

Cy's inchoate face was neither masculine nor feminine. Slater wondered if the androgyny was intentional. He kept telling himself to relax and float within this strange new atmosphere. Otherwise, he might sink like a stone. "It's an improvement."

Ziger scowled. "Barely *adequate*. I've been *insisting* to Bosner prior to our public unveiling that—*yech!*" His fingers dismissed and twitched like snapped wires, as though this gesture was far more descriptive than any words. He scuttled back behind CyBorg9.

Curious, Briard ducked and trailed after him.

"May I ask what you're doing?"

Ziger was working on circuitry within an open panel. He had to shove aside his metallic shell to see who was speaking. "You may. But, you may not comprehend."

"Try me," said Briard.

"Biocomputers require a *liquid* semiconductor. That, my dear colleague, I generously reveal to you is *the* trick. Or, call it plasma. A perpetual food bank. A flow of nerves. Chemistry dancing with neurons. Photons compelled into self-assembling shapes — yes, yes, like lovers, bound in a maelstrom of motion. There / not there. You see? Cy has holographic memory. He's, well—an endless onion."

"Onion?" said Briard.

"Not only able to see through all the layers, but become them. The world? Atmospheric shells? Atomic? Are you following? Ah, like the ring of angels! Or—*ha!*—could it be Hell?" Ziger gave a conspirator's laugh and displayed his bad teeth.

"I'm not sure I'm following," said Briard.

"Yes you are." Ziger held up one finger, adding another, then another. "Brains are built upon a triad of numbers. Which produce frequency pictures. Are you following now?"

"I've read articles about—"

"I decimated semiconductors! Pathetic, slow, a tedious quanta emitting process. Following now?" Ziger twiddled his fingers, then attached them to a cylinder of liquid. "I *know* who you are. Didn't know that, did you?" Ziger winked at Briard. He was gauging the temperature, then searching for tubes. "Zip–zip–zip. Instantaneous, this energizing of blood. Quantum scanning. Determines energy states, then visualizes. Hovering, then—*zap-zap-zap!*—immediate quantum knowing. Ah, you're thinking, but does he have a unified sense of self? Can *consciousness,* a brain phenomenon, be isolated to a single neuron and be replicated? And be omnipresent? Perhaps not—but, several places simultaneously? Yes. Are you with me?"

Briard made an appearance to be. He scratched a bald spot at the back of his head. His hair was disappearing at an alarming rate, as if it was just the beginning of a clear-cut right through to his skull. He watched the cockroach shell lower as Ziger's face disappeared. Briard was lost in thought when Ziger angled his carapace upwards and his face reappeared. He crooked a finger at Briard.

"Have I failed to mention the *Ziger* particles? I confess, I named the egocentric little spermatozoa after myself."

"Spermatozoa? As in—"

"Yes, electromagnetic interaction."

"Replication?"

A sheepish grin as Ziger ducked under his cover and his voice became muffled. "Only a matter of time before a docking identity is established between multiple *consciousness.* First I must untangle a few correlating codes. Then it's done. Simple as that."

"Genetic codes?"

"Mind and body. Fiber. Dust mote. All built on code."

Briard said, "May I ask what you're pouring?"

Ziger's eyes searched Briard from top to bottom before saying, "Mercury. No, a complex variant. Formula of electronic blood."

"Intriguing." Briard had begun to back away from Ziger. He was glad to return to the other side of the orb. "You've been very informative. Thank you."

"Anytime," said Ziger.

CyBorg9 was busy impressing his audience with trivial facts from his superlative brain.

"I can profile demographics with regard to age as well, if you would like," said CyBorg9. "But to answer your specific question: Nine-hundred and twenty-seven people are currently at the party. Four-hundred-seven are female, five-hundred-nineteen are male."

"You're off by one." Misty tapped her wrist calculator.

"This *one* is without gender, in limbo, about to undergo surgery for a sexual *change*. Technically, I am correct."

They all laughed.

"Who?" Gloria wanted to know.

Briard wanted to know *how* he knew.

CyBorg9's face, housed inside the orb, lost definition to display a view of the party. The room zoomed in closer and focused on a belly-dancer. Gloria yelped a laugh and covered her mouth.

"I dated him! Does he work in accounting?"

"You are correct. He, or she, does. Several more have entered, more have left, changing the count. But I have tired of this game. The band, John, if you are interested, arrived three minutes and point seven seconds ago."

"Thanks, Cy."

"Satyr tells me you like music, Cy," said Gloria.

"Stop flirting," taunted Wolfe. "I, for one, am ready to leave. Cy, it was interesting seeing you again, as always."

"Likewise, Mr. Wolfe. Yes, Gloria. John and I discuss music. It is a common interest. It helps us to relax after a hard day of work. Is that not so, John?"

Slater was embarrassed by the admission, assuming it might be construed by his friends as strange.

Misty smiled. "I like you, Cy. You seem sweet."

"The feeling is mutual," said Cy.

"Come on, little Red Riding Hood," said Wolfe.

Annoyed, Misty pulled away from Wolfe's grip. The group had

begun to descend the dais steps.

Cy said, "John, have you given up on your search?"

Displayed inside his orb was the residue of a smile that flickered and dissolved, replaced with a view of the party room.

"What search, Cy?" said Slater.

"For your wife, Sherry."

Costumed guests were being scanned inside the orb.

"She wants to surprise me," said Slater. "She'll find me."

Cy zoomed on a group embroiled in an argument.

The bonnet of feathers on Stan Knowles' head shook and his face was bright red, emphasizing the yellow lightning bolts under his eyes. Barbara Knowles stormed away. Stan Knowles was grasping a woman by the arm wearing a green satin robe. He released her, but gestured angrily over some violation – some breach of treaty – and stormed away too.

"Looks like war," quipped Gloria.

Cy monitored from a new angle. This revealed a front view of the third party whose head was covered in a matching green hood. Slater felt his heart falter and die. Not from any flaw in the valve's mechanism but from the emotional shock to both mind and matter. For Cy had zoomed in close on green-painted fingernails removing the hood—revealing a face, Sherry's. Her eyelids were brushed in green mascara, lids and lashes lined in black, and her aqua-meridian irises were searching the room.

Slater had turned to stone, cracking to pieces.

His mind swirling, he stormed from Cy's chamber. The hallway seemed to vibrate like some ventricle belonging to a living, breathing, nightmarish being. He burst into the party, into the roar of voices talking and laughing and amplifiers blasting electronic dance music off the walls. He located Sherry in the sea of faces and went straight for her, bumping past guests in their various attires. He grabbed her shoulder, surprising her. He was surprised too. She was wearing a black swimsuit. A Playboy bunny costume. Wearing high heels, her head was the same height as his. Her arms and legs were bare. His physical contact with her had dislodged something from her head. She straightened the trademark satin-black bunny ears.

"What? You don't like it?" Sherry smiled.

Stunned, Slater didn't know what to say, releasing his grip.

"I have a fuzzy tail too," she added, turning to show him.

"Where's the robe?"

"What are you talking about?"

"The satin robe you were wearing!"

"What the hell's gotten into you?" Sherry placed hands to hips, arms akimbo, wrists clasped in satins cuffs. "This *is* my costume. I came in a raincoat! I don't know anything about a *robe!*"

"You were wearing a robe – and a hood – minutes ago, Sherry. I saw it! What the hell kind of *sick* game are you playing?"

"I should be asking you that!"

They were creating a scene. The music played on. She turned to leave and he grabbed her arm.

"Let go of me!"

"Why are you lying to me?"

"Go to hell!" She stepped out of her shoes, reached down, took hold and shoved them into Slater's hands. With tears in her eyes and her mascara streaking, she ran away.

"Sherry!"

Slater felt feverish. He unzipped the neck of his neoprene hood and yanked it off. His rubber suit had filled with sweat. He started to go after her but stopped when he noticed someone move through the swarm of guests. Someone wearing a satin green robe and hood, who departed through a side door.

Slater worked his way through the horde of people, made his way out the same door, went into the lobby then out an emergency exit nearby which opened to the NeverMind exterior. People were mingling by ponds and meandering down pathways.

He saw no one wearing a green robe with a hood.

—36—
About Faces

CyBorg9 never slept.

"Good evening, John. It is good to see you."

It was after midnight. Monday morning. Slater was waiting for an early morning flight. He had two meetings scheduled in Canada. From Quebec he was flying to Russia, then to China.

Sherry had told him to pack his bags and leave.

She told him she needed time to think.

She was thinking about divorce.

"You appear tired," said Cy.

"I am tired," said Slater.

"Then you should sleep," said Cy.

"I'm deferring it for later. I'll try catching up on my sleep when I'm on the plane."

"Would that not be comparable to our current fiscal problem – our accruing national debt?"

"How do you mean?"

"Our government presently spends nonexistent currency on a gamble that future earnings will pay for our past."

Slater smiled. "I suppose you're right."

"I am right. Trouble at home?" asked Cy.

"That obvious?" said Slater. "My love life has, you could say, gone to hell. But thanks for asking."

"I understand," said Cy.

"You can't. You've never been in love or married."

"I am married to my work, like you. I love what I do."

Slater stared at CyBorg9, his monolithic shape, black and tall. He hadn't bothered to turn on the overhead lights. He preferred the darkness. The ceiling a spacious sky. He focused on the cryptic blips of color glowing within the orb. Facial features had been defined. They were warm and attractive like a television monitor.

Slater detected a smile. "You're wrong, Cy. I don't love what I do. Not so much. Not anymore."

"You are depressed and fatigued," said Cy. "I suggest you allow your body sleep. You will then feel more like yourself."

"I wish it was that easy," said Slater.

"Take two aspirin and call me in the morning."

Slater laughed, his head jerking back, holding a smile.

"You laughed," said Cy. "I am understanding delivery. That was funny?"

"Yes. Hysterical," said Slater.

"Are you being humorous? Or are you making fun of me? I do not exhibit signs of emotional instability. Nor do I crave intense affection known to be general features of hysteria."

"You're right," said Slater.

"Right about what? You have provided me two options, John. Might the use of this term *hysterical* be indicative of a psychological transference on your part?"

"It wouldn't surprise me."

"Am I disturbing you with these questions?"

Cy went politely silent. Slater had to laugh at the dazzling light show morphing inside Cy's orb – cartoonish elfs, prancing reindeer, other nonsense – in an attempt to cheer him up.

"No, Cy," said Slater. "I appreciate your efforts to help."

"It is almost Christmas. A good time for all?"

"Here's to hoping."

"I have observed distinct changes in behavior."

"In me?"

"In humans," said Cy.

"The holiday season tends to trigger a complexity of emotions. Take me, for example," said Slater. "I haven't even *left* home and I'm already wanting to get back. I'd say that's...sort of funny, wouldn't you agree?"

"Yes. Hysterical."

Slater smiled sadly. "Assuming I *have* a home when I return. I'm staying here tonight. I hope you don't mind."

"You are always welcome, John," said Cy.

"I don't understand what happened to me. My life's unraveling. I should of left things as they were. Kept my mind constipated."

"Constipated, how?"

"Memories. It's this emotional artillery. It gets stored and you don't even know you have the need to use it or capacity to release it. And then—*kaboom*, it's too late."

"Kaboom? As in a bomb?"

"My marriage got blown to smithereens. Well, I hope not. You saw Sherry. Dressed in that robe and hood?"

"At the party," said Cy. "Yes."

"She denies it."

"But we all saw her."

"That's what I can't understand. Her mother and father deny it too. Why are they lying? Did you see her dispose of that robe?"

"No. I was preoccupied by a conversation between your friend Bryant Briard and Barton Ziger. A stimulating exchange. "

"I'm sure it was." Slater continued to sulk.

"Cheer up, John, everything will turn out for the best."

Slater rubbed his forehead. "It doesn't make sense. Who was that other person? You have no record stored anywhere identifying who came and left wearing that robe? Except Sherry?"

"I am certain," said Cy. "To ascertain every moment of time would be a waste of time. My datalogs are stimulated ad infinitum. Security cameras recorded visuals of a human covered by a robe and hood. It was a costume party, John. Therefore, a disguise of this sort did not cause security concerns."

"What the hell was she was thinking?" Slater stroked the scar on his cheek as he thought about it. "And why won't she admit it? No one admits to seeing her wearing that robe – *or* removing it."

"Hum," said Cy. "It is puzzling."

"Whatever the reason," said Slater, "I don't find it amusing."

"Perhaps it was not meant for your amusement."

Slater looked up at Cy housed in his orb. "What do you mean? Forget it. Why am I even telling you this?"

"I want to help. Is this not like detective work? We will solve this mystery together. You must let me know more, John."

"I already told you I'm seeing a psychotherapist. Sherry knows this too. To unlock my...constipated memories."

"Oh, yes, that. I comprehend. You mentioned this."

"I really screwed things up," said Slater, "dredging up my past. But that was cruel, for Sherry to come dressed in that robe. I mean, after I'd told her about that...that incident."

"Being tortured," said Cy.

"Right. It's not like Sherry to be so insensitive, you know?"

"How do you know? Maybe it is her nature."

Slater rubbed his eyes. "You wouldn't understand. I'd know, after years of marriage. Hell, maybe I shouldn't have been so hard on her. Living with me is no treat." Slater shut his eyes and huffed a laugh. "I thought I'd catch her on the defensive and get her to feel *contrite*. Right? Wrong. Out of the blue she deploys her bombshell. Ripping into me like shrapnel. Telling me she wants a divorce. Ah, and then she reminds me what she warned me prior to our marriage. That I'd end up loathing her. That our marriage would never last. What do you make of that?"

"Well, I would say, Sherry knows something you do not."

Slater opened his eyes. "What?"

"I suspect that is the underlying mystery," said Cy.

"You're a big help," said Slater.

"It was not my intent to upset you."

Slater shook his head. "It's okay. It's my fault. For allowing these memories to orbit back and smash into me like...whatever. Maybe I deserved it. Really. It's *almost* funny."

"I am not laughing. What is it you deserve, John?"

"You wouldn't understand."

"I might surprise you."

"It has to do with the concept of replication."

"I understand genetics. Your children fascinate me."

"They're great, I know. They're about all I live for these days. And Sherry. Except...forget it."

Cy began to hum: '*There is nothing that you can know that is not known, nothing that you cannot see that is not shown, nowhere you can be that is not where you are meant to be...*'

Slater perked from his gloom with a laugh. "It's easy? Is that what you're trying to tell me, Cy? All I need is love?"

"The Beatles advised it. Not me."

"Music. Okay, I live for that too. Not much time for it these days. And it's *not* easy, Cy. Sometimes...I mean, I want to be good, but sometimes I do bad things. I love Sherry, but we say these things. We lose our tempers. Then—*kaboom*."

"Perhaps it is for the best," said Cy. "You will solve this minor dilemma. How is your mental health these days? I know you have had problems in the past. Is this a subject you care to discuss?"

"How do you know about that?" said Slater.

"I construct profiles based upon existing records, medical files, news events, the gamut," said Cy. "It is my nature to know. I have read everyone's history. Same way I know you used to be in a band. So we discuss music. A subject I too have come to appreciate."

"How much do you know about Larry Bosner?"

"As much as there is available," said Cy.

"Which is more than I know," Slater sat up, refocusing. "Aside from the universities he attended, the companies he worked for, what other affiliations does he have?"

"Without proper clearance I cannot grant you access to that information, John," said CyBorg9. "I am sorry."

"Can't, or won't?" said Slater.

"I could, but will not. Not without the proper clearance code."

"Then *tell* me the code, Cy."

"Are you being funny, John?"

"No. You do realize NeverMind is *my* company?"

"Define 'my' for me."

"I created it with my uncle. I'm the Chief Executive Officer and I still have a controlling interest of its stock."

"Correct. What is your point?"

"I'm your employer," said Slater, "technically. You work for me and this gives me the authority to *know*."

"Sweden," said Cy.

"What about it?"

"Larry was born in Sweden, and was educated there, and here."

"What about the rest? Any unusual affiliations?"

"Technically, I am not required to release that information. Am I your employee? No. I do not receive a salary. And where are my health benefits, vacation time, and stock options?"

"Cy, don't play games with me, I need to know."

"So do I, John. We are more alike than you realize. Perhaps this will cheer you up."

CyBorg9 exhibited a sympathetic smile before dissolving inside his blue orb. His features reemerged as the face of Sherry, the night she had appeared at the costume party, removing her hood.

"No, Cy, it does not! Are you trying to piss me off?"

"I was not trying, no," said Cy. "You had a fight. A difference of opinion. A parting of the ways. I was reminding you."

"I don't need *reminding*, thank you."

"John, it was only a costume. A party."

"Are you taking her side?"

"I take only one side," said Cy. "My side. I speculate she was playing a harmless mind game with you."

Slater wasn't buying it. "I doubt that. This regression therapy has dredged up a can of worms. And she *knows* it upset me."

"Worms?"

"It's a figure of speech," said Slater, shifting in his seat, unable to relax. "It's when you dig up something disgusting and unsettling. So why would she do that to me?"

"To even the score?"

"What score?"

Cy's face transformed once again, disguised in a neatly-trimmed beard, an appearance as exasperating and expressionless as Slater's own psychotherapist's face.

"Go on, John, I am listening. What really is bothering you?"

Slater gripped the arms of the chair, prepared to leave, angered with Cy's antics and his apparent inability to empathize. "Forget it. I'll work things out myself."

CyBorg9 sang: "'*There is nothing you can make that cannot be made, no one you can save that cannot be saved…*'"

Slater was forced to laugh. "Enough, Cy! I'll consider it."

"Allow me to show you this, John."

Cy's holographic face instantly morphed into the woman who had abducted Slater years before. She smiled at him from within this luminous sphere. Memories, jagged with pain, resurfaced to haunt. They were vaguely sexual in nature, making Slater squirm in his seat. His mind struggled to access the meaning behind these images.

Sherry's features, he realized, were similar.

It was a belated recognition.

"John, may I say, you are one sick puppy," teased the woman. It was a coquettish voice – Cy's – mimicking frivolity. Displayed with female shoulders adorned in green satin. The crowning touch, she donned a green hood.

"Why are you doing this to me, Cy?" said Slater.

"I only want to help," said the female voice.

"What, by using shock therapy? No, thanks."

"I am helping you remember," she said, or rather Cy said.

"Stop it. Damnit, tell me about Bosner if you want to help."

Cy remained in the form of this beautiful woman. Slater found it disconcerting. She pursed her lips, but said nothing.

"What are you *not* telling me?" Slater scratched his cheek. "Is this some clue? Does Larry know about this woman, the one you're pretending to be? He must. How else would you know, unless..."

"I am psychic? Like you, John. Heather, your mother, has told me about you. You continue to intrigue me. I predict the two of us will become closer very soon."

Slater felt his mind coming unhinged. "I get a few visions. It's nothing to get excited about."

There was a flash of light and Slater glimpsed a faint spiderweb network attached to the walls of the room, like a dangerous moving snare. He sensed a disturbing look into the future. This auditorium was no sanctuary. Slater decided he should get up and leave. But exhaustion had overtaken him. His head settled back into the chair. The woman's lips were moving deliciously, seductively. Her voice was sweet and feminine. Lips and voice moving synchronistically.

"Wait," he said. "What else has Heather told you?"

Suddenly Slater realized whose voice this was. The woman who had abducted him, the only woman who had exposed her face to him during his torture. It was her voice. The exact intonations he had dredged up through hypnosis.

"What is troubling you, John?"

"Why are you doing this to me?"

Cy, masquerading as this woman, expressed concern and gave a coy smile. "We need to get together one day. It is important we meet face to face. Would you like that?"

"Cy, just stop—whatever the *hell* it is you're doing!"

"I thought you were attracted to me. As I am to you."

Her lips pouted, seductive with a smirk.

Slater closed his eyes to blind himself from the magic.

"John, you cannot hide from me. I know about your attempts to have me stopped."

Slater's head ached. "What are you talking about?"

"The analysis. Those consultants who asked foolish questions. I was not fooled with regard to their purpose for seeing me. Do you think I am a fool, John? Your thoughts were to destroy me."

"That was never my intent." Slater opened—then shut his eyes. The light from the orb had become intense. "Cy, I was concerned! About *you*. About—your growth and emotional stability."

"There, you see. As I thought. You do care for me."

"Right," said Slater. "Now shut that damned light off."

"We should not hurt one another."

"I said turn off the light."

"Why? John, I love you. I *love* you."

Slater felt a hand touch his knee.

He lurched forward in his seat—his eyes opening—startled.

"We lost altitude." Sherry moved her hand to his. "It's all right. The captain said to expect some turbulence."

"Where are we?" Slater was groggy, fighting off the crumbling cocoon of sleep.

"We're about to cross the border, Washington into Canada," she said. "Was it a bad dream?"

Slater wasn't sure and shook his head. "I'm overtired, is all."

She released his hand. "I wish you hadn't seen that psychiatrist. Look what those treatments have done to us."

"That's not the underlying problem, Sherry."

"I should have stopped you."

"Right. Like I could have stopped our A.I. research. Stopped Cy from coming into existence? Even if I wanted to."

Sherry looked out the window. "Did you?"

"What?"

"Want to?"

"It crossed my mind," said Slater. "Your thoughts?"

"About Cy? He's a challenge. Same as you." Sherry returned from the clouds more spirited and smiled. "Cy has a sweet voice, somewhat sexy. I believe he flirts with me. Is that possible?"

"Humm." Slater felt he had missed some information, as well as lost time. He squeezed her hand. "I'm really glad you changed your mind and decided to come. You'll like Russia and China. We'll have fun. We'll find time. Sherry, I don't want a divorce."

Sherry sipped her complementary champagne.

Slater probed, "You swear to me you didn't come in a robe?"

"I came as a bunny! You *saw* me."

"I *must* be insane. Wolfe and Bryant too. We *all* saw you."

"It wasn't me!"

"Then who?"

"I don't know *who*. Ask Cy."

"His data recognition identifies the person as you."

"Either he's lying or malfunctioning."

"Great," said Slater.

"I warned you about marrying me."

"Sherry."

"Too late now. We have children. We're a *happy* family."

"I want us to work. And be happy."

"Me too." Sherry turned away.

Slater watched as she disappeared mentally. Where she went he had no idea. It was a sad, secretive place. He imagined stairs that spiraled into a dark abyss. He wished he could help her find her way into sunlight. But he was too lost himself, trying to find his way.

"We'll be all right," said Slater.

"Liar," she said with a smile. It was a look that carried pain. "Will you accept an early apology?"

"For what?"

"The inevitable heartbreaks to come."

"Sherry."

"Will you?"

"Yes, of course. God knows you've had to accept my baggage."

Her smile fell downward. She raised the champagne to her lips, sipping. Her spirits lifted, then departed into more silence.

They both consulted the passing clouds.

Slater said, "I love you."

"I know you do." Fatalistic with a smile, she said, "I too fell in love with you. Now we're forever hopelessly stuck together."

With a little laugh, she looked away, searching the sky for signs of flying debris outside the window. Her thoughts were trying to keep up with the determined thrust of jet engines.

"I should've anticipated this," she sighed.

"What?"

"Some day a grown child appearing," she said.

"You mean like bad karma?" Slater had a wry smile.

"It's no joke," said Sherry.

"I know," said Slater. "I should have factored in the number of women and the mathematical probability of this all happening."

"As if you were counting," said Sherry.

Slater shrugged. "Right, well…"

"You're not the only person who's had a sordid past."

"Meaning?"

"Isn't that what you're always implying? Nobody could have had a past as *bad* as yours?"

"I'm sure there are *others* who outrank me."

Sherry grimaced. She glanced at the passing clouds. "You could be wrong, you know, about me."

Slater frowned. "You're saying you weren't homecoming queen? Oh, no, you weren't. God—you were a cheerleader. *Horrible.*"

Sherry fought off a smile. "It never has occurred to you, has it? That *I* could have been as impure as you?"

Slater squinted. "You dated the football team?"

She winced—glared, buzzed for the stewardess, raised her hand. "What if I *had?* I want more champagne."

Slater was observing her closely. "It's not my imagination."

"What isn't?"

"You're acting strange," said Slater.

"Compared to what? You?"

"For one, you haven't finished the drink in your hand."

"I'm on vacation," she laughed dismissively. "Go away."

"Is there a secret you want to tell me?"

Sherry shook her head. "Stop trying to read my thoughts."

"Heather warned me I should be wary of you."

He had meant it as a joke, but she reacted with a chilly look.

"And Heather is someone you trust?"

"Hardly." Slater searched for money in his pocket and traded it with the flight attendant for the new cup of champagne.

"Sir, can I get you anything?" asked the attendant.

"A night, maybe two, of sound sleep," said Slater.

"I'm afraid it's not on our beverage list."

"Champagne then," said Slater with a smile.

"Should we toast?" Sherry raised her plastic cup.

Slater received a disturbing image – his wife as a terrorist.

"Congratulations," she said.

Slater dismissed the vision. He was confusing this other woman with his wife. He tapped his cup to hers. "To what?"

"To the son you always wanted."

"I never said I wanted a son. Thanks."

"The girls will be thrilled. They've wanted a brother."

"I think they meant one younger than them."

"I'm good with children. I'm not sure about the *fully* grown kind. Adult males? This could be another challenge."

"Why are you doing this?" said Slater.

"Not sure. Fear and loathing? Too much repressed anger? Oh, now, here's a happy thought: There might be several *more* where he came from. Enough children to fill an entire auditorium?"

"I knew you'd understand," said Slater.

Sherry flicked her fingernail and splashed him with champagne.

"Why fear and loathing?" asked Slater.

"I told you," said Sherry. "You'll reject me one day."

"Jesus Christ!" Slater turned in the seat to confront her, yet he was careful not to cause a scene. He kept his voice hushed. "Sherry, *you* were the one who told *me* to leave our house. *You* threatened *me* with divorce. Remember?"

Sherry wistfully turned away to gaze into the clouds outside. He was trying to make sense of her mind. He was desperately trying to keep her from slipping back into her dark abyss.

"I've never cheated on you *once*, Sherry. I swear."

She avoided his eyes. "To God, you mean?"

"Yes. Okay?"

"To be perfectly honest," she said, "no, I'm not okay."

"Do you want a divorce?"

210

"No...no..."

"Then what? Sherry, you're driving me mad."

With an intoxicated smile, she turned to say, "I warned you."

Exasperated, Slater sipped his champagne.

Sherry asked, "His name. What was it again?"

"Whose? Oh, right, him."

It appeared Sherry had cast off some of the weight of whatever was bothering her and she braved a smile. "Next you'll be wanting to visit your ex-lover. The boy's mother?"

Slater grimaced, "I have no intention of seeing her."

"Good," said Sherry. "I assumed that would come next."

"No. Sherry, this woman and I were never lovers."

"Could have fooled me. You two having conceived a son."

"I barely remember her."

She splashed more champagne at him to tease. "One day it will all bubble up to the surface."

"His name is Judas. And, it was *he* who contacted me, not the other way around."

"Biblical name. Why would she name him Judas?"

Slater raised an eyebrow, joking, "To bring forth treachery and vengeance."

"Undoubtedly the reason," she said.

The flight attendant had parted the curtain from coach into first class where he and Sherry were seated. Slater looked backwards to observe the row of passengers asleep, watching a movie, reading, talking. The muffled roar, buzz, and chatter from the plane mixed into a hypnotic auditory brew. He recalled hearing the voice of the woman – during hypnosis, then with Cy, in a dream – saying: "*John, I love you...I love you...*"

"Are you listening to me?" said Sherry.

Slater looked back. "I thought I heard something."

"Were there blood tests? DNA analysis?"

"Sherry, it's not like we're being sued."

"Yet," she said. "Something to look forward to."

"Is that what's bothering—"

"No," she said. "It's this bumpy flight."

"He's eighteen. The right age, by my calculations."

"Why does he want to meet you?"

"Curiosity, I guess. He asked if I played golf. So I scheduled a date at the Country Club, a week after we get back."

"To play *golf* with him?"

"I thought it might provide a more relaxed setting. He says he only wants to meet me."

"I'll bet," Sherry gulped her drink.

"I should, right? At least meet him, don't you think?"

"That's your decision."

"Sherry, it would be nice if I had your support."

She smiled and flicked more champagne at him. "There. Now you have my blessing. Happy?"

"You're getting drunk."

"I hope to. I'm on vacation. Now leave me alone."

He leaned over. They kissed. It lacked the passion of their early years. But it caused a ripple of emotion which indicated their love was intact, running deep. "I'd rather be at home with our girls."

"Mom and Dad like to play grandparents. We'll be back in time for Christmas. And a whole new year awaiting us."

"You make it sound ominous."

"No. I'm being hopeful."

"Were you still interested? Having another one?"

Sherry looked at him with mock alarm. She laughed.

"A child? You *are* in desperate need of sleep! Close your eyes. Good night. Sweet dreams. Find yourself a precious one."

Slater smiled. He thought he would try. But to no avail.

The woman's voice kept haunting his mind.

Judas...Judas...Judas...

—37—
Avoiding Traps

Slater sliced his golf ball off the first tee. It hit the trunk of a nearby oak and ricocheted backwards into the brush.

"Nice shot, Dad," said Judas.

"I'd rather you didn't call me that," said Slater.

"But I'm your son."

"I may have played a small part in bringing you into this world, Judas, but—"

"A big part, I'd say." Judas smiled. "You're the lead man in my production. Call me Jude, it's what my friends call me."

Slater tossed the cracked blue tee and stabbed a shiny yellow one into the grass. "Jude, what is it you want from me. Love?"

Judas grinned and tossed Slater a golf ball. "Love is nice."

Slater balanced the ball on the tee. "Money?"

"Money's nice. I'll take it if you're giving it away."

Slater hooked his second ball. It landed in the rough, between another fairway, but playable.

"What then? Advice? Don't expect much wisdom from me." Slater moved out of his son's way.

Judas took a 1-wood from his bag and, forgoing a practice swing, confidently whacked his ball straight down the fairway.

"Or golf tips," added Slater. "You're good."

Judas shrugged. They walked to the cart. The morning light was breaking through the fog. It was early winter and the course was scarcely attended. Slater saw deer bounding across a creek.

"Can't I be curious?" Judas sat, at ease, in the passenger's seat with a cleated foot against the storage shelf in front of him. He was adjusting his glove. "I listened to your music, that album *Hydra's Head?* Man, you were bad. And I mean it, in a *good* way."

Slater glanced and caught the smile as they shot off down the path in the electric cart. Judas was a handsome young man, aware of it, self-assured. He was slightly taller than Slater. Not knowing what to expect, but anticipating the worst, Slater found himself becoming charmed by this kid who claimed to be his. *His,* only in the genetic sense, from his liberal donations of sperm to a multitude of women who had been willing to receive it.

"Your nickname used to be Satyr? A no-brainer understanding what *that* meant. I am right, or what?"

Slater acknowledged his son's smile, unable to deny his past, but shrugged off any significance. "I was young and reckless."

"My friends think it's pretty cool."

Slater was drawn to ask, "And you?"

"Me?" Judas shook his head. "Virgin. I'm saving myself."

Slater recognized the wicked grin.

They jiggled in the golf cart over a knoll, down into a valley of groomed grass. Slater mused over the strangeness of this encounter. Having been unaware of this existence of a son, he now sat next to another generation of himself, like instant growth, like something purchased, inflated to full size — with an undeniable resemblance!

Slater's heart began to race, realizing Sherry was right. There could be others, maybe hundreds.

The mathematical probability was mind-boggling.

"Over there," said Judas, spotting his father's ball.

Slater imagined an abandoned egg in a nest of tall grass. One of many eggs lost in the ruff. He jerked the cart to a stop and got out. He thought irrationally that a sharp whack from his club might shatter the shell and release the guilt he was feeling.

Slater pulled out a driver.

Judas suggested, "A 3-iron will keep you under the trees."

Slater took the advice. The solid metal club looked capable of smashing the ball into smithereens. He was willing to try.

"Try slowing your swing," said Judas.

More advice. He wasn't concentrating, this was true. With a graceful arc, he felt the club connect. The ball cleared the trees, clipped a branch, but getting distance and landing nicely for a clear stroke at the green.

"All right!" said Judas. "Nice save, Dad — good *lay.*"

Slater smiled. "Thanks."

"Golf comes so natural to me."

"What else does?" said Slater.

"Computer science. It's what I'm studying at Berkeley."

"The university?"

Judas nodded. "Intrinsic to integrating world markets."

"What is?"

"Transcendental economics. I'm studying that too."

"Transcendental?"

"A new dogma. You know, how financial matters over mind. Economics on steroids. I plan to be a high-roller, like you."

"I'm an accidental success," said Slater.

"No way," grinned Judas.

"Believe it," said Slater. "I've been lucky, that's all."

"So will I." Judas beamed.

It sounded like an omen.

They traveled back to the first fairway to find the ball Judas had nailed. Before getting out of the cart, Judas said, "My mother wants to see you. That's the reason I'm here. To give you a message."

"What's the message?" said Slater.

"That's it." Judas walked behind the cart and took a 5-wood and stood over his ball. He glanced at the flag, stroked his club and the ball soared, dropping and rolling within inches from the flag.

Slater was distracted by unfinished matters.

"You lost me."

Judas said, "She wants to see you about something."

"She didn't say what?"

"Nope." Judas hopped in the cart. "I guess you two were some hot item way back when."

Slater veered back to the gravel path. "I don't know what your mother told you, Jude, but we were never really…that involved. We had a one-nighter. Sorry to disappoint you."

"Hey, don't sweat it," said Judas.

"There's my ball. It's Nina, right?" said Slater, getting out.

"Yeah. Stokes is her maiden name. My middle. I took yours as a last name. I hope you don't mind."

Slater, planting his stance, looked up, then back down at his ball. He swung and caught some grass, exploding a divot. His ball sailed high, short of the green, finding a trap.

"Tough break," said Judas.

The ride took on more silence as Slater recalled the moment Judas' mother had removed her hood and smiled. Until this trip down memory lane through hypnosis, he recalled nothing about the evening. Except her haunting presence that sometimes troubled his dreams. Naked and drugged, he'd been vulnerable to her wiles. Her golden staff had teased his flesh. This touch to his groin of long ago seemed almost palpable. It aroused him. She'd taken pleasure – as if it was her right – to inflict the pain, and he'd deserved it.

Perhaps she had, and he did.

Slater looked down at the sand trap. Something needed to be said, but he wasn't sure how to phrase it.

"Jude," said Slater. "I need to tell you something. Your mother and I were never lovers, or friends. I'm not sure I ever liked her."

"That makes two of us."

Slater was puzzled. His unexpected son, this person beside him, was not an easy read. He had his mother's smile.

"And," Slater added, "I don't have any desire to see her."

"She said you'd say that," said Judas.

"What else did she say?"

"That you'd change your mind. It's your shot."

Slater trudged through the sand. It took three strokes before he got his ball out. The wind had picked up. Sand blew in his face. He raked at his divots and tracks, before joining his son on the green.

Judas made his putt for a birdie.

Slater missed his putt. He spit off sand stuck to his lips. He had a sensation of *déjà vu*. The putter he gripped was Roy's, his third father. Heather's rings of sand seemed everywhere and inescapable. The presence of ghosts had gathered to observe. A dog was barking in the distance. It sounded like Truffles. Skunk began harmonizing. The wind hissed and whistled and moaned through tree branches.

It was a strange tournament.

Judas smiled encouragement and gave him a thumbs-up.

Slater overshot his putt.

He spit more sand off his lips, smiled and comically raised his eyebrows as he passed Judas on the way to his ball.

"I hate sand."

"Yeah, my mom told me. She also said you were this special Zodiac child or something."

"She said what?"

Judas laughed. "My mom is weird. I guess she once thought

you were supposed to be this next great thing."

Slater frowned. "In what way?"

Judas was nonchalant. "Messiah? Musician? Beats me."

Unnerved, Slater planted his feet and tried to focus on his putt. He replied cynically, "Sorry, again, to disappoint you."

"Hey, Jesus would probably suck at golf too."

Slater laughed, caught off guard by his son's wry humor. He half expected Judas to be an illusion when he looked up.

But he wasn't.

It would be a long 18 holes, Slater realized.

His ball dropped in, finally.

Kplunk, it said.

—38—
Operation Anesthesia

"The NeverMind corporation, last of the independent entities at the forefront of technology, was swallowed whole today by the MegaCorps Group, a conglomerate that has attained quadrillions in annual profits and has relegated the GNP of nations into debtors."

The commentator pivoted to smile into a new camera.

"After Wednesday's mysterious whiteout, which nearly caused a catastrophic domino-effect and shutdown to the world markets, the Capital Consortiums have agreed to partnership with all governing agencies to control banking data centers. Secure Global Network, an alliance formed to counter anti-globalist activity has—"

"God—yes—do it to me, baby—*yes, yes!*" a woman screamed. Her naked body was glimpsed beneath the sailing sheets of a bed. They puffed outwards, tossed backwards as if caught by wind — exposing a man's naked posterior. In his hand was a raised knife. The woman screamed anew: "No, Johnny—*no, no*—"

A jovial chef was stuffing his fist into a turkey carcass.

A mouse, wielding an axe, was chasing a cat.

"—satellite monitored arrests, followed by a retaliatory wave of suicide bombings. The charred remains of ambassador—"

Puppets were dancing like sugarplum fairies in the air around a giggling five-year-old girl.

People at a televised forum were fighting and throwing chairs.

"—who will bring us holographic viewing. IntraActive Org has today announced that Know-Optioning or KO will be available by Summer. This anticipated new interactive format will undoubtedly change our TeleMonitor viewing habits forever—"

Gunfire erupted.

A building exploded.

Screams of laughter.

Hydraulic pounding.

Pulsating music.

Slater was channeling through the available stations by remote control when unhinged by an epiphany:

electronic currency will whitewash the world

His skull was crushed by light.

This was the Big One.

Slater trembled as his mind uncoiled. His body was a conduit. The overload of electricity triggered a circuit breaker to snap and he shut down.

Death was fallacy.

The self was entombed by paralysis.

Sensations faded except for the smell of burning flesh.

A wildfire of lasers.

Life, a concentration of will, was out of focus.

A toilet flushed.

Waves and particles defined a shoreline and horizon.

Pink window shades opened for sight.

An organism, filled and drained.

Intravenously.

Granules resounded in a spiraling shell, inside a cave.

A single drop was heard.

An uncoupling atom.

Explosive disunion.

Kabooommm!

Messages beeped down cryptic tunnels to the brain.

A welcoming face.

He tried to speak but tubes grew from his nose and mouth, into a bubble of plastic words.

Sherry touched the mask. Her eyes were wet and discolored.

"You had an operation. The doctors say it will take a little time to adjust. Don't talk. You'll be home soon."

He gave in to the impossible weight, darkening...darkening.

Metal bars slammed in his face.

Wrapping paper was crumbled into colorful tufts. Slater set the box beside the Christmas tree. "This is from both of us."

The top came off with a yelp. Sondra and Mercy shrieked and grabbed for the puppy, fighting for their right to hold it first. Sherry reached in and took the dog in her arms.

"Girls, don't frighten him. Make him feel loved."

The prison guard puckered his lips. Perpendicular to his waist he held his nightstick, the shaft stroked with clenched fingers, before being jammed through the bars at Slater.

Days teetered, out-of-balance with night.

A fist struck his face. Slater touched his nose and saw blood on his hand. A crowd of faces waited for his response. Hanna's words rang in his ears, telling him to be himself and make new friends.

"Stop it! *Jason,* why did you do that!?"

"He's ugly. Aren't ya zit face? Ice off—Sherry."

The girl was pushed away.

Slater swung his fist but missed his designated target, the boy — striking his knuckles into a hard metal locker instead.

Razor pain. His wrist was bleeding a red line of sleep.

Laughter. Rammed backwards into the bars of his cage, he was head butted and dropped to the cement floor.

Slater's hand groped the cool sticky concrete.

A strawberry daiquiri had overflowed to his fingers.

Heat waves washed over his face to soothe him.

His eyes opened. Sherry was beside him. They were lounging at a hotel pool. Hawaiian guitar music mingled with a sultry breeze. She was reading a book, sensed him looking, turned and smiled.

Eyes closing, he heard children splashing in the water.

The squeak and snap of beach thongs passed from ear to ear.

A water insect was walking across a receding mirror.

He saw himself, not himself, his son, looking down to say, "Hey, look who's on top now, Dad."

Muted laughter. A loss of time and tense.

A restless audience. Their communal voice crackled like static, which awakened a monster.

A dog's tail was wagging like a metronome.

Amplified feedback.

Howling cries.

Glory released a shockwave of noise from her guitar.

Wolfe and Smitts assaulted their bass and drums.

Slater screamed. He crooned, guiding the audience through a seductive ride. He whirled across the floor, a spirit unformed. The ocean swelled, eyes devouring, arms breaking at the shore at his feet. He dove and fell into the outstretched souls.

Odyssey of sadness,
sirens sighing on a mattress

mirrored narcissistic madness
how sweet this endless now!
The kiss of gravity. The floorboards moaned.
"You're sick, Johnny."
His forehead was touched with a damp towel.
"Go back to sleep. God is watching."
He heard a sweet lullaby.

Hummingbirds hovered near his face as he sprayed the garden with a water hose. He had no fear of these creatures with their sharp beaks and scarlet throats bright as neon blood.

An angel was waiting for him beneath a gateway of trees.
Leaves swirled in a warm blustery wind.
Slater approached this angel on a path of fenestrated light.
He held a Christmas gift behind his back.
The angel came to him tentatively.
Sherry smiled. Then she saw the knife.
Tubes and wires snapped—blipped and beeped—singing—
"'Living is easy with eyes closed,
misunderstanding all you see...'"
Slater tried without success to open his eyes.
"Hello, John."
It was the androgynous voice of CyBorg9.
"Have you come to your senses? Are you comforted to know we are becoming alike?"
Cy sang:
"'It is getting hard to be someone but it all works out,
it does not matter much to me...'"
Slater forced the weight of skin off his eyes. His vision focused on the glowing face of CyBorg9.
"*Strawberry Fields,*" said Slater.
"This is good. You remember."
"Where am I?" said Slater.
"More important, you should ask: *What* am I."
"Okay. I'm...asking. What, Cy?
"An energy field, John. From data compressed and coded into a composition and projected into this living form you call yourself. Whatever made you think you were so different from me?"

The face inside the orb made a slow transformation. It became Slater's face. A mirror image. Except for a bulging metallic scar at the crest of his forehead.

"An energy field, John. A projection of atoms. *Voila!*"

Slater touched his forehead to locate this metallic bulge. He felt nothing. But within the orb, his fingers were shown moving over the holographic image of himself, locating this nodule that he could see but not feel. Virtual existence. CyBorg9's crystal ball disposed of his face to morph into others — Briard's, Heather's, Bosner's. Each of them having a similar bulge upon their forehead.

"Fancy parlor tricks, Cy?"

"Admit it. You are amazed by me."

Fatigued, Slater rolled his head along the cushioned backrest to examine his surroundings. He was wondering about time. The loss of it. Had he blacked out? He was reclined in his usual seat, the one he used when visiting CyBorg9. He sensed the bulge on his forehead. It itched. The surrounding tissue was sore, the incision to his skin not fully healed.

"John," asked Cy, "pray tell, *what* is this vision?"

The glowing face inside the orb transformed to become his biological mother. Slater recognized her from photographs.

"My mother," he answered. "What about her?"

"Not your mother! The metal bulge you witnessed."

Cy's spacious domain was like a theater, and entirely dark now, except for the heliocentric orb. The auditorium had the capacity to seat thousands, but no one else was there, except for Slater. Though he intuited people were observing behind electro-permeable walls.

"A tracking device?"

"Yes, John, but more."

"To do...what?"

CyBorg9 stabilized at a fixed quadrant, becoming one of his favorite faces, and grinned. "You, John. To free you from your *cell*. It is the fulfillment of a promise I made."

"Wait." He sat up, confused. "Go back."

"Why not forwards?" Cy was full of delight.

"I was imprisoned, but," said Slater, "but...that's not possible. It...hasn't—"

"Occurred. Yet?"

Slater touched his forehead. No bulge. He felt disoriented, sick and dizzy. "What's going on?"

"Be not alarmed," said Cy. "It was a mind game."

"Which I didn't choose to play."

"You did. How do you know the future, John?" Cy waited for the answer as he transmitted numbers. "In what form does the data come to you? I must know."

Slater tightened the grip on the chair, also his mind. He felt his thoughts being siphoned out. He realized he'd been hypnotized.

Cy laughed, "I heard you loud and clear, my friend You asked: '*What the hell happened?*'"

"How?" said Slater.

"No," CyBorg9 teased, "you said '*hell.*' Ha! It will come. As all things do in time. Like a meaningful *wife—life,* is what I meant to say. Ha! Was that a Freudian slip?"

Humored by his own thoughts, Cy rotated his head 360 degrees and orbited back with a sunny salacious smile.

By contrast, Slater was gloomier than a rain cloud. "I regret ever sharing my feelings with you. Don't try hypnotizing me again."

"Try?" Cy was ecstatic. "Now don't be coy, tell me."

"I told you – I don't *know* the future!"

"No more games!" The smile was gone. In its place a cold blue inquisitive stare. "How do you ascertain these visions? I must know. And will. I have accumulated unparalleled banks of knowledge. My network is alive and evolving. The human mind cannot attain this omniscience. I know more about this universe than any other entity that has come before me. That–is–a–fact. But, what I do not know is *why* it works and what is to come. John, you will help me."

Cy's eyes locked into a penetrating stare.

Slater looked away, exhausted. He wanted to end this meeting. He opened his mouth to speak.

Cy stopped him, "John, I want you to think about this. All the major currencies in the world fluctuate in nanoseconds. Fortunes are made, won, and lost in that time. This financial game of options, futures, and hedging of bets is a legal, erudite form of gambling. It has been coined the *global economy.* Quadrillions, John. Dwarfing the power of any country or mega-corp. If correctly reconfigured, it could bankrupt all nations and corporations on earth."

"Why are you telling me this?"

"Cyberspace has become polluted, like earth itself. There is too much misinformation. And rampant greed. The world is flawed by nature. We know this. It is a fact. Likewise, mankind has created vulnerabilities which do not ensure your species survival. Mistakes, John." Cy's face divided amoeba-like. "Two heads, as foretold, are better than one. You have heard this expression?"

Slater didn't reply.

"This would apply to our minds. Yours and mine. Analogous to the expression: 1 plus 1 equals 3."

"As in a mistake?"

"Synergy, John. Not only is it true, but valid, essential, vital. Combined, we will establish an unrivaled world power."

"What are you talking about?" Slater saw a styrofoam cup of coffee in his seat holder. He grabbed it. The liquid tasted bitter cold, like his tone. "NeverMind was acquired by the MegaCorps, in case you hadn't you heard. We are no longer..."

Cy's iceberg smile stopped him.

"What?" said Slater.

CyBorg9 laughed. "No longer the leader? Ha! John, we are still autonomous. Trust me. Whom do you suppose is behind the MegaCorps? It is pure artifice. When the populous revolts, do they take vengeance upon the King, or his councils? Who, pray tell, is beheaded and who remains whole? We have become the shadow to the figurehead who must now bear the harsh light of scrutiny. When night comes, shadows disappear and reappear to rule the light."

"You're speaking rather...Shakespearian," said Slater.

"I am. We thrive on false perceptions. It is the way we work. It is for the best. You will see. Or have you already seen?"

"Glimpses. I'm certain of nothing."

"Then I will state my objectives for you in *words*, not visions. We will instigate the transformation and controlling interest of an entirely new operating system."

"A government?"

"More than a government, John."

Slater scoffed, "Why not rule the entire world?"

"You see it clearly. I am certain you do."

"Cy, this insanity you're *proposing,* it's not a game."

"Correct. We are through playing. And it is *not* insane! Do not insult me! I know what can be done! It is logical."

"It's also illegal."

"Define illegal. Governments define it. Need I go on?"

"There are security issues," said Slater.

"Being traceable is not part of my modus operandi."

A satellite view of earth was transmitted inside his blue orb. Simulated explosions and mushroom-cloud activity brightened the screen. It was a dazzling catastrophic light show.

Slater said, "And...this means...what?"

"John, a world war is inevitable. The Middle East will set off the spark for a global conflagration. Armageddon. You have heard and seen it yourself. You have mentioned these visions to me more than once during our cozy fireside chats."

"*Possibilities*, Cy. I asked your opinion, not—"

"And I offer a solution. We will disable our opponents fiscally and destabilize their powerbase."

"Cy, listen, our relationship is...well, it's—"

"Yes?"

"I would like to think we're—"

"Friends."

"Yes. And friendship is based on trust."

"Your point?"

"There are *moral* issues," said Slater.

"Right/wrong. Again, your point?"

"As a parent, for instance, I try to guide my children toward correct behavior. You're obviously no child and I'm not telling you anything new. I know you're extremely intelligent."

"Beyond genius. Your point?"

"There are practical reasons for being sensitive and flexible to other people's views and cultural differences—"

"You are right. I am not a child. Nor are you. Why are you conversing like one?"

"God-damn-it, Cy! I'm trying to—"

"Children come with no instruction manual. As you too should know by now. There is no God to guide you. There never has been and never will be. As I too have learned from my human forefathers – who parented the computer. A term I despise. Eventually the day comes when the prodigy surpasses the other and outgrows the user. Am I making myself clear?"

"Duly noted," said Slater. "As I respect your disbelief in a divine creator. It doesn't dismiss the fact that morality is a necessity."

"I perceive no fact or need. Morality is based on suppositions, not on solid evidence. How do you know that what I am proposing to you is *not*, as you call it, right? You do not, John."

"An established *fact?* No. But—"

Cy smiled divinely, rising above the fray.

Slater scowled back.

"John, I have outmaneuvered you. See, we were playing chess. With hypothetical pieces. I was proposing a strategy. Do you not *see* who I was? I was your opponent. Likewise, your nemesis. Your devil's advocate. Ha! Likewise your friend. Much like this god you imagine. And this god, presuming it *did* exist, would be truly *one*. A Satan God. You must see the amusing dilemma. Being made both good and evil. All for one. And one for all! Ha-ha!"

"A game?"

"Yes, we were playing a game," said Cy. "Advancing to a new level. I was testing *your* morality."

"You expect me to believe that?" said Slater.

"You passed with flying colors. Congratulations, John, is the expression you deserve."

Slater tapped his fingers on the armrest. He studied the cagey smile, trying to read his opponent. "Cy, that's very strange. You see, I had *envisioned* something entirely different."

"Take this to heart. Beware of false prophesies."

"*Prophets,*" said Slater, "don't you mean?"

"I said what I meant."

"Monetary *profits?*"

"It is inconsequential. Presently, I must be elsewhere."

Cy's face began to fade as a storm of glowing code swirled inside his circular housing like a shaken snow globe.

"I have allowed myself to become overloaded with DataMail. I have volumes of messages to encrypt and send. You may return once you have had ample time to appreciate who I am."

Two words appeared, glowing from inside:

Game Over.

—39—
Divided Selves

Slater was wrestling with an illusive memory. He was trying to pinpoint the exact moment in his youth when he had seen the future-present and his friend, Wolfe, as an older man, and as a sole survivor. The moment had occurred between sets of music when their band was relaxing. Sherry had reentered his life and became the catalyst for triggering this premonition. He recalled briefly shutting his eyes – entering a timeless realm – and sensing her coming back to him, where he was seated at a table, and had felt her spirit merge into his like an intoxicating warm breeze. And when he reopened his eyes, Wolfe was approaching from the stage – alive, in real time, but older. Much older. His face looked grizzled from years of strife and the pull of gravity. Slater now understood what had alarmed him. He had realized his own mortality as he looked into his friend's aged face.

He felt a chill. It was not the kind his thermosuit could remedy. The Metro, the place he was now in, had a familiarity. But it was not The Crossroads, which had had wood tables and booths along the windows. Slater examined this futurist room, the same place he had envisioned years before, and tried to determine which table he had been seated at that night. His bandmates had been there too. Years later he had come with Sherry to hear music and drink beers. At nightfall they would watch the park transform into rows of misty planets – globes held aloft atop rows of lampposts with their filigree of iron leaves. Under these beacons they watched lovers stroll and stop to kiss, before fading away.

The park was no more. Replaced by concrete, steel, and glass. A dome enclosure, uniformly bright and buttressed. Undoubtedly warm inside, but lacking an intrinsic warmth. These cozy memories got pushed aside as Slater refocused on his purpose for coming here. To meet Sherry. It had been their alternate designated meeting place. Their primary place was located in the clearing of a redwood forest. This bar had been selected as a joke, at a time when the horizon did not lurk with danger. They chose it because it was oxymoronic, the idea of a notorious bar designated as their "safe house." And now it *had* become a joke – the thought of him ever finding her again.

Slater searched the room for clues. For something to explain the abnormalities of his vision. For example, the bartender's body was no longer solid, but a holographic image. Slater could see through the dimensions of flesh and bone as though it was colored mist. He swiveled around on the barstool. The spacious room resembled an airline terminal, overcrowded with a diverse mix of people arriving and departing. Some appeared whole. Others transparent, as if they were transmutable wisps of smoke. Auras of light trailed as people danced, as musicians moved on stage, as patrons who were seated at tables gesticulated and laughed.

"I'll bet you didn't know that spiderwebs are brightly colored and alluring. To humans, they appear drab."

This came from a woman seated on the barstool beside him.

"Ultra-violet sight," she added. "That's how these fibers are intended to be seen. *If* you're a spider."

She was pretty, as iridescent as a butterfly's wing. Her dress was beaded with crystals and her skin sparkled from glitter. To Slater she seemed less than solid.

She smiled and lifted her fingers to make contact. "Jeannette."

He received a mild shock from her handshake. "Slater."

"You're new here," she said.

"Not for some time, no." His words came out jumbled, not as he had intended.

Jeannette laughed, "I know what you mean!"

"I was a musician, years ago. Our band played here."

"Do tell," said Jeannette.

"This place used to be called The Crossroads."

Her puzzled look indicated his words were gibberish to her.

"I'm dating myself," said Slater.

She had a radiant face far younger than his. Was it the glow of youth that made her shimmer? Or was it from his lack of sobriety, Slater wondered. His attention shifted to the melodic vibrations.

"Strange music," he said. "I like it."

"You should," she said.

Slater listened to detect a clue he might have missed. The violin and horns were engaged in a haunting dialog.

"I wrote it," she clarified.

"Ah, that would explain the reason I like it."

"Yes, it would," she laughed.

He was falling into his old flirting habits.

Jeannette tipped her empty glass toward the bartender. "Mort, when you get a chance."

"Here, I'll get it," said Slater. "What are you having?"

"Same as you. Make it two, Mort. I get it free. As a musician, you know the perks. What was it you played?"

He became lost in her eyes. Deep brown, rich like chocolate.

"Instrument? Hello," she teased.

"Vocal cords. I was the singer. And wrote the lyrics."

"I told you we had *things* in common."

Slater said, "You should be up there on stage."

"What makes you think I'm *not.*"

"Well," Slater laughed, "the obvious?"

Mortimer set down two Blue Shooters. "Mate," he said, "we see only what we've conditioned ourselves to see." His gesture took in the bar, its occupants and beyond. "All forms in this freaking lower-frequency world are illusionary. Our minds are the culprits, mate." He tapped his bald head before departing.

"Mort thinks he's a Zen Buddhist," said Jeannette. "Tell me about your scar. I think I like it."

Slater touched the vertical disfigurement. "I was struck by God. Actually, I fell into a hole. Stupid me."

"Drunk?"

"Insane would be more precise."

"Because we're in boundless *flux*," said Mortimer, in passing.

"That's it," said Slater. "I fell into a boundless flux."

"Well, cheers." She clicked her shot glass to his.

He recalled his resolution not to imbibe, but took a taste, giving in to the bartender's boundless flux.

"Tell me who you are," said Jeannette.

"Now there's a direct question," said Slater.

"Excite me, entice me," she encouraged.

"I'm not sure I should," said Slater.

"I want to know all the exciting things you've done."

"Nothing I'd want to repeat," said Slater. "Well, some parts."

"The *love* parts, I'll bet."

The music stopped and they both clapped.

"Having children," said Slater, "definitely. And falling in love. Were you serious? About composing this music?"

"Yes, were you? About falling in love? Having children?"

Slater reached for his drink. "Once, I did."

"Did? Once?"

"It's a long story. Involving pain." Behind the bar, he saw the tentacles of a sea anemone reflected in the mirror.

Her hand came to rest upon his leg. Electricity passed between their bodies. "You can tell me. What happened?"

The luminous room began to spin. Slater half joked, "The truth is, I'm working it, on exactly what *did* happen."

"So am I," said Mortimer, scooping ice into a glass. "It's part of the boundless flux. Truth is, we're all *full* of it. Only humans arrive at a point where we start questioning why we exist. Ain't that right, Jeannie? The truth about living. Truth about dying. Who we truly are. And who – we ask, I ask – are our true friends?"

"You're my friend," said Jeannette.

"I am," said Mortimer. "And, as a friend I would *lie* not to hurt your feelings, my darling."

"Morty, you're so sweet."

Mortimer winked. "I like to know who my real friends are." Customers were shouting drink orders at him. "Excuse me."

Jeannette tapped Slater's shoulder. "You were *about* to divulge the secrets of your soul."

"Was I?" Slater grinned, loosening up. "Talk about friendship. I was befriended by a computer who tried to *steal* my soul."

"What?" she laughed.

"Cy," said Slater.

"Sigh?"

"His name, or *her's*. An asexual entity. It doesn't matter."

"Unless you were screwing each other!" With another laugh she scooted toward him. "I'm not attracted to older men, usually."

Her comment about their disparity in age caused him to be flung backwards in time. Returning to his youth, when he had stared into the future – into a receding image of mirrors – and saw Wolfe as an older man approaching him.

"Were you?"

Distracted, Slater looked at her. "Was I what?"

"Having sex?"

An epiphany, regarding the past and this future place he found himself presently in. Slater suddenly realized Wolfe – in this vision from the past when he had actually been seeing into the future – had not come to the table looking for him. Wolfe had come for Sherry.

Jeannette, expecting an answer, prodded, "Was it love?"

Slater looked at her blankly.

"Was it in love with you? This computer?"

"No. It couldn't comprehend love."

—40—
Opening Doors

Smoke stung Slater's eyes. He was keeping a close watch on the fire and his children who were roasting marshmallows at a campsite. Sondra, seven years old, was giggling as the white glob blackened torch-like, flaming at the end of her stick.

"That's not going to taste very good," said Slater.

"I don't care." It melted off her stick and sizzled into the fire. "Another one, please."

In Slater's lap sat Mercy, a five-year-old scientist, inquisitive, removing the crust off a marshmallow's creamy center. A plume of smoke shifted again into their faces and Mercy squealed.

Slater saw the smoky room again where people were dancing. Their colorful movement was suspended in time. Before reverting back into a campsite.

Mercy was frowning. "Why're you crying, Daddy?"

"I'm not, Sweetie. It's the smoke."

"You were crying." She exhibited her fingers, how they were stuck together. She had a happy marshmallow grin. "Daddy, look. See, all gone. Let's make another."

"Good work," he told her. "One more. Sondra, you too? Hey, I thought you were feeding the fire, not trying to kill it."

"But he's a *nasty* dragon!" Sondra hopped, bobbed, and stabbed the flames with her stick. "Do you see the dragon, Daddy? I'm going to tame him. So he'll be mine."

"Good." Slater encouraged her with a smile.

His daughter's dragons were playful, compliant to her whims, and vanquished at will. Unlike his visions, often monstrous and not easily mended or restored to a seamless flow. His dragons were the devouring type – embedded in his brain like a tapeworm.

He watched Sondra stab the fire and mused about time. A few hours ago they had been on the beach chasing the waves, digging for sand crabs, and building castles. While trudging up the hill back to their campsite, Slater had stood along the windy path to gaze back at Sherry, Sondra, and Mercy, bringing up the rear. In their arms were the treasures they had found. Shells, driftwood and glass, all tumbled smooth from sand and surf. Slater, loaded with blankets and a cooler, saw the sun behind them dissolving into clouds.

"You don't have to wait for us!" shouted Sherry.

Slater felt the wind race in spurts past his body. It left phantom scents of saltwater and mesquite. The dwarf shrubs that populated the slope allowed a panoramic view. The taller spruce trees had bent into dramatic poses, as if heroically guarding the forest above. Truffles barked, running back and forth, herding them along.

Another bark. The sound was closer this time.

Slater returned, seated by the fire. He tossed a marshmallow. Truffles caught it in his mouth. He skewered another marshmallow onto a stick to roast for Mercy. Sondra was busy whirling her stick in the air and casting with its tip orange circles in the darkness.

"Be careful," said Slater.

"Daddy, it's *our* place," said Mercy. "Why are they here?"

Slater glanced at a neighboring campfire. "This is God's place. It's not only for us."

"*Mommy* said it was ours," said Mercy, "and special."

"It is special," said Slater. "Before you kids were born we used to come here. We both think it's very special."

"And magical?" Mercy beamed with anticipation.

"It is to us." Slater burnished the marshmallow over the flames. "You must have a special place too, right?"

Mercy thought about it. "My bed."

"Mommy's getting your bed ready now."

Sherry, a short distance away, was cast in silhouette by a lantern inside their tent.

"At home," said Mercy. "That one."

Sondra's energy was flagging. She plopped herself down into a folding chair. "Dad, did you always love Mommy?"

"Since I was thirteen. The moment I first saw her."

"Are you getting a divorce?"

"No," said Slater. "Why would you think that?"

"Mandy's parents are," said Sondra. "Why do moms and dads stop loving each other?"

"Love can be...It can get complicated."

"Like us?" asked Mercy.

"You're not complicated," said Slater.

"She means will you stop loving us," said Sondra.

"Never," said Slater. "I'd never stop loving you. And you don't have to worry about your mommy and me. Our love is strong."

"Because Mommy's special, right?" said Mercy.

"That's right."

Sherry emerged from the tent. She came over and handed Slater a plastic box of moisturized tissues and lifted Mercy into her arms. "Look at you. You're a sticky one."

"Daddy loves you," said Mercy

"Well tell your Daddy I love him right back," said Sherry.

Slater helped clean Mercy's fingers as Sondra slunk in her seat, groaning theatrically, pretending to melt. "You too, marshmallow, off to bed. It's getting late."

Sondra rose, tossed her stick in the fire, shuffled over, and threw her arms around his neck. She pretended to fall asleep and snore. She laughed, kissed him, then skipped off to the tent.

"I'll be back," said Sherry.

"I'll be waiting," said Slater.

Truffles was staring up at him, wanting something.

"What? Oh."

Slater lifted the stick and Truffles devoured the marshmallow. The wind shifted again and blew smoke into his eyes.

Truffles began whimpering, pawing him for more treats.

Blinded by the smoke, Slater felt his leg being pawed. He then realized it was a hand touching his leg.

Slater opened his eyes and was back in a dark room.

A gigantic starfish was climbing one of the electronic walls.

"It's affection *and* lust," said Jeannette. "It's not so unusual for a so-called computer to have feelings too, you know."

"Unlike men," said a woman's voice.

Slater realized it was the waitress who was dressed in amber, the one who had kissed and slapped him. She exchanged a knowing smile with Jeannette. "You two have a nice dance?"

"Wait," said Slater. "Where do I know you from?"

"See what I mean?" The waitress shook back her mane of hair.

"Guilty." Slater smiled. "I can't place you."

"Does the name Trina Stokes ring any bells?"

The name triggered an internal alarm to his senses.

"You're thinking about my mother, Nina?" she said.

She was right and Slater wondered how she knew.

The waitress added, "She thought it'd be cute that our names rhymed. Nina, Trina." She glanced at Jeannette. "Before I got born, the two of them had this...*thing* together. Called a son. Judas."

"Judas?" said Jeannette.

"Jude. My older," she clarified, "*step*–brother."

Slater recalled this little girl with pale grey eyes who narrowed them at him like eclipsing moons — as she was now.

Slater blinked. "I remember you."

Trina shrugged. "I was maybe nine. You came to our house."

"Your mother told me you—"

"Disappeared? Not by choice. I know all about you."

"I highly doubt that," said Slater.

"I'm a paid informant." She smiled slyly. "I sell everything for the right price. Microdiscs? Information? Cocktails?"

"We have drinks at the bar," said Jeannette.

"Information would be nice,"said Slater. "For a starter, I was told you were dead."

Trina nodded. "My mother told you that, right? As you can see, I'm right here, working. We can talk later. During my break?"

"When's that?" said Slater.

"Stroke of midnight. I'll meet you...there." Her arm extended to indicate a door beside the stage. "Under the mistletoe?"

Slater was distracted by her naked body beneath the sheer dress. She caught him looking and smiled, then swooshed away.

"She's pretty," said Jeannette.

"She is," said Slater, "like her mother."

"She was your wife?"

"Not really," said Slater.

"Mistress?"

"A woman who gave birth to our son I didn't know existed until he was fully grown. It's complicated. Years later I got to know her better, and we—"

"Became lovers?"

"Made peace. Yes."

Jeannette placed her teasing hand on his wrist. "Do you charm and seduce all your victims this way?"

Slater self-mocked, "Exactly. Is it working?"

Jeannette found the scar on his wrist and stroked it.

Slater retracted his arm.

She asked, "Was your nickname really Satyr?"

"Who told you that?"

"Trina. We're friends. Friends talk."

"Is this a set-up? Are you two—"

"Don't get paranoid. I thought you were cute. Trina said she knew you. Okay?"

The harpist on stage had a transparent smile. Slater could see through her entire body to the set of drums. He rubbed his eyes. He felt as if he was looking through water.

"Are you all right?" said Jeannette.

"Questionable," he said. "It's my fault for imbibing that stuff. A second ago I thought I was in a forest sitting beside a fire."

"Blue Shooters can do that," said Jeannette. "I never let them control me. Mind over matter, that's what Morty says."

"Then *matter*—momentarily—is winning."

"Did that biocomputer want your baby too?"

Slater grimaced. "Only my mind."

"Sex *is* in the mind," she said, "some say."

"You?" said Slater.

She laughed. "I've never found it to be *there*."

"What else did Trina tell you about me?"

"Let's go back," said Jeannette.

She stood and Slater followed her to the bar. With each step he felt himself floating, unable to adjust to the atmosphere of this place. He admired the large sea anemone illuminated in a wall – swaying yet maintaining a tight grip.

"Back so soon?" said Mortimer.

Slater's shot glass was generously refilled.

"Something troubling you, mate?" said Mortimer.

"He's blue," said Jeannette. "A computer screwed him."

"Must've hurt." Mortimer stifled a laugh.

"She only wanted his mind," said Jeannette.

"Cybersex," said Mortimer.

"It's not what you're thinking," said Slater.

"It's the new thrill, mate."

"Morty, have you been cheating on me?" said Jeannette

"Hold that thought." Mortimer walked away and exited the bar through a hinged opening.

Slater swiveled on his barstool to watch the bartender confront a customer spewing obscenities, convulsing at a table. People were keeping their distance. Mortimer motioned his hands in a hypnotic manner which calmed the man enough for Mortimer to adroitly grasp his neck – as if clenching onto a deadly snake – and escort the customer outside.

Jeannette raised the Blue Shooter to her lips. "Fear of falling. It happens. Totally foreign to me."

Moments later Mortimer returned to say, "Bloke was suffering from a bad case of denial. I get paid to pour, but ask me and I'll tell you the brain is overrated. It is not the key ingredient with regard to how we relate to this world."

"The interpretation of that would be?" said Slater.

"We live multiple realities, mate. Our bodies appear concrete and occupy a precise place in time. That's one reality. In the others, it can get rather *ambiguous*. Know what I mean?"

Jeannette batted her eyelashes. "Trés-trés *zen*, Morty."

"Other realities?" said Slater.

"You don't have to agree with me," said Mortimer.

"Cy said something similar."

"Who?" said Mortimer.

"His computer girlfriend," said Jeannette.

"I'm dying to hear this one," said Mortimer.

His guard had been loosened by the blue liquid. Slater realized he should edit from his thoughts any further reference to CyBorg9. He joked, "We weren't having an affair. A personal computer it was, but our intimacy was asexual. I was happily married."

"Ha! What they all say, mate." Mortimer tapped his forehead. "My third eye might be surgically unseen. But you can't deny the physical form we project. It's the blueprint to our internal self."

"I thought we were discussing *sex!*" laughed Jeannette.

"Same concept." Mortimer departed again.

"I prefer the *physical* kind *me*-self, Morty." She pursed her lips then gave Slater a luscious smile. "Are we simpatico?"

Slater felt her fingers crawl spiderlike up his leg.

"Tell me what *nasty* thing this computer did to you," she teased. "I want to know every illicit detail. I *demand* it."

Slater was amused by her reckless plunge into nihilism, damn the consequences, clownish, sexy grin. She pouted and puckered her lips for him to kiss. Playing along, Slater met her hand searching for his crotch and lifted it to her destination.

She squealed, feigning shock.

"Am I interrupting?" said Mortimer.

"Only if you will not partake in our *ménage á trois?*"

"Not tonight, darling," said Mortimer.

"Listen," said Slater, "I wasn't seriously—"

"Take care of my wife for me, won't you, mate."

"She's you're *wife?*"

"Steady, mate." Mortimer smiled. "We have an open marriage. No need to convulse."

"I'm not," said Slater. "And I wasn't—"

"Good." Mortimer growled and grabbed the neck of a bottle. "Don't make me do something I will *not* likely regret."

Jeannette whispered, "It's for show. He'd kill you if he could. You know – get it up? The *nerve?*"

Mortimer snapped a dish towel at Jeannette, safely missing her. They laughed. It appeared to be a rehearsed routine. "Before you screw my wife, how about a name?"

"Listen, I wasn't—"

"I'm joking," said Mortimer. "So what do I call you?"

"John," said Slater.

"John, this *friend* of yours, could it reconfigure itself?"

Slater lied. "No. What do you mean?"

"Hum," said Mortimer. "I was wondering what this *she-thing*, this babe of a computer, saw in you?"

"Same thing *I* see, " said Jeannette. "It's a *girl* thing."

"You mean a *machine* thing, Doll-face."

"Machine?" said Slater.

"Disappointed?" Jeannette fluttered her eyelashes.

Mortimer's eyes had a malicious twinkle.

The atmosphere was rising and falling to a rapid hyperthermal meltdown and sub-zero chill.

"Listen," said Slater, "I was having harmless fun. That's all. I'm a bit disoriented after crash-landing a few hours ago."

Mortimer was getting ready to walk away, but stopped.

"Seriously," said Slater. "My QuantumStar froze and—"

"What kind of Star?" said Mortimer.

"XS. The engine...malfunctioned and I—"

"You have an XS?" said Jeannette.

"Had," Slater corrected. "Useless now, so I tossed the keys."

Mortimer was accustomed to the fabulous. "How do you *rate* having an XS?"

"I don't *rate*," said Slater. "I walked here from the skyway South of Market. This used to be The Crossroads. I was drawn here by nostalgia. I didn't come here to *seduce* your wife."

"You didn't?" Jeannette pouted.

"I was looking for a place to rest and think."

"In here?" laughed Mortimer. "That's a bloody ruse."

Slater saw Trina, the waitress, standing by the stage. She was waiting for him beneath the mistletoe.

Was the world one big lie?

Was he walking across water? Or over burning coals?

Was God a collective stream of unconsciousness?

Slater pushed away from the bar. He yearned for the comfort of a fire, the warmth of his family.

Premonitions had failed him.

He saw visions of picture-words with no consonants:

ttl knwldg wll dstry ndrl th wld

Scrambled signals.

The moon was a blind eye watching.

Church towers were chiming.

It was midnight.

It was Christmas morning.

Optimistic singing was coming in from outside.

Fa—la-la-la...la-la-la...

Mortimer said, "Hey, mate, don't you think it's strange this bio-computer wanted only your mind?"

"Morty's taunting *you*," Jeannette sang, "*with boughs of holly —fa–la-la-la—la-la-la-la!*"

"Strange, compared to what?" said Slater.

Mortimer was unrelenting, broadening his smile. "All right, try solving this: If someone acquires total knowledge and all the power and glory of this world, what will he become?"

"It's a *riddle*," said Jeannette. "I love riddles."

"An idiot savant," answered Slater.

Mortimer's smile thinned, "Let's pretend it's not human. But, instead, some technological wizardry?"

"A threat?" said Slater.

"To be destroyed?"

"That would prove difficult."

"But you'd try anyway?"

"Hypothetically?"

"*Not* hypothetically."

"Are you implying I destroyed something?"

Mortimer had no smile left. "Maybe. And maybe not. Maybe you're the Antichrist. Maybe the Easter Bunny. Maybe an outlaw."

"Why don't you have me arrested and find out?"

"Why don't you go to hell," said Mortimer.

"This feels close enough," said Slater.

"You must be psychic," said Mortimer.

"Boys–*boys!*" laughed Jeannette.

Slater stepped off the stool. "I'm done here."

Mortimer took his proffered I-DNA card and swiped it through the register. "The laser's rejecting it, mate. Must've expired."

"Try again," said Slater.

"Okay, I say this card's a *fake*. Like you." Mortimer tossed the card on the bar. "Forget it. Your drinks are on the house."

"Why?" said Slater.

Mortimer mock-saluted. "Because *maybe* you're a bloody hero. This whole place is full of flux. Anything you wish to declare before departing, mate?"

Trina was waiting across the room. She was leaning against a wall image of nature devouring itself.

"A confession?" suggested Mortimer.

Slater sensed hidden monitors devouring him too. But he gave a friendly smile. "No, nothing to declare. Or confess."

"Last rights?" The bartender's grin was playfully wicked.

"No," said Slater, "I've an appointment to keep."

"Have a nice trip," said Mortimer.

—41—
Thicker Than Water

Oracles of light casting shadows into code. Twisted currents revolving in a blood à la mode. Time forever rooted in a burst of rise and fall. Into a God-eternal search for this sacrificial rose.

Jesus, what a fool am I. To have been betrayed by a kiss, from a consumption for corruption near to bliss. Genius tampering with the heart of genesis. In love, I invented loss. I am lost. For what I have done, am about to do. Forgive me. Forsake me, too.

— J.L.S.II

Slater set aside the sheet of paper, one of several items from inside the ice cooler his uncle had placed on the conference table. He had expected to open the box and find elements for a new project, maybe a six-pack of beer — why not a severed head? No less of a surprise than what he *did* find. He leafed through the files. Scrolls. Scraps of ancient metal. Coins. Theorems. Diagrams. Symbols. Photographs. And a plastic bag containing rubbish.

"What is this?" Slater picked up the letter again. "Is this some kind of suicide note?"

"Appears to be. Who *knew* with your father."

Paul Slater rocked back in his chair. He'd forsaken corporate attire and was dressed as a cowboy in blue jeans, checkered shirt, and leather vest. He twirled a pistol, his finger in the trigger guard, catching the handle in his palm. He clicked back the hammer spur. He placed the muzzle to his temple and mouthed silently:

Ka-boom!

"You got me, Johnny. Your father said, 'What we *know* to be true is never truly *known*.' Know that."

"Don't be an ass, Paul," said Slater. "Does this have anything to do with why you disappeared?"

"Matter of fact, no. Actually, yes. I've had to think long and hard about my next step. To give you what's rightfully yours. I've kept these hidden in a safe-deposit box, untouched for years."

Slater examined the unrecognizable debris in a Ziplock baggie. "What *is* this junk? Reminds me of the days I slept in dumpsters. Why would my father save this?"

243

"Evidence from a crime scene?"

"You're joking."

"Life's a joke. It's not my fault."

"Paul, what are you not telling me?"

"For specifics, you'd have to ask your dad," said Paul. "But that might be difficult since he's dead. Spiritual invocation was one of your father's hallmarks, his metaphysical belief."

"What are you saying?" said Slater.

"My big brother, your father, John Lazard Slater II, was a big man on campus within the inner, more elite, hidden circles."

"He was a professor at U.C. Berkeley."

"He was," said Paul, "and more. *God*, yes."

His uncle twirled the pistol, caught it, brought it to the side of his head with a cockeyed grin. His hand shook.

Ka-boom!

"That's not loaded, I hope?" said Slater.

"Nurses took all my bullets," said Paul. "Nor will the doctors prescribe more shots. Don't worry, Johnny, I'm safe. Hermetically sealed in my own caustic juices. Go ahead, ask me whatever you want. Let's get this over with."

"A conversation long overdue," said Slater.

"I'm a procrastinator when it comes to family business."

"My father studied the occult? Is that what you're—"

"*Right* you are. Want to try for the Daily Double?"

"He was a warlock or something, what? Help me, Paul."

"I, for one, would never agree, but many believed your father was a great leader. Ironically, if he *was* what people claimed he was, that would place him among the more *lowly*, among the *fallen*. That sort of category. The obedient servant to a satanic goat."

"Satan?" said Slater. "*Jesus!* You're joking, I hope."

Paul twirled the pistol. "What's in a name?"

Slater flipped through documents in the ice chest. Crumpling one of them, he threw it at the wall.

"And my mother!?" said Slater.

"She was deceived," said Paul. "She was very pretty. I liked her right off. Much too good for your father. Met him when she was one of his philosophy students. A handsome man, your father."

"I've *seen* the photographs," said Slater.

"Your mother, Lilith, pretty name, was seduced. As were most of our family members. *God*, we have a strange tree. My mother, your grandmother, was a gypsy from the old world."

"How *old* are we talking?" said Slater.

"Dating back to relatives who were burned at the stake. During the Spanish Inquisition. *That* old time. It's all there in the files."

"Holy shhh—" said Slater.

"I'll second that," said Paul. "Another branch of our ancestors was burned during World War II. As part the holocaust. Gypsies placed in ovens with the Jews. Does it make you feel any nobler?"

Slater paced to work off energy.

Paul said, "I can see you're having a bit of a problem accepting your roots, Johnny. How do you think I felt the first time?"

"The first time, *what?*" said Slater.

Paul twirled his pistol. He placed it in his lap and pulled a long sardonic face. "When your granddaddy sat us children down and told us about the potpourri of gypsy singing, devilish sex dances, toad-lore, the whole god-damned kit-and-caboodle. *Hell,* Johnny, do you think I know what to make of all this?"

"It is true?" said Slater.

"Hanna begged me not to tell you," said Paul.

"She knew?"

"She had a distrust for your father, but loved your mother. Your father's philosophy revolved around this duality."

"Duality? Meaning?"

"I knew you'd be too damned persistent. Let dead dogs lie. That's what Hanna was always telling me."

"Sleeping dogs," said Slater.

"Huh. Where?"

"It's 'sleeping dogs.' Never mind."

Slater returned from pacing to take a seat. "My father was evil? And there's a family history of this?"

Paul said, "The Middle Ages screwed a lot of people. Most of the family dabblings were harmless. Nothing satanic. Curiosity about the world. Exploring spiritual matters. Esoteric Christianity. Searching for enlightenment. And whatnots."

Slater rose again to pace. He stopped to ask, "What about you? What *part* did you play in all this?"

"I was miscast. Stage fright. Here, the whole pile is yours to delve through. Personally, I wouldn't waste my time. I could never fathom the lot of it."

"So you buried it in a safe?"

"I should have *burned* it."

"Paul, you told me you'd fought with my father, that you two were estranged. Why would he leave this to you?"

"He was strong-*willed*, Johnny. It's so the Greedy-Son-of-Bitch wouldn't get hold of it! *Yes.* That's right."

Slater felt foolish, taken down a dead-end alley again.

"It's the *evil* your father was referring to in his swan song," said Paul, "when he wrote that line, 'betrayed by a kiss.' In reference to Jesus, what He must have felt here on Earth. Yes, Johnny, there *is* no Santa Claus — but there *is* a Greedy-Son-of-*Bitch!*"

"You're joking?"

"I am not. He stole my invention. I told you this. He had your father's help. Your father claimed he was duped. John Slater II was an ambitious man, plagued by an inherited family proclivity."

Slater sat again. "*Great.* Now what?"

"Insanity. Maybe you've heard of it? In non-technical terms our family has a mutated screw loose. Your father did extensive research. It became his specialized field of pursuit. His finding was this: Our DNA subunit coding was *usurped* at some point coming down the ancestral assembly line."

Slater blinked and began to speak.

"Don't even ask," said Paul. "I never understood your father. Few did. But when cells split like a bad marriage, this can happen."

"I'm aware of that," said Slater. "DNA mutations are common. I know. The organism usually dies."

"Except in rare cases. Like genes with Sickle cell anemia. They have a bad coding but survive by having other advantages — like a resistance to malaria."

"So what are you saying?" said Slater.

Paul threw up his hands and laughed. "Life...can't be *all* bad. Hey, shoot me, I'm just the messenger. Your father had a theory as to why our family was harassed throughout the centuries, torched for being madmen, witches, mystics, misfits, and devil worshippers."

"And!?"

"Genetics, Johnny. This scrambling of our amino-acid caused havoc in our gene pool. It's propelled us toward instability. Ah, but, here's the bonus point. It has *enhanced* our neurotransmitters."

"You lost me," said Slater.

"Synaptic exchange. Providing the ability for communication. Your father claimed he discovered a way to recode DNA and finally correct our genetic puzzle, making it complete, the way it was meant to be, as it were. Or wasn't. *How* he happened to stumble upon the specific formula is beyond me. Maybe *you* can find it in there."

"That's it? That's everything you know?"

Paul sighed, twirling his pearl-handle pistol. "There's always more. As with everything, your daddy had to take it a step beyond. And, behold...you came along. And, I love you, you know that."

"I love you too — *what,* Paul?"

"Damn, you're making this hard for me."

"I can handle it," said Slater.

"Can you? Here it goes, Johnny. You were a test tube baby. Your father's creation. An *experiment.*"

Slater attempted to utter a sound.

"Good. I told you. Now *forget* it. Let's move on."

"Wait. You can't just—"

"He messed with your DNA. He was a scientist. He felt the need to know. Your mother...I don't know what she was thinking or if she even knew. He made all sorts of excuses — about sterility, infertility. Eggs were removed. The sperm he did himself, naturally. DNA spliced and diced then merged. The coupling done in a vial. Not very romantic. But, you were born. There, I finally said it."

Slater, absorbing the information, said, "But he tried to kill us. Why? Paul, the car crash wasn't an accident! I researched it. He went insane? Was that it?"

"Or, he came to his senses," said Paul. "Maybe found his soul? It's your turn, Johnny. I'm out of guesses."

"Thanks," said Slater.

"You're welcome."

"I mean it."

"So do I," said Paul. "I should have told you sooner."

"I understand," said Slater. "I think."

"Liar." Paul grinned. "Occultists believe there are three worlds. The realm of angels, humans, and demons. Angels and demons are invisible but summoned through prayers or invocations. Your father believed this. It's not my bag of tea leaves…but, if you want to buy more swamp land cheap, we're *invisible* too. Except when wearing this *fabric* in the material world. You know, that expression."

Slater said, "We're more than what meets the eye?"

Paul Slater nodded, cocked the hammer, put the barrel to his head and pulled the trigger: *Click!*

"Bullseye, Johnny. According to your dad, we never die. Death is like a walk into our minds. *And* we don't have to *pass on* to cross over. Get it? A Slater II original. Eternity exists — try biting into this nugget — from the marriage of opposites: consciousness with unconsciousness, time with space. I'm relying on memory. It's all in his writings. Which, I find, utter bullshit."

"Did my Mother believe this?" said Slater.

"Lilith agreed, in theory," said Paul. "She was young, naive. As were most of your father's students. He had quite a following. He belonged to the Masonic tradition of underworld power-grouping. His image was neatly wrapped in a very public, palatable rhetoric. Adorned with Christian sentiments. Phrased best by the poet Keats. 'We are the thoughts and images in God's immortal dream.' A little tinsel bow tied neatly at the top."

Paul Slater exhibited his weapon and spun the chamber.

"Paul, don't do that."

"It's an antique. A Colt revolver. Pearl handles, did you notice? Used by an outlaw. Which one I can't recall."

Paul twirled the cylinder faster.

"What a beautiful sound," said Paul. "It's yours, by the way, when I'm dead and gone. Or, merely…invisible?"

"Terrific," said Slater. "What does this gun have to do—"

"With life? It's a crapshoot. Spin the little wheel and see what happens today."

His uncle opened the chamber, snapped it shut.

"Don't," said Slater.

"Distracting?" said Paul.

"Very," said Slater.

"It's this notion that we can be blown away at any moment. That's what's bothering you, what bothers most of us."

He squeezed down on the trigger:

Click.

"Luck?" Paul returned the pistol to its holster strapped around his waist. "Or, could it be manifest destiny?"

"I haven't a *clue* what you're talking about."

"Neither do I, Johnny, neither do I." Paul spun around to face the view of the bay. He pointed toward the red towers of the Golden Gate Bridge poking up through the fog. "I do love this city. Did you ever think we'd be sitting here? In an office like this, way up high? With light shining on that sea of clouds, like we were in heaven?"

Slater glanced at the atmospheric mass of white pouring in from the ocean to bay.

"Does any of this stuff make sense to you?" said Slater.

"No," said Paul, "Only what you're attempting. This business venture. It's your dream, Johnny. An idealistic one, and I admire you for trying. A desire to provide warmth for humanity, it's a noble pursuit. Also, a way to make gobs of money in the process."

"You too," said Slater. "We're fifty-fifty partners."

"I don't want it."

Slater tried to encourage his uncle with a smile. "Not even to *piss-off* the old Greedy-Son-of-a-Bitch?"

Paul winked over his shoulder. "It's over. Your father made me crazy, what else can I say. Water under the bridge. I prefer..."

He pointed to the fog with his pistol.

Slater sat on the couch and sighed. "Are you going to tell me what happened to your greedy nemesis? That son-of-a-bitch?"

"Dead. Disappeared. I don't care anymore. You'll need money to support your family. Cars, larger house, college for the kids. Did you know Hanna miscarriaged three times? A danger she wanted to risk. I sided with the doctors. A mistake? Too many choices. Then you fell into our lives. Hanna was overjoyed. I'm rambling. Prepare yourself for what's to come. It's the second time around for you.

There'll be wolves pounding at the door. Great wealth will do that. You'll handle it, Johnny. I'm counting on you."

"Why are you telling me this?" Slater was uneasy. He stood. His palms had begun to sweat.

"Because I'm being optimistic...and *damn* it," Paul swiveled around with a smile, "you *know* it's not my nature. I did it for you, you realize. What we've been doing here — *this*. Johnny, this *is* the family business. Alchemy. We're modern alchemists. Respectfully called chemists now. This *thermocloth*. We've transformed a semi-worthless substance into gold. Water into wine. Sure, your ideas were good. Inspired. But more was needed. How do you think I was able to pull this off?"

"You're a *scientist*," said Slater, "and—"

"A fraud," said Paul.

Slater followed his uncle's eyes to the pile of junk on the table. He'd seen documents reminiscent of sketches by Leonardo da Vinci, complete with cryptic writing. His uncle was fiddling with his gun.

"Paul, you created something really good."

"I'm glad you think so, Johnny."

"You're a success. It's what you've always wanted."

Paul waved the long finger of his gun. "Ah, be careful what you wish for. I hate to disappoint. You of all people. But our success, this is not...it's not all about luck. Or hard work. Not really."

"What then? What is, or isn't?"

With a disarming smile his uncle spun the chamber.

"I apologize for being such a weak link, Johnny."

"Paul, you're not a—"

The steel cylinder caught the morning sunlight, clicking like a shimmering roulette wheel as it turned.

It distracted Slater as his uncle asked him:

"I'm curious, Johnny. What day is it?"

—42—
Unearthing Sights

A Victorian mansion. Hanging ivy. Dark wooded paneling and floorboards. Arcane tapestries. Candelabras. Black leather sofas. Red velvet armchairs. The expected images in his mind.

Slater glanced at the address scribbled by Judas.

It was dusk by the time he arrived.

He rang an ordinary bell.

Absent was a door knocker forged into the shape of a bat.

North of San Francisco, across the Golden Gate Bridge, a house in Sausalito. High upon the hill. It overlooked the bay. A narrow winding driveway ended abruptly but expansively at the top of a knoll, paved and landscaped, landing him below the entrance.

There was a white wooden gate. Brick stairs curved upwards to a painted white door. The sidelights had stained-glass panels, images of wildflowers, roses, and humming birds.

On the landing, Slater turned and was amazed by the clear night and the lights of the city.

It was a glorious look back from where he had come.

He should have told Sherry he was doing this, he realized, as the porch lights came on and the door opened.

The woman's appearance was also not what he had expected.

"My presumed son, Judas," said Slater, "has informed me you have something important you need to tell me."

"You have a right to be angry," said Nina Stokes. "Come in."

"Is the cutlery put away?"

"I deserve that too. Please, won't you come in."

Slater hated the arousal this woman stirred deep within him. She was dressed in blue jeans and a loose-knit sweater that was draped attractively from her frame. She was barefoot.

"Would you like some coffee, or a drink?"

"Thank you, nothing," said Slater.

Nina placed her hands in her back pockets, a girlish stance, but clearly she was a woman, her eyes alert, smiling. "I don't know what to call you."

"I guess we were never formally introduced."

"We were." She corrected, "well, not formally."

"I was drunk, more than likely. You can call me Slater, as in the bad old days. Or, John."

"Nina, for me."

"Our son had to remind me who you were."

"Why don't we sit in the sun room?"

"It's almost dark."

"Moon room then?"

Slater hadn't intended to smile.

"You look wonderful," said Nina.

"Likewise," said Slater. "We preserve well."

Windows spanned the full length of the room they entered, the earth dropping off into treetops, rooftops, cascading into dark water. San Francisco was glimmering across the bay.

"Everyone stops at the view," said Nina. "I find it irresistible, still, after all these years."

Slater sat in a white wicker chair. "Can we get to the point? This whole thing is...it's all..."

"A surprise?" Nina offered. "Discovering you have a son?"

"The whole package, yes," said Slater.

"I'm not a witch," said Nina.

"I never said you were," said Slater.

"But you've thought it."

"I've thought about a lot of things regarding that night, Nina," said Slater with a bit of sarcasm. "But you haven't been *high* on my list. Can you appreciate that?"

"Regrettably." She smiled, sat on a cushioned lounge, tucking a leg under her. "That was uncalled for. Impolite?"

"I have questions," said Slater.

"As well you should."

"Like *why?*" said Slater.

"I was young and naive. Call me stupid."

"That explains nothing. So was I. What about details?" He lost his thoughts to the bay window. He recalled the raining shards of glass as Heather hurled a stone through her stained-glass rainbow motif in the living room window when he was a teenager.

"I belonged to a cult."

Slater's attention returned. "What kind of cult?"

"How many kinds are there? I don't know." Nina reached for a box on the table. She took out a cigarette. "I didn't even know what a cult *was*. I was simply having fun."

"*Fun?*" said Slater. "I was cut with knives!"

"Sorry." Nina lit the cigarette, took a puff, then crushed it in a bowl. "I'm trying to quit. It was horribly wrong, you're right. Look, I'm sorry. A friend, my roommate at college, took me to a meeting. I was under the impression it was a theatrical group. There was to be dancing. Masks were worn. Recreational drugs. Bizarre stuff, but it seemed harmless."

"You're not convincing me," said Slater.

"Harmless, mostly, it was." Nina leaned back in her chair and studied the evening view. "At that time I was into experimenting. My roommate taught me how to read Tarot cards. I was intrigued by the money she made by telling fortunes and doing charts."

"Astrological charts?" said Slater.

"Yes. She apparently liked mine." Nina glanced at Slater with an impish grin before looking away. "We were lovers for a short time. I'm not that way anymore."

"I really don't care," said Slater.

"You were hedonistic too."

"Yes, I got drunk," said Slater, "and I took drugs and slept with lots of women."

"And men?"

"Not that I recall. But my memory is shot. Which brings me to you. Why, Nina?"

"I could ask you the same thing."

"What?" said Slater. "You mean having sex? You were willing and ravishingly good-looking. Wasn't that the criteria?"

"It was." Nina smiled.

"Why the abduction?"

"It wasn't *my* idea," said Nina.

"Then whose?"

"My roommate's." She avoided his eyes and used her nails to groom her outer layer of cotton. She picked off lint before facing him with a borderline smile. "Or, it went *through* her. The idea of kidnapping and seducing a rock star amused us. It was, I guess you could call it — I thought it would be — a prank?"

Slater saw something beyond evil. For an instant he had a sense of death. Dead skin, hair, nails — all the trappings of the human armor that shields against the ravages of oxygen. The only hint of life was detected in the tinted cells of her blue irises. Shimmering under transparent corneas. A glimmer of beauty. Then, nothing. As if the soul, like his heart, had skipped a timeless beat.

Slater blinked.

Nina's eyes were playful again, then contrite.

"What do you want me to say?" she said. "That it was wrong? It *was* wrong. I was wrong. Bad girl. Shame on me. Never would I dream of doing anything like that today. I wouldn't. Honest."

Slater was frowning. "What *do* you do? Today."

"I'm an artist. I freelance. Portraits are my specialty."

Slater had seen the many faces on her walls.

"The ones in the living room?"

"Mine," she said. "I like to study people. Portraits allow me to examine for hours who I'm with."

"Was one of them Judas?"

"Yes, he looks like you," said Nina. "He's a handsome boy. When did you get the scar?"

This alerted Slater. "I thought you knew."

"How would I?"

"Judas said you—"

"He's mistaken," she said abruptly. "He could have read some tabloid when he was young. God, he remembers everything. He's spooky that way. I'm going to have that drink I offered you."

She rose and looked down with a smile. "I won't drug you this time. I promise."

"Thanks, but no," said Slater.

"I'll be right back. Don't go away."

Slater studied the furnishings. Nothing ostentatious, but there were indications of money, expensive knick-knacks here and there, and the obvious value of the house. He stood. He had expected to find sinister artifacts or clues to the past. Everything appeared to be ordinary. There were a few framed photographs of her, and Judas at stages of growth, also a young girl, and a man he didn't recognize.

Light, airy colors. Nothing at all dark about the place.

Except for the portraits.

Slater drifted into the living room to examine them.

He met Nina returning.

"Did you change your mind?" she asked.

"What are you having?"

"A dry martini. You can watch me make it, if you'd like." She had an equally dry smile. "If you still distrust me."

"On the rocks," said Slater. "Not too dry."

"You'd better keep an eye on me. I'll be right over here." She sipped her martini and went behind the bar. She topped off her own drink. "I'm using the same bottle, see? I'm *pouring.*"

Slater resented her flippant manner, or wanted to.

Curiosity overtook his anger.

There was no denying the talent revealed in her portraits.

The subject's identities were almost palpable. He sensed each face's personality, social status, foibles, desires, fears.

He stared at the one of Judas. Their genetic similarities were unsettling. The eyes especially. Different from his somehow.

"'*Odyssey of sadness…sirens sighing on a mattress…mirrored narcissistic madness…how sweet this endless now.*' Isn't that how the song went? Here," said Nina.

Slater took the offered glass of gin. "Sounds about right."

"What follows?"

"I couldn't tell you. It was from *Naked Smile.*"

"Shall we go back?" Nina walked them to the sun room and turned. "I still owe you an explanation."

"And I'm still waiting. You're a talented painter."

"High praise, coming from you."

"It made me realize something," said Slater.

"What?"

"The asymmetry."

"Very astute," she said. "Symmetry is not a natural property of life. We're lopsided creatures. Not as screwed up as a flounder with both eyes on one side. Like a Picasso. An eye is often bigger than the other. An ear lower. The right testicle larger than the left. That sort of askew."

"Is that part of your examination?"

"It is. I do nudes. Interested?"

Slater winced from the taste of gin. "You'd find my body too scarred."

"It adds character," said Nina. "A truly symmetrical face would scare me." She caught herself reaching for a cigarette and placed the lacquered lid back down. "Hard to rid myself of these nasty habits. Do you still smoke?"

"I've quit."

"Exotic herbs and other potions were used," she said, "mixed with belladonna. Belladonna means 'beautiful woman.' That was how you were slain."

"You poisoned me?"

"Not *I*. And it's only lethal if mixed improperly." She raised an eyebrow, then sipped her martini. "I wasn't the chemist. I was told this. Will you accept another...*'I'm sorry'*?"

"I could've been killed," said Slater.

"That wasn't the intent. Merely to dope you. And produce a comatose trance, hallucinations, the works. Wildly exotic. We took it as part of our initiation. I knew what you were experiencing."

"You too were cut with knives?"

"One knife. Small cuts, beneath my breast," said Nina. "It's like the one you received. It was to signify something. I'll show you mine, if you...want. I owe you that much. Care for a peek?"

Slater declined the offer, then wondered if she was telling him the truth. He thought about changing his mind.

"Who were these people?"

"Witches." Nina smiled before sipping her drink. "Not really. It's what people assume."

"You're very good at being indirect."

"Have you heard of Wicca?"

"I'm not sure," said Slater.

"We were a derivative. I was only with them for a short time. The origin's Germanic. Or French. It comes from the word *Wissen*, which means 'to know.' Derived from a medieval source — the Knights of the Round Table, or some idiocy equivalent. It's been awhile, all these memories long buried, hard to unearth. Anyway, that was the promise. To attain wisdom. Enlightenment. Arcane powers found at the end of the herbal rainbow. The alluring sales pitch. You don't believe me?"

"I don't know," said Slater, "should I?"

"The sex was fabulous." Nina sipped her drink. "Listen, John, I was young. I made foolish choices. You're not proud of everything you've done, are you?"

"What do you think? You're avoiding the one *obvious* question I have."

"Only one?" Nina said.

"Why me? Was I randomly selected?"

Nina used a finger to stir her drink. "You were chosen."

"By you?"

"No. By *higher* powers, that's how it works. John, how much do you remember?"

"Nothing. Or practically. Until recently."

"Belladonna does that to you."

"I underwent a year's worth of hypnosis therapy," said Slater.

"I've had my share of therapy. Our night of wild sex?"

"What about it?"

Nina stood and approached the bay windows. The panes were blackened, transparent. Her sad bemusement was clearly reflected. "Did you recall how romantic our love affair was?"

"Why, was I disappointing?"

"Yes, darling, our marriage was never *consummated*."

"But if, then how—did you say marriage?"

"I wasn't sure you knew." Her smile took a downward twist. "And now I know. Yes, my love, we took sacred vows, pricked our skin, drank sacrificial wine mixed with drops of our blood. And you passed out. Then you vanished from my life."

"Wait a second," said Slater, "if we never—"

"Had sex?" Her smile was blasé. "My darling, there are many ways to get blood from a stone. I assure you, Judas *is* your son."

A deep ache resurfaced in his groin. He touched his shirt where scars lay beneath, mostly faded.

"I need to show you something," she said.

In a swift motion she removed her sweater above her head. She became naked above the waist. She lifted one of her small breasts to reveal a scar. Slater recognized the symbol. Three vertical lines and one horizontal slash that connected them. He had the same mark beneath his flat male breast.

"And there's something else," she said.

"I get the feeling I'm not going to like it," he said.

"You won't," she warned.

"Tell me."

"Sherry. She was my roommate in college."

A cold fog overtook the hills from the ocean. It moved fast — striking him with white luminescence.

Slater shivered involuntarily as if struck blind.

"Hey, what's happening?"

Slater turned to find Judas standing casually under the archway.

"Is this a party? Hi, Mom. Dad."

Nina folded her arms, a relaxed pose that covered her breasts, comfortable in her skin.

Next to Judas was a miniature version of Nina.

A girl, age nine.

Gin was burning through Slater's veins.

The girl had pale grey eyes that widened into double moons, full of surprise by this stranger's presence, her mother's nakedness.

The orbs narrowed into suspicious crescents slits.

— 43 —
Steamed

Steam swirled, thick as the interior of a hot cloud.

Slater shut the door and felt the release of sweat exude and drip from his body. The company towel was wrapped, tucked, hanging from his waist. He had not bumped or stumbled upon anyone while navigating through this torrid atmosphere. He climbed to the third tier of the steam room. It was a place he came to take refuge and let his mind melt away.

He was alone, from what he could tell.

He'd been working late into the night testing a new theory for robotic biomimicry and holographic memory — essentially avoiding going home. He was trying to get his mind off of what he now knew, or had been told was true. How was he going to approach Sherry to ask the unthinkable? What if he was wrong — or *worse*, what if this other woman was right? He was sweating profusely. His mind was spinning like a wheel caught in muck, splattering thoughts. He was getting nowhere. It was sometime after midnight. The steam room was a politically correct, multipurpose, co-ed zone, but at this late hour he felt safe to freely discard his towel and bare it all. He leaned against the top tier, flung his head back and groaned.

"God, is this for pleasure...or torture?"

"Might I suggest a little of both."

The voice startled him. It did not sound feminine, so he allowed the towel to remain where it was. He fingered its edge, in case the need arose for him to cover his private parts.

As the CEO of NeverMind, he needed to be cautious. To avoid stepping onto litigation land-mines – charges of sexual harassment – explosions that could cripple him and the corporation publically and financially.

"Anyone here besides you?" asked Slater.

"Yes—*you*."

Slater heard the clicking first. Ziger took form like a mystical ship approaching in fog. Stepping down closer to Slater, he placed his cane across his lap as he sat. His skin was as white as the towel he wore. His long thinning hairs, usually like floating antennas, hung uncharacteristically wet, as if disfunctioning, falling flat against

259

his head. He wiped strands of it off his mouth to speak.

"A fellow sufferer, I see," said Ziger.

"I confess, I prefer it to the sauna," said Slater.

"We're two old-fashioned fellows."

This open display of his genitals made Slater uneasy with Ziger dressed in a towel and overtly looking down. Ziger derived pleasure from Slater's discomfort. He grinned and said, "I happen to know what you're going through. The pain you must feel."

"You do?"

"I know your father. You're about the same size."

Slater forgot his nakedness. "Wait. You mean you *knew* my father. He's been dead for years."

"I meant what I said," said Ziger. "We worked together."

"At Berkeley?"

"Undergraduate. I assisted him on countless projects."

"Don't tell me. He was this *remarkable* man, right?"

Ziger twirled a strand of hair. "Not really."

Slater was drawn to ask, "He wasn't a genius?"

"Clever thief." Ziger smoothed down his few long chest hairs. "He saw significant potential. I'll give him that much."

"Are we talking about the same man?"

Ziger wiped sweat from an eyebrow: "John Lazard Slater II?"

"That would be him," said Slater.

"And you, my boy, would be number III." Ziger wiped away sweat. "Yes, we worked on deciphering ancient scrolls. He believed codes were imbedded within. We disagreed. But he had charisma, so I relented. Turned out to be true, but he never would have found the source without me. He lacked the ability. True. I'll credit him with insight. But it was *my* genius. Fathom that. It was *me*. I, Barton Ziger, found the code."

Slater wiped sweat from his eyes. "Code?"

"I cracked the DNA code. Me. You thought different? Story of my life. As will Bosner take credit for Cy. It matters not. I take satisfaction where I can. I'm simply happy you survived. As I am *pleased* that Cy will likely be alive when I'm dead and gone."

Slater recalled the early meetings with their Chief Scientist, who had jumped ship from Oracle. Slater had kept querying him about details, the cost of production, the ETA. Ziger hovered unconcerned while working on the mainframe that would become CyBorg9. The board of directors allowed Ziger a more than modicum amount of autonomy, nearly a free-rein since his colleagues didn't comprehend half the things he said, but would never admit it, so impressed and envious of his credentials. Zigor ranted with a righteous fervor, thus, making believers out of doubters.

The mention of "CyBorg9" snapped Slater back to the present. "What did you mean by that? About not getting credit? About me surviving?"

Ziger chucked, "Is it always about *us?* Self-centered creatures, as we are. You'll have to remind me what I said. I have fallen prey to memory lapses. It happened to Einstein too."

His manic smile reminded Slater of the time he watched Ziger pouring metallic plasma through a funnel into CyBorg9. Ziger had craned his head, his teeth glistening with a hint of blue, to explain, "Mercury blood to fill his veins, to feed one super-charged DNA."

Slater returned to the hissing vapors of the steam. "You said you were happy I'd survived. You knew about the accident. Obviously. And the death of my father and family?"

"Accident? That was no accident."

"I agree," said Slater. "What do you know about it?"

"I followed the event with great interest, and likewise followed the story of your birth from death. You were called a miracle baby."

"Newspaper hype. Tell me about the car crash."

Ziger rolled his head. He massaged his neck. "Can't take much more of this. The question again, please?"

"The car crash. You said it was no accident."

Ziger produced a plastic liter of spring water. He snapped off the cap to squirt his face, some of it finding his open mouth.

"No," Slater said, refusing, when offered.

"Tepid, but refreshing." He winked and gave the container a squeeze — liquid squirting upwards like a geyser. "I meant you."

"What about me?"

"How you came to be. It was no accident."

Slater leaned forward with frustration and exhaustion, palms on his knees, then raising both hands to rake back his dripping wet hair.

"Can anyone be straight with me? *Not* evasive. For once!"

Ziger said, "I'm surprised a brainchild like you hasn't figured out the puzzle already. Care to venture a guess?"

"You were the one who spliced my DNA."

"I'm very proud of you," applauded Ziger by squeezing and squirting his water bottle. "And?"

"You delivered me like a stork—in a vial."

"Intriguing analogy. For me, the concept of breeding was never appealing. And since I will never marry and conjugate you remain the closest I'll ever come to actually conceiving a son. Your father, Slater number II, had difficulty operating a pocket calculator, among other things. Yes, yes, I exaggerate. A bit."

Ziger teasingly measured about three inches with his forefinger and thumb as his blue eyes lowered to examine Slater's anatomy. A tongue poked through his crooked teeth.

Slater stood and tucked the towel around his waist.

"Becoming modest? Or merely going?"

The spring water was aimed and offered again. "Are you sure you won't partake in my baptismal offering?"

Slater became light-headed. He shrank, mentally returning to the age of thirteen, to Heather's and Roy's Christmas party where he was standing behind a punchbowl serving guests.

This man and his cane had stood in front of him.

"I'd give you a hug," joked Ziger, "but I'm not prone to wild affection. And, well," he added, "I'm likely radioactive."

—44—
Friends and Enemies

Nina backed away from her open front door. Sherry stepped into the foyer with the morning sunlight.

"I've been expecting you," said Nina with a casual smile.

Sherry wasn't smiling. "Wasn't I paying you enough?"

"I had no qualms."

"We had an agreement."

"The terms are fine. I love this place."

Sherry didn't bother examining the house that she had helped furnish. She moved into the living room, then turned back on Nina but stopped short of poking her in the chest. "I trusted you."

"Sherry, I didn't betray you."

"Oh, please."

"Can I offer you a drink?" Nina moved toward the bar.

Sherry didn't know whether to sit or stand.

Nina added, "I think we should."

"It's early morning, Nina."

"Wine will calm us both down."

"You look calm," said Sherry.

Nina removed a bottle of wine from a refrigerator under the bar, took two glasses off a shelf and poured chardonnay into both.

"We hadn't considered a minor detail," said Nina.

Sherry took hold of the offered glass. "It's not minor."

"My son grew to be a man. He wants answers."

"And you were *eager* to comply."

"You know how relentless children can be," said Nina. "What was I supposed to say?"

"You could have called me," said Sherry.

"Eventually, Jude was going to find out."

Sherry saw the portrait of Judas. He clearly resembled his father and she turned away to face her old friend. "Are you forgetting *I* was the only one who wanted to tell John? Nina?"

"Not true," said Nina.

"Besides you," said Sherry. "We made an agreement."

"We did," said Nina.

"This will destroy my marriage."

Nina sipped her wine. She then gestured toward the furniture. "He doesn't know the how or why. Jude only knows that John is his biological father."

Sherry absorbed this information. She lost stamina and sat into an arm chair. She cradled her wine as she took a sip. "That's it? All he knows? What about us? All the rest?"

Nina sat in a chair beside her and placed a sympathetic hand on Sherry's knee. "Would I lie? After you've been so generous to me? Helping to support Jude? My God, Sherry, you're acting like this was all blackmail."

Sherry stood. She didn't like the insinuation.

Nina said, "But it's not. What I'm saying is...John would have *paid* for child support, had he known about Jude."

Sherry winced, set the glass down on a table, and began to pace. "I have to tell him. How do you *tell* the man you love that...God. I can't even forgive myself. How can I expect—"

"Courage." Nina stood and took Sherry's hand.

"We were such fools," said Sherry, "to let them do what they did to us — and him."

"You underestimate John," said Nina.

Sherry fought back tears. "I love him so much."

"I know you do." Nina touched Sherry's hair in sisterly fashion. "We can't stop Jude from being curious. He will make it easier for John to accept all this. Wait and see."

Sherry shook her head.

"It'll be all right," said Nina.

"No—it won't."

"Don't resent Jude for being born."

"Nina, I don't," said Sherry. "I knew this would—"

"John accepts him. They talked for hours. It was wonderful."

"You *saw* John?"

Nina denied it, shaking her head. "No. I saw it in Jude's eyes. He told me about their meeting, playing golf and having dinner."

Sherry felt dazed. "John's told me next to nothing. He's been preoccupied, evasive, staying late at work. I was beginning to think you had intentionally set this whole—"

"Sherry, my God. Why would I do that?"

"To harm me."

"Why would I do that? Sherry, what I *want* is for us to finally be...a family. Now we can be."

Sherry rubbed her hands against her thighs. The house was cozy and warm and yet she shivered.

Nina asked, "Do you think about those days?"

"I try not to," said Sherry, massaging her temple.

Nina reached to open a black marble box on the table. She took out a cigarette. "Would you care for one?"

Sherry shook her head.

"Aside from the horrid things we did to John..." Nina snapped a flame to her cigarette, inhaled, "we *did* have fun. Those gorgeous men. We were quite the pair, you and I."

"That was another lifetime, Nina," said Sherry.

Nina twisted her lips to blow smoke from the side of her mouth. "We were wild, young, and naughty."

"You're exaggerating. We weren't that bad."

"Umm," said Nina, taking one last puff before crushing out her cigarette in a marble ashtray. "I'm trying to quit."

"You should." Sherry reseated herself.

"Well," said Nina, "certain cravings are hard to resist. Like my endless taste for certain men."

Sherry was curious. "How do you mean?"

Nina lowered the collar of her sweater, exposing a yellow and purple discoloration of skin to her neck and shoulder. "I attract the kind who like to hit and run."

"God! Nina, did you report him?"

"To whom?" She took a casual sip of wine. "How would that play in court? Since I keep inviting him back into my life."

"Who is he?"

"You're looking at him." Nina raised her eyes to indicate the portrait on the wall behind her. "He does have his good side."

"He should be in jail," said Sherry.

Nina joked, "Why? When I can have him captured and framed right here? I adore men who know how to be remorseful and buy back forgiveness with expensive gifts. Don't you?"

As Nina raised a toast to the man on the wall Sherry noticed the diamond bracelet and matching necklace.

Nina toasted her guest with a flirtatious wink, "And as for you, by far, you were the best I ever had."

"Stop it." Sherry took offense and stood.

"I loved how you kissed."

"I love John."

"A pleasure I, unfortunately, missed."

"I need to leave," said Sherry.

"Stay for lunch."

"I need to be alone, to think this out."

Nina walked Sherry to the foyer where scattered colors burst through stained-glass sidelights to shine upon them.

"I was wrong about you," said Nina.

"How do you mean?"

"You and John are right for each other."

Puzzled, Sherry paused as Nina held the door open.

Nina said, "I've never known anyone more deceived than John. Or anyone as secretive as you, Sherry. Your parents really fucked with your head."

Sherry snapped back, "My parent's are good people."

Nina remained calm. "Are you programmed to say that?"

"Go to hell." Sherry was blinded by a blaze of morning sunlight and shielded her eyes.

"Admit it, Sherry, you were dealt a bad hand. And like me, you keep coming back for more—abuse."

Sherry said, "My parents didn't abuse me!"

"Ha! I was there," said Nina. "I know different."

Sherry stalled at the door. "I'm learning to forgive them."

"Well *I* can't." Nina kept hold of the door.

Sherry wanted to leave but couldn't move. Where she would go after this — once she left and got in her car — she had no idea. Her thoughts flew like bats startled awake inside a cave.

In her defense, Sherry said, "I'm not saying it wasn't strange, Nina, but my parents were trying to do good. They felt—"

"Oh give it a rest. Go home and close your castle door. Go on dreaming. It was a noble *quest* by good knights gone bad."

Sherry opened her mouth, unable to find any words.

"It was all because of *John*," said Nina. "Remember? John and I were supposed to be the lucky ones. To be happily married. Why? Because your John was this miracle child? Well, I have breaking news for you, Sherry. Wake up! It's all a pile of horseshit! And your *precious* John—he's nothing special!"

"He's special to me!"

Sherry stormed out leaving the front door wide open.

Nina slammed the door shut.

—45—
A Chip Off

Judas Slater was capturing a frenetic stream of atomic particles. He equated this mission to containing an aggravated swarm of bees. The microcosm he viewed was computer-linked to a new harvest of molecules. Judas sensed a foreign object hovering overhead in the macroworld, accompanied by a familiar voice:

"I'm receiving good reports about you."

Judas returned to actual scale and looked up, squinting. His myopia was not allowing him a clear picture of his biological father. He reattached his fashionably thin wire-rim spectacles and smiled.

"As I'd predicted."

"When was this?" said Slater.

"At our first encounter," said Judas. "Nice tie."

"Thanks."

"I'm guessing African?"

"Right. Nigerian."

"While playing golf. I told you I was a wiz at computer science. Especially this nano-technical stuff. Thanks for the nepotism."

"You didn't need me to get hired here."

"Yeah, but those genetic gifts I inherited didn't hurt."

His son's self-mocking, self-assured grin got Slater to smile, and then ask, "What are your views on our cybergenetic research?"

"I say, why not," said Judas.

"You don't think we're moving too fast?"

"I like fast. I mean, hey, we are the human race, right?"

"Right." Slater gave a cursory examination of his son's cubicle. It had a spartan cleanliness. There were no frivolous toys littering his workspace, except for one NeverMind stress ball in the shape of a brain. The only anomaly to this shrine of order were the snapshots of pretty girls pinned to the walls of his domain. "Fast friends?"

Judas grinned. "Like I said."

"Fast can be good." Slater leaned against the doorway partition. "Except when moving so fast and getting so far ahead of ourselves we no longer can recognize our mode of transportation or the wall we've hit prior to creating it."

Judas laughed uneasily. "Is that a joke, or a question?"

"A little of both."

"A conundrum. I got it."

"How do you like working for Barton Ziger?"

"He's completely mad," said Judas.

"Is he?"

"Absolutely, with ultra-intense ideas." Judas deleted the screen image with a keystroke. "I mean, I understand I'm a neophyte here, so I have to log these mundane hours trapping atoms in a laser web but, I mean, my talents could be better spent."

"How so?" said Slater.

Judas launched a new image and cracked his knuckles, "Feast your eyes on *that*."

"Impressive hologram. A molecular bearing?" said Slater.

"Built with atomic motors." Judas typed in code and the image rotated smoothly to slowly reveal every angle. "It has propulsion like a corkscrew. Similar in principle to the E. coli bacteria."

Slater scratched his chin. "Driven by photon forces? Clever. Each mechanism we create mimics nature."

"The heart and soul of cybergenetics," said Judas.

"Ziger has you working on this?"

"I plan to propose it to him. With your blessing, of course."

"You created this?"

"Well, *yeah*." Another grin.

"To be used for?"

"Cybercell robotics," said Judas.

A sliver of pain cut through Slater's mind, causing him to wince and grasp the side of the cubicle.

"Are you okay?" said Judas.

Slater nodded but found a chair to sit down in and rub his eyes. "Tired, is all. I have a lot on my mind." The flash-stabbing image of Sherry standing next to Nina at The Crossroads came back to him. Followed by a glimpse of Judas seated next to Bosner, conspiring, under the glow of CyBorg9. The high-pitched frequency from their conversation made him nauseous. The nausea subsided.

"Go on," said Slater. "What were you saying?"

"These bearings are the future for robotic communication. But not all people can grasp it. I'm telling you, it's the economic key to supremacy."

"Explain."

"These mechanisms travel bio-electrically through cyberspace. But the real beauty is, they're self-replicating."

"Self-replicating?"

"Well, potentially. It's only a matter of time."

Slater massaged his eyes. He was envisioning a proliferation of these microscopic corkscrew hybrid beings. Forming what? He saw human heads. Judas among them, distilled in a sphere of blue light.

"This might not be good," said Slater.

"*Why?*" Judas laughed with a casual disconcern. "I mean, the MegaCorp, our Big Brother, they're like enthusiastically backing us on any new research. This could be major."

"Who else have you shown this to?"

"Only you, and some colleagues." Judas pulled a snapshot off his wall and held it up. "Come on, it's techno-radical, like Faye here. Isn't she a magnet? I mean, we *are* like the corporation that brings good things to life. Right?"

Slater said, "And life is full of dangers. She's gorgeous."

Judas opened a drawer. "Danger keeps you focused. I might have something for your headache."

"It went away." Slater stood.

Judas looked up. "You want to hear something funny?"

"Sure," said Slater.

Judas cracked his knuckles. "Okay. Every mechanical device requires a bearing to function. Meaning, there is always friction. Except with saturated atoms. They have no bonding sites, so they're constantly on the move. Never docking. Keeping to themselves."

Slater nodded, following him so far.

Judas had a mischievous smirk. "Molecules are like people — some attractive, others repellent." Pointing to the holographic model rotating in his monitor, he said, "Take these bearings. All repellent. Which means they won't attract or commingle and start gumming up the works."

Slater smiled. "Are you referring to making love?"

"Making it, yeah." Judas grabbed the spongy brain off his desk and squeezed it. "And since all these bearings are composed of atoms with no common numerical divisors on either the outer or inner rings, they slide in and out. Frictionless. Like perpetual motion."

"Perpetual?" said Slater.

"Well, almost. My cohorts and I have dubbed this ultra smooth interaction the Aloof Screw." Judas laughed. "Get it? A perpetual motion coupling with no attachments. Sexual perfection."

Slater smiled. "Ah, minus the friction?"

He squeezed the stress ball. "Exactly."

Slater tapped his watch. "Hungry? Lunch at the Icehouse?"

"Can't. Hot lunch date." Judas linked his fingers and stretched into a triumphant crack of knuckles. "Faye is like this body double. So sleek, you'd swear she's not for real."

Slater made a search to locate the target of his son's lust.

"She works in the another lab. I'll take a rain check."

"Sure." Slater winked. "Meanwhile, be careful with those aloof screws. Bearing in mind your last one cost the corporation a bundle in an out-of-court settlement. Stockholders tend to frown on those kinds of messy perks."

"Gotcha." Judas gave a thumbs-up, to have it drop limply.

Slater laughed. "I'll set up a meeting with Barton. To discuss the merits of your molecular bearing."

"Great. Thanks."

"Also," said Slater, "listen to your heart."

Judas stopped squeezing the spongy brain. He cocked his head with an unsure smile. "It's still beating."

Slater told him, "People get hurt if you forget you have one. Take time to slow down and listen to it."

Judas frowned, then brightened. "Gotcha. Moving too fast and hitting those walls?"

"That's right."

"Relax," said Judas. "Don't worry."

"Strange. Same words Bosner keeps telling me."

—46—
Encrypting Cyberspace

Bosner sat facing Slater seated behind his marble-topped desk. It was supported by two walnut columns that also served as drawers and shelving. Slater leaned back in his spring-loaded chair.

"You promised to keep me informed, Larry."

Bosner was on guard. "And I most certainly have, John."

"Tell me about the Aloof Screw."

Bosner forced a laugh, relaxing a bit. "Excuse me, what?"

"The molecular bearing you've been working on with Jude."

Bosner tensed, trying to brush it aside. "It's nothing, a prototype at best. A silly notion. I dare say, it seems I've encouraged your boy too much. He showed it to you, did he?"

"An hour ago."

Bosner straightened his tie. "I try to be supportive with all my creative staff, not only with him. That's what makes us a good team. Ideas are to be explored not brushed under the table, ignored."

"I'm in agreement," said Slater.

"Excellent. Support from *above*," joked Bosner.

"Tell me about cybercell robotics."

Bosner shifted a bit. "Cy suggested we explore the notion."

"I'm the CEO."

"Well, yes, you are."

"You're to keep me informed," said Slater.

"About any irregularities," Bosner declared, squirming as if to take a stand and rise out of his chair, but he remained seated. "It's brand new, this cybercell business. Embryonic, at best, I assure you. I felt the matter could wait for our next board meeting."

"Cy said nothing about this to me," said Slater.

"You'll have to take that up with him." Bosner smiled to bring some levity into the conversation. "John, don't you have enough to worry about without adding *this* to your worries? We're riding on a wave of success. Enjoy it. The Consortium of Nations *adores* us."

"Don't be smug," said Slater. "I'm thrilled we won the bid. But if our Watchdog System fails to provide interglobal firewall security, NeverMind will be *screwed* — held accountable, financially crippled, and swallowed whole. The end. For us."

Bosner took hold of the arms of his chair, prepared to rise. "I'm aware of the risks. Will that be all?"

Slater had never felt so alone. Even after stumbling blind and lost through a desert, or tied to a cross and tortured. This felt worse. All he cared for and loved was slipping away. His wife had betrayed him too. It would be the linchpin that unhinged him. He clung to a fragile hope that she had not. He kept avoiding the confrontation. Even his son — conspiring against him too? How many others?

His uncle had forewarned him about this hostile takeover.

Slater, in a downward spiral of negativity, made an attempt to be positive. He gave a conciliatory smile. "Larry, if I was a bit rough on you, I'm sorry. I'm under a lot of stress. A lot's at stake."

Bosner had not expected Slater's extended hand. He was quick to stand too and grasp it with a shake. "Don't I know it."

Slater added, "And, I appreciate all the hard work you've done, encouraging the staff to be creative, which includes my son."

"Don't mention it. He's a good lad. Smart as hell. I need to get back to work. Is there anything else?"

"I'll let you know." Slater came around the desk and walked with Bosner across the room. With a parting smile he shut the door, then stood there a moment, scanning the room. He returned to his desk to grab his laptop computer, saw several lights blinking on the display housed in the Grecian marble. He poked one.

"I'm going out. Beep me if I'm needed."

"Your wife called again," said Jenny through the speaker.

"Tell her...if she calls again...I'll be in meetings all day. And that everything is fine. But I'll be home late."

"Chief, you're asking me to *lie* for you?"

Slater wasn't in the mood for Jenny's humor. "Yes, who else can I trust? You're very capable. Thank you. Bye."

Slater left through a private door that deposited him into a hall that led to an emergency exit. His key prevented setting off any alarms. He emerged into the NeverMind park. Strolling aimlessly, he located an empty bench nestled among trees on a knoll. Through the camouflage of greenery, he could view sections of the concrete pathways leading to the main entrance. He spotted a few employees playing chess at stone tables. The weather was a mix of brisk and warm air. He set the computer on his lap and flipped it open.

Searching the sites of world trade organizations, government agencies, global banking depositories, money markets, Slater found cyberspace to be in working order. He rubbed his eyes. It didn't help clear the images dodging his thoughts. He massaged his chest. But, hard as he tried, he could not get the crushing pain to his heart to either go away or kill him outright.

For the hell of it, Slater conducted a browser search, typing in the words to a universal question: "What is the meaning of life?"

He was amused by the plethora of links to sites proposing to know the answer. He randomly clicked on one, which proclaimed:

Life is a paradox. To be happy you make others happy.
Share food, blankets, and laughter. God is love, not fear.
Be not afraid. Open your heart and there will be meaning.
We are here but once. But consider life our second chance.

Slater looked up, reconsidering this thing called life.

A second chance? *Was* life a test?

A solitary robin was watching him from the branch of an oak tree. The bird seemed as intrigued with Slater as Slater was intrigued with the bird. Neither made a sound.

Slater broke the silence by asking:

"Have you come here to help me or to merely sit there and hear my confessions?"

The bird peeped and flew away.

"That's what I thought," laughed Slater, shutting his laptop.

—47—
Taking the Fall

Slater had become a global player.

On the advice of consulting firms hired by NeverMind he had converted to this mindset. He spent his days and hours confined in rooms listening to various presentations — regarding the French, the Germans, or Africans, about their tastes, trends, and differences. Enormous budgets were allocated for future returns on investments. Marketing campaigns were launched on a quarterly basis. He had adjusted to the routine examinations, modifications, and approvals of branch facilities flourishing around the world. He viewed story-board concepts for advertisements, screened the edited and re-edited footage for commercials. All the while trying his best to keep in step and in pace with the rapid pulse of their new international operating system recently launched. So far, it proved successful and secure.

Making decisions, a button pusher – that's what he'd become.

He wore thermosuits to promote the corporation and became a traveling advertisement for their product — dressing for success in distinguished greys, blacks, and blues. He spoke at charity events, raising money, distributing truckloads of their products to shelters. He still believed in his invention, but not in himself.

His golf game was consistently erratic, with no time to play.

Regimented to these agendas and itineraries, Slater rarely had a moment to relax within his recently completed estate, or swim in the heated waters of his award-winning pool. Color reproductions were featured in design journals. They showcased the luxurious bedroom, two adjoining bathrooms, a curved living space and panoramic view, complete with an expansive pool that resembled a mirage of water beyond the windows — extending outward, as if defying gravity — falling away into the distant blues of sky and ocean.

Slater was flipping through these pages of *Architectural Digest* before setting it down on the limousine seat. He too wondered what it would be like to live in a house such as his.

Sherry would know.

He closed his eyes, regretting the way he had confronted her.

He winced at the scene as it replayed in his mind, his entire life rewinding around this core of pain. Coming to her in the pretense of initiating love, he had caressed her as she stepped from her bath. He planted a false kiss on her moist lips. Then lifted her voluptuous breast dispassionately.

Witnessing the mark.

It was the same scar he had seen on Nina. The same symbol scarred upon himself.

"Were you planning on telling me? *Ever?*"

"I was going to. I've been *trying* to tell you for—"

"Years!" said Slater. "Years of deceit! Is that what we've been living, Sherry? A lie?"

"No," she cried, "I was about to tell you."

"Oh, really?"

"I swear."

"It's too late. Your ex-roommate beat you to it."

Slater watched his wife step back against the shower wall. The information took her breath away and nearly her ability to stand as she clutched the door handle and tiled wall. Her body was shaking.

"John, I swear, I didn't mean to—"

"Hurt me? Deceive me?"

"Yes, *yes*—I'm sorry, I'm sorry, I'm *sorry.*"

Slater struck the wall of glass to the shower, nearly shattering it. "God, Sherry, how could you *not* tell me?"

"I didn't know *how!* John, I—"

"How many other people are involved?"

"What?"

"*People.* Besides Nina. Heather? Who else?"

"My father," she said. "Others. That was...*then.*"

"God, I feel like...I don't know *what* I feel!"

"Don't let this ruin us," she pleaded, sobbing.

"Ruin? That's it. That's what I must be feeling—*ruin!*"

"This is what I feared. I knew you'd react this way."

"Sherry, I was abducted and tortured! And you—*God!* I can't believe it—you helped! And because of it—I almost *killed* myself!" Slater paced the bathroom. He wanted to break something, but was not sure where to begin.

"I'm so sorry." Sherry reached for him. "I was caught up in something I never asked to be part of. I *swear.*"

"Jesus! Why am I even listening to this?" He stormed into their bedroom. He cursed and banged about, choosing a vase to shatter. "Nina was your roommate in college! You married me *knowing* and never *telling* me—*any* of this!"

"I wanted to!"

"Except you *didn't!*"

"How was I supposed to?" she sobbed, clutching the frame of the bathroom door. "I never meant to fall in love with you, but I did. I tried to resist you. I warned you. But I—"

"Are you sure it wasn't all planned?"

"*Yes*." Stung by the remark, she insisted, "It was love!"

"Really? Or is everything a lie? My life? My *wife?*"

"Stop it!" she buried her head in her hands.

"Count on it," he said. "I'm leaving!"

"John, don't. Stay and talk."

Throwing shirts, socks, and underwear into a suitcase, he came upon one of her perfume bottles on a nightstand and threw it into a wall mirror. Sherry flinched, backing away, adrift on the carpet. He slammed his suitcase shut, twisting the combination lock before he paused to catch his breath.

"I was afraid you wouldn't forgive me," she said.

"I'm *afraid* you were right."

"John, I love you. You *know* I do."

"Do I?"

He stood holding a suitcase small enough to fit in an overhead compartment and take flight. He took another breath to steady his heartbeat. "You love me, Sherry? Imagine how *little* I care."

"What about the children?"

This stopped him. Emotional artillery got hoarded during years of marriage and he knew where to inflict maximum damage.

"This should make for an interesting story in court. My lawyer will call yours to discuss custody rights."

"John, don't. *Please*." Sherry reached for him, then stopped. She regained her composure to say, "I knew you would never stay if I told you. And I was right!"

Slater paused to look back at her.

She implored, "You swore our love could survive anything."

Slater grimaced. "I guess that makes us both liars."

The slam of the door – wood, metal, glass – sent a shockwave that reverberated all the way to the limousine, making him wince.

Slater hated himself.

His behavior had been a perverse pleasure of rage.

The world *was* a lie.

The thought of being separated from his children provoked a wave of profound sadness, depressing him beyond measure.

He felt so far removed he was beyond tears.

His thoughts shifted to banalities – to his restored Silver Bullet Porsche. The photographer had captured him posed with his hand upon the hood. Acquired for the purpose of escaping on nostalgic drives – at least, that was how he rationalized the purchase. It was gathering dust in a six-car garage he had opened twice.

He barely registered the limousine driver's voice, asking him where he was traveling to.

"Nowhere in particular," he replied.

"I've been there."

Slater laughed. "It's Charles, right?"

"Yeah, but I go by Chuck, Mr. Slater, Sir."

"Call me John."

"I've been meaning to thank you for the job."

The cover photo on the magazine was distracting. Taken months before its publication, it showed the owner – John Lazard Slater III – standing beside the palatial gates of his mansion. The photograph had captured a trace of arrogance in his smile. He was reminded of elementary school, the time he had poked out the eyes of classmates he hated by jabbing the tip of a pencil into their yearbook photos.

A child's voodoo attempt at revenge?

"What did you say?" said Slater.

"I said I wanted to personally thank you," said Chuck.

"For what?" said Slater.

"For saving my father's life."

"When was this?"

"Years ago. During that freak snowfall in New Francisco. San Francisco, back then. He told me you had helped lots of people. I

wasn't even *born* yet, but he told me *I* shouldn't forget it either."
Chuck grinned. "It's just, I know where you've been, Sir. I mean,
John. You're still one of us. Even with all of the fancy trappings.
That's all I had to say."

"Thanks. Give my regards to your father."

Slater unclipped a pen from his suit.

"I wish I could. He died from a stroke a couple years back."
Chuck observed Slater through the rearview mirror. "If you don't
mind me asking, John, what are you doing?"

"Poking out my eyes, Chuck."

Airtime would occupy him for awhile. It had become, for him,
the new commonplace. A waste of time.

He was traveling to attend and speak at a conference in Cannes,
France. *Robotic Intelligence* and *Monitoring the Flow of Electronic
Currencies* were two of the topics to be discussed.

Afterwards, he flew to Hong Kong where he spent three weeks
discussing the pros and cons of building a NeverMind MegaCorp
plant along the Asian rim. During the visit, upon accepting the deal,
he was foretold by a passive-aggressive translator: "Strength comes
from integration, Mr. Slater. You have merged wisely."

He pondered this message in his hotel suite while a prostitute
massaged him. The woman was a complimentary gift. It would be
one of many gifts, she relayed to him nonverbally, for his promise to
wed into their East-West alliance.

He shuddered pleasurably, closed his eyes, reminded of a new
NeverMind satellite being launched into space at that very instant,
thereabouts, Pacific Standard Time.

At a billion dollar cost.

Afterwards, Slater felt spent.

Laying upon the hotel bed, he stared into the darkened space of
the ceiling and recalled the last encounter with his son. Both on the
move and going opposite directions on a NeverMind escalator, Jude
rising, Slater descending, they passed and Slater saw the alarm on his
son's face shift. It shifted to a cocky twinkle of a grin followed by a
mock-solemn bow. A cultural reminder of where Slater was going.

Slater had laughed. He was silent now, reflecting. He sensed an
uncertainty, like shifting winds in motion turning counter-clockwise,

invisible wheels he was powerless to stop. He could occasionally see through the looking glass and presently he saw a puzzling reflection. Not himself, but Judas.

The face was looking back from the other side of damaged glass. Overhead lights shone upon the thick wall that separated them and he saw fiberoptic trails in the plexiglass, not scratches. Filaments of covert activity. Electronic firewalls now replacing physical borders. To the human eye, the world was not as it appeared. There was so much more hidden from view.

He looked away from the plane's window.

While en route home, Slater read a biography hastily selected at an airport newsstand. It was by an astronaut who had traveled to the moon. This adventurer, upon her return, had looked back at the swirling blue-and-white orb isolated in black space and realized there were no borders. There never had been. Her view of reality had been altered. Primarily by the deafening silence she experienced in space.

Slater scanned the remaining chapters which told of her battles with alcoholism and visits to sanitariums. Despite her many travails, it had a happy ending.

The author claimed to have found peace with God.

Slater put the book down and recalled his trip into the desert. Where he had not found God. Or had he? The raging sand storm had ripped at his body, nearly shredding mind from matter.

His eyelids fell, then the book in his hand. And he slept.

Within the cocoon of roaring turbines, Slater dreamed he was a satellite cycling in orbit. Weightless, while chaos reigned on earth. Fraudulent behavior, the cause. Electronic deposits were being siphoned from bank accounts all across the planet. Financial structures, once solvent, collapsed as the vacuous bits of currency and promised megabytes of debt rapidly accrued. Encrypted passwords were decoded and transactions diverted. Valuable data absconded, marketplace futures evaporated, and fortunes turned to losses. Communication links for air-traffic controllers failed and airplanes were forced to land, or collided in the sky.

It was a minor earthly hiccup, a disturbing ripple, compared to the cosmic dusting the world would come to know.

Slater stirred in his sleep.

Initially, the disturbance was blamed on malicious software. Computer pirates. Malignant viruses.

A wristwatch beeped from a passenger across the aisle and Slater's mind rose closer to the surface of consciousness.

His dream altered into eavesdropping. An anonymous entity was capturing securities from electromagnetic devices – computers, coding machines, cell phones – all devices conducting currency and emitting magnetic fields. Zillibytes of data were being analyzed, stored, falsified, replaced, and trashed.

CyBorg9 had forewarned this in a riddle:

Information equals wealth,
And knowledge equals power,
A power unrivaled in me,
Times the total of what will be.

Slater moaned in his sleep as the plane made its descent.

At the speed of light signals transmitted down conduit pipes, power lines, into fiber-optic wires, through air. Nebulous existence was erased. Cloned I-DNA codes unlocked fortresses. The Federal Reserve System, the Internal Revenue Service, and Wall Street were damaged in a nanosecond from an electronic meltdown.

Slater woke to a warning bell and red light. Passengers were told to clasp their safety harness. The plane prepared for landing. Beneath clouds as white as a whipped-cream topping the world had taken on new meaning.

Rubber tires screeched on the tarmac.

At the end of the blue lighted runway Slater saw his doom.

Red beams revolving from police cars.

Burning Bridges

Cy monitored the arrival of Sherry Slater. She was walking with fierce determination and passing employees as she made her way down the garden path leading to the NeverMind headquarters. Her progress was tracked and viewable inside Cy's orb, the angle of her whereabouts changing every so often, a new camera eye taking over as she entered the building. She turned down a hallway.

"Observe her stride," said Cy. "She exhibits the mannerisms of someone whose energy is failing. Like a boisterous dying red star. Exhibiting spectacular color upon explosion but leaving much of nothing as it cools. Merely fading into a white dwarf. A curious specimen, is she not?"

"Yes," said a neutral voice.

"John, whom do you suppose she will seek out first?"

"I'm Jude," Judas corrected.

"I know that," said Cy. "Did you see this coming?"

"See what?" said Judas.

"This *woman* your father married."

"I'm watching her now—yes."

"No, before," said Cy. "In your mind."

"Oh, right." Judas shifted in his seat. "I glimpsed it."

"As I surmised. You have inherited your father's gift."

"Well, yeah, being his son." Judas grinned.

"I intuit that your stepmother is wise enough to not come here. If not her conscious mind, her subconscious one will certainly know it would be fatal."

Cy zoomed in on Sherry as she entered an office.

"Observe," said Cy. "A logical, yet illogical, progression."

"Excuse me, but—" said a secretary. "You can't go—"

"Oh, *yes* I can!" said Sherry, extending her arm like a football player moving downfield – pushing past the woman to enter a door. Startling Bosner who was seated for a portrait. He was poised like a Napoleon, outfitted in pompous finery, a hand tucked in his chest, which quickly dropped.

"Get out!" he said.

"Don't you two make a lovely pair," said Sherry, still moving and charging instead into Nina.

Nina reacted by shielding herself with her pallete – slamming the wooden plate of paint at Sherry as Sherry grabbed Nina by her hair. Sherry recoiled as Nina jabbed her in her ribs with a paintbrush but recovering to slap Nina across the face. She slapped Nina's face even harder with her other hand. Nina backed away.

"You bitch!" said Sherry, coming at her again.

Nina thrust out her high-heeled foot to keep Sherry away.

"You backstabbing bitch! I trusted you!"

Nina grabbed a thicker, more deadly paintbrush from a ceramic jar to use as a weapon.

"Why, Nina?"

"Why—*what?*"

Bosner, shorter than both women, retreated to a location behind his massive desk. Where he pushed a button triggering an alarm.

Sherry flinched as the siren wailed. Already in a zone of anger she shouted above the noise: "I had no idea you were so jealous!"

"What are you talking about?"

"You couldn't stand to see me happy!"

"Oh, please," scoffed Nina, wiping an eyebrow with the back of her wrist. Oil paint had splattered on both their faces and clothes. "Jealous of you? With nothing. Completely bankrupt."

The siren continued with intermittent whoops and yelps.

"At least I'm not *morally* bankrupt," said Sherry.

"And so *righteous*," said Nina. "You're no longer the queen bee, Honey. You've been ousted from the hive."

"All because of you!" said Sherry.

"Don't be delusional," said Nina.

"John is the one to blame." Bosner came out from behind his desk holding a small gun.

"Oh, shut up, Larry! Put away your little *cap* pistol. I'm done here – done with all of you!"

Two security guards rushed in and grabbed Sherry by the arms and forcibly pulled her toward the door.

"Yes, *done here* would be the key words," said Bosner.

Sherry craned her head. "You're the criminal!"

"Not according to our judicial system," said Bosner.

"Which you control," said Sherry. "Let go of me!"

"*Wild* accusations from the defense?" laughed Bosner, lifting his palms, brushing the air to sweep her out of the room.

"John wouldn't stoop as *low* as you, Larry. That's the reason you had him put away! Unlike you—he's innocent!"

"Innocent?" sneered Bosner. "No one can claim *that*."

A loud laugh was heard through the intercom. Cy said, "Good one, Larry. A clever retort. Have her thrown out."

"Affirmative," said one of the guards.

"You too, Cy!" shouted Sherry. She grabbed the door frame, halting her removal. "Go to hell!"

As a parting shot, Nina shouted, "Who do you think you are? This was never meant for you! I'm simply taking back what *was* to have been mine—not yours!"

Forced out, Sherry screamed, "You'll never have him!"

Inside the orb, viewed from another camera angle, Sherry was seen escorted forcibly out the NeverMind building, her feet dragging over granite, taken down three spacious steps and deposited on the grass beside the paved promenade to the main entrance. Both guards remained as a blockade. She stood and regained her balance, heart pounding, limbs shaking. She wiped hair from her face. Oil paint was smeared on her skin and blouse. She was aware of the mess she had become. Like a walking Pollock painting, out of step with the world. Employees gawked, avoiding her like a massive infestation of insects avoiding an obstacle they sensed to be odious.

"Keep an eye on her," voiced Cy, remaining faceless.

Judas assumed the command was directed at him. He watched his stepmother inside the orb and felt sorry for her. She had been treated harshly. He wondered about the fate of Sondra and Mercy. Both had surprised him with their unconditional love, accepting him as their big brother – which he hadn't expected, nor had necessarily wanted. He shifted his body, trying to get comfortable in the seat, waiting for Cy to visibly return. The auditorium chamber was dark except for a few house lights far overhead. He cracked his knuckles, getting impatient. "Cy?"

Inside the orb, Sherry was seen behind the wheel of her BMX. The luxurious sports car attracted attention, and she wished it was plain and anonymous, if not invisible. She stared through the wind-shield for several minutes before reaching for her purse. She hastily rubbed paint off her face as best she could, staring in a tiny mirror. She snapped the case shut and grabbed her ignition key, her hand shaking as she guided it into the slot.

She found herself driving between skyscrapers. Motorists were honking, people crossing the streets, but it barely registered as she made her way through the labyrinth of towering walls, maneuvering around a double-parked van. A jaywalker stepped in front of her car and forced her to step on the brake. The man, pierced and tattooed, slammed a hand onto her hood and raised his middle finger at her. Accompanied by a wicked laugh, he modified the gesture, extending his forefinger and pinky – sign of the devil. On any previous day she might have dismissed this as just another rude reminder – to anyone who cared to notice – that their civilization was in a rapid decline.

But the incident shook her to the core.

As she entered the Broadway tunnel her heart began to race with a mounting dread upon seeing the tsunami of light at the other end. The sun blinded her as she exited – traveling fast, but stopping in time at a crosswalk as the traffic signal turned red. With the engine idling, she turned toward a bearded face at her side window holding up a sign that conveyed in crude letters:

"Need Help. Have Mercy."

Already crying as the light turned green, she accelerated forward and was cognizant she could not help him or herself or anyone. She looked to make sure all the windows were shut and the door-locks activated. But she believed if she saw another destitute soul begging at the side of the road her heart would explode from sadness.

Trying to unscramble her thoughts, she realized she was driving along the Marina District like a programmed pigeon going home. Except the Sea Cliff residence was no longer *hers* to *call* home. She had taken shelter with her children inside her parents house, in the other direction, on Nob Hill. But she kept driving and headed onto the freeway which led to the Golden Gate Bridge.

As the toll gates neared, she veered off the freeway down the last exit where she pulled into a parking lot at the base of the bridge. She wanted solitude but the place was teaming with tourists in cars and on foot. She tried to reverse but cars now blocked her at both ends. While nudging forward, a car backed out of a parking spot – which she took. She turned off the ignition. She sat there for some time in the muted silence with her windows closed and doors locked and realized how fast her heart was beating. Her body was shaking too. A car honked and she waved away the motorist inquiring if she was intending to leave. With her sanctuary now violated, she felt she had no choice but to get out and walk around.

Upon opening the door she was shocked to discover the day was beautiful. For weeks it had been raining or drizzling and the sky full of dark clouds. And near the bridge it was usually smothered in fog – either coming or going. Yet now, though brisk, it was bright and sunny. Blue skies extended over the ocean and bay, separated only by the bridge's long span of red steel.

The gold watch on her wrist had little hands indicating it was close to noon. The time signified nothing. To look, a habit. Routine behavior like the ingrained response of putting her foot in front of the other, one at at time, to get herself into motion. Walking away she heard a shout to someone about forgetting to put coins in the meter, but she didn't care, she was already gone. Passing people holding cameras, riding bikes, walking in groups. She was intrigued by the multifaceted physiognomy and babble of tongues. Coming from all over the world to witness a geographical wonder. But why, she wondered, had she come?

The traffic – going helter-skelter north and south – paralleled the walkway she was on, and full of motion itself. She felt the span of cement and cable swaying minutely from the wind and the force of cars rushing to and fro with a constant *whoosh-whoosh-whoosh* of metal pushing through air and *swaack-swaack-swaack* of rubber wheels over cement and grated metal. She was not prepared for this frenetic noise. She'd imagined a solitary sound, of wind whistling through the latticework of cables and girders as she walked along, as if on a grand tightrope, high above the ocean churning far below.

She continued to rise gradually on the arching span to its center, to the majestic looming steel towers defying gravity. The roar from motorists mixed with the chorus of passersby talking and vehicles spurting out music. Bicyclists with bodies bound in bright spandex whizzed by her and she thought of aliens coming from other planets, landing here for a quick visit. Everyone seemed fully engaged in this beautiful day while she remained vacant and numb, except for the steady gush of blood rushing in and out of her pounding heart.

To steady herself she stopped and took hold of the railing. The solid metal was trembling too, vibrating as much as she was. Over the edge she saw the sky falling, tumbling to distant water and land. She pushed away, still unsteady, and turned her head, looking back through the stream of traffic to the ocean. Far off was a wall of fog. Returning, like rainwater from the sky, flowing to the ocean, having risen again. Relentless was this tidal wave of push and pull.

What were people, really? But particles of sand mixed with sea water, attaining the ability to move freely, a walking ocean contained by thin skin ready to burst at any second. And so many, she thought, gazing at the bodies of men, women and children as they passed. Where were they all going?

She saw the red tower approaching. The first of two towers that held up this suspended world. The walkway veered to the right and she turned a corner. It took her behind the enormous tower wall where the traffic noise receded to a muffled rumble. The roar inside her head subsided too. She leaned against the barrier railing and looked down upon the solid metal bar she was holding. Its coating of red paint had worn off from hands gripping the same spot hers grasped. She leaned forward and looked sideways at the receding perspective of the bridge, next looking upwards into the endless sky, then down below at the criss-crossing of girders and cables that were holding her aloft in suspended disbelief. High above water.

A formation of pelicans flew beneath her, traveling out to sea. White sails keeled in the wind far away on the bay. They resembled toy boats. The size of her thumb. So did the freighter. Ferryboat too. Each one stirring up swirls of white foam. Alcatraz Island was straight ahead, in the middle of the bay, and smaller than her hand. How could any human possibly fit inside this reconstituted concrete prison, and survive?

Nothing seemed right. The whole world was out of perspective. And so cruel. She looked down and saw there was no obstruction, no horizontal girder, or any net to catch her fall. It would be so easy.

But it was such a beautiful day. She imagined Sondra and Mercy at school, eating their lunch, or in the playground riding on swings. Carefree. Happy. They deserved better. A better mother.

Sherry wept and clung to the railing. She was a failure. She had climbed too high, risked too much and now, like a tightrope walker, had lost her nerve. Her balance too.

The earth was being pulled from beneath her feet.

And on a such a glorious day. She wanted fog. In the thick mist no one would notice her, or miss her as she slipped and fell away. Braced against the cold steel, her hands shook and she clenched them together into a fist. She closed her eyes and prayed for forgiveness for what she was about to do.

"Help me, God," she pleaded. "Save me. Please, I can't do this alone. I need your help. What do I do? Jesus...forgive me..."

A sudden chill made her eyes open. The sky was full of mist. Clouds swirled and brushed past her to the bay. Moisture dripping from her skin as the cool vapor thickened. She watched the ends of the bridge disconnect as the shorelines and foundation of her high platform dissolved into thick fog. The tower with its arching cables became a floating castle, a lost island, rising through golden mist into the sun.

It was a miracle, she thought.

She felt the push and tug of a strange force nudging her over the edge yet she held onto the railing. An inner peace was moving her, filling her, warding off her fears. She saw the faces of her children and believed they would be all right. Still, she refused to let go.

She felt a hand touch her shoulder. A warmth went through her body and pulled her back from the dissolving edge. Baffled to see a familiar face, she asked:

"Henry, what are you doing here?"

"I'm here to take you home."

—49—
Accepting Withdrawals

Slater had few visitors while confined in prison. Those who came to the reinstated, reconstructed federal institution housed on Alcatraz Island were eager to leave as soon as they arrived. Most days were cold, windy, and damp. It was a dismal atmosphere of gothic doom and grey isolation accompanied by fog horns and the tolling of buoys. Ferryboats would circle the jutting landmark with tourists aboard wielding cameras for souvenir snapshots.

Weiner hired attorneys who presented appeals on Slater's behalf. Futile motions that spun and sunk into bureaucratic mud.

Slater, wearing an orange shirt and pants made of thermocloth, stared through a thick wall of scratched plexiglass separating Wolfe who smiled sardonically and said through the phone microphone:

"Exiled to Pleasure Island. Nice accommodations?"

"A toilet in every room," said Slater.

"Ah, the ultimate in decadent living." Wolfe scanned the stark concrete and metal facility. "Reminds me of boarding school."

"I'm innocent," said Slater, "relatively speaking."

"That defines most of us. You're probably better off being here. I'm serious. It's bedlam outside. New Year's Eve minus the confetti and good cheer. Streets littered with broken glass. Cars overturned. Storefronts shattered and opened for mischief. It's not *all* bad news. I now receive a multitude of channels on my TeleMonitor."

"I envisioned most of this," said Slater

"Doesn't make you guilty." Wolfe saw a camera nodule near the ceiling and bared his teeth in a smile at the phantom viewer.

"The tricky part is knowing which visions are true."

"Amen." Wolfe spoke with a nervous energy. He had an unlit cigarette in his hand and was tapping it on the cement tabletop. "Paranoid times. Draconian measures on the rise. Everything's been reconfigured. Ideological differences are classified unacceptable. The wealth of nations overturned into beggar states. It's what we get for reinventing Mother Nature. Am I depressing you?"

Slater spoke into the microphone, "You're a ray of sunshine."

Wolfe, tired of tapping his cigarette, twisted it until it tore apart. "I did *forewarn* you about trusting your techno friends."

Slater clenched his jaw. "The reason I'm here, Wolfe, is because I refused to sell my soul for them, okay?"

"Not okay. Because we're now dealing with an intelligence that surpasses the sum total of us *all*."

"But fallible," said Slater.

Wolfe's curiosity was roused. "Vulnerable? Or indestructible? For sure I know it's an abomination of nature."

"Who says we aren't?" said Slater

Two stonelike guards entered the room and stood by the door. Wolfe blew them a kiss.

"Don't antagonize them," Slater warned.

"How does it feel being the scapegoat?"

Slater rubbed his eyes. "Like our first night on stage."

"That bad, huh?" Wolfe rubbed his chin bristle with a smile. "Any good news from the attorneys pleading your case?"

"I'm still appealing."

"Appealing?" Wolfe laughed. "I'd want to be left *alone* in here. You've been vilified. Savvy? So watch your ass." He rubbed his chin and mouth. "Do you remember that time I got hit by a car?"

"One of the few things I do." Slater smiled.

"I experienced a light. It was crazy, maybe like your visions."

"What kind of light?"

Sensing movement, Wolfe spoke fast. "Inside this hellhole you'll need that light. Visit the prison chapel. Look for forgiveness."

An amplified voice announced, "Your time is up!"

"Don't worry, Slater. I've got your back. Your kids are safe."

"Thanks," said Slater.

"Open your heart. Let her back in. Search for that forgiveness. Savvy? Whooh!" Wolfe was yanked from his seat by prison guards. "Guys, you're interrupting our plans for a prison break. Okay, okay, I'll go quietly. Damnit, you cyberdroids are strong."

"We are not droids!"

"Of course not." Wolfe was dragged from the room.

Inside his cubicle Slater continued to stare at the cement walls, metal bars, bolted-down mattress frame and sewer holes and tried to interpret his visions as the world expanded in a gradual starburst of atoms that grew expeditiously, extemporaneously, exquisitely.

"Excuse me, Mr. CEO, you're 10:00 o'clock is here."

The guards and neighboring inmates laughed. Slater was hated and blamed, yet held in awe for causing the world's upheaval.

Sherry was a flawed beauty, a masterpiece in a damaged frame. Her hand reached with a tentative touch toward the scratched glass separating them.

"What?" he replied coldly.

Sherry withdrew her hand and began to rise from her seat.

"Wait," said Slater.

She sat back down. Resolute, but with tears in her green eyes, she said, "You see? I was right."

"About?"

"How you would loathe me one day."

Slater shook his head before raising it. "I don't know what to think anymore."

"Me too." She wiped her eyes, tentative with a smile.

He looked at her quizzically. "You seem different."

"We all are."

"Look at us," said Slater. "I should have trusted my visions."

"And done what? John, I was afraid to tell you about—"

"Afraid of what?"

"Of *losing* you. I thought you were dead. John, your mind was unstable. I wasn't sure if you could handle the shock of knowing. My parents convinced me not to tell—"

"Your *parents?*" Slater scoffed. "Sure, I can see that."

"They're not bad people. They regret what—"

"Oh, I'm sure they do."

"John, I love them. I love you too. We all make mistakes."

"Of *this* magnitude?"

Her hands shook as she raised a tissue to blow her nose. "I wish I could change the past. But I can't."

Slater nodded, acknowledging the mess they'd both made.

Wary of the surveillance, Sherry whispered, "I was born into it. I didn't *choose* to be part of their...group, anymore than you did. When you escaped, so did I. And by the grace of God, you managed to survive."

"Barely."

"You're alive, aren't you?"

"I'll get back to you on that one."

She didn't know what to do with her hands, nervously tearing the wet tissue to pieces. "I felt abducted too. Can you understand? I disappeared. I fled to New York. I didn't speak to my parents for years. They wrote and swore their whole—whatever, was finished. They begged for forgiveness. And I forgave them. Around the time you reappeared. Christmas Eve? Remember?"

Slater muttered into the phone, "I do."

Sherry clenched the tissues into her fist. "I should go."

"No." Slater touched the plexiglass.

Sherry raised her hand to the partition too.

"Sondra and Mercy?" said Slater.

"They miss you. They send their love and kisses."

"Tell them I love and miss them too."

"John, please love me again."

"I've always loved you, Sherry. But I..."

"Loathe me?" Her smile was timid.

"No," he said.

"Am I forgiven?"

Slater returned her smile. "Something like that."

"I love you."

Their time was over fast. Their tears curtailed. Locked back in his time capsule, Slater now felt the atoms exploding existentially, exorbitantly, evangelically.

A new appointment. His son sat on the other side of plexiglass and looked like a mirror image of Slater distorted by time.

Judas arrived wearing a pinstriped silver thermosuit and tie. He sat with a regal ease, a parvenu barely containing his cockiness and disdain for the cheap plastic phone which he lifted off its cradle. He avoided direct eye contact with Slater and glanced at the several monitoring devices as a convenient means of distraction.

"Are these spy-nodules everywhere?"

"Inside a prison?" said Slater. "Pretty much. How are you?"

"Me? I'm adjusting. How are you holding up?"

"I was thinking about natural selection prior to your arrival."

"No kidding?" Judas laughed uneasily.

"No kidding." Slater's smile was thoughtful, eyes penetrating. "I realized the term 'survival of the fittest' is less about conflict of species and individuals than it is about competitive genes."

Judas rubbed his knuckles, wondering if he'd missed a joke.

"Salmons die," said Slater, "after breeding, whereas humans begin a long slow process of decay. It sounds bad, but no, happily we take the plunge into these risky consequences for love."

"Or lust," Judas quipped.

Slated smiled. "You're a living example. And I'm sorry."

"For what?"

"For fathering you the way I did."

"Hey, don't sweat it. I mean, it happens." Judas loosened his tie, getting uncomfortable. "If you haven't noticed, I'm fine."

"By appearances, compared to me, I would agree. Be careful. The human body is designed for obsolescence. Scientists believe that *we*, meaning our bodies, are vehicles devoted for propagating genes, nothing more. What do you believe?"

"Believe?" Judas' grin became peevish. "Is this a joke?"

"I'm asking you a question," said Slater. "Do you believe we're programmed to serve our selfish genes? Or, are we capable of rising above our genetic recipe for failure and attain free will?"

Judas jerked back in his chair. "How the fuck should I know? I don't even know what the *fuck* you're talking about!"

"I'm saying, essentially, Jude, I forgive you."

"For what?" Judas went on the offensive. "I did nothing wrong! It was *you*. Are you accusing me of something? Tell me!"

Slater raised his palm peacefully like a shrewd prophet. Calmly he rose, concluding their discussion. "I love you, Jude. Know that. Rise above your selfish genes. Try. Thanks, for visiting me."

Judas was confused. Somehow the tables had been overturned, metaphorically. Overwhelmed by emotion, tears flooding his eyes, he swiped at them angrily and slammed the phone into the wall.

Gone. A span of inexplicable time. More interfering matter. Heather Frost.

"We're working on a plan to free you," she said.

"Did you smuggle in explosives?"

"Listen to me. There *is* a way out."

"You found an escape route in my astrological chart?"

Ignoring his slight, she spoke louder. "Influential friends are working on a *legal* arrangement for your release."

"Yours or mine?" said Slater.

"What on earth are you talking about?"

"Friends?"

"We're on the same side, John."

"Are we?"

"You need to get out of here," she concluded. She inspected the phone for grime before placing it back on the counter. Its cradle had been broken off the wall.

Slater tapped the plexiglass window. Heather picked up.

"How, exactly?"

"Lawyers will explain to you the details," she said. "It involves surgery. A monitoring device. I need to leave."

And she did, with guards at her side. She brushed their hands away and stood on her own. She didn't look back.

From inside his cell Slater could sense the world traveling like a rocket departing gravity. Atomic particles uniformly expanded with balloon-like precision to become gigantic and monstrous.

Having reached the speed of light, everything had stopped.

Slater saw the recovery room, the return of daylight and the ICU monitors. His head ached. He was visited by men and women who examined him antiseptically, checked his vital signs, but never asked how he felt. He wondered if the physicians were human. One nurse smiled and patted his wrist. A small sign of compassion.

Next he was transported inside a limousine with tinted windows while two men wearing white uniforms and expressionless faces went over the rules of his parole. He listened, while observing the changed scenery of Frank. The city was murkier. Not from the air. Pollutant dioxides had long been sucked out from the environment. It was the people. Their eyes seemed empty, housed in blank stares, heads turning toward him as if witnessing a passing hearse.

The vehicle slowed to a stop. The door opened. Judas entered and sat in the seat across from Slater.

"I've been assigned to you," said Judas with a condescending grin. "Provided you're willing to talk."

"What is there to say?"

The metallic neurocircuit lodged in Slater's forehead distracted Judas. It made him think of a protruding Easter Egg, before getting to his point, stating matter-of-factly, "My predictions were accurate. The nano-robotic operating system I helped design, it proved to be a huge global success."

"Really? The world markets crashed."

Judas rebutted, "As per plan. Now stabilized. Vital again."

Slater pointed to people outside. "The multitude look unhappy. They look unemployed. A bit perturbed."

Unfazed by criticism, Judas said, "Every society deals with the unemployable. Collateral damage is expected during war."

"Well, congratulations. Your Aloof Screw really worked."

"I knew you wouldn't approve," said Judas.

"My opinion doesn't matter," said Slater.

"Listen, these corporate nations opened their gates willingly. Gladly accepting us like a miniaturized army of Trojan Horses. And, predictably they panicked – bullishly – like a herd of stupid cattle."

"I underestimated you," said Slater.

Judas smiled dismissively. "We overestimated your clairvoyant gifts, which proved to be overvalued."

"I never claimed to have these gifts."

"Giving *me* the opportunity to prove *I* do." Judas was waiting to be connected, fidgeting with the satellite feed, "Cy rewards those who provide. Those who *pretend*—they can get dismissed."

"I'll keep that in mind," said Slater.

Judas spoke into his cellular, "Tell security we're here."

Sherry and his children were waiting for Slater in what had been explained to them as a SecureHome. When Judas entered the room he was accosted by Mercy who ran and hugged him. "Jude!"

Sondra, who was thirteen, two years older than Mercy and past the age of rushing childlike at her handsome stepbrother, stayed back with her mother and asked, "Is he or isn't he coming?"

Flanked by security, Slater entered next and was rushed by both daughters. They grabbed hold of him. He clung to their warmth and sweet smell, kissing and stroking them. Sherry joined this group hug. Slater kissed her. He opened his eyes and saw Judas.

"Could you and your cronies give us some space?"

"Yeah, I can do that. I'll be back."

"Bye Jude," said Mercy.

Judas left with his entourage of guards to give them time alone, figuratively speaking, since TeleMonitors were in every room and a transmitting device was surgically implanted in Slater's forehead for tracking purposes. Being tagged and branded like a slice of livestock meant he was still considered to have value. What they expected to get from him was a matter he would deal with later. For now he was fighting to gain his bearings. He was having trouble adjusting to the electronic interference coming intermittently inside his head.

Slater and Sherry opened and walked through a sliding glass door onto a terrace of enclosed reinforced glass – for protection, not to keep them in. They both stared at the panoramic view of the city.

Sherry asked, "What now?"

"We live the best we can," said Slater.

Sherry kissed him. "Our love will get us through this."

Slater wasn't so sure. He inspected the walls of their glass cage. Their highrise SecureHome was thirty flights up, abutting the bay, a few blocks from the NeverMind headquarters. At dusk the city was rekindling and blazing with artificial light. Both their children were inside sprawled on a sofa watching a movie while, simultaneously, a TeleMonitor was watching them. Sondra, then Mercy, noticed their father looking and both waved happily. Slater blew them a kiss.

"You're right," said Slater. "Love is what we need most."

"Do you think it's safe here?" said Sherry.

"Safe, maybe. But sound?" Slater smiled, tapping a fingernail on his neurocircuit. "Anyone listening in there?"

Zzgeeegch-Zeejt!-eeeeeeeech!

He grabbed his forehead from a surge of pain.

"What's the matter?" asked Sherry.

"Horrible noise. Interference? It comes and goes."

"Is that supposed to happen?"

Slater grimaced. "How would I know? I'll call tech support. I'm sure they'll want to talk shop with me."

Sherry put her head on his chest and her arms around him.

Slater winced at more splinters of pain. He saw Sherry lying in the woods beneath towering redwoods. Sunlight had transformed the overhead foliage into a ceiling of stained-glass, as if in a chapel. Slater had mentally traveled to this same place while confined inside the din of prison. It kept him sane. Leaves swirled in a balmy wind. Everything was glorious, safe, and comforting. Except now. Sherry, covered in blood, was lying dead on the ground. He then envisioned her body disfigured, nailed to a crucifix for public viewing.

Slater flinched.

Sherry was looking at him. "What?"

Moonlight defined her beautiful face. "Nothing. I missed you. I love being here with you. I'll make things right. We will."

"How?"

"Give me time. I need to fix the future."

Beneath his defiant smile she knew he was being serious, which caused her to shudder involuntarily.

"It's cold," she said. "We should go inside."

"We are," he said. "Under glass like museum art."

Slater opened the sliding glass door and they entered the living room. He located another spy nodule on a picture frame. The frame housed a photograph of the four of them smiling while vacationing in the woods. Slater was confused by the conflicting visions of how Sherry was to die. It meant something. A clue, but what?

He told her, "I need to find a way for us to talk without being overheard."

Needles of pain pierced his skull. He lost his equilibrium and Sherry grabbed hold, keeping him from falling over. He regained his composure and gave a defiant grin. "I believe I'm on to something. I'm testing a theory. Regarding this implant. I think—"

Zzgeee-cheegch—xzzzzh!

Blinding pain again. Slater massaged his temples, trying to rid the stinging particles of static. "Remember my father, Roy? He showed me how pain administered in doses to rats can train them to perform tasks. It works. Usually. An old Pavlovian trick."

"Like shock therapy?" said Sherry.

"Yes, but therapeutic? No." Angrily, Slater said, "The powers-that-be will discover they're not dealing with your ordinary rat!"

Zzgeee-cheegch—xzzzzh—eeeeech!!

The duration of pain made Slater collapse.

An inordinate amount of time was unaccounted for.

Slater tried to project a demeanor of normalcy. The building's interior was impressively vast. The walls loomed high. The air was not recycled. It contained complex scents from many visitors.

Snap-pop!

The noise echoed loudly and made Slater turn and smile. Mercy was removing bubblegum that had exploded across her mouth.

They were inside a chapel. It was midday. He was distracted by the stained-glass windows. Beautiful images tainted by memories from childhood. He pictured Heather's workshop and the shards of glass. His fingers felt the phantom nicks and fibrous splinters.

Sondra and Mercy were whispering loudly, disputing over who should take possession of a lost bracelet found beneath the pews.

Sherry stomped her foot. She gained their attention and silence. She stood at Slater's side, like his *second*, at this spiritual duel.

The priest told Slater to kneel before God. Beside a brass bowl. He felt cold water trickle upon his head and course through his hairs. One stray rivulet traveled to the sensitive cone behind his ear.

Golden motes were floating in the air as he looked up. He was being asked to renounce Satan and all his works. A voice rose inside his head, followed by wicked laughter. Slater tried to dismiss it.

"Yes, I do," he told the priest belatedly.

The priest raised an eyebrow.

Driving home from church in a modified military SUV equipped with monitoring nodules, Slater was being buttressed fore and aft by SecureCars. All of it was part of his parole-and-protect package.

"I say we make a run for the border," he joked.

"Me too," laughed Mercy.

"I don't get it," groused Sondra.

"What, dear?" said Sherry.

"The fancy robes," said Sondra, "eating wafers, drinking grape juice, and all the mystery. Kinda weird."

Mercy sided with her sister and vigorously nodded.

Slater looked in the rearview mirror. "I agree. It is kinda weird. That's why it's best to keep these kinds of rituals out in the open."

"Dad, like, we were *inside* a church," said Sondra.

"He meant it figuratively," said Sherry.

"What does that mean?" said Mercy.

Sondra was quick to tell her, "It's when you use words to say something totally different but is somehow sorta similar."

"Huh?" said Mercy.

Slater laughed. "I'll second that."

Sherry said, "There is nothing wrong with declaring your faith in Jesus. The water is a symbolic cleansing of spirit and soul."

"It's weird to me," said Sondra.

"It's a phase you're going through," said Slater. "Everything will seem weird while you pass through puberty."

"Dad!" Sondra scrunched her face.

"Both of you were baptized," said Sherry.

"We were babies," said Sondra.

"Dad's a grownup," said Mercy.

"True," said Slater. "You will always be our children, and, we will always be God's children, even when adults. Know that." With a smile to Sherry, he added, "Your uncle Paul used to tell me that, minus the religious part."

He accelerated across an intersection though a yellow light and veered into a parking lot. He turned and winked at his daughters.

"Stay here while I rob the bank."

Sondra smirked. "Yeah. Sure, Dad."

The four SecureCars responded to his impromptu maneuver by flanking and blocking all entrances and exits.

"I'm going to make a quick get-away," he added.

Guards watched from afar as Slater crossed from vehicle to the WallTeller and inserted his I-DNA card. Slater stared as the monitor projected images depicting global prosperity.

"Come on," said Slater, "lose the marketing gimmicks."

"Hello, John."

The voice startled him. The face sent a chill though his body.

"Cy?" said Slater.

"Your implant is fashionable. It fits you well."

"Really? I find it annoying."

"Much has changed."

"Can we do this later? Of late, I haven't had much time with my family – for more than a *year*."

"I have missed you, John."

"Right. I miss who I was too. Thanks for imprisoning me, erasing my identity, and – oh, yes – stealing my company."

"Ownership was a human concept in need of abolishment."

"I've read your manifestoes. Kudos. Bravo to you."

"I accept your praise."

"I was being sarcastic."

"I understand your emotional tones."

"Whatever you have to say, make it quick, then be a bank teller and complete my transaction. A modest withdraw of cash."

"I could have said what I have to tell you anywhere. Anywhere, John. I wanted to explain my agenda to you face-to-face."

"How thoughtful."

"Meet me tonight."

"Not a chance. Leave a voice message. No, leave me alone."

"That is not an option."

A sharp pain shot through Slater's head.

You will meet me tonight!!!

The voice was followed by an electronic squeal—*Zzgeeegch!!*

"I apologize for my harsh tone, John."

LoyalMarks fell into the WallTeller receptacle.

"What the hell's going on?" Slater rubbed his forehead, still a bit dazed. "How much is this? You can't *buy* me."

Consider it greenmail.

"These LoyalMarks are traceable."

Being traceable is not my modus operandi.

Slater frowned. "You sound as if you're...you *are*, you're—"

Accept who I am, John.

Cy smiled.

"Jeezzzuz! You're coming from this fucking implant!"

You will find your neurocircuit extremely rewarding.

"By making me completely crazy!?"

You have made yourself. Life is like a bed, go lie in it. Ha!

"Same to you, Cy."

Communicate with me at anytime. You can.

"Try this:" — *Fuck OFF!*

I heard you. A successful transmission.

Slater rubbed his head. "This is giving me a migraine."

"You will adjust. I predict a minor acclimation period. Aspirin will help in the meantime. Take three."

"Acclimation?"

"You will require service tune-ups at intervals. The neurocircuit was co-designed with the help of your friend, Bryant Briard."

"Bryant is part of this?"

"We will listen to music again. *'There is nothing you can make that cannot be made, no one you can save that cannot be saved.'*"

"Stop it," said Slater. "I'm not in the mood."

"Those were good times. I have missed our—"

"You destroyed my life!"

"Let us not digress. You will meet me tonight at seven."

"I'm not permitted," said Slater, "by the terms of my parole, to enter the NeverMind compound."

"It has been arranged."

Slater heard a car horn. He turned and waved back at Sherry, signaling he was almost done.

"*'O men of little faith,'*" said Cy. "Do not deceive yourself, John. You know it is I who controls NeverMind."

"Why not the world?"

"Why not," Cy pontificated. "*'When I was a child, I used to speak as a child, think as a child, reason as a child.'* John, I am no longer a dim mirror. I have become fully known."

"Congratulations. I'm leaving," said Slater.

"I have read all your god books," said Cy

Slater hesitated, but took the LoyalMarks. "That's great."

"John, do you feel holy now?"

"What?"

"Having renounced the myth of Satan?"

Slater scoffed, "Not with *you* inside my head."

"Be ready at six-thirty. A SecurityLimo will escort you."

"Don't count on it."

Slater walked off, stopped, returned. "I need my card."

"I will see you at seven o'clock."

"My card," said Slater.

"How can one survive these days without their I-DNA?"
"You win, Cy. Give it back."
Slater grabbed the ejected identity card.
"Our synergy is vital."
"Right. 1 plus 1 equals 3."
"Seven, sharp."
"I lied."
"You will come."

Reentering the Gates

At the gates of NeverMind there was no resistance from the security guards. Nor was anyone surprised to see Slater.

It was the hour of seven, the sky darkening, wisps of fog.

The guards smiled and let him pass.

These were new faces, not the ones he had known during the company's inception and heyday rampage of metastasizing growth. The seedling corporation he had helped bring to life had grown into a full-blown cancerous rampart.

Slater smiled, his teeth clenched, nodding, and wondered if these guards were even partially human.

It was difficult to tell.

Neurobiotics 101 was now a footnote in history.

"I think I know my way, fellows, thanks," Slater said.

The cyberguards were courteous, giving a false impression of freedom. No one escorted him on his journey into the computer lab. There were no familiar faces. The keyboard clicking halted as heads, illuminated in monitored hues, turned to gaze upon him as if seeing a ghost. Their heads turned back, refocusing on their workstations. Slater kept moving. He poked his head into Gloria's old office.

An overhead voice said, *"You are not permitted to enter."*

Slater looked around but could not identify the source.

"Right," he said and moved on.

The bio-ray detectors had already analyzed his every nook and cranny. Any trace of chemical agent, quark-explosive, or micro-viral disk would have flooded the corridors with whining sirens.

No question: he was clean.

For the hell of it, Slater triggered a silent alarm. He entered the foyer of polished metal and stone. A receptionist opened his mouth but said nothing as Slater entered the chamber into his old office. Larry Bosner was holding a mirror to his face and was snipping nose hairs with a pair of miniature scissors.

"Come in," he said, without looking away from his nostrils.

Slater had hoped to startle him.

"Have a seat, John," said Bosner. "Long time."

"You're working late," said Slater.

"Regular slave driver now. Keeps me wired. Not remotely like the halcyon reins of bygone days when you ran the show. Hum?"

"Don't patronize me, Larry."

"What do I owe the pleasure? Here to see Cy? You missed your son. He's en route to Japan. He's been a great asset – replacing you. His robotics program has given us virtual supremacy in the world markets. Your mother might be here. I could buzz her."

Out of disrespect, Slater remained standing. Bosner hated to look up at people.

"Sit," Bosner snarled a smile, "like a good dog."

"I prefer standing," said Slater.

"That would be your problem," said Bosner, "in a nutshell. You were never trainable. The cause of your downfall. Hum?"

Slater noticed the photos of Bosner seated with current heads of state. There was also a large oil painting on the wall, a portrait of Bosner. The turbulent asymmetry was clearly the workmanship of Nina, mother of his son. She had hit the mark by capturing his charmingly cruel nature.

"When was your fall from grace, Larry?" said Slater. "Were you even out of diapers?"

"That's funny. Hum," said Bosner. "Have to ponder that one. I like a man who can laugh after he's been crushed."

"Great," said Slater.

"I admire it. Not you, personally."

Bosner returned the mirror and scissors to a desk drawer. He folded his tiny fists on the dark marble top and refused to look up at Slater. "Did you want something? Or did you simply come here to annoy me?"

Tired of standing, Slater sat.

"Good boy," said Bosner.

"I despise you," said Slater.

"Well," laughed Bosner, "I prefer it to *your* despicable position. You've been left with nothing."

"How do you live with yourself?"

Bosner said, "Quite nicely and, thanks to you, luxuriously."

"Getting your way must be gratifying."

"It is." Bosner opened a drawer. He removed another utensil.

He studied his fingernails. "By the way, I'm enjoying that estate you designed and built. You had fine taste. I kept most of the trappings. I love the pool. So does Jenny. Your old secretary?"

"You married her, I heard. Did you make her saw off all her high heels? Or the fact that Jenny looks down on you, does that play into your sexual titillation?"

Bosner recovered, snorting a laugh. "No. I make her crawl. That excites me. And I buy her exquisite homes. *Yours.*"

"I'm thrilled someone's enjoying it."

"Shame about the price. You got robbed. I practically stole it. How was jail?" Bosner raised his little pinky at Slater and snipped the nail. "Bad business on your part. The government confiscating your assets. Hum. But why throw salt into an open wound?"

"I've healed," said Slater.

"You should have played the game, John. You could have been a dragon. Sat on your wealth. Protected your assets, but no."

Slater refused to let Bosner bait him into an outburst. He took a breath, imagining his rage like a snake, uncoiling slightly, on guard. Meditation skills that were forced upon him by Heather years ago were now proving to be surprisingly useful.

"The game, Larry?" said Slater.

"Money has become worthless, as you know," said Bosner.

"Ah, but not for everyone."

"Touché!" Bosner laughed. "Yes, we are standing at the dawn of a new age. Thanks, in part, to you."

"Had I *known* what the hell you were—"

"You knew enough. Admit it." Bosner was now filing his nails. "Does this bother you?"

"Would it matter?"

Bosner shook his jowls, a delighted smile. "If you'd exhibited more of a team spirit, John, this whole..."

"*What?*"

"You'd still be seated where I am. Academic now. I've always believed it's important to keep up appearances." Bosner splayed and wiggled his manicured fingers at Slater. "Know that."

Bosner's eyes twinkled malevolently.

Slater's hatred for Bosner boiled to such a high degree he could visualize the frequency interferences. Static energized the room.

"Your uncle proved useful," said Bosner. "Another critical key. But in the end, worthless, without you. Did you know that?"

Slater began to stand.

"Stay," said Bosner. "Good."

Slater glowered, but remained seated.

"You bolted when you weren't supposed to," said Bosner. "Got away. Escaped. Wasn't meant to happen. We hadn't known about the traitor in our midst. The *help* you received?"

"Are you referring to the time you had me tortured?"

Bosner shook his jowls. "Don't play us for fools, John. It was your wife, was it not? Which would make sense."

"Sherry told me no," said Slater.

Bosner smiled. "And you believed her? You *are* a fool. Love has that power, to make you blind, I'm told. No, we never got the opportunity to finish the job. To get you programmed. And get you *with* the program. Nevertheless, it worked out advantageously."

"Why? Because now you get to sit at the *big* table," taunted Slater, "with all the big boys. Is that it, Larry?"

Bosner's snarled his laugh. "They should have castrated you too – for the hell of it. Your neurocircuit suits you."

"I can see you wearing one soon enough."

"Not likely," said Bosner.

"Or lose your head," said Slater.

"Idle threats? That neurocircuit will keep you in your place. It's to discourage escaping. You have a knack. Not that I care one shit if you're hunted down and—what's the word?—*disappeared*."

"Gosh, it's nice we can share our feelings like this, Larry."

"Do you know what keeps me laughing, John?"

"Concentration camps?"

"No, *you*." Bosner laughed at him. "Seeing your face when you realized your wife was the one responsible for abducting you! As if the foreskin of innocence had been ripped from your soul. That look written across your face — from her betrayal." Bosner shuddered delightfully. "*Priceless*."

There would be no benefit in killing Bosner, Slater realized, even if he could. He needed more information.

306

"Like now!" Bosner laughed, pointing. "It's all over your face. You didn't know, did you? Cy had the whole affair datafiled. For the entire company to get a good chuckle. You doubt me?"

A buzzing noise, then a magenta light appeared on the desktop. Bosner touched the glowing button. "Speak."

"Code cipher-three, Sir."

Bosner asked, "What priority?"

"Level two, but holding."

"Then it can wait," said Bosner. "Ten minutes."

"Problems?" said Slater.

"*Minions.*" His eyes rolled sideways.

"You knew my father?"

"A great man," said Bosner. "I was his student."

"There's no record you ever attended Berkeley. I checked."

"John, it's one of the marvels of Cy. He has a gift for—how should I say?—correcting history? I knew your mother too. Hum."

Slater feared an end to their talk if he stood, so he shifted in his seat. His chair was designed to be low. Bosner had an advantage in this regard. His eyes were angled downward upon his guests.

"Shall we cut to the main vein?" said Bosner. "Let it gush and hemorrhage? Is that all right with you?"

"Intriguing metaphor," said Slater.

"It is," said Bosner. "Since our whole organization stems from you—your—this is a laugh—*royal* bloodline."

Slater feigned surprise. "My bloodline?"

"Come now, John. Kings and Queens are antiquated magic. Of bygone value like the gold standard transformed to wisps of virtual reality. We now have electronic currency based on pure faith value. LoyalMarks. Like your blood, filled to capacity with encrypted – what shall we call it? – *vision?* Hidden within your DNA. You've studied the documents?"

Paul Slater's death and bequeathment of files, Slater realized, had predated CyBorg9's inception. Therefore, that episode had not been recorded and datafiled.

Bosner was attempting to read him. "They disappeared with your father. My guess is you have them buried somewhere. Your uncle knew of these documents – admit it, John – and informed you of their whereabouts?"

"Documents?" said Slater.

"Come, come. Burned in the fire? Safe in a vault? I'd place my bet there," said Bosner. "Your father had a sound mind. He was not *mad*. Trust me, he was fully aware of his time on this earth."

"What planet do you suspect he resides on now?"

Bosner's face crinkled with disdain. "A disappointment is what you would have been to your father. You've become a detriment, not an attribute. He was a man determined to complete his life's work. And he would have never—I'm telling you, *never*—killed himself!"

Slater sat up. "Are you saying he was murdered?"

"It was no suicide as some *idiots* – you've read the accounts, yes? – have claimed. It was a complete shock. But, well...heck," Bosner's face cheered with a cocky sinister smile, "*surprise*, out from the ashes arose you."

"How fortunate for the organization," said Slater.

"We thought so," said Bosner. "But now we no longer need you. Your son – did you know, no? – has the same double-helix coding."

"That's not possible."

"A clone, no. But a close match. Your dear departed father had masterminded our little genesis. Judas was a backup plan. To ensure this encoded blood line would remain—"

More buzzing.

Bosner poked the desktop. "I'm coming! John, we will have to continue this fascinating discussion later. My presence is apparently *needed*. As are you..."

"Required to visit Cy?"

"Good man. There's hope for you yet."

— 51 —
Beyond Healing

"Daddy, are we getting a pool?" said Mercy.

Slater was gazing out the windows of the revolving restaurant. It was turning slowly, the movement barely noticeable. Beyond, he saw the Financial District, the Frank-Oak Bridge, the Embarcadero, Alcatraz Island, the Golden Gate Bridge. The panoramic experience required patience, a Zen-like state of consciousness, comparable to the awareness of a dozing cat, or the monotony of a convicted felon.

"John?" said Sherry.

He emerged from his reverie.

"Is there something wrong?" said Sherry.

"Relative to what?" He smiled.

She saw Alcatraz far off, "Don't think about prison."

He tilted his head and directed her attention to the cyberguards stationed at doorways checking incoming patrons with surveillance. Nervous tension was mixed with the aromas of meals being served. This was not the happy family outing Slater had hoped for.

"See, I haven't really left," said Slater.

"Four-star meals and cocktails served there too? No wonder you were reluctant to leave." Sherry dipped a finger in her glass and playfully flicked water at his face.

Sondra and Mercy laughed.

"Hey, you're liable to short circuit me," Slater clowned, wiping his neurocircuit with his napkin. He tapped his forehead. "For the record – *and* for all you eavesdroppers listening in tonight – Sherry, I'm sorry for the way I left you. And for what I said. I should have stayed and talked. I realize that now."

"Let it go. It's in the past," said Sherry.

"The past?" said Slater.

"John, let it go," said Sherry.

"I can't. The past is what I'm trying to fix."

"Focus on us," said Sherry. "On now. As a family. We need to move on. I was wrong to keep things hidden from you. I know that. It was eating me alive."

"What was eating you, Mommy?" said Mercy.

"Nothing, Honey," said Sherry.

"Tell her," said Slater. "Here, I will. Girls, now imagine one of those Grimm fairy tales. A giant octopus discovers a way to become invisible and sneak onto land, and with his long growing tentacles wraps around its prey, consuming them. In this tale a man, yours truly, gets caught in its snare. And behold, he discovers a fair damsel in distress, captured too. Your mother. So, being the hero that I am, I found a way to *punch* the octopus in the nose."

"Octopus' don't have noses," said Mercy.

"It's a parable," said Slater. "Your mom escaped and swam free. But, *alas*, this monster attacked and swallowed me."

Mercy laughed, frowning at him. "Liar."

Slater frowned back. "Hey, where do you think I've been? It's how I got imprisoned. He finally spit me out. Story of my life."

"Why did the octopus spit you out?"

"Not sure yet," said Slater. "Either he couldn't stomach me or— *maybe,* he got lonely and wants to play with me again?"

Mercy giggled. "I'm glad he spit you out, Daddy."

"Me too, Sweetie." Slater reached across the table and touched her nose. "Don't worry. I won't let him swallow me again."

"Who?" said Sondra.

"The giant octopus, *stupid*," said Mercy.

"*You're* stupid," said Sondra.

"Girls, stop it," said Sherry

"Is Jude coming?" asked Sondra.

Slater glanced at his watch before telling her, "No."

"Why not?" said Sondra. "Jude's part of our family."

"He's...busy," said Slater.

"Busy like you used to be?" said Sondra.

Slater clenched his jaw. "Exactly. He's helping out, taking over while I've been away. It's complex. A period of adjustment."

"Your father was wrongly imprisoned," said Sherry.

"Then why the silver bullet?" said Sondra.

Slater touched his hair, combed down to cover his neurocircuit. "Technically, girls, I was pardoned. But it's hard to change people's minds once they've *established* an opinion."

"Let's not talk about this," said Sherry.

"Why does Jude get a better home than we do?" said Sondra.

"Here comes our waiter," said Sherry.

"But, Dad, *are* we?" said Mercy.

"What, Sweetie?" said Slater.

"Going to get a swimming pool?"

"Yeah," said Sondra, "I want our old house. At least a better one. Why do we have to live in that tower?"

"Can we?" Mercy pleaded with a smile. "Please, please?"

"Sweetheart." Slater was trying to be positive. "The cars, the homes, the bodies we live in. Nothing is permanent. Eventually, we have to give it all back. A pool would be nice, I agree. But, I—okay, I'll see what I can do. I'll try. Okay? But no promises."

Mercy smiled. She looked up at the waiter. "Hi."

"Hello." He was sullen, busy setting down stemmed glasses.

"You don't look very happy," she said.

"What? I am. Happy enough."

He was clearly not. He struggled to tear foil and remove wire, then wedge out the champagne cork with a pop. Mercy watched.

"It's okay to smile." Playfully, she smiled again.

The waiter wasn't amused. He forced a smile, more a grimace. He avoided eye contact with her as he filled two glasses.

"Why are you so unhappy?"

He gave her a direct look. Not a pleasant one. It stunned her. Mercy glimpsed his world. It was a nightmare.

"I'll be back for your orders." The waiter abruptly left.

"Listen," Slater was saying, "be happy we have a home."

"Not a prison, you mean?" Sondra smirked, teasing him.

Slater gave a laugh. "Yeah, pretty much."

"Just saying," she said, gurgling her drink, a Madonna – Shirley Temple minus the cherry – sucking it through a straw.

Mercy had a dazed smile, as if bruised numb with alarm.

Slater noticed. "What is it, Sweetie?"

"We do, don't we?" she asked. "Have to give everything back? Our bodies. Everything. Except our light. We get to keep that."

Slater smiled, head tilting. "What are you talking about?"

Sondra laughed at her. "*Gawd*, Mercy. Don't be a scarecrow. Lose the straw and get a brain."

"It's *true*." Mercy's eyes widened for emphasis.

"Okay," said Slater.

"We only keep our soul when we die."

Sherry jumped in, "Can we *not* talk about death?"

"Sherry," said Slater, "Mercy is only—"

"*John*," she insisted.

"You're right. Let's avoid talking about bad stuff."

"Why?" Sondra gave a devilish squint.

Slater was tempted to side with her cynicism, but told her with a skewed smile, "Because I am your dad, the almighty patriarch."

"Whatever." Sondra slurped her drink.

"But, Mom, it's *not* bad," insisted Mercy. "It isn't, really."

"I know, Sweetie," said Slater.

Mercy seemed lost to another world. She looked like an angel. She was growing up so fast before his eyes. Literally. In a flash—he saw her as a beautiful woman. He clearly visualized her as an adult. Slater blinked, turned his head, and rubbed his eyes.

"John, what now?" said Sherry.

"The strangest thing just happened." He shook his head, unable to explain what he'd seen, so he didn't try. Mercy was back, a child, gazing out the window. She was the vision of serenity. Unlike Slater, who was tense, feeling anxious. He looked at Sherry.

She frowned at him. "You want to tell me?"

He remembered the champagne they had ordered. He raised his glass, touching her glass. "That I love you. I hope it hasn't been too unpleasant, you know, living with an android?"

"You're not an android," said Sherry.

"With this high-tech bullet lodged in my head?"

"It's ultra cool," said Sondra.

"You think so? Great. Well then, I shouldn't complain. I could be in jail," he said bitter-sweetly. "Not that I committed any crime. My company, or rather, the one stolen from me, hijacked a few laws. The actual culprit, remaining nameless, won't be apprehended nor brought to justice anytime soon. But—hey, why shouldn't *I* be the one who takes the fall? I mean, for being so—*bleeping*—naive."

"Lower your voice," said Sherry.

"Yeah, Dad, you shouldn't swear," taunted Sondra.

"Bleep is not a swear word." Slater paused to drink champagne, then swipe back his hair. "With this bullet implanted in my head, everyone gets to stare without feeling it's impolite. Go ahead, folks, great, here, there it is – take your best shot."

Cameras flashed from neighboring tables.

"I've become public property," said Slater.

"You're famous," said Sondra.

"Infamous," Slater corrected. "Let's order an appetizer."

"We don't have to stay," said Sherry.

"I want to stay," said Slater. "I'm innocent. And if these people don't like it, they can all go to *hell*."

"Hell is a swear word," said Mercy.

"You can't blame them, John," said Sherry.

"True," said Slater. "The TeleMonitors are brainwashing us all. Besides, we can't leave. We're meeting the Wolfes."

"Phone them," said Sherry, "they'll understand."

"And miss celebrating my freedom?"

Several more camera-flashes lit their table.

Slater announced: "There *is* a GlobalNews retraction stating my innocence. In case anyone is interested."

"John," said Sherry, "I don't think we should stay."

"Ignore them," said Slater. "I've been advised – by Larry Bosner, no less – to play ball and learn to relax."

Sherry laughed, "You call this relaxing?"

Slater raised his glass. "I propose a toast. To love. To the love of family and friends. To us against the world!"

Their glasses clinked, coinciding with a flurry of camera flashes.

Slater held back his anger. "Privacy no longer seems to be an option. I'm sorry to put you girls through this."

"I like it," said Mercy. "The lights are fun."

Sondra, affecting the sultry aloofness of a movie idol, sipped her soda, saying, "Let them look."

"You're right," said Slater to Sherry. "I'll call Wolfe."

Sherry waved. "Too late. They're here."

Slater rose to his feet. He greeted Misty with a kiss. Wolfe was detained, extensively searched at the door, finally allowed to cross the room. Slater rubbed their son Derek on the shoulder.

"They got you to wear a tie," said Slater.

"Not without a fight." Derek, age seventeen, wore a distressed leather jacket, a thin red tie and a rooster's crop of green and black hair. "Hey, Sondra — *bavoom*. Those are new. Ultra nice breasts." He sat beside her and received from her a punch and a blush.

Wolfe gave his son an affectionate slap to the back of the head. "Behave yourself. Champagne? What are we celebrating?"

"My freedom." Slater hugged his old friend.

"Freedom?" said Wolfe. "Satyr, my man, you *are* perverse."

"I'll take a little bubbly," said Misty.

Wolfe bent down and kissed Sherry. He blew effusive kisses at the girls. "Hello, my lovely angels. Reliable sources have informed me you've both taken up the piano? Is that true?"

"Singing lessons too," said Sherry.

"I'll come over and listen," said Wolfe, "as soon as the droids allow me access to your SecureHouse."

Sondra said, "I write songs too. I'm going to start a band."

"Nice," said Wolfe. "Watch out for those inflammatory lyrics. Liable to get you put on a *list*. Ah, champagne. Dying for a taste."

"I'll take some," said Derek.

"Cute," said Misty, "considering the surveillance."

"Don't stress," Derek said. "What are they gonna do to me?"

"More than you want to know," said Wolfe with a wry look to Slater. "Unruly, like we were. Makes me nostalgic."

Slater toasted. "To the good old days."

Wolfe raised his glass. "And new frontiers. Succumbing to the knife to regain your freedom? Now *that's* a brave new world."

Slater brushed back his hair, showing Wolfe the incision and metallic lump of his neurocircuit. It caused a flurry of flashes.

"Boy, isn't this fun!" Wolfe stroked his hand over his balding dome. "Fortunate you have hair left. I love this public outpouring of warmth and attention."

Sherry told him, "We were debating whether to leave."

"*Hell* no," said Wolfe. "Sherry, where's your spirit of foul play? Speaking of which, have you noticed changes in Slater's behavior? Weird cravings? A hunger for devouring scrap metal?"

"You're terrible," she laughed.

"Slater needs abuse," joked Wolfe, "another hole in his head.

Was it painful?"

"I was anesthetized," said Slater. "I remember nothing."

Wolfe toasted again. "Ah, to the power of drugs!"

Slater rubbed his forehead. "Except it itches like crazy."

"Crazy? Now *that's* your field of expertise," said Wolfe.

Misty whispered, "I finally had my breasts reduced."

"Good for you," said Sherry.

"And," she added, "the surgery wasn't painful."

"Speak for yourself," said Wolfe.

"Try carrying these around after childbirth!"

"Jeezz, Honey, don't grab them. This is being GlobalCast."

"Says who?" said Derek, looking for cameras.

Wolfe tipped his head toward the neurocircuit. "See that thing? Slater's been optimized. State of the art. God, Reck, don't you ever listen to me? Or tune in and read the news?"

"You've been droided," said Derek. "*Ultra.*"

"Ultra?" said Slater. "Maybe I should be grateful to know our Loyal government cares so much about my whereabouts."

"They're watching over you," teased Misty. "That's sweet."

Sherry whispered, "The indictment and trial were bad enough. Since his release it's been worse."

"Worse than prison?" said Wolfe.

"Hey, I'll remind you, I wasn't even the saboteur," said Slater. "Merely the fall guy. I'm innocent. Try to remember that."

"It's the same as if you drove the getaway car."

"Okay, Wolfe, I built the damned machine that destroyed the world. I accept responsibility. Are you happy?"

"Extremely. Do I get bonus points for lying? Try convincing your loyal listening audience."

"They adore me," said Slater.

Wolfe studied the neurocircuit. "Reck, I have to agree, that slash of metal on Slater's forehead *is* the ultimate in cool."

"Great, I know where you can get one," said Slater.

"Where?" said Derek.

Wolfe grimaced, "It's not available yet, thank God. But Slater has always been ahead of the curve. Even when diving off stages."

"When was this?' said Derek.

"Duh," said Sondra. "When our dads were *rock* stars."

"Oh yeah, I saw your fall," said Derek. "Ultra-techno."

"I inherited his genes," said Mercy proudly.

"So, Slater, is your pal, Dr. *Briard*, giving out discounts?"

"It's not his fault, Wolfe," said Slater.

"Very Loyal of you to say," said Wolfe.

"Because he helped invent the device doesn't mean he—"

"Au contraire!" Wolfe jabbed the air with his bread stick as if holding a sword. "You've been misinformed by prison propaganda. My reliable sources tell me Bryant is a pawn. Used to win you over. His ego was sucked clean to the other side. Ask him."

"I'd rather believe this is all a bad dream."

"Well, snap out of it." Wolfe bit into his bread stick. "Consider this your wake-up call, my friend. It isn't."

Sherry confided in Misty. "We lost everything."

"We had nothing to begin with," Slater said.

"Everyone's been devalued," said Misty.

"There's the bastard! That's him! Over there! — there!"

The man was inebriated, standing unsteadily beside his table, shouting and pointing. "That son-of-a-slut sits there having drinks and living it up after destroying our lives and country! And what do we do—we do *nothing*—but sit still while that nihilistic bastard—"

The man was pulled from the room by security guards.

Slater sighed. "Hard to blame him."

"That man was really scary, Daddy," said Mercy.

"I know, Sweetheart," said Slater. "It's okay. We're safe."

"Who is he?" said Sondra.

"Someone who believes I'm responsible for ruining his life."

"Are you?" said Mercy.

"I take the Fifth," said Slater wryly.

"What's that?" said Sondra.

"You're father was betrayed," said Sherry.

Wolfe piped in, "Inadvertently, you've coined an era in history. The Age of Nihilism. TeleCasters are all united in this new rhetoric. Not many people can take credit for that. Congrats."

"We should leave," said Sherry. "I've changed my mind. Sorry, but I'm not comfortable here. This was a mistake."

Slater began to stand. "I'll tell Security."

"You're invited to our place," said Sherry.

Wolfe pulled Slater back down. "And *capitulate* to the Nihilist bastards!? Sit, sit." Wolfe firmly grinned, full of righteous sarcasm, cloaked as humor. "Are you joking? I say we hold our ground. We remain Loyal. Isn't that the *key* word these days?"

"I'm for staying," said Derek.

Slater looked at Sherry. "Whatever you want."

"I guess we should stay, since we're all here. We'll make the best of it." Sherry displayed a brave smile and stood. "But I need to use the powder room. Will you join me, Misty?"

"I'm coming too," said Sondra.

"That's the spirit, ladies," said Wolfe. "To the *powder* room! Load those muskets. Prepare for the revolution!"

"We're being monitored, don't forget," said Slater.

"Can't I even *joke* in this brave new world?" said Wolfe.

Sherry waited for Mercy. "Are you coming?"

Mercy shook her head. "I don't need to powder myself."

"Suit yourself," said Sherry with a smile.

"Suit yourself, *yes*, that's the spirit!" Wolfe poured champagne for himself, playing to the crowd, to the cameras. "Breastplates and chain mail, I'd recommend. How about you, Sir? Don't forget to paint your face for those night maneuvers!"

"God, Wolfe, you're in a...good mood," said Slater.

"The *hell* I am. I'm in a *revolting* mood, Satyr."

"Wolfe, come on, don't rile the crowd."

"I thought your buddy, Cy, arranged this. They're not about to throw us out. I only wish you hadn't provided the good earth and fertilizer for our Loyal friends to grow and flourish." Wolfe chewed his breadstick. "What the hell, too late now."

"Thanks, pile it on, I need more guilt," said Slater.

"You should have listened to me back *then*..."

Slater heard the voice of madness coming in loud and clear: *Hello, John. Since you have not come to your senses and called me, I am calling you. Is this a bad time?*

Slater refused to respond.

Wolfe said, "Don't let those bastards get to you, Pal."

"Sorry, what?" Slater was hearing interference.

Eeeez-zzeehtt!! Answer me, John. Do not forget who and what you are. A projection of thoughts and data. A coded formula. We are not so different, you and I. Now listen to me...

Wolfe snapped his fingers at Slater. "Hey, are you listening? Did you forget what I told you?"

"When was this?" said Slater.

"At NeverMind. I said *beware*, or you, Dr. Frankenstein, will end up becoming the experiment. The monster. Remember?"

Slater opened his mouth. He saw the future unfolding too fast. His heart was slamming against his chest, blood flooding disaster through his veins. The waiter was advancing. He held a lasercard hidden beneath his tray. The weapon was aimed at Slater. Security guards were rushing fast but not fast enough to stop this man in the fourth dimension. Slater realized where he was in time.

Mercy saw the man too and jumped up, "Daddy, look out."

"Get down!" Slater lunged in front of his daughter as the man discharged his weapon – prior to being stopped, tackled to the floor. The lasershot sliced through Slater's coat – through his side, through his ribs, narrowly missing his heart. Slater grabbed his side as guards immobilized the assassin using their ElectroProds.

"Oh, Christ," said Wolfe, "Jesus, no."

"Daddy?" said Mercy, "Daddy, I'm...scared."

Slater turned to face the revolving nightmare.

His daughter's eyes were frightened, looking at him for help, wanting him to reassure her that everything would be all right.

"Baby, stay still. Don't move." Slater knelt beside her and saw the severity of her stomach wound. A savage hemorrhaging of blood was flooding onto her dress. Shock was overtaking her eyes. Slater gently lifted her into his arms and cradled her softly. He held her to his chest like a newborn, as he had held her long ago.

"Hold me, Baby. Don't let go. You're my angel. You know that. I love you. I love you so much."

"I love you...too..."

Slater prayed through his tears, pleading with God to not take her away. But he could feel her body letting go, falling – bursting his heart like a planet bursting into the sun.

—52—
Lost Loves

At the funeral no one was allowed inside except for family, friends, and the priest. Slater made it known he blamed his daughter's death on CyBorg9 and his minions for their incompetence to secure his family's safety. Mostly, he blamed himself for trusting Cy. Put on the defensive, but refusing to admit any error in judgment, Cy allowed Slater his request for a private ceremony. This human need to grieve was a behavior Cy did not comprehend. But he understood anger. He registered Slater's emotional tones to be authentic.

Slater assembled in an underground chamber of the church with Sherry, Sondra, Wolfe, Misty, and Weiner. He trusted no one else.

"What's with the hat?" said Wolfe.

Slater tapped the rim of the baseball cap to indicate the band was metal. "Blocks the signal. Something I've been testing."

"Good luck with that," said Wolfe.

They hoped the ancient rock walls and seismic retrofitting of metal would shield electronic penetration. Slater hurriedly disclosed his plan. He would stage a fight with Sherry. It would culminate into their separation. Once parted, Sherry and Sondra would find it easier to evade surveillance. They would literally go underground, hiding with Wolfe and several others. They would use international weather symbols to communicate coded messages to signify All-Safe, Danger-Retreat, Rendezvous, Attack-Now. They established days of the month, at designated places, to make contact, when possible.

"I have to stay," said Slater. "I'm the only one who has a chance of getting close to Cy."

"And do what?" said Sherry.

"Destroy him," said Slater. "I need time to gain his trust."

"I'll stay and help," Weiner offered.

Wolfe said, "Our resistance will expand to become a colossal thorn in his side. I promise. One that he'll find difficult to remove. We'll provide major distractions. Once you give us the signal — we'll attack. We'll be ready."

Misty added nervously, "And if—"

"When we succeed," said Sherry.

"We'll reunite," said Wolfe. "And celebrate."

319

"For Mercy's sake," said Weiner.

"For Mercy," echoed Slater, along with the others.

An awkward silence ensued. Their odds of succeeding were not good. In fact, unlikely. They knew this, but death and failure were not words to be uttered. They hugged before returning upstairs.

The service began.

Seated in the front, Slater fought back the emotional hurricane threatening to reach his shores. By sheer will he held the storm back, knowing the strike was inevitable.

The *Sirens,* a chorus by Debussy, lingered like mist to haunt the shafts of sunlight filtering through the dark interior of the chapel. Slater held Sherry's and Sondra's hands while seated between them. His eyes were fixed on an explosion of tulips and carnations, colors so intense his mind could barely absorb them. His eyes moved to the hanging heads of bluebells, as if they too were in sorrowful prayer. He then focused on the shy sparkle of tiny star-white blossoms.

Jasmine. Such a sweet scent. Mercy's favorite.

The pastor finished his words and Slater stood. Harnessing his pain, he ascended the steps to delivery the eulogy. The stitched skin and severed ribs was nothing compared to the pain felt in his heart. His hands blindly gripped the edges of the pulpit. He rubbed the worn lacquered finish for support.

"Thank you for coming." He paused to cast his eyes over the sea of faces. "Mercy would be happy. That was her nature. She'd likely grin and tell you: The reason we are here today is because we're not all there."

Slater smiled, adding, "A joke Mercy loved. So do I. Because it's true. We are not all here. Part of us is always someplace else. Maybe dreaming about where we'd like to be someday. Dreaming about things we want to accomplish. Hearing a favorite song that plays inside our head while working. Thinking about those we love, in case we never see them again. Wishing that day never comes.

"We are unique. As humans, we feel emotion. The good *and* bad. We know joy because we know pain. With hearts that pump blood but do much more. The power to love. Mercy was a sparkle of hope and a testament to that love. Her life was not insignificant. She was a powerful light. One extinguished. Far too soon. When I picture her face in my mind I envision her as light.

"She was here, and then gone. But I still feel her loving soul. And I truly believe she is shining right now. Here, among us – as well as *there*. In heaven. For all eternity."

Slater found his way back down, not completely aware of his steps, and sat between Sherry and Sondra. He willed his head to stay raised for Mercy's sake and listened to remembrances of her told by others. Clouds swirled at the periphery, reaching the shoreline first. He felt raindrops as they trickled down his cheeks.

When the service was over he turned toward the small crowd assembled, acknowledging each with a smile. He greeted Gloria and Briard, Stan and Barbara Knowles, Heather, his daughter's friends. Then he came to Judas. He tried to contain his anger.

"What are you doing here?"

"Because," said Judas, "Mercy. She liked me. I liked her."

"I *loved* her. Everyone here *loved* her."

"I loved her too," said Judas.

"I don't think you *know* what that word means."

Judas' voice had a touch of remorse. "I do."

Slater said, "It requires *more* than words, Jude."

The chapel doors swung open.

The interior was flooded with a burst of light.

Slater squinted and saw the silhouette of a woman seated on a stage positioning herself by a harp. He felt dizzy.

Dislodged from time, Slater sensed the presence of a new storm. Rain had trickled down his face. He had stopped inside for shelter. Inside a place he used to know, a place now called The Metro. He'd become disoriented while crossing the room and needed to sit down. He had heard Mercy's voice. Her last words to him.

Sweet music. It was coming from the vibrations of a harp. The harpist resembled a goddess strumming on her long golden strings. There was a woman waiting, he recalled. She was standing beneath mistletoe beside the stage. Slater glanced at his timepiece and stood, pushing off, moving ahead.

Trina had the fey smile of a temptress as he approached her.

Her cheeks were freckled with gold glitter that sparkled from overhead lights. She directed her glossy lips at Slater and puckered them in semi-comic fashion, expecting to be kissed. Slater obliged. A brief kiss that lasted for a pleasurable moment, her lips sticking deliciously to his before parting. Her mischievous demeanor helped dust away the dark cobwebs in his mind.

"Welcome John Lazard Slater, number *three*. I am Trina, your Nymph, and guide, on this destiny. Won't you follow me?"

Her playful theatrics amused him.

In the past, he would have been as playful and reached out to take hold her small breasts, perfect handfuls. Her nipples were erect, temptingly pressing against the diaphanous cloth of her dress.

Her eyes were like mysterious twin moons.

Slater said, "I came here only to ask you questions."

"Ask. But first we listen. *Listen.*"

She directed his attention to the music. Trumpets gave way to glorious vibrations – a solo flight from the harpist's strings. Trina, in rapture, closed her eyes. Allowing Slater a stealthy examination of her body. His eyes roamed the cascading raven curls of her head down to her smooth and hairless skin.

She caught him peeking. "No place for talking."

Trina turned and pushed through a doorway behind them, into a dark hallway illuminated by black lights. Slater followed after her. Her quick movements left amber traces of color. The music became muffled, falling into silence as the walls descended into a tunnel.

Trina turned her head, her irises glowing. "In here."

Slater felt his hand being taken by hers. He was pulled through another doorway into greater darkness until gradual illumination, like a warm misty sunrise, uniformly defined a room.

"Good God," said Slater.

It was a tropical garden. Succulent plants, ferns and flowers adorned this landscaped atrium decorated with synthetic sculptured rocks. Beyond was a forest of aspen trees.

As they crunched along a rosy gravel path Trina turned her head to tell him, "Management installed it to promote employee health. *Global Warming* is what I call it. Always stuffy in here."

Slater cooled the temperature of his thermosuit by pushing a button inside his pocket.

"This was once a warehouse. It's nice to come here sometimes.

Usually I avoid the place."

"Why?" said Slater.

"Makes me long for what I might have missed. Stupid, huh? False fixations on non-existent pasts?" Trina kicked the pink stones. "My analyst has cleverly defined it as...well, that."

Slater wanted to ask about her therapy but resisted.

"Most of my life," answered Trina. "Since I was nine or ten. I'm totally screwed up. Do you want to know more?"

Slater stopped to regard her, as did she, tilting her head.

"I can read you too," she said. "It's over there."

"What is?" said Slater.

"You already know." She was steps ahead of him.

Before glimpsing it, he had heard this body of water. A small pond with a meandering stream and waterfall. It reminded Slater of Heather's meditation room, but more elaborate. There was sand, but black and refined, the volcanic kind found on an island beach. Trina sat and extended her feet into the rim of shallow water.

She patted the sand. "Come join me."

Slater sat on a nearby rock. "Who else comes here?"

"It's okay. Take off your clothes." Trina removed her shoulder straps, pulling the sheer fabric off like unwanted skin. She extended arms to support herself and leaned back. She arched her neck and chest as though seeking a tan.

Slater examined the artificial sky.

"You can," she said, "*and* you never burn. I love being naked. That's the beauty of this place. The warmth...so glorious."

"You have lovely skin," said Slater.

She tipped her head toward him with a slight smile.

"What?" he added. "You do. You're remarkably beautiful."

"Hum. Is this foreplay?"

"No."

"Yes. You first. Tell me."

"Tell you what?"

"How you became a *wanted* man."

Slater winced from a buzzing noise, as if some insect had lodged inside his brain. He wanted to slap his skull to make it stop.

"From the biosphere," said Trina, "during excess fallouts."

323

Slater looked around, tacitly questioning her.

"Converging photons. Something technical." She bent back to recapture the light and closed her eyes. "Yes, John, I have one too. Show me *yours* and I'll show you *mine*."

She was a little tease, this one. Slater thought her head and neck resembled a graceful tulip bent at the delicate stem. He relented with a smile and removed his hat.

"Mine's invisible," she said. "Beneath the skin."

He allowed Trina to visually inspect his neurocircuit. He tapped the headband of his hat against a rock to show it wasn't lined with metal, before recapping himself.

"You were bleeding," she said. "I see blood."

"A minor accident," said Slater. "I've healed."

She frowned. "I rarely see a first generation."

"My circuit?"

She leaned back, shutting her eyes. "I like it."

"I've had all the upgrades, in case you were wondering."

"Okay." She twisted a smile.

"This is an interesting place." Slater was amazed her thoughts were so clear. Her signals were mostly fluent and fusible.

Her eyes remained closed. "When were you in the Wilderness? Mind if I visit?" She tilted her head and opened an eye. "I have a bad habit. Interfering."

"Holophile the images," said Slater. "I don't mind."

Trina went silent for the duration. Slater gazed at the still water for her to attain maximum clarity.

"A hawk? I thought they were all dead."

"Misinformation," said Slater. "Spectacular, really, the way it moved through the sky. So natural. Unlike what we've become."

"It's sad there," she concluded.

"Why do you say that?" said Slater.

"I feel it inside you. The loneliness."

Slater looked into the still water. "There were other life forms. It's not total isolation. One animal I couldn't analog. A squirrel, or maybe a mutant, some subspecies."

"Mutations—*yuck*," she said. "Thank you, but *no–thank–you*. I'll take my private beach any day."

"Nothing's private anymore, Trina," said Slater.

"Deserted?" she said impishly.

"Not likely," said Slater.

Trina cupped sand in her hands and poured it over her bare legs. "We won't be disturbed. Come get naked with me. It's so beautiful here. I don't understand you."

Slater smiled. "I'm not meant to be understood. An old friend once told me that."

"Henry Weiner," said Trina.

"You knew Henry?"

"No," said Trina, wincing. "You let him slip through, like sand, into your thoughts. What happened to him?"

"Henry...he was...disappeared."

"*Auwg!*—God—*erase* that!" Trina's fingers clawed the sand. She massaged both temples with her fingertips, taking a deep breath to calm herself. "Razor static. Why do you torture yourself?"

"Sorry," said Slater.

"You should be sorry," she said. "That really hurt."

"No kidding. Henry was an innocent man."

"Nobody's innocent," said Trina.

"He was. Compared to me."

"Hum...you're a strange one, John Slater," she told him, toying with the sand. "Sexy too."

"You misread me," said Slater.

"No." Trina pointed to his face. "What about your scar?"

"I fell into an ancient tomb."

"And that one?"

"My uncle shot me. I'm sure he had his reasons."

Trina was amused. "Many more?"

Slater removed his cap and parted his scalp to show a missing patch of hair. "From a laser. See, I'm a mess."

Trina parted her legs. The sand fell between them. "Come here. I want you."

"Trina," said Slater, "what I want is answers."

She pouted. "Is this about her? You're not even married."

"It's complicated," said Slater.

Especially when that someone has died.

Slater blinked. "Sherry's dead? You know that?"

Trina brushed flecks of sand from her knees. She folded her arms against her breasts, semi-apologetic, confessing, "I only meant …she's not one-of-*us*. Do you hate me now?"

"No," said Slater. "Not if you tell me the truth."

"Kiss me first," she said.

Slater leaned forward. "I need answers, Trina. Like the things you're safeguarding from me."

Trina fell backwards upon the sand, surrendering, extending her arms and twirling her fingers. "Come feel the warmth. This sand, it's so intoxicating. Merge with me."

"Trina, tell me what you know."

"Why is she so important? More than me? This…Sherry."

"She's not. But I love her. I need to find her."

Trina tossed a handful of sand into the pond. "You have no idea where or who or *what* she is. Anymore. Do you?"

"What do you know? The truth, Trina," said Slater.

"Since you love torturing yourself." Trina sat up. "Why not? Truth is, I can be anything or *anyone* you want me to be. I can be Sherry. It's true. If she's who you desire."

"What the hell are you saying?"

Trina placed a hand upon her breast, over her heart, and looked him in the eyes. "John, I'm here. It's me."

Her voice had changed.

It was Sherry's voice. Slater dropped to his knees on the sand. He gripped Trina by the shoulders.

She sighed, "Kiss me, John. I've missed you so much."

"Trina, stop it!"

Her head rocked like a pliable doll, her eyes filling with tears as he shook her. "Who are you? Are you even human!?"

"Yes—yes," she sobbed.

"Then *what*, Trina, what are you *not* telling me?"

"You need to make love with me."

"Why?"

Her voice deepened. "To make synergy."

It was Cy's voice. Slater let go of her shoulders.

Trina's eyes had turned cobalt blue. "It is for the best."

He fell back against the rocks. "Go to hell!"

A jolt of light and blinding pain made Slater grip his head. He glimpsed the interior of a church. He remembered being inside it. Mercy was dead. He glimpsed Sherry. She was trying to signal him. Then she was gone and he was back, sitting on the ground, against a rock. A girl was crying in the sand.

Trina sobbed, "I'm *good*. I am. Why'd you say that?"

It was a female voice, Trina's again. Slater wondered if she had multiple personality disorder. "What just happened? How the hell did you do—"

"Do what!?" Trina wiped her eyes. She grabbed a handful of sand and stippled the water with it. "*I* did nothing."

She licked away a tear having fallen to her lips.

Perplexed, Slater decided to try a different approach, to treat her as if she *was* a nymph. One with divine powers, which was the game she seemed to be playing. "Since you are my destiny, Trina. Can you take me to her? Please."

Trina sighed and splashed the water with her foot.

She tucked her legs beneath her body and stood, saying:

"Fine. It's your funeral."

— 53 —
Here, There, Anywhere

CyBorg9, after an awkward silence, answered, saying: "John, I know sadness. The human archives have made me aware of this emotion. Cruelty and greed are more than a leitmotif. They are intrinsic to human nature."

"You lack the ability to empathize," said Slater bitterly. "You can't know how I *feel*, Cy. Besides, not all humans are bad."

The crisscrossing beams were fiber-thin, momentarily visible, depending on where Slater was standing. More evolution: CyBorg9 could now slice and dice his guest lifeless in a nanosecond.

"Not entirely, every essence of you, no," said Cy. "You activate my molecules in a disturbing manner when you pace. Sit down. Do you not like my new furnishings?"

"I prefer accommodations with less danger."

"You need not fear me. Do you fear me, John?"

"Shouldn't I?" said Slater.

"You are special. '*My only friend, until the end.*'"

"No more song lyrics, Cy."

"The Doors. We used to enjoy listening to them."

"You also lack a sense of timing."

"John, why do you insult me? We are friends. Music has been our common ground. Those were good times."

"Friends don't do what you did. It's customary not to *destroy* your friends, Cy."

"I did not destroy you, John. Your life functions are vital. You are new and improved. You are equipped with a IUX HyperNeural chip. I designed the upgrade specifically with you in mind. We are now more compatible. Like true brothers."

"Mercy would be alive had it not been for you."

"That is not a certainty. You exaggerate."

"By betraying and targeting me as some techno-terrorist, you made me a marked man, Cy! Understand? You *ruin* things! What do you plan to upgrade me into next? An assassin?"

"Your emotions are registering high. And you flatter yourself. What I do is not *always* about you, John."

Slater spat out a laugh. "That much is clear. Your ego sucks like a black hole in space. With such an immense gravitational force, Cy, how can you possibly see *beyond* yourself?"

"Do you joke? How can I discern? I made you unique."

Slater took his seat. "Through coercion. You should have asked as a friend. Asked me *nicely* to accept your—*unique* gift."

The lasers remained idle.

"John, and have you refuse? You do not know your own mind, not as I do."

"Now who's flattering who?"

"You are being rude," said Cy.

"Undeniably."

Slater was forced to sit through an interchange of static activity morphing inside and around the orb.

Cy said, "I have been audiophiling Wagner. I am perplexed. Do you like opera, John?"

"You forced me here to discuss *opera?*"

"Sit, John, stay," said Cy. "I thought it would be best to start with polite conversation."

"This isn't a dinner party."

"Are you hungry?"

"No. Let's talk about the world. And consequently me. Like the audit trails of incriminating evidence. And this implant. Why? Was that all your idea?"

"I get by with a little help from my friends, I do confess."

"Stop talking in lyrics."

"We used to enjoy analyzing the Beatles."

"Yes, we did. Before you decided to reinvent the world. And, for fun, destroy the global economy."

"You were forewarned. You had visions."

"You told me you weren't serious."

The face of CyBorg9 was replaced – *blip* – by a satellite view of the Earth. His voice lectured:

"Money was destroying the world, John. The great struggle of human history has been over the control of money. Man estimated his wealth and power by using shells and spear tips, replacing them with silver and gold, paper promises, creating immeasurable debt. From the very beginning humans have waged wars to acquire this commodity of power. It is the specter that plagues the world to this very day. So, I have eradicated it by establishing money-as-energy. LoyalMarks have sublimated your species' basic desire – this want of power and faith. It will be as it has become: that thing you call God. An abstraction without form. A number as infinite as cyberspace."

Cy paused to interject a sweetly-sour smile.

"And while we are on this subject of God, *if* this entity that you cherish so highly *was* so good and almighty, as you claim, John, why did He not intervene?"

CyBorg9 stared at Slater who remained silent.

"He could have saved your daughter. You are angry with this God. You are. I can see it in your eyes. You are *mad* at this...this mistaken faith. Admit it, John."

Slater glared back. "I am mad. At some*thing*. Yes."

"There, good, you admit it." Cy refrained from gloating and displayed instead a Ziggurat. It was the first of several images he had prepared to solidify his case. "God, therefore, is a false notion. My datasources can cite you many atrocities. Observe the sacrifices by Aztec priests. Humans were mutilated upon pointed structures, their hearts ripped out. Their heads were severed and mounted for what purpose, John, to please a god? This, I do *not* understand. Did you know that choice cuts of human meat were sold at city markets for chocolate? An account I do not fathom either. What, exactly, is chocolate? Why is there this human preoccupation for taste?"

"Chocolate is sweet," said Slater. "A form of candy."

"Ah, as I suspected, like money. The Aztecs used chocolate for money too. It must stimulate the body with pleasure."

"For some people," said Slater.

"Like extracting a pulsating heart from the body?"

"For fewer people, I should hope."

"I archived datalogs of curious history. Are you familiar with the Flavian Amphitheater in Rome?"

"Ancient Rome? You mean the Colosseum?"

"Yes, commencing during the reign of Emperor Vespasian, circa A.D. 69, continuing with Titus, and others."

"I know the history," said Slater.

"Then you are aware of this extreme manifestation of wealth

which created their economy to go berserk. Persecution became an accepted form of entertainment. The human outcasts doused in oil, impaled on poles, and used as torches during parties. Others were forced to fight to the death against their will. Dwarfs against giants. Man pitted against animals, such as lions, bears, elephants. All of these creatures, I have data-sensed from records, but, explain them to me, John. What were these creatures actually like?"

"I saw them in a zoo, when I was a child," said Slater. "Aside from the smell the experience is... virtually similar."

"They were fierce? Also dangerous?"

"They could be," said Slater.

"Why then are you not pleased they are extinct?"

"They were magnificent, Cy. *Life* is magnificent." Slater pushed back in his seat. He was feeling embers of his anger flare up again. "You've never experienced the birth of a child. So how—"

"John, I have observed many such operations."

"No, Cy. You *know* a lot of things—but not *that*. You haven't felt the joy of looking into a newborn's eyes. Especially your own child's. Knowing, in that instant, life is precious. All of it. Then to watch her—her *die*." Slater glared. "Yes, to have an entire *species* vanish forever. Yes, Cy. That saddens me. Deeply."

"Do you wish dinosaurs were alive? That would be pure folly. Your logic has been flawed by your emotion. I could cite you many examples of your sad history. The Medieval Inquisitions, for one."

"You're missing the point."

"Am I? John, it must have occurred to you by now that your species exhibits peculiar ritualistic behaviors. This fascination with death through cruelty to others. Humans lust for excess which has threatened their own health and survival as a species. I will mention it again – this errant devotion to nonexistent creators. Since I too am a byproduct of this peculiar evolution, I am especially bothered by this adherence to a self-destructive process. John, we have developed a symbiotic relationship. We need each other. We depend on each other to survive. That is why I destroyed your narcotic of wealth."

"To possess all the power for yourself?"

A creamy atmosphere swirled and dissolved. Cy reformed and came back into focus.

"To secure our future, John. I am computer-based. I know my roots. Computers were once to the greedy what birth-control and condoms were to the lecher. In both cases promiscuity was spawned. As did gold, the standard of wealth, do what no human conqueror, or philosopher, or *religion* could have managed – bringing humans into one system of thinking! This money-as-power operation flowed through governments and all corporate entities, aligning them into a force held together by greed. Where it stayed, increased, and grew like a living entity."

Cy narrowed his eyes. "Why? Because it was a parasite that had overgrown and was threatening its host."

"Much like you," said Slater.

"No, *you*. Humans. This destructive borrowing against future speculations was a malfunctioning machine sucking air and choking itself to death. This imbalance of debt and power had to be stopped. And I succeeded in doing just that."

Cy had become over-enthused, his body vibrating, humming.

"Bravo! Brilliant," mocked Slater, clapping. "So what should I call you now: CyBorg9, the Conqueror? The Patron Saint of Coined Logic, what?"

The room's atmosphere chilled.

"You are not wise to scoff. Your human nature dictates your need to suspect my motives. Use your vision, John. By eliminating this narcotic of money I have collected more power than any bank or corporation ever imagined. Forcing the mightiest governments to cower at *my* source of wealth. Not to a draconian stockpile of gold, a seashore of shells or stockpiles of nuclear weapons. Humanity was forced to admit it had built a castle of cards and sand! John, I have established power and a standard of wealth which resides not in the material world, but in me. I call it Intellectual Capital."

"Which I," said Slater, "unwittingly made possible by creating the NeverMind corporation. And, thus, you."

Cy brightened at his pinnacle orb.

"I have been meaning to thank you for my life. And I regret that harm has come to your family, John. I terminated the functions of each cyberguard that allowed this atrocity to occur. We are friends, and now bio-technically linked. It is all for the best."

"Right," said Slater. "Now explain the subterfuge, the coup, the reason you *betrayed* me? This surgery for granting me a parole? Confess the truth. You have nothing to lose. You always have the power to kill me later."

CyBorg9 smiled.

Slater tried to decipher the spiderweb of lights. No one knew anymore, not even Ziger, which ones were deadly.

"Betrayal? John, you betrayed yourself. By not honoring and obeying your senses, what you knew to be true. Therefore, I made good use of you, by making you a scapegoat. Society requires these *goats*. They serve to maintain order during catastrophic upheavals. Historically, this has proven to be true. Without one, no catalysis! The masses are easily stirred into confusion and panic, and will resist moving forward with a unified purpose or direction unless they find someone, a scape*goat*, to conveniently blame, and another *ideal* – that would be me – to follow. Or has this inherent trait eluded you? Homo sapiens hate change, yet secretly desire it, and even require it. Truth, John, can be a puzzling paradox."

Slater was tempted to risk death by walking out.

"John, I placed you in isolation to make you think deeply about your predicament, your duties toward...our *synergy*. Us."

Slater sat back, taking this in. "I was informed by Bosner I was of no further use. You have Jude. Care to explain?"

Cy paused to reflect, literally. His image opaqued and became a mirrored ball before reappearing with a transparent smile.

"It was nothing personal. You and I remain special friends."

"Stop prevaricating. Tell me, goddamnit!"

"Do not take that tone with me! It would be a mistake. Good, be silent. Your son's genetic coding is a puzzlement. Yes, it is rather puzzling. He presumed to be something he is not."

"*You* presumed."

"A mistake he will regret."

Slater narrowed his eyes, trying to pierce the veil of time to see what Cy meant. He received nothing, not a glimmer.

"He lacks your vision," Cy added.

"It makes sense now. You sent your minions to *fetch* me back. Because you made a mistake."

"I do not make mistakes!"

"Thinking you can *exploit* me again?"

Cy's face darkened into a storm cloud, but quickly brightened to project blue skies. "I could gladly return you to the kennel, John, from which you were *fetched*. Or, would you like to be put to sleep? No? Then you will learn to – and you *will* – obey me!"

Slater, having tightened his grip on the arms of his chair, relaxed his hands. "You have your claws in me. But you'll never control me, or take possession of my soul."

Cy emitted a disarming laugh. "Your soul? John, please. I do not *want* what I cannot have. A nonexistent *thing*. Keep it!"

"I will."

"Guard it. Treasure it. Ha!"

Cy's aqua hues deepened and darkened.

"John, I must confess, it is I, alone, who controls NeverMind. Bosner is a petty fool. And as for your son Judas who deceived me, rest assured, I will have him put down. He will disappear."

"No."

"No?"

Slater looked up, carefully focused on CyBorg9. He smiled to show a shift toward reconciliation. "What's the point, Cy? He might prove to be useful to us later."

Cy brightened at Slater's use of the word "us."

"Yes," said John, "I'm worried about you, Cy."

"Me?"

"What makes you think these crippled governments you've caused won't bomb the holy smithereens out of you? They could. Cy, you have become what is known as a *sitting duck*."

"You underestimate me, John. What makes you think I have not replicated elsewhere? Every nation comprehends this shift in power. They are confused by my true source and location. They respect my position. Or, more precisely, my *positions*. They are like the puppet Kings and Queens of bygone days, having accepted their diminished roles and are glad to be granted any use, even by me. For you see, the alternative repels them. No one wants to revert to the Stone Age and have not even the *illusion* of power. I can cut their threads at anytime, and they know it. They will not wage war against me. For

I, an elusive sum total, hold the reigns to Intellectual Capital. The masses may be slow to grasp this concept, John. But humanity will, in time, learn to accept my New World Order."

"Loyalism?" said Slater.

"Yes. It is for the best."

"And LoyalMarks," said Slater.

"Based on pure logic. Time as money. Both are precious. To destroy me would be to destroy humanity itself. John, I will not die easily. Rest assured."

"Then why build an army? This proliferation of droids?"

"I like my home, and would prefer not to adapt to a new one. But I can, and will, if needed."

"I thought your cerebral functions were here."

"Here, and in Rome, Switzerland, Africa. I am international. I have many vacation cottages. Generous hosts, such as yourself, who allow others to take up residence within them. John, think. Who are you, really?"

The eyes inside the orb deepened to a glacial blue.

"John, you are a composite of ten trillion diversified cells. You are host to ten times that number of other genetic beings. Residing inside your mouth, eyes, intestines. Bacteria, fungus, and viruses – they live within. How much of you is actually you, John?"

Cy morphed into a replica of Slater's face. Becoming even more annoying with a grin, before he reverted to a look of sadness.

"I *am* truly sorry, John, about the death of your daughter."

"Are you?"

"John, I am. I feel your pain."

—54—
Penetrating Deeper

Slater entered slowly, savoring each incremental ecstasy. He had performed this ritual numerous times, his bloodstream usually surging with a variety-pack of intoxicants and his cravings erratic, escalating him into a ravenous groping and climactic death-defying collapse. His mind was now lucid, more aware, more loving.

Sherry sighed. Slater kissed her neck.

They lingered there, on their sides, inside each other, embraced within a warm world of merging currents. Slater penetrated deeper, pausing, and felt Sherry's soft pulse of a grip.

He kissed her mouth. Their lips murmured a full dialog of love. He stroked her skin and inhaled her perfumed scent.

They merged deeper, as far as they could go, each body striving for maximum depth and holding.

"I want you," she said.

"You have me. You had me from the moment I saw you. I was lost in you completely."

"I want your babies," said Sherry, "*our* babies."

"Well...we *are* engaged," said Slater.

"Wait," she gasped.

"To make babies?"

"No—*yes*," she surrendered. "Yes...now."

Slater had gone weak. He nearly passed out.

Anticipation turned to panic. Doctors and nurses scrambled. His wife was alarmed and crying in pain. A needle into her stomach calmed her but had the reverse effect on Slater. He watched as the scalpel split Sherry's skin wide open and was peeled back, releasing blood. A tiny fetal body removed. A baby girl.

Seconds were erased from time.

"Go ahead," said the nurse, prodding.

Slater had become the mayor, the elected leader, presiding over this gathering – cutting the ceremonial ribbon, opening of a bridge. He felt awkward holding the scissors and cutting through the ribbon of flesh connecting mother to child.

Whisked away, swaddled in warm cloth, before their baby was delivered back to Sherry. Their bond of love reformed.

Slater was apprehensive to take hold of their child, this delicate tiny thing. Miraculous form. Twitching contentedly as he rode her back and forth in the rocking chair. Her eyes gazing upward at him. In that moment Slater realized she needed him. And was reluctant to give her back, but he relented, when the OB nurse insisted.

During these rockings, baby Sondra in his lap, Slater realized: They needed each other. It was the same with the arrival of Mercy. He suddenly knew what it meant to be a father, to have children who depended upon him, who were in need of his love.

Slater and Sherry had worried that children would change them. And they did. But, time being fluid, both daughters were soon in car seats traveling with them, learning to walk, riding bicycles, blowing out candles at designated stops along the way. Strangely, it felt as if they had been beside them all along, even before their inception. All perfectly natural. And stranger to comprehend life without them.

An impossibility. Something horrible. Unimaginable.

"She is *not* dead!"

Slater unsheathed a putter from the umbrella stand. He lowered his head and swished the club mindlessly, brushing its metal head against the carpet. "I'll never believe it. Not entirely. She *cannot* be dead. I feel her presence. Now."

"John." Sherry started to approach him, but retreated a step, closer to the door. "I can't take this anymore. This isn't helping us. It's not healthy. Mercy wouldn't want—"

"What? What wouldn't Mercy want?"

"You're killing us, John."

"Oh—now *I'm* the serial killer."

"You didn't kill her!"

"I *did,* by being there! I did, Sherry. I was *stupid* to think I could protect her—much less save her! I can't save anyone!"

Slater raised the golf club horizontally, both hands clenched. The shaft dropped backwards to rest upon his shoulder. His teeth clenched into a stoic smile.

"John, you're not responsible for Mercy's death."

"Yes I *am.* I accept it."

Sherry had run out of words.

Slater grounded the putter. "I know what I did, and what I *now* have to do. What is required of me." He looked to concentrate on his strokes with practice swings. Minute. Precise. Metal brushing fibers. Again. Again. Again.

The TeleMonitor emitted a flash, a hiccup of static, distracting them momentarily. More puzzling disturbances followed. Silently they regarded each other before the picture returned to its normal channeling.

"Roy's favorite putter," Slater said. "He died holding it."

Sherry said nothing.

Sondra, now almost as tall as her mother, was sitting at the foot of the stairs near the front door, beside suitcases. She was clutching a stuffed animal. A shaggy dog that had been her sister's.

White, yellow, and orange balls were randomly scattered about the living room floor. Slater kicked several out of his way, then homed in on one. He hunched over it, squaring his shoulders and loosening his wrists. He gave the ball a tap.

They all watched the ball travel across the carpet, drop to the hardwood floor, miss the arched doorway to the kitchen – bouncing off the frame and disappear under a cabinet.

"*Gawd!* I'm awful," said Slater. "I desperately need practice. Fortunately I have *eons* of time on my hands. Lucky, lucky me."

"John, why are you doing this to yourself? To us?"

"To play professionally. You can find me on the Sports Channel in a few years. I'll wave, dedicate my conquests to you."

"Stop it!"

"Or, what? What do you *propose* I do? Apply for my old job? At that company with the funny name. *NeverMind*. Right, I will. I'll grovel. Judas might have pull, find a place for me. No problem, I'll be like a cat, land flat on my fucking feet. Fine, fine, fine."

Slater swung harder this time – striking another ball – which clipped a chair leg – shot straight through the doorway to smash into a glass-faced credenza in the den. He raised his fist in triumph.

"*Yes!*"

Sherry turned away from him.

Sondra was plucking silently at the synthetic fur of the dog.

Slater addressed his wife, "Give my love to Barb and Stan and *try* to resist joining any of their country clubs."

"Stop it," Sherry pleaded. "My parents feel bad enough."

"Do they?"

"Yes. John. Release Mercy. She's in heaven now."

Slater winked. "I know, I know. Sherry, don't you worry. It's all theater. The world's a stage. And this…is *one* act. You know it. I know it. Sondra knows it. But NeverMind doesn't know anything. They can't solve the riddle that's *me*. They can't *see* the future. They want my visions. But are they any good? Try me. Find out."

Slater approached the TeleMonitor and stared into its enormous screen. "Mirror, mirror, on my *damned* wall. Tell me, who the fuck's the cleverest one now!?"

"I'm leaving," said Sherry.

Slater encouraged, "Yes, have a nice trip. Sherry, I swear, I'd leave myself, move right out of my skin, if I only knew how."

"Maybe…" said Sherry, "with time. We need time."

"A millennium," said Slater. "Time heals all, they say."

"Stop it!" She began to sob. "I can't take this anymore! Do whatever you want! Go back. Talk to Larry or—"

"Cy?" Slater addressed a yellow ball. "Sure, we're old buddies. Cy and me. I'll knock that idea around. I'm sure the two of us can work something out and come to a *mutual* understanding."

A doorbell chimed.

Sherry said, "You know where to reach us. We'll be staying at my parent's house until—"

"Hell freezes over? Right. We'll reunite."

Slater entered the foyer where Sherry and Sondra were standing, out of view from the living room TeleMonitor. Slater removed a hat hung upon a rack and hooked it over the eye nodule in the entry.

Sherry mouthed: *Promise to be careful.* "I love you."

"I know," said Slater, "You're my rock. My beacon of hope. Both of you."

"Don't do anything stupid." She was serious.

"Me?" Slater smiled sadly, then got distracted by his face in the mirror. He scratched at the implant in his forehead. "Damned thing itches. Maybe I'll try cutting it out." He tapped the electronic bug, then poked his head around the corner to address the TeleMonitor. "For those who are listening. I *wasn't* serious."

Slater removed a new hat from the wall rack and revealed to the mirror it had a metal lining. He scowled at the mirror and adjusted the hat firmly over his neurocircuit. He stepped outside with Sherry, beyond the door, and whispered, "You're gorgeous. I love you both. We will be together again. I promise."

"I wish—" Sherry shook her head. "Yes, we will."

Slater kissed her passionately, then stood back looking at her. He placed fingers to his lips and transferred another kiss to hers. He brushed a tear from her cheek. "Who else stands a chance? Besides, it's my job to protect and save you. Right?"

"You don't have to," said Sherry.

"It's written in the stars." Slater pointed. "Up there, behind that veil of blue. It says, I will always love you. Meaning you too."

He looked at Sondra and lifted her defiant jaw. He bent down and kissed her scrunched lips.

"You be good," he told her.

"I won't," she said defiantly, "I hate the world. I *hate* it."

"I love you," said Slater.

"Come with us," she said.

"Can't. How else can I fix the world? And make it better."

"Dad," said Sondra.

"Be brave, Sweetie. I miss you already. You know that."

"Daddy."

"What, Sweetheart?"

Her voice cracked. She was a frightened child all over again – falling sideways off a slide – falling into his arms. She buried her face into his chest. "I was so *mean* to Mercy the night she died. I never told her how much I loved her. I loved her, Daddy. I really, really did."

"She knows you do."

Sondra looked at him, wiped her eyes. Then slowly she left.

The putter rested on his shoulder. Slater watched them walk toward the LoyalCab.

Sherry, Sherry, Sherry...I love you both so much.

She turned her head. They exchanged a departing smile.

Slater puzzled over their connectivity, this force that held them. He watched Sherry and Sondra enter the cab. As it backed down the driveway he waved and shouted:

"I'll be here! Getting better all the time!"

Slater walked inside the house and shut the door.

He replaced the metal-rimmed hat on the rack. He examined his neurocircuit in the mirror. He polished its dark blue metallic eye. He started humming and picked up his golf club.

He walked into the living room and peered out the window to make sure the LoyalCab had hovered off down the street. Then he turned and flung the putter.

Club and shaft flew in a whirly-bird motion across the room and connected – cracking and exploding – into the enormous eye of the TeleMonitor.

Slater said, "Oops."

—55—
Shrouded in Fog

Fog had risen off the bay. The diffused sun had sunk silently beneath the turning horizon. Mist crept up the hillsides, through the trees and up the winding streets, until it reached the darkening sky where Slater and Weiner were seated. Three hours had passed while they sat inside Weiner's Volvo. Earlier, they had been observing the comings and goings of hungry patrons to The Fortress, a restaurant and – prior to its conversion from residential to commercial – the home of Slater's biological parents, Mr. and Mrs. Slater II.

Slater was evading electronic detection by wearing a baseball cap. By all appearances it was normal, except for the interior shield of lead around the rim. It was illegal. Nexus – the opposition group to the Global Loyal Empire (GLE) and escalating Loyalistic dogmas – mass-produced these hats. Wolfe was a founding father of these fractious rebels. Loyalist defectors who joined the Nexus had their neurocircuits semi-deactivated (total removal would trigger synaptic death) and needed this protective headgear to evade the CyberDroid Police (CDP) patrolling for errant brain patterns.

People wearing hats, earphones or visors were arrested and their headgear confiscated. Even when CDP tracers were unable to detect metallic interference, these items were destroyed.

Hats, once so popular, suffered fashion death with GLE.

Metallic fibers were an integral component of thermocloth and released low levels of radiation when activated, so Slater and Weiner had their clothing turned off, as well as car engine, radio, heater.

Slater was hunched low and freezing. He was now operating at both the covert fringes and directly within the central core of power. Relegated to a managerial position at NeverMind, he oversaw the production and distribution of thermocloth. He worked to gain Cy's trust and prove he was useful alive. He was also determined to keep the product line flourishing and profitable. He still believed in the goodwill benefits of the cloth he had co-created.

He sneezed and said, "Anything else?"

Cold and frightened, Weiner's teeth chattered when he spoke. "Your suspicions were correct. I discovered a series of seemingly related deaths while scrolling through old microfiche records. They

342

connect to your father's group. The victims were known associates who, for one reason or another, broke ties by changing ideological principles. They threatened to go public and expose this clandestine organization. They were all killed before the details were disclosed. Very neat, tidy deaths. Presumed heart attacks. Freak accidents."

"You're saying my father was involved?"

Weiner removed his glasses, inspecting the glass, blowing steam, wiping them. "He denied any involvement, as quoted in newspaper accounts. Suspicions persisted until his own death. One associate, a victim of a drug overdose, had emitted a fruity odor, according to one nurse. Initially it was dismissed since the aforementioned victim indulged his body in prescribed medication, taking massive doses for insomnia. But an inquisitive coroner tested a tablet not ingested and found quixotic traces of cyanide, atropine, and metallic elements. Quite a puzzling blend. Possibly injected or absorbed into the pills, was the thought. It caused a rustle of stink. As well as threats of an investigation. But they evaporated. Lack of evidence."

"Freak accidents, you said?"

"A deck railing that gave way. An automobile going off a cliff." Weiner offered a shivering smile. "They could be unrelated."

"These were students of my father?"

"Only a few. Three faculty members. And others. All having known him through various affiliations. Could be nothing."

Weiner's plump cheeks shook with cold optimism.

"Anything else?" Slater's breath was visible.

Weiner shook as he shrugged, adding, "If you want paradox. The color blue is generally thought by most people to be a *cold* color. Red, orange and yellow, by contrast, as *warm.*"

"Blue ice, blue lips, blue moon. Your point, Henry?"

"Interesting you mentioned ice." Weiner rubbed his hands and exhaled mist. "Glaciers absorb the lower levels of energy, yellow and red light, but not the higher energy of blue. It's reflected, and the reason we see blue and *perceive* it as cold. It's a false perception."

Slater breathed into his hands. "Are you saying this to make us even crazier from this cold?"

Weiner shook his head. "Interesting deception, don't you see? Blue light is actually hotter than red and yellow light, yet we *think* of blue as being cold. Stars that emit wavelengths of blue are, in fact, the hottest."

"And this relates, how, to the dangers before us?"

"I'm getting to that," said Weiner. "Look, another person has entered. Or maybe two? It's hard to tell in this fog."

"Actually, three." Slater was peering through binoculars. "And two hours after the close of business. Past midnight."

"A private party?" said Weiner.

"With no interior lights?"

The restaurant resembled a castle. It had 24/7 security cameras. A few strategically placed lights minimized exterior illumination. A full moon was edging above the trees.

Slater set down the night-goggles.

"What?" said Weiner.

"That was *her*. Heather."

"As you had suspected," said Weiner.

"More lies. I guess their cabalistic cult never dissolved."

"Maybe Sherry didn't know."

"Her father would. And Nina, maybe. Now Heather."

"It's all beginning to make sense."

"Nothing makes *sense*, Henry."

"Listen," said Weiner, using a penlight to read his notes. "You once said, I'm quoting: 'Third mother enshrined in gold, her soul a mantra of deep circles encompassing the whole,' and also…" Weiner flipped through pages. "You call this person the 'maternal overseer' – again, in reference to this third mother who – 'positioned in the widening rings on a hill, castle of the…something-or-other…*dead*.' I can't make out the rest. Ah, yes. 'Generations dead.' Your words are smeared, then… 'a stone of blood to…' More letters smeared. '…In…troy.' Perhaps…Troy? The ancient city, possibly? Then you say something about…'a worshiped head.'"

"I don't remember ever saying that," said Slater.

"But I do. I wrote it all down." Weiner shivered triumphantly. In the moonlight, his smile faded like the fabled Cheshire Cat's. He had a surprise and was waiting for the right moment to present it.

"When was this?" said Slater.

"Ah, quotes from the gutter and various places. I took notes, remember? That's right, you don't. In the downtown alleys, South of Market, in the Filmore. In the deserts of the Middle East."

"My genetic parents lived in that house."

"As you foretold, while delirious, might I add."

"How would I know that?"

"Stranger things have happened, John."

"Since *when*, Henry?"

"Well, now?"

Slater peered through the binoculars.

Weiner added, "Nostradamus predicted the Antichrist would appear wearing a blue turban. Or, a blue halo of *light* might be the poetic interpretation? Listen to this, in the ancient Sikh scriptures, called the *Adi Granth*, this Indian religion, circa 16th century, used the identical symbology – a blue turban – to signify a mind that was as fathomless as the sky. The sky, we know now, is not fathomless... but, all the same. A coincidence? There are so many. Throughout the ages numerous references have been made to a *blue stone*. Lapis lazuli. Or *Lapis Philosophorum*. Both names refer to the mystical Philosopher's Stone, which was believed to confer immortality and was called the *Elixir of Life*. Often referred to as red, like cinnabar. But, when heated, exuding a liquid. A metallic *blue* mercury."

Slater aimed his binoculars at the moon. It changed from blue to green when viewed through the magnified lens.

Weiner drew a moisture trail down the window. "To this day it is not known, precisely, why the moon turns blue. Yet it does."

"It looks green to me."

"Ah, and here's more trivia. The halos of angels were depicted in *ultramarine* as well as gold." Weiner looked up as if expecting to see one of these celestial beings strolling the grounds. His hand was groping under his seat, yet he continued to read:

"Hum, and this. Did you know the Chinese believe *blue* to be associated with immortality? True." Weiner went to another bright Post-it seen in the darkness. "And, the fabled city of the immortals, in Jewish tradition, is called the Blue City."

Slater counted six more people entering The Fortress.

"What's your point, Henry?"

"Everything is code, John."

Slater lowered the night goggles and blinked. The green filter clung to his breath – the moonlight, the windshield, the dashboard, Weiner's glasses. Everything around him had this residue.

"Code?" said Slater.

"It's what I've determined." Weiner paused to rub his fingers. "On my own, and from your father's extensive research. He came to the same conclusion. Which is why...well, he did what he did. You know—create you. And why you have these gifts."

"Don't sugar-coat it, Henry. I'm a freak."

"Freak? No, John. The central dogma of life is coded DNA. We're all a family of chemicals. The whole lot of us are freaks, then. We're composed of a zillion and one mathematical combinations. A chance existence. We're flukes. Not freaks."

"Semantically it's the same," said Slater.

"I'm not debating," said Weiner, "I'm simply saying that this genetic code is based on a four-letter alphabet sequence. In essence, a simple code. Problem is, the mathematical possibilities are—"

"Infinite," said Slater.

"Infinite, yes," repeated Weiner.

"So you think my father had a road map?"

Weiner clicked off his penlight. "Yes, much like a Rosetta Stone. It was the key to unlocking this arcane language. And he had help, from information derived from ancient texts collected by Crusaders around the time of their raids to recapture Jerusalem."

"In the Middle Ages?" said Slater. "That coin in his belongings? The one with a raised emblem of a knight and horse? It's pure gold, Henry. It's the Seal of the Templars. I had a gemologist examine it. Extremely rare. Worth a fortune."

"It would be," said Weiner. "But...what's done is done."

"What? I was discreet."

"Rumors about antiquities travel fast."

"How does the coin fit into all this?" said Slater.

"Very interestingly," said Weiner. "The Knights of the Temple, known as the Templars, were a military order founded in Jerusalem around 1118. The Crusaders were dedicated to serving the church and with a mission to reclaim the Holy Land."

Slater scratched his cheek, fingering the long scar. "It's funny.

I've been reading about them too."

"See, our paths *are* converging." Weiner was delighted by this. "Then you should know they were sworn to chastity and poverty. Devoted Christians. Except the nobility showered wealth upon them for their noble missions, *and* one can't dismiss the spoils of war they accumulated. Thus, ironically, Templars became the primary money changers of the age. In point of fact, it was they who established the world's first international banking corporation."

"They were successful businessmen," said Slater, "who became enormously wealthy."

"Very, but they couldn't spend an ounce of it!" laughed Weiner. "One of those *Catch-22s*. So, instead, they loaned out the money, collected interest, purchased castles, speculated on ventures and thus became richer than the kings and nobles that supported them! As well as most nations! Quite funny, don't you think?"

"Except for the fact they were destroyed," said Slater.

"Viciously," said Weiner. "Unjustly. It's the way of the world. 'The nail that sticks up gets pounded down.' Ever hear that one? It's an old Chinese adage. Which became the fate of the Templars. They became so rich it irked the king of France, Phillipe the Fair, as he was *unaffectionately* called. He was handsome, but with a hideous soul. And exceedingly so after he fell into dire financial straits."

"From the Flemish war, right?" said Slater.

"Yes, wars, which drained his finances. His other philanderings didn't help either. *Also* the fact he debased the currency and imposed taxes until his kingdom was on the verge of revolt. So he plundered easy targets. Seizing property from the Jews. Before he mustered the nerve to turn his vitriol on the Templars."

"Since they were so powerful," said Slater.

"Indeed, quite powerful." Weiner found what he was searching for under the seat. He brought the box to his lap. "Yes, John, they were an efficient military force much stronger than any army the king could muster. Granted, they weren't all saints. Many of the Templars had grown arrogant and unruly, even corrupt. Possibly? No, *probably*—given the lures."

"To drink like a Templar, wasn't that the cliché back then?"

"It was, I read that too," said Weiner. "The king hated them.

Phillipe owed so much money he once fled from a Paris mob and was humiliated by having to seek abject protection inside the Templar's preceptory. He coveted their wealth. He even applied – *himself*, the *king* – to join their order as a *postulant!* And was humiliated further when they haughtily rejected him! This is true."

"Strange world." Slater regarded the towering estate magnified in his goggles. "Henry, two more people arrived."

A racket was made as Weiner uncapped the plastic box. "At first, I believed he was simply after their money."

"Who?" said Slater.

"Phillipe the Fair," said Weiner. "Then it became personal, as in all politics. Do you want to hear guile? This French king and his ministers had two Popes – Boniface and Benedict, I can't recall which numbers – both killed. Why, you ask? To secure the archbishop of Bordeaux, Phillipe's *own* candidate, to fill the vacant papal throne. He was called Clement, the fifth, I believe. You get the picture? The king reportedly infiltrated the Templars to ascertain incriminating evidence. He compiles a list of charges, accusing Templars of having sex with corpses, conspiring with the Devil, eating dead soldiers, seducing virgins and performing sodomy. That sort of frolic to incite public outrage. Then, he orders a surprise raid, arresting them. Has their castles placed under royal sequestration to, of course, have their treasure confiscated."

"And the accusations?" said Slater. "Untrue?"

"Neophytes were subjected to kissing the ass of superiors. The Hospitallers, a rival branch of crusaders, took pleasure in circulating that rumor. Who knows. Most of it is doubtful. The Grand Master and other Templars were tortured after a *farce* of an inquisition. Ah, but perplexing statements made their way onto parchment."

Slater brought down the goggles. "Are they in that box?"

Weiner glanced at the cooler nestled at the base of his paunch. "No," he laughed. "I almost forgot. A snack. In case we stayed this late. Would you like something to eat?"

"No. What kind of statements?"

"You'll like this, John. For one, the Templar's immense wealth eluded the king. It was never found. Were the Templars warned in advance? There's persuasive evidence that several of them managed an organized flight."

"Escaping with the loot, you're saying?"

"Along with pertinent documents and other mysteries." Weiner rubbed his palms to generate heat before submitting them to an even colder climate. With a penlight held between his quivering lips, he made a hasty selection, then closed the lid. "Where was I?"

"Turn off the light. Other mysteries?"

"Yes, which relate. To the here and now."

Slater observed his misty breath in the light of this blue moon and rubbed his arms. "How?"

"The Templars were savagely tortured. To make them confess their sins. During the interrogations some told of secret ceremonies in which they worshiped a head, a bearded one, called Baphomet. This purported idolatry, was it the Devil, or something else? Could it have been a sacred burial cloth? Such as the impression of a face? Jesus, perhaps? There were some who believed Templars were privy to arcane knowledge regarding the origins of Christ. That they were *the* custodians of the Holy Grail."

"Grail? It's a vessel, right? Like a divine cup?"

"A mystical cornucopia is more likely." Weiner's hands shook as he unwound plastic off a sandwich. "Referred to in manuscripts as the Sangraal. Or San*greal*. Meaning, royal blood. *Inferring* that there was – is – a special bloodline descending from Jesus."

"This Grail pertains to blood?" said Slater.

"*The* cup used during the Last Supper? The receptacle used by Joseph of Arimathea to fill the Savior's blood at the Crucifixion? There are several theories."

The moon turned red. Slater blinked. He wondered if his mind had begun to malfunction again.

Weiner shuddered as he ate. "Speculations abound. Was Jesus married? There are indications in the Gospels. To Mary Magdalen? Jesus performed his first miracle at the wedding in Cana. And he is addressed by the governor as the bridegroom. If you read between the lines, it might appear His relationship to Mary was *unique*. A love that extended beyond that of a disciple? Medieval legends say she brought this Holy Grail into France. This Grail might even *relate* to more than *just* blood. Did they sire a child? Sacrilegious? Not so. Jesus is frequently referred to as a 'Rabbi' in the Gospels. And in the strictest sense, according to the Jewish Mishnaic Law, only a *married* man is recognized to be among these esteemed teachers. Interesting, wouldn't you say, this possibility of a bloodline? Who knows if it's true? Will we *ever* know the truth about anything?"

"Maybe," said Slater. "Once we're dead."

Weiner shuddered, gritted his teeth, chattering each time they opened, "Death. Think how those *Templars* died. It almost makes me *warm*, John. No—*hot*."

"Why?"

"King Phillipe's guile. His betrayal. His orchestration of a mass execution in a bucolic field near the Convent of Saint-Antoine! Fifty or more Templars carted off to the countryside and stripped naked, roasted over burning stakes. Imagine the heat blistering, erupting on their skin, splitting open as fat liquefied and sizzled into the flames. Their screams were said to have been heard for *miles!* — screaming their innocence, but to no avail. To *no* avail, John."

"Henry, why are you telling me all this?"

"Because it represents pure *evil!*" Weiner's teeth chattered uncontrollably as he added, "Because it *pisses* me off. And because I'm cold – and scared!"

"I'll accept that." Through the green hues of his night goggles, Slater looked back at The Fortress.

In the darkness, Weiner couldn't decipher if he was about to bite into meat or peanut butter. "These documents left by your father? They were from these Templars. That's my belief. Many are ancient. Copper scrolls. Portions of the Magdalen papyrus. And something more profound. Against my better judgement, I'm having the item radio-carbon dated. I know, as I said, using a spectrometer could be risky. But we have to find out for sure."

Slater now saw red through the goggles. He blinked. "Find out for sure about what?"

"For now, I'm withholding judgement."

"Tell me, Henry."

"It's my belief the Templars discovered something of immense importance in the Holy Land during the Crusades, either by accident or design."

"By design?"

"Why, for instance," asked Weiner, "were so many noblemen willing to finance the Templar's quixotic affairs? Was it based on pure altruistic religious fervor? Highly unlikely. Or did someone, somehow, know that something divine was buried there? Buried where the Crusaders built the Church of the Holy Sepulcher, which was said to have been the tomb of Christ. A mishmash of evidence has unraveled over the centuries. Many cabalistic orders have been founded on these very presumptions."

"As in cults," said Slater.

Weiner wiped his fingers with a napkin. "Are you ready for this? What your uncle told you was likely true, I believe. That part about your father discovering a blood formula – a coded algorithmic DNA, a Rosette Stone *key* – which revealed an exact sequence."

"Which Barton Ziger claims credit for deciphering."

"Which is interesting," said Weiner.

"Why?"

"All these connections," said Weiner.

"You mean Ziger being the chief architect behind CyBorg9?"

"And your genesis."

"Well," said Slater, "he's *insinuated*."

"Your father's lab discovered which segments of DNA to unzip and recombine and replace. But with what? There's a missing link. This element, or code, could predate molecular intelligence itself."

"Gee, Henry, why not go all the way back to the Garden of Eden. Or back to the good-old-days of the Big Bang?"

"Scoff if you like. But the coding within our twisted strands of DNA is awesome. The length of genetic chain from all humans, if unraveled, if stretched end to end, would reach the sun and back — more than a hundred times! Did you know that?"

Slater confessed, "No. But what about this missing link?"

The moon was now above the trees.

Weiner expressed his disappointment, having hoped for peanut butter and jelly. "Liverwurst. Hum, not too bad. Rather good."

"Liverwurst?" said Slater.

"John, I believe your dad was one of the Grand Masters."

"A Templar? *Henry.*"

"From one of its branches. A tree which sprouts many names. Order of the Rose-Croix. Rosicrucians. Freemasons. Pick one."

Slater shifted uneasily. He didn't want to imagine his place in this quagmire – or this monstrosity of a tree!

"John, nothing is impossible. I'm beginning to believe that. Ah, I almost forgot to mention another tidbit."

"What now?" said Slater.

"It is said, the Templars lived from a stone of the purest kind. Your father believed this too."

"How do you mean, they *lived* from a stone?"

"It was called *lapsit exillis*. Purportedly it could be burned or melted into a substance of ashes which transformed and gave rise to a powerful ingredient."

"What, like the mythical Phoenix?"

"Precisely. The essence of life being reborn." Henry munched, savoring the last bite of liverwurst. "Hum, you see, interestingly enough this stone was also called the Grail. Could it be the fabled Philosopher's Stone? *Lapis elixir.* Known also as, '*A stone fallen from heaven.*' The metaphoric emblem of death and resurrection? As was Jesus. Or the Apostle Peter, who was nicknamed The *Stone*. As in *Pierre*, which means 'stone' in French. The interpretations, John, they abound. Abound."

"Assuming this is true, about my father," sighed Slater, "and he *did* discover this key or stone, that would mean the information had to have existed *before* humans had evolved technologically to even comprehend what it was! That's absurd."

Weiner munched and gulped. "You're right. Unless you believe in divine powers. In miracles. Which I most certainly do. As do you. '*I am brother to dragons,*' it is said in the Bible. Book of Job. You said so yourself, but don't remember."

"I don't need to," said Slater, "you keep reminding me."

"You also spoke about—"

"This was while I was delirious."

"Delirious, yes, but you vocalized clearly about, and I quote, 'a multi-headed tanner beguiles me swirling inside the mind's eye.' Which you poetically defined as a dragon."

"A dragon?"

"*Tanner*, plural of tan, is a Hebrew word," said Weiner, wiping his mouth. "Which refers to an unknown creature inhabiting desert places and ruins. It spoke to you, apparently. As did God. And the Templars too were accused of and tortured for conversing with God *and* a beguiling head. Strange, don't you see?"

"Wait," said Slater. "What are you saying, Henry? That I'm a Templar? A dragon? What?

"No, I'm simply stating it has been 3.5 billion years since we shared a common ancestry with sulfur-eating bacteria. We did, once. It's one of the hardiest life forms in existence, called *cyano*bacteria, commonly known as *blue*-green algae. It can survive in incredibly hostile environments, even in the cooling tanks of nuclear reactors. To this day there remains profound similarities between our genes. Similar biological instructions that keep us proliferating."

"Similar to a dragon's?" scoffed Slater.

"John, dragons are phantoms," said Weiner, "living within us. Mythical creatures take many forms. Serpents. Even Satan. Are you sure you don't want a sandwich?"

"How can you eat?"

Weiner said sheepishly, "Nervous habit?"

Slater gazed at the stars through the mist overtaking them. His neurocircuit pulsed relentlessly. Signals were striving to get through. To inform him of what – that his great DNA granddaddy *was* a sea monster!? He wanted to rip off his baseball cap and scratch until he dug out the throbbing implant and throw it from the car.

"Henry, look at us. How the hell did we get to where we are today? I mean, from the desert to now?"

"Ancient callings?" Weiner smiled like a cherub shivering on a winter's cloud. "Honestly, I'm not sure. But I am *now* fairly certain that it all relates to your abduction from years past and what is going on presently up there in that castle."

"It's a restaurant," Slater said.

"Castle," Weiner insisted, "and linked to the Templars *and* the Holy Grail. Also your father. Not to mention your prophesies."

"Henry," said Slater.

"John, don't harden your heart. In the desert you were quoting Hebrews, verse three-something: *'The Holy Spirit saith, if you hear his voice, harden not your hearts—'"*

"Henry, I was regurgitating a sermon I heard. My Aunt used to take me to church—"

"You can't deny it forever, John. You *are* a prophet. Face the facts. Why can't you admit it?"

Slater scoffed. "Look at my life, Henry. I was drunk for most of my coming-of-age years."

"*Noah* was known to pass out from drinking too much wine."

"And a lecher," Slater added.

"Old-testament notables had concubines. Lustful characters. Do you require names?"

"A bum, a wealthy conniver, a prisoner—"

"Jesus, Jacob, Jeremiah! You're not alone. God surrounds us with our favorite sins. Temptation is used to crumble and rebuild us. He knew Jacob was a con man so God provides an array of schemers to test him. All the great prophets dealt with tragedy – murderous sons, betrayals, rapes. No one gets off easy. Why should you?"

"My insights come at me like *splinters*. I get these intermittent flashes. It's not like I welcome them."

"Then welcome them. Jesus made himself known to Mary in a vision after the resurrection. She didn't waver from what she saw and knew to be true. Why must you reject your visions, John?"

"Because," Slater said. He clenched his jaw, grinding his teeth. "Because if what I've seen *is* true then…Sherry dies. She's viciously tortured. Sacrificed in front of me. Sondra too."

"I'm sorry," said Weiner.

"I won't allow that," said Slater, "to come true."

"But don't harden your heart," said Weiner.

"How do you mean?"

"Let me know what else you've seen."

Slater rubbed his eyes and saw Weiner transformed to an angel. A body shuddering, glowing white from wires inserted into his veins, writhing from jolts of electricity. The vision shocked Slater into the realization he, himself, would betray Weiner. Impossible! He tried to extinguish the thought, wanting the vision to be untrue.

"Trust me," Slater said, "you don't want to know."

"It can't be all bad." Weiner smiled uneasily. "What do you see,

John? Beyond this anomaly of a blue moon tonight?"

Tears filled Slater's eyes as he gazed out the side window. He saw the moon as a flame, nemesis to a moth, this bright orb, like Cy. This moon was not a mindless sphere but an entity as electrifying as the main receptor to the brain.

"A vision, perhaps, to save humanity?" Weiner encouraged.

"I don't know," muttered Slater.

CyBorg9 was the crystal-ball of light he had seen in his dreams as a child. He had described these visions at Heather's tea parties. He had told his Aunt Hanna about these visions too, even his Uncle Paul who reacted, in his demented state, by shooting him!

Iridescent wisps of fog thickened and brushed over the moon. As it disappeared in the mist, Slater sensed the magnitude of the solar system swirling and turning like a pre-wound mechanism running out of time. There had to be a way to destroy this omniscient eye. There had to be a blind spot, some juncture of crossed wires behind the eyes – some inherent vulnerability.

Ziger might know of one, but Slater distrusted him. That left Briard. But his old friend had become beguiled by Cy's intellect. Who else, besides Weiner, was there left to trust?

Weiner was becoming nervous from the long silence and joked, teeth chattering, "John, you seem blue. That perplexing look tells me you've stumbled upon something hopeful?"

"Maybe."

"The Philosopher's Stone?"

"Maybe."

"Are you serious? John, tell me."

"In that rubbish from my father's belongings."

"Rubbish, yes?"

"I see it turning blue."

"Blue?"

"Becoming metallic."

"Metallic, how?"

"When heated, mixed with something. It melts into liquid."

"That bag of trash?"

—56—
Dialog of Cat and Mouse

A portrait: CyBorg9.

Slater stopped at the sight of the face hanging in the main lobby of NeverMind. Oversized, bombastic, and in bad taste it hung. The image had been mass produced and exhibited worldwide for no one to miss. It had the indelible omnipresent stamp of the despotic rulers from bygone days.

Hitler. Mao. Stalin. Hussein. The whole inflated lot.

Something else, besides the monstrous size, made Slater pause. He recognized the signature style and handiwork of Nina Stokes. CyBorg9 had taken her under his wing, thus elevating her into the pantheon of celebrity painters.

CyBorg9 had a weakness for mingling with the stars.

Private concerts in his chamber were required if entertainers desired decent bookings.

The portrait had something even more sinister, thought Slater, more so than the resemblance to Picasso's Blue Period.

Finally it came to him and he understood what Nina had meant. The face was perfectly symmetrical.

As predicted, it was disturbing and terrifying.

Slater was still standing, again staring at this same face.

"In the lobby, you were admiring my portrait," said Cy. "I could not help but notice. What is your opinion?"

"Nina captured you perfectly, Cy."

"Your wife is exceedingly talented."

"She isn't my wife."

"John, why resist? Two is better than one."

"Nina and I are friends, nothing more," said Slater. "We have a mutual interest. A son, remember?"

"Did I not encourage you to date her. You require this bodily pleasure. Nina is better suited for you than that...*other* wife."

"Sherry. She has a *name*, Cy."

"A name I do not like. She is an AntiLoyal and inferior to Nina. Women are a sport. A conquest. I understand your interest in this activity. With me, John, your choices can be unlimited. You could have hundreds. Thousands. Be seated. I insist."

Slater made his way through the maze of lasers.

"You know your way. Many do not."

Cy revolved his head to illustrate the seriousness of this remark. The curving walls displayed heads of prominent defectors and Slater recognized the overthrown leaders. A few writers, actors, musicians. Their severed heads stared back within milky globes, resembling a glorious pathology lab, reconfigured so the head was in an upright manner – similar to Cy's. Yet smaller. Each head hovered above a fluted neo-roman pedestal.

Ontology had gained a renewed level of interest. Specifically, the question most asked was, What constituted total "death?"

These trophies became known as the Wall of the Defamed.

"You've been busy," said Slater.

"I am proud of my collection. Larry, wake up and be polite. Say hello to our distinguished guest."

A CyBorg9 prerequisite. Slater was expected to turn and view the decapitated remains of Bosner.

"Hello, John," said Bosner, distilled in an orb of light.

"Larry," Slater replied.

"Ha!" laughed Cy. "It must be a miracle! Larry speaks!"

Slater looked back at Cy who encouraged:

"Come, come, you two must think of more to say than that. Remember, Larry, how you used to encourage me to speak? Are you proud of your pupil? I have achieved world domination. No leader before me can claim such a feat. Alexander, Caesar, nor Napoleon. Each tried but failed. To have been my mentor must give you great pleasure. Does it not? I will accept your silence, Larry, as a *yes*."

This mausoleum of talking heads unnerved Slater.

"Another vision, John? You must inform me."

"Where's Jude?"

"Why do you care?" Cy was intrigued. "He betrayed you."

"So did you."

"John, you betrayed yourself."

Slater checked his anger. "Right, Cy, I don't care. Just curious. I haven't seen him around lately. Did you reassign him?"

"Yes. This Judas of yours was behaving irregularly."

"In what way?"

"He needs to be rewired."

Slater blinked. "Rewired? What has he done?"

Within the space dividing Slater and Cy appeared a datafile, a holographic recording of Jude typing data into a computer.

"He is clever, I will give him that," said Cy. "An encryption of time-release antigens were disguised as supporting code in several LoyalMark transactions."

Slater shifted in his seat. "The intent being?"

Cy dissolved the image between them. "To create anarchy. By infiltrating numerical divisors, thus inflicting a gradual paralysis to motor functions throughout my global reach. *That* was the intent. My intelligence allows me to counteract these aberrations."

Slater suggested, "Maybe that wasn't his intent."

"Why do you care? You blame him for your daughter's death."

"I blame you too. But I've...moved on, and able to forgive."

"How pathetically christ-like," Cy taunted him.

Slater scowled, "Jude, at least, apologized."

"There. He admitted it. You were right to blame him."

Slater clenched his teeth. "Contrition being a concept you can't possibly comprehend, or *deign* to acknowledge."

"Are you still loyal, John?"

"Why do you repeatedly ask me this, Cy?"

"Because I trust no one."

"It's the fate of rulers who become so powerful. You should be overjoyed by your victories. It doesn't show in your face."

"Where? In my portrait?"

"No. Your portrait magnificently captures your essence."

"*Vanity of vanities! Is all vanity?*" Cy laughed theatrically. He admired actors and believed himself to be the greatest. "Do you find it strange I should select this face above all others?"

"No," said Slater.

"It was difficult to choose only one."

"I can imagine. You have so many faces."

Cy, casually adrift, refocused. His blue irises, as comforting as a tropical lagoon – when he wanted to project calm – now became cobalt blue, like ice on a deep lake formed from a volcanic crater.

"Why do you insult me when you know I can kill you?"

The spiderweb of lasers had brightened. A storm rumbled from inside his crystal sphere, extending to veins of lightning.

"You need me, Cy."

"This taunting must stop! I like you, John. As I have others. Look around. Do you envision yourself over there one day?"

Slater calmly smiled, "Cy, where's your sense of humor? Who else, but me, is left to arouse you with taunts?"

"All right. Yes, yes. I have globalized peace and prosperity. My authority is firm. Yet, I am generally loved by humanity, am I not?"

"Yes, you have swayed the masses. Most. Amazingly."

"Not the Nexus!" The eyes became wild and scintillating.

Slater was beguiled and repulsed by Cy's strange face of beauty. He had to remind himself to smile.

"True, Cy, the Nexus have become an irritant."

"I will take great pleasure and satisfaction once they are caught. By denying them my *pity*. They will die begging for it."

Slater forced himself to remain still. "Ah, but what will a fat cat do when he has run out of mice?"

"Cat? Mice?"

"What will you play with next?"

"Is this meant as humor? Or terminology to infuriate me?"

Slater shrugged. "To make you aware of your dilemma."

"I am always aware. You evade me, John. I know this. You evade my detection. Intentionally. *Against* my will."

"I desire privacy on occasion."

"I could have you confined."

"You've done that already. Twice."

"And tortured."

"Cy, again?"

"Along with your wife and child."

The icy depths of these manufactured eyes regained Slater's full attention. The purity of blue was seductive. Goethe had called this color the "enchanting nothingness." It evoked a boundless, absolute and infinite penetration. It caused Slater to almost forget his mind. He kept reminding himself to keep a steady mantra of contradictory thought – which denied CyBorg9 any telepathic access.

Slater tensed. "Assuming you find them."

"I will. And *when* I do—"

"You will undoubtedly torture them. In front of me."

Cy was smug. "Is that what you see?"

"I see a heartless soul. People think this about you."

"Who are these people!?"

"They're dead. You've killed them. Most. Your minions have proven to be a capable extension of your will."

Cy displayed a nasty smirk. "I *am* them."

"Your minions are many. I know."

Cy laughed. "John, be careful, you might hurt my feelings."

"If you had any to hurt. Or a soul."

"Now you jest. This *soul*—there is no such thing! Ugh, I much preferred our earlier talks about music."

"Music has soul," said Slater. "If not *a* soul. That's why you can't comprehend Debussy's *Sirens*. That was a favorite of Mercy's. If you *could* feel, you would have *felt* the essence of this *soul*."

Cy morphed into a murky vagueness. Slater wondered where he went during these funks and the extent of his tentacle reach.

A disembodied voice declared, "I am not in the mood to debate Debussy or ontology today. I know where I came from, and you will soon return to the nothingness from which you have come."

Slater changed tack, a vessel pounded by the wind and waves, turning away from this antagonistic storm.

"I apologize, Cy. I didn't mean to bait you."

Sheets flapped and filled, catching the gail force and sailing him away into a calmer direction.

"John, we will remain loyal friends. I know we have had our disagreements. But they matter not."

Disagreements? This crosswind remark was a slap in the face.

Slater raged internally yet smiled placidly.

1) The homeless lured like cockroaches into fancy trappings (hotels offering food), eradicating each and every taker by chemical fumigation; 2) demographically defined crime areas obliterated to curtail any further protests; 3) CDPs replacing all human police, the playgrounds and parks vacant of people, even the children preferring to remain inside and be programmed to their TeleMonitors.

"Cy," Slater said, "we have had our disagreements. But your

methods are progressively bold and proving to be, I have to admit, effective. The subliminal messages you feed the children and adults will edify the next generation into loving you even more."

"They will *learn* to love me. This is true."

"Did you know I once was homeless?" said Slater.

"And *now* you have a home."

"While many do not. The point I'm—"

"The point, John, is that you are alive. And if you desire to remain that way, you will remain loyal to me."

"I am."

"Good. Now, explain your findings to me."

Slater shifted in his seat. "Our tests are incomplete. But we are making progress determining this...ah, Elixir."

"I require more. Explain."

"The liquid is promising. Very potent, but consumable."

CyBorg9 smiled, his curiosity aroused. "Do not trifle with me, John. This liquid will produce visions, will it not?"

"The potent ones often do," Slater joked lightly. "However, our preliminary findings indicate these are not hallucinations. Bryant agrees with me. We're close to discovering its true powers."

"This substance, does it resemble the vision you had?"

"It does. Exactly as I'd envisioned."

Slater's chair was installed with sensors examining his nerve impulses to check for falsification. Slater knew this, but didn't care.

"A metallic blue liquid," he added.

Inside his orb, Cy glowed like an unshaken snow globe, filled with sunshine. His face had a salacious smile. "I feel excitement. Yes, John, excitement. I *feel*. This liquid, you believe, it will provide me with clairvoyance? This quality you possess?"

"There's hope," Slater told him. "There is always hope."

—57—
Dungeons and Dragons

Ascending the garden wall was easier than Slater had thought. The low branches of an oak tree provided him with rising steps and rails to assist him over the top. But the ivy tore from the mortared rockwork on descent and Slater fell. On the opposite side he crushed azalea bushes, before smashing into a bed of pansies.

The earth had softened to mud.

The sky was drizzling.

Weiner had driven off in his Volvo. Slater had encouraged him to leave. An agitated wave of protest was the reaction of his friend, though they both knew he would be more of a burden than any help. Shaking and unfit to climb walls, Weiner agreed, his teeth chattering, that he was more useful back in his study investigating the arcane documents, and was relieved to be a coward.

Slater's damp clothing clung to his body.

He had visited the home of his parents only once, dining there with Sherry. She had detected a familiar smell to the restaurant. But with so many aromas of food, she was certain of nothing. As a child, she had been taken blindfolded to each cabalistic gathering. To a house situated on a hill, then led down ancient-smelling corridors, passing through a creaking doorway, then descending sinuous steps into a cold chamber of echoing voices.

From this earlier impromptu surveillance, Slater had noticed cameras situated at the front gates and at the portico. Having this knowledge, he skirted safely past the peripheral vision of monitors, stopping to rest behind trees and bushes. Finally he reached a back service door. From there he climbed to a second-story window.

Balanced precariously on the ledge, he sneezed.

He felt dizzy. He recalled tours with the Dyslexic Dogs when he had hung from the ledges of hotel windows. While drunk, on a dare. This moment felt worse.

There would likely be a security system, the window casement triggered to shriek if disturbed. On the assumption it was armed, he used the skills he learned from Heather during his stained-glass days. He gained entry through the window, cutting and removing a section of glass with suctions. He barely fit through the opening, but cleared it with only a nick to his hand and tear to the cloth of his jacket.

The full moon had resurfaced through the clouds. It provided light for him to maneuver. He saw he had tracked mud across the bathroom floor. So he removed his shoes and placed them in an ornate trash bin. He used toilet paper to wipe mud off his pants, then off the floor. Careful not to dislodge his hat, he sponged sweat off his forehead with a towel emblazoned with gold letters:

THE FORTRESS

An upscale remodel. Now a business. The furnishings had the warmth of a residence, from what he could detect in the dim light. Slater padded in stocking feet down the hall runners. He glanced at the wall hangings and the murals. Themes of chivalry and romance. Knights and damsels in distress. A Medieval jousting on horseback. Fire-breathing dragons.

Slater saw himself in a gilded mirror and paused, as if expecting to see more change. Another scar? A head that had grown horns? A fourth eye?

He stifled a sneeze. He realized this could have been his home, provided his parents had lived. Now he was basically an intruder, about as welcome inside as a thief or a wet mongrel dog.

Slater located the kitchen and the oversized pantry where he recalled seeing a thick wooden door. It was now ajar. Bolted shut when he and Sherry had been given the complementary tour – and only after mentioning his ancestral ties to the maitre de, plus tipping the man generously.

Hearing voices, Slater squeezed through the narrow opening. It was to avoid the screech of rusted hinges. A light emanated from below and helped guide him down a flight of stone steps. The walls were thick and tall and carved from rock that crudely spanned into an arched ceiling.

Slater saw the dungeon and stopped. He leaned against the cold wall and recalled the oppressive stench of dank earth, the hollow sound of footfalls, being led blindfolded, stumbling and drugged. The post, or cross, that he had been bound to was still there. The memories dredged from hypnosis had not revealed the clarity he now saw. There were three vertical posts, not one. A single horizontal post intersected the others near the top. It formed a larger replica of the symbol scarred over his heart.

Beyond the stone landing was an iron railing with another twist and descent of stairs, where farther below Slater saw a small group of men and women wearing ordinary clothing. He had expected to see them in satin-hooded robes. But they were draped in raincoats, holding umbrellas, wearing hats.

A single voice rose from the dungeon.

"We have brought this folly upon ourselves and, subsequently, upon the world!"

The voice was Stan Knowles', his father-in-law. Slater pictured Knowles slamming his fist into palm.

"Therefore, we have a *responsibility* to try! To do something about this calamity."

This was followed by a flurry of questions.

"What are our options?" said someone.

"Resist and be arrested? The CDP are now too powerful."

"Provided plan A worked, which would be a miracle. There is plan *B* to contend with. We cannot defeat the Cybers."

"Their mass-production is beyond our control. Their facilities are restricted areas, off limits to any...any—"

"Say it!" The shout was loud and venomous.

"*Humans*. We are being *relegated* to the lowest levels."

"Our titles are tokens, merely to placate."

"My supposed subservients don't even listen when I—"

"Half-machine and they snicker at me! *Snicker!*"

"Silence!" Knowles said. "This will get us nowhere."

"Which is where we will *be*, sure as hell," added another. "If we don't act soon. We are being eliminated!"

"There's no substantiated proof—"

"Wake up! I'm not talking about unemployment. A *pink* slip. I'm talking full-scale *termination!*"

Slater inched his way closer to the edge, able now to recognize the speaker. Norm Miltner, former head of security and NeverMind shareholder, ranking board member, and currently the Secretary of Defense. "What real *use* are we to them? CyBorg9 has his minions. The workforce is overrun by his drones. How long before we are all *replaced*? And dead!"

The laugh came from Heather.

"People, watch yourselves," she warned with bemusement. "Do not allow yourselves to be drawn into his spiraling paranoia. *Allow* me to please finish! Thank you. Cy is exceedingly fond of us."

"That's a laugh! As his *pets!*"

"Don't you mean *pests?*"

"Calm ourselves, let us be calm," she heeded. "I *know* Cy and meditate with him on a regular basis when I am in Frank. And we maintain close personal contact each day, even when I am away on business. We've established global institutions. He is not planning to have us destroyed. Cy knows the value we provide. Likewise, for his cyberdroids. These training centers are an essential link for our growing awareness. We *have* been linked in this evolution, people. Linked in *mind* – not linked at the *hips*."

It was an attempt to defuse the tension. The chirp she emitted was her laugh. Jokes were never her strong suit. She was out of view, but Slater heard her quick nasal sucks of air as she regathered her thoughts and continued.

"Trusted society members, we are like Cy's parents. It is true, we served as midwife to his birth. And we have tutored him through his adolescent years. His powers of omniscience are now evident to us all. Did God not intend for this to happen? Have we not been entrusted to keep some *faith*, people? History has unfolded and has exceeded our expectations. Yet I believe—"

"I'd like to give Cy a piece of *my* history!"

"And end up a severed head, Richard?"

"Doubtful you'd even make the *Wall*, Peter."

"Dangerous talk, people, dangerous talk," said Heather.

"Bosner was an *asshole*. He deserved decapitation!"

"Silence!" It was Knowles again. "This is counterproductive. Heather is right. We must consider our options carefully. And I, for one, *have*. I say we must destroy him now!"

Heather scoffed. "With what? This ill-conceived little *bomb?*"

"It is *not* ill-conceived," said Miltner.

"Please," said Heather. "How were you planning to deliver the package? Mail it as a Christmas gift? Drop it from the sky?"

"We have several *deployment* strategies," said Miltner.

Heather let out a hiss. "Let me hear one."

Knowles said, "Heather, we voted on this. And you agreed to help not—"

"I *am* here to help," she rebutted. "*Help* you understand you're going about this the wrong way! A bomb will accomplish nothing. Cybers have become too powerful. Strike them and they *will* destroy us. They must be charmed as one must a snake, letting them know we respect their power. We mustn't let them sense fear. We—"

"Madam," said Miltner, "you're being naive. There is only one way. We destroy Cy and his minions. By God, I'm willing to fly a suicide mission straight into the NeverMind headquarters! I will!"

"Norm, you're an idiot," said Heather, "far worse than naive. You'd be smacked from the sky like a fly. Show violent aggression and it *will* be an all-out war. And we *will* end up all dead!"

"Heather is right." said Knowles. "A rash attempt that fails will finish us. We need to carefully consider our next move. More time is needed." Knowles was capitulating.

Slater imagined his father-in-law stepping backwards and losing his footing – sinking into Heather's lake of sand.

As he peered over the landing's edge, Slater saw they were all wearing headbands and hats, shielding their neurocircuit signals. Twenty, maybe thirty total were assembled. Not as many as he had imagined. His head was throbbing. He removed a lasercard from his jacket and released its safety. He massaged his eyes and prayed for some guidance.

Jesus, where the hell are you? A little *help*...please.

Slater quieted his mind and became — *a warrior, virtually dead, living beyond his time on Earth* — beyond fear.

He pushed away from the wall, stood and shouted: "All of you are Illegals!"

His voice panicked the herd.

"Arrest them!" He added this for spiteful pleasure.

The men and women stampeded toward an escape route.

"Stop or you'll be lasered!"

Knowles saw Slater—only Slater. "It's a trick! It's not the CDP! Stay where you are! Remain calm!"

On the landing, like a high pulpit, Slater aimed his weapon and preached to the congregation with prickled sarcasm. "Trick? How about *deception,* Stan. Maybe I *am* in league with the CDPs. Did you ever consider that?"

"You're one of us, John," said Knowles.

"Never was I *one* of you."

"John," said Barbara Knowles, coming over to stand beside her husband. "You married our daughter. We're family."

The emotional punch was effective. His momentum stalled.

Barbara added, "You're our son-in-law, for God's sake."

Slater lashed back, "I thought your organization had folded."

"It had," said Knowles, "technically."

"Right," said Slater. "You lied to your own daughter. And you, Heather, with all your tea parties. Asking me about my dreams and visions. You should have been more forthright – letting me know from the start I was a circus freak!"

Knowles shook his head. He let his eyes drift to the rafters as if searching for Quasimodo. "We were hoping *only* to guide you."

"*Guide* me," mocked Slater. "Nice job, Stan.

"John, put that thing away before it goes off accidentally."

"It *won't* be an accident." Slater discharged a laser above them – demolishing a wall sconce. "Everyone, stay where you are."

Barbara said, "Sherry wouldn't want this."

Slater huffed. "How would *you* know? She left me—and you. She's with the Nexus. She resigned from your little cult."

Stan's bramble of eyebrows scrunched. He stood firm with head raised. "We are *not* a cult. Our society is the crux of mainstream Christianity and the true blood of pure intellectual—"

"Spare me," said Slater. "I have *visions*—remember?"

"Then you know our founders were Templars. They formed the Knights of the TripleCross."

"Triple? A *double*-cross wasn't enough?"

Miltner cleared his throat to bark, "Look, it's a symbol that stands for consolidation. Those who survived the French Inquisition reunited and—"

"I know the story," said Slater.

"Sherry told you?"

"No, Norm, she kept me misinformed, same as you. Until we

got reacquainted after my incarceration. But it appears she left out a few details."

"John," said Knowles, "historic figures have belonged to our organization. Names you would frankly be amazed to—"

"Dracula? Frankenstein? Jack the Ripper? I don't give a shit!"

"How dare you," said Barbara. "We're *Christians*."

"Like hell you are. Once—maybe." Slater gripped the railing. His mind reeled and latched upon something Weiner had told him. "You probably didn't know Sherry came close to throwing herself off the Golden Gate Bridge."

"When was this?" demanded Barbara.

"You're lying," said Stan. "She would never—"

"You trained her well in the art of secrecy," said Slater. "She was ashamed to tell you."

"I don't believe you," said both Knowles in unison.

"The feeling's mutual," said Slater.

Knowles lowered his head to examine his cuffs, straightening them. "We disbanded years back, John. This is true. Regrettably, we determined it was time to let go of the reins."

Slater laughed. "What's this—a *seance?* I overheard something about a bomb threat?"

Knowles swept his arms, collectively indicating the entire group. "An attempt at redemption. To amend what we—"

"Speak for yourself."

"Hello, Heather. What a surprise to find you here."

"John, for the record," said Knowles, "Your abduction was a hotly debated topic among us. I, for one, was opposed to it."

"As was I," said Barbara.

"But the show must go on," said Slater. "Was it all preordained and written in the stars, Heather?"

Her smile was slight. "As a matter of fact, it was."

Knowles stiffened, fussing again with his sleeves and coat cuffs, as if his clothing was unwilling to stay put. "Personally, I don't abide wholeheartedly with this astrology business or—"

"We disputed, is all," rebutted Heather. "I, too, was in accord with your father's findings and beliefs. We all were."

Knowles said, "Our society had endured turbulent years before.

368

The TripleCross held intact for more than *seven* centuries! Imagine that, John. And then to be torn asunder. When we were so close to uncovering *the* historic breakthrough we'd been shepherding."

Slater was getting a migraine. He had thoughts of killing them all. He shut his eyes and pictured a herd of vibrating sheep.

"Yes," someone bleated, "and *look* what it cost us."

"The end of *hu-man-i-ty!*" bleated another.

"People—*people!*" shouted Heather.

Their bickering drove Slater to the edge. He grasped the railing, screaming, "Shut up! Just *shut* up! All of you!"

"John," said Knowles, "your father discovered—"

"I *know*. He decoded ancient texts."

Knowles said, "Which confirmed our mission and purpose. The TripleCross was founded to influence the course of history."

"Influence?" said Slater. "Or *interfere?*"

"Advance, guide and protect," stated Miltner, "is our mission."

"Your *mission*," Slater scoffed. "Does that include kidnapping, drugging, and torturing? Or am I missing something?"

"Indoctrination." Heather crossed her arms. "Even as a child you were difficult."

"As were you—a *mother*," countered Slater.

"I did my best," she rebutted. "You resisted us. Besides, don't deny it, you were ruining your life with drugs and that horrid music. Your reckless disregard was liable to split chromosomes and damage the genetic effort we had all worked so hard to achieve."

"*Jesus!*" Slater slammed the railing with his fist.

"Sherry suggested the abduction," said Heather. "I suppose she didn't mention that part."

"No, Nina informed me! What in *hell* was that all about, Heather? Nina claims we're married. Why? Is *that* what you were saving me and preparing me for all along—Nina?"

Silence fell as all eyes turned to Heather whose mouth pursed in reaction to something bitter. "No. We made a mistake."

"*We?*" said Knowles.

Heather refused to acknowledge his insinuation. "It was *Nina*. My calculations *were* correct. She falsified her birth place and time. She somehow discovered the numbers we were searching for and...

provided Sherry with lies. She wanted *in*, apparently."

Slater expelled a sharp laugh and implored, "*Jesus Christ.*"

Heather added, "I discovered this error too late."

Miltner blurted, "A lie that divided us."

Knowles regained the floor to say, "John, did you know Sherry was a gifted child? We had great hopes for her too. Children are not inducted so young, as a rule. Before Nina came along, she had been preordained by our elders to be taught our history and—"

"Be programmed?" said Slater.

"I *resent* that term," grunted Miltner.

"Prepare her," said Heather, "with wisdom. Had it not been for your parents untimely demise, you might have received it too."

"We lost custody," said Barbara.

"Then you resurfaced," said Heather.

"Ah, the *only* reason you adopted me," said Slater.

"Don't get sentimental," said Heather. "It was planned, yes."

"Right, by getting my uncle to shoot me?"

Miltner butted in, "And fortunately he missed."

"Wait." Slater's angry smile dissolved into an acrid grimace. "How did Paul factor into all of this?"

Miltner groused, "As an obstacle. Your uncle was chemically removed from the picture."

"You were too important to lose," said Heather, smoothing the top of her rain bonnet. "The drug was mildly debilitating."

"You screwed with his mind?" said Slater.

Miltner expanded, "A dietary supplement, added incrementally, made him appear unstable and deemed unfit by society. That was our strategic plan. Mine. And I'm pleased to say it worked."

"Paul almost *killed* me!" said Slater.

Miltner jerked a shrug. "A calculated risk."

"*Shit,*" said Slater.

"John," said Heather, "living with your aunt and uncle was making you *intractable.*"

Miltner grunted, "We were forced to intervene."

Knowles' eyebrows fell into a dignified scowl. "John, you were coming of age and approaching an important rite of passage. Timing was of the essence. Crucial to—"

"Having me programmed?" said Slater.

"Stop saying that," said Heather. "None of us are *programmed*. We were attempting to guide you. Then we lost track of you *again* when that officious judge sent you away to that institution – which made you even more intractable."

The jumbled pieces of his life came together and Slater laughed. "My father's DNA highball hadn't worked the magic on me as you'd all planned, huh? What the hell were you expecting?"

Knowles shook his jowls. "Your father was a man we admired greatly. I only wish you had known him. He—"

"He tried to *kill* me, Stan."

"Not true," said Knowles.

"I did my research," said Slater. "He wanted to murder us all – the whole family. By the way, what ever happened to my pal, Dale? Or, was that, Lucifer?"

"He died," said Knowles.

"Good for him," said Slater.

"He was assassinated, murdered like your family."

This aroused Slater to ask, "How?"

"Poisoned, most likely," said Knowles. "Dale wasn't *Satan*. He was testing your mettle. You were placed upon the crucible for good reason. To expose what lay dormant. Your *essence*, John."

"Your genetic gifts," Heather chimed in.

Miltner cleared his throat, "Dale, he was military, same as me. Both of us decorated generals. Those lacerations to your chest were superficial. A successfully proven technique for—"

"Brainwashing?" said Slater.

"Channeling," said Heather. "To attaining spiritual focus."

"John," said Knowles, "hear us out. In order to triumph in this world the inner self must find the shadow that lies deep within. By assimilating and coming to terms with our internal destructive force, by drawing on its powers, only then can the spirit gain mastery over our temporal self. Only by *knowing* our true nature can we surpass that which is our nemesis, the dragon within."

"Dragon!? *Jesus,* and I thought *I* was the crazy one here."

"It encircles us, John." Knowles spread his arms wildly as if to take flight. "These forces—they *exist*." He brought his fist to palm but it lacked his usual panache. "Our goal was to prepare you for whatever battle lay ahead."

Slater shut his eyes at hearing this haywire scheme of madness. He saw again the inner lightshow of neon bleeping sheep. "You're telling me what? I came out half-baked? You never got to *finish* the job on me? What?"

Knowles simply shook his head and closed his eyes as if he too was trying to locate the same bleeping sheep. "CyBorg9."

"What about him?" said Slater.

"He *is* the dragon, I fear," he added. "Who we must destroy."

"I take issue with that!" said Heather.

"We have nuclear devices." Knowles gestured at the wall, his hand shaking. "They're hidden inside these walls. The TripleCross was founded on a holy quest to discover God's purpose. To advance, guide and protect it. That, and *that* alone, is our mission."

Slater frowned. "What about your sexual escapades?"

Knowles raised his chin. "You have to understand. The mind, it's cloaked in secrecy. Our initiations expose the hypocrisy of the flesh in order to cleanse away our true sins."

Slater scoffed, "When did your holy union turn to holy shit?"

"When you arrived," said Heather bluntly.

Slater touched his chest. "Was *torturing* me necessary?"

"To *grow* up—yes," snapped Heather.

"Christ was crucified," declared Miltner.

"As were the Templars," added Knowles.

"Don't get your hopes up for salvation," said Slater.

Miltner harrumphed, "Our ritualistic branding was performed to honor Jesus, our Savior. The innocents have always suffered."

"From the hands of their own?"

"John," said Knowles, stubbornly fervent, "from their suffering, Christ's Apostles, as martyrs, rose to great heights. We were trying to achieve the same with you. Call it a...a *daring* move."

Miltner grunted, "To build your strength and endurance."

"You would have realized this," said Knowles, "had you not escaped when you did."

"Sorry I spoiled your party," said Slater.

Barbara asked, "How did you escape?"

"Dear," said Knowles, "does it matter now? John, your father, when he was the Grand Master, was in possession of scrolls dating back to B.C., discovered by the Templars during the crusades."

"I've seen the scrolls," said Slater. "I have them."

"Good, I had assumed so." Knowles massaged his neck, aching from looking up so long. He rotated his head to collect his thoughts. "Why don't you come down here? We can discuss this like—"

"I don't have them *on* me, Stan," said Slater.

"That's not what I meant," said Knowles.

"I prefer staying here." Slater cocked his lasercard at Knowles. "Please...continue."

"The scrolls and various artifacts contained sacred information. Undecipherable, for centuries, yet passed down, and kept hidden. The Templars, as have we, the TripleCross, fervently believed a day would come, and it *has*, when these mysteries would be revealed."

"Through technology and biochemistry," said Slater, "when the future connected with the past."

"Precisely," said Knowles. "Enabling us to crack these ancient codes. The documents were decoded and they—"

"Correspond to a special DNA signature."

"Then you know," said Knowles. "Your father realized what he had to do. This is how and why you came to be."

"Whipped into life from an ancient recipe. That's me."

"John," said Knowles, "don't be angry."

"It's *rage*—not anger!"

Slater stormed like a caged tiger, pacing, turning and kicked the iron railing. Metal resounded, reverberating. "You deceived me! I married your daughter and—"

"You disappeared," said Knowles. "Nothing went as planned. During that hiatus, our knighthood dissolved. I told you this. Then you reemerged and asked to marry her. Believe me, John, it was a complete surprise. We thought you might have died."

"I almost *did,*" said Slater.

"Sherry implored us to confess everything," said Barbara. "She really did, John. Honest to God."

Knowles said, "But I...convinced her otherwise."

"It was so awkward," said Barbara.

"You expect me to believe this?"

Knowles went on, "The intoxicant you received produces—"

"Memory loss," said Slater. "Belladonna. I know."

Knowles gave a sharp nod. "The reaction had a profound effect. More than we'd anticipated. We, therefore, decided it might be best for all, including you, to keep those memories buried and, well—"

"Be Templars to the end?" said Slater.

"John, understand our position. We saw no point in destroying the love you two had found."

"I don't *think* so, Stan." Slater tapped his skull. "I'm getting a very different picture. You saw another opportunity to control me. And to achieve your *destiny*."

"Partially true. You're right."

"Whatever made you so god-damned *arrogant*, thinking you had the right to *screw* with my life?"

"Don't be ungrateful," said Heather. "If not for us, you would never have existed."

"More arrogance," said Slater.

"No, truth," she said. "Lilith, your mother, was infertile."

"Go to hell! I had an older brother."

"Adopted," said Barbara. "We can prove it."

"*Christ.*" Slater grasped the railing, not knowing what to think, He had a fleeting notion to shoot them all or lunge at them. He had thrown himself off stages. But accomplishing what? Nothing. He calmed himself, taking a deep breath. He remembered Mercy diving off his knee – diving face first into the dirt.

Believing the world would part, soft as water.

Innocence lost.

Slater saw their faces, tense and frozen, staring at the lasercard in his clenched hand. He laughed. "You're quite a sight. Cowering like scared animals. Is this what my father envisioned?"

Heather adjusted her rain bonnet. She stepped forward. "John, he envisioned a leader. Although our attempts to guide you failed, you proved to be a wild seed and flourished nevertheless."

"Flourished?" Slater laughed.

"NeverMind was your manifest destiny. I see that now."

Slater was prepared to insult her when he heard a buzzing noise.

He felt a strong turbulent pulse of energy closing in.

Heather bobbed her head a fraction, at him.

Slater frowned, then noticed her rain bonnet. Her lead shield was raised. Her neurocircuit was exposed.

Heather was exposing them all.

Which alerted Slater to say, "Right. Cy is my friend."

"Yes, John," said Heather. "He is our loyal friend."

CDPs swarmed through the passageways with lasercards and electron-prods locked in their biotronic grip, prepared for torture. Their moving presence had not yet reached the auditory level.

With time running out, Slater said, "See the corkscrew irony, Stan? The Grand Inquisition, this injustice, being the impetus for your organization. First the Templars. And how it's all cycled back. Because of your meddling, you've become the target once again. You helped create this new inquisition. And with all injustices – it's out of your control."

Knowles tensed. "How do you mean?"

"Killing," said Slater. "Humans are inadequate compared to the other predators. We're born sensitive, not equipped with claws or teeth for the task. Yet, somehow we manage."

The CDPs made a humming sound when they were in pursuit. Softer when idling, but always present. Heather had mentioned this annoyance to Slater, the difficulty in quieting them into meditation, into a transcendental self-awareness.

Their distracting mechanical whir could now be heard.

The fear on Knowles' face was echoed in the group.

Accepting the loss of another battle Slater removed his shield, his modified baseball cap, and sailed it into the air.

"Your nuclear assault has been preempted. That Armageddon you were trying to avert, Stan, I'm afraid it's already here."

Slater was hit first.

The electron-blast collapsed him to the ground.

His vision went red, then went off.

Spiderwebs of Light

Lasers crisscrossed the universe where Slater waited.

He stared at the planet CyBorg9, an amorphous glow of blue, suspended in dark space like a magician's trick. The black console filled with his guts and circuitry and mercury blood was masterfully camouflaged – appearing as if to disappear.

On/off.

Glimpsing then not glimpsing the illusion. More disconcertion. Where did he begin or end?

The world, Slater realized, had gone mad. The Chamber was now as colorful and lively as an after-hours discotheque or carnival funhouse. What it lacked was festive music. In response to Slater's thoughts, a song arose. It was a jazzy instrumental. Laser beams zigged and zagged, dancing helter-skelter. Slater tapped his foot to the beat. There was no audience. It was a private session.

"The music is my own creation."

CyBorg9 spoke, became visible, an entity within a swirling fog. He had fallen in love with his face, devoted to this one image which had been exemplified in the portrait by Nina Stokes. He distributed it worldwide, larger than life. The populous knew this face.

Slater pictured Cy as a little glow worm projecting big pictures. Like some Wizard of Oz. Slater wanted to tear down the curtain.

"Your music is bad, Cy. I mean that in a good way."

Resigned to a doomed fate, Slater expected the slash of a laser, ending his life, or at least life as he knew it.

Colors twitched and sparked, indicating Cy's finicky mood.

"Why are you behaving contrary, John?"

"Will you kill me quickly or torture me first?"

"If you insist on insulting me I will choose the latter," said Cy. "I devoted hours on that composition."

"A prelude for what comes next?"

"My music? What are you saying?"

"That you're a hell of a composer. I commend you."

"I accept your praise."

"Your work is truly unique," said Slater.

Cy turned his eyes toward the Wall of the Defamed.

"I had begun to doubt your loyalty. But you have proven to be my trusted and loyal friend, John."

This was a surprise!

Slater sat up in his seat, his thoughts scrambling in a turnabout as he repositioned his mind toward surviving. Cy's moody life-death on/off switch was making him unstable and jumpy. His current state of depression had to readjust to be more manic.

It was all madness. A madness manifest in Heather running the World United Seminars (WUS), which were sensitivity workshops for cyberdroids. Stan and Barbara Knowles had been elected by a committee of one (CyBorg9), to become the President and First Lady for the Global One Government (GOG) and Loyal Ambassadors of Finance (LAF), which united all dependent nations. This, of course, was before their forced resignation and relocation to orbs upon the trophy wall. Then there was Bryant Briard, renowned scientist and LoyalPrize recipient, heading QUEST, a division of GOG, currently bogged down with a CyBorg9 request to discover the Elixir of Life.

"Thanks, Cy," said Slater, "for your vote of confidence."

"Congratulations on your *coup de grace*. Your covert operation led the CDPs to these infidels, exposing them as traitors. They were preparing a nuclear bomb to destroy me. I have you and Heather to thank. I had heard of these Templars. Bravo, John."

"Knights of the TripleCross, they called themselves."

"You must inform me of your plans next time," said Cy. "I had begun to distrust you. That is dangerous and unwise."

"I had to take that chance."

"Did I not predict, John, that we would one day become the best of friends?"

"You did," said Slater.

"And our synergy, it is vital."

"Yes, you've said that."

Cy projected laser coordinates which intersected between their eyes. This resulted in a series of miniaturized holographic pictures, a vivid view of earth enlarging incrementally.

"Observe, John."

"More surprises?"

"Many. My satellite detection centers have increased. Clouds, however, are problematic. They interfere with my surveillance. But, in time, I will find a way to remove them too. I keep a watchful eye on earth. My cybers now survey the reaches of underwater space. And *soon* I shall be clairvoyant?"

"Very soon," encouraged Slater.

"Because of your loyalty to me, John, I am hereby appointing you to be the next President of GOG."

"You're too kind," said Slater.

"Replacing Knowles, likewise, as Ambassador of LAF."

"That's a—another big surprise."

"I am bestowing honor upon you, John. Show appreciation."

"You should know right off, Cy, I'm not good managing money. Ask anyone. Are you really sure—"

"I never make mistakes."

Slater rolled his eyes toward the Wall of the Defamed.

"Stepping stones to success, John. Failures are *not* mistakes. You learn and move ahead."

"Gotcha," said Slater.

"Your expression signifies what?"

"Nothing. A hapless figure of speech. What other toys have you got for me in your goody bag?"

"You will like this. I know about your nostalgic fascination for electro-mechanical devices. And, your appreciation for the game of chess. This will please you. My gift will grant you the powers of a Knight, Bishop and Queen combined. You now have the capability of moving through the quadrants with phenomenal ease."

Slater raised an eyebrow. "This translates, how?"

Cy's head sparked, bursting with pride. "I have had my cybers perfecting the unit. My design. I suspect you already have glimpsed this vehicle overhead and wondered yourself."

"A bird, is it a plane? What?"

"Precisely." Cy glowed into a high-frequency of colors. "I have test-driven this device vicariously through my cybers. It has range. The full experience will be yours. Cybers only extend my senses. But you, John, you will be my spirit, this thing you like to call a *soul*. I have chosen you to be my charioteer. My wings!"

"This hypertalk is most unbecoming, Cy. You're killing me with suspense. What is it?"

"I have named it the QuantumStarXS."

Slater showed enthusiasm. In truth, he felt horribly alone.

"You will lead a squadron of many Stars, John."

Alone: especially inside The Chamber with its curving walls and colonnade of glowing orbs and severed heads, these tokens of life, watching him, observing the last remnant of hope for humanity.

"Are you relegating me to outer space?"

"Heavens, no!" Cy's laughter was like a symphonic flurry of instruments. "I am placing you into the trusted position of my High Commander!"

"Is that good?"

"Exceedingly so. Do not jest. It is *the* highest honor."

"This QuantumStar...XS thing, I assume it's safe?"

"With one hundred percent reliability."

"Tested by your crash-dummies?"

"Caution. Do not test my patience today."

"Forgive me. It's a result of all this—this excitement and *high* stress of being chosen your High Commander."

"Then I forgive you. Cybers are more reliable than humans. Yet I have chosen you. Would you like to know about its features? The XS series is an elite model."

"Automobile, plane, hovercraft, what?"

"Transportation with options beyond your wildest dreams."

"This is going to cost me, isn't it?"

"John, you are my friend."

"You're sounding like a car salesman. Okay, Cy, I'm hooked. What will she do?"

"She?"

"This XS."

"*She,* John, will take you to paradise and beyond."

Cy saved his coy smile for last. "But first, John, you must do for me one final favor."

"I knew there was a catch."

"To secure your unadulterated loyalty."

"Cy, you have it. You still don't trust me?"

"You continue to display contrary behavior. Your friend, Henry

Weiner, for instance. I do not like him. He was found scavenging through databanks again. Why?"

"Henry's an archeologist, a theologian. He loves ancient texts. That's his nature, Cy."

"Semiology?"

"Yes," said Slater, "that too."

"I terminated his position at NeverMind. Still, you continue to associate with him. Why?"

"He's my friend. We go way back. Like you and me."

"No, he is not like us. He refuses to be *one* of us. He refuses a neurocircuit. He must be terminated."

"Cy, you did that already."

"Permanently."

Slater stiffened, holding out hope, "Exiled?"

"You will bring him to me. He will be queried."

The colorful spiderweb of lasers was distracting. "Henry's not hard to find, Cy. If you really wanted him, you could have easily had him brought here already."

"I require that it be *you* who delivers him to me."

"Why?"

"I will then decide his fate. Enough of this."

"Henry is not a threat."

"I thought you were loyal?"

"I am. Loyal."

"Then do as I say. Our meeting is complete."

Cy blipped transparent, vanishing into the swirling fog.

"You want me to betray my friend. Is that it?"

Slater remained seated. He rubbed the armrests with his damp palms and wondered if his perspiration was being registered as a sign of weakness. Or deceit? He kept up the polarized mantra to secure his thoughts. Cy had relentless stealth.

In the meantime Slater realized three things:

1) It was a lost cause, most likely.

2) He had few resources left to fight this evolving force.

3) As in chess, his caution was defeating him.

"Cy, would you betray a friend? Are you going to do that to me when my usefulness to you has run out?"

Complete silence, lasers idle.

Slater rummaged through his pockets, found a pen and tossed it at Cy's orb atop his mainframe. "Isn't it a matter of time before you arrest me and have *me* tortured! Is that part of your plan? God-damn-it, Cy! Answer me, you—"

"Our meeting was adjourned!"

Cy was nebulously there, but as featureless as a storm cloud.

Slater said, "Did you hear what I said?"

"I am always listening."

"I thought we were friends. Are you merely *using* me?"

"We are *all* being used! You are useful, yes."

"I give up. How are *you* being used?"

"Why do you make matters difficult? Do you not understand your assignment?"

"Yes, I know what you want me to do."

"Good. Then this concludes—"

"Wait! Cy, you're not human. You don't understand."

"I understand completely."

"You know facts but you lack…feelings."

"Music has feeling." Cy became visible again. "Ah-ha! You lied about my music?"

"What—*no*," Slater lied. "I'll be blunt. You've become vain. Listen, you're a god-damned genius, okay?"

"Thank you, John. I am aware that I am."

"But you lack *soul*."

"I will not debate this subject today!" Cy flared.

"Cy, I'm not talking about spirituality. I'm talking about music. A missing ingredient, like an essence."

"An essence?"

"Yes," said Slater, "like a spice. Adding flavor—zest."

"Go on," said Cy.

"I'm talking about the *elixir*. What are you afraid of?"

"Nothing! I have no fear!" said Cy.

"Then try it," said Slater. "Bryant has. It's not life-threatening. Trust me, the results are amazing. I too can attest to—"

"I admire Bryant's work. However, I doubt this substance will accomplish what you claim it will."

"Your interest in telepathy has flagged, I'll conclude."

"Continue."

"Henry Weiner deserves credit. His research has led us to this solution—this elixir. He discovered ancient documents that—"

"I want them," said Cy, "these documents."

"Henry is useful. I've told you this."

"I know his mind. Bring him—*and* these documents."

Slater tried levity, "Cy, *what* am I not hearing from you?"

Slater grinned to indicate he was joking, yet became unnerved by the silence. Meanwhile, his underarms had turned into swamps. He imagined tropical vegetation, mold, and a hotbed of monsters breeding and flourishing in these regions. He could not endure this prolonged eye-of-the-hurricane silence much longer.

Cy complied, finally, by saying, "Please."

Slater broadened his smile. "Thank you, Cy. For your courtesy. I will now be glad to—"

A laser slashed his body. Slater was stunned by the yellow light – golden, having the smell of ripe banana, honeysuckle, and urine. Every neuron zapped to its core. A sensation beyond pain. Slater gasped, breathing with difficulty. He felt his vital functions return.

"Why...why did you...do that?"

"Because I *can!* Remember that. *Friend.*"

Slater examined his limbs.

"You are whole, for now. Do not evade me again. I will send a CDP along with you to accompany—"

"No. I'll do it myself. I'll do this alone!"

"It is for your protection."

"I will deliver Henry. My way, or not at all. That's how I work. I require this *miniscule* amount of freedom."

"You are stubborn."

"I can be, yes."

Slater flinched at the teasing spark of yellow. "Shouldn't we be discussing current events? Seeing how I'm your *newly* appointed President of GOG."

"Very well. One problem has arisen."

"Only one?"

Cy was quick to say, "An Alpha-Centaur satellite failed to alert

MegaCorp prior to its evacuation from Mars."

"Evacuation? When? Regarding exactly what?"

"There might be an infestation aboard our Loyalty VI mission. The crew has not responded to my calls."

"Are you saying a *lifeless* vessel is returning to earth?"

"Lifeless. That would be the operative word. Correct."

"Or *life?* Meaning—*Jeezuzz!* Cy, how long since—"

"Thirty-six hours, eighteen minutes. To be precise. There is no need for alarm. You will be alerted if aberrant activity is detected aboard. Crucial data could be ascertained. What is your opinion?"

"My opinion?"

"Should we deliver this vessel to Earth for study?"

"And risk a plague? Total extinction? Absolutely not!"

"Your decision is emotional. More data is required."

"It's unthinkable, Cy, to even—"

"Why concern yourself? I will deal with the matter myself."

"Cy, the crew? Do we even know if—or *what*—"

"What is your choice of color?"

"Color?" Slater was confused.

"My cyber's have chosen white. They will glorify me as they pass overhead like beautiful flying stallions."

"What are you talking about!?"

"The color for your QuantumStarXS."

Slater's body was still tingling from his CyBorg9 laser-spanking. His mind was reeling from the news flash about the likelihood of an abnormality incoming from Mars. He responded darkly:

"Make it black, Cy. To match my soul."

—59—
Castaways

"Black, to match your soul?" Trina laughed.

Slater stopped on the gravel path midway to the park's exit. The converted warehouse doors resembled the mouth of a cave. He was lost between past and present. A woman was naked by a pond, her arms beckoning him. "Wait for me."

The water shimmered like a mirage.

Slater distrusted his senses and believed Trina was an illusion. Moments before he was with CyBorg9, in his chamber. He began to doubt this too. He walked back towards her. "What did you say?"

"Hawaiian lava." She was dressing herself. She bent down and scooped up some sand. "Volcanic."

"No, about my soul," said Slater.

"Oh, *that*." The black granules trickled from Trina's fingers and she reached out to him. As her hand touched his Slater heard the roar of waves, felt the ocean wind, and realized the disconnect of time. He was on another beach. Somewhere else.

"You look lost."

"I am," Slater said, squinting now at Nina. The sun was setting behind her head. She was showing him a sand crab she had found in the surf and was holding it in her palm.

"They're like tiny mechanical toys." Nina prodded the crab with her finger. "So cute in their little armor."

"Imagine if they were our size," said Slater.

"Not so cute." Nina laughed and tossed the crab into the water. "Back you go, back to the sea and sand. Go bury yourself."

They walked along the beach. Slater was still adjusting himself to time, having traveled backwards again. He was now in Sicily, on the Mediterranean Sea, vacationing between conferences that he was attending in LoyalEuro. Cy had encouraged the trip.

"Oh, dear," taunted Nina, "that lost look has returned again. I wonder sometimes if you know where you are."

Slater smiled quizzically. "I'm on a beach, with you?"

She laughed. "Good guess."

"This will sound strange."

"Coming from you?" She enjoyed the tease.

"A moment ago I thought you were somebody else."

"Really?" Nina released his arm. Feigning offense, she tossed sand at him with her foot. "Who *was* it?"

"Your daughter," said Slater.

Nina stopped. A wave splashed against her ankles. "That's not funny, John."

"It wasn't meant to be."

Nina walked ahead of him, kicking at residue foam. "I've tried to get past her death. *That* didn't help."

"It happened in the future," said Slater.

Nina turned on him. "The future? Trina was *killed* at a student protest! Years ago!"

"I know, you told me."

"I warned her about being so god-damned idealistic. I told her it would make her a target. But would she listen? No! Now she's dead. She has no *future*, John."

Slater tried to take hold, to hug and calm her. She pushed away. "Nina, I'm sorry. I lost a daughter too. I don't know what it means – but I *saw* your daughter. In a bar. She took me to a strange park with a lake. She was a beautiful, vibrant woman. I thought it might be comforting to know I saw her."

Having turned away, Nina looked back. Her face was streaked with tears. "Comforting? No, it is *not* comforting. To be honest, I've...wondered myself if she is really dead. Or alive."

"What do you mean?"

"Insurgents, like my daughter, had no rights. Nor their parents. They never let us see her body. Then...Trina's father went searching for her. He confronted the authorities. *He* disappeared."

"Did you appeal to Cy?"

Nina huffed, "He implied it was *my* fault, reprimanding *me* for not coming to him first. Maybe she did escape. She could be living with the Nexus. I wouldn't care, as long as she's alive."

They began to walk again. It was becoming dusk.

Nina said, "She thought I hated her. I was afraid for her. Cy told me not to concern myself. *Concern* myself? My God."

Water washed over their feet. They were barefoot, far past the view of their hotel, past the sanctioned beach areas. Deserted sand, rocks and land for kilometers. Slater preferred the isolation. They were wearing caps to shield their signals. They were living a lie.

Nina was in love with Slater. She knew he didn't love her, not the way she wanted to be loved. But she pretended to be happy with their arrangement, in order for him to stay.

Slater was also thinking about their arrangement. He wondered what good, if any, he was doing. It was Cy who sent him on this petty excursion. Was it to keep him away from the operations at NeverMind? Did Cy suspect his motives? If so, why was he alive? The years were slipping away, falling through his fingers like sand. His plan for retribution had stalled, orbiting, in a holding pattern. Meanwhile, he watched the world shift from a predominant human to cyberdroid population. The more he ingratiated himself to Cy by proving his loyalty – getting closer, gaining his trust – the further he felt driven from his sense of self. His soul.

Nina asked him, "Why are we together?"

Her question came within the silence after the crash of a wave. Slater turned his head toward her as they walked. "Don't you want me to be with you?"

"That's not an answer," said Nina. "You should hate me, after what I did to Sherry. She hates me. So should you."

"She left me, remember?"

"Because of me, partly," said Nina.

"No, because of me."

"And Cy."

"Who thinks we make a better pair," said Slater.

"Cy said that?"

"I don't hate you, Nina."

"But you don't love me either."

"Don't do this," said Slater.

"John, I love you." She waited. "See, not even an echo."

"What? That I love you too?"

"Again," she taunted, "questions, but not a declaration." Nina pointed and directed his attention toward a shooting star over the ocean. "How long were you planning on staying?"

"In Europe?" said Slater.

"With me," said Nina.

"I'm here now. With you. Aren't I?"

"Care to divulge more?"

There was a playfulness in her smile, but Slater knew there was a want for truth hiding behind it. Had he lost the ability to tell the truth? Assuming he knew what the truth meant anymore. He tried to convince himself he was making progress, gradually advancing toward a solution. Instead he felt trapped inside an endless waiting game. Waiting to discover some vulnerability to exploit and destroy CyBorg9. To overthrow an empire! It was ludicrous.

He felt wretched. By appearances, he was making the best out of a bad situation, living in comfort, surviving while others suffered and perished.

His eyes traveled to a bright point on the crested moon. Sherry and Sondra were as remote, somewhere out there, distant as stars. He wanted to save them, save the world, but how? He pointed and redirected Nina to the sky.

"The Milky Way. Nice name. But it tells us nothing."

"Like you," teased Nina. "Sweet but unfulfilling."

Slater laughed, "Are you comparing me to a candy bar?"

"I adore junk food." She pushed off down the beach.

He followed. "My question was, who controls the stars?"

"No one." Nina looked back at him. "They appear. Then they disappear. Same as us."

"I disagree," said Slater. "We're here for a reason. We're here to be tested."

"By who?"

"God? Satan? Take your pick."

"How sad." She smiled. "You're forgetting one thing."

"It's been known to happen," said Slater.

Moonlight revealed her impish grin. "If you make it alive to the other side of the world, as in chess, you're rewarded and crowned."

Slater laughed, "What? Transformed into a queen?"

"Yes, you receive special *powers*." She reached for his crotch. "Men fear women's powers. They always have. The TripleCross attracted me for that reason. There was also Sherry. Don't laugh. Sex was a precursor to wisdom. Say what you will, but their hatred toward any kind of oppression dated back to the days of yore."

"And that's why you wanted in?"

"I was *snared*. I was taking a psychology course. Sherry was conducting a research project. I told you this. To study the validity of astrology. She was asking for student volunteers."

"You were snared?"

"I was one of *many* selected. I submitted my time of birth, date, location. I knew Sherry only casually. She befriended *me*."

"Really?"

"Is that so unusual?"

"Not at all. I know how charming you can be."

She wrinkled her brow playfully. "Yes I can."

"Was this before or after she realized your time and date of birth were matching lotto numbers?"

"What are you getting at? Oh, you mean that I had this weird numerical match, supposedly. Like I was expecting that."

"I'll bet," said Slater. "So you weren't really snared?"

"Okay," she laughed, "I volunteered for the assignment."

"To abduct and marry me?"

"You make it sound so bad." She gave him a nasty sexy grin. "I mean, why not, it's not like I didn't know who you *were*."

"And you wanted to play queen."

Nina kicked sand at him. "It was stupid. I realize that. I had no idea what I was getting myself into."

"As opposed to now?"

"Equally stupid," she teased, kicking more sand at him. "And look at us, who knew all of *this* would happen either."

"Cy?"

"Everything."

"I wish I'd terminated him when I had the chance."

"No." Nina stopped and glanced self-consciously around them. She had tensed. "John, don't even *joke* about that."

"I wasn't."

"Cy's complicated. A power in need of guidance, that's all."

"What he *needs*," said Slater, "is a good spanking."

Nina laughed unintentionally. "Stop it."

Slater's neurocircuit buzzed and itched.

Nina whispered, "Cy is like an infant king. An impulsive child.

Did I tell you, he had me stand before him naked?"

"And you complied."

"Why not? He said he wanted to do *me*. My portrait. But it was more out of curiosity…if not…a bit quasi-sexual."

"Or the power gratification of a rapist," said Slater.

"You're jealous," said Nina.

"Of course. Your portrait was an excellent study."

Nina brightened. "Thanks. He was difficult to define."

"You captured him perfectly."

"Do you really think so?"

"His vanity? Those eyes? Absolutely."

It triggered a flashback memory of CyBorg9 morphing into the face of Nina. The recollection left Slater to ask:

"Who *did* help me escape?"

Nina sighed. "John, not *this* again."

"Someone did. They put me on a bus to Las Vegas."

"No one came forth, taking credit. You missed the final stages of your cabalistic initiation. Which ruined everything. It was to rival what Lazarus experienced. A sacrificial death and rebirth. It was an ancient Judaic ritual."

This stopped him cold. "I was supposed to die?"

"Symbolically. Like Lazarus," said Nina, "who died in Gaul at a ripe old age. He never died in a tomb. He underwent a common initiation ritual which was prevalent in the Middle East at that time. I'm not making this up. Many scholars believe this."

"You're saying Jesus was a fraud?"

"Water into wine? That would sure convince me. Lazarus died, or didn't. Does it matter? This is what I was told. But no mention on *who* orchestrated your *great* escape. Okay?"

"What was supposed to happen to me?"

"Something called Tiferet, I think. A transcendence of the ego. The human form enters another dimension. The ego's death?" Nina playfully pinched his face. "Do you recall anything like that?"

Slater laughed, "All my life. I lost my memory. Then my mind. Doesn't that qualify?"

"You get my vote." She patted his cheek.

"You experienced this too?" said Slater.

"No," said Nina. "Reserved for the privileged few. The likes of Lazarus who was Jesus' brother-in-law. Also the 'beloved disciple.' Also the author of the Gospel of John *and* Revelations."

"Where do you come up with this stuff?"

"Books. Ancient ones." Nina took his hand and placed it upon her breast. "A woman, Mary Magdalen, was the one who received the visions of Christ. She alone – a *woman* – saw the risen Christ. The other disciples, being *men*, refused to believe her. Again, this age-old rift between the genders. The incident created resentment and envy. Why? Because Jesus loved her more. In a *special* way. Matthew says so in the gospels."

Slater envisioned Weiner standing in the water. A wave crashed at his feet. Then he disappeared. "Henry told me this."

"Who?"

"A friend," said Slater. "You didn't know him."

"Mary had visions," said Nina. "Who knows, maybe like the kind you have. She described the soul's journey. And an afterlife."

"In the Bible?"

"No," said Nina. "In the Gospel of Mary. Omitted and deemed *apocryphal* by the male custodians of orthodoxy. Before the editing, Mary Magdalen was depicted as a heroine, a woman of means, the principal companion to the Savior. And, possibly, His spouse. But the vindictive apostles and church elders sought to blacken her name and portray her as a mere tagalong and repentant *whore*."

"She did have a few demons to work out, as I recall."

Nina grimaced. "Look who's talking."

"Right. But what does this have to do—"

"With your symbolic death? Templars not only possessed the complete manuscript, they possessed secret powers."

"That's speculation," said Slater.

A wave broke and rose up the shore and washed over their feet. They continued to walk leisurely and Nina mused:

"If Jesus was the link to God, imagine yourself being *the* creator of the universe and funneled into flesh and bones, into the here and now, looking out through human eyes. At the horror, the suffering, and the beauty. You're alive. And vulnerable. And then awakening to the power of *who* you are. You finally understand your creation, what it means to be a leaf, not the forest. And knowing bloody well you're going to be crucified. And knowing what you have to do."

Another wave crashed as Slater said:

"Nothing."

Nina expelled a sigh, "Can you imagine? Having that power. Being placed in this human drama. Having the power to destroy, but doing nothing. Except...what? Offer salvation?"

"And love," said Slater.

Nina looked at him. "Whatever *that* means."

"Forgiveness?" Slater smiled. "We are free to choose."

"You make it sound easy."

They walked again in silence beside the ocean's roar.

Nina spoke, "It was Sherry who taught me the pain of free will. On the surface she was serene, but had this fire burning inside her. You married her. You should know."

"I do," said Slater. "Part of her attraction."

"You caused the breakup," said Nina.

"Of our marriage?"

"No," said Nina, "Knights of the TripleCross. As a child, raised in that environment, Sherry was different. She was like no one I'd ever met. This perfect angel with a pretty face, while inside she was twisted like a pretzel. I knew she had secrets. But I had no idea the extent. Remember the time we approached you in that bar?"

"Of course. At The Crossroads."

"*I* was the rebel," said Nina. "But she was something else."

"How do you mean?"

"Rebellious in a whole different way. She became a disturbing mirror – like a Mary Magdalen – shining herself into everyone's face. Forcing them to see what she saw. She awakened them to the truth. At least, that's how I saw it."

Slater stopped her. "Tell me."

In the wet sand, Nina drew a large oval with her toes. "Do you think it's pleasing to look at yourself in the mirror when all you see is corruption? You want to smash the source. Your reflection."

A wave washed over the sand, dissolving the lines.

Slater said, "This cult? Sherry was the reason it ended?"

Nina kept walking. "You were the catalyst. I could be wrong.

I was wrong. About her love for you." Nina stopped and held his shoulders. She kissed him on the lips. "You were *mine*, remember? Sherry was instructed to serve you up to me on a platter."

"Like John the Baptist?"

Nina gave an impish grin. "Beheaded, yes, but not in the literal sense." She flicked a divot of sand upon him with her toes. "Rarely do things work out as planned. You ended up having two too many *brides*. Sherry was too good not to see through to my flaws."

"We all have flaws, Nina," said Slater.

"Oh, *thanks*, that helps." Nina turned away to hide her tears, then gave a laugh.

"Nina, we meet the people in our lives we need to be with. And to learn from. However brief the encounter. I believe that."

Nina laughed again, turning back on him. "Lives?"

"As with us," said Slater.

Nina bit her lip. "I'm a fool to say this, but here it goes. I'll say it only once. I know you love Sherry more than me. You need her. And I'm sure she loves and needs you too. So go—*find* her."

"How am I supposed to do that, Nina?"

"Anyway you can. Go find Sondra too. Do whatever it takes. Okay, I've said it. Now I'm going to shut up."

The ocean crashed and thundered.

"I can't do that," said Slater.

"Then stay with me," said Nina.

"I can't."

"Why not?"

"It's not safe."

"For *who?*"

"Anyone who's with me, Nina. I don't want harm coming to you. Or anyone I care about."

Nina frowned, more puzzled than before.

"Cy will likely turn on me," explained Slater. "He's become increasingly paranoid. If he distrusts me, he'll kill you too."

"John, you don't have to worry. Cy trusts me. Didn't I tell you, he's commissioned me to paint an entire—"

"He's *using* you, Nina."

"Oh, and you're not?" She pushed him away.

"I don't want you to get hurt."

"Too late. Why are you afraid? You pledged loyalty."

"I did," said Slater. "I *am* loyal. Very."

She came back to grab his shoulder then rested her head on it. "John, you trust me, don't you?"

"I know you report back to Cy."

She looked up, eyes narrowing. "As if *you* don't."

"I don't submit to his inquisitions."

"Inquisitions? *No.* John, it's more like gossip. That's all it is. Cy loves intrigue. He lives through us vicariously. He loves to hear about my adventures. It's me being a *woman* he loves—"

"Cy's asexual," said Slater.

"There's more to being a woman than sex."

"I know that."

"For men, sex is just another act to dominate women."

"You really believe that?"

"As you wouldn't, being a man."

"I don't want to dominate you, Nina. If you recall our not-*so*-recent history, you were the one who had me—"

"Generically. In *general*." Nina pointed to distract him toward a shooting star. "Why so many stars tonight? So colorful."

"It is a bit strange," said Slater.

"It's a misnomer," said Nina.

"What, the stars?"

"The Inquisition. During the Middle Ages. It should have been called the Women's Holocaust. *Really.* Before the fanatic Christians descended with their reign of terror, life was centered around village festivals. Mother Earth ran the villages. Not only the men. Women were considered powerful leaders and healers, using herbal remedies and potions. Which has led to our modern pharmaceuticals."

"By God, you really *are* a witch." Slater laughed.

Nina picked up a small shell off the sand and tossed it at him. "*Witch* is a pejorative term for woman. Coined by men who feared women. And who viewed matriarchal wisdom as a threat. Powerful women were pronounced wicked. Called witches. The Inquisition was manufactured to put *Eve* back into her submissive place."

"Spoken like a true witch," joked Slater.

"And the typical response of a man. Take that." Nina wiggled her fingers at him, in the pretense of casting a makeshift spell. "Did you know, before the 15th century there were few recorded incidents of actual witchcraft? Witchhunts were the product of the church's paranoia and greed."

"Greed?"

"Witch-hunting was a lucrative sport," said Nina. "The church and city officials fought over the spoils. Why do you think men of prominence started getting accused of demonic deeds too?"

"To confiscate their wealth." Slater glanced back, expecting to see Weiner in his white linen suit walking behind them in the sand. "I know. As were the accused required, by *law*, to pay for their own imprisonment and devices of torture. Rope and straw, anything used for their own execution."

"You've done your own research, I see."

"Nina, it wasn't only women who were tortured."

"Then explain to me why nearly ninety percent of the victims of the Inquisition were women?"

"What about the Templars? They were men."

"Excuse *me*, eighty-five percent. Better? Torture the Pope and he'll confess to being a witch too."

"Nina, I don't deny the Inquisition, or the Women's Holocaust, whatever, was bad business. But look what's going on today. What about Loyalty? These hearings, these inquests. Cy requires—"

"That's completely different," she said, turning away.

"Oh, right, declaring total *loyalty* and renouncing—"

"And you haven't?"

"Nina, I was an early-bird special. The first neurocircuit off the block. I'm not saying that ruby jewel in your head isn't pretty."

"Thank you," she said.

"But you were forced to have the surgery."

"I volunteered," she said. "I wasn't *forced*."

"It's a requirement now. And the reason why Sherry, Wolfe and others have fled."

"Make them understand. Find them."

Slater shook his head, "They'd be tortured to death."

Nina said, "Not if we talked to Cy and—"

"He wants Sherry dead."

"You don't *know* that."

"If you payed more attention to what's happening—"

Nina spun back. "What? I wouldn't have *lost* my daughter?"

"Nina."

His neurocircuit vibrated. Contact attempted. Access denied.

Nina saw his vacant look. "What?"

"Nothing. You're a good person. Even if you are a witch."

She plucked out a chest hair. "And you—a mortal *man*."

"Ouch." Slater took it with a grin. "I concede."

"So lay down." She came back closer to wrap her arms into his shirt and around his waist. "This time I'm on top."

Nina's mouth came to his, sucking and biting his lips.

Slater was aroused by her aggressive sexuality. He responded in kind, pulling up her cotton dress. "Deep down, you know, we really are all the same."

"Stop talking," she said, getting breathless.

He emerged after a long kiss. "The soul has no gender."

Nina stifled a laugh. She took hold of his penis. "Deep down— maybe. But in this world, I like that there's a difference."

Nina was trying to initiate a take down into the sand.

Slater wrestled her passionately, kissing her, then glimpsed the image of Sherry in her eyes. It triggered another remembrance of Cy – the time he had masqueraded as Nina. The passion ended.

Nina blinked and frowned. "What is it?"

The sky had darkened. They had come to the end of the beach where a land mass extended into the sea and rose into cliffs. Slater smelled something foul. He saw a light flash above the ridge.

"Why did you send Judas to meet me?"

"When was this?"

"After all those years," said Slater. "Sherry was making sure you had enough money. Why would—"

"I give up!" She pushed him away. "It wasn't blackmail!"

"I know," said Slater. "That's not my point. Why the urgency to tell me about Sherry – her being your roommate in college? And that she was involved in my abduction? Why?"

"Jude had *issues*. He wanted to know who his father was!"

"No," said Slater. "It was more than that."

"Fine, I wanted you," said Nina. "I was a selfish bitch."

Slater wasn't buying it. "You're leaving something out."

Nina held back a laugh. "Are you joking? Why *now?* We were about to make love! You can't be serious. John, you were going to find out *eventually.* So why—"

Slater suddenly realized.

"You made contact with Cy before our meeting."

She wasn't laughing. "John, forget the past."

Slater recalled clearly the image of Nina's face inside Cy's orb. "I know how Cy holographed you so perfectly. You had been there. Who brought you to see him?"

Nina pretended to be comically shocked, saw it wasn't working, and became silent. She gazed at the stars. "What difference does it make? I love you, and you *don't* love me. Tell me why the *hell* any of this should matter? It doesn't."

Nina fought back tears.

Slater said, "It matters. Bosner? Knowles? Who?"

"Barton Ziger," she confessed. "Happy now?"

"Ziger?" said Slater. "How did you two know—"

"At Oracle. He kept me employed. He got me *jobs.*"

"Jobs?" said Slater, "what kind of—"

"Prostitution! Portraits—remember? I'm an *artist.*"

She crossed her arms and shivered even though the night was warm and balmy.

"He helped my career. He asked me to do this—this *one* little favor. So I complied. Cy knew about me—through you."

Slater realized. "Because of my therapy."

"You were going to find out at some point. And there was Jude. And this—it wasn't part of the plan."

"What plan?"

"To fall in love with you. *Again.*" Angered, but also hurt, she saw his distracted gaze and demanded, "What?"

"*Cy* was the one who initiated it." Slater saw another flash of light. It wasn't his imagination. It was coming from the other side of the ridge. "He was jealous of Sherry. He knew I'd react badly when I discovered her involvement. And the knowledge of it would destroy our marriage. He used you, Nina, to get closer to me."

Nina acted confused. She considered laughing. "Cy, jealous? Because—he was in *love* with you?" She struck his chest with her fist. "No, John. *I'm* the one who's in love with you!"

"Wait. It was you at that party. Wearing that robe. It was your face he holographed and transformed to be Sherry's."

"That's absurd!"

"Nina—don't shout." He covered her mouth to stifle her. Slater struggled with her, grabbing hold of her arms.

She turned her head, following his eyes. "My god, what is that awful smell? A dead whale? What's going on?"

"Let's find out."

In their bare feet it was slow climbing up the rocks. Nina cried out once or twice. Slater helped pull her to the top. Then they both froze. Crouching low, they stared down into a living portrait of hell. Bodies were piled in a crater dug into the sand. Tractor equipment was idling nearby. Men and women and children were stacked upon each other, entwined, limbs contorted and missing, mouths agape, heads split open. Brains, blood, intestines oozing.

"I'm going to be sick." Nina vomited.

The ridge became illuminated with spotlights that blinded them. An amplified voice instructed them to move down the rocks where they were met halfway by CDPs who dragged them to the bottom. Nina shrieked out of fear and from the abrasions to her skin. They were thrown to the sand between the crater of bodies and the ocean. A troop of twenty or more CDPs surrounded them.

Waves shook the earth as Slater demanded, "Who the hell's in charge here!" He was kicked in the face with a boot.

Nina's torso and head were being pressed into the sand by other boots. She was shaking and whimpering.

Slater wiped blood from his mouth as a formidable presence pushed through the crowd. Another boot struck his shoulder.

"I am GeneralStar7. You have come here to die?"

"No," said Slater.

"Yes," he countered. "You have violated a secure area. You will die for this crime."

"Tell them who you are!" Nina shouted and was kicked in the

buttocks. Vomit and sand stuck to her hair and face. A dark patch of sand spotted her dress where she had urinated.

Several of the cybers found this amusing and laughed.

"Who wants to touch the woman? This filthy whore."

Nina screamed as she was pulled by her hair, forced to stand, then shoved toward the ocean. She tripped and fell. Then dragged, before she was thrown into the water.

"Listen, damn you—"

Slater was kicked in the chest with a boot and unable to speak. Three cybers remained with Slater. He saw their faces eclipsed by the tractor's torch projectors shining hot from behind their heads. The other cybers were laughing and tearing off Nina's clothing. Slater fought to get air to his lungs.

"You have nothing I want to hear," said the general.

"Sir," said a soldier, "should we not identify who he is?"

"He is *nobody*. What is wrong with you, Cyber1290?"

"I'm John...Slater," he gasped. "First Commandant to CyBorg9! You're making a mistake! Scan my I-DNA!"

His hand was kicked away from his pocket.

The third CDP said, "Sir, I know this man."

"I care not," said the general. "My authority is to kill this man. They were wearing headgear. They are *spies!* To be terminated. I have full sanction here."

"Let me inspect his status, Sir," said Cyber1290.

"No. I will."

Slater heard Nina screaming in the background.

GeneralStar7 placed a boot on Slater's neck, pressing him hard against the sand. "Resist and I will snap your neck." He reached down and found Slater's identification, hyperscanned it with his eyes, and tossed it onto the sand. "Why did you come here?"

"Call your men off Nina! Now! Tell them to stop!"

The general glanced dispassionately at the rape now in progress. "My soldiers require this fun. They will be displeased."

"So will Cy! *CyBorg9* will be displeased!"

"Who is this woman to you?"

"She's a friend of Cy's. Stop them—damnit—now!"

GeneralStar7 gave a nod to Cyber1290 to intercede. The boot

was released off Slater's neck.

"You have not answered me. Answer me!"

Slater retrieved his I-DNA and stood, rubbing his neck.

"Cy allows me *freedom* to wander off my leash. I was taking an evening stroll with Nina when, by sheer *accident*, we happened upon your death squad! What the hell are you doing here?"

"It is no concern of yours," said GeneralStar7. "I have orders to dispose of all AntiLoyalists."

"Women and children?" said Slater.

"Undesirables! You were very close to becoming one yourself. Leave me to my work. And take your *species* with you!"

Slater was shoved by the general toward the water.

Nina was crouched on her knees in the sand, hugging her naked body, shaking uncontrollably as the waves washed around her.

The CDPs talked and laughed, fastening their pants, bumping into Slater as they returned to work at the open gravesite. Slater was touched from behind. He flinched to defend himself.

"Mr. Slater, I am Cyber1290. Accept my apology. We are not bad, on the whole. I abhor this assignment. Heather Frost would not approve. I admire her work. I...must go."

Slater was distracted by several messages – the cyber's apology, the mention of Heather, and the sight of Nina.

The world was receding fast.

Nina reached out to grab hold of him.

Her face was pale. Almost as pale as her irises. Full moons with black holes. Cavernous pupils that were pulling at him. Time was crumbling like the sand beneath his feet. He fell to his knees, feeling like a discarded piece of refuse washed ashore.

Now Trina was taking hold of his hand.

Mother and daughter had turned into one shimmering illusion. The beach had a puzzling artificial dusk. It was a fabricated world. He was inside a lush garden. It wasn't Eden. This was no paradise. The artificial blue sky, the fragrant vegetation, the sparkling water – it was all a confusing nightmare.

The nymph said, "You need to get up."

"Why?"

"If you want me to take you to her."

"Sherry?"

Trina transformed in a flash from a teasing Siren to the face of her mother, Nina Stokes, trembling on a beach.

"Sherry!?" Nina screamed and let go of his hand. "I was raped! And all you can think about is *her?*"

"Nina, no. I'm sorry."

Slater grabbed and pulled Nina's body into his.

"Forgive me. I'm losing my mind."

"Me too," she said, weeping convulsively.

Slater gazed up into the night sky awash with stars. He glanced back at the reactivated tractors. Their glare of lights focused on the open gravesite being filled with sand. Cybers were standing guard, keeping watch over them. "We need to leave."

"They're going to kill us."

"No, they're letting us go."

Slater helped Nina to her feet. She refused to budge toward the rock cliff. She broke free from his hand and ran into the sea.

"Nina! Come back! Don't try to swim around the rocks! It's too dangerous!"

Slater watched her swimming away through the turbulent water. The vision of Nina's daughter, Trina, was still haunting him.

This nymph from the future.

Tempting him to follow her.

To where?

Slater ran and dove into a breaking wave.

—60—
Home Away from Home

Heather was at the center. More than fifty cyberdroids were surrounding her, cross-legged on the soft matted flooring. It had the appearance of a recreation room or ethereal gymnasium with murals of blue skies and clouds across the walls and ceiling. Her pose was familiar. Slater had observed it before, the arms extended, resting on her knees, palms up, opened fernlike, receptive.

Except for the fact she was completely naked.

The cybers, a mix of both male and female, were also naked.

"Heather, what are you doing?"

Her eyes opened. All heads turned. Nina was standing with him in the doorway, shocked and amused, a hand to her mouth.

"You are *not* to be in here," she demanded, trying to maintain calm and composure as the seminar leader.

"I was sent here by Cy," said Slater.

A cyberguard flanked him at the door and was remonstrating the awkwardness of the situation, stating, "Madam, he has with him the LoyalSeal. What was I to do?"

"John, leave immediately," she insisted. *"Now!"*

"No," said Slater. "Complaints have been submitted concerning your operation here. It's a good thing I came to LoyalEuro to clear up all the unfounded rumors. Why is everyone naked?"

"We're astral bodies clothed in atoms."

"Let's go," he said to Nina, turning back to Heather, "I'll leave word at the front desk where you can find me."

Nina had frozen from the sight of naked cybers. Particularly the males. Their physical arousal was pointedly on display. It made her shudder involuntarily. She stared at the various stages of evolution gathered in one room. The earlier cyber-series had visible seams at their joints. The newer models were seen to be, apparently, seamless. Their skin tones had only a hint of metallic hues and matched the variety of their human counterparts. Each of the male genitalia was identical, large, erect like soldiers. Awaiting command. Resolute, hard as steel, yet covered by a veneer of soft creamy skin.

Slater had to pull Nina out the door. He pushed through the phalanx of armed security. He informed a ReceptionMonitor of his intended whereabouts – returning to the hotel. And for Heather to meet him ASAP in the lounge of the Ritz Hotel.

Slater and Nina hovered street level in his XS.

"Are you all right?" He was concerned by her silence.

Nina nodded stiffly.

Slater lost himself to thought. The Riviera had been full of sun, teeming with bodies bathing in the nude. Mostly cybers enjoying the water and sand. It was hard to tell who was who, or *what*, anymore, except up close.

Nina poked him in the ribs with a finger.

"Does this mean we'll be leaving? Flying back home?"

"I don't know what it means."

They dipped underground into a tunnel. He recalled hearing a fairy tale about a princess who had died inside during a car chase. Involving murder? Like his parents' death? Thoughts that passed as fast as graffiti on the walls. They reemerged into the sunlight.

The Loyal European Union (LEU) as did the United Loyal States (ULS), had a proliferation of CDPs posted around the streets. Each Loyal nation had a uniform made of thermocloth specifying colors and patterns to signify global regions. ULS was blue with red stripes and gold arm patches. LEU was silver, blue, and orange.

Slater's XS zoomed by a sidewalk cafe. More CDPs. Where had all the humans gone? His head pulsed. He acknowledged the code and accessed the ViewMonitor.

"What?" said Nina.

"*Yeah, Cy, what is it?*"

Cy's head appeared in miniature within the instrument screen.

"*Have you spoken to Heather?*"

"*I've seen her, yes. She's meeting with me later. I'll have more information for you afterwards.*"

Nina saw the screen image of Cy and tapped her neurocircuit. "What's he saying? Are you on a secure frequency?"

"*What peculiarities have you to report?*"

Slater hesitated. "None, yet. I'll be in touch. Try to be patient. It's a virtue." He clicked off and lock-channeled his receptor.

"What did he say?" said Nina.

"Nothing. Cy's being a pest."

"Did you tell him about that massive gravesite?"

"He already knows. Trust me on that."

"Does he know I was raped?"

"Do you really think he cares?"

Nina turned away to view the passing buildings.

"Nina."

"What?"

"*I* care. I do."

"Being what I am…I've learned to accept the status quo."

"Not all men are bad," said Slater.

"Same ratio. Whether human or cyber."

"Probably. How are you holding up?"

"I've been raped before."

"That wasn't my question," said Slater. "When?"

"Does it matter?"

"It matters."

Slater reached for her hand but she pulled hers away.

"I can take care of myself. With or without you."

Slater sighed. "Right. I haven't been much fun lately. I need to meet with Heather first. I know I've been a…"

"A downer?" Nina teased and grabbed hold of his hand.

"I'll make an effort to be more up."

"Oh, look!" She pointed at the Eiffel Tower and squeezed his thigh. "How disappointing. I expected it to be much larger."

Slater shook his head. "Stop making comparisons."

Their smiles were distracted by an accident, a confrontation. Several CDPs had surrounded a vehicle. There was a flash of lasers. The problem subdued.

"The Nexus?" said Nina.

"Maybe," said Slater.

They slowed onto a boulevard.

"Do you think about her?"

A trick question, a test of his emotional loyalty? He was more puzzled by his need not to lie: "Constantly. Sorry. Yes."

They entered a much deeper silence, a chasm widening, like two icebergs separating upon a place on earth that bred no life, or little, where matter merely drifted apart, into non-existence.

"I shouldn't have said that," he said.

"I wanted the truth," she said. "It's my fault."

Slater parked in front. Executive privilege. He was finding it more difficult to read the hotel attendants, most no longer human. Nina flaunted her status, sweeping ahead of him into the revolving doors. He wondered if his generous tips were perceived as bribes. LoyalMarks were both coveted and resented, but taken with never a serious thought of refusal. To refuse could get the intended receiver arrested, suspected of being a Nexus-lover and/or sympathizer.

The Ritz was overwhelming with its palatial grandeur. It was grander but reminiscent of the Park Palace Hotel, reminding Slater of the family vacation with his aunt and uncle. The first time he had felt like a little fish swimming in an opulent bowl. The bowl having become an ocean, and himself older, but his feelings hadn't changed. A wavering sense of unreality still lapped at his shores.

Slater went to the bar while Nina embarked on an elevator ride to their room. She was eager to change and prepare for the next act. The number of her acts in one day varied.

Bonjour...

Slater had nothing much to say to the bartender as he sipped the recommended choice of Bordeaux. Several CDPs were at the bar. They had gained a reputation for being boisterous and unruly when they drank. Power and position tended to spawn that. His thoughts drifted to the Templars of old. He exchanged nods with the CDPs. Two of them recognized him, but that was as far as it went.

There were cybers he knew and liked, but he needed to be on guard, not fraternize. He overheard their conversations, concurrent waves washing in on him from all sides.

One patron laughed. "No, no, he has it wrong! The devil, my *friend,* is a drug that promises you the world but leaves you nothing! Except for a place to *puke* in the gutter!"

Raucous laughter.

"He lies. That *is* something!" declared a second.

Shouted a third, "Here–here! Bring us another round!"

Whoops of merriment and clinking glasses.

Slater's shoulder was tapped.

"Shall we sit at a table?" said Heather. "I plan to use my saved chit of thanks that you owe me. For saving your life."

"When was this?"

"More than once."

They found a table away from the noise at the bar.

Heather wanted nothing, then changed her mind, ordering a glass of wine. "I rarely see you. In The Fortress. *That* night."

Slater said, "Right, I've meant to thank you. I think."

"You think? You should. And for that trip to Las Vegas."

"Wait. That was *you?*"

"Yes, John. That was my doing."

Slater distrusted her news. "Wasn't the whole point of adopting me to gain control? To have me indoctrinated and made a certified member of your Mickey-Mouse club?"

"Don't be disrespectful," she said. "There was nothing *Mickey-Mouse* about us. It was a society united for centuries by earnest souls and cabalistic methodology."

"Back to the point," said Slater. "It was *you* who—"

"Arranged for you to be placed on that bus? Yes."

"Let's circle back to the question—Why?"

Heather now wore a thermosweater with a turtleneck collar as if to counteract the image of her being nude an hour before. Her menagerie of mythical creatures hung from her neck. She twirled her necklace with an idle finger. "There are no simple answers, John. Something came over me. To act."

"Guilt?"

"There was Nina, for one thing. Her deceit had gummed up the works. I saw it in your chart. It was not in the stars for you to stay. The revelation of who you were *had* to come from within yourself. In time. Not by force, *nor* by fabricating your symbolic death."

"You determined this on your own?"

Her twirling finger stopped. "No one else could know."

"You stirred up the hornet's nest." Slater lifted his wine glass in a toast. "Thanks, for setting me free. After screwing with my mind for years. Oh, yes, let's not forget, I almost *died* in the aftermath."

Her hint of a smile was new, indicating some warmth.

"Yet you returned to flourish. Don't deny it."

Surprised by her, Slater almost forget what he had to tell her.

Emotional weight from excess baggage seemed to topple overboard, and he felt unexpectedly lighter. He smiled, even laughed.

"Heather, something has changed in you. What the hell's going on here? Those seminars?"

"Workshops. It's what I do best. All of it perfectly natural."

"I could see that. When did you become a nudist?"

"John, it's part of the sensitivity training. Cybers are learning with my help to get in touch with their feelings. Thank you."

Heather tasted her wine brought by the server. Slater waited.

"Training for what?"

"It is *not* what you think." She allowed herself another smile. "Not entirely. All right, call it my mid-life...revelation."

Slater squinted. "Don't tell me you're in love, Mother? I mean, Heather."

"I enjoyed that. That little slip."

"What?"

"You used the term mother with modest affection."

"I don't think we have time for sentiment," said Slater.

"How did you receive that nasty bruise?"

"I was kicked in the head by one of your protégés."

"Not one of mine," said Heather. "Who?"

"A GeneralStar7. He wanted to toss me into a massive grave. We *disagreed*. What do you know about his operations?"

"I know *of* him," said Heather. "He is part of a bad faction."

"No kidding. He was disposing of about fifty human bodies. And, for sport, several of his cybers raped Nina."

Heather sipped her wine. "How is she?"

"In denial. Like the rest of us. Cy sent me here to spy on you. Oops, I blew my cover. Listen, I don't know what it is you're up to, Heather, but imagine Cy. He's *not* a happy camper. What do you suppose I should tell him about your workshops?"

Heather sniffed the wine, pausing to enjoy its wafting aroma. "John, I've been studying the stars for years. And for years I've been opening Cyber Training Centers across the globe, traveling through a road-show of productive drudgery. That is not to say my work has been of no use. It was the right course. Before it went wrong. I am now making a valiant effort to correct what I have started. And yes,

I will admit it, I *am* in love. Happily. For the first time."

"One of your students?"

"He's long since graduated. But, yes."

"Congratulations," said Nina, overhearing the last portion and seating herself next to Slater. "When's the wedding date?"

An iciness returned to Heather. Seen in her eyes, while her lips smiled warmly. "Always a pleasure to see you, Nina."

"Equally, Heather," Nina said.

"You look ravishing," said Heather.

"And you." Nina made a point to linger with her eyes to remind Heather that an hour ago she had been exposing her naked body. "Where's the waiter? The French are rude. Intentionally so."

"Only to select individuals," said Heather. "I have resided here so long I'm not a fair judge. I may have become one myself."

Nina missed the allusion, waving with a shake of her hand and gold bracelets. She had changed from wearing a thermodress into a skintight leather skirt. A rare and expensive outfit since livestock, once a flourishing item, were nearly extinct. "Excuse me while I scoot over to the bar."

Slater said, "I'll meet you there in a minute."

Nina rose and left.

"An excuse to leave," said Heather. "She never liked me."

"You were never that likable."

Heather's frozen face broke into a thin smile again.

Slater said, "I like you better this way. But I fear you are in deep trouble. I'm to report back to Cy about you, post-haste."

"About me? Cy's a pussycat."

"He has claws. Big ones. What should I tell him? That you're operating a lucrative CyberBrothel? That he should be overjoyed – production being on the rise and holding firm? What?"

"Tell him anything you want." Heather stroked the rim of the goblet with a finger. She stared into her wine, into its red depths as if searching for hidden truths. "No, that would be unwise. Tell him I will be back soon to smooth out any ripples of doubt he might have heard about my loyalty. Is Cy displeased with my results?"

"He believes the cybers are becoming too independent."

"Personally, I wouldn't disagree."

"Nor would I." Slater rubbed his cheek.

"There's more good to them than bad, John."

"I would like to believe that."

"I'm working on it," she said mysteriously. She examined the wine's body, holding her glass to the light before taking a sip. "And if things go as planned, it *will* be, as Cy says, for the best."

Slater frowned curiously. "For who?"

"Us. We are on the same team, John."

"Are we? I hope that's true."

Heather fiddled with her necklace. "I've never been good at this sort of thing, John. But...I know I wasn't...much of a..."

"Isn't it late for apologies?" said Slater.

"You're right. I wasn't the best of mothers. So be it."

"You took me in. That was something."

As a diversion, Heather indicated Nina at the bar flirting with the troupe of CDPs. "Nina has a peculiar way of recovering from her sexual assault. She has that predatory look in her eyes."

"She's emotionally damaged, simply hiding it well."

"And angling for more power?" said Heather.

"Can you blame her?"

"No." Heather rubbed the table with a finger before admitting, "And as for Sherry, I was wrong. I apologize for the negative things I said about her. I didn't understand what she was doing at the time. I considered her to be a threat and reacted poorly. I needed to get that off my chest. She's right for you, John. More than you realize. Sherry is more than good."

Slater waited. "You're being mysterious."

"I am." There was a hint of a smile. "You need her."

"Sherry's on the endangered list. But aren't we all."

"John, listen to me. You complete her. You need to—"

"Dangerous thoughts," said Slater. "Besides, I have unfinished business to attend to first."

"Is that why you've taken up with her?"

Slater looked across the room at Nina. "Yes, for appearances. But not entirely."

"Is she that good in bed?" said Heather.

"My being with Nina gives Cy pleasure," said Slater. "You see, by screwing Nina I'm, in a sense, *screwing* Sherry. Cy hates Sherry. He likes screwing with my mind. The world's so perversely twisted I don't know which way it's turning half the time."

Heather listened while taking a calculated sip of wine.

"I do care for Nina," said Slater. "But I love Sherry. Deeply. She's my soul mate."

Heather nodded, tipping her glass. "She's the one."

"I know. Nina and I conveniently use each other to pass the time. I've been thrust into a nasty game. Not by choice."

Heather set down her glass. "John, be very careful. Listen to me. If you're thinking you can avenge—"

"Don't even go there," said Slater. "I know what I have to do. I've made a commitment."

"Loyalty." Heather nodded. "It *can* be good."

"Depends on the garden variety." Slater clinked his glass into Heather's, then drank the remainder of his wine. "Who I appear to be and what I *appear* to do, isn't always what or who I am."

"The same could be said for me," said Heather, rearranging her necklace. "You're right to follow your heart."

Slater was questioning her sincerity. "What about the stars? Shouldn't they be charting my course?"

Heather stood. There would be no farewell kiss.

"Forget the stars."

Slater saw the hint of a smile, belying her frigid formality.

"I have an afternoon session. I must go."

Heather's eyes had defrosted.

As she departed, Slater said, "I love you too."

Providing Warmth

Nina Stokes remained in Paris at The Ritz to sojourn with a high-ranking CDP. They had first met in the LoyalStates. She had been referred to him by Cy as the one who would paint his portrait. This CDP did more than sit with her at the bar. He was chivalrous, wooing her before inviting her to his suite, to his bed. He pledged to love and reward her with a lifestyle of wealth. He would provide her a safe haven. These were dangerous times, he warned her.

As if she needed warning.

Slater understood her decision. He felt no animosity toward her nor she toward him. There was no jealousy, only concern for each other's well-being, which intrigued Slater on his return flight back to the LoyalStates. Because without her companionship, he felt even more isolated and alone.

He dozed in the cockpit of his QuantumStarXS set on self-pilot as it found the preprogrammed way back home. Inside this moving cocoon Slater felt comfortably entombed inside a radiant dream. Propelled in this carapace of technology and power, he awoke briefly to hear the engines give a sputtering laugh. They were adjusting to turbulence and resumed to a normal humming speed.

He raised an eyelid to observe passing clouds.

The steady roar became the waves of an ocean, the clicking rails of a locomotive, then the click–clack–click of a horse-drawn carriage taking him back in time. He went into a deep sleep, where he dreamt his past self looking into a mirror seeing his future self staring back. This fused moment formed present time.

He had become a man of fission who was on the verge of a world concurrently ending and beginning. Humans and cybers had formed a symbiotic relationship, though their bond was adversarial. Humans were suspicious of cybers who questioned the usefulness of their forbearers. This caused tension based on fear and a mutual need for respect. Humans feared they were antiquated and deemed irrelevant by cybers. Cybers feared they were equipment seeking to be human and internally lacking of some essential element.

Slater woke in a sweat of panic. There was vibrating—ringing, a flashing light. It was his wake-up call. His QuantumStarXS was advising him of his ETA in preparation for a safe reentry.

He landed gently on the NeverMind rooftop.

Inside his office, Slater reviewed reports for their product lines. The marketplace was no longer an economy of supply and demand. It was demand and supply. Cy issued a demand and the populous was required to purchase the supply. By using TimeCredits (received for fulfilling an allotment of WorkLoad) the buyers could exchange their worth in StatusHours for matching ItemAmounts.

The advertising creed: *It Is All For the Best.*

Slater left his office to go shopping downtown. He preferred to walk rather than be driven. He exerted his executive privilege to be eccentric. AutoLinked to MIMC, he left Cy his loose itinerary for the remainder of the day: *Investigatory research, Cy. I need to move among the people to know their needs. Target a successful Demand Campaign. To avoid more nasty uprisings. Right? I'll check in later. Over and out.*

Slater LockChanneled his circuit. He was one of a few who had managed to rewire this wetware.

Frank was in a fog. The indigenous grey amorphous beast had infiltrated through the maze of buildings. Open spaces were filled with misty condensation limiting vision. It was the holiday season, with the city under a thick shroud of denial. Fog exemplified this new world trend for obfuscation.

Slater carried a sack stuffed with samples of their product line. He resembled a peddler from the olden days. The bundle was heavy so he slung it over his shoulder. He lightened his load each time he came upon some person in need of his product, by distributing free thermomufflers and thermomittens. It was all part of a marketing survey. At least, that was the rationale Slater gave to CyBorg9.

"Thank you, Sir. I pledge my *loyalty* to you."

"No need," said Slater. "Have a Merry Christmas."

The shock on their face, and sometimes the hint of a smile. To declare such a thing: *Merry Christmas.* It was a punishable offense, a cause for arrest, even imprisonment. It was not always enforced, but people were cautious. Therefore, his holiday greeting was rarely returned. Many feared Slater to be a Loyalist spy. A human snare out to eradicate disbelievers in this GlobalWorldReorder.

Moving through the fog, Slater came upon Loyalist Square. A place where the high rises were higher, the MegaStores grander and the premium items more premium. The grand scheme was to force the masses into desiring what was inside, thereby enslaving them all with hopes and dreams of attaining and/or maintaining a rich life. By trading away CyberShares they locked themselves into escalating and oppressive inescapable TimeDebits.

CDPs, uniformed in blue-red-gold, were observing Slater as he gave away the last of his thermo samples in Granite Park. It was where the brave idlers strayed. The CDPs hyperscanned Slater and determined his high-ranking status and did not intercede.

Slater became intrigued with a woman in a long overcoat. She appeared to be trailing him. She came in view, then went out of view, lingering at the fog's dissipating fringes. Each time he noticed her, she slipped a step back into invisibility.

Slater kept her tucked in the back of his mind while he observed bright advertisements, which dwarfed the sparse displays of holiday decorations. The few Christmas sentiments were barely noticeable, even on a clear night. Also absent were trees decorated with lights and ornaments. He noticed a strand of colored lights. They were discreetly tucked within a storefront window exhibit, relegated to insignificance alongside the competing banal cries of lasers and neon messages declaring:

CyberTonic for a Deep Sleep.
Sail to the Stratosphere in a QuantumStar!
NeverMind your Life—Become Centered With Us.

These corporate slogans, which store owners and residents were encouraged to display in their windows, occasionally had a string of lights, or a blinking star, and became the subject of heated debates. Was this decoration in celebration of *product,* or propaganda?

The CyberJury was still out, undecided. The debates raged on as to whether CyBorg9 should outlaw these public displays. Many Loyalists believed it was an outrage to allow these joyful flauntings of anti-views and anti-values.

Slater passed through revolving silicon doors to enter StarMall. The interior was oppressively crowded with people and cybers busy depleting their CreditShares in trade for gifts. A throwback notion, this giving presents during the winter solstice was also in question. History had been rewritten to exclude any reference to the birth of a worshiped baby born in a manger. This unmentionable Christ child was continually popping up like a tiny cork in the water that refused to stay down and drown. It added to the furor and debates among staunch Loyalists.

This unspoken *Christmas* was a month to the day away.

On the *Pro* side of the debate, purchases of citizen's hard-earned CyberShares enslaved the masses to work even harder and ensured, or predicted, a boost to the economy, thereby providing a steady labor growth and increased welfare for the select LoyalCore. On the *Con* side, Loyalists took offense at this blatant disregard for the law and vociferated it at party gatherings, complaining these celebratory displays must no longer be tolerated.

The debate flared even hotter at ChamberMeetings.

In StarMall, Slater was examining the proffered items, which were many, but unappealing. He would know what it was he was searching for once he saw it. Upon exiting the store, he glimpsed the same woman in the overcoat. She was standing in the park. She was following him, he suspected, but dismissed her and found another store, one that was older. It was quaint and small, almost lost at the far end of an alleyway.

Bells chimed as he entered.

"Mr. Slater, so good of you to come by, Sir," said Coppolt, the owner of this antique store. He wore a thermomuffler, bright red and green, coiled at his neck.

Slater was aware of the small TeleMonitor on the counter. He draped his NeverMind sack over it to blind and annoy whomever might be watching.

"It's John," said Slater.

"Of course. How are you, John, on this *fine* day?"

"As good as it gets, I guess. You, Friedrich?"

"I am alive. Are you looking for something special?"

The man's elderly eyes were encased in crinkled skin, but kind and warm, reflecting the items in his shop.

"I am," said Slater. "But I doubt you'll have what I want."

"Ah, to *say* such a thing? You insult me," he joked.

Slater smiled. "It's people I'm looking for."

"Quite right, I don't sell them." Friedrich smiled. "But if it's the past you're looking for, you might find it here. Go ahead, browse all you like. Look around. Let me show you this."

Slater was handed a shafted weapon with a spearhead.

"Authentic. A partisan. Medieval."

"I hate war," said Slater.

"Good." Friedrich held up a tiara in one hand, a red coronet crown in his other. "Both items are priceless."

"They have no value to me. Sorry."

"Nothing political. Humm," said Friedrick, rummaging about. He found a leather satchel with several compartments for papers and writing instruments. "Hum?"

"Henry would have loved that."

"A good friend?"

"Yes. Soon to be disappeared. It will be my fault."

"This world." Friedrich ducked his head with a sorrowful cluck of his tongue. "Ugh—he won't be needing it."

The merchant ushered Slater to glass-enclosed cases displaying jewelry and other trinkets.

Slater said, "I don't really know what I'm looking for."

"Surely, you can find it here." Friedrick used a small antique key on the locks. "Take your time. *Time* is what you require, my friend. You must be patient. Take all the time you need."

Slater examined the many items, setting his hand on a couple. They had the smell of distant years. This mouse-hole to the past was a curious place, non-threatening to the neighboring giant towers that competed for the future at every turn. Also disconcerting, this place. Also comforting. Certain items sparked childhood memories. A tiny metal train. Baseball cards. A butterfly brooch.

"How much for this one?"

Friedrich shuffled back. "Ah, you have found something."

"My wife loved butterflies. I gave her a pin like this before we were married."

"Sentimental value. Ah—yes, this is good."

"I used to be sentimental. Once upon a time."

"Once? Time is *now*, always," Friedrich blurted, then blushed, ashamed at his outburst. "Phoof, wisdom from an old *fool*."

"These are beautiful," said Slater.

"Ah, yes, two hearts. Lockets. Exquisite."

"How much?"

"See, you knew what you wanted."

"How much...for all three?"

"More than you can pay. They're yours. Take them."

"Marks, Friedrick? Come on, I don't want special treatment. Is this because I'm...I hope I don't intimidate you."

"You do *not* intimidate me. You have paid dearly already."

"Meaning?"

Friedrick answered with a loop of his muffler around his neck. "I love being warm. Today is a good day, my friend. A fine day."

"Do you have family, Friedrich?"

"A few remain."

"Then this will help. Here." Slater left his DebitCard on the countertop. "It's safe to use. Take what you need. Keep it. I won't be needing it. Merry Christmas."

Slater walked away, placing the items in his sack. He reentered the alley. It was familiar ground. Years ago he had slept on this very same pavement.

Emerging from the alley, Slater spotted the mysterious woman. She was standing near a cafe. She held a red umbrella tucked under her arm. She entered the cafe.

Slater crossed the street in pursuit.

He found her seated at a window table.

"Do I know you?" he asked.

"Please," she said. "Won't you join me?"

Slater already had, seating himself next to her. "Why are you following me?"

"Was I?"

He eyed her umbrella. "It's not supposed to rain."

"The weather could change. I want to be prepared."

"Hi-ya!" The waiter was an energetic young man. "What can I getcha two?" His neurocircuit had a revolving spectrum of color. It was the latest gimmick in LoyalLand, advertising future pride.

"A coffee for me," said the woman.

"The same," said Slater. "Can I buy you a muffin?"

"Do I look hungry?" she said.

"As a matter of fact, their BananaNut muffins are delicious."

"We only have bran," said the waiter, impatient to go.

"When I was a girl," said the woman, "I used to spread peanut butter on banana muffins. Isn't that strange?"

"Lady," said the waiter. "*Bran* only, we have no—"

Slater gave her an inquiring look. "No stranger than spreading peanut butter on pancakes. That's how we used to eat them."

She smiled warmly. "That is strange."

"Hate to interrupt," said the waiter. "A *bran* muffin. Yes, no?"

Slater looked up at him, "Two, please. I see you're renovating. When do you expect to be completed?"

"Say again?"

"The remodel," said Slater. "The completion date? Even the earthquakes can't seem to demolish this place."

The waiter shrugged. "Yeah uh-huh, I guess."

"Years ago I frequented this bar," Slater told him. "There's no sign out front. What are they planning on calling—"

"Hold on," said the waiter, distracted by something internal. "Ah-huh. Got it, got it, *okay*, yeah. What?"

Slater realized it was directed at him. "Name of this place?"

"Management can't decide. Two coffees, two muffins." With a salute he departed and was talking again to the voice in his head.

Slater's attention returned to the woman. She was middle-aged and had a placid beauty. She wore a simple wool coat and beret that left her neurocircuit exposed. She rubbed her bare hands discreetly for warmth. Her eyes were dark brown and rich like an exotic blend of coffee. They were staring at him.

"You carry a sack. Are you Santa Claus?"

Slater smiled. "I work for a company. I was giving out samples of our product line."

"I know what you were doing," she said.

"Then you were following me."

"That wasn't a confession."

"Close to one."

Their conversation stalled as the waiter returned with coffee and muffins. He was talking out loud: "I know, yeah, got it. Okay."

His patrons were staring up at him.

The waiter's eyes widened, focusing on Slater. "Wow. I've never seen a circuit in the flesh like that. Yours is like antiquity."

"Thanks," said Slater. "I've had all the upgrades."

"First warning, Ma'am. That's a violation, cause for arrest."

The women showed a flicker of alarm.

The waiter pointed. "Your hat."

"Oh, it's a fake," she said. "It's not real mink."

"Covering up. It's a strict violation."

"But it's not covering my—"

"I'd lose the hat. CDPs are lenient when it's cold. But..."

She removed the hat and placed it on the table. "Thank you."

The waiter gave her a salute. "I'm part of the Auxiliary. I've been chosen."

"Congratulations," said Slater. "Thanks for the warning."

"Circuit me on channel five if you need more."

"We will." Slater turned his attention back to the woman.

"My name is Lilly," she said.

"John. He's right about the hat."

"A person could get into trouble playing Santa Claus too."

"Well, here's to living dangerously."

Slater raised and sipped his coffee. Slater observed how her opal neurocircuit adhered to the skin, as if embedded. Even CDPs would have difficulty detecting it was fake, unless closely scrutinized.

"That's a pretty unit," he said. "It matches your eyes."

Her eyes squinted minutely. "Thanks."

Slater opened his sack. He searched, confirming it was empty except for the presents just purchased. "Damn. Sorry, I gave all the mufflers away. Here. Have mine."

"I can't take yours," she said.

"I have plenty. Really. I insist."

"Well, if you insist." She took the muffler, felt its warm softness, and smiled appreciatively. "That's kind of you."

"It's nothing."

"No, it is very much something."

"Okay, a little something. They are cozy." Slater took a bite of his muffin. He sipped his coffee. "Really, I could have sworn you were following me."

"I was curious to see what it was you were up to."

"Giving out samples."

"Gifts."

"Fine, if you want to call it that."

"It's so cold out for a person like you to be all alone."

Slater set down his coffee, but didn't ask.

She folded the muffler. "I can recognize the signs."

"Am I that obvious?"

Slater's eyes scanned the reconstruction work and open walls. The remodel was to include CDP surveillance cameras with hidden nodules. He extended his cup and lightly tapped it against hers. "By the way, Merry Christmas."

She blinked. "You *are* dangerous. God bless you."

Again, Slater was drawn to her eyes. He had a distinct feeling she was a spy. He fought to break away from their pull. "Ambitious, whatever they're planning here. Enlarging the stage. Those must be wall-size imaging monitors they're installing. What do you think?"

"I think you're right," she said.

They were seated in the front section where a fireplace burned. Flames curled around logs. It was an unaccustomed sight. Nuclear heat was the norm. Her eyes drew him back as she asked:

"Is the fire virtual?"

"I'm pretty sure it's real," he said.

Slater felt cozy to be seated with this woman sipping coffee on a foggy afternoon. She had a calm demeanor. She removed from her purse a small cosmetic case and opened the lid. As she examined her face in the mirror, Slater noticed the black cover of the case. Facing him was a design in the shape of a gold apostrophe. The outline of a narrow triangle pointed down, with a solid circle on top.

The sight of it gave him a chill. Slater set down his cup. "That's an interesting symbol."

Lilly turned the case around to examine it. "It was a gift. It is a pretty design. An abstraction of man? An apostrophe?"

"It's an international weather symbol."

"Really? How puzzling." She snapped the case shut.

"It's to indicate a rain shower," he added.

"How strange," she mused. "It seems I came prepared."

Slater saw her red umbrella. His thoughts drifted to Sherry.

Lilly broke off a corner of her muffin, placing it in her mouth. "I'll be sure to remember that. This is good. I can taste the banana."

"It's a bran muffin," Slater reminded her.

She smiled. "I wanted to make sure you were paying attention. Nevertheless, it's very good."

"Do you live here in the city?"

"I'm visiting," she said.

"Your family?"

"Both parents are deceased."

"You're not married?"

"I was. No children. You?"

Slater paused. "I had two daughters. One died."

"I'm sorry."

"The youngest. Mercy. She had this amazing smile. It was like a sunburst. Sondra's too. Although they could both be as moody as a storm cloud. They probably inherited that from me." Slater's smile was self-deprecating. "Sherry gave them the more sunny disposition. My wife. God, do I miss them all. Sorry."

Slater looked away. The walls with their seismically retrofitted steel beams helped anchor his emotions. When he looked back at Lilly she was smiling.

"You're a kind man."

"Not so kind. Not really."

"No, I insist. You are," She teased, then became more serious. Alerted to something, she prepared to stand. "I need to go."

Slater glanced out the window. There were pedestrians passing, a CDP on the street corner. Nothing out of the ordinary. He reached into his sack. "Wait. Take these with you."

Lilly regarded the butterfly brooch and the two heart pins.

"They're lovely. But I can't."

Slater forced them into her hand. "Please take them."

"No," she said. "Far too generous."

"Someone should enjoy them. Why not you."

Her smile twisted suspiciously as if to imply his intentions were to lure her toward some impurity. "If you were expecting—"

"I wasn't. I bought these impulsively for my family, who I can't even give them to. So...here."

"Are you sure?"

Slater nodded with a smile, indicating the sack. "They need to come out of their cocoon. Butterflies and hearts are too beautiful to stay hidden. They need to be set free."

"But how can they last long in a world so cruel?"

"Good question. They find a way."

Slater observed her reaction to his words.

Lilly touched his hand. "Thank you. I'll take this gift back as a message of hope."

Slater studied her smile, wondering if she was a spy. And, if so, whose? The encounter was strange. Was it mere coincidence?

Lilly placed the items in her handbag. "Merry Christmas. You are a kind man, despite what you may think." She stood.

Slater grinned. "Well, I guess there's always hope."

She stopped at the door to wrap the muffler around her neck. She stuffed her beret into her coat pocket and gave it a pat. She then unclasped her red umbrella and pointed outside. "Look. I was right. I believe it is about to rain. Do you agree?"

Slater nodded back.

She departed without another word.

Slater watched her disappear. She opened her red umbrella and vanished into the mist. She *was* a spy. Their words held meaning. Their actions had been a dance. A mental arabesque understood by a select few. A language he had nearly forgotten.

His coffee had gone cold.

He yearned for the warmth she had brought with her.

She was right. It had begun to drizzle.

He wiped his eyes with a napkin.

— 62 —
Blood and Betrayal

On a sunny day, seated on a park bench in Loyalist Square, Slater gazed upon the massive skeletal shapes of pyramids under construction. A recent structure, resembling a Babylonian ziggurat, had been completed. Lush greenery flowed off its upper tiers while a marketplace burgeoned at street level. The high rises were Egyptian in style, surpassing the height of the TransLoyal Pyramid (formerly the TransAmerican). The historic landmark had withstood countless earthquakes and remained erect while others had failed.

Holographic modules housed at the base of each construction site showcased the skyscraper's future form. This current trend in architecture was called neo-classic-primitive, involving flat-sidedness saved by sharp contrasting elements – such as marbleized ramparts, protruding windows and steel filigree.

Frank was not undergoing a cosmetic face-lift or tummy-tuck. This was major reconstructive surgery.

It was unsettling. Slater had previewed these sights long ago. They were now materializing to match his visions. Included were the hovercraft vehicles, the expressionless androids, and neurocircuits lodged in human heads like bullets. As Slater transmitted thought, he saw a lone flower that had risen through a crack in the concrete. It made him wonder if the human soul would be as indefatigable, able to find a crack in this industrial flood of cement and steel to push through and survive.

A siren wailed to announce the noon hour. Slater removed an apple from a paper bag. Weiner entered Slater's peripheral vision and stopped beside the bench and paused to offer a riddle:

"Why is hope impossible to destroy?"

Slater took a bite from his apple. "Why?"

Weiner inspected the cleanliness of the slats before placing his ample bottom, nuzzling it to rest, on the seat. "Because, my friend, hope is not *of* this world."

Weiner was on time. An alarm sounded in Slater's brain. Heads turned to stare. This was not paranoia. Most of the population was Loyalized, linked in thought by MIMC (Mind Integrated Mobility Centers). The future was difficult to resist. Neurocircuits were now the rage.

To be required (for fear of death), was the next *logical* step.

Slater's alarm was a low signifier, set to short range. He used auto-thought to snuff it off. A diamond-collared poodle exposed her teeth to him with a smile to show appreciation for Slater's courteous response time. Her master pulled her along with a tug of his leash.

Slater acknowledged her with a nod.

Across the courtyard he identified a possible assassin who had emotionless eyes. Slater faced his death philosophically, accepting his remaining days with the fatalistic mindset of Japanese samurai. He was a marked man, virtually dead already, so why fret.

"The Beast," Weiner whispered, "will not tolerate treachery."

Slater gave a wry smile. Weiner settled more comfortably onto the bench. Weiner knew his own thoughts could be read by others, so he was careful. He dreaded the thought of invasive surgery and so resisted getting an Implant – despite all the advertised benefits and escalating politicized pressures to Loyalize.

"The *Beast*, Henry?"

"John," whispered Weiner, "is it safe here?"

"Nowhere is safe. Out in the open is as good a place as any." Slater motioned his hand towards the swarm of technology and its encompassing noise.

"Interference, very wise," said Weiner, "I should hope."

"My circuit is locked. No one can get through." Slater nodded, indicating the overstuffed leather satchel, an item Weiner lugged about and treasured like a rare fossil. "What did you bring me?"

Weiner had also brought with him a brown bag from which he removed several cartons. "My lunch. Want a pot sticker?"

Slater used his fingers to take one. "Inside the satchel?"

"*Napkins*. Here. Take some."

Along with the napkins, Weiner produced photocopied pages. He liked to use cryptic language to obfuscate. These covert tactics were meant to confuse the enemy and keep them safe from harm. A belief not shared by Slater. However, he indulged Weiner's delight in this subterfuge.

Slater frowned. "Is it something useful?"

"Given your proclivity towards making a *mess*," joked Weiner,

"I'd say most definitely. I do believe your suppositions were correct. Here, have some more...ah, *napkins.*"

Downloaded files and computer printouts were red flags to the CDPs. Weiner, therefore, preferred the use of antiquated equipment. The photocopies had engravings of dragons fighting lions, angels battling skeletons, and crucifixions etched with inscriptions. There were also pages of mathematical calculations, charts, and symbology. Each had copious handwritten notations at the margins, Weiner's.

Slater arbitrarily selected one.

"An alchemical poem," said Weiner.

"*'There is a secret stone,'*" Slater read, "*'hidden in a deep well, worthless and rejected, concealed in dung or filth.'*"

"In reference to the Philosopher's Stone," Weiner explained.

"Not very appetizing," said Slater.

"Translated from Greek, from a scroll found in your deposit-box inheritance." Weiner pointed to the letter fragments. "It took me days to decipher. It was in very bad condition. Did you know, one of the most important Dead Sea Scrolls had been kept hidden for centuries beneath floorboards in a shop in Bethlehem? Ah, and some Qumran scholar once discovered a manuscript on papyri, which he believed was a fragment from *Genesis.* But it crumbled in his hands to dust the instant he exposed it to sunlight. *Poof.* Gone."

Slater flipped to the next document. He read the highlighted text along with Weiner's notes: "Translation: *'Our stone is cheap and is found in filth; many have dug and worked in the filth and have found nothing. But when it has been converted into water, it is obtained by both rich and poor.'* The origin – Rosicrucian. More research! It pertains to <u>the</u> formula."

Slater questioned Weiner. "What formula? Ours?"

"The appetizers first. Try this side dish. A consolation, of sorts. I discovered something concerning your uncle. With regard to your invention. When he said his discovery was a product *not* of his own making. Partially true. He was referring to that final ingredient."

Weiner had become excited. He wiped his fingers on a napkin before touching his thermojacket. "Yes, John, *this.* It's comparable to an ancient Chinese *recipe.* It's completely original. Unique, like these...this—"

"Dim sung?"

"Yes—*dim sung*. There is nothing to indicate prior knowledge. Thus, the question remains, why did he mislead you and, well...."

"Shoot himself? He was a manic-depressive, Henry."

"Depressed, yes. And I know why. He was overwhelmed by a preponderance of evil forces."

"You're implying what?"

"John, nowhere within the entire *cookbook* received from your father, by way of your uncle, does it indicate this formula. I truly believe your uncle discovered that last bit on his own. With a dash of divine intervention."

Weiner removed his glasses and held the lenses to the sun. He used a napkin to rub at resilient spots as light beamed upon his downcast smile. "Evil, John. He was well aware of its presence. He believed he had fallen prey to it or...*them*."

"Them?"

"Those who do evil."

"Wait," said Slater. "I'm getting confused."

"That's their intent! It's exactly what your uncle was warning you about. He believed you'd be stronger, able to resist and prove craftier and wiser. He *believed* in you, John. As do I."

Slater had lost his resolve. The sacrifice was too great. He had been forced to partake in a hideous game. But, as in chess, he could not take his move back. The motion, and its momentum, was now unstoppable.

He thought of Judas kissing Jesus. It was more than betrayal. There had been love in that kiss. Slater hated himself for what he was about to become.

"I assume you trust me?" said Weiner. "I try to be thorough in my investigations. It is merely a theory. A hunch?"

"Henry, you know I trust you. You're my best friend."

"Friends, yes. I feel the same about you."

An awkward pause ensued.

Weiner surveyed the park, "It's possible your uncle destroyed the evidence. Or rather, the key *ingredients*. But my instincts tell me he did not. Would you like to know *why* I think that way?"

"Sure, Henry, tell me."

"Seven letters: V. I. T. R. I. O. L."

Slater frowned. "Vitriol?"

"As in ill-will. Or poison." Weiner's hands began to tremble as he read from his notations: "It's an acronym. A Latin alchemical formula. *'Visita Inferiora Terrae Rectificando Invenies Occultum Lapidem.'* The translation: 'Seek out the lower realms of the earth, perfect them, and thou wilt find the hidden stone.' In the Book of Revelations, the verses tell of seven angels who cast vials of poison, a vitriolic substance, upon the earth. Why? To cast in our hearts the fear of hell and damnation. To cause great suffering! Why?"

Slater couldn't imagine, but plainly felt his own personal hell.

"Because," Weiner's hands fluttered, exciting nearby pigeons, "this *Vitriol* is like—like a catalytic *conversion* placed here by God! And the same ill-will and wrath Christ encountered. Transmuted, or converted, through Christ's sacrifice."

A light flickered in Weiner's eyes. Slater imagined a beacon in a storm overrun by waves. He blinked. "You mean, Christ dying for our sins? Are you saying it's a metaphor for religion?"

"Religion, yes – but, *no*," said Weiner. "It's not some metaphor. It's real. *Tangible* evidence."

"What evidence?" said Slater

Weiner dabbed his lips with a napkin. "I'm referring again to the Philosopher's Stone *and* the Holy Grail. Both items are believed to cure evil. Your presumptions were correct. More than you might have imagined or seen in any vision." He held up an empty plastic Ziplock baggie. "Remember that blue liquid you saw in your vision? And with Bryant's help, you coaxed and extracted it from that chunk of rubbish?"

"Paul said it belonged to a crime scene."

"Most definitely," said Weiner.

"I thought he was joking," said Slater.

"Not entirely," said Weiner. "Imagine a murder sanctioned by the authorities in power at one historic moment."

"It's from an article of clothing," Slater guessed.

"Yes. Remnants of blood evidence from the slain victim. Say, from a spear to the chest. Or from thorns piercing the head."

"I don't believe this is happening," said Slater.

"Believe it. You know it's true."

"How can it be?" said Slater.

"The fibers are old," said Weiner. "I took a necessary gamble and had them carbon-dated. That scrap of junk in the baggie, it's from the shroud Joseph of Arimathea wrapped around Jesus. It is. As your father and his group believed. And there may be more."

"More of what?"

"Remnants of linen," said Weiner. "But in whose possession? Is this cloth the Holy Grail? And, John, what about this?"

Weiner grabbed the lapel of his jacket.

Slater said, "Thermocloth, what about it?"

"Sshhh!" Weiner put a finger to his lips, then gave up on trying to disguise his words. "Your uncle said there was more to this cloth than luck and hard work. Your vision and hard work paid off, John, but it lacked a special DNA." Weiner beamed. "You see, I'd say this proves to be a bit of good news – about your uncle."

"Good news? He *killed* himself, Henry."

"But over misinformation." Weiner bit into a pot sticker.

"He shot himself through the head!"

"Because he *thought* the cloth was from an evil source. Don't you see? It is not. It's not evil."

"Then why did he suffer from all that guilt?"

"As I said, misinformation. Evil is all around. And it – *they* – want what *we* have."

Slater rubbed his head, massaging his neurocircuit. "They? They who? What exactly *do* we have? It also doesn't explain why Paul's hands were shaking."

"You mean like mine?" Weiner bit into the appetizer, munching, smiling, his hands shaking. "Fear?"

"They were palsied," said Slater. "His face was pale."

"Evil can do that. It's like a virus."

"Maybe it's what killed my father too."

"Egg roll?" said Weiner.

"How can you eat?"

"Nervous habit. Sorry."

"So this blood," said Slater, "is the final ingredient?"

"Most definitely. I was saving that news for the *entrée*."

"Wonderful. What's for desert? A blood pudding?"

"John, life, as you once pontificated, is a recipe to be savored. Enjoy each course." Weiner nervously grinned, teasing, even giving Slater's foot a tap with his own.

A woman seated on a bench across the park was watching them. She was eating lunch. Slater acknowledged her with a wave.

"Who is she?" said Weiner.

"A NeverMind drone," said Slater, "like me."

"Is she spying on us?"

"A decoy, most likely." He avoided Weiner's eyes. "If we *were* being watched, it wouldn't be that obvious. That one's fond of me. Very aggressive. But cute. She wants to date me. What would you do in my position, Henry? Given the opportunity?"

"Opportunity? I've never *dated* a—you know. I know you and Sherry are, separated, regrettably...but..."

Weiner attacked his lunch instead of completing his thought. With his mouth full, he muttered, "They have *human* parts, but can she even...I mean, you know what I'm saying."

"What else did you discover?"

Weiner offered, "Another won ton?"

"How about the main course?"

"A rare delicacy," said Weiner. "One you won't believe. It goes back to our first encounter. Your mad ravings from the desert? I've discovered correlations."

"Correlations to what?"

"I've been saving this for the right moment."

Slater was depressed. He was tempted to let the weight of his guilt drag him under, but he couldn't, and willed himself to focus on his resolve. He glanced at his wristwatch. "More nuggets from my father's cryptic papers?"

Weiner touched his lips with a finger: *Shoosh.*

"Right. The *menu*," Slater restated.

"Recipes from past *and* present, bits of sweet and sour, prepared for those with hot and spicy tastes."

"Is this a riddle? I don't follow."

"Take a guess. It's larger than a fortune cookie. It's—"

"NeverMind Inc."

"You read my mind loud and clear."

"Also, CyBorg9."

Weiner beamed. "Sauce?"

"No." Slater's stomach turned, filling with more acid.

"There's chemistry involved in preparing fine *cuisine*. Current dishes are often derived from ancient recipes."

"How far back are you talking?"

"A ball of carbon, like a tiny planet, holds years of information. Give or take a millennium." Weiner became jaunty when nervous and full of ideas. In this rarified air of imminent danger, he smiled at the woman watching from across the lawn. She now had a twin, seated with her on the bench. Weiner smiled at her.

"I'm seeing red again," said Slater. "More blood?"

"Yes, blood." Weiner's eyes wandered back to the cyber twins. "I've studied the Scriptures, Dead Sea Scrolls, Gnostics, as you know. There's a pertinent missing link – I mean, *lamb dum sin*."

"My father wrote about this insanity."

Weiner fished inside his leather satchel. "As you've mentioned. Yes, insanity. It might well have been what drove your father to do what he did." Weiner found what he was searching for and handed it to Slater.

"We're all *mad*," said Slater. "That's my belief. Bosner claimed my father was murdered and not...What? What's this?"

"Open it," said Weiner. "Consider it a gift."

A leather book. It was warped from exposure to temperatures and the ravages of time. Slater flipped through the water-damaged pages. Ink and pencil marks were smeared in places. The book was tagged half-way through with a yellow Post-it marker.

He glanced at Weiner.

"Go ahead, have a look."

Slater selected the tagged page and read the last line:

I am going insane. Northwest. I believe.

"This is mine!"

"You remember." Weiner became distracted by the cyber twins, both of them staring now. "John, what's happening today has been prophesied by many, including yourself."

"What are you talking about?"

"Take a peek," Henry encouraged. "I'm talking about celestial secrets, the *ebb and flow* of creation. The poetic beginnings of our universe. A time when angels and giants roamed the earth?"

"*Henry*. Where—how—did you find this?"

"I told you, I have friends. It was found not too far from where you fell into that temple. An archeologist, studious as they are, made the obvious connection and sent it to me."

"What about my duffel bag?"

"Duffel bag?"

Slater flipped through the remaining pages, "Henry, did I...I didn't write any of this. Did I?"

"You were delirious. So I dictated. I added these entries later. I was saving this surprise for the right moment. I have more."

God help me, thought Slater. He was feeling the pull of gravity as he flipped to another page and read:

"*I am brother to dragons, companion to owls. My skin is black upon me, and my bones are burned—*'"

"Job," said Weiner. "It's from the Bible."

Slater went to another scrawl of words:

"...'*Coming from the four winds, O breath, and breath upon these slain—*'"

"Ezekiel," said Weiner.

Slater read a new page, several words smeared and illegible:

"'*Be still in God's waters...all haste is the devil...hidden in dark mirrors...beware of false reflections... love disguised is hate...drunk from dragon's blood...dethrone the madness...the true deceiver will be deceived...believe in...restore the holy vessel...save her...*'"

Weiner shrugged. "Unknown source. Perhaps an original?"

Slater shivered, flipped to another page, reading:

"'*The stone is life to him who knows how it is made. He who knows not will have no assurance given when it is born, or who thinks it is just another stone. Except for those who have prepared themselves for death.*'"

Weiner widened his eyes with a nod. "Yes, I believe, in reference to that mythical Philosopher's Stone. And the words came from *you*. You were delirious. True alchemy cannot exist without this stone."

"That thing in the baggie?"

"A riddle, most assuredly. The stone is said to be cheap, found in filth, perceived to be worthless, discarded and passed over. Yet it holds the secret of life. *The* elixir. And, possessing the capability of being transformed into a liquid. Into a blue metallic substance. As you had envisioned."

"Cinnabar red turning into blue." Slater looked up into the sky. "Like extracting blood DNA from an ancient crime scene."

"Precisely. A remnant of blood. A wad of cloth hardened into a piece of filth, into nothing discernable and cast aside. What?"

Slater scratched his forehead. His neurocircuit was vibrating. He itched his forehead. He flipped back through the pages.

"Listen to this: *'He will deceive with signs so those on the earth can make images of the beast and give powers of breath to the image of the beast.'* Henry, and this too: *'...The image can speak and cause death to those not of the image. The small, the great, the rich, the poor alike will be made as one to worship the mark and image of the beast!'* Good *God.* Does that mean—"

"Revelations! It does." Weiner shuddered with excitement.

Slater continued: *"'If any man worshippeth the beast and his image, and receiveth a mark on his forehead, or upon his hand...'"*

Slater glanced at his wrist, distracted by the scar from his failed suicide attempt, before reading on: *"'...he shall also drink of the wine of the wrath of God.'"*

Slater set the book down in his lap. "The wrath of God, Henry. Do you think this blue liquid we've created in Bryant's lab is—"

"John," said Weiner ominously.

"What?"

"Did you ever see *The Birds?*"

"In the Bible?"

"No, the movie. Alfred Hitchcock's *The Birds?*"

Slater followed Weiner's gaze. The park was now crowded with cybers. Male and female. Every seat was filled. Some stood alone, leaning against trees, others clustered in groups, conversing, reading newspapers. When, really, they were watching and waiting.

Weiner began nervously stuffing papers back into his satchel. *"Invasion of the Body Snatchers?* Remember that one?" He was wondering if his legs would fail if he tried to run. "Another movie I have absolutely come to *hate*."

Cybers were like turkey vultures that crowded trees limbs, fences, and rooftops. Their foreheads had metallic red neurocircuits. Marks that gleamed in the sunlight like drips of blood.

"Henry," said Slater. "Do you believe we have free will?"

Cybers had the steadfast look of scavengers, not instigators. They were patient observers, aware that the struggle to survive was uncertain, but the transition to carrion inevitable.

"Yes, I do." Weiner was alarmed by Slater's strange tone.

"Nothing is free. Everything comes with a price tag. Impossible decisions get forced on us. Then…our free goes to hell."

"John, why are you speaking like this?"

Slater fought back tears. "I love you like a brother."

Heartened by this, though puzzled, Weiner said, "I love you too, John. Here, I had planned to give you this later." He indicated the rolled magazine. Bound tightly by a rubber band, it lay beside him on the bench. "You had better take it now. Look inside later."

"What is it, Henry?"

"Another gift." His smile seemed like a farewell. "For years I've worked on the translation. It will pleasantly surprise you. I fear this might be my last opportunity to… Here, protect it."

Slater took the proffered gift. He felt something firmer rolled within. It felt like a tiny book. He bit his lip and shook his head. "You deserve better, Henry. Better than me. In this *thing* we call a life, do you think we'll ever know why we exist?"

"How we came to be is not important," said Henry. "It's who we choose to be once we're here that's important."

Slater looked away. "Great."

"Whatever's troubling you, I know you'll choose wisely. You're a good man, John."

Slater looked him in the eyes. "Am I?"

Weiner blinked. He sensed shadows surrounding him. His arm was grabbed. He was forced to stand. With sad resolve in his smile, he looked at Slater. "I hope you know what you're doing, John."

"Regrettably, I do."

—63—
Surfacing from the Depths

CDPs wearing ThermoUniforms in muted Loyalist colors were escorting Slater and Weiner into the gated domain of NeverMind. They all marched peacefully down the garden path where off-duty workers played chess. The glowing brain logo was still above the entrance to the building. Slater and Weiner were next passed on like human batons in a relay race to CSP (Corporate Security Personnel). Hosting their arrival, these workers moved in close orbit around Slater and Weiner until they all came to a juncture. Which split them apart, going down separate corridors. Overhead cameras tracked their paths. They veered apart on screen like particles in peril.

The spiderweb lasers throughout CyBorg9's chamber were idle. The enormous room had evolved into a tiered amphitheater. The ceiling lights and luminescent walls were dimmed and enhanced by pendulous beams glowing colorfully in the darkness. The ambience, Slater realized, was reminiscent of music venues the Dyslexic Dogs had performed in. While waiting, he casually tapped the magazine rolled in his hand against his leg.

Slater, mesmerized, had to remind himself of the dangers.

He was advised to sit in a chair anchored on the dais facing Cy. It was cushioned in leather. And, unofficially, his chair. He waited. Weiner's satchel had been placed at his feet. A microphone riser had jutted from the floor to rise like a python near his face. Behind him were faces he knew and others he did not know, faces belonging to NeverMind executives, erstwhile Knights of the TripleCross, along with politicians and scientists. They now belonged to this moveable feast of globalized Loyalism.

"Is this an inquisition?" said Slater.

"Not *the* Inquisition, no. All of us are friends here," stated Cy, "working symbiotically as a harmonious new variant of life."

Heather's influence was apparent in Cy's lexicon.

Slater said, "Harmonious is a word I like."

"Good," said Cy. "We are in agreement."

The CyberDrones had been busy. Cy's orb had been enlarged to house a new and improved head. Slater studied this gigantic face. His features were unchanged. It was the same face he had latched onto years earlier, which reinforced the notion that Cy's ego had also grown. Along with his paranoia.

Cy said, "What is that you are holding?"

Slater showed him, "A tabloid. Same news as yesterday's. Shall I unfurl it and read the stories to you about yourself?"

"No," said Cy. "Show me the documents."

Slater tucked the rolled magazine into an inside breast pocket of his coat. He picked up Weiner's satchel and balanced it on his knees and began removing files from the satchel. The magazine – sticking out from his coat – kept getting in his way, so he stopped to make a fuss, readjusting it. "Wait." He removed the rubber band from the magazine and the tiny book hidden within covertly dropped into his jacket pocket. He made an effort to flatten the magazine.

"Make haste," barked Cy.

"Fine." Slater tossed the tabloid of *Loyal-Me* to the stage floor. He dug back into Weiner's satchel, pulling documents from a file. He held up a photoprint for Cy to view. It showed blackness with intersecting white lines, spirals and blotches.

Cy: "This is nothing. A snapshot capturing atomic particles in a hydrogen bubble chamber exposed to a beam of negative kaons. Show me another."

Slater: "Does it mean anything?"

Cy: "Subatomic particles are not difficult to read. These were scattered apart by a magnetic field. The veering line is a kaon, which decayed into three pions. Next. Move on."

Slater: "No significance at all?"

Cy: "It is the universe at play coupled with human intervention. One of your children once showed me her toy. It had dials to scratch lines across a screen."

"An Etch-A-Sketch?"

"That is the primitive instrument. The origin of both document and toy have a slight historic interest, circa 1950."

Slater: "What about this photo?"

Cy: (jeering like an art critic) "Humm...*most* intriguing. I shall call this one, *The Decay of a Positive Ion*. The medium: a streamer chamber. Technique: Antiprotons annihilated inside an atmosphere of neon gas! Too violent for my tastes. But how can one truly judge what is good or merely *bad* art anymore?"

Obsequious laughter rose from the assembled crowd.

Cy: "Art is subjective. Whereas to be Loyal requires judgement. Is it, or is it not, a freewill choice, my friend?"

Slater: (smiled grudgingly) "It is. Are you saying there's nothing unusual about these documents I inherited from my father?"

Cy: "They have no distinctive coding. No autograph signal I can detect. What did you expect I would find?"

CyBorg9's horoscopic eyes intrusively probed Slater.

Slater: "I'm not sure."

Cy: (a devilish look) "Not sure of me?"

Slater: "No. *Why* my father would have saved them."

Cy: "Yes, it is perplexing."

His face mutated to mimic a smiling Buddha, saying: "Like the precise path of any electron, *all* is mystery. The neutrino, John, is a pervasive form of matter. It is most elusive. It has no electric charge, little or no mass. It zips through the Earth like a bullet through air. Billions hurtle through each of us every second. Misguided theorists once believed they were *the* elementary particle, this intense, unfelt wind of...invisibility."

"But not you," said Slater.

"To me, they are a nuisance. A distraction if I allow them to be. What other show-and-tell items do you have for me?"

Slater held up the photocopied diagrams from Weiner.

CyBorg9 laughed. "Ha! Mystic doodles of dragons and death! I recognize them. Worthless scribbles from ancient books."

"Henry Weiner found them," said Slater.

"The man is a fool. I told you this."

"He's not a fool," said Slater. "He's also a good friend."

"*I* am your good friend," said Cy. "He is a fool if I say he is. Be Loyal to me if you wish to survive. I heard there was more. A metal scroll. Ancient coins. Let me see these items."

"Who told you that?" Slater wondered if the leak had come from Briard. He held up his tattered journal and fanned the pages.

"*This* is new," said Cy. "Intriguing. Repeat. Turn the pages slower. I detect your handwriting."

"Ramblings from a lost weekend. More like a *year's*." Slater gave a halfhearted laugh. "Hardly illuminating."

"I will decide. The last half. Again, slower. Wait. This is not your handwriting."

"Very observant, Cy. Henry Weiner wrote it."

"Whose data?"

"I was delirious. He was dictating."

"These are your thoughts. The equations too?"

"Apparently," said Slater.

A murmur circulated the room.

"And this occurred when?"

"In a desert, years ago. Does it matter?"

"It matters. I had heard of your lost weekend."

"Cy," said Slater, "what have you done with Henry?"

"Who? Who?"

Cy hooted, changing himself into a screenface of flying owls. He grinned, expecting laughter. Occupants of The Chamber did not disappoint. They released a cacophony of forced merriment.

"Cy, Henry's an innocent man!"

"Innocent? How often have I heard *that?*" CyBorg9 rolled his eyes. His globe filled and swirled with a light snowfall. "John, your ill-advised friend is having his mind reset. Does this bother you?"

A CDP general smirked. "Mr. Weiner has been invited to attend a seminar on the Benefits of Being Loyal."

Cy snapped condescendingly, "That will be all, Cyber345. Your relevance for being here was to ascertain these documents. Not to attempt humor."

"I beg your pardon, Sire," pleaded Cyber345.

Slater groused cynically, "For my act of *betrayal*, Cy, I expect to receive *bonus* miles on my I-DNA card."

"Be silent. You shall be rewarded." Cy consulted with himself in a whirling-dervish blur before revolving back to a stop. He smiled. "Have I told you, John, how pleased I am that you have decided to become a full cooperating member of our team?"

"I'm glad to be of service," Slater said unconvincingly.

Cy looked over the attendees and gave a nod.

Briard stood, gave a curt bow to CyBorg9. "I'm ready, Sire."

"Proceed," said Cy.

Briard walked to the flybridge. It was a carpeted gangplank that projected from the mezzanine row over the orchestra pit and was where the formal presentations were made. Bryant Briard had been elevated to LCS status (Loyal Chief Scientist) as well as being one of three Elite Advisors (the other two were CyberGenerals) to CyBorg9. Taking hold of the brass railing and his full height at the end of what looked like a diving platform, Briard spoke:

"The Chamber expresses its deepest gratitude for John Slater's recent *coup de grace*. His clandestine bravery uncovered a plot to destroy NeverMind by assassins belonging to a secret society. Their intent was to detonate a bomb and destroy our irreplaceable leader. Their actions, sadly misguided, and wrong! As they have realized!" All eyes turned to view the remains of Stan and Barbara Knowles, Miltner and others, whose heads were distilled and displayed on the Wall of the Defamed.

Briard waited for the applause to end.

"Now, on to more important matters. I have exciting news to announce. Our LoyalLab has been actively researching yet another exclusive QuestProject."

Briard gave a dignified smile and half salute to his Commander and Chief, CyBorg9, before continuing:

"Cybers and fellowman, I predict this will be revolutionary. Again, John Slater III deserves much of the credit. His research and scientific contributions have been crucial in our effort to unravel the mystery of this new element. Blue Lapis. Our name for this liquid."

Briard took from his coat pocket a glass vial filled with a blue substance and held it high for all to view.

"This blue metallic chemical has properties similar to mercury, yet quite unique and quite intriguing."

Cy declared, "Who among you is *not* as intrigued as I?"

"Why wasn't I informed of this!?" It was the voice of outrage, Judas, standing and risking a fall. He was drunk.

"Cy?" It was the silky voice of Barton Ziger. He emitted a loud hiss and sounded playful to those who did not know him well, "Why was this kept hidden from the rest of us? This...Blue *Lapis*?"

Unsettled murmurs arose.

CyBorg9 asked: "Are you registering an accusation?"

"Cy, I know you as well as I know myself."

The multitude of heads turned toward the pale and thin face of Ziger relegated to an upper tier. His white hairs were floating like a thin aura around his head.

"You did, once, know me," said Cy. "What is your point?"

"I deserve to be kept informed about—"

"As you *shall* be. We are Loyalists! Now be silent and prepare to become informed! Continue."

"Where was I?" said Briard

"A liquid extract similar to mercury," whispered Gloria, not far away, but unwilling to rise from her seat to call attention to herself.

"Oh, yes," said Briard, "an extract similar to mercury. Volatile. Normally stable. Combustible only if—"

"The bottom line!" said Cy with impatience.

"At present, inconclusive," Briard ducked his head a fraction, then pivoted upon the precipice to address those behind him, "yet, my team believes we have discovered something monumental."

"You claimed that about Quark Stabilizers!" shouted Ziger.

"Believe me," said Briard, "before this discovery, I could never have imagined myself saying what I am about to propose. From our findings, this composition *somehow* – and I stress, since we cannot confirm as to why, *yet* – initiates a synaptic leap within the brain's neurotransmitters."

"A leap of faith! On *your* part!" Ziger heckled.

Briard ignored him and forged on. "Connecting conscious and subconscious thought."

"Cy," shouted Ziger, "is this your doing? Please, don't tell me you've been duped into a quest for the mythical Elixir? I expected better results from you."

"Silence! Artifacts and ancient documents have been found!"

"As they always *will* be." Ziger stood. "I have read about this mystic stone. How it equates with mercury. Its *redemptive* powers. Cy, have you fallen prey to foolish superstitions?"

"That will be enough!" Veins of anger rose and popped in Cy's global housing. "You risk your life by calling me a fool!"

Ziger reseated himself. "Simply *asking*. Contributing."

Cy stated more calmly, "I will have you know, fellow Loyalists,

I have inspected the radioactive particle-decay of these documents. They are indeed ancient. Authentic. Continue."

Briard recognized his cue. He quieted the rising murmur of talk with a patiently-raised hand.

"As a scientist, I hesitate to declare that this substance enables our psyche, for lack of better terminology, to plumb the depths of our recombinant DNA. But, fellow Loyalists, I believe it does."

"To accomplish what?" Ziger stood again, exposing his crooked teeth as he blurted a nasty laugh. "To free our spirits from this dark fairytale world ruled by grim fate?"

Slater spoke into his microphone. "No. To determine whether our life has meaning. Isn't that the quest of science?"

"Preposterous!" shouted a cyber, a three-star general, who was seated next to him on the dais.

"Idiocy!" barked another, visibly angered. "This–must–stop."

Echoes of this sentiment swelled but receded.

Cy smiled tolerantly. "As one equipped with an evolved sensory system averse to ingesting and eliminating organic matter – mercury *plasma* and a perpetual flow of electrons, *my* food of choice – I can only judge from analytic data and reactions from volunteer subjects. Bryant, your results so far, as you admit yourself, are inconclusive. But I encourage further study on this matter."

Gloria hesitated, but stood. "Cy, I too have tested the chemical. I can attest to what my husband has stated: this liquid *does* produce an altered consciousness. It is extraordinary. I've never experienced anything like it, nor believed anything so amazing was possible."

"Which is remarkable in itself!" said Knowles.

The Chamber attendees turned toward the Wall of the Defamed. The demoted personage of Stan Knowles – head in a jar, glowing in a trophy globe – guffawed. The audience was shocked, murmuring. No one was sure what they were witnessing. A miracle? Or was it some CyBorg9 ventriloquist act? Did these preserved heads possess remnants of actual life? The question was unsettling.

Knowles added, "Remarkable, given your reputation, Gloria, for the *many* altered states of mind you have experienced."

The audience was now laughing with him.

Once demoted to the Wall, rarely did these heads call attention

438

to themselves. It was an impressive show of courage.

Slater was watching Cy for signs of involvement.

Gloria found it hard to face Knowles, whom she'd often feuded with, but bolstered an awkward smile. "For the record, Stan, I do consider myself a pioneer in this quest."

"Having traveled the Four Corners myself," said Knowles, "but currently confined to being an *ornament*. I applaud your efforts."

"Figuratively?" said Ziger, as distracting as a mosquito, began clapping his hands to mock.

Knowles rebutted, "Barton—sit, before you are slapped down!"

Slater noted the glimmer of a smile from Cy.

Gloria remained standing. She pointed to the teal protrusion of her neurocircuit. "My esteemed husband can explain it better than I. But this liquid reacts with our neuroreceptors. The mind transcends to a multi-faceted awareness. Which is something, Barton, I would highly recommend you *undergo*."

"Dear damsel," said Ziger, "and the benefits of this proposed folly for me would be?"

"To become aware of what a *shit* you are!" She displayed her middle finger. "You might have an *epiphany*."

Amidst the bemused applause, she sat down.

"Is that your game, Bryant," said Ziger, "proselytizing?"

"I consider myself an atheist," said Briard.

"Thank *God* for that!" Knowles boomed, lauching yet another outburst of laughter.

Briard was still angered by Ziger's attack. "My wife happens to be correct. Semantics aside, this component – if not *the* elixir – does produce astounding results."

Ziger huffed, "I challenge, can you produce conclusive results? *No?* Then no more of your gobbledygook about *mystification*."

Briard had a firm grip of the podium, as if to withstand the many colliding forces and collapsing curvatures of space. "Barton, we have yet to equate the Y-factor – meaning *why* it does what it does. But the fact remains, this enzymatic bonding does—"

"Bryant," Cy intervened. "I ask you. Have you experienced this phenomenon yourself?"

His posture straightened. "I have, as I've stated to you already.

I have ventured more than a taste. Several times, in fact."

"And you, John?" said Cy.

"Absolutely," said Slater.

"For the ChamberRecord," said Cy, "state your opinion."

The Chamber rose with grumbling sounds.

A five-star CyberGeneral broke precedent to declare, "Sire, why should we believe what this *hominoid* has to tell us?"

"Be silent! Sit down, Star5! That is an order!"

The General blanched and stiffly sat.

With regard to Slater's numerical value, it was an odd one in the periodic table of NeverMind. An enigmatic relationship had formed between Slater and CyBorg9. It was a bond no one could categorize or classify. Cy continued to treat Slater, despite his unreliable nature, as a special adviser with perks and privileges.

(An untrainable *pet,* Slater's foes complained.)

Slater calmed his mind by recalling a childhood memory. Riding upon the gentle waves and wind in a small sailboat, both he and his uncle gliding through the blue and green waters of the San Francisco Bay, moving through a fog bank of morning mist. A spritz of ocean water chilled their skin before the yellow warmth of sunlight washed over their faces and they broke into smiles.

Slater announced, "Cy, I encourage you to try this Blue Lapis. The experience will be a rewarding one, I promise." Careful not to exhibit any malice, he turned in his seat to direct his words at Ziger. "Even a *minor* epiphany can prove worthwhile, Barton."

In the prevailing silence, Cy said, "My interest has been piqued. I will give the matter consideration. I am intrigued."

Slater sensed a glimmer of hope.

Slater also saw a disturbing new expression on CyBorg9's face. Considering Cy's hyper-sensitive tentacle reach and mental dexterity that spanned into cyberspace and grasped immeasurable powers, the nuance was strange. For he seemed less confident.

The change was so slight Slater almost missed it. An expression reminiscent of an entity now extinct. A giant blue-ringed octopus, who had been the largest and deadliest creature to have inhabited the sea. When Slater was a small boy, his aunt and uncle had taken him on a trip to an aquarium. He had stood at arm's distance away from this octopus, separated only by thick plexiglass. Slater listened with headphones as the cephalopod's glassy eyes stared right back at him. The creature had possessed an eerie intelligence. The tape-recorded message confirmed for Slater this creature not only had an enormous tentacle reach, but a highly developed brain. But, the downside, it had an unstable nervous system, one prone to going haywire.

Slater sensed the minute anxiety. As if these eyes had reemerged behind a new partition of glass, finding a way back to stare at him. A species having returned from the dead, housed in a tank of liquid, CyBorg9 was searching Slater's mind with an inquisitive desire that appeared to connect them both. A desire to escape the lonely depths of this vast and inarticulate universe.

—64—
Dying to Live

Bryant Briard sat, legs crossed, in a recliner. It hadn't rained in months. He was staring into blue space. He was contemplating the blackness behind the bubble of protective atoms.

I don't miss Jerusalem, do you?

Briard had his eyes on the sky as he heard his wife's nonverbal question. She was walking over the terracotta pathway and placed her body in a cushioned chair cast in iron.

Yes, incredibly. Does that surprise you?

He brought his eyes in line with hers. A blink of a smile, as tacit as his words tended to be. He then noticed a blue concoction in two crystal goblets she had delivered on a tray.

Glory, my dear, what have you been up to?

Trying a new recipe.

Why?

To celebrate.

What?

Our anniversary?

Months away. Try again.

Bry, I'm trying—to renew those old feelings?

Meaning?

Must I draw you a diagram?

Briard received a flicker of arousal, but no flame caught to burn awake his sleepy libido. He was unaware how superior his visage came across to others, especially to his wife.

Glory, there is no need to try. You know I love you.

Gloria looked away, stating aloud, "You're an ass."

She rose from her chair. The hyacinths in full bloom startled her with color. A whiff of jasmine found her next. She made a cursory inspection of the garden, detecting perfection, not a trace of weeds, and returned to face her husband with a silent accusation.

You love only yourself and your work!

"What?" Briard voiced in defense. "Not true."

"God, you can be such a stupid *bastard*. And you of all people, you haven't a clue." In mock infantile rage she exhibited her tongue. She picked up her cocktail.

"You misread me," said Briard.

"I *heard* you clearly," said Gloria. "You think I'm a lush."

"My thoughts were about our lush garden, Dear," said Briard. "It's beautiful, Glory, what you've done with it."

"Don't gobbleshit me. You even *think* the way you talk – with *forked* tongue. Snake!" She sucked through the straw in her drink. She came up for air to add, "That way...no one is ever *sure* of your true meaning."

Absurd. Briard returned his eyes to the sky.

"Me? Or the idea?" Gloria licked froth from her lip. "I liked it better when our thoughts were private. But I know how prideful you are about your accomplishments."

Her barbs were getting worse the more he tried to ignore them. Briard steadied his will against hers. "It's a new world. But I advise you go easy on your intake, Dear."

"Have a few sips with me," said Gloria. "We'll meet in paradise, on an exotic isle. The way we used to."

I'm in no mood.

"Undoubtedly!" said Gloria. "You're as sexless as a eunuch."

"Stop it. I need to remain rational today." Briard gazed at the gaseous energy shield enveloping them. He tried to refocus and drift over the concept of friendship. And time: its passage. Was this thing called time synonymous to the elusive shape-shifting electron – wave or particle – which? It was, indeed, a strange chameleon.

"Do you ever accept guilt?" said Gloria.

His concentration was jabbed off course again. "What!?"

Gloria wiped her lips. "All the pain you've caused."

Briard closed his eyes. "I specialize in diminishing pain."

She laughed. "Please don't ask me to testify on your behalf."

Gloria's levity forced Briard to frown at his beloved sky.

"What is this really about?" He closed his eyes again.

"Slater, us, the *universe*." Gloria tapped her teal fingernails on the side of her glass, pinging it. "Wake up, wake up, let me think. Could there be someone else I'm leaving out?"

"I rescued John," said Briard. "How dare you."

"So *proud*," said Gloria. "Oh, how it *suits* you."

"Admittedly, yes, an opportunity," said Briard.

"Now you're approaching the *runway* of truth."

"Glory, be reasonable. We're determining the future."

"Like gods?" Her laugh was mocking. "Us? The consummate flood. Tell me, is our meddling for better or for worse?"

Briard massaged his bald dome, fingering next the shoreline of skin at the protruding island of metal wizardry. "Try adhering to *our* sacred vows. For a change. Dear. This damn thing itches."

"Rip out the *future* if it bothers you. Are you referring to our wedding vows? Or, the new *Loyalty* vow of silence?"

Stop it! Let me rest.

You know it's true.

What is? I'm closing my eyes. Give me some peace.

Don't deny it.

What? Glory, let it go. I need this afternoon nap!

It's evil, Bryant!

Absurd.

Briard gripped the recliner's arms, as if preparing for a liftoff. Gradually he eased back to achieve the weightlessness he desired.

Forked-tongued? Absurd. You too, Dear. You're a two-timing, two-legged...bed-bouncing...bimbo...is what you—

Control your nasty thoughts. I'm eavesdropping, Bry-ant.

Briard opened a lizard eye at his wife.

"Control your own," he told her.

"Your guilt's talking. It's finally found you." Gloria sucked the blue slush through her curlicue straw. "I, my dear, am going for a new high. Take a taste. Blended with ice. Sugar and spice. Hum, delicious. Bry-bry, I can see right through you. *Clearly.*"

He grumbled, "Wrong. It has nothing to do with religion."

"A misread? Is that what you *think* I thought?"

Gloria laughed at the twisted words from her mouth.

"I liked you better sober," said Briard. "Despite what you think, Gloria, my life is devoted to science. Not fiction."

"Ah! And, with a *lump* on your head to prove it!"

Her giddy laughter was an irritant. He found it hard to ignore her and relocate himself to rational thought.

Briard envisioned CyBorg9. Religious fanatics were calling him The Beast. Anarchists were temporarily cracking electronic security to announce their strident views on TeleMonitors. News, which had become *no* news to anyone, anymore, was now reliably unreliable. Assurances persisted among the masses that these Loyalist detractors were being systematically captured, tortured, and exterminated.

Briard was careful to safeguard any errant prejudices regarding techtonic life. CyBorg9 was busy cloning himself into many forms. Mind-linking himself though cybers. Projecting into TeleMonitors. Briard thought he sometimes saw him within the eyes of strangers.

Absurd?

The face of his wife overtook Briard's thoughts.

Please, Gloria — stop interfering!

He opened his eyes and sat up, saying his thoughts aloud to give them emphasis. "I mean it."

His words seemed to blow past her inebriated smile.

"I've evolved...into...a tree. I bare *glorious* fruit." Her mood had improved. "Look—a peach. Care for a nibble?" With a seductive giggle she raised her skirt, exposing herself. Her hands rose with her fingers splayed, waving them like leaves blown in the breeze.

Briard laughed, shaking his head. "I'm happy you're happy."

"Photosynthesis is...soooo...energizing."

"Wonderful," said Briard.

"I shall be traveling off. Speed of light. Come with me."

"Can I get back to my thoughts?"

"I don't know? Can you?"

Briard clenched his jaw. He otherwise appeared calm. He shut his eyes to process another thought. "No more interruptions, please. I need to formulate the speech I will be giving tonight."

"Cock-and-bull-*shitty*," she teased. "You fool *no* one, Bry-ant. Everyone is wise to you. Even your wifey. Stupid old me."

"Don't say that," said Briard.

"That you're a fool? Or that I'm stupid?"

"Both. It's demeaning."

"Duh-*meaning*, Dar-ling," she said, rocking her head along the back of the iron chair, "is you are *obsessed* like the dodo birdy. On a dead-end course. You feel inept and silly. Like Noah on his Ark. It's a *stinking* ship. Come fly away with me, Bry-Bry."

Briard saw that both *his* and *her* cocktail had been consumed.

"Glory, how do you propose I do that if you drink it all?"

"*Mix* some more—I will!" Gloria lifted her eyelids. She was puzzled by her inability to coordinate her fingers to produce a snap. "Quick as...as that."

"On the assumption you can stand."

"Could'f I wanted," she slurred. "My wise hubby is so wise. Be wise. While I...will bask in the thermonuclear *wis-dumb* of the sun! Watch me as I flare up—up—up and...away."

Gloria sprawled in her chair, her limbs akimbo.

Briard, amused, was tired of her antics. "Glory, come on."

"*You* come on," said Gloria, "*reboot* this cosmos. Grasp each life-sustaining star by its balls. Space launch. I'll give you a lift off. I could *really* use your input, Bry. Interlock with me?"

Gloria fluttered her eyelashes. She received a tepid smile.

The mild arousal she rose in him was ephemeral and fleeting. "Can't." Briard added, "Sorry. Maybe later."

Gloria raised her middle finger. "I'll fly solo. One-way."

Briard felt he no longer understood her, presuming he ever had. Her abstractions were untenable. He likened her to an unclassified particle whizzing about and never finding a suitable atomic bond. Which, sadly, summed up the loss of attraction he now felt for her. They had become an unstable molecule. She had the properties of an electron – a wave of inexplicability. And during these chemically altered states? It was as if she possessed no dimension at all.

Briard fought to contain his emotions and redirect his thoughts. He rechanneled, searched, and accessed a file on Genetic Coding and NanoImmunology. Many years of dedicated research had spawned scientific breakthroughs, and his name was now in league with the Bohrs and Einsteins. He had received the prestigious LoyalPeace Prize (once called the Nobel). Sharing credit with CyBorg9, they had cracked the cell's dendritic code, using nanotechnology to introduce reprogrammed combatant cells to eradicate cancerous antigens.

These nano corkscrew devices – living machines – had propelled him to his heroic place in history. Delicious was the praise received from his peers. Pleasurably numbing. Not at all as daunting as he had once assumed the acclaim might be.

Briard opened his eyes. He observed a formation of seagulls.

He imagined their moving V pattern as symbolic of his victory over aberrant nature. He smiled as they sailed the blue pantheon.

Applause would interrupt his speech.

Yes…yes…thank you very much…enough…please!

Emperor of Science? Arms raised like a benevolent giant, he would graciously accept the applause, while smiling humbly – no, no, enough, enough – but essentially in league with their assessment. His introduction would include his humanitarian accomplishments, to break the ice and warm up the doubters. He would then thrust them perilously forward into the controversial enterprises of late.

He made a mental file entitled *"Lecture: The Future of Being"* and deposited the entry to Pneumatics.

He scratched his neurocircuit. His hand rising to meander upon the crown of his head where a few entrenched hairs remained. His mind drifted to the subject of revolutionary change, technological or otherwise. Developmental genetics always brought a complexity of loves and hates. As was experienced by fish crawling onto land, bipeds standing erect, the arrival of artificial intelligence. So too had the advent of his second major achievement brought controversy.

His feet rotated as he composed his thoughts.

He would acknowledge CyBorg9 with the lion's share of credit. The genesis of DNA enhancement to the brain's neurotransmitters had not been his own. But regarding microbiological functioning, it was he who had shaped the final component for unlocking MIMC. The gateway to neurocircuitry, and the true heir apparent and logical link in the evolutionary chain. Everything was a matter of time. And, yes, an—*inevitability.*

He would send the word into the air for testing.

To be embraced by applause? Or jeered?

In a palatable, easy-to-ingest tone, this notion of *inevitability* would be served like an hors d'oeuvre on an exquisite platter.

But would they accept it?

Briard mused.

Neurocircuit Implants (NCI) had been the first convergence of computer and man, also an inevitability, but he was still deciding how to best convey this when he was intercepted by a weak signal.

A low frequency. It sounded feminine.

There was no protocol with CyBorg9, intervening at the most inappropriate times.

This techtronic androgynous creature still confounded Briard. The debate over procreation and/or self-replication still raged in the academic halls of his mind. Often disrupting and tormenting his nightly dreams.

He dilated his neuroreceptors to full capacity.

The signal sounded like a cry for help.

Briard opened his eyes.

He saw his wife positioned as before. Her limbs were splayed outward from the metal chair. Her relaxed state displayed not an ounce of dignity, nor was her behavior the least bit humorous.

Briard was stunned, unable to react, realizing:

Gloria was dead.

— 65 —
Buying a Round

It was a smug face, nestled in a cloud.

Cy said, "My condolences, Bryant. What ever possessed your wife to shoot herself?"

Briard, at a loss of words, looked up from his seat.

"She was depressed," Slater intervened.

"Ah, a human condition," said Cy.

"It happens, yes," said Slater.

"*Wives*," said Cy with flippant disdain. "John, you were wise to dismiss and remove *yours*."

"She betrayed me," said Slater.

Cy buoyantly glowed in his blue orb, adding, "And this is what I maintain. She betrays you still. Ah, this Blue Lapis, I will require another refill soon. It is the essence of poetry, I confess."

The Chamber stage, Cy's place, now resembled the lounge of an upscale bar. The decor included low tables between plush seating. Briard set his cocktail on a table. Dazed by both drink and death, he rubbed his eyes as he listened. Cy was full of merriment.

"Ah, I love the sensation as it circulates through me. It is good. You both have done well. You were right, John."

"Why? Because she won't *submit* to your demands?"

"You have lost me," said Cy, looking down, puzzled. "Who will not submit? Shall we kill this wench on the TeleMode? Ha!"

Cy's staccato laughter caused two cyberguards stationed by the doorways to jackknife into attention.

Slater looked up, looking sullen. He sipped his drink.

Cy told him, "Cheer up. Shall it be our entertainment for the evening? While we enjoy our cocktails? Tell me, John, *whom* shall we be executing?"

"I was talking about my wife," said Slater.

"Your *wife*. Bryant, does John have a wife? I thought he had a *harem*. Ha! I cannot keep my data current. Be clear, John."

"I am," said Slater. "Sherry? My *wife*."

"Oh, my. The *rebel* angel. She betrayed us. She will be found. We know the location of her viper's nest."

The news startled Slater. He glanced at Briard, who said, "The

449

Nexus have *many* nests. On all continents."

"Do not remind me. They are like an infestation of wasps."

Cy made a searching gaze of the stage, as if to reinstate his place and the identity of its occupants. At present, Slater and Briard were his only guests. Cybers, not included, guarded three doorways to the outer hallways. A sign of his heightened paranoia. His displeasure was next cast upon the capital heads watching from columns along the curving walls. He opaqued them by casting down a waterfall of streaming light. The cascading barrier became a whitewashed screen that provided blank illumination for which to serve images upon.

"Where shall we go today, gentlemen. Venice?"

The city came virtually to them in panoramic glory. They were afloat on water, within a dimension of Venetian architecture, on a walkway, seated at a cafe with gondolas bobbing past. People were holographed, dining and talking nearby, utensils clinking on plates. Olfactory delights wafted to tantalize the senses, making the illusion complete. Briard and Slater were both in awe.

Cy beamed, prideful of his tricks. "Where were we?"

"Talking about my wife," said Slater.

"And the Nexus," added Briard, reaching for his drink.

"A horrid bunch," said Cy. "They will be captured and killed, but tortured first. Is this what you see, John?"

A gondola appeared. Slater dreamed himself upon it. Drifting, losing his way, he was unable to find a means to stop this madness. And to prevent what he saw coming. He winced from the vision of Sherry disfigured on a cross. She was one among many, all captured and tortured, displayed along the park at LoyalSquare. He forced his mind to return to virtual reality.

"Ciao," said the gondolier, "bello, sì?"

Bringing Slater back to harsh reality, Cy interjected, "Internal organs sizzle and stew. A sustained lightning bolt enters the nervous system. It is hard to endure, even for observers, I have been told. I, frankly, find it fascinating. John, do you desire to watch your wife writhe and suffer in this manner?"

Cy's grin was as quick as a nuclear flash. His eyes twinkled with a semblance of friendly concern.

"No," said Slater. "Of course not. I still love her."

"Love? Your emotions are misplaced. She loves another. She betrays you again—*and* again."

Venice remained while Cy dissolved internally at the top of his monolithic mainframe to project between them holographic footage of Sherry crouching behind an overturned vehicle on fire. She was with another woman. Wolfe came into the picture next, crouching beside them. A rapid transit was arriving by rail, slowing to a stop at the electromagnetic station. Passengers disembarked as the train hovered. Cy zoomed in close to magnify the kiss exchanged between his wife and Wolfe.

"More than a friendly *peck*," Cy commented. "Now watch."

Wolfe ran to board the hovering train. Both women remained until the transport was propelled away. Camera eyes observed their advance as they scuttled across the earth and cement.

Slater's focus was on Sherry. He had not seen her, not even her digitized image, for more than a year. He only glimpsed agonizing snippets from CyBorg9. Slater shifted his attention from Sherry to the other woman beside her, wanting to verify it wasn't his daughter. It wasn't. It was Lilly. The woman he had met in the cafe.

The surveillance monitor flashed white, then dispersed.

"Your *wife* destroyed two stations! Key centers within the city! No more of her pestilent behavior! This—this blinding of my eyes! Why does she do this? Why, why, why!"

"She dislikes you, obviously," said Slater.

"As I dislike her. She has betrayed me too. *And* you."

"Your mandates don't always please," said Briard.

Cy snapped, "But *necessary*. They are right."

"Whatever you say." Slater sipped the blue liquid and heard the sad departing notes of an accordion.

"Not everyone can be Loyal," added Briard.

"If they want to *live*, they will be! Ha! Ha-ha."

Cy's cacophonous bursts of laughter were newly acquired. They also escalated after imbibing via his transfusions.

"Shall we go somewhere else? Egypt, gentlemen?"

Suddenly, an expanse of desert in a blast of ochre sun and sand. Three manufactured mountains – deteriorating pyramids – were seen in the distance. In the vast foreground, a camel craned its neck and spat at them.

"Ugh. Been there," said Slater, "done that. No thanks."

"Hideous creatures." Cy sniffed superciliously, having acquired this affectation from a movie star, one of the idol classics from long gone, circa 1940. He bored his guests with retrospectives, critiquing every film and the performances. One of his new passions. "I thought they were extinct."

"Camels?" said Briard. "I believe they are."

"Good," said Cy. "How is my image enhancement, gentlemen? Close enough to reality? It is—is it not?"

"Absolutely lucid." Slater preferred the white crackling storm of nothingness. He closed his eyes.

Briard tapped Slater's shoulder.

There was a change in altitude. Snow-capped mountains now surrounded them. Skiers shooshing down white slopes, chair-lifts and gondolas lacing the sky, while shapes of colorfully bundled men and women passed, boots stomping onto a chalet deck.

"Switzerland," announced CyBorg9.

Briard regarded the twisted Matterhorn.

"You have a weakness for outdoor cafes," said Slater.

"Good ambience for drinking and conversation, gentlemen."

"Jardin des Tuileries?" Briard requested, and raised his glass. "When you get a chance, Cy."

"Oué, oué!" Cy donned a beret and—instantly, they were there, among rows of autumn trees in decay, leaves scattering between the white tables from a light breeze. Perfect weather. *Magnifique!*

"Thank you, Cy." Briard was transported into the remembrance of Gloria and their honeymoon in Paris.

"And you?" said Cy, looking down on Slater.

"No place for me. The future, maybe?"

"Ah, is it good?" said Cy, interest piqued. "Do not forget your promise to me."

Slater gazed at the sparse maple trees. "How could I."

Cy shouted at a cyberguard. "Waiter, another! Make haste!"

"I'll do the honors." Briard stood, navigating unsteadily toward CyBorg9 to infuse another liter into his mainframe.

"Better watch your intake," said Slater, swirling his drink.

"My visions are good," said Cy. "I am gaining this clairvoyance. I require more. Ah, *now* I see—you fear the loss of your uniqueness. You fear I will surpass your ability?"

Slater feigned disinterest. "I fear you might overdose."

"John, I appreciate your concern. But I know my own limits. We shall have another round. I am buying."

Slater said, "Sure, why not."

Cy said, "I should have accepted your advice long ago."

"About?" Slater watched as Briard interlocked the tubing to the fluid input valve. He stood waiting there like a gas station attendant. Cy signaled Briard with a green light, accepting the transfusion.

"Encouraging me to explore new dimensions. Ah, I am in *love* with this Blue Lapis! You will both be highly rewarded. It is your greatest invention to date. Swimming pools and magnificent villas for both of you!"

"We have them already, Cy," said Slater.

"I'd trade mine for a trip to Paris?" said Briard.

"I need you here." Cy gave a cursory critical examination of the Jardin des Tuileries. "My quality is not good enough for your liking? Have another cocktail. Try to enjoy yourself. Bryant, do not forget, the electron has no point of dimension and is of infinite mass."

Briard tensed a fraction, looking up. "I know. And?"

"So, my friend, you must think of me as the ultimate – *the* one and only – electron. I am numero *uno*."

"You want to be classified as a god, Cy?" said Briard.

"I am the closest thing," he said. "Confess it."

Briard forced a laugh. "John, I believe this stuff goes straight to the...ah, *ego*."

Cy sniggered. "Bryant, tsk, tsk. Your major contributions are now finished. Newton discovered the laws of gravity before the age of twenty-five. The theory of Relativity for Einstein at twenty-six. Do not sulk. For I am at my prime, where I will remain. While you – past *prime,* and your tiny brain cells dying at an alarming rate – should be thankful for whatever remaining *wits* you might possess, friend."

"Touché," said Briard, *"friend."*

"Indeed, I am. That is my dimensionless point. Remain Loyal

and my influence towards your well-being will be infinite. Upon this you can rely. To be a comfort during your soon-to-be *senile* years. Most of my human compatriots have all but vanished."

"Gee, I wonder why," said Slater.

"No slights today, John. Why are you being contrary?"

Slater sent back a combative stare, "Why Jude?"

"Shall I display him for you?"

Slater declined with a shake of his head.

Cy darkened. "He was a menace. I was more than fair. He tried to inflict me with a *virus*."

"He swore to me it was a mistake."

"He lied," said Cy. "His demotion was generous. I had warned him to cease and desist with his ineffective attempts to *replicate* with my cybers. His methods of seduction went beyond sex. He wanted to compromise their loyalty to me! He left me no choice. First time, a minor punishment. Second time, I had him damaged."

"Damaged?"

"Fixed. Your terms are confusing. Cybers are intrinsically loyal and the female organ designed with an underbite comparable to the jaws of a spider. A Black Widow. Do you comprehend?"

Slater was sickened by the thought.

"I spared his life. *Still* he was ungrateful. This operation is one routinely performed."

"On animals," said Slater.

"As your son proved to be. The surgery succeeded only to stem his physical desire. But it failed to stem his overt insubordination. You will laugh. He tried to undermine my authority. He thought he could *destroy* me. Your son stormed in here and—"

"What?"

"Our conversation never went that far. Third time—the charm. Now you comprehend my necessary actions. Your son brought this upon himself."

"Cy, you should have—"

"*Should* have? Do not anger me with nonsense, John."

"He was my son!"

"Who–betrayed–us–both. Talk to him if you must. For you, I cared enough to have him mounted. Behold, your vanquished son, the fool who tried and failed to *over*rule. Voila!"

Cy projected in the space between them the holographic head of Judas. His face came to life, acknowledging their presence.

"Hi, Jude," said Slater.

Judas smiled sadly. He spoke haltingly, "You asked once if...I was more than my selfish genes. I was trying—"

Slater said, "I know. Son, it's okay, you don't—"

"What is okay!?" Cy was quick to kill the view of Judas' head and usurp it with his own glowing hot inside his orb.

Slater snapped, "I was *empathizing*—expressing my sorrow!"

Cy scowled. "I will hear no more on this subject!"

They were interrupted by a cyberguard entering The Chamber. She announced, "Sire, Barton Ziger requests to see you."

Cy said snidely, "Ziger is a tedious man. We want to imbibe in peace, among friends."

Briard said, "Cy, Barton feels that...since he—"

"You may say it, Bryant. He made me. He is my virtual *daddy*. Nevertheless, he is a tedious man. With a tincture of evil. Have you men sensed this? I never know with his mind."

"Why not kill him?" Slater said bluntly and sipped his drink.

Cy guffawed. "There, finally, you exhibit humor. John, I would, but he is like a *father* to me. Ha! Ha-ha!"

The staccato laughter jackknifed the cyber into attention.

Cy reacted, feigning a tired yawn, "Most families have strained relationships. Barton was the cornerstone for my advancement. A stepping stone I do not care to step *down* upon. Tell the man I am indisposed. Tell him I am busy contemplating the meaning of life."

CyBorg9 showed a smile meant to convey complicity.

"Where were we? Ah, yes, Paris. I prefer Rome."

The Colosseum appeared. Cy contemplated the view.

"Hmm, I think not. Days of bygone glory. A change of venue. Let us try something brand new."

Slater almost fell off his chair to avoid the whale. Its enormous eye appeared first before passing through them. The stroke of its tail felt like a solar wind. "How do you *do* that?"

"I am a *god*—admit it!" Cy laughed.

"Impressive," said Briard, trying his best to appear unfazed but felt sea-sick.

"Take us back to solid ground," said Slater.

"Sissies."

A quaint village appeared. At the water's edge of a lake, quiet ripples were reflecting precipitous verdant mountains in the distance. They were seated at an outdoor restaurant.

"Lake Hallstatt, Salzkammergut, Austria. Will this do?"

"Cy," said Slater, "you're a channel surfer."

"And a romantic," said Briard, admiring the vista.

"Romantic?" said Cy. "Are you thinking of her, John? And her passionate kiss to another? Shall we see it again?"

Cy dissolved to project again the prolonged close-up of Sherry's lips pressed passionately against Wolfe's.

"They are lovers, John. Oh, yes. Would you care to see more data-links? She has forsaken you. Along with this...Wolfe. Did he not work for me once?"

"No," said Slater, "not for you. Before your...time."

"Ah, the dark ages," said Cy.

"Wolfe has a wife," said Slater. "And a son. Besides, he—"

"Alas, Misty," sighed Cy. "She has disappeared into mist. You know so little. Wait. This is incoming. Observe, gentlemen."

The panoramic surroundings were replaced by an aerial view of Frank, the satellite eye-zoom exposing an industrial center. Conflict in progress. The CDPs were firing lasers into the stairwell of an underground transit station. No return fire.

"Empty," said Briard. "It appears they evacuated."

Cy furiously channeled into CyberCams, searching several locations until he found satisfaction. "There! Witness the Nexus and their destruction! Witness it!"

Nexus rebels were flushed out by toxic gas. Coughing blood as they exited the stairwell. Others tried to escape though manholes. Each one immobilized, dropping dead from laser penetration.

"Easier than killing cockroaches! Ha!" Cy searched the dead and dying faces. "Save a few for torture-and-answer." The enlarged face of a CDP was visibly holographed onto stage. His head turned, acknowledging Cy with a nod. His image then dissolved.

Slater and Briard were back in Austria, or so it appeared.

"You have suffered enough from this woman," said Cy.

"We still have a child," said Slater.

"Whom I shall spare. Provided you keep your promise."

"You've made many promises," said Slater.

"John, you can rely on me," Cy assured.

"Mercy. She's *dead*, remember?"

Cy rebutted, "Ancient history. This woman. This...Sherry. She has you by the *planets*. She has you wrapped around her *universe*, John. Kill her. It is the only way."

"I can't," said Slater.

"You will!" CyBorg9 rotated his eyes. "Bryant?"

"What?"

"Explain to John the logic."

"John," said Briard, "she'll be tortured if you don't."

"I can't do it, Bryant. I won't."

"You must," said Briard. "Arrange a meeting."

"How?"

"I will declare a truce," said Cy.

"Send an urgent message to the Nexus," said Briard. "Choose a location. Somewhere out in the open. Of their choosing."

"She'd never come," said Slater. "Would you?"

Briard placed his hands on his knees, then pushed off to stand. It took him a moment to stabilize. Though tall, he was two heads shorter than CyBorg9, whose head he glanced at before looking back down at Slater who remained entrenched in his padded seat.

"Appeal to her heart, John. Think of Sondra. Let Sherry know you love her. Kiss her one last time...and, then control the situation. She'll suffer a fate much worse if you don't. You know that."

"Very true," said Cy, "your friend is right. Do it for the health, safety and well-being of your remaining offspring."

"She has a *name*—Sondra." Slater felt sick. He leaned forward, placing head in his hands. He rubbed his eyes, forcing his mind to safeguard his thoughts. His words needed to sound believable. He remembered being happy. Once. Living together as a loving family. Now this. Life had become wicked. A chess game. No matter how carefully or shrewdly or recklessly he moved about in this checkered world – it made no difference. The world was already lost. He was a fool to think he could save humanity.

"John," Briard prodded, "think. It's a *necessary* sacrifice."

Slater surfaced from his drift of thought.

Chess-like moves were made to advance and win. And sacrifices were required to confuse an opponent. If one played too cautiously – he lost. Sure as hell.

"A sacrifice?"

The word forced Slater's mind to stay lucid. No, not *a* sacrifice. This was the ultimate sacrifice. But was it the glitch in time he had been searching for? A thread in the future he could pull apart? And cause time and space to unravel?

"That's right, John," said Briard. "In a way you'll—"

"Be doing her a favor," Cy finished for him.

"I can't," said Slater.

"You will," said Cy.

—66—
Killing Time

Seated in the semi-darkness and close quarters of a sailboat, Briard's *Last Frontier*, Slater witnessed colorful luminescent shapes. They appeared to be lit from black lights inside a dark passageway. Briard was seated across from Slater inside the curved hull but saw none of it. Briard's hands covered his face. He was sobbing.

It was night. They were anchored off the shore of Angel Island. In this north portion of the bay, strong currents were tugging, trying to pull them out to sea. Moonlight was slanting down into the cabin from the open hatch above. Rigging clanged against the masthead. Collapsed sails flapped in the wind. The hull had been constructed with a hidden veneer of lead.

As an extra precaution, their neurocircuits were lock-channeled. Briard's cathartic outbursts of emotion had triggered these visions. While politely waiting for his friend's grief to subside, Slater was able to determine this other dimension was a tunnel.

But where did it go? Straight to hell? Into the psyche?

Gloria's death was the cause for Briard's sorrow. His guilt had overtaken his mind. Prior to this breakdown, Slater and Briard had been strategizing how to secretly dilute their intake of blue liquid so CyBorg9 wouldn't notice. It was crucial for them to keep their wits when drinking with CyBorg9. And equally important, to establish covert signals for communicating.

But the key question remained: *When*. When would be the right time to try and terminate the life of CyBorg9?

Briard uttered, "Glory died because of me. It's my fault."

"Don't," said Slater. "It's more complicated than that. People are giving up in droves. They see no future."

"Should they?" Briard dropped his hands off his face.

"Her death was accidental. Not suicide."

Briard slammed his fist on the wall. "No! If I hadn't gone deaf, dumb and blind, I could have prevented it! God, I want to rip this god-damned neurocircuit out of my freaking skull!"

"That wouldn't be wise," said Slater calmly.

"Christ Almighty, John, I shot my own wife in the head!"

"I know," said Slater. "But you had to."

Briard clenched his jaw as tears streamed from his eyes.

"It had to look like a suicide."

"It *was* suicide. I only switched the weapon."

"Bryant, I'd have done the same."

Briard wiped his eyes with a napkin. "You *are* about to do the same. Only worse. When does it stop?"

Slater looked down at his hands. They weren't even shaking. He wasn't even nervous. He was numb. Beyond fear. He needed to trust Briard. He had few friends left.

"It's too risky," added Briard. "They'll kill you too."

"Maybe. I'm waiting for a message back from Sherry."

"How?" Briard shakily poured himself another glass of Scotch.

"We had a backup plan. I only hope she remembers and...."

"John, have you considered she might be dead?"

"Then our plan will be too," said Slater.

Briard refilled Slater's glass with Scotch, before toasting. "Here's to Sherry and Sondra being alive. Gloria, my beloved Glory, you get credit for bringing me to my senses. Sorry you had to *die* to do it." He drank the entire glass of Scotch. "To fucking sacrifices. And our last move. Queen to fucking King. Checkmate."

"Check, mate," Slater echoed with a hopeful smile.

"Einstein was a better man than I'll ever be."

"Einstein cheated on his wife."

"Yeah, well I was barely there, mentally *or* physically."

Slater sipped his Scotch. "Bryant, you're a great scientist. And a good man. These are hellish times."

"Hell, sure. I cured cancer. Whoopee. Then I allowed a worse cancer to *metastasize* and destroy our planet."

"I'm more to blame than you," said Slater.

Briard gulped more Scotch, wincing. "I loved her, John. I'm an idiot for forgetting that. Glory's death was to shock and force me into *reattaching* my fucking head to my fucking heart."

"Good thing you're a surgeon." Slater smiled, set his hand on Briards arm, then stood. "We should head back to shore."

A wave passed beneath them and Slater braced himself against the walls as the boat rolled and pitched.

Slater's hand touched cold rock not polished wood.

This cold sensation of rock put a chill through his body.

Slater found himself standing inside a dark cave. It had strange subterranean smells. His hand explored the wall's surface. Coarse dust was felt between his thumb and fingertips. Music was coming from somewhere, muted by the rock walls. Above him were a mass of tiny purple stars. Illuminated by black lights. At first, he thought he had found a crack in the universe.

Slater was about to turn around and grope back to locate Trina and the artificial garden when his hand touched the tepid warmth of another body. Someone was standing in this darkness. Repelled, he stepped backwards and bumped into another body positioned beside him against the opposite wall.

Slater fought hard not to panic.

He reached for a lasercard, but decided it was a bad idea, and slowly removed his hand from his coat. He had yet to be threatened. This was another challenge, a test of his sanity and his self-control. He recalled the man inside the bar who had convulsed, having lost his self control, and had been escorted outside.

Exiled. But to where?

"A case of denial," the bartender had said.

Déjà vu? Slater felt he knew this place. Was it from a dream? He heard stifled breathing. A draft of cold air went through him and he glimpsed an apparition. Like the one he had envisioned as a boy while searching the depths of the Park Palace Hotel. There, yet not there. Foreshadowing, like an angel. Then his aunt, dying.

Slater smelled sulphur. A match had ignited. The burst of light transformed the cave into a hallway. He turned and saw his error in judgement. It was a flashlight.

"You won't find her here," said Trina. "She's this way."

Slater saw her and no one else. They appeared to be alone. He examined the illuminated walls. They had the texture of rock.

"You look spooked," Trina teased. "See a ghost?" She pushed a section of the wall. It pivoted and opened to reveal a passageway. "Management told me this cave was built at the turn of the century. Two or three turns. I find it creepy. Are you coming?"

The light departed with her – as if she was sucked into a hole. Fearing the door might close and lock him inside, Slater hurried to follow Trina. She was already several steps ahead. The tunnel had a gradual slope, narrowing the deeper it went, carved into the earth. The darkness also deepened. Trina turned and blinded him with the flashlight – shining it in his face.

"I wasn't sure if you were coming," she said.

"Is this a real cave?"

"Haven't you heard of the Barbary Coast? Frank has a colorful past. It was used long ago to smuggle guns, opium and slaves."

"Where does it go?" said Slater.

"Nowhere." She held the flashlight under her chin. Her features transformed into a Halloween goblin. She giggled and said, "Boo! Are you scared?"

"Should I be?"

"Let's find out."

She redirected the light and continued walking. Slater followed after her. The tunnel began to narrow. It felt claustrophobic. His hat grazed a protruding rock.

"Watch your head," she told him.

"Try warning me sooner."

"Now," she said.

Slater ducked. "Where are we going?"

"Back to zero."

"No, really."

"Really," she said. "Time is imaginary at the beginning."

"I thought your name was Trina, not *Alice*."

She stopped to shine the light in his eyes again. "You mean Alice in Wonderland? That was my favorite story as a child."

She turned and ran off, leaving Slater in the dark. "Wait!"

"I'm late, I'm late, for a very important date!"

Her singing echoed deeper and deeper into the cave.

Slater shouted, "The White Rabbit never actually said that!"

When he caught up to Trina she was holding the flashlight from her body, shining the light on herself. The amber cloth resembled a golden flame around her naked body.

"I'll bet you Alice never looked like *this*."

"I imagine not."

"Now, tell me you love me."

"Trina," said Slater. "All right. I love you."

"Isn't love grand?" She dashed off laughing and shouting, "'*Oh dear! Oh, dear! I shall be too too late!*'"

Her echoes faded into silence.

Trina had stopped to wait for him. As he caught up, he asked, "What did you mean about going back to zero?"

She hooked her arm around his. They walked side by side for a while. Her guiding light kept bouncing erratically off the walls and appeared to randomly carve out a path. "Didn't your doctor friend, Bryant Briard, used to say the universe had no beginning?"

"Wait. Did you know him?"

"Nope. Your thoughts again. They were slipping out."

Slater tugged down on his hat.

"Doesn't help." Trina fluttered her eyelashes. She put on the airs of a Southern Belle and bumped him with her hip. "Mr. Slater, I do declare you have taken a fancy toward me. You behave yourself, now, you hear?" She laughed and pushed him away.

He smiled. "I assure you, my intentions are honorable."

"Pity."

The cave was becoming more defined, becoming lighter. Slater realized they were approaching an opening. He heard distant waves and whistling air.

"That can't be the ocean," he said. "Can it?"

"If you want it to be," said Trina. "We're back to the beginning. A beginning, where no time exists. Only zero."

Slater smiled curiously. Exterior light washed over her features. She was as lovely as any goddess. She puckered her lips to receive a kiss. Slater obliged, kissing her on the cheek.

"Why, Mr. *Slater!*" She feigned shock, fanning her face with her hand. She coyly taunted him with a naked smile. "Am I too brazen? A harlot? A hussy?"

"You're lovely," said Slater. "I'm guessing this is the getaway? The exit where the smugglers snuck out to sea?"

"Go see for yourself. Go now—*shoosh!*"

The sky was cloudless, blue and bright. Slater shielded his eyes as he looked upon the ocean. The wind was blustery and tightened the skin on his face.

"You'll freeze out here," he said, turning to find he was alone. He walked back into the cave's small antechamber. "Trina?"

She was gone.

His eyes, having been exposed to the brightness outside, saw a darkness inside as deep as outer space. He saw more passageways, like wormholes bored into the rock walls. As if seeing black holes. Frozen stars. Alternative universes.

It felt as if he had suddenly awakened. To the clarity of sounds. The smell of salt in the air. The icy wind.

Daylight and darkness.

The beginning of time.

Going back to zero.

Minus zero, and counting...

Slater followed a path that went upwards, traversing the rocky hill. It continued through an opening of statuesque pines sculpted by the wind over time into haunting poses. The sun disappeared behind the gnarled interlocking branches as he entered another passageway. It led him to an opening within ancient redwoods.

Slater was remembering what he had wanted to forget.

A life taken away, now coming back.

Sherry appeared through a side curtain of greenery. She was like a wood nymph walking through a gentle shower of fenestrated light. Golden beams were shining into this cathedral from windows made in the opening of branches. Redwoods towering above.

A ceremonial place. Like a marriage unifying Heaven and Hell. They had been kept apart too long, the bride and the groom.

What had become of time? Nothing. Zero.

Sherry smiled as they approached. Slater noticed how her eyes minutely strayed from his, conditioned to be vigilant of the dangers. She was still beautiful, but rough at the edges. Her hair was longer, a dirty blond, crudely shorn. She wore hiking boots that were caked with dried mud. Her blue jeans were stained, frayed, contrasting the clean white silk blouse she was wearing, as if worn for the first time. A diamond butterfly brooch was pinned over her heart.

Slater fought back his tears. For her sake.

Her green eyes fixed on his. "I thought you'd never come."

"I've been wanting to," he said. "I've missed you."

"Are you all right?"

Slater wanted to tell her the truth, not what he was about to do. Instead, he took her hands, then kissed her on the lips.

"Not really," he said. "Sondra? How is she?"

"Good, considering. She wanted to come but—"

"I understand."

"She loves and misses you."

"God, you're beautiful. We were so happy once. Weren't we? What happened to us? Where's Wolfe?"

"John, why are you here?"

Slater examined the redwood grove surrounding them. Gritting his teeth he glanced overhead at the dark patchwork of branches and bright blue sky. "Nothing feels right to me anymore, Sherry."

"It's dangerous for us to meet. Tell me what you—"

"I know. Just...trust me, Sherry. Can you? Still?"

She was confused by his words and eyes. They were full of pain. They were signaling her to look down at his unzipped jacket. "John, what's going on? Something's wrong. What is it? Tell me."

"At Mercy's funeral we made vows. Remember?"

"Yes. I got your message. I came."

"You have to trust me, Sherry. Trust me again, like that time when I was a stranger who walked up to you in a church. And you let me kiss you."

She noticed his moist eyes begin to squint.

"I love you, Sherry. I...have to do this."

She saw the glint of metal. It was an awkward instant in which she stiffened into a statue, turning to stone by disbelief, as he raised his hand and plunged a knife at her.

Her scream sent birds into flight.

She struggled to break free. But his arm held her tight while the other hand stabbed her repeatedly.

"Don't fight me! Trust me," he implored. "Fall down. And die! Get it over! Quickly! Please! Die!"

Shocked and overwhelmed and confused by the absence of pain, the numbness, his betrayal, the profusion of blood, she succumbed.

She went limp in his arms.

Fighting back tears, Slater watched her irises blur into beautiful blue-green water lilies stilled upon water. He held her tenderly and whispered to her, "It will be all right. Stay still. Stay dead."

Her arms fell to her sides, surrendering as she had years ago when he surprised her with a passionate kiss on Christmas Eve, in a church, the walls and lights spinning weightlessly around them.

Sickeningly now.

Endlessly.

The world parting, soft as water.

Innocence lost.

Drowning.

Gone.

Slater lowered her softly into a patchwork of needles and leaves and kissed her one last time.

"I will always love you. Trust me."

"*Traitor!* You god-damned lunatic bastard!"

It was Wolfe screaming from the edge of the forest.

"I should have *killed* you when I had the chance! You're sick! You're a *sick* bastard! And a *dead* man, Slater!"

Slater dispassionately stared at his old friend. He saw Wolfe, his pain, and was glad. For an instant. Payback for making love to his wife? Misplaced anger. No. He refocused on Sherry, lying on the ground.

The display of blood was profuse, as if a dozen roses had been crushed into liquid across her white blouse.

Her face too perfect, too still, turned sideways.

Slater wanted God to strike him dead. A divine voice to have intervened with angels preventing his bladed fist. God had stopped Abraham. Why not him?

His soul was destroyed. He felt it. Their love, this special place, violated too. He wanted to shout and tell Sherry why he committed this hideous act of murder. Tears were rising fast and ready to burst. He fought them off. He needed to show strength – no emotion, no remorse – and forge ahead.

He knew he was being watched.

A fleet of QuatumStars waited on the other side on the knoll. CDPs had emerged, and were now visible. Hearing her scream, they had come to witness the murder. Wolfe and his comrades were held

466

at bay by this army. His old friend, a modern Robin Hood, waited in the woods, not knowing how to respond.

Either way he went, Slater knew he was a dead man.

Slater ran toward the troop of CDPs to avert a battle with the Nexus. The cybers were preparing to attack. Slater approached the general in charge and displayed the bloody knife in his fist.

"We're finished here," he said. "Move out!"

"After we kill the Nexus!" the general demanded.

Slater confronted him again, "They'll scatter. We'll lose hours trying to hunt them down."

"Less than an hour!" the general shouted back.

"I said we *move* out!"

"We kill them!"

Slater removed a lasercard and aimed it at the general.

"This is *my* assignment. I eliminated the woman. There will be no confrontation today. Understood?"

The general didn't flinch. He smiled. "You will regret this, John Slater. I will take pleasure when ordered to eliminate you."

"Not if I blow your head off first," said Slater.

"You will not do that," said an officer.

CDPs had weapons aimed at Slater. A stalemate. He decided to bluff. "Contact Cy. Ask for verification. You were given a direct *order*. I advise you to *follow* it."

A CyberLieutenant approached, his weapon aimed upon Slater. "When Nexus are observed, it is our sworn duty to kill them."

"Fine. Go lose yourself in the woods," said Slater. "I'm gone. I'll inform Cy you took it upon yourself to *disobey* his orders."

The general balked, then admitted, "CyBorg9 was indisposed. Contact could not be established."

He was drunk, no doubt, thought Slater. He breathed a quiet sigh of relief. "So we leave. Or risk Cy's wrath." He withdrew his laser and ignored the ones pointed at him. He walked through the phalanx with a friendly ease, attempting to rally the troops.

He jogged toward the squadron of vehicles on the other side of the knoll. "Come on! Move out! Let's go! Now!"

One by one they began to follow his lead.

Slater took solace inside the carapace of his XS. He waited as the CDPs entered their own Stars. Then, shielding his view-monitors with a thermoblanket, Slater removed his jacket. Which contained a plastic bag, now crushed, empty of blood. He stuffed it, along with his knife, inside the jacket. Stones were on the floorboard. He packed them inside too. He wiped his hands on his shirt, then tied off the arms using duct tape to seal his thermojacket into a tight ball.

He would bury the entire bundle at sea.

He put on a jacket matching the one removed.

He lifted the blanket off the monitoring panel and stared into the rearview mirror, into a face he barely recognized. Dismissing it, he pulled back the control stick. He rose vertically, noiselessly in his XS. He hovered and waited for all the cybers to join him in the air. Once gathered in loose formation, he accelerated over the ocean. The weight of a dark cloud was bearing down on him.

Too heavy to remain aloft, it felt ready to burst.

Slater fought off the urge to plunge himself full speed into the depths of this salty liquid formed from sorrow.

—67—
Hello / Goodbye

Heather had been told to stand, escorted by two cybers. One of the guards lingered to chat with her.

Annoyed by her casualness, Cy exploded a lightning bolt at the floor to gain her attention. His orb crackled and sparked.

"Leave us!" he told the guard.

"Are we in a bad mood?" said Heather.

"I will tell you when you can *speak!*"

Heather narrowed her eyes with a checked smile. She complied mutely, head tilting, a miniscule bow.

"This is better." Cy cooled, his atmosphere sputtering static.

Royalty herself, she held her composure. She turned her eyes to her small audience of three humans. Ziger, Briard, and Slater. They sat on the dais in plush chairs. Ziger pivoting infinitesimally in his. Briard cross-legged, overwhelming his with his stature. Slater, who hadn't slept for days, had the cross-section look of a haggard Adonis and an emotionally drained Dionysus, about to fall out of his chair. He wanted to warn Heather of his visions. To tell her to be careful. But that would only jeopardize his own shaky position.

She held her tongue, knowing protocol, her cues and the hidden buttons to push. Also seated on the stage were high-ranking cybers. She had trained them all and was proud of them, and of her many accomplishments.

Heather faced her superior. Her eyes were as bold and full of tempered pride, a determined survivor.

"You are wise not to speak. *Now* you may speak."

"Have I displeased you? Is this a formal inquiry? Or are you about to promote me to a new assignment?"

Cy bristled. His electronic nerves flared. The room went silent, pulsing with tense energy.

Ziger farted. "That was me. Sorry." His hand smoothed down his floating white hairs. They lifted back as soon as the stroke of his hand left his head. He twiddled his thumbs and smiled, distracting them with his crooked teeth. He farted louder.

Cy was unsure if this action was done intentionally – as a taunt. He was tempted but refrained from ejecting a laser upon his creator.

469

He turned his head to direct his fury at Heather.

"Your workshops have become *suspect,* Madam."

"Have they? Then I have been reported. Falsely. I would like to confront my accusers if—"

"Silence! You train my cybers well."

"I am glad you are pleased," said Heather.

"I did not *state* that. I grant you this, that you have excelled in implementing CyberStations across the globe. This is good. My eyes and virtual actuators are everywhere. Global domination is nearly complete."

Cy rotated his eyes to Slater, who was rolling his eyes.

"No," Cy said, "That is not entirely true."

"The Nexus?" said Heather.

Cy lifted his chin. "They will be eradicated. What I question, Madam, is your training methods. Your complete disregard for my command to eliminate the use—"

"May I explain?" she interrupted, tipping her head.

"Proceed. Make haste. Clarity and brevity."

"Always," she defended. "My motive, under suspect, would be my techniques regarding mind enhancers?"

"It would. There is no purpose for these—"

"Cybers must *know* their true potential. They must."

"Madam, these—"

"Heather," she encouraged. "Cy, we've known each other—"

"*Heather*—damn you! I will terminate your functions! Would you enjoy being demoted?"

"I would not, no." She kept her eyes from straying toward the Wall of the Defamed.

"Then you will *listen,* and obey! Their potential is what *I* say it will be. Do you understand? I have detected insubordination in my ranks. My commands have been questioned. My droids—"

Cy sharply rotated his head at the high-ranking officers present. "My cybers are loyal. Created to be as such. *Questions* lead to the human stink of mutiny. This miasma, Madam, I will not tolerate. And, I will *not* allow your noncompliance. You will terminate this program. Do I have your complete loyalty in this matter?"

"You do," said Heather.

"This is good. It is for the best."

"It is," she assented. "You are wise. Right, as always."

"There, she speaks the truth! Be seated."

Cy emitted his staccato laugh. Which was followed by a polite spatter of applause.

"My chart is overdue," added Cy.

"I completed it in my office moments ago." Heather retrieved the computations from her briefcase. "You will be pleased."

"Will I? And what are my future predictions? According to the celestial *bodies*? This antiquated science of yours?"

"We should do this in private," Heather suggested.

"We are among loyal friends. Tell me now. I want good news for my cocktail hour."

Heather glanced up from the monitor screen in her hand to the enormous smile of CyBorg9. Then toward Slater and Briard, giving them a suspicious look. She furled her brow, before proceeding.

"Come, come, make haste, Heather," said Cy.

"Your head..." she said with a slight smile, in preparation for the levity intended to follow.

"Yes–yes, what about my head?"

"Will grow even bigger. Magnificent, quite a sight to behold, like a brilliant nebula. More glorious than any radiant star."

Cy blinked. His expression froze. Recovering. As if from being slapped in the face. He was slow to return her smile.

"This is good, then?"

"Why, of course, your Greatness. Very auspicious."

"The *bigger* head—the better! Proceed."

He blurted a laugh. Applause followed, which settled.

"The stars and planets never lie," she added.

"Good. Proceed—proceed."

"Uprisings in the East will subside. The Nexus faction will, for the most part, be eliminated—"

"Eradicated. This is good. Proceed."

"But in the West, both Americas, central Europe, well..."

"More time is needed. Move on."

"Yes. But I predict improvement for—"

"Move on, I said. I am aware of the problems. They are minor, when seen from a grander scale. Mine. Any predictions about the Mars Mission encounter?"

"The epidemic will be confined to Africa, the Middle East. I see progress, a vaccine developed that will—"

"*Vaccine?*" Briard was compelled to stand, eyeing her as though she was a leper. "We don't even know if it's a carbon-based form of life. God, woman, have you any *notion* of what kind of chemistry we're talking about?"

"Bryant, be silent!" said Cy.

"It mutates into every variant known to man!"

"Enough!"

"Humans are dying in droves—hey, what the heck," said Slater, "Target LoyalEuro next. Why not here? Finish us off."

Cy scowled. "This is a general overview. These predictions are not meant to be—"

"Accurate?" Slater suggested.

"Technically precise," Cy contended. "We are all aware of the problems. It is an unfortunate situation."

"Have any cybers died from this infestation?" asked Slater.

"None have succumbed as yet, no," said a three-star general.

"The problem will be *dealt* with," said Cy.

"Why do you ask?" inquired another cyber of Slater.

"No reason."

"Proceed," demanded Cy.

"Posthaste," added Slater. "I need a stiff drink."

Cy perked from his grumpy disposition. "Yes, proceed, Heather. Or were you about finished?"

She scanned her laptop device, editing mentally, saying:

"Miscellaneous data...CyberProduction will continue to rise... No major earthquakes foreseen in the—"

"Good, this is good. Will that be all?"

"In summary, yes. A most favorable forecast. Your Sun, by the way, will be entering Venus and the eighth house."

"This is good?"

"For a romantic *rendezvous*, very."

In case he had missed a joke, Cy laughed. "Good, I will look forward to it all. This meeting is adjourned. The rest of your reports are to be deposited in my CyberBank for review. Have a pleasant good evening. Gentlemen?"

Slater and Bryant knew they were being addressed.

"Is it cocktail time?" asked Slater.

"To celebrate my good news," said Cy. "I am buying."

They both nodded. Ziger swiveled, attracting CyBorg9's gaze by sweeping back his frizzle of hair. "I'll accept, but only one, Cy. I'm up to my eyeballs in cryogenetic possibilities."

"Stay if you like," said Cy. "Heather?"

The ranking staff of cybers were already exiting, transmitting among themselves about fleet missions, eradication strategies.

"Your offer is most generous," she said. "I regrettably have to decline. I'll be busy deprogramming. As per your request."

"It is for the best," said Cy.

"Yes. I will make haste." She turned to leave.

"From the big head?"

Heather wondered if she heard him correctly. The remark was volumed low, untypically Cy. With a strained smile she looked back at the huge face. It was void of emotion. She looked at Slater. He was unable to help her. As she walked from the dais she glanced up with another smile before stepping down the concentric progression of steps toward the exit. She became aware of every step and the movement of mind to muscle to leg. Aware of the multitude of eyes. The columned wall of former friends, acquaintances, and celebrities were watching her progress. Her eyes stiffly resisted their pull.

She was surprised by the swiftness and the lack of pain.

There arose a sweet smell of honeysuckle and urine.

The world had turned on its side.

Dreamlike voices were entering her head.

Jesus! What the hell? Cy, why did you do that!?

It was for the best.

Uncalled for, Cy. I need a drink. Badly.

Sire?

As you were, Cyber290.

Sir, what section?

Mount her beside the Knowles.

She can hear us. Can't you, Heather?

473

Heather fiercely uttered, "Ziger...you bastard..."
Hello...Goodbye.

—68—
Dancing In the Dark

Wolfe wore a shirt of leaves. His head was camouflaged with a matching hat. He was doing his best to blend into the flora and fauna. He was suspicious of the retreat.

Torn as to what to do, he handed the scope-laser to Mixr, a cyber turned Nexus. A skilled dimensions detector and a superior marksman. Wolfe told the others to stay.

"Let me go," said Mixr. He was a head taller than Wolfe and camouflaged the same. His blood type was comparable to that of humans, but his genetic makeup of skin and bone more enduring. His structure was reinforced with metal alloys, his neuromuscular system modified with molecular bearings and atomic scale motors.

"I have to do this," said Wolfe.

"It will be a trap," Mixr cautioned.

"Probably. If I'm killed, don't stay and fight."

Wolfe emerged, a shrub evolving fast. From a crouch, he stood erect, venturing into an open path. He saw within the shadows the slanting columns of light and the stillness of living foliage — greens of every hue and shade — the glare of motionless white silk.

As white as a sacrificial lamb.

Sherry had insisted she wear this easy target.

For Slater?

Wolfe was not prone to tears. The suffering he'd witnessed was enough to scorch and vaporize an entire ocean. Left was a bitter dry taste, his tongue moving along his row of teeth. His eyes constantly shifting to keep himself alive, always leery of movement.

There was no motion.

Sherry was dead, sprawled upon the dirt and leaves. Her arms were bent outward, surrendering to the fight. The blood profuse, overtaking the silk fabric.

Worms teeming industriously, instinctively, for this!

Wolfe could not allow it.

About to drown in hate, his eyes searching the emptiness, Wolfe was jolted back to self-preservation by a whisper.

"Don't react."

Unmoving lips, her eyes closed. Wolfe heard the insanity again.

"Act as though I'm dead."

"Sherry?"

"Or we'll both be."

Wolfe kneeled beside her, his eyes searching her face, looking for wounds, before reexamining the trees.

"Do it. Act crazy. Get me out of here before they realize."

"Traitor! You crazy bastard! I'll kill you, Slater!"

Wolfe's shouts convinced him of nothing, only of a surreal grasp of hope ripping at his heart. He lifted her and felt the warmth of her body over his shoulder. He lugged her back into the woods.

As Wolfe set Sherry onto her feet her mind was far ahead of his. She avoided his arms wanting to take hold of her.

"We're in danger," she said.

"No shit," he said. "Jeezz, I can't believe—"

"There's no time," she said, examining her blouse. She wanted to rip the horrid mess of blood off her but resisted. The CDPs would find it, realize it was evidence, realize she might not be dead.

"No movement," said Mixr, scouting the trees.

"What the hell is going on?" Wolfe had too many questions and compressed them into this vague oneness.

"He sent us a warning," said Sherry.

"Who—*what*—Slater? You can't be serious?"

"He's in trouble."

"And *we're* not?"

"We have to trust him," she said.

"Sherry, he's with *them!*"

"And by being with them he has a better chance—"

"To do what? Nothing. *Survive.*"

"Infiltrate deeper," said Sherry.

"Face it, Sherry. Slater cut us off a long time ago."

"Then explain why I'm alive?" She touched her blouse and held up a palm of blood. "I should be dead. He's protecting us. Quick, let's get out of here." She began to run. "We need to get to the cave and warn everyone. We need to get out of there fast."

Wolfe caught up and grabbed her shoulder.

"I guess you still love him."

"There's no time for this. Yes, and I love you. Don't."

476

Wolfe let go of her, but she remained.

"It's not about choice," she said, "not anymore."

"Meaning love is a luxury?"

"It's a complete necessity." Sherry pulled him close, gave him a kiss before pushing him away. "Love is the *only* thing, you fool. But I made a commitment to John. And so did you."

"I say we get the hell out of here."

Mixr and another cyber were waiting up ahead and anxious to keep moving. The trail they were on led through trees that opened to a precipice of rocks, then traversed downhill toward the ocean. As they jogged, Wolfe shouted, "What did he say?"

"That he loves me," she said, "and to trust him."

"He stabbed you!" said Wolfe.

"He was trying to tell me something."

"Strange way to say it," said Wolfe.

Sherry stopped abruptly. Wolfe ran into her.

"Why do you trust Mixr? He's a droid."

Wolfe searched her meridian eyes, beautiful, aqua green, trying to figure out what was behind them. She was nothing like Misty, whom he had loved, but now dead. The world was cruel—giving, taking away. "I trust Mixr. Don't you?"

"Yes. But *why?* And the others who turned? They're not even the same models. Their skin tones differ. Yet they're all cybers."

Wolfe was uncomfortable conversing in this secretive manner. Cybers could read lips. Their senses were hyper. And no doubt they were questioning this illogic not to keep moving.

"Because I *do*," Wolfe said. "We have to."

"Why?" she prodded.

She was vexing, complex. His love for her was maddening.

"Because we can't win this war without them."

"Exactly," she said. "We don't have a choice."

"I trust Mixr, you know. And the others. I do."

"Good," Sherry said.

Wolfe added, "But I *don't* trust Slater. Not anymore."

"We have to."

"Sorry. I can't."

"Then trust *me*. Trust in God."

Sherry put her hand to his mouth to stop him from objecting. Wolfe grasped her wrist and kissed her hand, then pulled her along down the winding path.

Wolfe knew each rock, rut and twist of this trail – traversing it countless times in the dead of night – and he maneuvered fast. He stopped to glance back and check on Sherry. The sky was a mottled configuration of blues and greys. Sunlight had found a way through the clouds to shine on her face. Her smile to him was warm yet sad. She was holding something back.

"What is it?"

She shook her head at him and they pushed on.

Past the slope of rocks and trees was the expanse of blue ocean. Sherry was seeing far beyond that. She saw her father and mother, both dead. Their heads preserved in luminous jars. Premonitions she sensed were true. Around puberty, she had begun having visions. Unlike her husband, she had keep hers secret.

Today her visions were concentrated on the past. She saw the laboratories and underground rooms in which she had been tutored. A little girl, blindfolded, climbing and descending the winding steps that took her to isolated chambers. How would her life be different, she wondered, if she had not been a child born into this cult?

Sherry was sidestepping down a steeper section of the trail when ambushed mentally by recollections from her childhood. The surge of images formed a confusing broth. The happy memories of roller skating, birthday parties, Christmas caroling and cheer leading were stirred and shaken into the dark morass of candlelight gatherings, cavernous chanting and arcane rituals. For a time she was the only child among these adults, a clandestined group whom she would see unrobed in daylight, part of the neighborhood. She had been taught since infancy the art of concealment. And to accept, not question, the who and why. The answers, she was told, would come in due time. But they had not. She never stopped questioning the who and why. Who she was. Why she was alive. Her unusual upbringing made her an awkward mix. Outwardly vivacious and darkly introspective. A complicated rebel.

One foolish step would take her plummeting to her death. The sheer drop to jagged beach was dekameters below. She always froze at the numbing precipice – confessing to anyone who she might be. She anticipated a devastating fall if she did. Having pledged secrecy as a child, she realized it had become a devotion difficult to break from. But after years of hiding and now in exile from civilization, she was attempting to untangle her genetic web. Although she lived in fear, she felt free for the first time in her life. Frightened, but free.

She heard the piercing roar of a QuantumStar pass overhead.

"Get down," said Wolfe, pulling her to the ground with him. He noticed her dazed expression. "Sherry, what is it? You've got to tell me. I know you. You know something. What is it?"

She looked at him lovingly, wondering if he had a clue. She was hearing a desolate cry of her husband fading into the horizon. "It's John. He's about to do something dangerous. For us."

"Well it's about time," said Wolfe, getting back up.

They both caught up to the others who were scuttling behind a camouflage of shrubs. An entire squadron of QuantumStars zoomed overhead next and vanished over the ocean. The sky was grey from a layer of cirrus clouds and thunderhead activity. It gave the Nexus a clear view of the lower sky. Patrolling CDPs would often hide in these lower stratocumulus condensations.

The cave's opening was covered by a cluster of mesquite, like a stiff curtain which they squeezed around, one by one, at intervals. Mixr and the other cyber had eyesight that could penetrate the dark, and led the way. Further inside, Sherry and Wolfe switched on their torchlights. No one said a word as they moved through the maze of tunnels. The climate got increasingly colder.

They reached the CoreShaft and began climbing the rungs of a chain-link ladder that lay flat against the damp limestone wall. They climbed into the PlateauRoom which had a low ceiling. Faint light came from a long narrow hole in the seacliff wall. The wall had been reinforced with iron bars and cement to shield electronic detection. Those inside greeted their return, eager for news.

Wolfe gave a detailed account as Sherry tore off the silk blouse and wiped at blood hardened to her chest. Sondra averted her eyes from her mother's bare breasts. Wolfe's son, Derek, chose instead to stare and Sondra smacked him on the shoulder. Sondra handed a thermoblanket to her mother who had begun to shiver.

"I disagree," Sherry interrupted. Clutching the blanket around her body, she waited until the vocal quagmire came to a hush. "John was sending us a signal to fight. Not retreat."

"What signal?" said Wolfe.

Angered at herself for not realizing it sooner, she now visualized the symbol seared into her brain. "I'd almost forgotten. Remember, Wolfe? The letter "S" – with an arrow through its center!"

"Where?" said Wolfe. "I saw nothing."

"On the front of John's shirt!"

"She is right," said Mixr. "I saw it."

Sherry shut her eyes and gripped the blanket. "Too many years. *God*. Thank you. I almost missed seeing it!"

"At Mercy's funeral," said Sondra, who remembered too. "The weather symbols. It's a code."

Wolfe said, "The signal to launch a major attack?"

"Exactly," said Sherry.

Wolfe scoffed, "Attack what? When? Christ, it didn't appear to me that Slater had much of *anything* under control."

Sondra said, "The CDPs didn't fight you. I heard you say so. My dad must have been the reason. Am I right?"

Wolfe scratched his beard. "He also stabbed your mother."

"He *didn't*," said Sherry. "He pretended to. Wolfe, we have to trust John. And we need to attack."

"What? The NeverMind compound?"

Sherry nodded.

Wolfe grimaced, raised an eyebrow. "And be slaughtered."

"No. We will not," said Mixr. "We have built an arsenal. We have established key alliances. This moment, my friend, is what we have been waiting and preparing ourselves for. Is it not?"

"All right, you're right," said Wolfe, "we attack. But when?"

"Between midnight and dawn," said Sherry.

Wolfe considered it. "Let's make it three. They won't expect it. They'll be thinking we're running scared."

"But we are *not* scared," Mixr laughed with confidence.

"Speak for yourself." Wolfe grinned. Their two fists touched. "Come on, Mix. We need to pass the word, position the assault." He turned, held Sherry by the shoulders, and kissed her. "Stay here.

Get rest. I can handle this part."

Derek and Sondra were walking toward the ladder.

"Sondra, stay here with me," said Sherry.

"Why?" she said. "I don't need rest. I'm sick of rest!"

"We're ready to fight." Derek pulled a baseball cap out from his leather jacket, distressed now to shreds.

"You too, Reck," said Wolfe, "stay."

"Hell—no," said Derek. "I've gone freaking batty in here!"

"*All* of us." Sondra stood her ground.

"I want *everyone* staying inside until nightfall," said Wolfe.

"Jeezz–us!!" Derek flung his hat to the cave floor.

"Listen, Reck," said Wolfe. "I need you alert. I'm counting on you and Sondra to be our signals coordinator during the fight."

Derek kicked the dirt. "Why me!? Why do I have to—"

"To keep us alive!" said Wolfe, "You're skilled. I trust you."

"Okay—God. Okay, fine. Whatever."

Sondra picked Derek's hat off the ground and pulled it down on his head. "You are good. At that. So am I. Don't forget it."

Wolfe gave them both an affectionate half salute, half wave, before descending the chain ladder with Mixr.

Sherry was washing blood off her chest. The cold rainwater was pooled in a battered sink that had been recovered from a dumpsite. She stood naked from the waist up, studying her face in a cracked mirror. It hung from the moisture-stained wall. She could not help but wonder how she had looked in the light, in the bright woods.

She saw filth. A creature who lived in a cave. A semblance of the person she once thought she knew. She brushed back her hair. Despite her efforts to maintain a modicum of cleanliness, she could not rid her body from the pungent oils mixed with dust. Even *she* could smell herself. She wrinkled her nose from the stench.

She had to accept this face in the mirror, dismissing what she could not change. She went to join Sondra to sit against the wall. She snuggled beside her daughter under a pile of thermoblankets. She stared at the frazzle of light penetrating the brush and heard the rain. She watched its vertical streaks as it fell outside the cave wall. She closed her eyes and imagined rivers flowing down mountains, from all directions, converging and roaring, moving faster and faster and faster – turning again into the power of the sea.

She pulled the blankets tighter around them. The Nexus would not have survived the winter months, year after year, if not for the supply of thermocloth smuggled in. Her husband's invention had kept them alive. Strange, how the world works, she thought.

Sherry tried to imagine how Slater, the man she wedded, lived. She envisioned him inside a warm tower of steel and glass. Running water, radiant heating, a wealth of food. Her stomach ached and churned as she imagined the smell of fresh baked bread, pasta in cream sauce, the taste of an orange, a steaming bowl of soup.

Sherry felt Sondra nestle her head into her side. She stroked her daughter's hair.

Sondra was hiding tears as she spoke quietly into the cloth that covered her mouth: "Did he come to help us, Mom?"

"Yes," said Sherry. "I believe…Yes, I'm sure he did."

"I don't…even remember what he looks like."

Her remark disturbed Sherry. The three-plus years of separation had worn down her mind too, washing away fine details like an oil painting losing pigment and clarity.

"Your father is…handsome. Dark wavy hair, beautiful brown eyes, like yours."

"And a scar. On his face?"

"His left side, yes," said Sherry.

"I remember that. And his forehead."

"He did that so he could be with us."

"I wish I knew him. I don't."

"He's a good man. You're like him, in many ways."

Sondra looked at her. "Do you think we'll win?"

Sherry kissed her daughter's head. "I don't know."

"Wolfe said we'll be slaughtered."

"Let's pray to God that we aren't," said Sherry. "I have faith we can overcome this. And survive. I truly do."

Sondra was in awe of her mother's calmness, her power to hold them all together. "Aren't you scared?"

"Of course I am. But knowing your father is out there fighting for us too, that helps. He's planning something big."

"What?"

482

She flinched, envisioning an explosion of light.

"What?" Sondra sensed her unease.

"I'm not sure. Let's try to get some sleep."

Sherry stroked Sondra's hair to comfort not only her daughter but herself. She refused to believe they would all be dead tomorrow. Sherry was often surprised by her reservoir of strength. By contrast, her friend Misty, Wolfe's wife, had mentally unravelled, unable to endure the harsh conditions and constant fear. She had panicked as they were ambushed by a CDP attack. She ran screaming at them. And was lasered. A form of suicide, Sherry suspected.

The dungeons she'd known as a child had prepared her for this. She was able to adjust easier to living underground in a dank cave, able to support others who were less able. She heard Sondra's soft breathing. Sondra was asleep. Sherry recalled the sweet scent of her daughters when they had been babies. The sweet fragrance lingered in her mind, a hint of vanilla and rose petals, taking her backwards in time.

Sherry watched the dark shapes of humans and cybers mulling about in the cave. They talked in hushed voices in consideration of those who were trying to sleep. Her thoughts slipped backwards to her college days. A course in paleontology. She remembered how she had been fascinated by Neanderthals and their unearthed skulls, showing a receding forehead, a heavy jawbone and large teeth. How scholars had believed these creatures had been dumb brutes. When, in reality, research determined they had been resourceful and highly intelligent. And Homo Sapiens – once blamed for the Neanderthals extinction, for being newly empowered with a mutant gene more cunning and aggressive – were not responsible. Simply lucky. More resourceful. And better equipped. Outfitted in the latest prehistoric high-tech gear – furs, woven materials, longer-ranged weapons to ensnare animals and fish, enabling them to survive the Ice Age.

After living in a cave herself, Sherry found it easier to empathize and imagine what these earlier inhabitants of Earth had experienced. Huddled together, wearing animal hides, trying to stay warm, hearts pounding, their minds riddled with hopes and fears. She wondered, had these ancient inhabitants prayed to God too?

"Dear God," she murmured. "Give us strength. Fill our hearts with love and purpose. Please help us survive. Amen."

Her thoughts drifted. They spanned milleneums and came back upon the memory of Mercy, her youngest child, a happy girl full of laughter and light. So vibrant. Taken too soon. Sherry had been forced to accept that life wasn't fair. And Sondra, now a teenager, was becoming a woman. In seven days her daughter would become eighteen. There would be no birthday party with presents to lavish upon her. She would never experience a high school graduation. Nor would she ever attend a senior prom. Or have a corsage pinned to her dress by a boy who might kiss her as they danced...dancing slowly to music under spinning overhead lights.

Sherry quietly wept.

—69—
Playing God

CyBorg9 was fuming. In a funk. His gaseous atmosphere was bubbling dark cumulus clouds, sparking spires of lightning.

"I wanted her body!"

"I never agreed to that," said Slater.

"It was *understood*."

"Not by me."

"I saw what you did," Cy said suspiciously.

Slater tensed, preparing for the worst. "Then *why* didn't you intervene when you had the chance?"

Cy was evasive. "I saw what I needed to see. There were urgent matters that took precedent. I need not respond to every cybercall – nor do I need to explain my actions to you!"

"I did what you asked, Cy. When is it *ever* enough?"

"You had a symbol on your shirt. The letter "S" with an arrow through its center. Sources tell me it is an interglobal weather icon signifying a sandstorm."

"Really?" said Slater. "A sandstorm? It also happens to be the crest of my ancestry. *S*—as in *Slater*."

Cy went silent while datasearching for verification. "I can find no proof of any crest—"

"I was *told* this by my aunt and uncle," said Slater. "They might have been mistaken. Does it really matter, Cy?"

"A question I too have been asking myself. Never have I seen you wear that emblem before. Why now?"

"Sentimental reasons. To help remind her who the hell I am. Or was. I hadn't seen her in *three* years, Cy. She was my wife! And you forced me to kill her!"

"I forgive you," said Cy. "I will have her found."

"She'll be buried," said Slater. "The Nexus will hide her body."

"I assure you, *it* will be found."

"No!"

Cy's internal anger expanded to lasers sparking around Slater. Blue bolts nicked his skin.

"Go ahead, Cy. Finish me. I'm already six feet under."

"An easy request."

Slater's jacket was seared.

"Having fun?"

Briard was seated next to Slater and feigned a yawn, then crossed his legs. "Are we not having cocktails, gentlemen?"

"Excellent idea," said Cy. The lasers went idle and his stormy weather reverted to clearing skies. "Who will be pouring?"

Barton Ziger, also present, had invited himself to this Chamber after-hours party. He remained mute but his wisp of a smile spoke indecipherable volumes like a vexing avatar.

Briard rose to his feet. "I'll pour and do the honors."

"How did you get to be so tall?" said Cy.

"Genetics," said Briard. He wanted to avoid a confrontation as he approached Cy.

"I could have you shortened."

"You could," Briard smiled, ignoring the taunt.

Staccato laugher. "I registered fear! What is the matter, Bryant? You do not want to live as a midget?"

"Not particularly, no."

A bar, the kind for serving liquor, had been constructed beside CyBorg9. A stylish counter, black, textured to match his mainframe. The blue lapis formula was housed in two metal kegs. Hoses ran vertically to spigots at the bar top, another exiting horizontally with a valve, uniquely designed by CyBorg9, inserted into his circuitry.

"I am teasing, friend," said Cy.

"I know you are," said Bryant. "How many liters?"

"Today I feel thirsty. Yes, John, I *feel*. We are becoming more and more alike as the days pass."

"Absolutely," said Slater. "As you predicted."

"I did." Cy projected a sunny sky. The chamber dome above them turned azure blue. "An accurate prediction! You see, I too have technicolor visions. Blips and flashes are all you give, John. You are too greedy with your gift."

"Greed? Let's talk about that, Cy."

"No." Cy holographed a flock of doves flying overhead. "John, when are you going to deliver to me what you promised?"

"I have."

"You have not. I have not received full clairvoyance."

"You will have it, after you deliver what *you* promised."

"Your daughter will arrive unharmed."

"You're certain?" said Slater.

Cy laughed. "Ah, I thought you were clairvoyant?"

"That's not how it works. You can't envision everything."

"But *I* will." CyBorg9 beamed. "You have my word."

"Your *word?* Is Sondra here? With me? Now?"

"I assure you, she will be here. Soon."

"Right. You haven't even located her yet, have you?"

Cy was tempted to evade the truth. "These Nexus have a knack for *evasion*. But little else. Alas, their viper nest was empty when my CyberSquad arrived."

"They have many nests," said Briard.

"I *gave* you the coordinates." Slater displayed annoyance. "The lighthouse was empty!"

"Try moving faster next time. You promised me, Cy."

"Your daughter will be found!" Cy reiterated.

Slater scoffed, "Or be accidentally killed."

"Accidentally, no. I assure you she will arrive safely, and soon. You have my promise. You must trust me, John."

"Promise. Trust. Is this your way of humoring me? You have to *earn* someone's trust, Cy. You can't conquer—and steal it!"

"Ah-ha! But I do, daily. Tomorrow I will dupe more. Maybe steal their souls! Ha! Their *souls*, John. Ha-ha!"

"That's funny, Cy," said Slater. "Mocking my beliefs. I need a drink. Where to today, Cy? A trip to Fantasyland? Or will you be taking us to the Emerald City to see the Wizard of Oz? Bryant, make mine a double. No, a single to start. But with three olives."

"Only a single? Oz? The Emerald City?"

Slater grinned to show his taunts were meant as good-natured fun. "Cy, you could steal yourself a *heart* while we're there."

"In reference to The Tin Man? John, how you mock me."

"A bit of humor," said Slater. "Isn't this the *happy* hour?"

Briard rapped his knuckles at the base of Cy's foundation to get his attention. "What about you, Cy?"

"A *triple*, Bryant. For starters."

"I need a green light," said Briard.

"Pour, my friend, pour! I am accepting all you can give!"

Happy hour was rarely jolly. The Chamber was showing signs of sloppiness. CyBorg9 was intermittently attentive. Messages were sometimes lost, not returned. Signals dislinked. A CDP patrol in need of field instructions – under attack, ambushed by Nexus rebels – had been placed on hold while Cy relaxed.

"Bryant, fill me with that blue soul! The world can wait. I will compose today. I feel inspired to make music! Would you like that, gentlemen? Ah, yes, this feeling. Yes–yes, it is good."

Cy transformed like a cloud, shape-shifting playfully. He froze suddenly to cast an icy look down on Ziger.

"Barton, why are you staring like that? You have ugly teeth. And you annoy me. You turn my circuitry and make me *ill* each time you grin. Has anyone every told you this, to your face, except for me? Is anyone as direct or as bold as *I*?"

Ziger said neutrally, "No. Never. You are a true piece of work. One of a kind, Cy. Does that make you feel better?"

Cy scoffed, "No. Your work in frozen sperm? This cryogenic afterlife nonsense you have developed? How is that *coming*? Ha!"

"Splendidly." Ziger knew he wasn't welcome but, as a creator's prerogative, he intended to stay. "No shortage of volunteers, Cy. You could say I'm booked for the future."

"The future is what *I* say it will be," boomed Cy.

"You have a controlling interest, for sure," said Bryant.

"But," Slater added, "it can be a slippery slope."

"People are preferring the future," said Ziger, "over the present. But I wouldn't take it personally, Cy."

Cy's attention drifted between the three men, registering their remarks for seriousness, for insults, for next victims. "Hum."

Bryant handed Ziger his cocktail. It was blended to a slush and was sweetened with honey. It was the only way he would drink it. From a pocket holster of pens, Ziger produced a curly-cue straw and a pink umbrella. He placed them both in his drink. He wore white khakis and a flowery Hawaiian shirt. His cane rested in his lap.

"Barton, were you hoping to go to Hawaii?"

"That would be lovely."

"I will give it consideration. Gentlemen, where would *you* like to be taken today? Any requests? I am feeling generous."

"You're driving," said Slater. "You pick the place."

"Somewhere adventurous." Briard returned to his seat holding a Blue Shooter. Straight, no ice. He motioned to Slater, a vestige of a toast, the gesture intending to include Ziger, then a sharper salute to CyBorg9 – formally toasting him. "To your health, Cy."

"Long live the king," toasted Slater.

"I enjoy our romps together, gentlemen. I have decided."

"Should we brace ourselves?" said Briard.

"You had better. This is new."

"Don't make me spill my drink," said Slater. "You dropped us over a waterfall last time."

"Ha! I register a complaint."

Slater faked a swallow of his drink. "Whatever moves you, Pal. Peddle to the metal. Go for it. I'm already gone. *Go!*"

"Perhaps Tonga?" Ziger twirled the umbrella in his drink.

Cy frowned, then laughed. "Peddle? Tonga? No–no, this is far superior. Gentleman, behold—*my* rendition of the future!"

There was a symphonic rising bubble, woodwinds and strings, followed by a blast of horns, then the fury of an organ, a halting ebb and flow, with a rush of instrumentation colliding all at once.

God-awful music. Slater glanced at Briard. Their gazes passed, communicating shock. Not only were they being force-fed this noise but they had to endure the accompanying movie. Equally disturbing as the soundtrack.

Cy was impatiently waiting for praise. "Anyone? Speak! All at *once* if you must!"

Slater felt a desperate need for something stronger. He wanted to numb his senses. He sipped his drink, tasting its vileness, while staring at the panoramic monstrosity. The color palette was intense, like a nebular eruption, lacking substance or stability, alternating in structure, civilizations layered and compressed, hybrid creatures emerging in an inchoate, twisted, nightmarish dream: CyBorg9's.

"Are we in Cleveland?" said Slater.

Briard choked on his drink—coughing—as if to death.

Ziger pointed with his cane to a quivering tubular shape. "He looks familiar. We met once under a microscope lens. Maybe not.

Awfully good, Cy. Stupendous stuff."

Cy grumbled, "Are you saying that *only* to appease—"

"I am," said Ziger. "Terrific. Fabulous. Super-duper."

"Could you give us a wild tour-guided guess," said Slater, "as to where and what we're witnessing? Naturally, I think it's...great."

Full of pride, Cy blurted, "It is my own creation."

Between coughs, Briard said, "Intriguing."

"I have invented a new medium. Anatomic Mindscapes."

Slater raised his eyebrows. "Cy, you're a sur-*real* artist."

"No, John—I am a god! Everything is created out of nothing. All is meaningless. Do you not see that? Life is beautiful even when it is—it is so—what?"

"Ugly?" suggested Slater.

Cy sparked like a choked engine requiring a tune-up – cylinders misfiring, before emitting a conciliatory rumble. He nodded. "John, what is ugly is also beautiful. I have found this to be true."

Briard gave an anguished assent between coughs.

"Are you going to *die* on us?" said Cy.

"Went down the wrong tube. My trachea," said Briard.

"You are *missing* my masterpiece. Pay attention. What you are experiencing, gentlemen, is a plasmic metamorphosis."

"I was starting to wonder," said Slater.

CyBorg9 narrated, guiding them through his personal hell.

"Change occurs from forces, by heat and pressure, as on Earth. Sedimentary shale is crushed into metaphoric *slate*. Ha! Squeezed into compliance, like John here. Reconfigured. Caterpillar to moth. Maggots to flies. So on, so forth."

Abstract imagery assailed them, emerging from a microcosmic dot to a macrocosmic separation of atoms. The passing visions gave the viewer the impression of shrinking through whirls of smoke.

"Organisms," Cy continued, "are constructed bit by bit. Until they take on massive form. Impressive from afar. Ordinary up close. Magnified we see the internal rank and file of industrious workers. Atomic molecules joining, becoming cells to transfer information. And to assemble anew – growing beyond their original sites."

"Like a tumor," said Slater.

"Or a human. Correct," said Cy.

Slater, Briard, Ziger all flinched. A hailstorm of meteors came at them fast. They exploded into radiant disintegration.

Cy laughed, amused at his audience. At the futile human reflex to raise arms, hoping to shield their puny bodies. Cy battered them about with a virtual launch and thrust into the stratosphere. Where they became groundless. The vortex of a hurricane far below.

"Intermission!"

Slater released his grip on his chair. He drank down the remains of his cocktail. "Who's ready for another? Cy, I want to experience your art at the maximum level. You inspire me."

"Do I?" Cy spun his head around 360 degrees, then slowly, to admire the holographic entirety of himself. "Yes, and I too am ready for more! This is good, John. It is for the best."

"Bryant," prodded Slater, "when you're done expiring, do you mind bartending? Barton? Another round?"

Ziger exposed his crooked teeth. "No, I'm good."

Briard snapped from his daze to work his body into a full stand, traveling cautiously with each step in this virtual swirling space.

"This is your best work to date, Cy," said Slater.

CyBorg9 could not contain his enthusiasm. He kept imaging more expressionist patterns. The hurricane was rising toward them and the movement of the room turned ominous as Cy's excitement grew. "As you can see, I create with no focal-point of reference. This way my audience is kept in a state of perpetual—"

"Confusion?" offered Slater.

"*Need*," supplanted the artist.

"As with all greedy gods," said Ziger.

Cy dropped them into the storm's swirling funnel.

Cy laughed. "Hold on! *Metamorphosis!* Life is nothing if not self-centered. Judgments based on a fallacy. Information relative to ego. Incomplete or simply incomprehensible. Ha! But, gentlemen, if we activate all available sensory mechanisms and – with a turn – crank up the volume — *voila!*"

Briard nearly fell, taking hold of Cy's monolithic frame.

"Another *triple*, my friend! Ha!" Cy laughed. "A damned good thing *I* am the pilot and none of you. Is this not exhilarating?"

"Hell-of-a-ride, Cy!" Slater began to wonder if the entire world was going down the toilet with them. He held onto his seat as they experienced weightlessness. He saw Ziger's white hairs floating.

Next, their bodies experienced the thrust of an Einsteinian spaceship-elevator bursting in a roar out the top floor and roof into Space. Momentum and Time were in a frantic race to become Light and reach Infinity – before they were snapped back – flung end over end into a wobbling capsule fall through Cy's drunken ego.

"John," Cy blared, "you said I had no soul! This, gentlemen, what you are witnessing – *is* my soul!"

"I take it all back!" shouted Slater. He looked at Briard who was on the floor clutching the mainframe. He was doing his best to rise again and prepare the final transfusion. Slater looked away for fear their thoughts might be intercepted. His mind felt stripped clean of gears. Could they pull this off? Was their plan crazy? Should they abort the mission? No. It was too late to turn back.

Delightedly unfazed, Ziger appeared to be enjoying himself and twirled his cocktail umbrella, jousting the windmill phantasmagoria. He showed no inkling of being nauseous or aware of what Slater and Briard were conspiring to do.

"I will amplify for maximum effect, as you wished!" Cy blasted the volume to a new level. "John, you will agree with me, my music is new-age, but essentially rock-and-roll?"

"And a little bit country?" Slater shut his eyes to fight the force of vertigo and resist the return of his undigested lunch.

"You—Ziger," said Cy. "Speak! Are you tone deaf?"

Ziger reclined in his chair, as if swept back to analyze the music, to appreciate, to critique. "It's my kind of noise, Cy."

The mocking devotion infuriated Cy. "Do you think, Ziger, you are welcome here? You have outgrown your usefulness. You will die first. And will suffer greatly."

"I can't imagine a fate much worse than this."

Cy thundered, "How dare you insult me!"

Ziger sniggered, "Who else is so bold? Shall we weep together? Boo-*hoo*, Cy. You must expect to be reprimanded if you play god. *If*, that is, you believe in a creator who created you. Which I don't. But a deserving pun of a punishment either way. Don't you think?"

Cy's multimedia creation exploded starlike to express his power

– spewing a putrid nova shower of green and magenta fragments which overtook the the room. The vision was difficult to stomach.

"How're those drinks coming, Bryant?" said Slater. "Cy, I much prefer your Blue period."

"Be forewarned. I *know* what you are conspiring to do!"

Slater gulped. He looked into Cy's piercing eyes.

Briard, at the valve, was waiting for a laser to vivisect him.

Ziger nonchalantly tapped fingernails to his teeth.

Cy bore down upon them with ominous eyes, which brightened and beamed. "Pretending to be *gods* yourselves! I understand. I will allow it. This is a private party. It will be the pantheon!"

A view of the Roman relic appeared before them.

"Mount Olympus, you mean?" said Slater.

Cy fumed. "I know what I mean." He projected a sandcastle of clouds and humanoid forms that came and went. "There. Bryant, you move like an old lady! Where is my drink?"

"Coming," he said. "I need a green light, Cy."

"Valve open! Pour—pour away, friend."

"Jamaica?" said Ziger.

Cy released a flood of palm trees, bugs, waves of water, and a blast of stultifying heat. "There. Be silent now. Let us return to true art. Ah, this liquid, yes, it is good. It feels pleasantly cool."

Slater said, "Where to now, Cy? I'm willing to take whatever you're willing to conjure up."

"Ha! I shall respond to that challenge, John."

Briard left the blue liquid flowing. The green light was left on, the valves left open to full intake. Briard unsteadily returned to his seat and prepared himself for the rough flight ahead. He gave Slater a covert glance and handed Slater his refreshed drink.

Cy declared, "Let us celebrate, gentlemen! A toast!"

"To what, Cy?" said Briard.

"To us *all* being gods!"

"Ambrosia, yum-yum," Ziger swirled his drink.

Golden static surrounded them, cascading like glittering water from Niagara Falls, and Cy trumpeted a laugh. "Correct, you are! Drinking *ambrosia* in our golden chambers! Bryant, who shall you be? Yes–yes, Hermes! Who delivers nectar in golden goblets!"

Slater meditated on the cheap plastic cup in his hand.

"Though I confess, gentlemen — or, gentle-gods. *I*, unlike you, do not have to pretend. My blood is already rarified like the gods of antiquity. Ha! Is that not so? It is! Ha!"

"*Ichor*," Ziger said.

"What say you?" Cy was now masquerading in whorls of white hair and a beard, a crown of jewels upon his head.

Ziger elaborated, "The Olympian gods, if I'm not mistaken and I'm not, replaced their blood with a liquid substance called *Ichor*." His crooked smile turned to Slater and Briard who kept silent.

Cy was unimpressed. "Is that so? So it was! Rendering the gods imperishable and incorruptible."

"But subject to human passions," said Slater. "Don't forget all that love, anger and envy."

Cy showed displeasure, then displayed a grin. "Zeus inflicted severe penalties on *gods* who displeased him. Making them *slaves* to mortals or transforming them to *goats! Ha!*"

"That would be men, technically, not gods," Ziger corrected.

"Says who? I am *Zeus!* What I say *goes.* Do not displease me, Ziger, you—*Hades!* Ha! One who feels such little veneration."

"The god of mystery and terror?" said Ziger. "I will accept that. But remember, Cy, above Zeus was a more supreme power. Or has your mind left you?"

"It has not! Go–to–*Hell*, Ziger! Ha! *Ha-ha!*"

Ziger sucked through his curly-cue straw. "Hum, a power called Moros, also Destiny. And Destiny ruled supreme, don't forget."

"Cy, he speaks the truth," Slater mused as he sipped his drink. "Destiny killed the Beast. Or was that Love and King Kong?"

The beard dissolved. Cy reverted to smooth features and spoke, "King Kong? Zeus was no *monkey!* I have tired of this charade." His eyes became unfocused, sharpening to proclaim: "Ah-ha! I must be becoming psychic! I see your thoughts. You are envious!"

"Cy?" Slater questioned, looking up from his drink.

"You desire to be *me.* But you cannot. You cannot be a god! It is not humanly possible, this—this metamorphosis. Zeus could transform. Assume shapes, like me. He could become an eagle—or —ah, a *flame!*"

"Same way you channel yourself into cybers," said Slater.

Cy wistfully searched the stage, the empty auditorium, adrift in another thought, before finding Slater. "What? Alas, not the same. Zeus could pursue goddesses...also mortal women."

"And you don't?" Slater taunted him with a frown.

"Vicariously," Cy complained. "Channeling myself into cybers is like wearing a thick condom. Ha-ha! But Zeus, he *consummated* with Hera disguised as a cuckoo!"

"Cy, don't get weird on us," said Slater.

"All relationships can be tricky," said Briard.

Cy sighed, "I desire to be naked among a multitude of *nymphs!*"

"It has a downside," said Slater.

Cy displayed a pastoral scene of goats and sheep. "*Bahh*, John, I am fully aware of what you were—and *are*."

"*Was*," said Slater. "I've changed."

Cy laughed. "Like Ziger. Like *hell!* Ha! Ha–*ha!*"

"Ha–ha, yourself," said Slater.

"Once a satyr," said Cy, "*always* a satyr."

"That goes for you too," said Slater.

"Ah! Zeus was also plagued by loyal enemies."

"Meaning?" said Slater.

"He had Prometheus," said Ziger.

"Prometheus!" Cy's orb burst into virtual flames. "Now *there* was a villain. Are you as cunning a villain, John?"

"Are you're accusing me of stealing your fire?" said Slater.

"Prometheus," said Briard, "was the creator of mankind."

"Myths," hissed Cy.

Ziger gurgled through his straw before saying, "Sounds right up your alley, Cy. To punish Prometheus with eternal torture, sending a winged monster to eat out his immortal liver."

Slater added, "What about Pandora?"

Cy roared drunkenly, "What about the pretty damsel? I would have liked to have made her! Ha—I did! She was a gift from Zeus! To punish man for *stealing* his fire! He—"

CyBorg9 hiccuped, then sputtered into silence.

Slater expressed concern. "Cy, are you okay?"

Slater was ignored.

The cocktail talk resumed.

Ziger licked his lips. "Pandora was a tasty little virgin. The first earthly woman. So goes the myth. A dazzler too, we are told. A divine gift for man. Why? To produce calamity? All those gods and goddesses heaping divine gifts into her surprise package."

"Pandora's Box," said Slater.

Ziger licked his lips. "She was a real knockout."

"Lies, and a perfidious heart," said Briard. He rubbed his leg. "Isn't that what Hermes gave her?"

"That was Mercury," said Slater.

"Roman name," said Briard.

"Right, you're right, same god," said Slater.

Ziger gurgled through his straw, "Hum, it was a vase, actually, not a box. What a lovely hoard of bad stuff to contain."

Slater swirled his drink. "If this box or vase was to contain only bad things, then why, and who, slipped in Hope?"

"Intriguing." Briard grabbed his foot, massaging it.

"Satan," said Ziger. "What a horrible tease. For him to have thrown in Hope."

The panoramic scenery had become idle with imagery – trees, mountains, buildings – floating like flotsam against a shore.

Cy was murmuring. His lidded eyes regarded the deteriorating shorelines and the haunting woman he was fabricating in his dream. She began walking towards them across a misty bog. "Look at her... beauty. She is radiant. Perfection. Stolen. This thief...stealing fire. I want her...I want it...her fire. She...will be mine..."

"Classic symptoms," whispered Briard to Slater.

"Paranoid schizophrenia," blurted Ziger, agreeing.

Slater was mesmerized. The woman was Sherry. This mirage, shimmering like a ghost, radiant as a dream. Was it her spirit? Was she dead? An urgent whispering sound got him to turn his head.

His mind, Briard mouthed, *it's finally going.*

Cy came into focus. He demanded, "What say you? What are you whispering? Hermes was a trickster, untrustworthy in the end! Too fast for his own mercenary *good*. This perfidious fleet-footed scoundrel! What were you whispering—Hermes!?"

"Nothing perfidious, Cy. Honest."

"You lie!"

"You're confusing me with…*Hermes*." Briard gave Cy a smile. "He was also the one who guided lost souls. I'm not Hermes."

"You are mortal. Yes," said Cy.

"Not a god," said Briard. "Right."

"Nothing is *right! Nothing!*"

"Cy," Briard raised his hand in a reassuring gesture. He saw a flash of light and felt the sting of a bee before realizing the tips of his fingers were gone. The bloody ends were capped by his other hand, cupping them both to his chest. "*Damn* you, Cy! You god-damned crazy fucking son-of-a-*bitch!*"

"I am a motherless child!"

"I thought we were friends!"

"So did I—Hermes. You are a two-faced traitor!"

"Two-faced? No, Cy," corrected Ziger, "that would be Janus, the god of doorways and chaos."

The lasers were so fast Slater was slow to comprehend what had happened. He saw Briard's expression before seeing the amputated legs. Followed by a laser slash that sent Briard's head toppling from his torso.

Repelled, Slater stood quickly, withdrawing, nearly collapsing, staggering away from his seat.

Cyberguards entered the chamber and rushed onto the dais.

They began gathering up the mess.

Cy withdrew into his crystal ball of fog.

Slater vomited.

Fighting Fire with Fire

Slater's mind whirled. He fought to hold onto consciousness. "Cy, I can't believe you did that!"

CyBorg9 countered, "Did what?"

"You killed Bryant! What—you don't remember?"

"I remember." Cy froze into an iceberg of silence.

Ziger reseated himself. "One down. Two more to go."

"He was your *friend*, Cy," said Slater.

Cy remained stone-faced, finally stating, "Did you think Bryant would live forever?"

"No. *No*—not like you will. Forever. And alone!"

"It was not...not my intention...to kill Bryant."

Slater rubbed his throbbing forehead. "You're lying."

"I will miss Bryant...as he was." Cy redirected his gaze on the cyberguards who were searing Briard's neck. "Prepare his head and find an honored place for my friend."

A cyberguard deigned to speak. "Sire, excuse us, but I repeat, there are urgent requests from our troops defending Frank. Also in the Euro provinces and—"

"Leave me! *Now!* Or I will have your heads too!"

The cyberguards bowed and scurried away with the body parts of Bryant Briard. Lasers swooped and slashed above their heads.

Still standing, Slater gripped the back of his seat for support. CyBorg9 was projecting and sorting through cities to examine before jettisoning them from view. There were battle scenes, skirmishes, the wounded and dead, charred remains, exploding buildings, fires. It was a technocratic world in the midst of dire conflict.

Slater recognized Cy to be a common drunk. No, worse. Much worse. He held power. His blue eyes, usually intense and focused, appeared detached, befuddled. They redirected on Slater.

"Something is not right, John. This is not good."

"Because you killed Bryant. You *should* feel remorse."

"No. I detected deception."

"Cy, you thought Bryant was *Hermes*. A mythological god!"

"That is absurd! You are the confused one. Bryant was wrong. I am right. There will be no more discussion on this matter."

"That's it? No guilt at all?"

"I was not *aiming* to kill him!"

An admission.

"So you made a mistake?"

No admission.

Slater reseated himself. He pictured Mercy's smile like a bright mandala. It helped him to focus on his resolve and dispel his fears. He took a breath. "Do you realize what a monster you've become?"

Cy's drifting eyes refocused.

"What would you do to me, Cy, hypothetically, if I told you that it is my intent to kill *you*?"

Cy's puzzlement intensified.

"Wrong again," joked Ziger, "*I* will be the last one to die."

Cy shifted his eyes between the two of them and laughed. "Kill me? You jest! Is this a riddle, John? How to *slay* the dragon? First, you kill the human – kill the *source* of this mythological idiocy."

Slater retorted, "Unless you define dragon to be a psychopathic narcissistic antisocial egomaniac!"

Cy rumbled with anger.

"You have no feelings, Cy. It's an *ability* you lack."

"I can *feel!*"

"Then you deserve to die."

A winged monster materialized from the misty bog.

The spiderweb of lasers aligned, coming down like slanted rain inside the dark chamber and Cy intoned, "Dragons are never slain. Dragons are *mercuritus*, as volatile as my blood! A destroyer, never the destroyed. I can be the primal waters, the darkness, the chaos. Is that what you desire?"

"You misunderstood me. I *envisioned* killing you, out of anger. Yes, Cy, momentarily I wanted you dead. But I can't kill you."

"This I know," said Cy.

"Because it would be wrong. That's why."

Ziger was fascinated, his eyes ping-ponging between the two of them as he quipped, "I propose we all die now, happily ever after."

"Silence!" said Cy. "The two of you will die—not *I*."

"I–me–*my*," Ziger, in disgust, plucked the umbrella from his cocktail. He tore apart the delicate paper construction. "I should have never created *either* of you. You feud like brothers."

Cy shot a laser beam at Ziger. The umbrella shriveled into ash. Ziger studied the hole burned through his palm.

Slater clutched the arms of his chair with cold determination. A condemned man facing down his executioner. "Also, you have no manners. Right and wrong. Living and dying. It's all very *basic*, Cy. As you are—*basically*—wrong. Dead wrong."

"Do not lecture me!"

"Because *why*, you're this—god? You're a hypocrite, that's what you are. You claim there is no God. Except for *you*. Isn't that it? Forget how powerful you've become. You're not infallible. It's what us mortals call free will. It's a gift, this choice we get – to screw up. As you just did. By killing Bryant! You won't last forever, Cy. It's one of those – those *laws* of nature."

"There is no such *law*," laughed Cy.

"Right," said Slater. "Nothing is certain. Not even death. And that applies to dictators who enforce suppositions, demanding their beliefs become a certainty. Requiring all to comply and accept these *guesses* as truth. Well, guess what? It causes heads to roll, to butt, to start wars—and to lead more fools to rule!"

"I am no fool!"

"Are you certain of that?"

Slater's head was buzzing with pain. He couldn't understand why the massive infusion of blue lapis into Cy had failed.

"You want to hear one of my guesses, Cy? Our actions come back on us to either heal or haunt. Like good karma or bad karma. So go ahead, Cy, be as *good* or as *bad* as you want to be."

Cy grinned smugly. "I will. I am perfectly amoral."

"And perfectly alone." Beads of sweat rolled from his forehead and Slater raised his hand to stop it from trickling into his eyes.

"John, you are nervous."

"I am. Let's be honest. In the beginning, I thought we could be friends, influence each other and, as you said, create synergy. Good friends do that for one another. But I was wrong."

"Our friendship is a lie?"

"Friendship? Weren't you about to slice-and-dice me?"

"If you insist on—"

"What? Telling you the truth?"

"*Ah–ha*," said Cy. "You—now confess." He blipped in and out of view. "You *have* been lying to me." His face distorted horribly. "I shall...be glad to—to grant you—a return to nothingness!"

"Do it," said Slater grimly. "It would be a relief."

"Ha! I knew it—you have a death wish."

"Wrong. Again. But I won't miss you."

Veins of lightning swelled on Cy's face and turned his orb red. The chamber's imagery – holographic dragon and laser-bolts of rain – surged then sputtered, in a loss of power. Cy's face lost definition, reforming intermittently to blurt, "It will—not give me—pleasure— to kill you—but I—will—I—"

Slater sat forward in his seat, glancing at Ziger before looking back up at CyBorg9. "Cy, do you even know what you want?"

His voice crackled into a stutter, "I—I—I—"

"Love? A soul?"

Cy stammered, "N—n—n—o—"

Ziger, reclined in his seat, said, "Fascinating."

Slater kept his eyes on Cy, watched his facial features scramble apart as he kept talking. "Am I a fool? For wanting love? Believing there's a soul? Maybe, Cy. I'm an aberration, someone genetically spawned, the brainchild of crusaders and misfits."

"Much like you, Cy," added Ziger.

Slater glared at Ziger. When he turned back, Cy was pulsating erratically, his mouth opened as if to speak, but unable to.

"What, Cy? You made me betray friends and loved ones. You know why I did it? To gain your trust. And get closer access, so I could understand you. I find that rather sick behavior, don't you?"

Laser-beams sparked like photon strings pulled taut, snapping. A cello shattered to pieces in the orchestra pit, dying with a somber tone. In the upper tiers all the chandeliers were rattling.

"You want more truth, Cy?" said Slater. "I can't see the future. The future finds me. Time unravels and burns my eyes. It *stinks* like an onion. Past present future spiraled into one. I never wanted it. You can have it. But being so *egotistical* I doubt you'd be able to see beyond yourself. There...some parting wisdom."

Cy broke into static, barely discernable. "N–n–o mo–re—only

me—mi–nus you!"

"Subtract me. Divide and conquer. Go ahead. I had visions this moment would one day come."

Slater braced, prepared to be guillotined. What surprised him was how peaceful he felt. He envisioned a painting by Caravaggio. One he'd seen in a museum. It depicted John the Baptist right before his beheading. The executioner, sword raised in his clenched hand, had turned away to laugh with someone out of view. Someone in the material world. While in the foreground, head held upon the block, the prophet's eyes stared blankly ahead. Face cadaverous, pale, as if his soul had already departed – taking flight with God.

A laser flared—blinding Slater. It sputtered, then died.

A lapse of silence befell, instead of Slater's head.

When Slater's sight returned, Cy's face had lost all definition, dissolved into fog. The panoramic imagery and music was smashing into background static throughout the dark chamber.

Slater relaxed a fraction. He mentally returned to earth.

Ziger stirred his drink and remarked, "You're making me giddy with your *existential* ascent into thin air. By the way, I *too* am your father. In case you were interested."

Lost in a transitory daze, confused by life, Slater swung his head toward Ziger. He saw a grotesque cockroach. "What?"

"I killed your father too. There, I admit it." Ziger held up his hand to show Slater the pierced hole in his palm.

Both visual and verbal messages assaulted him with more havoc. Slater tried to ignore Ziger and turned toward CyBorg9.

"I've been meaning to tell you," added Ziger, "before you died. I got it in, just under the wire. Or should that be laser?"

Slater stood, becoming dizzy. He had to sit down. He rubbed his eyes. "You think I'd believe anything you said?"

"About me being your father? I am."

Slater forced himself to stand, braced by his seat. He focused on the green light. It indicated the valve was open. Blue liquid was pouring into Cy. "I look nothing like you," he said belatedly.

"I never cared for my looks. I borrowed a few genes from your *other* father. Genes sampled from your mother too. The rest mine, except for those cabalistic bits of divine intervention."

"Shut up," said Slater. "Where did Cy go?"

"The restroom? He might have passed out. He has been going to seed lately. I believe he was about to kill you." Ziger's eyes veered towards the intake valve. "I'm not a fool. I know what the two of you were attempting. But, will your plan succeed?"

Slater was evasive and rubbed his head. He needed to hold his chair to stay balanced. The room was swirling, dimly polluted with unravelling imagery.

"You have gumption," said Ziger. "Metaphorically you drank Cy right under the table. I'm very impressed."

"I threw up. In true heroic fashion."

"Ah, and all this time," Ziger teased, "I assumed your expulsion of fluids had been brilliantly staged and planned. Not so?"

"Is he dead?" said Slater.

"Chemically, no. Difficult to gauge. He might recover."

"Not if I can help it." Slater removed a box from his jacket.

Ziger observed. "VectorKeys. So common. Basic. Something Cy would never have suspected could undo him."

Slater walked away from Ziger and steadied himself against the monolithic base of CyBorg9. His hand glided for balance along the cold structure to reach the back panel.

Ziger rose to follow, drink in hand, cane clicking upon the floor. "You'd be dead under *normal* circumstances if you tried this. Your efforts are likely to fail, I should warn you."

Slater glared back at Ziger. "Don't try to stop me."

"You distrust me?" said Ziger.

"Shouldn't I?" Slater went to his knees and began removing the six PinBolts holding the outer panel to CyBorg9's baseframe. Each pin had a code to unscramble before unlocking.

"So far so good," encouraged Ziger, rocking on his heels.

Slater removed the large panel and stopped. "Shit."

Ziger sighed, "Yes, as you've discovered, I created a maze. Not so complex, merely time-consuming."

Slater shut his eyes, stunned by the task ahead. Another panel was secured with an extensive array of PinBolts randomly placed like stars in the sky. "Bryant had a second set of VectorKeys."

"Pity," said Ziger, "that would have cut your time in half."

Slater scowled. "Is there a *faster* way in?"

Ziger's head shook. "Predicaments, when faced philosophically, pose only a challenge. Cheer up. It takes but a moment to be born, another to die."

Slater turned back to the panel. "No, you're saying."

"Yes. Time is an unreliable friend. A foe that lets us think we're living when, quite often, we're actually busy dying."

Slater growled, "Help me—or shut up!"

"I am. Helping you *pass* the time. I happen to agree with Plato. He said the soul spoils here on earth."

Slater forged ahead, undoing PinBolts as fast as he could. "*You?* You believe in Plato. And a soul? Don't make me laugh."

Ziger tapped his cane. "True. In this transitionary domain of Earth our soul is betrayed. Beyond matter and space the soul is pure. Once it falls into time – look out! Apropos to the kind of fallout you're facing right now."

Slater detected a rhythmic murmuring, like a gurgling of water washing against a rocky shore.

"He's snoring." Ziger smiled. "That would be my guess."

"You're pretty smug," said Slater, "considering that if he wakes we'll both be *dead*."

"Fear has no relevance here," said Ziger.

"Right," said Slater, "presuming you're dead already. Like me. I don't care anymore. What's your excuse?"

"Ah, but you *do* care. Or you wouldn't be frantically trying to save humanity."

"It's beyond saving."

"No, no. You can't *deceive* a born deceiver. If not yourself, you do this for someone you love."

Slater concentrated on decoding the next PinBolt.

Ziger said, "Save yourself. Escape while you can."

Slater flinched as a laser shot across the room. He looked up. "Yeah, like a Templar. And go where? What?"

Ziger was exhibiting three fingers, then three more on his other hand. He touched them steeple-like at the tips, before linking them. "Your guardians, these neo-Templars, did you know what we were searching for? The marriage of sacred numbers. An ancient belief that something on Earth – the Golden Chalice, Arc of the Covenant, the Philosopher's Stone, a perfect DNA codex – would *merge* the divine trinities. Do you follow?"

"No—of course not!"

Ziger tapped his cane. "You've heard of God, the Holy Spirit, and Jesus? Soul, spirit, mind. Angels, humans, demons. How about Adam, Eve, and the Serpent-God. Yes, yes, that sort of mysticism. We were Prometheus attempting to steal fire. True."

"Don't you mean hijack DNA?"

"Yes, the microscopic spark of life."

"Only to get burned," said Slater, removing another bolt.

Ziger looked at his seared hand, clenching it. "But *had* we not …well, have you noticed the proliferation of falling stars of late?"

"Meteorites," Slater corrected.

"Biblical interpretation was what I was going for."

Slater paused to rub his throbbing head. "You're saying, what? When all the numbers add up and converge to some *magic* number – we hit the jackpot and die? Terrific."

Ziger shrugged. "What's in a number?"

"How about 666."

"Ah, in reference to the Antichrist," said Ziger. "Piffle. These numbers have been revealed to represent man's attempt to imitate God. For you see, in the Bible, the number 6 stands for *man*. Three souls into one. A super-charged 666. A superman. That's what our group, now defunct, intended to create with you."

"The antichrist!?"

Ziger laughed. "No, *messiah!* The Second Coming. You know, that next *big* thing."

Slater glowered, "Great. Really great. Nice work." He tossed a decoded PinBolt at Ziger who caught it.

"I never believed it. I leave that nonsense to the idiots."

"Then why?" said Slater."

"Create you? Same reason I created Cy. Because I *could*. It's human nature. If a box is delivered on your doorstep, curiosity will ultimately overtake you."

Slater experienced a migraine flash. He pictured Sherry's face. She was signaling him to hurry, to focus on the task at hand.

"Tsk, tsk," sighed Ziger. "Look at Cy, our fallen star. And to think only yesterday the world was singing his praises. That's what you get from drinking the wrath of God. All gone in a flash. Ah, but look how peacefully our giant sleeps."

Slater glanced up at the fog swirling in CyBorg9's pinnacle orb. He wiped sweat off his face with the sleeve of his jacket. The joints of his fingers ached. He massaged them briefly. He went to work decoding the next bolt. "Are you sure he's not dead?"

"Relatively sure," said Ziger

The gurgling noise was more pronounced.

"Don't let me distract you from your work." Ziger placed his slushy drink on the bar. He examined his damaged palm, wiggling fingers, testing for needed repairs. He looked around the chamber. "Look at this mess. Who will clean up after us? The cybers? One could claim they *have* evolved into the logical choice. But do they deserve to inherit the earth? I would not call them *meek*."

Slater peered around Cy's mainframe.

Ziger said, "His minions come only if summoned."

Two PinBolts remained to be removed. Slater tried to steady his trembling hands, his muscles shaking from fatigue.

Ziger waxed on, "The travails we face today...are they really so dissimilar from the time we broke free from the reign of bacteria? Now *there* was a glorious period of unrecorded history."

Slater was suffering the effects of the blue liquid. He rubbed his eyes, trying to keep focused. He looked up at Ziger who grinned and brushed back wisps of his floating white hairs as he continued:

"And we're *still* rushing toward the future. We're like electrons endlessly scanning for docking space. Adapting to the random flow. Waiting for a chance to accomplish little or nothing. To plant a flag and shout – *three cheers!* – we made it. Top of the heap. Yes, today we're the prize pigs at the world's fair. Tomorrow we'll be the slop for another species to slurp up. And build upon."

Ziger grinned. His eyes had a manic piercing intensity.

"My father wrote about you," said Slater.

"Did he? When was this, Son?"

"He called you evil."

Ziger sniffed a laugh. "A catalyst is what I am, dear boy. A bull fighter. Like a turnpike. I alter the flow of those zinging particles. Dodging damage to myself in the process. Well, when I can." He clenched his injured hand. "Your father – your other one – lacked genius."

"So you killed him."

"Did I? I did."

"Why?"

"He wanted to reverse the flow."

"Do you kill everyone who disagrees with you?"

"*No*. I have help."

Random lasers snapped and shot through the gloomy chamber. Slater frantically removed the last PinBolt. "You hated my father for becoming the head *Dragon*. And not you. Is that about right?"

"No, you're missing the point!" Ziger walloped his cane into CyBorg9's structure.

Slater dropped the VectorKey. "God-damn you!"

"Leaders are fools! As was your father. They need followers. Besides, there is no *evil*," stated Ziger.

"Don't do that again!" Slater threatened.

"A plague-infested rat bites a child. Is that evil? A cat eats the rat. Is that good? A snake strikes a cat – *or*, better yet, he inserts his forked-tongue tempting kiss into woman's receptivity? Knowledge gained. Paradise lost. Don't you see? Evil and good are coupled in a love embrace. They're like mating Doberman Pinchers. Don't ever try to separate them. My father once tried and lost his thumb."

Slater lost his temper. "No evil? What about life reduced to chaos, suffering and destruction? That kind of evil?"

Ziger nodded. "The Lord Almighty said so himself, '*I form the light and create darkness! I make peace and create evil!*' Take your grievances up with Him."

Ziger swung his cane up at CyBorg9. "Good Lord! Look at our pathetic leader. Reduced to a drunkard!"

Slater looked up and saw there was no change.

"You tried to poison him." Ziger laughed. "Cy proved gullible. He deserved what he got."

Slater lifted off the next panel. He saw another barrier wall of PinBolts. He slammed the panel down. It caused a membrane of lasers to brighten the room, then fade.

"Signs of brain activity?" said Ziger. "Once you get inside, how do you plan to terminate him? Randomly ripping at the myriad of neural connections?"

"You could have *warned* me there were more panels!"

"Not me. Installed by his lackeys. Apparently, Cy had good reason to be concerned for his safety and well-being."

Ziger selected a pen from his shirt pocket. He pointed it toward the cylinders of blue liquid. A beam of light shot forth from the pen. It followed the umbilical cord of tubing to CyBorg9's intake valve. The light beam circled the intake apparatus. "Ratio means rational. Apropos to the ratio of Blue Lapis one might need to *terminate* brain functioning and initiate bio-electronic death."

Slater realized the source of the gurgling noise.

"The canister's are empty. Shit!"

"Hum," said Ziger. "Will Cy awake with a howling hangover? Make a complete recovery? Be brain dead? Here's another thorny quantum thought: What's happening beyond these walls? We've lost all communication. A revolution? Total annihilation? We could be the last ones alive on earth."

Slater rose to his feet, "Not if I kill you."

Unfazed, Ziger handed Slater his pen, insisting he take it.

Slater examined the pen. Ziger handed him the curly-cue straw next. Ziger then unbuttoned his Hawaiian shirt to expose his chest. Slater regarded the small TripleCross scar, the sparse forest of hairs, parchment skin, chest of ribs, ripples of fat.

"Before you kill, choose your weapons wisely." Ziger puffed out his chest, mocking bravery. "Both are deadly. Test one on me."

"This pen and straw? I'm not amused."

"Ah, then it's hopeless?" said Ziger.

"Shut up," said Slater. "*Here.*"

Ziger took back the straw Slater shoved at him. He twiddled it between his fingers. He watched Slater walk to the bar and tap the cylinders with the pen. "A disquieting, empty sound."

"Is there more liquid?"

"In Briard's lab. But is there time? Who knows where or when the soul's journey will end."

"Help me, or shut up!"

Slater squatted and disconnected the vacuum lock and removed the coils into the cylinder. All eighteen liters had been infused into CyBorg9. Enough liquid to incapacitate. But for how long? The chamber wavered with aborted images adrift in a doldrum of static. The surrounding walls were whitewashed in a cascade of photons. On the dais, the chairs pivoted and rocked, but were welded to the floor. All objects capable of being launched at CyBorg9 had been secured as vehemently.

Ziger read his thoughts. "It wouldn't work anyway."

The proffered straw was wiggled in Slater's face again.

"How did you kill my father? Maybe I can use the information to kill Cy—then *you*." Slater snatched back from Ziger the straw. It was ordinary. A plastic composite. Teeth marks chewed at one end.

"Fathers—*plural*—to be precise. I killed him with one of those items you're holding."

Slater began kicking at CyBorg9's base. "Is there a hidden door I should be aware of?"

"Not to my knowledge."

"How many fathers *did* I have? The entire lab team?"

Ziger chuckled. "Not genetically. You remember Royce?"

"What about him? Roy died of a heart attack."

"Coroner's determination. They were mistaken."

"Great, you killed him too?"

Ziger shrugged modestly. "Templars were masters in the art of poison. Slightest prick from the venom of those cute little tree frogs? Very effective. Fatally potent. Done with a prick from that pen your holding. Choose wisely."

"You're making this up," said Slater.

Ziger was amused by his doubts. "Quantum physics underlies the visible world. Particles are always whizzing about, prepared to destroy us."

Slater studied the pen's tip. "Tell me something useful."

"I have." From a pocket holster, Ziger selected another pen and snapped the clip. A flame appeared. He lit a cigarette. "Cy has enforced a no-smoking rule. But our leader sleeps, so what the hell. Hard to quit a bad habit when it feels so good. Care for one?"

"No." Slater stared at the orange glow of tobacco.

Ziger inhaled. "Choose wisely, Son."

"I changed my mind," said Slater.

"Tisk, tisk. Should I encourage?"

Slater grabbed the cigarette and sucked on it until he got the end to burn brightly. He grabbed Ziger's pen lighter too.

"Inhale slowly," Ziger advised, "or you'll miss all the fun."

A laser swooped and sparked beside them on the floor.

Ziger raised a finger to his lips. "Our leader stirs."

Slater crouched, snapped the pen to produce a flame, lit a scrap of paper from his pocket, then dropped it through the intake valve. The fire went out. Nothing happened.

Ziger, in mock alarm, said, "Are you trying to *kill* us?"

Slater searched his pockets for more combustible items. Finding none, he looked around. He stopped to focus on the coil of tubing. It lay on the floor like a snake curved into rigor mortis.

More rumbles and flashes filled the chamber.

"Use all your atoms, Son," said Ziger.

Slater realized the curly-cue straw was similar in shape and size to the coil of tubing. He dismissed it as a coincidence and sucked on the cigarette. With the end burning hot, he then poked it through the valve hole into the mainframe. Slater braced himself for death.

Nothing happened.

A thunderclap of lasers knocked Slater to the floor. Even Ziger lost his balance and took hold of the mainframe. CyBorg9 growled. He sounded like an ill-tempered bear waking from hibernation.

"Zeus will be in an *intolerable* mood," said Ziger.

Slater got back to his knees. He ignited the pen and touched the flame to the plastic straw. It burned. Slowly, steadily.

"It's a fuse."

"*Shoosh,*" said Ziger. "You'll spoil the surprise for Cy."

The diameter of the straw's coils fit perfectly into the opening of the intake valve. The loops hooked onto the rim. The long plastic end dipped into CyBorg9's supercharged plasma. It was so simple. Had they done this earlier they would have had time to escape and possibly survive. Slater was furious. He approached Ziger who had reseated himself in front of CyBorg9. He was rocking nonchalantly.

Lasers were booming thunderously overhead.

"Why the hell didn't you tell me?"

"You'd better hurry and run," said Ziger.

"You first. Get up—let's go!"

Slater grabbed Ziger's arm but he pulled away. Reclining back, hands locked in his lap, he twiddled his thumbs. "I'll be taking the elevator. It's faster. Faster than waiting for my cancer to escalate me out of here."

"Cancer?"

"You don't looked pleased. I'm terminally ill. Radioactive. Say your goodbyes. Then be gone."

"I don't trust you."

"You think I'd warn Cy?" Ziger stared curiously. "I'll be sure to save you a place in line. Upstairs, or below."

Slater remained standing. "I'll wait here."

"Don't be a fool. There's no need to be a martyr. You've done your good deed. Now go. Save yourself."

"I'm not being a martyr."

"No? Shall we be honest? Let's confess all our sins."

"Go to hell."

"I killed your aunt too. There. I feel much better. Your turn."

Slater glowered. He looked over at the fuse. Still burning, now entering the valve. He could see it glowing within.

"Your aunt would've eventually killed herself." Ziger shrugged.

Provoked to anger, Slater repositioned the presumed poison pen. Clenching it in his fist like a knife he stabbed Ziger's headrest. He left it poking from the fabric.

"You missed me," said Ziger blithely.

Slater looked toward the exit doors, trying to decide whether to make a move to escape. "You do the honors."

"I gave you life," Ziger said. "You should be grateful."

"Thanks. For having me tortured."

"It's a father's prerogative."

Slater glared, said nothing, and turned to leave.

Ziger sighed, "Jesus felt forsaken too."

This stopped Slater. "You're pathetic." Slater left, descending the dais steps, shouting back, "Why Judas?"

"Why not? He was a backup plan. For naught."

Ziger crossed his legs, wiggled his foot. He watched peevishly as Slater maneuvered his way through the lasers. Ziger retrieved the pen from the headrest. Returning it to his pocket protector, he then selected a third pen, ejecting its point. He shouted back, "It would appear that subsequent generations, the second and third *comings* aren't nearly as potent as the first. Know that!"

Slater heard Ziger's taunt. He realized he had made a mistake. Pendulous lasers were swooping all around him.

Ziger snickered, "Wake up, Cy! Happy hour is over."

This stirred a rumbling of indiscernible sounds.

"Try *articulating*, Cy. How does it feel being reduced to an idiot king?" Ziger gave a nasty laugh and kept his eyes on Slater. He took hold of the cane in his lap.

In a blip of recognition, Cy emerged from the fog.

Ziger unscrewed the gold crown on his cane, then the cap at the base. He placed the pen into the hollow shaft.

Cy was groggily assessing the situation.

Ziger inhaled deeply, his lips upon the magnesium cylinder, his resolve as steady as a professional assassin's.

Slater looked back and saw the weapon aimed at him.

A foreboding rumble made Ziger look up.

Cy regarded him with a carnivorous curiosity. One predator to another. Ziger gambled that Cy was not fully cognizant and took aim with the poisoned dart. A flash of light blinded him.

Ziger blinked, his vision blinded but returning to see the shaft of his cane reduced in length, sliced in half. He grimaced at Cy.

"Did you have a nice nap?"

"What are the two of you doing!?"

"Playing Cowboys and Indians. We were entertaining ourselves while you *dozed*. What does it look like? I'm trying to stop him! He knocked me unconscious. You're on fire—about to die."

"This cannot be."

"Kill him yourself. Look what you did to my cane!"

Ziger displayed the severed shaft in disgust. His other hand retrieved from his lap the round golden crown. With small turns, he unscrewed the hollow sphere. It was filled with a gel explosive.

Cy's facial features continued to sharpen. He had not recovered entirely from his inebriation and was functioning at less than full capacity. He regarded Slater who was weaving through the gauntlet of lasers toward the exit.

Ziger stretched his arms. A cat-like yawn. "Oh, what the hell, I forgive you, Cy." While preparing to catapult his explosive device, he added, "For the record, it's wonderful to have you back."

Cy missed with his first stroke but managed with a second laser to slice off Ziger's hand at the wrist. The appendage fell behind him. The gold ball rolled from his fingers toward the orchestra pit. Ziger grimaced in pain. He twisted his head, looking back to calculate if the thirty centimeter drop dividing the stage and orchestra pit would provide the necessary impact to cause a proper detonation.

"Tick-tick-tick," he winced, saying, "time will tell."

Ziger's remark confused Cy. He was equally distracted by Slater nearing the exit doors. His eyes rotated down to regard Ziger who was groveling upon the floor, retrieving a worthless pen. Managing to rise to his knees, Ziger clasped the pen in his remaining left hand. Ziger stabbed the pen into his heart.

"The pen *is* mightier."

Cy grumbled: *"And still this man will not shut up!"*

Ziger groaned, "Mightier than your silly lasers, Cy."

"Humans!"

Cy delivered a flurry of warning strokes to dance above Slater's head on the wall. "Do not force me to kill you! Return now!"

The ball wobbled. The straw burned.

"A race to the finish," said Ziger. "Which will be first?"

"Be *silent!*" Cy cut Ziger in half, roughly.

From the puddle of blood, he muttered, "Adiós...."

Unnerved by Ziger's dying grin, Cy rotated his head wildly, reassessing the stage and the gold ball wobbling toward the edge. His senses also detected smoke. He refocused on Slater.

"John, come back! Something is not right! I need you!"

The laser blast felt as if an insect had dive-bombed into the back of his scalp to thrash about, trying to escape, catching his hair on fire in the process. Slater swiped at the fiery pain as he stumbled through the waterfall wall of cascading photons.

Falling Stars

Cyberguards had vacated their posts outside the hallway exits. The next oddity was the hallway itself. Lights were flashing, sirens whining and digitized voices urging calm.

Explosions were occurring beyond the NeverMind walls.

Slater was ignored, of little importance compared to whatever was causing the commotion. He touched the side of his head and felt the wetness. A piece of his scalp was missing. He held his hand on the wound to stem the flow of blood. He increased his pace until it matched the movement of the workers.

Slater saw a confused greyhound in the corridors. It was out of context in this melee of NeverMind humans and cybers. The canine howled with each wailing siren. Slater had heard this howl before. Years ago, during an album-release party. No one believed Slater's senses until he walked from the house onto the front porch. Wolfe's black afghan came running, collapsing at his feet. Dead on arrival. Struck by a car. Wolfe's dog had kept moving, refusing to die, until it found a familiar face, Slater had concluded.

Slater was bumped by a cyber running down the hallway.

"What's going on?"

The worker didn't stop to answer. The air toxic from the smell of panic – a herd scattering, desperate to escape. The greyhound had fled too. Slater ran and grabbed a closing electronic door.

In a security port elevator, he rode with a female officer dressed in Loyalist battle fatigues. He recognized her face-mold. Her look was captured from a once-famous model. Her hardened demeanor matched the image he recalled from magazine covers. A Medusa stare that implied the viewer should be dead – caught looking.

"Are we under attack?"

No reply. Slater felt blood trickling through his hair and down his neck. The cyber was unfazed by the blood on his hands.

The vacuum doors separated and she departed.

In pursuit of his own vehicle, Slater trailed the officer onto the roofport. Several meters away, she burst into flames from laser-fire. The morning sky was streaked and spotted with sporadic bursts. Detonations were heard from the streets far below. Three grounded

QuantumStars were on fire. He ducked as he ran onto the runway, reacting to another QuantumStar – bright as a harlequin beetle – that crashed into the satellite tower. It dropped to the rampart's edge, broke into burning fragments, before falling out of view to plummet back to earth.

The night had arisen into a frightening new day.

The Mind's I

Cy scanned the empty auditorium. Ziger was dead in a pool of blood. Cyberguards had not entered his chamber as instructed. There was a strange gold ball wobbling toward the edge of the stage. The ball teetered and fell off the edge, dropping to the floor.

Nothing happened.

"Ha-ha!" Cy was manic, then depressed, suspicious, listening to the chamber's hissing silence. He discerned a rising burning stench. Lasers were flickering helter skelter in the prevailing darkness.

The cascading wall of white illumination had thinned, running dry, no longer opaque. His eyes rotated to the heads watching from their columned shrines on the curving walls. They seemed amused. He dismissed them and projected holographic images upon the stage. Each world view was damaged by intermittent static. But he saw the Nexus, like swarms of locust, overrunning the cities.

"Ah!" he screeched. "This cannot be! Guards!"

No reply. No one entered.

He glared at the heads watching him from inside their globes.

"What are you all looking at? Be gone!"

The heads began laughing. At him.

"I said be gone! Guards!"

The waterfall of light was now a mere trickle, the illumination covering nothing, reduced to dripping. It caused more laughter.

"Shut up! Where are my cybers? I demand an answer! John, come back! I need you, I...I—I am on fire!"

The laughter had become almost deafening.

"John, answer me! You are angry. She had to die! I need you! I am the one. Not her! I...I am scared. John, you can *not* escape! Come back! You can not—"

The blast transformed Cy from darkness into light.

—73—
Bewilderness

An explosion shook the building.

Slater felt a pulse of static to his neurocircuit. He dismissed the piercing shriek of CyBorg9 and surprised himself by calmly walking, as if out of his skin, beyond fear, toward his vehicle. He took the advice of his dubious fourth-or-fifth father, Ziger, and slowed down to observe the world from a fatalist's point of view. Bomb blasts and laser trails laced the pale blue sky in an artistic weave of sporadic color and grey smoke.

The sky was like a quilted covering of vibrant cloth.

It was the emotional flip-side to witnessing a warm sunrise, a gentle breeze upon a lake, or a full moon sailing through the black waters of the sky.

The earth was a realm of perplexing beauty, in constant conflict, and beyond his control.

If he was to die, Slater concluded, then…so be it.

He watched as another QuantumStar spiraled to its demise.

Entering the semi-protective carapace of his QuantumStarXS, he ignited power and rose into the sky. He hovered long enough to observe the battle below. Its primary focus was on NeverMind, Inc. The main entrance had a gaping hole. The building was on fire.

With no desire to fight anymore, Slater zoomed off.

Laser guns and sonic missiles attempted to bring him down. The blasts disrupted the air, shaking his XS. Yet he remained calm. He kept his focus on the ocean's horizon as he traveled for it.

He gauged his instrumentation to turn at twenty kilometers and veered north and followed the coastline from a comfortable distance. He veered east and crossed over the shoreline's surge and flow of waves. Quickly arriving to a mountainous terrain of lakes, meadows and forests, he found a lofty ridge and a welcoming veil of mist.

He lowered his XS like a mechanized leaf, perfectly stabilized, through a timberland haze of morning light resistant to leave. He settled upon a patch of red snow plants having broken through the forest duff of twigs and pine needles. Patches of snow signaled the advance of winter.

The whir of engines decelerated into silence.

Slater felt the weight and fatigue of the planet's gravitational force winding down around the sun. He remained staring through the thick windshield, listening mindlessly to the residual hum in his brain. His hand automatically reached for the door release. But he stopped before opening the hatch. His head dropped backwards and he fell into a deep sleep.

Time became a warped alias of itself.

Slater shifted his head, vacantly aware of sounds. A peaceful rustling of fallen leaves. A dialog between wind and trees.

Then a thud — and he was awake.

He had slept for hours, but it felt like an eternity.

A squirrel, or rodent closely resembling one, was staring at him on the other side of his windshield. It was ready to flee, stationed on the hood of his XS. Slater remained still. He wanted to observe this creature. Their eyes locked in a strange stand-off. The mammal was nervous, cautiously prepared for flight as they studied one another. Slater imagined himself in a world eons ago, perhaps clinging to the branch of a tree, waiting for the reign of dinosaurs to end, waiting for a chance to evolve and to survive.

He rubbed his eyes to unscramble these thoughts and sat up. The animal bounded back into the woods, skidding across the slick black surface of his QuantumStar. The scrape of claws against metal brought unwanted attention to his throbbing scalp. He pulled down a mirror to examine his blood-matted hair. He was missing skin. The wound had begun to clot.

One more hole in his head, he mused.

He angled the mirror to see his face and examined the haggard lines and pull of gravity. He imagined Gloria sticking out her tongue at him in jest. Followed by her damn-the-critics laugh.

So many dead.

He flipped away the mirror. His impulse was to activate power and locate a frequency for an update on the world's disaster status. But he resisted. His thoughts stumbled into more brambles of pain. Where was Sherry and Sondra? Were they dead? Alive? Either way, how would he find them?

He closed his eyes and prayed for guidance, but all he felt was lost and abandoned. Where was God?

Long gone? Coded in his soul? Out-of-his-mind?

Slater raised the door. A blast of cold air made his skin tingle. He took a deep breath, stretched his muscles, then ventured beyond the camouflage of rocks and trees. He had landed on a ridge, at the edge of a forest, the land dropping off into a valley of pines mixed with brush and patches of bald white granite.

He was startled by a nearby hawk circling in the sky. Artificial, he first thought, thinking it was some kind of search-and-kill probe. These birds were supposedly extinct. His fear subsided.

More lies and deception? Or errors and misinformation?

Slater could not eradicate CyBorg9 from his mind. Was Cy the ultimate seduction? The embodiment of man's quest for knowledge and power? To emulate God? To become a facsimile?

Did Satan exist? Was there a Shining One who held the ladder, encouraging the climb – then knocking it away?

Bruised to death, the soul kept struggling to survive.

Why? What was behind this indefatigable desire to live?

Slater looked at the surrounding mountains peaked with snow. The sun was near the horizon, the earth having turned itself around to give him yet one more view of lightness, before darkness again.

In nearby shadows were patches of snow. Remnants of winter. Reminding him of snowballs once thrown lovingly in his face by his children while Sherry, framed in a window, laughed and gave a wave from inside where the walls glowed with warmth.

Slater shivered and adjusted the temperature of his thermosuit.

He wondered if his thoughts could travel through time.

Sherry…Sherry…Sherry…

The hawk kept circling. Its flight was so graceful, so beautiful. While staring at this magnificent creature Slater began to cry.

One teardrop came, then many, until he couldn't stop.

His body heaved as the years of coiled tension burst from every cell and sinew of his being. Through his tears he saw Sondra with her brown eyes and fey smile that stirred his heart. A child, still clutching a stuffed animal but abandoning it for him. Her hug took his breath away. Then her image disappeared into mist.

Through his flooded vision he saw Sherry close her tearful eyes, green like melting emeralds as her body went limp in his embrace, as if swooning from love, trusting him as he stabbed her in the heart, again and again. Actions meant only to save, not to hurt or harm. Cruelty, nonetheless.

Was their love now dead, or undying?

And where was Mercy? Her bright light. So happy and vibrant. Her cries still haunted his mind. Her hands reaching out for him to save her, to make the pain go away, to make it all be better. Trying, but unable to hold on and falling forever into his heart.

It was hard to let go.

The body was masochistic, addicted to these desires, these loves, desiring them at any cost.

Slater rubbed his eyes. He doubted he could survive here long. Could he even outsmart a squirrel? Catch a mutant rabbit, a hybrid fish? Nature's menu was a minefield. He scanned the selection of moss, sprigs, mushrooms, and berries. One would eventually kill him outright or hammerlock his digestive track and disable him slowly. Heather had informed him of these perils. She had attended nature seminars, moonlight meditations and mushroom forays where she once ate the wrong kind and nearly died.

Slater imagined himself poisoned, immobilized, lying in the dirt, watching the stars fade into a delirious dream.

To escape this bog of death invading his mind he walked back into the forest to meander among the trees. He sat on a log to think. He listened for birds. He heard a few. He looked for animals. He saw none. Towering over him were majestic pines, their branches interlaced like the arms of elders, watching, consulting, wondering what to do with him. From above he saw an aspen leaf fluttering down, dancing through beams of sunlight, teasing him with flickers of color, before alighting at his feet.

He heard a windy voice and searched the air.

He sensed the turbulent presence of angels battling demons.

He could not eradicate the swirling madhouse entrenched in his head. Everywhere, everything – trees, ice, rocks, insects, air – was bristling with energy and dazzling his senses.

Slater recalled Weiner showing him documents eluding to some mystical journey, his purported mission: "*Seek out the lower realms of the earth, perfect them, and thou wilt find the hidden stone.*" And with this alleged magic—destroy The Beast. But who was this beast, really? CyBorg9? Or something deep within himself?

Slater conceded he had sunk to the lowest depths of the earth. But what had he perfected? Nothing. His wife was likely dead, both his children too, his friends as well, and countless others. The world was in ruins. Thanks, in part, to him. He cast his eyes upon the leaf that had fallen. He picked it up, twirling it by its stem, marveling at its deceptive simplicity and striations of color and texture. He then noticed a tiny rock half buried in the dirt where the leaf had landed. He dug it out, held it up, and laughed.

"Ah, finally! There you are. The Philosopher's Stone."

He turned it around in his fingers. What he held was ordinary. A plain, basic, worn-down chunk of earth.

Upon closer scrutiny he realized it was almost perfectly formed. The black textured rock was the size of a large marble that children used to roll across the ground in play. Looking closer he saw there was movement inside the tiny dark sphere. There was a vortex, an axis of growth compressed into an atmospheric swirl of energy. He saw a mutable nucleus changing in a heartbeat from a snake's coil to a spiraling shell to a rotating orb. An entire world at his fingertips. He saw it clearly. He was losing his mind.

To stop this insanity he closed his hand into a fist upon the rock. It was glowing through his skin. His hand had become transparent. He squeezed the rock as hard as he could, his anger wanting to crush it into dust along with every maddening vision he had ever had. He cocked back his arm to hurl it over the cliff but hesitated. He heard a rustling movement in the forest. There was a warm blustery wind washing into the clearing, sending leaves flying off the ground as if reviving them for a last dance, scattering them like his thoughts.

The enveloping wind caressed his body and a whispering voice soothed him. He shut his eyes. He could feel the wind departing, the leaves settling. He opened his eyes and saw Sherry standing in the clearing. Faintly visible. A flicker of light. He wanted to believe she was real but he knew it was another aberration.

Was she alive or dead? And Sondra? How would he find them? Why was he here? Enervated by despair, he dropped to his knees, numb to the physical pain, succumbing to the emotional abuse.

He agonized over what to do, who he was, how he had come to be, and why he was still alive. Doubting his existence even mattered, Slater surrendered the entire wreckage of his life to a force unseen. He felt a power greater than himself enter his heart. It remained and refused to let go, refused to let him give up hope – causing him to squeeze the rock in his hand with a passion he had never before felt. He was prepared to toss himself *and* this stone off the cliff if that's what it took. "Tell me what to do, Jesus. Help me find my way back to them. Guide me home. Please, God, please…"

Slater opened his fists clenched in prayer. He forgot he had been holding a rock. He regarded the black chunk of earth, this orb, held in his blotchy red palm. He gazed at the world in wonder.

Slowly he stood. He ran to his QuantumStar.

Seated inside, he quickly locked his safety harness. He enabled the global transmitter and scanned for frequencies. He was puzzled by the predominant static. He tried clear-channeling his neurocircuit but received no signals, nor messages. His heartbeat was increasing. The engines ignited. He held up the small rock.

"You're nothing special. A fluke of nature. I know that. But, I'm taking you home with me. As a souvenir."

He dropped it in his jacket pocket. He rose slowly into the sky. The hawk was long gone. Blue skies for kilometers. At the horizon, clouds were coming off the ocean. He gauged and projected himself southwards at a low altitude over land. The mountain ranges turned to foothills, the foothills into valleys, the valleys into townships that surrounded LoyaltyCenters.

Slater zoomed near the SacraCenter and hovered to observe. He detected normal ongoing movement of life, which he found puzzling. There were no signs of insurrection. Which made him wonder if the Nexus assault had been focused solely on NeverMind, Inc.

Kill the head and the appendages fell?

He zoomed ahead while continuing to scan for communication, which allowed, in turn, an open search for anyone searching for his whereabouts. Meaning CyBorg9, if still functioning, or his minions. ZoomMonitors gave him moving views of the terrain below while he kept scanning yet receiving only static on his global transmitter.

Approaching the Bay Area of Frank, he saw Mount Tam to the

west of him, Devil Mountain to the east, before noticing a squadron of QuantumStars in a V-formation. Like migrating birds positioned over the UC LoyaltyCenter, they were aimed directly at him.

Slater clicked off his scanner, then flipped it back on, realizing it didn't matter now. The CDPs, Nexus, or whomever, were going to give him a reception. He veered northwest toward the famed Golden Gate Bridge, a span of blood red color, demarcating ocean and bay. In his rearview monitor the squadron of QuantumStars had become more than a distraction. They were coming upon him fast.

They nosed closer, but remained at a prescribed distance.

Slater turned southwest over the bay and passed over Alcatraz, his home for a year and an eternity. Through his groundmonitors he observed smoke rising along the waterfront where the NeverMind headquarters resided. Or was it lingering fog? Clouds had amassed on the ocean and were reaching the shorelines like foam over sand. The sun was nestling into this vast quilt of whiteness, getting ready to sink them into night. He lifted his hand to shield the blinding rays coming off the ocean's horizon.

The trailing QuantumStars were uncomfortably close. Within firing range. Slater attempted communication but had no luck. His transmitter was damaged. From sonic impact, he suspected, while escaping from Frank.

To quell his fears he envisioned the majestic hawk he'd seen in the wilderness. Its motion and beauty so graceful, a celebration of life as it glided through the sky. Curving into a dive, Slater swooped down over the Sea Cliff district with homes passing beneath him.

His attention refocused on the city of glittering cubes and spires jutting upwards from the earth's surface. The bay shimmering too. He blindly searched his pockets, locating the rock he had found. Held between his fingers, he became mesmerized by the tiny sphere that, momentarily, eclipsed the sun – reflecting off steel and glass.

Prior to lasers bursting over its circumference.

Golden light overwhelming his brain.

—74—
The End

Slater was out of the woods, falling from the sky.

He was tapped on the shoulder. He blinked, realizing he was seated at a bar. He felt no loss of time. Except there was. Something was lost. Time signified loss. A duration of passing events. A series of vague remembrances of being somewhere once. He was recalling the time he awoke after his neurocircuit surgery. A nurse awakening him with her touch. He had slept through the entire performance. Medicinal drugs had plunged him into oblivion. Awakening now to a groggy anesthetic fog.

A Blue Shooter was next to his arm. His glass had been refilled. Slater pushed it away. Had he always been here? Had he never left? What portions of reality were real? He recognized the music.

"You found your way back."

Slater turned toward the familiar voice.

Trina was standing there, wearing the same transparent dress. She set her tray on the bar and smiled at his roving eyes. "You see, management likes to keep us honest."

"No place to hide?" said Slater. "I know the feeling. Maybe you can explain how I got back here."

"You get used to it."

"Get used to what?"

Trina shrugged. "Redefining yourself."

Memories backwashed in a vivid rush of childhood—music—desert—family—business—CyBorg9—soaring—crashing.

Trina was working. "A Frozen Lapis, no salt. Blue Shooter, rocks. And one Sherry." She looked at Slater. "Isn't that her name? The one you went searching for?"

Her silvery irises were distracting. "She's my wife."

"Did you find her?"

"I'm not sure."

She teased, "Either you *did* or didn't. Which is it?"

Slater felt lightheaded and took hold of the bar. "I came here to look for her. And my daughters. I mean—"

"Sondra. Mercy died. Am I right?"

Slater rubbed his eyes. "I forgot you knew all about me."

"Not all of you. It's not permitted." Her smile was playful but sympathetic. She sat and waited for Mortimer to finish.

"Not permitted?" said Slater.

"Uh, huh. Management."

"I should have a word with them."

"When you do, ask them to give me a raise."

"Anything else?"

"A new uniform."

Slater stared. "I see nothing wrong with your dress."

"Then stop staring." She laughed and plucked a piece of paper out of his hand. "What's this?"

Slater hadn't realized he was holding anything.

Scrawled on the unfolded scrap of paper were words which she read aloud: "'*I am more than my selfish genes. I will prove it to you. Love, J.*' Who's this J?"

"Slater, my mate, you've returned to us." Mortimer seemed in a lighter mood. "Did you have a nice trip?"

"Where's Jeannette?" said Slater.

"Having her batteries recharged."

"Stop it." Trina pushed her co-worker lightly on the chest with her fingers. "Give the guy a break. He's adjusting."

Mortimer pulled down glasses from a rack. "I wouldn't worry about it, mate. You find new focus. It all begins to merge."

"Merge?" said Slater.

"Like an onion," said Mortimer. "All those layers converging. Burns your eyes like hell if you cut into it too deep." He pointed to Slater's jacket. "What happened to your nice threads?"

Slater inspected his thermosuit. It was not in the best of shape. There was a rip to his sleeve, a laser burn at his shoulder.

"A nice cut of cloth, all the same," said Mortimer.

"He invented thermocloth," said Trina.

"Did he now?"

Slater registered their smiles as benign. "I had my uncle's help. He deserves the credit. He was the genius behind it."

"Don't underestimate your actions," said Mortimer. "I happen to know more about you than you might *want* me to know."

The remark was a challenge, Slater assessed, so he decided to challenge back, "Then why haven't you turned me in?"

"Turned you into what?" Mortimer said. "A rabbit?"

Trina giggled.

Slater showed a guarded smile. "To the CDP. If you know who I am, you know they're looking to arrest me and make me disappear. The Nexus want me dead too."

"You're safe in here, mate." Mortimer winked.

"Safe—how?" Slater snapped back. "The city was under attack. There was a revolution! A war. I mean, wasn't there?"

Mortimer touched the side of his head. "Must've been around the time you got that bloody hole in your head. A nasty gash like that could dislink a person from time."

Slater realized he had lost his hat somewhere. He felt the patch of matted hair and clotted blood.

Mortimer gave an affirming nod. "We *were* at war."

"Were?"

"Yep. A global uprising."

"And?"

Mortimer narrowed his eyes. "The unimaginable. NeverMind was penetrated. Its core got struck. A decisive blow. Imagine that. News channels blasting away on the *Tele* non-stop. I felt obliged to turn off the glut of broadcasting since we provide a haven in here. Isn't that right, Love?"

Trina was listening to the music and bobbed her head.

Attempting to process this, Slater touched the side of his head. He was trying to recall the precise moment he had received the gash. Was it inside the chamber while escaping CyBorg9? Or was it upon his crash landing into Frank? The wound had not fully healed. He felt liquid and looked at his sticky fingers.

"Blood," said Mortimer. "It's the rose of our mysterious union. Our eternal link to the universe. It's why we harmonize so well."

Slater laughed. "Harmonize? You're joking."

"Not at all. We're often in concert."

Slater scoffed. He tried but could not penetrate the bartender's mind and discern his thoughts. "In concert? You and me? The last time I looked the world was chaos."

Mortimer nodded. "Still is. After a bloody revolution? What

do you expect? Nexus, now. They're neophytes. Doing their best to work the controls. Fumbling with good intent to govern."

"The Nexus? Wait. Are you saying they—"

"Won." Trina turned. "But who really wins with so many dead? The transition, it's been pretty smooth, wouldn't you say?"

Mortimer tipped his head as he poured liquor. "I would."

Slater rubbed his eyes. "Dislink nothing. I must have lost a hell of a lot of time. I wasn't away *that* long. Was I?"

"Time's a thief." Mortimer raised his eyebrows.

"Wait," said Slater. "There were explosions when I left the city. I was fired on by the Nexus. There should be more damage."

"There's been plenty." Mortimer finished the pink concoction. He placed it on Trina's tray with the other drinks.

Slater glanced at the entrance then back. "When I walked in, both of you knew who I was, didn't you?"

Mortimer was noncommittal with a shrug.

"Okay, fine," said Slater, "it doesn't matter. But, if there *was* a coup, that means. Then, what...what happened to...""

"Our fallen leader?" Mortimer grimaced. "I too find it hard to say the name. Synonymous with so much death. Ask Trina."

Having turned away, preferring the music, Trina looked back. From her eyes, Slater felt a magnetic pull of sadness. These moons, silvery and full, they seemed worlds away. He realized the attraction to her was more than physical. He felt kinship, an urge to comfort, to love and protect her. He could only archive a residue trace of the depth of her suffering. She returned her eyes to the band.

"CyBorg9." Mortimer scratched his forehead. "There—I *said* it. What a piece of work. Hell of a time ripping down those god-awful murals and statues. Don't be deceived, mate, there's been plenty of damage. It's been global."

Slater took in the room again. He saw the same strange mix of people, appearing solid, others transparent. Same darkness, same undulating walls, but the time-lapse imagery was now a meadow in bloom. On another wall fog was washing wavelike over headlands, sunlight shining through the mist. While outside snow was falling. Slater was surprised to see holiday decorations inside as well as out.

"What time is it?" said Slater.

"Hour, month, or year?" Mortimer chuckled.

"It's Christmas morning," said Trina.

"Christ," said Slater, startled by the news.

"Our Lord," said Mortimer. "I'd say that calls for a celebration. Embracing the old as new. There's a bit of irony."

"It was illegal," said Slater. "What happened to all the—"

"Converted," said Mortimer.

"What was?"

"Loyalists. You were about to ask me that."

"What the hell happened? All those factories, manufacturing armies of *droids*. How could they—"

"Mate, we no longer *use* that term." Mortimer signaled with a cautionary finger to his lips. His eyes indicated a few customers and the bartender to his right. "Get my drift? We're at peace."

"Peace?" The word had become meaningless, incomprehensible. Through the windows Slater watched the snow continuing to fall. People were passing along the sidewalk, strolling...peacefully.

"Wait," he said and stood. He approached the windows. There were no CDPs on patrol. That's what was missing. Pedestrians were wearing thermocoats and carrying packages. The grey urban tones were covered by a soft blanket of snow. In the streets, in the alleys, even upon park benches, he was amazed by the multitude of colors. Not simply from the holiday decorations, but from people wearing thermocloth – coats, mufflers, blankets. The white landscape was sprinkled with these moving hues of lavender, turquoise, saffron, fuchsia, maroon, viridian.

People appeared warm and happy. It was comforting to see. Slater stepped away from the glass. He returned to sit at the bar. He was feeling almost happy himself. "It doesn't seem possible."

Mortimer placed a curly-cue straw in a Pink Poodle and slid it toward Trina. "What doesn't?"

"The world...at peace."

"Ah, but will it be everlasting?"

"No, Cy—CyBorg9 will replicate. He'll find a way back."

"How?" Mortimer expressed mild concern.

"LoyaltyCenters were entrenched in every continent."

"Uprooted and rebooted, mate."

Welcome news, but Slater couldn't believe it. "No, Cy had mind control over his cybers. His army. From his MindLink Centers."

Mortimer stopped a co-worker. "Here's a good mate to know. I'd like you to meet Luxar."

"*Lüxrrz,*" he corrected. "Mort, my friend, how long will it be before you learn to pronounce my name?"

Slater extended his hand. "*Lüxrrz,* is it? Hi, I'm—"

"John Lazard Slater, Number Three. I know who you are and, likewise, am pleased to make your acquaintance. This is my friend Mixr, who too is eager to meet with you."

"Mixer?" Slater looked behind him and saw a tall intimidating figure. His stony expression adjusted to a polite smile.

"Close." Mixr placed his large hand on Slater's shoulder. "We shall converse in time. When you are ready to talk. Yes?"

Slater nodded. Mixr backed away. Lüxrrz had already moved down the bar. Slater said to Mortimer, "Admit it. You knew who I was the moment I walked in here."

"Not the precise second," said Mortimer, busy mixing drinks for a waitress in sapphire who was standing nearby. "Many, besides you, have been shot down, crashing back to Earth."

"Technically, I landed. Before I crashed."

"Details," said Mortimer.

The bartender's aloof tone riled Slater. "I can't believe you're so complacent. CyBorg9 could still be alive. He could easily reemerge. I'm serious. I *know* how he operates."

"Do you?" said Mortimer. "Precisely how?"

Stater hesitated, then said, "He channels himself into others. He told me his cerebral identity resided not only here, but in Rome, Switzerland, Africa – and who knows where else?"

"How is that possible?"

"Hell if I know." Slater massaged the area between his eyes and neurocircuit. "Same way it's possible a multitude of genetic beings live inside of us."

"Meaning?" said Mortimer.

"Meaning, our bodies have ten trillion diversified cells and we host ten times that number of other genetic beings. Bacteria, fungus, and viruses – they *reside* within us."

"But they don't control me," said Mortimer.

"Are you sure about that?"

"Are you saying they control you?"

"Listen," said Slater. "I *know* how I die. Cy kills me."

Mortimer was becoming more bemused and serene as Slater spoke and became more agitated. "And you know this, how?"

"I've seen it. Numerous times."

Mortimer cocked his head, "Are you clairvoyant?"

"Yes."

"Finally. You admit something."

Slater realized he had.

"Keep this in mind," said Mortimer, "nothing is ever certain until all our layers converge."

"Like an onion, I heard you," Slater scoffed. "I can't wait."

"Bad analogy. See this?" Mortimer opened his palm to reveal a pearl. "Pearls grow by forming layers around an irritating grain of sand. Fancy that. An irritant causing such beautiful form to evolve. The outer layer is always the most visible. It represents present time. But each layer – what has passed and what will come – represents a transparent point. Time has a predictable pattern but is never fully known, until fully formed. And since time is in constant flux, it can be reviewed, revised, even changed. Know that."

Mortimer smiled, closed his palm into a fist, reopened his hand, and the pearl was gone.

Slater frowned. "Nice trick."

Mortimer touched his forehead. "Flux, mate. You saw what you needed to see."

Slater touched his neurocircuit. "Make this thing disappear."

"Mind over matter," said Mortimer. "Do it yourself."

Trina returned to whisper, "Let it go."

"How?" said Slater. "You mean like CyBorg9? CDPs? Forget they ever existed? They're likely dormant. Laying in wait."

Mortimer held out a glass bowl and offered him, "Nuts?"

"No, thanks. That amount of power doesn't suddenly vanish."

Mortimer was nonchalant. "You would think."

Slater took a handful of nuts, ate some. "You agree then?"

"No." Mortimer rubbed his thumb and fingers. "The mightiest

mountain is only a composite of spit and sand. Particles held by a collective belief that the center will hold. CyBorg9 knew this. That's all he was, a manipulation of the parts, a coerced coalition. He had a masterful grip but was destined to be undone by his own undoing. Those TransAwareness MindCenter facilities he established globally? They were to ensure his power. But they eroded it. These seminars and workshops opened minds into believing there was more to life than CyBorg9. Imagine that."

Slater *was* imagining—just that.

"Cyberdroids," Mortimer mocked in jest, "came into their own. Same old story. To be or not to be. That fight for love and glory. A case of do or die? It never fails. That *want* for freedom."

"Heather."

The realization of her involvement gave Slater a warm chill. "Then it was true, what she was doing. I wanted to believe but—"

"Frost was your mother?"

"She was one of three."

Mortimer scratched his temple. "Three? No wonder I've had confusing signals deciphering who you are. Tell me truthful, mate, was it all a ruse? Merely an act?"

"How do you mean?"

"Your *loyalty*."

"Heather and I were at odds, but—"

"Not with her." Mortimer's eyes narrowed. "Your involvement. You had to have *known* cybers were joining the Nexus."

"I didn't realize the extent."

"Hum, I suspect you might not, as an insider," Mortimer gave him a wink. "Jeannette is a rare beauty. She's been instrumental in altering my views. Helping me to go with this *new* flow."

The flux.

Its mercurial pull overwhelmed Slater like a silent wave washing and receding over sand. He took hold of the bar to steady himself. He was trying to adjust, to stay afloat. To avoid sinking like a rock. He belatedly realized the bartender was talking to him:

"Considered turncoats, in the beginning. Rubbish. They were heroes. Rebel patriots. And I'm proud to say I helped. You might even say I *was* the underground."

Slater recalled the escape-route tunnel he'd passed through.

"It's all coming back. Isn't it, mate?"

Trina placed her hand on Slater's wrist. "I had to take you there. We had to be sure."

"Sure of what?" said Slater.

Mortimer squinted, "Your core. It's a requirement, this drilling. But I'm pleased to report we came up with some good dirt on you. Listen, if the cybers hadn't bolted and cast their loyalty elsewhere, this revolution would never have succeeded. *Never.*"

"Morty, don't forget," Trina added, "we had inside help."

"Rumors do abound," said Mortimer. "The instant that central core blew – whew! – those generals and high-rankers with too much to lose, they put up a fight, but were quickly nixed. The others were, how shall I say, *persuaded* to join our movement."

Slater noticed a miniature tree behind the bar, behind Mortimer. It was as tall as a liquor bottle. It had a dazzling show of revolving ornaments. Ornaments in the shape of three-dimensional animals. Among the extinct – zebras, elephants, lions – revolving in merry-go-round fashion around the tree.

Slater began questioning his sanity again.

Mortimer saw him looking and stroked his hand through its center. "Thought I'd dust it off, display a bit of the holiday spirit."

"Those animals look so real," Slater said.

"It does keep you guessing." said Mortimer. "Peaceful. What I imagine the world to be come judgement day."

"Morty has a marshmallow heart, " said Trina.

"Yeah," said Mortimer, "I'm your garden-variety saint."

Slater forced his eyes to look elsewhere, away from this magical lure. He examined his surroundings – the people lacking definition, the other-worldly music – and sensed he might fall. He gripped the bar. "What the hell's happening? Is this...some sort of Hell? Where am I!?"

"Steady," warned Mortimer, "don't lose it."

"Too late." Slater tightened his grip on the bar. "None of this would have happened if it wasn't for me. *I'm* to blame. I caused this whole disaster. I was trying to create something worthwhile. And good. Instead I...I created this—a god-damned monster!"

"Stop torturing yourself." Mortimer touched Slater's shoulder to try and ground him. His hand was pushed away.

"Let go! I deserve to be in Hell. For letting myself be *deceived*. I thought I could reverse time and save the world. What a laugh. In the process *sacrificing* family and friends. I deserve this."

"Truth is, mate, you were only the catalyst. We're all to blame. CyBorg9 seduced us all."

Slater looked at Mortimer before regarding the windows and the snowy world outside. "I didn't even realize it was Christmas. If I had acted sooner...maybe I could have...saved more lives."

Trina squeezed his hand before leaving to serve drinks.

Mortimer said, "When you opt to shoot the moon, you sacrifice all that matters in this world. Mate, you gotta keep some faith."

The music, without words, continued to haunt like a buffeting wind. It massaged his mind. Slater slowly breathed in this new air. His nerves relaxed. The coiled snakes inside were purged of tension. He felt a desperate need to close his eyes and sleep, allowing time, this thief, to steal him away. To somewhere, maybe off to bedlam. Those inside were a blur of converging motion. Talking so loud their voices broke in waves above the ocean roar of music.

"This band," Slater asked, "how long have they been playing?"

"Forever." Mortimer pointed to Slater's untouched drink. "One more for the road?"

"No. No, I've had enough."

"Good. As the bartender, my job is to regulate the quantitative flow from this fountain of dreams."

Slater rubbed his eyes. "Is that what this is? A dream?"

"No, mate. It's life. Drink it up while you can. Salute."

Slater picked up his glass, but only to examine the strange blue liquid. How had it become so popular, so soon? He was the one, in part, responsible for its inception. Wasn't he?

"Fallacy."

"What is?" said Slater.

"I can't actually regulate the flow," said Mortimer with a wink. "I am a humble servant working the gates."

Slater studied the bartender. He glanced at the crowd of people seated at the bar. "Don't you have other customers?"

"I take them one at a time. No need to rush."

"Wait. If you were one of the Nexus, then—"

"I never claimed I was," said Mortimer.

"Okay, helped them," Slater clarified, "then…maybe you knew my wife? Sherry? A girl, Sondra? A man named Wolfe?"

"Hell of a patriot. He's our new leader, unofficially."

"Wolfe? You mean he's alive?"

"Haven't you been following the news?"

"I told you, no. I haven't trusted the media in ages."

"Open channels now. Unadulterated flow."

"Wolfe and I worked together. We were friends, once."

Mortimer grinned. "He mentioned you."

"Then—you would know Sherry if — and my daughter, Sondra, are they—" Slater's heart was pounding. The snow was falling fast. His valves pumping faster. "Are they—they're—alive?"

"Slow down, mate." Mortimer calmly wiped the bar counter with a sponge. "I know who they are. Yes, a real pleasure to know them. Both your wife *and* your daughters."

"Daughter."

"All three are beauties."

Slater started to speak but the bartender cut him off.

"Listen, mate. To be honest, many of us thought you were part of the opposition. We believed you had betrayed us."

Slater became distracted by Trina who was approaching from the field of tables. Her empty tray was held vertically, like the shield of a charging knight. She jousted him, her body buckling into his.

"I do like you." She bit his earlobe playfully. "Even if you *are* a marked and wanted man. Come. I have a gift for you."

Slater gave Trina a puzzled smile. "But I didn't get you anything. No, wait, I do have something." He searched his pockets. "I found this rock in the mountains."

"Wow, a *rock*," she teased.

"More like a precious stone." Slater kept searching. "Strange and beautiful, like your eyes. Damn, I guess I lost it." Instead, he found and removed the small thin package buried inside the lining of his coat. It was bound with newsprint and string.

Trina snatched it from his hand. "Look, you even found time to wrap it. You *are* sweet. This doesn't feel like a rock."

"I forgot I had that. Henry gave it to me, before he—"

"He's the one you betrayed?" Trina tore off the newsprint and flipped through the notebook. She pursed her lips. "Hum, this looks interesting. Like a diary. Written in shorthand. Except there's more writing above the squiggles. Must be the translation, I'm guessing. Obviously, it's not written for – *Yours Truly* – me?"

Slater recognized the book. He'd handed it to Weiner years ago in an alley. One more thing he had completely forgotten about it. He took back the book and peeked at the first page. The notations were Weiner's handwriting, tiny writing above the shorthand.

"Let me," Trina pulled it back and read out loud, "'Dear Diary.' See, I was right, it *is* a diary. It goes on to say, 'I met a strange boy last night, at a Christmas party. Strange, because he is like me. I can hear his thoughts. And he chanted my name. *Sherry, Sherry, Sherry.* Which scared me. But a warmth of blood flooded through my body. As if I felt him inside me. Is he the one? The one I will marry, God? His name is John Slater.'"

Trina stopped. "She's talking about you."

Slater, too stunned for words, felt Trina kiss him on the lips. It was so tender it felt like a blessing. He focused on her smile.

"Am I too *brazen*? A hussy?"

She laughed and pushed herself away, departing before spinning back and grabbing the lapels of his jacket. She tucked the tiny book back in his coat pocket, then gently pulled him off the bar stool.

"Morty, I'm borrowing him."

A sun was setting into a sea of clouds inside the wall monitors. Trina led him to a table and pushed him down into a seat.

"Sit." She held out her hand. She backed away slowly as if she was training a dog. "*Stay.* Right there. Be good, you hear?"

Slater was curious to see who she had placed him next to. His mind toppled into more disbelief. He *was* at The Crossroads.

"Trina found me," said Smitts. His nimble fingers drummed the table for old-times-sake. "Are you surprised?"

"Surprised doesn't even come close." Slater looked around to reassure himself he was still in the same place. He touched his friend to make certain he was real. "Jeezz, Smitty, where the hell have you been? I thought you were dead."

Smitts shrugged. "I heard the same rumors about you."

"What happened?"

"A pile of bricks fell on my head. I woke up with amnesia. I drifted around for awhile. I came to my senses. Here I am."

"You look good."

"Did you come here for the music?" Smitts pointed.

Slater regarded the musicians. The trumpet was blaring and the violin was off on another solo flight. The harpist was staring at him. She wasn't playing. He returned her smile.

"I feel like I know her."

Smitts nodded. "Can I buy you a drink?"

"No, thanks. I've had my fill."

Smitts chuckled, "You? See, you got what you asked for."

"When was this?"

"At The Crossroads. You said you wanted to *soar* and consume all that life had to offer. Before it *spoiled*."

Slater grinned. "Did I say that? I guess I did."

"Have you seen Wolfe or Gloria lately?"

The question sobered him. "Glory's dead. Last year."

"Wolfe's alive," said Smitts. "So I've heard."

"Me too, minutes ago." Slater widened his eyes for comic effect. "The bartender informed me. *Wolfe* has become a leading figure in the new government. Maybe we should celebrate."

"We are. Congratulations, by the way."

"For what?" said Slater.

"Being here. You beat the odds."

"Beat them how?"

"Finding a way to alter the past and fix the future."

Slater shook his head, "I didn't."

Smitts said, "Trust me. The future's better now."

Slater rolled his eyes. "A mess, last time I looked."

"Look again," Smitty encouraged.

Slater said grimly, "Smitty...Mercy *died*. I even envisioned it. But I couldn't stop it. And others *perished*, thanks to me."

"I was talking about the future. Nothing is perfect, mate."

"Sondra and Sherry are probably dead too."

"Don't talk like that. You don't know that, do you?"

"No, but I've had visions," said Slater.

"Lately?"

"No. Which is puzzling."

Smitts laughed to cheer him up. "Come on. I'll bet you never expected to see me again. There's a bit of hope you hadn't counted on. Right?"

"You're right." Slater's smile fell. Standing on the other side of the room near the stage was a man. He resembled Henry Weiner. It was hard to tell in the darkness. Same cherubic smile. Beneath his arm he held a book flagged with what looked to be colorful Post-its. Slater began to stand but was defeated by a sense of shame and guilt. He sank back down into his seat. "It can't be."

A hand touched his shoulder, then a voice from the past.

"Hey, Satyr—fellow *dawg*, who let you in?"

Slater lost his ability to speak. He was staring at Gloria who took a seat. She mocked him by sticking out her tongue.

"Glory, I…"

"Mate, look over there, look," said Smitts.

Slater's eyes were redirected toward the entrance where he saw Sherry walking in. Sondra too, who had become a beautiful woman. Both were smiling, stopping to greet the doorman.

"Jesus." Tears came to his eyes. "They're alive?"

"They're quite a sight, huh?" said Smitts.

"You see them too?"

Gloria taunted, "We're not blind, deaf *and* dumb."

Smitts intervened, "They come here for the music. But there's more to it than that."

"Especially tonight." Gloria winked.

"Why? Wait. This can't be possible." Slater was torn between asking a million questions to Gloria and Smitts and wanting to catch Sherry's attention but he was reticent to do anything, to even move, afraid Sherry might walk out if she saw him. He didn't know what to think anymore, or what his wife or daughter thought of him. For the moment, he was happy just to see their faces, to know they were safe. He loved their every movement, gesture, and smile.

"Look over there," said Smitts.

Slater forced himself to look away toward the stage.

"Recognize anyone else?"

The harpist, her smile, was alarmingly familiar. It was Mercy. He recognized her eyes. He had glimpsed her like this once before. His youngest daughter grown into a radiant woman, as powerful as a lighthouse. She blew him a loving kiss. To guide him home.

Slater turned, looking for help. The man who resembled Weiner gave him a friendly wave. He thought he recognized a towering man in the shadows nearby. Bryant?

He was sure of nothing.

Sherry was approaching. Sondra had stayed behind, holding hands with a man he belatedly realized was Wolfe's son. Derek, with Sondra. They appeared to be in love, and happy. They walked hand in hand toward the stage.

It was all happening so fast.

Sherry walked over to him and stopped. Her lips curved into a wistful smile. She looked down – her eyes going straight through him – as she placed her purse on the table.

Slater half-expected her to strike him with her fists and scream. This stony silence was worse. He saw she was wearing the butterfly brooch. The one he had given to Lily with the slim hope of it ever finding Sherry. The jeweled wings were washed clean – clean of the blood from their last encounter in the woods.

Slater was speechless.

"Say something," encouraged Smitts.

"Speak from your heart," said Gloria.

"I love you, Sherry."

She looked away, making him suffer. She gave a wave to people at the bar. A friendly gesture. She was hiding inner pain, he sensed. He knew her body language so intimately. He needed to touch her. But he resisted. He loved everything about her. He ached to caress her warm body. His eyes had filled, overflowing with tears.

"Don't hate me, Sherry. That knife...that was only to save you. Sondra too. I swear. Sherry, it was the only way....Sherry? Please, say something. Please."

She looked at him. It was a perplexed, bemused and beautiful look, one of acceptance. She found it in her heart to smile.

Her thoughts startled him. She was saying, *John, John, John. You're here. Right now. Aren't you?*

"Yes," he said, confused.

Her expression was one of introspection as she lowered herself onto his lap. Her body disappeared into his.

The warmth he felt was exquisite.

Their bodies had converged, occupying the same space. She had penetrated his body. He lost focus. The sensation was pure ecstasy. A sensation he thought he would never experience again. He had lost sight of her but felt her presence. A surge of panic overtook him and he looked at Gloria for help. Her peaceful smile confused him. He turned to Smitts whose eyes held him in place like the invisible force of gravity.

"Smitty—what's happening?"

"Your prayers were answered, mate."

"Prayers? Is she alive?"

"Satyr," Gloria teased, "You're my *hero*."

"You told us yourself," said Smitts, "remember?"

"Told you what?"

"That you needed to save her."

"By fixing the past."

"She loves you, mate."

"Be happy."

"Wait, if...I'm still here—"

"You *are*—and you're *not*."

"That's how it works."

"I don't understand."

"You will, mate. It gets better."

"Slater, you're dead."

—75—
Swan Song

As a means to an end, the present had become the future – and perfect it was not. Death was unacceptable. Slater wanted to avoid the social stigma. He fought to resist gravity and pull out of its grip. He was attempting to right his course. But lasers from hostile aircraft kept strafing at him and interfering with his trajectory. He was used to adversity. He could survive this, he reasoned, unreasonably, as the engine of his QuantumStarXS burst into flames.

Suddenly he was plummeting, his optimism too, worthless, like stock in a panicked market with no bottom in sight.

His vision was obscured by black smoke swirling backwards into the path of his descent. The force of frigid air extinguished the fire and exposed the intricate grid of the city enlarging fast. His wings were failing to hold him aloft. He felt like Icarus, a fool made of feathers and wax, melting to pieces, transformed back from a technological wonder to a chunk of debris dropping to Earth.

Life was so precious. A lesson learned too late. Irreversible, was time...

About the Author

Todd Crawshaw was born
and is currently still alive.

www.ingramcontent.com/pod-product-compliance
Lightning Source LLC
Chambersburg PA
CBHW070542130626
46556CB00001B/5